"... The angelic letters series is absolutely stunning and enchanting. I did not want to do ANYTHING other than read and find out what happened next. Thank you for sharing such a magical journey with us, not me..."
LINDA

"... God has truly blessed you and at the same time He has blessed us, your readers, with your gift."
CRYSTAL

"... I don't know if I've ever read any book that has affected me so much before. They are truly a blessing and I look forward to reading them again! Never have I read a book twice."
LESLIE

"... With tears in my eyes, I want to thank you for all I received from your books. Love, Healing, and my beautiful little butterfly angel."
SUSAN

"... I have loved reading your books and cannot wait for the 5th...The suspense is killing me. I also enjoyed the spiritual connections throughout the book."
LENORE

"... I have never experienced the feelings of joy, sorrow or even anger when reading a book. I've read all 4 Editions. I'm not a big reader but when I started reading these books I could not put them down. I was touched spiritually.
BETTE

"... What a tremendous series of books – 'The Angelic Series' – there is not a dull page in all of the many pages of each book! – and yet simplistic, real, touching, captivating but also spiritual, clean, and such wholesome content – and I could go on! Thank you for providing this sort of reading.
LORAINE

"... I have absolutely loved reading all your books and find the life lessons that you thread through you're story so very meaningful and heartwarming!
BETTIE

"... It would be such a blessing if everyone would read these books, believe and put into practice the values taught...The books are so well written and easily capture you. Thank you for writing these beautiful, heart touching books.
EMILY

"... I have read a great deal of books by authors from all over the world but none held my interest like this series. Just could not lay them down until I finished them. Even took 2 days holidays just to read...
ESTHER

"... Your series of books are the first I've read in 30 years of not reading. I've loved every moment of the 4 books. I am dying to find out what is going on!! TERRY

"... I have never put so many sticky notes in works of fiction, to go back and remember how clearly you illustrated passages from the Bible through your characters. It was like a series of riveting homilies. Very influential! SUSAN

"... I just want to let you know that your Angel books have been so inspiring to me. I have read each one at least four times! DIANE

"... Words are inadequate to express how much I have enjoyed your "Angelic Series." So inspirational and your way of writing make it pure artistry. SUSAN

"... Never before have I been so moved by an Author's work. I had such a difficult time putting the books down. Their lives, your words, consumed my thoughts so completely. RUTH

I have not read a series as captivating and real as this one. I am an avid reader and often have two or three books on the go at once. However, when reading your series, that was the only book I could read at the time..Wonderful writing... BECKY

"... I read to my husband every night before we go to bed..We laughed, cried, sympathized, empathized, and felt the changing emotions throughout all 4 books. To be able to captivate your audience so easily, you obviously have a wonderful grasp of life and faith. Thank you for bringing such clarity into our lives... ELIZABETH

"... Your books have me riveted and they are some of the best books I have ever read. Please accept my congratulations and highest praise of your work. ANITA

"... Books are very inspirational. I had to remind myself to breath when reading book 4. I'm on the edge of my seat wondering what happens next. NOREEN

"... I am not an avid reader however, not only has this series captured my interest, I was spellbound, and just could not help myself by devouring one book after the other until I was left hanging...When is book five coming out? LORNA

"... My friend recommended them to me and I can hardly put them down. Best books I have ever read. Loved them... LAURIE LEA

"... I'm sure so many have told you what an inspiration your books and words have been, emotionally and spiritually. How they have brought tears, laughter, sorrow, joy, intrigue, suspense - a virtual basket of emotions. I have never read books that have moved and inspired me like this series. Thank you DAWN

"... The Angelic Letter books are a blessing, full of lessons for all ages. .. CATHERINE

"I just finished the 4th book and I really, really loved it! Wow, it kept me on the edge of my seat! It put me in a perfect state of peace and love at times right when I needed it most!!! Thank you for the beautiful books KAMLA

"... Thank you for the heart moving stories and thank you for allowing the LORD to move upon you so mightily that you are able to pass on those beautiful words and bless countless others. You have a powerful gift. BLESSINGS... WENDY

"... Love the books, and they are an inspiration to me. I have been through every emotion reading. They are so different than anything I have ever read. ROSALBA

"... They are without a doubt some of the best books that I have ever read....the spiritual messages are inspiring & uplifting. GRETA

"... Your books are without a doubt life changing... I had totally lost myself, put my spirituality on the back burner and now am proud to say, I am coming back... it feels good, it feels free. SHARLENE

"... Although this is not the genre I usually read ...once I started, I couldn't put them down. I enjoyed them more than I ever thought possible. Your writing is phenomenal; to a point that I could visualize everything you described. IRENE

"... My mother absolutely loves your books!! She is in her 80s and rarely finds such passion for reading so I wanted to thank you for this! MARISSA

"... Your story was a real page turner, read all 4 books in a couple of weeks. A lot of laughs, tears, and lessons. KATHLEEN

"... Your writing makes me feel as though I am right there with the characters living the life with them...I have gone with only limited amount of sleep sometimes because I want to see what happens next.

ANITA

"... I love your books sooooo much ...I am encouraging everyone I know to read them.

PATRICIA

"... Your books have helped me through very difficult times and that is why I am very sad that I am almost finished with book number four.

VICTORIA

"... Have enjoyed your first four books very very much cannot put them down. It is hard to believe that they are fiction.

NOLA

"... Your books are absolutely amazing! They have touched like a book never has. I just finished reading your latest one and am clinging to the edge of my seat needing to know what happens next! And I have to admit it brought me to tears more than once.

SARA

"... Thank you for your breathtaking story that encompasses so many valuable spiritual life lessons so delightfully told.

CATHERINE

"... I have never read such wonderful books! The story had a profound effect on me. I can't wait to read the rest of the series.

MARY

"... Love reading your Angelic Letters Series. Have read books 1 - 4 and am in the process of beginning a second time because I cannot do without the characters in my life. They are all so special and inspiring ...

BERNADETTE

"... I have read books 1 to 4 and I wonder when book five is coming as I can't wait to have it in my hands. I love the story, thank you, sometimes I call people Jenny that is how much it has impacted me.

DIANA

"... First I have to say how much I love your books, they are so well written. I was just wondering when your next two books from the Pewter Angel series is coming out?

NANCY

Please write to Henry at: henry@henryripplinger.com or visit www.henryripplinger.com for more information about Henry's work and art. We would love to hear from you!

ANGEL PROMISES
FULFILLED

ANGEL PROMISES FULFILLED   H. RIPPLINGER/2014

Also by **Henry K. Ripplinger**

THE ANGELIC LETTERS SERIES
Book One....Pewter Angels
Book Two....Another Angel of Love
Book Three....Angel of Thanksgiving
Book Four....The Angelic Occurrence

OTHER WORKS
If You're Not From the Prairie...
(Story by David Bouchard, Images by Henry K. Ripplinger)

Coming in future from Pio-Seelos Books:

BOOK SIX OF THE ANGELIC LETTERS SERIES
The House Where Angels Dwell

THE ANGELIC LETTERS SERIES,

Book Five

——— ✷ ———

ANGEL PROMISES
FULFILLED

1988 -1989

HENRY K. RIPPLINGER

Best Selling Author of Pewter Angels

Angel Promises Fulfilled is a work of fiction. Names, characters, places and incidents are either the product of the author's imagination or are used fictitiously. Any resemblance to actual events, locales, business establishments or persons, living or dead, is entirely coincidental.

Library and Archives Canada Cataloguing in Publication

Ripplinger, Henry, author
       Angel promises fulfilled : 1988-1989 / Henry K. Ripplinger.

(The angelic letters series ; bk. 5)
Best selling author of Pewter Angels.
Issued in print, audio and electronic formats.
ISBN 978-0-9917102-6-3 (bound).
ISBN 978-0-9917102-8-7 (audiobook).--ISBN 978-0-9917102-9-4 (epub)

       I. Title. II. Series: Ripplinger, Henry. Angelic letters series ; bk. 5.

PS8585.I565A836 2014   C813'.6   C2014-901661-1
                                               C2014-901662-X
                                               C2014-901663-8

Author photo: Bruce Vasselin, Designer Photo
Cover concept and design by Henry K. Ripplinger
Cover design and production by Brian Danchuk Design
Page layout by Human Powered Design

Pio-Seelos Books
Ph: (306) 731-3087, Fax: (306) 731-3852.
E-mail: henry@henryripplinger.com

Printed and bound in Canada by Friesens Printers
March 2014

This novel is dedicated to my readers.

Thank you for your love, loyalty and

commitment to the Angelic Letters Series!

ACKNOWLEDGEMENTS

MANY READERS HAVE asked me if there was a Jenny in my life. And I say, yes, just as there is a Julean in my life. They are both packaged up in the woman who has always been my one and only love; my dear wife, Joan. Thank you honey, for giving me the inspiration for the two main female characters in the story!

Thank you, too, Joan and Jen Howie for reading through the manuscript and catching errors in spelling, punctuation and grammar.

To Tracy Jacknife and Jody Ripplinger, thank you for proof-reading, editing and helpful suggestions. Very much appreciated!

Once again to all of you, my heartfelt thanks for making my writing the best it can be!

And as always, I thank the Lord for the gift of this story. I am thankful daily for His inspiration and guidance through His angels and Holy Spirit and divine providence... every step of the way!

For God so loved the world, that He gave His only begotten Son, that whoever believes in Him shall not perish, but have eternal life.

JOHN 3:16

"There will be more joy in heaven over one sinner who repents than over ninety-nine righteous persons who need no repentance."

LUKE 15:7

"See what love the Father has given us, that we should be called children of God."

1 JOHN 3:1

"You will seek Me and find Me, when you seek Me with all your heart."

JEREMIAH 29:13

"I am the way, and the truth and the Life; no one comes to the Father, but through Me."

JOHN 14:6

"A new heart I will give you, and a new spirit I will put within you; and I will take out of your flesh the heart of stone and give you a heart of flesh."

EZEKIEL 36:26

"Every one then who hears these words of mine and obeys them will be like a wise man who built his house upon the rock; and the rain fell, and the floods came, and the winds blew and beat upon that house, but it did not fall, because it had been founded on the rock."

MATT. 7:24-25

PROLOGUE

A THOUGHTFUL MAN ONCE said, "In the beginning was the Word, and the Word was with God, and the Word was God. He was in the beginning with God. All things were made through Him, and nothing was made without Him. In Him was life, and the life was the light of men. And the light shines in the darkness, and the darkness did not overcome it." John 1:1-5

My dear friends, as much as we are able with our finite minds, we need to understand life as a whole. See the big picture; why we are here, what our purpose is, the natural order of how God created the world with its laws and principles of life and that we live for eternity not for the present world. When we truly believe that the Word became a man and lived among us and that He is the Son of God; that He came and died for us to pardon our sins and when we fully understand and appreciate the necessity of His teaching for three years before He was crucified...

When we fully comprehend that we must be reborn in the spirit, repent and accept Him as our Lord and Savior and that He truly is the way, the truth and life...then, that is when our life begins to take on meaning and purpose. When we understand the big picture, we will discover we are in the world but not of the world. We will want to see the world through His mind and eyes. We will know why we need Him and must follow Him. It is the only path to life and freedom and inner peace, my friends; all other paths lead to dead ends…to death.

It all seems so simple and straight forward and yet, so many have not found or chosen this path! Why is it that this world seems more appealing than our eternal life with Christ? When I was granted those precious few moments on the other side I could see in an instant into the hearts and minds of humanity and of my closest friends. I recall discussing the visions I was granted to see from that heavenly perspective with my protector as if it were yesterday.

"It is easy to see, Zachariah, why there are so many differences between people on earth and why it is that some can live in peace with themselves and others, while still so many subject themselves to a life filled with worldly values, problems, confrontations, worries and all sorts of mental concerns and depression."

Zachariah nodded, his warm brown eyes reflecting compassion for the human dilemma. "How one perceives his world is crucial to his well being. All sorts of good and evil are played out in the mind's theatre. Clearly, the battleground in which man lives out his life is in his mind. And since all men have the gift of free will, the choices they make based on how they see and think about situations that come their way determines their emotions and reaction either for better or for worse."

"Yes, yes, we are what we think and how we think is determined by all the experiences of our past that bring us into each and every present moment we live."

Zachariah nodded, a momentary silence fell between us.

I gazed at my protector still in awe over the vision I just witnessed how from the moment we leave our mother's womb the journey of our lives begin. Learning first from our parents, family, then friends, and teachers and combined with our hereditary nature we acquire emotional habits, good and bad, and a self image of who we are. We develop fears, and values, prejudices, hurts, joys and sorrows…. Yes! Through the billions of choices we make based on all that went before continues to shape our lives and determines our quest for happiness and inner peace. On any particular day and given moment we may find ourselves a million miles away from the world of Jesus, and other days just on the doorstep and occasionally we may enter. This is how it is for each of us.

Zachariah broke into my thoughts with an insight I was just contemplating. "What many do not realize is that how they see their world is different from the world others see because of all the things in their lives that brought them to this moment in time as well. Each man creates his own world and is different from all other men. All too many believe that how they see a situation is the same as how another sees it, but this is not the case."

I was about to speak but Zachariah went on. "An awareness of this helps to make a man more compassionate and understanding of another. No-one is perfect and each man's world view is made up of much faulty thinking and conditioned emotional reactions, misunderstanding and hurts. For better or worse a man brings his good and bad traits into each situation he encounters. Reality is perceived through what each person brings into their lives."

"So true, Zachariah, that's why open, honest communication is so important to clarify our perceptions to each other. I have noticed that over and over during my life. So often we are left to our own thinking and analysis of what is in the minds of others and their motive. How could he or she do this to me? And yet, when we understand where they were at and see the situation from their point of view, even if it is flawed, we can then accept why they did what they did."

This time it was I who nodded as I couldn't speak. I could see how the minds of mankind churned with self righteousness and pride. Tears of sorrow surfaced as my heart pained to see the many conflicts in families; children angry with their parents, wives against husbands, husbands against wives, unforgiveness in so many hearts and misunderstandings of all sorts. Where, oh where is the love, the forgiveness and understanding? How can we let days, months and years go by and live in the past over some hurt that may have been over some reaction due to one's perception of life at that time? A past hurt or slight is only a thought kept alive by playing it over and over in our minds… for what purpose!? Such a heavy price to pay for the sake of getting even, being right or justified. We are all imperfect. Why do we act superior to one another and condemn the speck in our brother's eyes and fail to see the log in our own?

I could see in the vision before me that Jesus is absent in so many homes which further compounds and impedes man's search for meaning and purpose. Prayer, kindness, repentance lacking in so many lives, it is no wonder so many flounder and do not see the path that leads to life and inner peace.

Zachariah knew my thoughts and softly spoke words of hope and encouragement. "Had not the Lord become man to live and die for humanity the vision you see would have been the life of all mankind. There would have been continual strife and darkness and death would have been the end to man's existence."

I barely heard Zacharias' words when there before me appeared the good news, the coming of Jesus to pay the price for our sins and open the gates of heaven. I was spellbound as I saw Jesus standing on the mountain side giving the Sermon on the Mount that I had read so many times before in Matthew's gospel. His words were filled with love, compassion and forgiveness, teaching us to live through His world, His mind, His thinking! "Blessed are the poor in spirit, for theirs is the kingdom of heaven. Blessed are those who mourn, for they shall be comforted. Blessed are the meek, for they shall inherit the earth...." My heart began to overflow with gratitude as the light of the Word; its truth and justice swept through my spirit.

"Oh, if only we would all come to Him, repent and commit our lives to Him! How much more peace would fill our existence!"

Romans 12:2 illuminated my mind like a flashing marquee:

'And be not conformed to this world: but be ye transformed by the renewing of your mind, that ye may prove what is that good, and acceptable, and perfect, will of God.'

"Yes, it is easy to see from this perspective that the degree to which we accept, commit and obey His teachings is the degree to which we live in the real world that prepares us for eternity. It is the degree to which we grow in peace. It is the degree to which we become peacemakers and beacons to lead others into the light. It is the degree to which we help Jesus fulfill His great commission to bring all mankind into the kingdom of heaven."

"Why is it Zachariah that many know this truth, yet still live on the fringe of it all and so many abandon it all together as if unattainable? Yes, it requires effort to be obedient to His teachings and to yield our will to Him, but in my own life the rewards of living for God is immeasurable."

"You are a fine example of living such a life of being in the world but not of the world... You have realized early on that it is impossible to do God's will on your own strength. Daily I have seen you on your knees asking for mercy and forgiveness and inviting the Master into your heart to live through your life. It is because of the way you have chosen to live your life that your example has brought many people to the Lord. You have been a beacon of light for Jesus. You give others hope and instill faith."

I nodded gratefully, "I have only been a light to other's by God's grace and strength! As St. Paul says, 'It is no longer I who live but Christ who lives in me.' It is only by abiding in Christ that we can live as God intended. He is the vine, we are the branches. By remaining in the vine steadfastly, we grow in the light moment by moment until the day we die. When we are hurt, we forgive, when a lie is convenient we say the truth, when we are tempted to judge, we accept. We are obedient to Jesus' teachings. We show kindness, patience, goodwill, peace in every situation we find ourselves. All our thoughts, words and deeds must have a spiritual side."

My kindly guardian smiled approvingly, "Yes, man must take up his cross and follow Jesus daily. There will be times when the struggle is great, the temptations so powerful that man slips into darkness. That is why God sent the Holy Spirit and His Angels to continually help us. God understands man's frailty and how easily he is lured back into worldliness and worldly ways of thinking. Every moment is a decision to live for Christ or himself. Every time man yields his will to God and allows Jesus to live within him, he develops a new habit of living for Christ and weakens his old habits and nature. Although his tendency for self is always present, it is through his choices and sincere efforts that he receives God's grace and strength to grow ever closer into the mind and heart of Jesus."

"Yes, Zachariah, it is as you have said, when man sees the big picture and how he fits into the scheme and plan of the heavenly Father that is when he begins to live in the light of the real world. He now lives with meaning and purpose with eternity ever in his sight."

CHAPTER ONE

HENRY SPED DOWN Pasqua Street heading south. His heart was racing and pounding so hard, he thought for sure it would explode out of his chest. Beads of perspiration were beginning to roll down his forehead, trickling into his eyes. He brushed them away with the back of his hand.

"Oh, Jenny, please hang in there." Geez, for months already he could have been seeing her. *Marjorie's house was less than a mile away from the Santa Maria Home, for Pete's sake.* He remembered when he called the care home and asked about her. If only he had challenged the nurse on duty at the time, that he was more than family and had every right to see her. Perhaps if he had gone down there and pleaded with them or had asked them to ask Marjorie if she would see him.

But that's the past, Henry. What's done is done. Henry reached up and clutched the angel pendant once again.

"Oh please, guardian angel, get me there on time."

The light had turned yellow as he approached the intersection of Dewdney and Pasqua. He hit the gas and sped through but rather than slow down he kept increasing the gas…

"Oh, no…" he heard a siren and looking into his rearview mirror, he saw a patrol car almost touching his bumper.

Henry slowed and pulled over, his heart almost in his mouth. He knew better than to speed, but it was a life and death situation.

Henry rolled down his window as the officer approached the car.

"Can I see your driver's license, sir?" the officer asked.

Henry already had his wallet out in anticipation of the question. He deserved a ticket and wanted to get it over with as quickly as possible.

"Did you know you went through a late yellow light? It was well into the red by the time you got through the intersection."

"I'm sorry officer. I was so close to the intersection I decided to go through… I was going quite fas…"

"That's exactly right. You were going fast; too fast. I was sitting on Dewdney waiting for the light to change and saw you barreling down Pasqua and after you went through the light you didn't slow down either. Seems to me you went still faster."

"I know…but I can explain. I just learned that a girl I knew and was very fond of 30 years ago is very ill at the Santa Maria Home and apparently her case is terminal. I was hoping I could see her before…well before something happens to her…" Henry didn't even want to think that Jenny might be dead.

"That may be, but in trying to get to her in such a hurry, you are putting yourself and others in danger."

Henry nodded, clearly guilty, yet hoping the officer would simply give him his ticket and let him go.

The officer turned to go back to his squad car and write up a ticket when he noticed who Henry was. He came back to the car.

"Say, are you Henry Pederson, the artist?"

"Guilty again, officer, I am."

"I can't believe this. We have one of your prints hanging in our living room. My wife and I got it when we married five years ago. It's the one of a boy and his dog standing beside a dugout behind the barn in a farm yard. He's tossing a stone across the water to make it skip on the surface. I used to do that all the time."

Henry appreciated the fact that the police officer had a piece of his art but desperately wanted to go. He simply smiled and nodded, not wanting to get into a conversation.

"I know you're in a hurry…look, I'll give you a warning this time."

The officer tightened his lips and tilted his head as a sign he could change his mind but before he could, Henry said, "I promise, officer, I'll be more observant of my speed. Normally I am, it's just that I want to see Jenny before it's too late."

"You said she is in the Santa Maria Home?"

"Yeah," Henry nodded.

"Okay, look…follow me."

The officer hurried back to his car. No sooner had he started the vehicle, he turned on the siren and proceeded down Pasqua towards the care home. Henry followed and waved to the officer when they got there.

Just as he pulled into the Santa Maria parking lot, he saw Camilla run out of the care home crying. She looked so upset… She ran to her car and before Henry could even get out and run to her, she sped away even more in a hurry than he was to get here.

What was she doing here? Who was she visiting or seeing?

He wondered if she had ever found out if she was adopted or not?

Henry thought about going after her and explaining what he just found out about Marjorie, but he was more torn to see Jenny.

He hoped that Camilla would drive more carefully and not get caught speeding like he did. Geez wouldn't that be something if she got caught by the same officer…another dangerous Pederson!

The lady at the reception desk looked up as Henry burst through the door. He slowed to barely a walk.

"Good morning," he said, as he resolutely walked past the desk. He had already been detained once and he couldn't deal with another interference. Henry caught his breath and blurted, "I know the room number of the patient I want to see."

He was glad Father had given him the room number, otherwise he might have been held back again or told only relatives were allowed. The elevator doors opened up just as he got there. He stepped inside and hit the number four button several times.

"Who are you going to see?" the lady at the reception desk hollered, as she chased after him.

"A very close friend—"

The last part of the sentence was cut off by the closed doors and simply echoed within the confined elevator. Henry shifted from one foot to the other, wanting to help lift the slow elevator as it climbed past the second and third floor. His heart hammered inside his chest. Beads of perspiration formed on his forehead.

Sweat under his armpits rolled down his sides, joining the wetness of his undershirt soaked from the sweat off his back. It was as if he stepped out of the shower and put his clothes on without drying first. Exhaustion from the roller coaster of emotions was closing in. He breathed deeply to ward off a dizzy spell.

Finally, the elevator bounced to a stop and the doors opened none too soon. Cool air from the air conditioner on the fourth floor gushed into the stuffy elevator, offering Henry some relief. He grabbed the lapels of his jacket with both hands and flapped them back and forth. Along with the cool blasts of air to his face and chest came a growing nervousness.

"What if she doesn't recognize me or is upset with me for not writing?" Hopefully she got his letter like he got hers. He recalled Mr. Sarsky's secretary saying she sent his letter to Jenny at the same time.

One thought after another buzzed through his mind...

He shivered.

Only one nurse seemed to be on duty at the nurse's station and she was busy writing something behind the raised counter. Henry slowed down and tried to soften his footsteps, checking the room numbers as he proceeded down the hall. Room 453 was just to his right so room 455 must be at the end of the hall.

As he passed the station, he sped up. The nurse looked up and called out, "Sir, excuse me, sir."

Henry pretended not to hear her and quickened his pace as much as he could. He heard her bumping into her desk and a chair tipping over. To see Jenny was his mission, he'd deal with the protocol of patient visits later. He read the number outside the room: 455.

As he turned in, another nurse was coming out carrying linen. Henry bumped into her, almost knocking her over in the doorway.

"Oh, I am so sorry," he whispered.

He rushed into the room and looked over to the bed.

Instant panic swept through him. He staggered backwards and bumped into the nurse from the nurse's station who had finally caught up to him.

"Oh no," Henry cried, "I'm too late."

His heart thumped, ready to burst. The sight of seeing an empty bed was too much...

Jenny was gone!

CHAPTER TWO

"WHERE IS THE morgue?" He demanded, hoping he could still touch Jenny's hand, or kiss her lips before the warmth left her body. The nurse who burst in was ready to scold him, but rather put her hand on his arm. She could see Henry was on the verge of panic.

"It's okay, sir, she is not in the morgue."

Before the nurse could go on, he blurted out, "Where is she, then!?"

"Please calm down sir. She was taken to the Grey Nuns' Hospital early this morning and placed in palliative care. Are you a relative?"

"She is not dead then?" Henry asked, not answering her question.

"She is gravely ill, but was still functioning when she left this morning."

"Then I must get over there, right away." He turned towards the door. The nurse he bumped into on the way in was standing near the door holding the linen in her arms.

"I'm so sorry for barging in like that, I hope you are fine."

11

"Yes, I am fine, but who are you?"

"Oh, I am… I am Jenny's boyfriend," Henry said, as he rushed out of the door.

"You're the second person within a half-hour who was trying to locate Ms. Hamilton, that first one claiming she was her daughter!"

Henry only heard part of what the nurse said as he ran down the hall.

The two nurses stepped out of the bedroom into the hallway and saw Henry frantically hitting the elevator button. The older of the two rolled her eyes in disbelief, "It's a little too late for romance, isn't it?"

CHAPTER THREE

FATHER TURNED OFF the light switch in his room and walked out of his bedroom. He was about to make his morning calls to all of his brothers and sisters in Christ, as he did every morning. The care home attendants sometimes referred to him as Doctor Sunshine. Not only did he exude an aura of light, the words he prescribed shone into everyone's spirits, lighting them up with radiance. One could immediately tell if Father had visited one of the residents by the smile and light in their eyes.

"My gosh Father, you sure look handsome and debonair this morning," said Nurse Frowler. "And that yellow geranium in your lapel…wow!"

"Thank you, Dianne, I just feel it's the right time to get dressed up a bit. This is going to be a special day for me."

"Oh, what is happening?"

"I'm not sure yet, but we shall see. You have a nice day now, and I just want to say how proud I am of you, by the way you look over all your sheep. You are so caring, and the Lord will bless you richly for that."

"Why, thank you, Father. I really do love them all."

"Yes, it shows and they feel it too. They are always a little sad when you have your two days off. They immediately miss the love you give them."

Dianne's face turned a little pink as she blushed over Father's outpouring of good words.

"Well, thank you again Father. That sure makes my day."

"And mine too, just to see your smiling face."

Dianne's face turned even rosier.

Father walked down the hallway towards the chapel, stopping at each room for a brief moment. When he came to Edith's room he stopped at the doorway and peered in to see her sitting in her chair. Edith was perhaps his favourite resident, if he was cornered to admit to having one. She was in her nineties and still very spry. He loved the way she would go on and on, always friendly, kind and of good cheer. Her face was covered with laugh lines and over the years, they had worked their way over the rest of her body that seemed to jiggle along with her laughing. All of the exposed skin on her neck, hands and arms was shriveled and wrinkled. She reminded Father of a raisin. He smiled only briefly at the thought and then quickly reflected compassion. He could see she was not in good humour.

"Good morning, Edith, how is that tooth abscess?"

"Oh Father, not too well," she replied, holding her hand to the side of her cheek.

Father divined her suffering. He could see the pain in her eyes and walked over to her side. "The Lord will heal this Edith, trust in Him with all your heart. Perhaps He wants you to suffer like He does, for all the sins of mankind. Offer your pain and sorrow up to Him."

Father raised his hand and put it against her hand that was favouring her cheek. "Oh, heavenly Father, You have told us that where two or three are gathered in Your name, that you will be present amongst us. We ask you to accept the pain and suffering of our sister, Edith, and offer it up to You, that it may not go in vain. But we now ask You, Father, to heal our sister.

"Give her peace and rest. Fill her to overflowing with Your love. I ask You, Jesus, in Your name and by Your stripes that You heal our sister. We ask this, Father, and we trust in Your mercy. Thank You, Father." Father Engelmann then made the sign of the cross over Edith's hand just outside the abscessed tooth.

"Thank you, Father. I do believe it is feeling better."

"Thank you, Jesus," said Father. "Just trust in Him, Edith, He won't let you down. I will see you at Mass this morning; we will sing praise and glory to our Father. He is all good and holy."

"Yes, I am looking forward to the Mass, Father, it starts my day out so nice."

Father winked at Edith, turned and left.

"Good morning Johnny, know how to play that new song, yet?"

"No problem, Father, it came to me as easy as pie. I'll play it at Bible study later this morning. Hey, what's with the new duds, going to a wedding?"

Father smiled, "Yes, I just might be."

"What do you mean 'might be'?"

Father kept on smiling, like the cat that swallowed the canary. He just winked, raised his hand and waved as he strolled along, "See you at Mass, Johnny."

"Wouldn't miss it for the world, Padre."

Father's presence in the care home was a godsend. The transformation that took place was almost immediately miraculous. Many of the residents, who would normally just sit around, watch a little TV and sleep most of the day, were now fully awake, raring to go. It was like they had discovered the secret of youth. Most of them seemed years younger, more alert than they had been for years and years. Prayer at all meal times, Mass every morning, Bible study and singing daily, alternating between morning and afternoon, were activities that rejuvenated their hearts. In between, were exercises and crafts that the care home provided, further stimulating their lives.

In addition to all that, they had established a buddy system, where one resident of better health and mobility would look after another less able. It not only helped out the staff, but by the end of day, the residents were really tired, not out of boredom or to hurry to their death, but really honest to goodness tired from the day's activities.

Perhaps what was most beneficial was the increased human contact. The neighbours who initially came for the Mass, were so overtaken by the residents that they stayed to visit afterwards and became good friends. As well, more and more relatives and children were visiting due to Father's tours and speeches and the monthly magazine. As Johnny would say, "Boy, things are really hopping around this old joint, Padre!"

After Father got everything prepared in the sacristy for the morning Mass, he went into the chapel and knelt down before the altar. He crossed himself and began to pray. There were so many needs, so much suffering. He prayed for Henry, Jenny, and Camilla that the good Lord would restore their lives and grant their wishes. He felt overwhelmed by the circumstances in their lives and knew that out of turmoil, tragedy and heartache, some good had to come.

Finally, Father prayed for people to replace him, to take charge and keep up what had been started. After almost an hour of praising and thanking the Lord for His blessings and mercy, Father sensed it was time for breakfast. The clock on the wall proved him to be correct. He once again crossed himself, genuflected, and walked out of the chapel.

He heard the loud chattering as he approached the dining room. Father liked to hear his sheep babbling. It was healthy. He even enjoyed it when two or three of them would get into a heated discussion. A little anger and passion was good for the soul. It got the blood moving.

When Father walked in, everyone was present and seated. As soon as they saw him, howling, hooting, and whistling erupted. Angie dropped an egg in the kitchen and ran into the room to see what was going on. She'd never heard such carousing.

"Are you all drinking orange juice or what?!" she asked, with a chuckle.

"So Father, what's the occasion?" asked Helen.

"Yes Father, what's going on?" others asked as well, almost in unison. All attention was focused on Father and his different attire.

There was a long silence. Father didn't know what to say, he had an idea of what was going on, but wasn't certain. Also, he didn't want to alarm anyone.

"You haven't found a girlfriend, have you?" Johnny blurted out, breaking the ice and giving Father an answer to everyone's interest in his tan suit.

"Yes, yes, Johnny, that's right. I was thinking about my sweetheart. Next week will be our anniversary. If my wife Anna were alive, we would be celebrating our 78th anniversary."

"Oh my," muttered several of the residents.

"I thought I would try out the wedding suit I wore when we married, to see if it still fits."

"Well, it looks great on you, Father. You are a very handsome man," said Angie, as she turned and went back to kitchen. Not a moment too late as one of the frying pans was overheating and a little smoke drifted out into the dining room. She almost slipped on the broken egg on the floor as well.

Johnny's remarks seemed to pacify everyone's interest in the suit and before any more prodding took place, Father said, "Let us say grace.

"In the name of the Father and the Son and the Holy Spirit...," Father began.

The Catholic residents crossed themselves like Father, while the three or four of them who weren't Catholic politely and respectively bowed their heads and brought their hands together in prayer.

"Dear heavenly Father, we ask you to bless the food our sister Angie has so lovingly prepared..."

Angie rushed in again just as Father got started.

"And, oh Father, I specially ask You to pour out Your blessings on us all. Help us to realize how important each and every one of us is to each other. Help us all to look after one another and not wait for others to start. Let us all take initiative. We are all so capable and each of us has something to offer. There are so many needs, so much hurt and suffering, give us the strength and fortitude to do Your will. We are all leaders, all capable of taking charge in some way. Grant us, oh Lord, to be beacons, not only for this day, but for the rest of each and every one of our days that You give us. We ask this, Jesus, in Your name. Amen. In the name of the Father and the Son and the Holy Spirit."

Father said the prayer with such fervour and pleading that a long silence fell over the room. If it had not been for Johnny, perhaps more people at the table might have figured out what Father was trying to say.

"Hey, Angie, let's get on with it, I'm starving and I need a lot of energy to play that piano, you know, and keep up with all these teenagers!"

"Yeah, yeah, just for that outburst, you will be served last," countered Angie, as she scurried back into the kitchen.

Everyone unfolded their napkins and adjusted their chair in preparation for breakfast; everyone, except Margaret. She reached her hand out towards Father. Father saw it coming and extended his hand towards hers. Not everyone noticed or heard the exchange which followed when their hands touched one another.

"I shall miss you dearly, Father."

They just stared at one another as tears welled up in their eyes.

Chapter Four

Henry dashed out of the elevator and raced past the reception desk, towards the front door. The receptionist had called security and was talking to the commissionaire.

"There he is," called the nurse, pointing her finger at Henry, as he rushed by.

"It's okay, I am just leaving. I have the wrong hospital...sorry."

Henry ran to his SUV, clicking the unlock button from at least twenty feet away. He jumped into the truck and fumbled with the keys. Finally, he inserted the right one and the SUV roared to life. The tires squealed as he backed out of the parking stall and screeched again as the SUV thrust forward.

As he headed north on Elphinstone Street, the first intersection was a four-way stop. Two other cars, one heading east and the other west, arrived just seconds before he did. Just as they proceeded to enter the intersection, Henry pressed on the gas to beat them. They slammed on their brakes just inches away from Henry's SUV. Horns blared as he slithered between them, like a fish wiggling between two rocks. He dared not look either way, just kept going as fast as he dared to go. He was in a race, not just against time...but death itself.

The speedometer read eighty kilometers per hour as he approached another car inching its way down the street. Normally he wouldn't pass a car on an outside lane on a residential street, but the other driver was just going too slow, totally out of sync with his revved up body. Henry could sense his guardian angel cautioning him to slow down, but the desire to get to Jenny was too overpowering. Without further thought, Henry swerved out into the other lane to pass the car just as they both approached another intersection. Suddenly, Julean stood on the road in front of him, the palm of her right hand was raised, signaling him to stop. He slammed on the brakes just in time. He closed his eyes and cringed as the screeching vehicle passed through her and came to a stop. When Henry dared to open his eyes, a frightened elderly lady gazed at him with fear written all over her face. Henry suddenly realized why the car next to him was going so slow. The elderly lady was walking across the crosswalk. A quick glance at the driver told the story. He was glaring disgustedly at Henry, shaking his head. Henry tried to look apologetically at him, but it was all for not. The driver's lingering expression of disapproval, told Henry he was not accepting his plea for vindication.

"Oh, my God." It came to Henry that he had seen this scene before - that day when Jenny crossed Victoria Avenue and a blue Chev pulled out from behind a slowing van. The man in the Chevy was impatient, too. Jenny should have been killed and the lady in front of him shaking her cane might have been as well if it hadn't been for her guardian angel.

"Oh, thank you dear guardian and Julean…" Henry whispered as he wiped his brow with the back of his hand. The thought of harming the elderly lady would have been devastating!

As soon as the pedestrian crossed the street, Henry hit the gas and sped away, but more cautiously. In less than 30 seconds he had caught up to the slow driver, again. He was so tempted to overtake the other driver once more, but this time heeded the prompting of his protector. The driver ahead of him slowed further, aggravating Henry all the more. Finally the driver signaled to turn at the next intersection. Henry dared not look, as he sped past him. He could only imagine what he was thinking and saying. The worry and fear that he might be too late to see Jenny alive, was his only justification for risking such reckless driving.

"Get a hold of yourself." Henry chastised himself as he sped along. He hoped the police officer that gave him a warning less than half an hour ago wasn't in the vicinity.

"Hang on, Jenny, I'm coming."

Absently he thrust out his hand almost waiting for her command, "Quickly hold my hand."

Please, God, keep her alive, please, heal her. We've waited so long for this. The thought made him think about Father Engelmann. If anyone can get a miracle he can. Henry grabbed his car phone and while glancing up and down as he drove, dialed the number. The phone rang and rang, but there was no answer.

AFTER A HEARTY breakfast, one by one, the residents rose, picked up their plate and cutlery and took it into the kitchen. Ever since Father started to say Mass in the chapel, everyone wanted to attend, including the cook and other staff. To speed things up and help the kitchen staff clean up, everyone pitched in.

"Service to others is what the Lord wants," Father preached almost daily. "We are servants and helpers to the Lord. Every thought, word and deed we perform either helps or hinders creating a better world. And as we each give to one another we become more loving and kinder."

The residents were always on time for Mass. In fact, many of them came earlier to lift up special intentions and prayers for the world . Also, if they didn't arrive on time, they would have to sit at the back, as many neighbours in the community began attending too, and wanted to be up close. Word quickly spread how this elderly priest was transforming the care home and how loving he was. Many people nicknamed him 'Pope Engelmann the First.'

Johnny was already at the piano.

Father prayed with fervour as he began to say Mass, calling everyone to service, that they all needed the Lord's strength and guidance. He was trying to prepare his flock for his eventual departure and that they could get along without him. Father knew that this might very well be his last Mass at the Lord's altar.

HENRY TRIED SEVERAL more times to reach Father and finally concluded he must already be in the chapel saying Mass. He hated to disrupt Mass, but Henry considered this a spiritual emergency. He called the main number for the care home.

"Nunnery Care Home, this is Dianne, how may I help you?"

"Hi, Dianne, it's Henry. Father Engelmann may be in the chapel saying Mass. I really need to speak to him. Would you please call him to the phone? It's urgent."

"Oh my, I think Mass must be just about over. I will go check right away!"

Henry heard the receiver clang on the desk and running footsteps recede.

Without realizing it, his speedometer approached seventy. It was way too fast and he knew better. He swerved back into his lane suddenly realizing how far he had drifted over.

"Come on, Father, please hurry." After what seemed like an eternity, he finally heard voices and footsteps approaching.

"Yes, thank you, Dianne. Hello, Henry, what is it?"

"They have moved Jenny to an intensive care unit at the Grey Nuns' Hospital, I'm on my way there now. I'm sorry to interrupt your Mass, but I need your prayers. I think I'll die if Jenny were gone before I get there. Pray she stays alive, pray for healing…"

"Yes, yes, Henry I will pray, all of us here will pray. Just be careful and don't drive so fast; just slow down. Dear Father in heaven, let Henry know You hear his prayers, all of our prayers and that You are always there ready to help."

Father's words comforted Henry and he eased up on the accelerator. Finally he caught his breath. Father could sense it. "Yes, that's good, Henry, slow down, everything will work out fine. Trust in the Lord with all your heart and don't lean unto your own understanding."

Henry recognized the Scripture Father was quoting and began to repeat it. "Yes, Father, I know I need to trust Him. I'm just about at the hospital. Oh, Father, pray for me, for us, for a miracle. I will call you later as soon as I am able to."

"Yes, Henry, I am anxious to know what happens."

"I am too Father. Bye for now."

"Yes, good-bye, Henry. Say hello to Jenny for me," Father added, trying to be optimistic that Jenny would be still alive.

Fortunately, the traffic was light. Henry only had to wait for one set of lights as he arrived at the corner of Elphinstone and Dewdney Avenue. He turned left on the green arrow and ignored Father's advice to slow down. Fortunately, no pedestrians or police were nearby. Within seconds he was at the hospital, pumping his brakes enough to slow and turn into the parking lot.

There was a line up at the pay station. Rather than get into line, he sped past to the emergency entrance and parked his car in the ten minute drop off area next to the entrance. He knew he would be longer than 10 minutes, but was willing to pay a ticket, even have his vehicle towed away.

This was an emergency.

In a sense, he was dropping himself off. Bordering on a heart attack, feeling a stab of pain grip his heart, should his dear sweet Jenny no longer be alive.

CHAPTER FIVE

ATHER WAS VERY concerned about Henry after he hung up the phone. He rushed back to the chapel. The residents were deep in prayer when he returned. They were seated in a semi-circle around the front of the altar. Father felt like a teacher with a group of elementary school children before him. They were all so obedient, so kind, so polite, so childlike, and so eager to help.

'Unless you become like a child, you will not be able to enter the kingdom of heaven,' flashed into Father's mind, as he gazed at the class before him.

Father had just been ready to give the final blessing before he was interrupted by Henry's call. He decided to tell his flock of the urgent need to pray for a special healing. He began by sharing the incredible story about Henry and Jenny. How they met when they were young, how they were separated and kept apart; how their love letters to each other were kept from them time after time and destroyed. Yet despite others' efforts to keep them apart, despite the passage of time and even their marriage to other mates, still, in the recesses of their hearts was a first love that just would not fade away.

Then, Father shared the almost unbelievable angelic occurrence of how Henry recently bought a house which included all of the belongings and furniture of the previous owner. And, how over the past few months he began to discover that he actually bought his sweetheart's home. He told them about Henry's evidence that confirmed that the lady he bought the house from was really his childhood sweetheart, his first love.

Unfortunately, she was now in the hospital dying of cancer. Henry was rushing over to see her and he just called to ask them to pray to keep her alive. He so much wanted to see her.

Father also told them of Jenny's desire and wish that she be kissed by Henry before she died. How fervently she prayed to her guardian angel to grant her this last wish. He told them that he had known of her prayer for weeks, but didn't know until today that the lady he had been visiting was Henry's teenage sweetheart. Father's voice pled with the Lord as he told his brothers and sisters in Christ the incredible narrative.

There wasn't one of them that weren't moved after Father finished his story. It was like a fairy tale that deeply touched the hearts and minds of everyone in the room. It made them recall their first love, their affairs, their lovers, and thoughts which some of them still entertained. Father knew that their age was no detriment to their understanding of passion and the yearnings of love. What was inside was as real and as alive and as young as the day they were born.

Romance and passion is timeless, ageless. He saw it in their eyes.

Many cried; some were angry that Jenny's parents had destroyed the letters and over the various circumstances that kept them apart. And everyone was amazed at how, in the end, they were brought back together in this inconceivable way, guided by their guardian angels.

When Father summoned them to pray for a miracle to keep Jenny alive, they all took this task seriously and began to pray with a fervour Father had never witnessed before. Henry could not have asked for a more seasoned group to pray for him and his beloved. They were not timorous or novices in this business with the Lord. Their faith was like tinder ever ready to be inflamed with spiritual power. Father knew the kindling his warriors were made of and the childlike faith they possessed, completely devoid of doubt. And no sooner had he begun to fire them up with the Lord's words than their faith began to smolder.

A holy fragrance like incense lifted and infused the air.

"Oh, Lord," Father prayed. "What things so ever ye desire, when ye pray, believe that ye receive them, and ye shall have them. We lift our sister, Jenny, up to you and thank you for restoring her body."

"Yes, yes, we thank You, Lord," many of the residents chimed in.

"In Matthew 9:29 we are assured that nothing shall be impossible unto you—"

"Yes, Lord, You alone are all powerful—"

"And Mark 9:23 confirms that if thou canst believe, nothing shall be impossible unto you."

"Yes, Yahweh. Hallelujah, Lord," they rejoiced. "We thank you for healing our sister, Jenny." Many were already praising in tongues and lifting their arms.

"We know that according to your faith it will be done unto you," Father continued. "Our faith is complete, we trust in Your word—"

"Praise you, Jesus. We thank You, Jesus," Edith chimed in. "You have come to give us life and give it abundantly. We claim your promises—"

"Where two or three are gathered in Your name You shall be amongst us. We feel Your presence."

"Hallelujah…"

"And John 15:7 says, "If ye abide in me, and my words abide in you, ye shall ask what ye will, and it shall be done unto you."

With each Scripture Father and the various members quoted, the spiritual power inherent within the words infused their spirits, taking possession of their very essence. The powerful force in their exuding faith was palpable; the air vibrated between them.

But it was the words of Mark 11:22-23 that brought them all to their feet.

"Verily, I say unto you," Father boldly commanded, "Whosoever shall say unto this mountain, be thou removed, and be thou cast into the sea, and shall not doubt in his heart, but shall believe that those things which he saith shall come to pass, he shall have whatsoever he saith!"

The response from his warriors was instant and wholeheartedly resounding. The hurricane of praise, singing, and rejoicing was deafening. It threatened to lift the very roof off the chapel!

CHAPTER SIX

ANGIE LOOKED UP at the monitor and then at Peter. She held his hand as he laboriously breathed his last breaths. His two children, mother and several friends were circled around the bed. The doctor said Peter was in the dying moments of his life...a matter of minutes. Several of his organs had already shut down and a bluish tinge covered his once robust ruddy skin.

"Angelika where are you...? Peter uttered as his hand searched for his dear wife's hand.

Angie immediately clutched his, "I am here, Peter. You haven't called me by my full name in a long time."

"I have always loved your name. You have always been an angel to me...so accepting of my faults."

"You are too hard on yourself, Peter. There is no other man that could have made my life more complete. And, yes, I do like it when you call me by my Christian name rather than the way my friends have shortened it."

Peter squeezed Angie's hand and squirmed painfully more of a guilt ridden conscience than of the physical body. He began to mutter...

Angie strained to hear his last words.

"Forgive me, Jenny, for what I did. I pray you find our daughter and she forgives me too…Oh, Father, I have sinned so grievously…"

"Peter, the Lord has forgiven you. You above all people should know the Lord's compassion and endless mercy. A sincere repentant heart is always heard by the Father. He erases our transgressions and forgets these sins. They will never be used in our final judgment."

Tears emerged from Peter's eyes and rolled down his cheeks. "…it was good for the Lord to let me see my daughter. I know it is Camilla, Henry's daughter-in-law. It eases the pain in my heart when Henry told you that Camilla thinks she was adopted. My heart and soul told me that it was so even though she claimed other parents…"

His blood pressure was falling. The monitor recording his heart beat was faltering…a steady line showed, but then a blip and then another. Peter strained to utter what could be his final words…

"Angelika, it is right for you and the children to know Camilla and include her in our family. She has the right to know her father and step-family…thank you for accepting my past and the child that I fathered…without you and your love I would have died a long time ago…"

The blip on the monitor fell and a steady line ran across the screen…then a blip came back. It was hopeful for but a moment…

Chapter Seven

"OH, JENNY, PLEASE hang on," Henry repeated as he ran towards the emergency entrance of the Grey Nuns' Hospital. His heart was thumping, ready to burst.

The doors automatically opened and he ran through them into the large, open lobby. Immediately, off to his left, was the admittance office. He knew he would have to go there first as he didn't have a clue where intensive care was or even if Jenny was still alive. The lady at the desk looked up at him as he anxiously asked what room Jenny Hamilton was in. She quickly scanned the sheets in front of her as she ran her finger down the list.

"I don't seem to have a Jenny Hamilton, but I do see a Marjorie Hamilton was admitted this morning."

"Yes, yes, that's it! What is the number?"

"She is in palliative care, unit Five West, room 505. Take the elevator at the end of the hall. Here, I will write it on a slip of paper for you." She picked up a pen and began to write the number, but Henry was long gone, already at the elevator, mashing the button.

Finally, after what seemed like an eternity, the elevator doors opened and he dashed inside. He didn't realize when he stepped into the elevator it was going down and so instead of taking him up towards Jenny's room, he descended towards the morgue and file storage in the lower level.

"For God's sake, I hope this isn't an omen of where Jenny is!" Henry muttered as he repeatedly pressed five. Finally, it started to go up and climbed non-stop to Jenny's floor.

Henry stepped into the foyer and looked for direction. A large sign on the wall in front of him read:

> PLEASE REPORT TO THE
> RECEPTIONIST DESK
> BEFORE VISITING ANY
> PATIENT ON THIS FLOOR.

Just below and off to his right were two other signs. Rooms 501-505 was on one of the signs and pointed to the left. He didn't bother reading the other sign. He turned down the hallway and ran straight ahead towards the nurse's station.

"Uh, oh. How do I get past this one?"

As he approached the station, he didn't see anyone. He could use that as an excuse and go directly to Jenny's room. He rushed past the station to room 505 near the end of the hallway to his right.

His heart raced in anticipation, in addition to exertion. This was the moment he had waited for, for so long. He only wished it weren't under these circumstances. A mixture of emotions— fear, anxiety, excitement, wonder, exhilaration— swept through as he stood at the door. Would she even recognize him? He had changed, lost most of his hair...probably looked so ragged...

For Pete's sake, just go in!

Henry inhaled deeply and as he was about to enter, a nurse emerged from room 504 across the hall and saw him.

"Excuse me, sir," she said, as she reached his side. "I'm sorry, but you're not allowed to go in there. Did you check in at the nurse's station?"

"Nobody was there and since I knew the number to Jenny Hamilton's room, I thought I would let myself in."

"Are you a relative of Ms. Hamilton?"

"No, I am not, but I am a very close friend. In fact, I once was her boyfriend," Henry added, thinking that would bear more weight.

He was wrong.

The nurse studied him for a moment and then said, "Would you please come with me to the counter?"

"But, I have to see Jenny before it's too late." Henry pleaded.

"Only her husband or immediate family is allowed to go in there. Please come with me."

The nurse turned and walked to the station. Reluctantly, Henry followed. Once there, the nurse took out a form from atop of her desk and a pen from her pocket. "What is your name, please?"

"It's Henry…Henry Pederson."

"And you say you are her boyfriend?"

"Yes, that's correct." he answered abruptly. Here Jenny was dying in room 505 and he was being interrogated with these mundane questions.

"Please, nurse," he gasped, "I must see Jenny. How is she? Will she make it through the day?" He stared at her with a look of pleading and grave concern on his face.

"As I said, Mr. Pederson, only her husband or relatives are allowed."

"But, I bought her house and I now know who she is…"

"I'm sorry, but rules are rules. They are for the benefit of the patient."

"But, you don't understand, I am her boyfriend, we probably should have been married…"

Henry wasn't thinking clearly anymore and he could tell by the look on the nurse's face that what he was saying didn't make any sense. Time was wasting and he really didn't want to get into the whole scenario of buying her house and discovering Jenny's diary and so on, so he kept emphasizing that he was her friend and possible boyfriend.

"What do you mean possible boyfriend? Are you or are you not?"

Frustration and anger were pushing at the urgent feelings swarming inside of him. Jenny was dying and here he was caught amongst hospital rules and regulations and he didn't know how to quickly resolve it all and get to Jenny's room.

"Look, I bought Ms. Hamilton's house and she turned out to be the same person who was my girlfriend over thirty years ago and I know she is critically ill and I have to see her…can't you understand?"

"Thirty years ago!" she said in disbelief.

"That's right. There isn't time to explain it all to you. I know this sounds ridiculous, but this is just one of those rare circumstances in life."

Just then, an older, more mature nurse walked into the station. She wore a different coloured hat and Henry noticed that in addition to her name, Nurse Johnson, her name tag also identified her as the supervisor.

"What's going on here, Elsie? Is there a problem?"

Elsie motioned the head nurse to the side. Henry could hear them whispering back and forth and every now and then Nurse Johnson would look up at him. Finally, the head nurse gazed at Henry and gave him one of those analyzing, dissecting stares and walked over to him. The expression she wore appeared understanding and hopefully...relenting.

"You're Mr. Pederson, the artist, aren't you?"

"Yes," he replied, looking somewhat embarrassed in the position he found himself in. Yet, he was relieved in a sense that his notoriety might be helpful in this case.

"I've been into your shop many times and I just love it there."

"Thank you," Henry said, and instantly got the conversation back to the urgency of the matter at hand. "Could you please make an exception in this case, Ms. Johnson?" Henry asked more personally, hoping that might carry some weight. "I know this all sounds so strange, but I just have to see Jenny."

"You mean, Marjorie?"

"Yes, Marjorie, Jenny, they are both the same person!"

"Are you related to a Camilla Pederson?"

Now what? What on earth does my family history have to do with this? Time is wasting.

"Yes, yes, she is my daughter-in-law." Henry blurted, revealing his impatience.

"Well, she came in minutes before you did claiming that she just learned that Ms. Hamilton is her birth mother and had to see her, as well."

"What!?" Henry's expression changed from frustration and pleading, to puzzlement, then wonderment. He recalled his conversation with Father Engelmann earlier when they contemplated such a remote possibility. This entire matter was getting crazier and more unbelievable by the minute.

Nurse Johnson looked at her colleague and said something which not only interrupted Henry's thoughts, but got his immediate attention.

"His first name seems to fit the letter, as well."

"What name? What letter?"

"Well, when Ms. Hamilton came in this morning, she refused all medication and life support, all she requested was that I read a letter to her. It was a lovely letter and it was signed by a '*Henry*.' She studied Henry, her expression asking for a response.

"Yes, yes, that's me. It was a letter I sent to her just before Christmas in 1956, along with a pewter angel."

"That's right! The entire time I was reading the letter she was squeezing a metal angel at the end of a chain around her neck—"

"Don't you see, I just have to see her? Please, may I go in?"

"Follow me."

Nurse Johnson turned and led Henry to Jenny's room. She turned into room 505 and held the door open for Henry. His racing heart threatened to choke him. He reached up with his hand and brushed the few hairs on his head to straighten them. Of all times to be concerned about his appearance; he knew he looked wilted.

Would he recognize his Jenny?

As his eyes adjusted to the soft lighting, a tiny figure outlined the sheets on the bed. There were no tubes coming in or out of her body. The blue bandana she was wearing had slipped off her head revealing sparse golden wheat hair. The blue bandana immediately triggered a memory. He had seen a similar one before... yes, the person being wheeled out of the care home on a gurney by ambulance attendants the day he brought Father Engelmann to the Nunnery. He had touched the person's hand as the stretcher went by and had felt such a surge of electricity flow through his body. He had often wished he would have taken a closer look at who that person was. He wondered now if...

Henry stared at his beloved. There was no mistaking it...

It was Jenny.

She appeared in perfect peace and calm, just waiting for her Maker to come and take her home.

Henry's heart immediately went out to her—

"Dad, you came too!?" asked Camilla, as she got up from a chair near the side of Jenny's bed.

Henry was so focused on seeing Jenny, he had forgotten that his daughter-in-law was also in the room.

"Oh my God, Camilla, is…is Jenny really your birth mother?"

Camilla nodded, tears in her eyes. "Yes…she is my mother. I just found out yesterday."

Henry heard part of what she said, but his mind could not cope with that issue at this time. He was immediately drawn back to Jenny and overtaken by the sight of her.

There she lay like a dream that had finally come true.

Camilla stepped back making room for Henry to get closer to the bed. Her mind was buzzing with so many questions. The most urgent of them all was, *was Henry her father?*

Both Matti and Chloe were on the other side of the room so Camilla moved to the foot of bed. Matti could see the sorrow and worry in Camilla's face. Even though she had just met Camilla, Matti instinctively moved to her side and put her arm around the troubled girl.

Camilla started to ask Henry the question burning in her mind, but then was overtaken by the expression growing on his face…

Henry had moved into another world. He was totally oblivious to all the women in the room… except his Jenny.

The ladies watched on in awe as Henry sat on the chair next to Jenny and took her hand into his.

Camilla wondered what the connection was.

Nurse Johnson saw Camilla's bewilderment and went over to her and whispered, "Apparently they were teenage sweethearts and haven't see each other in thirty years."

Camilla had discovered that, but just to hear it now in this critical moment sent her reeling. "Oh my gosh, could it possibly…!?" Camilla tried to muffle her voice with her hand as she looked at Henry and her birth mother. The deep love between them was palpable. Henry must be her real father and…that would make Jeremy, *her half-brother*!

Matilda could feel Camilla's growing anxiety. She drew her in closer trying to calm her trembling. Matti was still unaware of what was troubling Camilla besides just discovering her real mother in this condition.

"Oh, Jenny," Henry slipped his other hand under hers; an indescribable exchange of love flowed between them that required no words.

It was spiritual.

A light surrounded them like the day they met and gazed into each other's eyes.

"Good Lord," muttered Matilda.

If only he could pick his beloved up, hold her and make her well. He ached to kiss her, hug her, and tell her how deeply he loved her.

After all these years it had come down to this. Their love, always thwarted by someone or some event or circumstance, was now threatened again as death beckoned at the door, waiting to separate them once and for all. Tears welled up in Henry's eyes and he began to sob; sorrow for Jenny and himself overtook him. If only he had learned earlier that Jenny was free they could have spent so much time together these past few months.

Jenny's breathing slowed. Camilla gasped and the other ladies shuffled as if to brace themselves.

Matti whispered, "Now Jesus, You do Your healin'…I be counting on You!"

Regret that he had not come sooner compounded the pity Henry was feeling. All that was left was precious moments, perhaps a minute or two at the most.

Chapter Eight

THE DIRECTOR OF the Nunnery Care Home was sitting in her office finishing some paper work, when she heard chanting. As soon as she opened her office door, she heard an electrifying sound— a strange humming filled with a static charge.

What on earth is going on? I hope Father isn't going overboard.

Doris strode down the hall to the chapel. Though she was a Catholic, over the years she had fallen away from her faith and hadn't been into a church for a very long time. To show her neutrality and acceptance of all denominations, she even refrained from going into the chapel. Now she regretted not attending at least once in awhile; perhaps she could have been alerted to potential problems.

As Doris approached the chapel, something stirred deep within her. A pulsating glow emanated from the doorway, like flickering bright candles. The charge in the atmosphere pulled her, tingled her skin, raising the hair on her arms. She slowed down, afraid to go on, yet compelled to do so. It was as though she were being drawn by a powerful magnet and unable to escape its field. The closer she drew, the louder the singing and chanting became, the brighter the light glowed and the more irresistible the attraction.

Cautiously, she peeked in. The light in the air enveloped her and welled up within her being. The chapel she knew of before was gone. She was entering holy ground. Instantly she was uplifted and awestruck by the scene in front of her.

Father and his warriors were surrounded by a shimmering aura of holiness. The nimbus hovering atop the heads of Father and Edith was exceptionally bright. Their faces shone with brilliant luster; sacred flames leapt from their eyes. Some were dancing, others singing and praying in tongues, and still others almost insane with praise. It was as though they were drunk without wine, totally immersed in a mad rapture.

Many who could barely raise their hands to feed themselves were free of their arthritic pain and tossed and waved their arms about as joyous children playing and dancing in a schoolyard. Johnny was out of his wheelchair and so deliriously happy, he was jumping on the canvas seat of his chair trying to thrust himself higher to his Lord.

They had thrown their hearts out of the bounds assigned to mankind and onto the doorstep of heaven. They were filled with the power of the Holy Spirit. Just a little further, Doris thought, they would mount up with wings as angels and fly into the celestial air. The entire holy assembly had transcended ordinary existence and entered the kingdom of God with perfect faith and belief and expectancy that their prayers would be heard and answered.

As this ethereal vision swept over Doris, she was instantly smitten by the Holy Spirit. Her legs forthwith gave way and she fell to her knees. Holiness washed over her and unbidden tears streamed forth like a gushing waterfall. Strange, wonderful, incredibly melodious sounds bubbled out of her rapidly moving lips. Praise and thanksgiving filled her mind and heart as tears of joy streamed down her cheeks. She raised her arms and outstretched them towards heaven.

"Thank You, thank You, Lord," she cried. Her life flashed before her. She saw how far she had fallen short and yet the Lord had given her a glimpse of what awaited those who loved and served Him. Doris bowed her head in worship and then prostrated herself on the floor before her Holy God in outpouring gratefulness for his infinite mercy and forgiveness.

CHAPTER NINE

M ATTI CONTINUED TO hold Camilla at the foot of Jenny's bed. Chloe stood quietly sobbing at the head of the bed, her hand touching her beloved auntie's shoulder. Henry sat on the other side of the bed holding his dear sweet Jenny's hand.

Nurse Johnson looked on at the moving love scene reunion before her. She had witnessed many deaths and sorrowful scenes, but this touched her toughened heart. Nurse Johnson was moved to tears, as well. She was going to suggest they all leave to allow Ms. Hamilton to rest. But Jenny was already in a coma and their presence wasn't invasive. Besides, having loved ones near her as she left this earth would be more comforting. Nurse Johnson always felt that people in a coma were more alert and awake than was thought.

The warm light coming from the lamp on the end table gently illuminated Jenny's face. Even though it was pale and sunken, Henry recognized his Jenny, his dear, sweet Jenny. Long, luscious eyelashes fanned out from resting eyes, sparse golden hair in the mellow light framed her soft oval face and her heart shaped lips still the same, drawing him. As ill as Jenny was, not even the savage attack of the cancer could take away her beauty. Yes, she was a sleeping beauty. Henry yearned to kiss her.

"Please open your eyes, Jenny," he murmured in earnest, so desiring to see and look into her soft blue eyes.

Her breathing seemed strengthened from moments ago, clear, shallow, and rhythmic, not raspy as someone ready to die. Henry was hopeful, thankful. Perhaps Father's prayers were helping. She just may come out of her coma.

Nurse Johnson was surprised to see Ms. Hamilton still alive. She didn't expect Jenny to last more than an hour or so after she'd arrived at the hospital this morning. She began to understand what it was that may be keeping this critically ill woman alive. She wanted to comfort Henry somehow, put her hand on his shoulder, but she couldn't move. The growing aura of light in the room transfixed her.

Henry looked on at his sleeping sweetheart, burning the image of her deeply into his mind, not knowing for certain how long this heavenly image would last. His swarming thoughts slowed down from all the incredible discoveries and revelations from the past two days to warm tender memories of the summer they shared, down to just his deep, deep love for his first love.

He willed for her to open her eyes, longed to hold her, ached to kiss her. Slowly he crept up from his chair and leaned forward enough to feel the warmth radiating from her skin. He so wanted to kiss her lips, but was afraid to constrict her breathing. His lips settled softly and tenderly on her forehead. A tear rolled onto her cheek. He withdrew and gently wiped the tear away with his forefinger.

"I love you, Jenny, now and forever," he whispered as soft as a cloud. A tingling sensation ran through him and through Jenny. She stirred and her eyes flickered.

Matti tightened her hold around Camilla as both quietly gasped. Chloe brought her hand to her mouth to hold back a hopeful cry...

They all could feel the ardent love flowing between the two lovers before them. The aura of light surrounding them glowed brighter. It was so intense and burning... so passionate it was palpable. The room brightened further and felt strangely, wonderfully warm; the air was charged with expectancy.

Jenny stirred again, reluctant to leave the dream she was caught in. Her heart merrily danced as Henry entered Engelmann's Grocery Store. She smiled as he hit a stack of salmon tins over the floor; this was her chance to meet him. She squatted down and picked up a tin, desiring to give it to him and gaze into his eyes…

She felt his lips on her forehead drawing her now into a reality more real than all of the dreams of her past. She dared to let go and open her eyes, but was afraid there was just emptiness. Yet, she sensed his presence and frantically searched the room, until suddenly, his green eyes gazing so lovingly into hers, came into focus. Instantly, a spiritual energy traveled the length of the gaze they shared, uniting their souls once more as it did in that incredible moment when their eyes first met and their love was born.

Chapter Ten

CAMILLA, SO TOUCHED by the reunion, let out a burst of pent up tears she could no longer hold back, breaking the spell-binding rapture they were in.

Henry smiled as he gazed into his beloved's blue sparkling eyes, still full of life even at the doorstep of death.

Jenny's face relaxed and all tension left her body as the presence of her first love swept through her.

As they gazed at each other, they were so moved, that the world around them vanished like a mist. Slowly, her lips parted and she smiled, sending Henry into ecstasy. Instantly, he recognized the smile that he so dearly loved and had burned indelibly into his mind's eye over thirty years ago.

With the soft voice of an angel, barely audible, Jenny whispered, "Oh, Henry, after all these years, you kept your promise and came back to me. I always knew you would…"

Her voice trailed off; she had expended all of her energy to utter those words. Slowly she raised her right hand and brought it to her chest just below her neck. Her fingers moved with great effort, as they made their way into the opening of her gown. A silver chain caught the light in the room and reflected back to Henry. The chain slipped through Jenny's frail, feeble fingers until she caught the dancing angel in her hand.

"I've worn it ever since the day I received it," she murmured so softly, Henry had to lip read most of the words.

"I am wearing the one I received from you too," Henry whispered back to her. The angel almost flew into his hand as he reached inside his shirt. He dangled it in front of Jenny and then brought it close to the one she was holding just inches away. Jenny released hers and also held Henry's by the end of the chain. They were identical twins, an incredible miracle that only a deep love could bring. The angels twisted and glowed and sparkled as they intertwined and kissed.

Camilla once more let out another burst of emotion.

Nurse Johnson shuffled from one foot to the other entrapped in the rapture of it all.

"Oh, Jenny, I love you so. I love you so very much." Henry whispered through tears.

"I love you, too." Jenny could only form the words with her lips.

Henry ached to hold her. He wished he could kiss her and instantly it came true.

Jenny was harbouring the same desire, revealed as she softly spoke, again. "I prayed to my guardian angel over and over again, that you would come to me and give me a kiss before I died."

Instinctively, without hesitation, he bent down, closed his eyes, his lips searching for hers, anticipating the fulfilling expression of their love that was held in abeyance for years and years. What both of them wished and prayed for over and over was about to be fulfilled. Henry felt Jenny's warm breath as she slightly parted her lips. Lovingly, he responded and ever so tenderly, gently, softly, their lips touched, sending them both into a world of utter ecstasy. It was like the kiss they had on the day Jenny told Henry she was leaving for Ottawa— the world stood still and the devastation of their impending separation momentarily vanished. The kiss was all they could remember and hold on to, to relive over and over in their minds and hearts.

But this kiss was now transcending that moment.

The blissful moment of touch they were lost in now held the dreams and hopes of two people separated in time, but desiring to be reunited, again. It was a kiss that was not forgotten, only suppressed in the recesses of their hearts. It was a touch that carried a love that could never be extinguished. A kiss relived over and over again only as a fantasy, as a dream, but now…finally…as a reality.

"See there now, the good Lord put healing power into that kiss," murmured Matti.

All those present were witnessing a rare and wonderful moment between two people deeply in love. It was hard to believe that Henry and Jenny hadn't seen each other for over thirty years. They had desired this moment so deeply, it was as if the separation of the past was crammed into but a moment of time, and their love a continuation of just yesterday; fresh as a drop of dew caressing the petal of a rose. They no longer saw Jenny as ill or about to die or Henry as an older man. The externals vanished before their eyes and what emerged was a vision of what life is all about; *the essence of happiness, joy, beauty and all that is good in God's kingdom comes from love.*

We are made out of love and for love… it is all about love.

After what seemed like an eternity, Henry withdrew his lips from Jenny's and began to straighten up. Jenny was still clutching her pewter guardian angel as she gazed at Henry.

"It was always my deepest prayer to see you and my daughter…" Then turning to the angel in her hand she whispered, "Oh, thank you, thank you for granting me my wish, my heart's desire. Perhaps I will see Camilla from a window in heaven"

"Oh, Jenny, your other wish has been granted too! Camilla is here as well."

Jenny tried to raise her head, but was unable to do so. Camilla quickly slid from Matilda's embrace and came to her mother's side next to Henry. Tears of joy flowed from their eyes as they gazed at one another. They were speechless, lost in time.

Chloe took a Kleenex and reached forward to dry Jenny's tears and then her own.

Jenny stared at her daughter and then at Henry, still finding it hard to believe that her prayers had been answered. The knuckles of her hand clutching her angel turned white as a candle.

"Oh, Camilla, I knew my guardian angel would bring you to me too. You are such a lovely lady…"

Fresh tears flowed once again as she gazed at her two loves before her. In that moment, Jenny was living what most people are only allowed to live in a whole lifetime. In spite of her grave illness, a joy, peace, and happiness spread through her. Jenny's eyes glowed and shone like a mirror.

Both Henry and Camilla saw the growing sadness of their faces reflected in Jenny's eyes. An awareness of what was about to come grew within them. An awareness that someone they so dearly loved was going away.

Henry could feel an unseen force pulling at his beloved. He had felt it before and then miraculously it left to fulfill Jenny's wishes… only to return with greater strength.

Camilla sensed it, too. She began to pray and plead with God. "Please, please, leave her here a little while longer."

"Oh sweet Lord," chimed in Matti, "You be forsaking me… no! I don't believe this…do Your healing, sweet Jesus…"

"Oh Auntie, please don't leave…" Chloe murmured. "I won't be able to bear it."

Jenny looked up towards Henry and then to her daughter, with wistful eyes yet filled with such fervent love that an inner luminosity shone through her pale face like the top of a burning candle. An aura of light enveloped her that drew both Henry and Camilla towards her. They leaned closer, their yearning trying to hold her, their tears spilling over onto her gown.

A radiant smile crossed Jenny's face. She wanted to speak, but no sound came from her lips. They did form a word that Henry was able to make out.

"Quickly…" It was a word so dear to his heart, one that he dreamed of and had so much special meaning for him.

"Hold my hand," he finished for her. He squeezed her hand which he was holding, trying desperately to keep her even though he could feel her slipping away.

"Oh, Jenny, please don't go, don't leave me, again. Oh, God, please leave her, heal her. Father Engelmann, help me, speak to God, please."

Jenny closed her eyes and she let out a long slow sigh. Her chest fell and didn't rise, again.

Jenny was gone.

Henry's heart almost stopped as he looked down upon his dear sweet Jenny. He leaned over and kissed her forehead and eyes, hoping his spirit would go with hers.

"Oh, Lord, not now," he pleaded, again. "Please, Jesus, please bring her back, please. Please. After all these years, not this, please. Oh how can You allow this?" He even dared to ask…

"Have You no heart?"

Matti cried deep within her spirit. *Oh Lord, I jus don't believe You be forsaking me.*

Chloe stepped aside as Nurse Johnson bent over and felt Jenny's wrist. Then she raised her hand to Jenny's neck and touched her artery... then shook her head, confirming what they already knew.

Camilla, overwrought by learning of her new relationship with her father-in-law, her husband, and now the untimely death of her birth mother, burst into tears, "Oh, Mom, how could you leave me... and Henry, how can you be my real father?"

Henry was so absorbed in Jenny's passing that he failed to hear his daughter-in-law's words. Matti suddenly realized Camilla's dilemma and went over to comfort her and explain...

Camilla tore away from Matti's hold and fled the room.

"That poor girl thinks Henry be her father which makes her husband her half brother." Matti turned to Chloe, "I best be going to help that child. She be one confused young lady."

As Matti made her way out of the room she hollered back, "You all don't worry none over Jen. She be coming back... I just knows it!"

Nurse Johnson shook her head and made her way over to Henry who was lost in a daze of despair. She softly whispered to Chloe, "Perhaps say your goodbye and then we best leave him."

Nurse Johnson touched Henry's shoulder, patted it and left the room.

Chloe, overcome with sorrow, bent down and buried her face in Jenny's side and wept.

Henry was unaware of Chloe's moaning. At that moment, all he felt was complete loss and utter despair, even more so than when Jenny departed for Ottawa all those years ago. Henry shut out all heaven and earth. Nothing had meaning anymore.

Chloe raised herself up and thrust her arms around Jenny. "Oh, Auntie, I will miss you so much. You were always a mother to me...Oh, Auntie, I love you...what will we do without you?"

Chloe straightened up, took one last look through tear filled eyes and left the room.

Henry squeezed his eyes, trying to expel the tears so he could see his Jenny more clearly, hoping against all hope that she would open her eyes once more. But her long lovely lashes remained still; she was gone, gone into eternity like a passing summer breeze, now free, while he remained imprisoned in his anguish.

Gradually Henry became aware of a growing stillness. Normally, there would be the sound of monitors, but since Jenny didn't want any kind of life support machines, the only sound he was aware of was that of his breathing. The adrenalin that had supported him time and again that day was gone, leaving him totally deflated. Complete exhaustion swept throughout his body, he needed to rest. He hung down his head and then fatigue slowly made its way upon his arm and hand which was still holding onto Jenny's hand. He didn't want to let go of her and had no stamina or energy to stay alert.

Self-anger grew within him as he drifted in and out of consciousness. At least six months ago he felt the urge to visit Marjorie while she was in the Santa Maria Home. Imagine, for six months they could have visited and shared their lives together, getting caught up, giving each other joy and pleasure, filling the void, the emptiness in each of their lives. How foolish he was to have neglected such a once-in-a-lifetime, golden opportunity. His second chance at love had come down to just these few minutes, just a few words, holding each other's hand and only one kiss, a final kiss.

"Oh, Henry, why did you leave it to the last minute? You're always putting things off and now you're getting what you deserve." That had always been his downfall, losing precious time that could have been so rewarding and enriching. "I could have lived two lifetimes in all the time I wasted deciding what to do." He screamed at himself.

Total weariness was at the doorstep; his eyes closed and he began to slowly drift off. He relived kissing Jenny, savouring her lips as he would for the rest of his days. Getting up and kissing her again would no longer be the same and besides he wanted to remember and feel it over and over again as he did just minutes ago when she was alive. *At least death waited until they kissed.* He could be thankful for that. Yes, their guardian angels watched over them, fulfilled their wishes, their hearts' desire. And just as Jenny clutched her pewter guardian angel before she died, Henry reached up with his free hand and searched for his. It was still hanging outside of his shirt ready to fly to his dear sweet Jenny, his dear sweet Jenny, his…dear…sweet, sweet…Jenny…

CHAPTER ELEVEN

As father left the chapel following the most powerful prayer meeting he'd ever seen, his legs could barely carry him down the hall. He knew his time had come. That it was his turn to see the Lord. The weariness he had been feeling over the past few weeks seemed to have reached a peak.

He had given his all to the Lord, not just in servitude for so many years, but his physical body. He had pledged his life in exchange for Jenny's so that his son and she could have the life together that they'd been denied.

He wobbled into his room for his Bible. The light that he'd noticed hovering around him over the last little while seemed brighter— as if the closer he got to heaven the more intense the light became.

Bible in hand, he walked into the sun room, periodically stopping to lean on the wall for support and rest. His favourite chair waited for him in the sunlight. His weary body found comfort and rest in the soft cushions.

Father took a deep breath— he knew it would be one of his last, as he felt the life draining out of him. He knew he wasn't far from seeing his Anna. He opened his Bible instinctively to the 23rd Psalm.

"The Lord is my Shepherd. I shall not want. He makes me to lie down in green pastures. He leads me beside the still waters. He restoreth my soul." As Father read these words, his eyelids closed.

THE DAY NURSE starting her shift came in to check on Peter. She was surprised to see him still alive. She smiled at Angie as she passed and said, "He's got a fighting spirit." The nurse patted her back and left. "I'll be in shortly to check again."

Angie didn't look at the nurse but simply nodded and softly whispered, "Thank you, Florence."

Peter's breathing was shallow. Angie felt so helpless and wished with all her heart that she could do more. She would miss her husband. He was such a good man. She recalled the day Peter confessed his deed to the parish. They thought that would be the end of their tenure at the church, but instead it only increased the love that the parishioners had for Peter. His openness, honesty and transparency precipitated many to share their transgressions. Sins and deeds that many were ashamed to reveal, opened up and received healing and the freedom that comes with forgiveness.

Peter was authentic inside and out. He showed his humanness and touched the hearts of others. Angie felt at times the parishioners loved him more than she did. Many were in the hallway now praying for him. The church was also packed with others praying.

"Oh, dear Jesus, hear our prayers. Let him lead the parish longer and train a predecessor. Let him see his daughter, Camilla. Let them reconcile. Please, bring Jenny and Peter together in peace, as well. His heart and soul yearn for such a healing."

Angie squeezed Peter's hand and bent forward and laid her head on her arm and wept. The day nurse came back and changed one of the IV bags. As she left, she stopped at Angie's side and rubbed her shoulder.

Angie straightened out once more and continued to pray. The faith in her words began to reflect a loss of hope.

"Oh, Lord, if it is Your will to take Peter home, You know the desires of his heart. He holds such a deep love in his heart for his daughter. His prayer would be that she would feel his love in spirit. He is such a Godly man. Grant him the peace of knowing that his life on earth was worthy and acceptable to you. Grant him peace that surpasses all understanding so that as he breathes his final earthly air, he knows in his heart that all is well with You and Jenny and his daughter, Camilla."

The monitor began to beep, startling Angie and those present. The nurse rushed in and made an adjustment on the wires leading to Peter's chest. The noise stopped and the blips continued, slowly… laboriously.

Chapter Twelve

"Perhaps I will lie down for awhile," he said to his mother. He could hardly believe that he didn't smell the potatoes and fried onions when he came into the house. He had just met the girl of his dreams and wondered if this is what it must feel like to be in love. Henry left the table and trudged to his room. Maybe he was suffering from the same thing his Uncle Ron had when he met Aunt Darlene. He recalled his mom saying that it had been love at first sight and that Ron had been lovesick for her. It would be at least another hour until he would call on Jenny and take her to Balfour Collegiate. He decided to lie down, but still exhausted from the roller coaster emotional highs and lows of the morning, he drifted quickly off to sleep.

As Henry lay there dreaming of that day in the hospital room, still holding Jenny's lifeless hand, he entered into another dream with visions of Sleeping Beauty. He was running through the woods and arrived in a clearing filled with heavenly wildflowers. There in the middle of the meadow lay his Jenny, asleep on a bed of white daisies like the Sleeping Beauty. He knew as Prince Charming, his kiss had the power to bring her out of her deep sleep. Henry ran towards her, but a man wearing a hooded black cloak was coming towards him, his arms outstretched, trying to stop him.

Henry's body shuddered when he had first dreamt that horrible nightmare while waiting to take Jenny to Balfour so long ago. He tried to snap out of it now, just as he had back then, but the dream held him firmly as he felt the grip of the hooded man. The man had no face, no life, *it was Death*.

Rigid and hard, his arms strong, he thrust Henry to the ground and sped towards Jenny. Henry scrambled to his feet in quick pursuit, "I should have known you would come for her. I was warned of this day. I must get to Jenny! I must hide her, kiss her, and keep her from you. Stay away, stay away!"

But Henry was no match for the swiftness of Death; He was way ahead and already at her side. Henry stopped, his chest heaving, catching his breath, desiring to have one last look at his beloved before she was whisked away. As Henry's somber gaze fell from the darkness upon the light of his Sleeping Beauty... she was no longer there...instead, in her place, was a man in a tan coloured suit, with a yellow flower in his lapel.

Henry recalled the dream so vividly now and as he drew nearer to the site, he should have known who it would be and what had happened. There on the bed of daisies, lay his beloved friend, the one who was always there for him...even now unto death...

"Oh, Father Engelmann, have you given your life for her? For us?" Henry searched the meadow...

"Where is my dear sweet, Jenny!? Jenny, Jenny where are..."

"Mr. Pederson, Mr. Pederson. Wake up."

Henry abruptly raised his head, but his arm wouldn't follow, it was asleep and he couldn't move it. Henry was perspiring profusely, and startled; horrified. Jenny lay before him dead and Nurse Johnson was standing over him, shaking his shoulder.

"Were you dreaming? You were shouting so loudly, I heard you all the way from the nurse's station."

"Oh, I'm so sorry," Henry said, finally orienting himself to what had transpired. "Yes, yes, I was dreaming, the same dream I had dreamt way back in 1956, the day I had met Jenny. It was so real, I had to kiss, Jenny, but *Death* held me back... a good friend of mine gave his life... Oh, I'm sorry, Nurse, I shouldn't be burdening you with my silly dream."

"Oh no, that's fine, I understand. Times like this can be very trying and dreams very revealing."

Henry gazed at the nurse still half caught in his dream, wondering if he could go back and search for Jenny. His entire arm began to tingle down to his hand, which was still holding Jenny's. All feeling was gone. He could no longer discern the warmth or coldness or stiffness of her hand. The strength in his arm had left him as well, and he was completely unable to remove his hand from Jenny's. A part of him had momentarily crossed over with his beloved.

"My arm's asleep and I can't get my hand back," Henry said sheepishly as he looked helplessly towards the nurse.

Nurse Johnson stepped forward, took hold of his arm with one hand and pried loose his grip on Jenny's hand with her other. It came free, but was lifeless, and just hung there, limp in the nurse's hand. It gave both of them an eerie feeling, what it must be like to have one's blood stop flowing through your veins. The nurse began to rub his arm and move it up and down encouraging the blood to flow.

"There, does that feel better?" Nurse Johnson asked, studying Henry and waiting for his response.

"Yes, it does," Henry wiggled his fingers, opening and closing his hand.

"You've been in here a long time, Mr. Pederson, I was beginning to get worried about you. You have slept for over an hour."

"Really?"

"Yes, I checked in on you almost a half hour ago and you were sound asleep. I decided to just let you rest until I heard you shouting."

"Well, I am glad you heard me and came. It was the strangest dream and it seemed so real, like Jenny may have come back to life, if I was just able to find her, kiss her. Kind of silly, isn't it?"

Nurse Johnson looked at him and smiled and tilted her head to the side as if to say, *anything is possible.*

"That was some kind of kiss you and Ms. Hamilton had. It certainly touched my heart. It made me think about a lot of things…" Her voice trailed off, not wanting to get into her private affairs. "Well, we have to move Jenny's body shortly, Mr. Pederson, I will leave you for a few minutes to say your good-byes and—"

"Yes, of course, Nurse Johnson, I understand. Thank you for allowing me to stay for so long."

"Yes, I am so happy that Ms. Hamilton came out of her coma and was able to talk to you and Camilla. Your reunion and farewell was so beautiful, I am still touched by it all. I will never forget this. Thank you for letting me share your experience."

Henry didn't respond. He had known Ms. Johnson was in the room the entire time, yet he had been so caught up in the moment, he'd been oblivious to her presence.

"The lady from Jamaica, I think her name is Matilda, did such a wonderful job in consoling your daughter-in-law. Coming to the hospital to find her real mother so critically ill and to think that you fathered her would be so overwhelming."

"Oh, my… is that what Camilla thinks?"

"She did. In fact, when I witnessed you and Jenny kissing and all, I thought that was the circumstance, as well. However, Matilda explained that was not the case and when Chloe came out, she too, confirmed that you were not the father, but some other man was. I thought I would pass that along to prepare you for what is ahead."

"Yes, thank you for sharing that. It is a relief to know that Camilla knows all the true facts."

"Do you know a James Hamilton?"

Henry wrinkled his face, "Not personally, but I do believe that is Jenny's former husband. Why do you ask?"

"He was phoning most of the day wanting to know how Ms. Hamilton was. I guess he took Jenny's passing very hard. In any case he asked us to pass along a message for you to call him."

The look on Henry's face grew more puzzled. He simply nodded.

Nurse Johnson went over to the window, moved the drapes slightly to the side and opened the window. Henry knew her intent was to bring in some fresh air and help revive him and bring him to his senses.

"We will see you in a little bit, okay?"

"Yes, I will be out in just a moment."

He watched as Nurse Johnson left the room and then turned his gaze back to Jenny. She looked as if she were asleep; so peaceful and still. A breeze gushed through the open window, tossing the plastic drape even more off to the side. It felt good against his hot, clammy body. The light coming through the partially exposed window struck across Jenny's face and spread almost down to the outline of her toes as the increasing wind continued to open the curtains wider. It almost seemed as if the wind and light were trying to give life to Jenny's body. Oh, how she loved the elements; the wind, butterflies, the rain and especially the sun, were her dearest friends. She so loved life and loved to frolic in it. Henry smiled as he recalled the pleasant thoughts.

Even though Jenny was gone, he sensed her presence stronger than before. He felt as if she were in the room, flying around, carried by the wind, dancing in the light entering the room. He surveyed the room, turning, looking into each corner and then raised his head towards the ceiling. He quickly repeated the pattern, hoping to catch her off guard and fully expecting to see her. He often read that when people die, their spirit leaves their body and floats about, looking down at themselves lying there and all the people in the room.

"I know you are here, Jenny. I feel your presence." He looked at her body lying in the bed. "No, I know you're not there, anymore, but I feel your spirit."

Quickly, he looked up again, hoping to catch a glimpse of her and bumped into the end table, almost toppling the lamp. The drawer was open; a letter shimmered with light inside. He just knew it was his even before it took it out.

It was the last letter he had sent to Jenny in 1956, the one Nurse Johnson had read to Jenny earlier that morning. Jenny must have read it often by the looks of it too. It was beginning to tear at the folds and the edges were soiled and tattered. Somehow it survived the carnage of all the other letters he sent to her father.

Amazingly, the last one he received from Jenny also survived. It looked similar in wear and tear to Jenny's. He still read it almost every day. It was inside his breast jacket pocket next to his heart; it felt unusually warm. He reached inside and brought it next to the one he was still holding. Instantly, a warm glow emitted from their union. It was almost as if two lost friends had found each other. Henry could feel the joy and love coming forth. The letters were not inanimate objects, but seemed to possess human qualities. Unbidden tears welled up in his eyes at the sight and feel of it all.

At long last together, *they truly are angelic letters.*

The angels on high had brought the letters together as they did Jenny and him. It was the *promise of angels fulfilled*. They had answered their prayers albeit the reunion had been short lived.

Henry tucked the two letters back into his pocket and walked over to Jenny. Strangely, he no longer felt sad at the sight of her lying there. She was gone and so it seemed, was the mourning he'd felt earlier when she departed. She was dead and yet alive, although invisible.

Could Father have given his life for Jenny?

The nightmare he had was so real and it would be something Father Engelmann would do. When Henry had recalled that nightmare so many times over the years, he had thought the man in the tan suit, wearing the yellow flower in his lapel was Father. The thought was absurd and yet when he looked for Jenny laying there on a bed of white daisies, there was Father Engelmann. He was certain of it.

Henry gazed lovingly at Jenny. Her lips drew his. They felt strangely warm as he bent over and kissed his Sleeping Beauty for the longest moment.

Glancing upwards, he surveyed the room again. Her presence was so strong, but where was she? He glanced at Jenny. An awkward feeling inched through him, confusing perhaps, but not frightening; rather, he would have to say, quite comforting.

Chapter Thirteen

Nurse Johnson was heading down the hall towards him as he left Jenny's room. She studied him and was surprised how revived he appeared.

"Well, you seem to look a bit more rested."

"Yes, the little nap did seem to revive me somewhat"

"The girls all left. Your daughter-in-law wants you to call her as soon as you are able. Matilda and Chloe are staying at the same hotel and left their phone number where they can be reached."

Nurse Johnson took the slip of paper out of her pocket and handed it to Henry. "I also wrote down Mr. Hamilton's phone number for you as well if you care to call him."

Henry took the note, looked at it, nodded and put it into his pocket.

"The ladies are a little concerned about the funeral arrangements. Apparently Mr. Hamilton wants the body flown back to Ottawa. He wants to have some kind of a State funeral for his wife… or rather former wife. I thought I would pass that along to you."

A silence passed between them. Henry hadn't thought of burying Jenny and the place of her interment. He hoped that she would be placed to rest in Regina and not away again in Ottawa.

Oh, God, not again…

"Yes, it does seem right for her to be buried back home…" His words trailed off. They did not reflect at all what was in his heart. He wanted Jenny with him, never to part again. Perhaps she could be buried next to the plot that he had reserved for himself beside Julean.

Wouldn't that be something, buried between the two loves of my life?

"I'll discuss it with the girls and either they or I will make the necessary arrangements. One of us will be in touch with you later today, or first thing in the morning. Thank you again for letting me see Jenny."

"I am glad I let you in, as well," replied Nurse Johnson. "It would have been a mistake had I not done so. And I will warn you, when you talk about funeral arrangements with Matilda, you may be in for some strong objection to that kind of talk. She wouldn't accept Ms. Hamilton's passing. She fully believes that Jenny is going to be healed, even in the face of an obvious death. She thinks Jesus is tending to other business today. 'Maybe it's a nice day in heaven,' she said, 'and He's gone fishing in one of them there streams. Same thing happened when Lazarus died,' she went on, 'He was busy at that time too, and didn't hurry home. But when He did, He woke that man up and Lazarus walked out of his tomb after four days! Yes, ma'am, He will be doing His healing in His own way and time, you just wait and see.'"

Nurse Johnson smiled and then added, "I hope her faith won't be affected too much by all this; she is such a strong, powerful lady for the Lord, but in for a disappointment, I'm afraid."

Henry nodded once more and smiled. It made him think of Father Engelmann. Those two could be two peas in a pod. He would have to phone his mentor as soon as he got home and let him know what happened.

Henry could feel Nurse Johnson's stare behind him as he walked away. But even more so, he felt Jenny's presence. It was so real and palpable, almost as if another person in real life were right beside him. He was still in a daze, not really knowing what to do next. The farm is usually where he wanted to go after a hectic day; the quietness of the country and nature always soothed him.

And he still felt somewhat drained and exhausted by the roller coaster of emotions he felt so far and yet, it was Marjorie's house that seemed to beckon him. Yes, he thought, perhaps a shower and nap there is what he needed more than anything.

As he strolled towards the elevator, the word 'quickly' popped into his mind. Jenny said it just before she passed away. Each time he thought of it, he felt compelled to complete the phrase that accompanied it.

"Hold my hand." Henry turned to his left expecting to see Jenny, but there was nothing, just the wall of the hallway with a picture here and there along the way. The phrase came again, only stronger this time, along with an irresistible compulsion to reach out for his sweetheart's hand. Henry raised his arm and opened his hand as if she were there extending her hand to him, as she did so many times during that memorable summer. He felt silly and yet it felt so right at home and… so wonderful.

As the elevator descended, Henry thought of the conversation he had had earlier that morning with Father Engelmann. He felt certain it was Father and his prayer group's prayers that kept Jenny alive long enough for them to see one another and kiss before she died. Jenny was so ill, so weak, she could barely speak. Prayer can be very powerful, Henry thought. He was glad that he believed in it. He was surprised that he was not upset with God for not healing Jenny totally.

And the dream… what did it mean? It seemed so real to see Father lay down his life for Jenny. I fully expected Jenny to wake up and be healed. Maybe it's in her spirit life that she has come back?

The elevator stopped abruptly, interrupting his thoughts. His hand was still extended as he left the elevator and walked across the lobby to the front door. It was crowded, and most people dodged his arm thinking perhaps he had a cast on under his jacket, while others bumped into it. Henry tried to pull it in, but it just felt so heartwarming and soothing, like Jenny was striding along next to him, her warm hand in his.

The bright sunlight was blinding as he stepped into fresh air. He drank in a deep breath of air and then another, it felt good to be outside, almost hot enough for him to take off his jacket. Most of the snow had melted and it looked like they were in for an early spring.

As soon as Henry got to his vehicle, his arm suddenly fell back to his side. Once seated and strapped in, however, he reached out his right hand to the passenger seat. He turned, but the seat beside him was empty except for Marjorie's diary which he'd brought with him from the farm that morning.

"Oh, God, I hope I'm not losing it like at Marj—Jenny's place." Jenny couldn't be beside him...*could she?*"Henry shook his head and backed out his SUV, narrowly missing someone who he hadn't noticed. As he made his way to the street and off to Marjorie's place, the word 'quickly' entered into his mind, followed immediately by, "Quickly, hold my hand."

Henry looked beside him, but nothing was there. Yet, he couldn't help himself; he slowly extended his right arm and grabbed hold of a very warm, comforting hand and together, their hands settled on the diary.

Chapter Fourteen

IN MAKING HER final rounds before her shift for the day was over, Nurse Dianne Frowler peeked into the chapel to see if Father was still there.

"Holy Toledo!"

It looked like a battle field. The chairs, usually arranged neatly in rows and facing the altar ready for the next day's Mass, lay all over the place. Song sheets were strewn all about as well, and Johnny's wheelchair was lying on its side, several feet from the piano and neither Johnny nor anyone else was in sight.

"What on earth happened?"

She had heard them singing and hooting as they sometimes did when they got carried away, but this was so unusual for them to leave the chapel in such disarray. And where would Johnny be without his chair? Could he have possibly been healed? The group had been exceptionally loud today.

Dianne quickly picked up the sheets and righted the chairs. She knew Doris was concerned about Father's prayer sessions and if she saw this, she might cancel the Bible studies. That would be devastating to the residents.

As Dianne made her way back to the station to sign out, she

noticed Father sitting in his favourite chair in the sun room.

"Good-bye, Father, see you tomorrow."

Dianne kept walking down the hall and then stopped, "That's funny. He didn't say good-bye like he usually does." Dianne turned and walked slowly back to the sun room. Even before she got there, an ominous feeling gnawed at her stomach. She forced herself to peek into the room. He looked asleep and as usual, clad with that slight benevolent smile on his face. He appeared in perfect peace. His head was tilted back on the high back of his favourite chair, with his eyes closed and his hands holding the Bible on his lap.

"Father, I'm leaving. Father...?" she called louder. Was he asleep or... she gazed at his chest, looking for some kind of movement. *There was none.* Slowly, she walked towards Father, her eyes glued on his chest and then his eyes, his hands, searching for any sign of life, a flicker of the wrists, eyes, anything to relieve the dread building up within her.

"Oh, God, no. Not Father Engelmann. Oh dear Lord, we need him so much..."

Tears welled up in Dianne's eyes, she was too choked up to say anything or call out for help. "Oh, Father David, we love you so much."

Hesitantly, she went over to Father and put her hand on his cheek. He must have just passed on, he still felt warm. She let her hand fall down onto Father's. Unhurriedly, she wrapped it around Father's wrist and felt for a pulse. She knew none would be there; it was more a reflex action from her nurse's training, following procedure. She had seen death before and knew what *it* looked like, but more so, *felt like.* The oppressive feeling sweeping over her was confirmation enough that Father was dead.

She stared at the beloved priest for a long moment and then bent down and kissed him on the forehead. "Good-bye, Father, I loved you as much as my own dad."

The conversation she had with him earlier that morning came to mind. He'd known he would meet the Lord, today. His wedding suit was a clear sign. "It's going to be a special day for me," he had told her. "Yes, he knew," muttered Dianne.

The open Bible on his lap caught her attention and when she walked around behind him, she wasn't surprised to see it open to the 23rd Psalm:

"The Lord is my shepherd; I shall not want;
He makes me to lie down in green pastures.
He leads me beside the still waters.
He restores my soul;
He leads me in the paths of righteousness for His name's sake.

Yea, though I walk through the valley of the shadow of death,
I will fear no evil;
For You are with me.
Your rod and Your staff, they comfort me.

You prepare a table before me in the presence of my enemies;
You anoint my head with oil;
My cup runs over.
Surely goodness and mercy shall follow me all the days of my life;
And I will dwell in the house of the Lord forever.

Dianne could barely read the last sentence, but she finished it from memory. Tears obscured the writing. She retrieved a tissue from her pocket and wiped her eyes and the tip of her nose.

"Yes, Father, you were a shepherd, too. You looked after your flock and now He has prepared a table for you. Your cup will run over and you shall rest in the house of the Lord, forever."

Just below the bottom of the page lay his bookmark, which must have slid down from the open Bible. She reached over his shoulder and picked it up. It was a narrow elongated stiff cardboard covered with a plastic coating. A golden frayed ribbon was tied through a small hole at the top. It had the prayer of peace by Saint Francis of Assisi printed on it. Father had recited it every day at the close of the prayer meetings and the Bible study. Not only did he read it, he had also been a living example of it.

Lord, make me an instrument of Your peace.
Where there is hatred, let me sow love;
Where there is injury, pardon;
Where there is doubt, faith;
Where there is despair, hope;
Where there is darkness, light:

Where there is sadness, joy.

O Divine Master, grant that I may seek not so much to be consoled
As to console;
To be understood as to understand;
To be loved as to love;
For it is in giving that we receive;
It is in pardoning that we are pardoned, and it is in dying that
We are born to eternal life, Amen.

Dianne's eyes filled with new tears. She wondered if this was the last prayer he uttered before he passed on or was it the 23rd Psalm?

"Oh, Father, you lived the life of a saint. You were just like Saint Francis. You brought such love into this home. How fortunate we all were to be blessed with your presence. *What are we going to do without you?*"

Weakness inched its way through Dianne. It had been a long day for her to start with and now this. She plopped herself down into the chair beside Father and let out a long sigh. She leaned forward towards Father and placed the bookmark back onto his Bible. She thought about keeping it as a memento, but thought better of it. It was Father's, and he may have willed it to someone already and maybe he was watching.

As Dianne sat there gazing at the man she loved and respected so much, she thought about the time when she had applied to work at the care home in response to an ad in the *Leader Post* paper:

Wanted: a very special, kindhearted person, sensitive to
the needs of others, and willing to care for seniors as if they
were your mother or father. Please apply to the Nunnery
Care Home, with a resume.

It was an intriguing ad. She'd always had a special place in her heart for older people and felt prompted to apply. It was the best decision she ever made.

First, Doris had interviewed her, then Father Engelmann. It was unusual to be interviewed by a priest. He was so kindly. But behind those friendly eyes, he analyzed every inch, thought and nuance she made.

Fifteen minutes into the interview, Father stood and said, "Yes, yes, Dianne, you are the answer to our prayers. Please wait here a moment." Father had left and returned with Doris a few minutes later to tell her she'd been hired.

Dianne accepted on the spot. Father Engelmann had been standing in the wings, with that sweet benevolent smile of his.

On her first day working at the care home, she thought she was in heaven. She couldn't get over how full of life and love the home was, how everyone mixed, how friendly and loving they were to each other and how much they were like a family. Some didn't have families anymore and were all alone, but through Father's example and encouragement, they began to love each other and care for each other so much. They more than made up for the lack of family. And the families and relatives that did come were so touched with the presence of love and peace in the care home, that they actually came to be filled.

Once people experience what love can do, they see what their hearts are really longing for.

"Thank you for hiring me, Father, I know it was your influence that made Doris pick me from the several other nurses that were much more qualified."

"It's not your credentials, Dianne," Father used to tell her. "*It's what is in your heart that is important.*"

Dianne smiled and gazed lovingly at Father. "You were such a strong leader, yet you always encouraged us to lead, as well. But who now is going to carry out the Bible classes, do the bingo, card games, the sing-a-longs, visit the hospitals and other care homes, and the magazine you started and... oh my gosh, the Masses?"

Mrs. Dance rolled by in her wheelchair. She stopped when she saw Dianne sitting beside Father and wheeled into the room. One look at Father and she instantly knew in her heart, Father was gone.

"Oh, Lord, what will we do without him?" she murmured.

Dianne was so engrossed in her thoughts, that she didn't see or hear Mrs. Dance at first, until she said, "He's gone, isn't he?"

"Yes, Frances, he has gone to be with the Lord."

Frances slowly rolled her wheelchair up beside Father and placed her hand on his. Tears welled up in Frances' eyes.

"Well, I better get some help and call the ambulance," said Dianne.

"No, no, please don't move him, yet," pleaded Frances. "Let's tell the others and bring them here. Perhaps they may want to say good-bye, too."

"Of course, that's a wonderful thought, Frances. Would you please tell the others? I'll stay here with Father."

Mrs. Dance grasped the wheels of the chair with her feeble hands and with all her might, thrust them forward. The wheelchair sprang to life and sped down the hall, weaving from side to side, almost toppling over. As Frances whizzed by Elmer's room, she shouted, "Come to the sun room, quick. It's Father. He needs us." And on she went, from one room to another, like a town crier or a messenger of the Lord, telling all, that their beloved shepherd had gone home.

One by the one they came, some were already in tears, sorrow and joy written all over their faces. Without even being told, many sensed Father's passing even before they entered the sun room. A few who didn't know were frozen in shock. Everyone comforted each other. To most of the residents, though, to die was not a sad affair. It simply meant one was passing from their earthly life to greater life with their Lord. However, they would miss their dear friend and consoler deeply.

Soon the entire house gathered around Father in the sun room, except for Johnny. After the prayer session that morning when Johnny discovered he was healed, he and all the others rejoiced and went outside with him to see him run up and down the block and then around it. At last count, he was running around the block for the fortieth time. Helen was waiting for him to come by the care home and call him in.

The late afternoon sun had travelled far to the west, flooding the room with warm light. It gave Father such a saintly aura and reminded the residents not only of the light he had talked about seeing for several days, but also the bright nimbus surrounding him during the prayer session that morning.

Much like they did when they had their sing-song in the chapel, the residents encircled Father and fell into prayerful silence. Suddenly, the front door slammed and in ran Johnny.

Sadness and shock covered his face over the news. His gaze

never left Father as he entered the sun room. He slowly walked over to Father, knelt before him, laid his head on his knees and wept.

Dianne, still sitting beside Father, was deeply moved by the love these two men had shared. She reached over and stroked Johnny's shoulder and was further prompted to take Father's Bible. As she did so and laid it on her lap it fell open on Jeremiah 31:13. It was a reading that Dianne knew she had to share with the group, whose hearts were also weighing so heavy in the wake of Father's passing. Dianne read the Scripture and then let the Words do their healing:

> *"I will turn their mourning to joy,*
> *Will comfort them,*
> *And make them rejoice rather than sorrow."*

The people knew instantly it was a message from Father and their hearts lightened. The silence was broken as someone spontaneously started to say the Lord's Prayer: "Our Father, who art in heaven..." Soon the entire assembly joined in.

After the Lord's Prayer, another resident started to sing "His peace is flowing like a river...flowing out of you and me...flowing out unto the desert, setting all his captives free. His peace is..."

After the six verses, someone started another song and then another one. On it went, for over an hour. By the end, everyone including Johnny was clapping and singing and crying; *their sorrow had turned to joy.* They all were hoping for some miracle, expecting Father to get up and join along like he usually did at the prayer meetings.

But, Father just sat there, still, his eyes closed with that smile on his face as if to say, *"Thank you, my brothers and sisters, and farewell."*

Father may not have been there physically, but there was no doubt that he was there in spirit. *They all felt his presence.* Like during the prayer meeting they'd had for Henry and Jenny, the air was thick and heavy with the Holy Spirit, soothing and comforting them.

They streamed by him, one-by-one for the last time. Some touched him. Some kissed him on the forehead. Some whispered to him a private prayer or farewell and some just silently walked by.

Slowly the room emptied as each went to their rooms to be alone with their own thoughts and memories of Father, how he reached out to them and to their every need. He knew what was in their hearts and souls. He was considered their friend, confidant and spiritual mentor. *He was their saint.*

Finally, the sun room was empty except for Father and Dianne and Carey, the other nurse on duty. The bright sunlight that entered the room earlier was gone and Dianne sensed that Father had left too, to go to his heavenly home.

Finally, Dianne spoke. "Please call an ambulance, Carey. I'll stay here until they arrive."

Carey stood there momentarily, trying to soak in the reality of Father's passing. Tears gathered in her eyes, and as she slowly backed out of the room, it was as if Father was speaking through her, "You'll have to take Father's place, Dianne. The residents may not make it without you."

Carey's comment struck Dianne's heart and instantly she sat up recalling the parting advice Father offered to her that morning. "They need you, Dianne, more than you will ever know."

Dianne got up and stood in front of Father and smiled through her tears, "Even in death you will guide us and let us know what we need to do." She patted his shoulder, "I will miss you terribly, Father, and...I love you so much. Please help and guide me to carry your torch, your light and encourage all the others to do the same."

Dianne remembered she needed to fill out some forms for the ambulance attendants. She stopped at the doorway, turning to look at Father one last time, then threw him a kiss with the tips of fingers. Father's last words echoed through her mind as she walked spiritedly towards the work station with renewed faith and determination.

CHAPTER FIFTEEN

THE NEXT THING Henry knew, he was standing on the landing to the front door of Marjorie's house...or should he say, Jenny's home. Exactly how he got from the hospital to here was all a mystery to him. He was so overtaken with the events of the day that all the present moments since leaving Jenny at the hospital, were filled with thoughts of the past or anticipations of the future. There was simply nothing left for the present.

Henry reached into his pocket for the key and yet decided to simply walk in. Somehow, he sensed that keys and obstructions were easy obstacles to overcome. He turned the knob and the door he had locked yesterday afternoon when he left for the gallery, simply swung open. To make a hot pot of chamomile tea and relax was his top priority as he entered the foyer. The drawer to the round antique table where he had discovered Jenny's diary was still open. Perhaps he might read some more of the diary when his tea was ready, but then he remembered the diary was still in his SUV.

I'll get it later.

The kitchen was bright as it captured some of the afternoon sun now lavishing the backyard. The gazebo was probably flooded with sunlight like it had been the day before.

On his way to the kitchen window, he picked up the electric kettle at the end of the counter to fill it with fresh water. He turned on the tap and absently looked out the window to see if the bouquet he saw yesterday was still there. Not only were the flowers there, but more greenery seemed to have been added. Water overflowed from the kettle into the sink. He poured some of the excess out and turned off the tap.

Was the angel's basket filled with more flowers? He set the kettle down and gazed out again. His attention shifted. There was someone sitting in the gazebo and… it looked like *Jenny!*

"That's impossible!" Henry leaned forward and looked again. "It must be Camilla. Sure, she probably wants to talk to me about our relationship, if I really am her father." The tea could wait.

He walked through the back patio doors, to the edge of the deck. It looked like she was writing in a book and she seemed a little old to be Camilla, but it must be her. It was just the way the light was hitting the gazebo and casting a shadow over her.

Henry followed the steps down at the end of the deck and slowly walked along the winding lane. Thyme strewn along the walkway filled the air with a strong wonderful fragrance. With each step, he became more confused. First it looked like Jenny and then Camilla. *They looked so much alike.* Perhaps the herb wafting up into the air was affecting his senses.

When Henry was about ten feet away, he expected his heart would explode through his chest, yet he was amazingly calm. The lady looked up and Henry was utterly stunned. It wasn't his daughter-in-law basking in the sun and writing in a diary.

It was Jenny!

She looked beautiful, no longer frail and pallid. Rather, her complexion was robust and radiant. The warm breeze in the garden gently fluttered her golden hair. Instantly, Henry grew excited as he viewed his first sweet love with longing and desire.

"Could I still be living in the fantasy I created?" Henry wondered. He shook his head and rubbed his eyes… it must be a mirage… but then the beautiful vision spoke.

"Hello, Henry. I've been waiting for you." Jenny said, her face full of loving compassion.

"But… but… you're… dead, how can you possibly be sitting here, when less than an hour ago I was in the hospital holding your hand… while you quietly slipped into eternity?"

I must be dreaming!

Everything looked so beautiful and the air smelled so… so, exhilaratingly intoxicating! When he left the hospital, he was so exhausted and now he felt like he could fly. No stress, no worry, just an incredibly unexplainable peace. Henry looked at Jenny again. She wore a beautiful smile, tilted her head and broadened her smile further. He couldn't believe this. It seemed like Jenny and he hadn't even been separated. Time seemed so different. Like there was no time. *It was timeless!*

Jenny wrote for another minute, then closed the cover.

"Is that your diary, Jenny?"

"Yes. And it is the one you discovered in my secret hiding place. I knew you would find it."

"But—"

"How did I get it when you left it in your SUV?" Jenny said.

What was the point of answering or asking? How was this even happening? He just stood there dumbfounded.

Jenny smiled. "I took it from your truck if you have to know. I had to write in the diary about Camilla; that she is my daughter and married to your son Jeremy, and that she is part of our family tree and heritage. We are the only family and relatives left. J.J. needs to know of his step-sister and that Camilla is James Junior's aunt. One of my dying requests to God was that my secret be known and not carried to the grave. J.J. and Camilla have a right and need to know one another to keep our heritage intact.

"I also wanted my son to know that I love him dearly and that it will be my eternal prayer that he forgives me, as I have him."

Just as Henry was about to speak again, Jenny continued. "And, about the flowers in the angel's basket and the fragrance in the air?"

Henry nodded and smiled.

"Well, the flowers are truly a miracle Henry, a gift from my dear guardian angel."

"I knew it, Jenny. It just had to be a miracle and I knew our angels were involved!"

Jenny smiled, her teeth whiter than fresh fallen snow. "And the fragrance in the air, well, that's down to earth if you'll excuse the pun. You will find I took two pots of herbs from the window sill in the living room. I threw thyme all over the walk, even the bench I am sitting on. I'm in love with the smell of herbs. When you walk on the thyme, crushing it, it releases the fragrance you smell. That's why I sit on it, too!" Jenny laughed.

Her laugh sent Henry into another world. He hadn't heard her laugh for over fifty… flaps of an angel's wings. He instantly recalled the day they met and he walked her home. She laughed then and he loved it. Even more so now!

Jenny knew what Henry was thinking and they both laughed again over his confusion with timelessness and memories of when they met.

Finally, Henry was able to get a word in edgewise before she read his thoughts. Or, was she just letting him say something?

"But, Jenny, I still don't understand how you are here. Why are you not dead and how is it I can see you? What is going—?"

Jenny got up and walked towards Henry. First, she tenderly kissed him on the lips, sending his world spinning. Then, on flat feet again, she stood in front of the love of her life.

Before Henry returned to earth, buzzing with incessant questions, Jenny put her finger to his mouth and whispered, "Ssh. Before this day is over, you will understand everything. In the meantime, just trust me."

Henry hardly heard a word his sweet Jenny said, he was drowning in her clear blue eyes. She looked so radiant, he yearned to hold her and never let her go.

Jenny smiled coyly and fluttered her eyelashes.

"Come, Henry, I want to show you something." She extended her hand. "Quickly, hold my hand."

CHAPTER SIXTEEN

JEREMY WATCHED THROUGH the living room window as Camilla drove up the driveway. He strained to see her face as she got out of the vehicle.

She was crying.

She closed the car door and hurried to the house. Jeremy quickly went to the front door to greet her. He hoped and prayed his dear wife had been able to talk to her mother and find out some answers to questions about her birth that had been so troublesome to her. It would be devastating if she hadn't.

Jeremy opened the door and Camilla immediately fell into his open arms.

"Oh, Jeremy, she's gone…" was all Camilla could say before bursting into tears.

Jeremy held her tight and rubbed her back consolingly. Tears surfaced to his eyes in sympathy. "It's okay, honey, it will all be okay."

Slowly he turned her towards the stairs and together they walked up the small flight into the living room. Once there, Jeremy turned towards her again and drew her tenderly into his chest.

Slowly, Camilla's weeping subsided and Jeremy gently asked,

"Were you able to talk to her…?"

"Y…yes," Camilla said between sobs. "She was in a coma when I got there. Two of her friends were in the room. I remember one from Father Engelmann's anniversary party, Eddy's bride's sister. Her name is Matilda. The other was Jenny's niece, Chloe. Oh, Jeremy, it was so painful to see my mother lay there waiting to die. I didn't know if I would ever be able to speak to her or for her to see me. I prayed so hard for her to wake up…even if it were for but a moment. But she just lay there. We all were watching her chest slowly rise and fall. There were no monitors so it was the only way to tell if she was still alive from one second to the next."

"It must have been so hard for you, Camilla…"

"But then your dad came in. I said hello to him but he was so transfixed on Jenny lying there he hardly knew I or anyone else was in the room. He immediately went to her side and held her hand. The love between them was so strong, Jeremy. I thought for sure he was my real father. *Who else could it be?* Then he got up and kissed her forehead. It was all so emotional…a light seemed to surround them; the love between them was so strong. And then her eyes flickered… we all held our breath. Even the nurse on duty gasped… I heard her mutter…'unbelievable'

"Jenny opened her eyes as if searching for the one who had kissed her and when her gaze locked with your father's, the aura around them brightened even further.

"It was supernatural, Jeremy… I can't explain it."

"Geez…" Jeremy slowly shook his head.

"It made me think even more that Henry was my biological father. Only my real dad would love my mother that way."

Camilla broke loose from Jeremy and took a tissue out of her sweater pocket and blew her nose.

"What happened next was unbelievable, honey. Jenny asked to be kissed… that was her constant prayer to her angel over the years. They both were wearing pewter angels around their necks. I think they were gifts that they had given to each other. It was all so beautiful how the angels sparkled and touched one another and when Henry and Jenny kissed each other, it was as if time stood still. We all were so swept up into that moment of love; as if we were all at one with these two lovers. It was so tender, so loving, so beautiful, Jeremy…" Camilla broke into tears again.

"You said she was gone…what did you mean? It sounds like she was alive and still is."

"Just moments after they kissed, she talked about me and that I was a part of her daily prayer to her guardian angel to see me and be re-united with me. It was then I rushed to her side and told her that I was her daughter. We looked at each other for the longest moment. I could see myself in her. I knew I had found myself and where I came from. I knew she was feeling the same thing. I wanted to kiss her and hug her and be hugged by her. I wanted that for so many years…It was such a happy moment, but I knew it wouldn't last…"

"What do you mean, honey?" Jeremy wanted to know.

"When I looked into her eyes there was such love, yet an unexplainable sorrow. She knew that she was being pulled away. Both your dad and I could immediately sense this power. It was greater than the both of us. Try as we might to keep her with us we could feel her slipping away. I could feel your dad tighten his grip around her hand as I was holding it, too. I never prayed so hard at that moment… and then, she slipped away…"

Camilla looked up into her dear husband's eyes. She shook her head from side to side and brought her hands up and formed them into fists and cried, "It was too much for me bear. To see my biological mother for just a few minutes and the thought that Henry was my real father and that you were my bro…"

Camilla couldn't finish. She buried her head into Jeremy's chest and sobbed uncontrollably.

Jeremy was at a loss for words. He tenderly held her and rubbed her back as soothingly as he could, wondering if it was true: was Henry Camilla's father?

Slowly Camilla regained some composure to go on. "I ran out of the room and was going to come home but Matilda, Eddy's wife's sister…" Camilla gazed into Jeremy's eyes for confirmation that he knew who she was talking about.

He nodded and Camilla went on.

"She called out to me as I was running down the hallway and took me into the waiting room. She sensed what I was concerned about and wanted to explain what she knew about my birth. She thought Jenny would do that, but under the circumstances since Jenny had died, she felt obligated to inform me of my past."

"Well…is it Dad…?"

"No, it's not your dad… thank God…"

"Well, then who?"

"Matilda is almost one hundred percent sure that it is Peter, the man that also was at Father's anniversary."

"Yes, I remember him; he was Eddy's best man, right?"

"Yes, but what seemed to confirm it for certain was when Jenny's niece came out and sat with us. She explained it all. She told me that one evening when Jenny and your dad went out to a movie, they were confronted by a group of boys on their way home. The boys overpowered your father and took Jenny to the park…"

Camilla couldn't go on… "Oh Jeremy, I hope it's okay with you…"

"Honey, there is nothing that would ever stop me loving you…"

Hesitantly, and gently he asked, "Was your mother assaulted by Peter?"

Camilla couldn't answer, she just nodded.

Jeremy pulled her in. "Oh, Camilla, I love you so much. I am so happy you were conceived… It was clearly not the most desirable way for it to have happened, but it did and I am the luckiest guy in the world to have you."

"Oh, Jeremy, I love you so much too."

Jeremy drew back and held Camilla by the shoulders as he gazed lovingly into her cerulean blue eyes. He raised his hand and brushed a tear rolling down her cheek. He moved his head from side to side to stress how very much he loved her. "Camilla, I love you with all my heart," he said once more, as he gently drew her close again and tenderly kissed his dear sweet wife's forehead. They held each other tightly for the longest time. Camilla rested her head on Jeremy's shoulder, as he broke the tender moment and said, "I'm so glad those two ladies were there to explain it all to you. Dad would call that God's divine providence, for sure."

"Yes, it is amazing how this all turned out…if only Mom wouldn't have died, it would have been so wonderful. The ladies were so supportive and understanding. God couldn't have placed me in more consoling hands. They were like two angels. And the way Matilda spoke of Peter was so kindly and uplifting. She said he was such a nice man when she talked to him at Father's anniversary. She said that he seemed to know who I was and that he dreamt of me, wishing he could find me and know me… She said he was filled with so much feeling and love. She could tell that it came from his heart.

"Chloe, Jenny's niece, said too that the boys had been drinking and not in control of their senses. Even though that certainly doesn't excuse what they did. Chloe added that Jenny, my Mom, had completely forgiven Peter. Mom wanted only beautiful memories surrounding my birth. And Jeremy, I feel the same. I feel no ill will towards him… perhaps I should."

"No honey, your feelings are being true to you. I don't understand how a man could do that…even if he was young and drunk, it makes me mad just thinking about it. You know I love you, Camilla, it doesn't take that away. It was wrong what Peter did and it's not every woman who could forgive someone who did that to her. It must have been very hard for your mother to forgive, but it seems that by forgiving, she was freed from the past and any resentment in her heart. I am so glad that you can feel that freedom in your heart as well."

"I am worried about Dad. He seemed so filled with despair when Jenny died. His entire world seemed to collapse. I must have talked at least an hour with Matilda and Chloe and he still was in the room with her. I wonder if he's worried about me that maybe I think he is my father. Oh, Jeremy, I have to call him and see if everything is okay and explain it all to him."

"I love you so much Camilla, I am so happy you were able to see your mom, even if it was for only a few minutes. *Lifetimes can be lived in precious moments like that.*"

Camilla nodded and forced a smile. She dried her eyes and went to the phone. There was no answer at the farm, so she called the gallery. Justin said they hadn't seen their father all day. He was gone even before they got up. Justin gave Camilla the phone number to the house on Hill Avenue where he seemed to spend so much time. Camilla called there and let it ring until the call disconnected. As a last resort she called the hospital and finally was able to get through to palliative care. Fortunately Nurse Johnson was still on duty.

"Hello, Ms. Johnson, this is Camilla, Jenny Hamilton's daughter…"

"Yes, how are you doing, Camilla?"

"I am doing better. I'm at home and my husband is with me."

"Oh, that's good. We need the love and support of our family and loved ones at times like this."

"Is Dad, I mean Henry still there…? do you recall who—?"

"Oh, yes, I know Henry. No, he left well over an hour ago."

"How was he when he left, did you see him?"

"Yes, we had a chat both in the room where Ms. Hamilton was and later when he left. He fell asleep for over an hour. I woke him up from a dream he was having. I think the rest did him good. It seemed to revive him, somewhat."

"That's good to hear. He seemed filled with such anguish and despair when Jenny died. I am worried about him."

"Well, if it's any consolation he seemed to be in better spirits when he left. He seemed to know where he was going and what he wanted to do and yet… he did act sort of strange when he walked away from me towards the elevator… People sometimes do strange things in circumstances like this. Try to find him and perhaps spend the evening with him."

"Yes, I understand what you mean. We will keep checking around for him. Thank you so much for your time and for also being with us during my Mom's last moments."

"Camilla, I was so fortunate to be with you and the others. It all so touched my heart."

Camilla hung up and turned to Jeremy. "Your dad seemed so despondent when I was there, like he would do anything to be with Jenny. He should have been at one of those places I called. You don't suppose he would do something… to himself?"

"God, no, Camilla. Dad would never harm himself…"

Just then the phone rang, startling the wits out of both of them. Jeremy looked at Camilla with fearful eyes and then rushed to the phone.

It was Justin.

"Slow down, Justin. I can't understand you." Jeremy looked at Camilla. Her face and entire body language screamed desperately towards her husband.

"What did Justin say?"

"He's crying so hard I can't understand him, Camilla…the police just called… I think it's something to do with Dad…"

CHAPTER SEVENTEEN

IN THE FLAP of a hummingbird's wings, Jenny and Henry stood in front of an accident scene just down the block on the corner of Hill Avenue and Elphinstone Street. A huge crowd was already gathered and growing.

Two of three police cars blocked the traffic heading east and west on Hill Avenue. An ambulance was parked in the centre of the intersection alongside a fire truck. The paramedics were examining the driver of a large moving van who appeared unhurt except for being shaken up a bit. Another paramedic was working beside two firemen trying to install the Jaws of Life inside the doors of a SUV lying on its side.

Two police officers were trying to keep the growing crowd back, many of whom were wearing looks of horror, others shook their heads and still others speculated as to what had happened.

A third officer was interviewing an eye witness and making careful notes in his notebook.

"I couldn't believe my eyes. I was sitting in my car at the stop sign waiting for this moving van coming down the Avenue to pass by. He seemed in a hurry and appeared to be going above the speed limit. At the same time across the street, I saw this red Escalade heading towards the intersection. Although it was not going very fast, it made no effort whatsoever to slow down or come to a stop.

"Just a few seconds before the van entered the intersection, the Escalade went through the stop sign and fully exposed itself to the speeding van. My God, I could hardly believe what I was seeing. There was a loud bang. The Escalade lifted off the road, landing on two wheels and rolled over at least twice before coming to a stop not more than ten yards in front of me."

By this time, a crowd had gathered around the officer and the witness. His hands twitched and waved as he described the accident, his face wore his shock vividly.

"Just look at it," he added, as he pointed to the crushed SUV lying on its driver's side against the concrete.

Henry could barely make out the driver behind the wheel and a bloody arm and hand partially exposed through the open sun roof.

"There was no way that guy was going to walk away from this one. There was no way the moving van could have missed or swerved or stopped in time. Like I said, both the moving van and the red SUV entered the intersection just a second or two apart. Unfortunately, the guy in the Escalade made it first."

A strange feeling crawled up Henry's spine as he listened to the witness describe the accident to the police officer. The red SUV looked familiar. Then it dawned on him.

"Hey, that looks like my Escalade, or whatever's left of it."

"It is your SUV, Henry," replied Jenny very softly, squeezing his hand at the same time.

"Oh my God, that's me they are dragging from the SUV! What's going on here?"

Jenny remained silent, knowing he would soon understand.

"Now I remember. When I left the hospital, I was in a complete daze. Everything was a blur. I really wasn't in any condition to drive and I remember trying to decide if I should walk or take a cab. I felt so drained though, I just wanted to get home, have a cup of tea, relax and try and figure out all that happened to me this morning."

"Do you remember holding my hand?"

"Yeah, it felt so comforting. I hated to let go when I got to my SUV."

"I was consoling you Henry, preparing you."

Henry looked at Jenny appreciatively and went on. "I got into the Escalade, turned on the key, opened the roof vent and backed out of the hospital parking lot. Someone yelled at me from behind. I turned just in time to see a man standing there, shaking his head. 'Watch where you are going, you almost hit me,' he said. It was a good thing I was going slowly.

"I apologized to the man and then cautiously proceeded out of the lot. And yeah, I reached out for your hand, again. It felt so soothing and comforting. When Dewdney Avenue ran into Elphinstone Street, I turned right and headed south."

Jenny stood silently beside Henry, tightening her grip on his hand, giving him the support he needed to go on.

"I was only about a half mile from home and felt confident that I could make it. The man in the parking lot kind of jarred me to my senses. As I drove, my mind went back to the scene in the hospital room. It was incredible to see you lying there Jenny. To learn that you were Marjorie Hamilton, the owner of the house I had purchased; that you and she were one and the same, my teenage sweetheart, my first love. It was unbelievable how destiny brought us back together after all these years.

"Without realizing it, I had picked up speed and as I entered the intersection... out of the corner of my eye, I saw the stop sign that I always stop at, but... preoccupied with so many thoughts, I passed it. My foot instinctively hit the brake, but by this time I turned to see this huge truck headed straight for me."

Jenny's hand tightened around his as it finally hit him.

"The last thing I remember thinking was, Oh my God."

Jenny turned and looked tenderly into his eyes. Very softly, she confirmed what Henry now realized. "Those were the last thoughts, the last three words you said in your earthly life."

Henry shook his head, his eyes widened, "I still don't understand. Why am I still here and how is it you are here too? Are we not both dead? Shouldn't we both be in heaven or...some place...?"

Henry hoped against all hope that they weren't in the other place.

"We are dead in an earthly sense, but our spirits are still very much alive." Jenny said assuredly. "I was quite confused about it all, too, but I think perhaps I am beginning to understand what is going on. My guardian angel, Hannah, thinks something special may be about to happen in our case, too."

"Happen in our case?' What do you mean, Jenny? And, where is your guardian angel?"

The moment the last syllable fell from his lips, he became aware of an aura of light behind Jenny. Henry had seen it around Jenny when he saw her in the gazebo, but now, with the awareness of his own death, the light grew brighter.

"Unbelievable," Henry muttered.

Jenny stepped aside, allowing her beloved to see her guardian angel in full. "Henry, this is my guardian angel, Hannah."

Henry squinted his eyes, trying to adjust to the sudden brightness, as they were introduced. Hannah's beautiful white wings moved ever so gently and her spirit shimmered, expressing excitement at making his acquaintance.

Hannah appeared much younger than Jenny, her face completely smooth, her cheeks rosy and full. One look at her eyes and Henry immediately knew where Jenny got her cerulean blue eyes from. Hannah's were the same, as clear blue as the most clear blue sky one would ever see on a sun-filled day. Her long, flowing hair was golden, much like Jenny's, but even more so. Her robe was pale blue and fit Hannah loosely. A white cord was tied at her waist and Henry's eyes followed the ends that hung down. Golden tassels terminated the hanging cords, but it led his eyes down to her petite feet peeking out from the bottom of her robe.

A mixture of amazement and awkwardness at this meeting swept through Henry. As soon as he extended his hand, Hannah raised her arms and moved towards him. She slid past his extended arm and instead gave Henry a tender hug. Electrifying warmth spread through his spirit, which began to glow much like hers. And then, for the very first time, he heard an angel speak.

"There is no formality here, Henry, only expressions of love."

Hannah backed off and gave him the most beautiful smile his eyes had ever seen, besides Jenny's, of course. Henry smiled back, the only response he knew to all of this.

"What is still confusing you, Henry, is that you and I are at different stages in our eternal journey. When I passed on at the hospital, my spirit passed out of my body and floated up to the ceiling of the room. I saw you and Camilla and Nurse Johnson tending to me. It was so good to see Matti and Chloe there as well. I called out your name, I wanted so much to let you know that I was okay and that I would love you, forever, but you didn't hear me. I went from one corner of the room to the other in the hope you would see me. Several times you looked up right at me. I waved and called out to you, but all to no avail."

"I knew you were there, Jenny, I could feel your presence, but I couldn't see you."

"I kept waving until I saw a light coming towards me, drawing me to come to it. It started to pull at me and I followed it. The love and peace coming from the light was so wonderful I had to go. You were calling out to me, searching, I didn't want to leave you and Camilla, but the attraction was so strong and compelling. The light slowly spiraled into a tunnel ever so bright. It surrounded me, overwhelmed me, and drew me in. My sense of space and time vanished. There was nothing relative that would provide any kind of orientation. The only sense of movement I had was that the light got brighter as I progressed further into it."

Jenny's eyes brightened and glowed. A love Henry had never sensed before radiated towards him as she described her progress into the tunnel.

"The light became so intense my vision was impaired; I closed my eyes lest I be blinded. And just as I could no longer withstand the brightness, I felt myself withdrawing. Some loving force was pulling me back. My acceleration into the light was decelerating. The feeling of love and longing was so strong, that even heaven had to relent and yield and honour such a mighty calling. I heard singing and praying and crying, pleas to God to heal me and to unite us together. I saw Father Engelmann and several other elderly people that I didn't know at all, praying so earnestly and with such fervour on my behalf that my heart overflowed with gratitude and love for them. I felt the love of Chloe, her father and so many others praying, as well. And then there was Matilda, her love and faith was so strong and determined and Father Engelmann's plea to take his life for mine… it all reversed my progress into eternity."

Jenny paused and gazed tenderly into Henry's eyes and said, "But in the end, it was your prayer, your unrelenting commitment and the earnestness of your love for me that pulled me completely out of the tunnel."

Hannah, who was standing directly behind Jenny, flapped her wings excitedly and nodded.

Like a flash of lightning, the thought occurred to Henry that if Jenny had a guardian angel and he could see her, then he must have one. He slowly turned his head and looked behind.

After 47 years, Henry finally saw his guardian angel in spirit.

"Hello, Henry, my name is Gabriel," A broad smile covered his face.

Henry loved him instantly. He could sense Gabriel wanted to greet him as Hannah did but hesitated, giving Henry time to adjust to seeing him.

Henry stood speechless. There before him, stood his spiritual guide. This was the angel who had been assigned to look after him, protect him, guide him through thick and thin, his soldier, his hero— his guardian from the moment he was conceived. Henry knew in his heart it was he and Hannah, who in the end brought Jenny and him together. How… could he show his gratitude…?

Gabriel knew Henry's thoughts. His robe shimmered like Hannah's as he approached Henry. Henry knew better than to extend his hand, rather he raised and opened his arms, stepped forward and fell into the arms of his strong protector.

Jenny murmured approvingly behind him and Hannah's wings fluttered in excitement and joy.

Gabriel patted Henry's back as he released his mighty, yet tender hold of him. "It was a joy to look after you Henry. Your heart was good, even though at times you took too many risks. It was always a challenge finding ways to bring you back on track."

Henry's mind immediately tried to think of those times when he misbehaved, had impure thoughts, gambled in the stock market and bordered on sinning…

Gabriel looked at him compassionately and forgivingly, "I understand all those times. It's all part and parcel of your humanity. God gave you a free will. He knew some of the choices you would make and they would not be wise or for the best. The Holy Spirit unceasingly prayed for your salvation and instructed us, His messengers, how to lead and guide you to come back to God the Father. And you unfailingly did, right to the end."

Henry looked at Gabriel and beamed.

"For most of my life I just knew I had a guardian angel,

especially when I met Jenny."

"Yes, both Hannah and I remember the moment you two met. We were exuberantly excited for you both."

Hannah fluttered her wings and gazing at Henry, she added, "You and Jenny were such a perfect match... almost heaven made!"

"And when Jenny moved to Ottawa," interjected Gabriel, "Hannah and I felt your pain very deeply."

Henry looked at Gabriel and then Hannah appreciatively. He detected sorrow in their eyes at the thought.

Jenny turned to Hannah. "I've often wondered about that day when I left Mr. Engelmann's grocery store and a car almost hit me when crossing Victoria Avenue. I occasionally dreamt about it. It was you that saved my life?"

"Yes, Jenny, it was a close call, but I moved you out of danger's way."

Jenny floated over to Hannah and hugged her.

"It was Henry's prayer of love to put a protective shield around you as you crossed the busy street that alerted us to be extra watchful that day," added Gabriel. "We are quick to respond to prayer and acts of love." Gabriel and Henry gazed at one another and smiled.

"It's our job to protect and guide you as much as possible... at times we are allowed to take such exceptional measures." Gabriel turned to Henry and continued, "There were so many times when you drove home tired after a busy day at the gallery that I had to nudge you to stay alert at the wheel. You had many close calls that you were unaware of."

Henry recalled the several times his car window unexpectedly opened, blasting him with a sudden gush of wind, keeping him awake. Gabriel knew Henry's thoughts and smiled, acknowledging that it was during those times.

Henry knew he would never know from how many dangers Gabriel had delivered him, or how much of his salvation was also actually due to his holy protector. Henry floated over to Gabriel and hugged him again.

Henry patted his protector's shoulder and pulled away. "I remember talking to Mr. Engelmann about angels one time and he quoted Exodus 23:20, that God sends an angel in front of you, to guard you on the way."

"I like the one in Psalm 91: 11 and 12," added Jenny. "'He hath given angels charge over thee; to keep thee in all thy ways. In their hands they shall bear thee up: lest thou dash thy foot against a stone.' How much closer and caring can an angel be?"

Hannah responded to what Henry and Jenny said by darting up and down and side to side like a hummingbird.

"An angel's task is very full and relentless. We are forever by your side protecting, warning and earnestly exhorting you at times. I must admit there were some days Jenny, with all your bubbly spontaneity, when sleep came none too soon and I was able to rest my wings."

They all laughed.

"So, were you responsible for Henry purchasing my house?" Jenny asked Gabriel.

"Yes, it took very little prompting to remind Ben Walker of one of his favourite clients. Ben is a true real estate salesman at heart and just a nudge spurred him into action to contact Henry. When Henry's son Jeremy didn't buy the home, it immediately opened the door for Hannah and I to help Henry revive his feelings for you, his first love, as we had many other times when the opportunity presented itself and did not infringe upon anyone's free will."

"I just knew you were involved Gabriel," Henry said. "The moment I stepped into Marjorie's—er, Jenny's house, I felt right at home. The furniture, the fragrance in the air, books, recipes… everything reflected my tastes. How I began to confuse Marjorie with Jenny only to finally learn they were in fact the same person!"

"We were a little concerned about your state of mind," Gabriel chuckled.

"Isn't that something, Henry?" Jenny chimed in. "We were beginning to live a life we could have lived… albeit not together, until now."

Jenny kissed Henry's cheek, then let go of his hands and stepped back. She turned and looked towards the guardian angels and then back to Henry. "They were present all the time helping us. Hannah started to tell me earlier how they tried to get us back together time and again and weren't able to do so until, today. It is in part for this reason I was allowed to come back and get you."

Hannah and Gabriel fluttered their wings.

Jenny's eyes brightened as did the nimbus above her head as

she gazed lovingly into Henry's eyes.

"Remember, Henry, some matches are made in heaven and perhaps marriages, too. Even though we missed out on earth, I believe our greatest joy is yet to come."

"But, Jenny, there are no marriages in heave—"

"Ssssh. Just trust in the Lord and don't—"

"Yes, I know, don't lean on your own understanding," Henry finished. "I now see I will need to rely on this passage in my spiritual life, as well."

"Hannah told me there is someone else we have to get. Someone you love very much."

"Who?"

"Father Engelmann. I think it is all part of God's plan. Perhaps, Father will be the one to marry us, either before or after we get to heaven."

"But, Jenny—"

"Just trust in the Lord, Henry."

Once again, Hannah nodded.

What Jenny said suddenly hit Henry. "Is Father Engelmann dead, as well?" Henry recalled his dream and what Jenny had just told him. "I dreamt that Father gave up his life for you so you could live…if that is the case, for what end? You are still dead and…so is he!"

Jenny looked at Henry and smiled; rather than answer his queries, Jenny said those wonderful words, those four magical words, "Quickly, hold my hand."

Without any hesitation, he reached out for her hand. The instant their hands touched, there was a huge flash of pure white light, brighter than a bolt of lightning, and their spirits, along with their guardian angels, were gone.

Chapter Eighteen

I'll get Josh from the back yard and meet you at the car."
Within seconds, Jeremy took hold of his son and told his friend
to go home. Camilla was already waiting for him as he got to the
front driveway. After strapping Joshua and then himself in, he
squealed back out of the driveway.

As they raced down the street, Jeremy began filling Camilla in
on the conversation he had with his brother.

"Was the officer certain that Dad was killed in the accident?"
asked Camilla.

"Yes, apparently the SUV is totaled. They used the Jaws of Life
to get him out."

"I can't believe all this is happening, Jeremy. Mom…now Dad,
all in the same day, what is going on?"

"Well, let's get to the accident scene and see if we can still see
Dad and do what we can." Jeremy refused to believe his dad was
dead… it couldn't be true!

Jeremy reached across to Camilla, "I know this is almost too
much to bear, Honey, but we have to hang in there."

"And what about Justin, he needs us to be with him, too. Maybe
you should drop me off at the gallery."

"There isn't time. It will take at least a half hour to get to the accident scene through the traffic. I'm sure Justin will tough it out until we get there."

Camilla squeezed her husband's hand.

"I know Dad would be praying at this point if it were one of us."

Josh piped up unexpectedly from the back seat and said, "Let's say the guardian angel prayer for Grandpa. You always tell me to say it for Grandma when I go to sleep."

Jeremy turned to Camilla and shook his head. "I didn't think he was listening to all this. Amazing what kids hear." And then raising his voice slightly, he continued, "But yes, Josh, that's a good idea, let's say a prayer to our dear guardian angel to take a message for us to God to please bring Grandpa back to us. Yeah, let's ask God for a miracle; to heal him!"

"Is Grandpa going to get better, Mommy?" Joshua wanted to know.

Camilla looked at Jeremy. The full impact of all this hadn't really registered on either of them. It all seemed so surreal, as if they were in a daze. They would have to see Henry's body to put some finality to all this.

"Grandpa was in an accident, Josh. We are going there now to see what has happened." Camilla turned to Jeremy and shrugged her shoulders. In a low whisper she said, "We will have to explain what happened to Josh tonight or at the accident scene…"

As they sat there frantically waiting for the lights to turn green, a small voice from the backseat filled the car with a quiet peace and hope…

"Angel of God, my guardian dear… please help Grandpa." said Joshua.

And then, after a pause, "Mommy? What comes after my guardian dear?"

Jeremy was too choked up to say anything.

With tears in her eyes, Camilla continued the prayer, coaxing her little boy along…

"To whom God's love commits me here, ever this day be at my side to light and guard, to rule and guide. Amen."

CHAPTER NINETEEN

After Father Engelmann died, his spirit left his earthly body and floated up and over to the far end of the sun room. From that vantage point, he could see everything in the room. Zachariah, his guardian angel, was by his side. Father had communed with him so often and intimately over the years that it was just a matter of seeing and meeting him spiritually to know Zachariah completely.

Zachariah was much like Father had always visualized him to be. His light brown hair was long and he wore a beard of the same colour. Streaks of white hair grew out of the top of his forehead as well as from his beard. It gave Zachariah a wise, timeless look, almost the perfect complement to Father Engelmann's appearance. He wore an amber-coloured gown with a tan rope that hung from the back of his neck, crossed in front of his chest and tied to a similar cord wrapped around his waist. His shoulders were broad and strong, and growing out of his shoulder blades were two huge white wings.

Zachariah was a good eight to ten feet tall if you measured him to the tips of his wings. His overbearing stature could have been intimidating, if it wasn't for his clear, friendly eyes and benevolent smile. Overall, his beaming countenance exuded such a gracious kindheartedness that it made Father Engelmann want to fly into his powerful arms.

Zachariah loved his commission to protect, guide, and watch over Father. Of all the 1147 people Zachariah had been assigned to over the years, David Engelmann had to be his favourite. On the whole, Father had been easy to look after. His life was built on the solid rock of the Word that withstood all the tempests and storms of life. He was a good man, a holy man, and the odd time his foundation quivered was when his stubbornness and impatience got the best of him.

Zachariah held a colossal fondness for this reverent man of God and regretted the fact, that as soon as he delivered David Engelmann to the Lord, his mission would be over and he would be reassigned to some other living soul at the moment of their conception.

David and Zachariah were about to talk over occurrences in Father's past, when they were interrupted by Nurse Dianne Frowler entering the sun room and seeing Father in his chair. It only took her a few moments to realize Father Engelmann was not just asleep, but permanently so.

Father was moved by her grief over his passing and the tender way she kissed his forehead. And what moved Father even more, was how all the residents came and gathered around him and sang and prayed.

Father noted the many healings that had happened that morning and immediately praised the Lord for His kindness. During that morning prayer session, Edith's abscessed tooth was gone and the blessing didn't stop until all her teeth were restored. She was shocked when her upper plate fell out as new teeth emerged! The cut to Angie's finger while preparing breakfast was instantly healed. Margaret no longer needed the hearing aid Father had bought her, and Elmer's lifetime wish for hair to cover his baldness, now looked like a hippy in desperate need of a haircut.

And to see Johnny run and jump about like a merry child, brought such joy and waves of euphoric exhilaration to Father's spirit, Zachariah had to place his hands on Father's shoulders lest he shoot off into the far reaches of heaven. The Holy Spirit was sure a-movin' in that morning's prayer session!

Zachariah struggled to control his wings from lifting him off. The sight of seeing Father so elated over his sheep and their blessings moved him more so than the miracles themselves. That is what he so loved about Father, always giving, always wanting the best for others, always happy for them, always… loving.

Until now, Father hadn't known that angels could cry. His tears of joy were already pooling on his lap and even more elation swept through him as he felt Zachariah's tears cascade through the fingers of the angel's hands resting on his shoulders. Father smiled. It was the reason why many times he felt extra gladdened for having done a good deed. His protector was rejoicing with him. Father reached back to his shoulder and put his hand over his guardian angels' and patted it. The burst of affection they shared brightened the sun room with glorious light, startling the residents below them.

"You have affected and influenced the lives of many, many people, David. The Lord is well pleased with you and what you have accomplished with the talents you were given."

Father turned and nodded, almost bowing.

As Father saw Angie scoot off to the kitchen to check on the roast for the residents' dinner, he was surprised that the wonderful smell was not making him hungry. It made him think, "Do angels have regular meals, Zachariah?"

"You're aware of the expression, 'you can't live on love'? Well, that may not be true for people on earth, but it is true for us. When we hear a kind word or see a nice deed, it's like having a snack. An act of forgiveness or acceptance, well now that's considered an hors d'oeuvre." Father chuckled. Zachariah turned to him and continued, "In your case, David, just look at my size! I'm feasting all the time. Since looking after you, my wings have put on over fifty pounds!"

Father laughed and Zachariah joined in.

"Now that my appointment with you is coming to a close, I will quickly shed this excess weight when my new assignment begins."

Father looked up at Zachariah. "Oh?"

"There's a learning curve that most people follow. Slowly they quit hitting their head against a brick wall or tire of going in circles and eventually learn to depend on their Lord, to accept, to forgive, to believe… to love."

"Yes, yes, Zachariah, I have seen much of that and in myself, as well."

Zachariah chuckled. "Over 1500 years ago I almost shriveled up, I lost so much weight. The Roman soldier I was assigned to at the time engaged in a lot of things that caused me much concern and worry. But as is usually the case, as he neared the end of his time on this earth, he began to change. On the day of his passing, he was so relenting, forgiving, and sorrowful for his deeds and misgivings, I put on over fifty pounds!"

Once again, they shared a huge laugh.

"There was one other time, David, I must share with you."

Father smiled, his eyes twinkling with delight.

"Just last century, I attended to a man who enjoyed sips of wine in much excess... actually, in considerable excess. Most days I could keep my distance from the intoxicating fragrance of it all, but the poor man needed close guidance and careful watch, requiring that I be near and... good heavens, some days I could not fly straight and nearly broke my left wing!"

Father roared. He had not reveled in such an enjoyable conversation in a long time. He was surely going enjoy heaven.

To his right, just off to Zachariah's side, Father saw a bright light. At first he thought it was the aura surrounding Zachariah or the late afternoon sun coming through the sun room windows. But the light was much too bright. It was the brightness of at least ten suns put together. Had he not been a spirit now, his earthly eyes would immediately have been blinded. He felt strangely attracted to the light, yet remained stationary. He knew it was his passageway into eternity, yet he remained put.

Even as Zachariah and he were enjoying each other's company he was wondering why he hadn't as yet crossed completely over into God's kingdom. He was honoured that the Lord had taken his life for Jenny's, but why was he still there? He turned to discuss this with Zachariah, his long dear trusted friend with whom he constantly communed with over the years.

"What is the hold up, Zachariah? Why are we not going to heaven? Have I done something wrong? Is the Lord purging me for some sin I have committed and not confessed?"

"No, no, David, it's nothing like that. You have been a good and faithful servant."

"Well, then, tell me what is it? I am so anxious to go to the other side and see my Anna and parents and—"

"Well, the truth of the matter is, you have done too good of a job. Over the years, there have only been a handful of people who have disrupted what was written for the destiny of each and every person who is born. The precise time when he comes into the world and the exact time he leaves has been known for all time and is written in stone."

"I don't understand, Zachariah." Father wrinkled his brow and looked confused and impatient, a lingering bad habit from his earthly days.

"Well, let me finish. David, we are presently in a state of limbo. Where we are now, there is no need for hurry."

Father smiled shamefaced, not surprised by Zachariah's quick and keen perception.

"The truth is David," Zachariah went on, his voice as warm as the sun, "that all the Masses and prayers you said over the years for Henry and Jenny and that prayer session you had in the chapel this morning... well, that was a humdinger; very powerful. All of us were quite moved to say the least. In fact, all of God's many mansions vibrated with tremors that in earthly terms would have gone off the Richter scale with ease!"

Father laughed, again. "I have to admit, Zachariah, it was a doozy. Those warriors of mine really got into it, didn't they?" Father beamed.

"Yes, they certainly did, even the Holy Spirit was surprised by the release of His power. The greater the faith and earnestness of the prayer, the greater His Spirit is felt. It is at times like this, David, when heaven and earth begin to touch one another. And I must add, you and your group did touch down, this morning, indeed."

Father looked deeply into Zachariah's clear, warm, amber eyes. The depth seemed to go on forever, impossible to read.

"So, what does all this mean, Zachariah?"

"Well, like I said, there have only been a few times throughout history when the pre-destiny of someone is changed. Lazarus is perhaps the one best known. He had passed beyond for four days and the Lord out of compassion for his friend, restored his life. Some say he was in limbo, but we know better. Lazarus had actually crossed the threshold and the Lord changed his destiny! This may very well be one of those times."

"Are you saying my fate may be changed?"

Zachariah's hands shuffled first this way and then that way, his wings mimicking every movement. "Well, there is more to it, David. Right now you are in a limbo region where we are still trying to decide what to do with you. Besides the depth and intensity of your prayers and the laying down of your life for Jenny, there also is the fervent depth of the love Henry and Jenny have for one another, their desire to be with one another, to marry one another. Their love is a rare thing and was a match that the heavens played a part in. You've heard the expression, 'theirs was a match made in heaven'?"

Once again Father looked puzzled. He'd always thought that expression was nothing more than fluff.

"Do you remember the day when they first met in your store and they were picking up the salmon tins that Henry knocked over?"

"Yes, yes, I could see it in the boy's eyes how smitten he was by that pretty young miss."

"Well, both he and she were more than smitten." Zachariah reiterated. "When they looked into each other's eyes it was not just a human attraction going on between them, but a spiritual one, as well. Both their guardian angels were so caught up in that union that a part of their heavenly energy surged along with the gaze Henry and Jenny shared, adding much greater force and impetus to their earthly attraction. Not only were they intoxicated with affection, with friendship and love at first sight, but their hearts were wounded as well."

"Love at first sight does happen," concurred Father. "It is difficult to embrace how it works, but how could their hearts be wounded? Does love not cause pleasure and even ecstasy?"

"Yes, it does appear as a contradiction. Humans sometimes describe it as an oxymoron. Something so pleasurable it causes pain. It's like the love I have witnessed which you have at times for the Lord. Over the years, I marveled how you longed for Jesus so much you ached in pain. While your love grew for the Lord over time, the passionate love between Henry and Jenny was instant."

Father's eyes brightened, a sign of comprehension, but his expression still looked perplexed and so Zachariah went on.

"Poets, artists and writers over the ages have tried to explain and portray this phenomenon of love at first sight. William did a fine job in Romeo and Juliet. Ah, that Shakespeare, the Lord blessed him with such a brilliant insight into human nature; wait until you meet him, Father. But I digress, Eros, in Greek myth—or perhaps better yet, Cupid, for example, the God of Love in Roman mythology (often depicted as a cherub with a bow and arrow) metaphorically explains what has happened in Henry and Jenny's case quite well.

"When those two young people locked into the gaze they shared that first time, imagine Cupid shooting his love tipped arrows along their gaze, right into their eyes and straight through to their hearts, piercing and wounding them. But because of the added impetus of their guardian angels' heavenly energy, the arrow, so to speak, went beyond their hearts, penetrating their very souls, deepening their love, deepening their wound, uniting them spiritually. Instantly, they were sick in love for each other, yearning one another, not wanting to be apart for a single moment."

"Yes, it is as you say, Zachariah. They desired to be with one another every moment and on the day they parted, it was as if the world had come to an end. I recall Henry mentioning that he felt as if something were caught in his eyes. Yes, yes, how Henry agonized and pained for her. Not just for a day, a month, but years; until this very day. Normally when things don't work out in a rela-tionship, it usually passes after a few months and certainly a year or two. Yet, time, distance and all the impediments that life thrust their way, could not squelch that love."

"That is a fact, David," concurred Zachariah. "The sorrow and pain Henry felt was the same with Jenny. How their guard-ian angels wept and reached out to their respective charges. They knew had they not added their spiritual ardor to Henry and Jenny's captivation at that moment, perhaps their pierced hearts, in time would have healed and as you just noted, they could have went on as most other humans do in similar circumstances. But alas, their wounds never healed.

"For years I witnessed how their protectors worked in earnest to get them back together, to correct what they had caused. But no sooner had their angels opened one door, life with its twists and turns closed it. Just look back at all the events: their final letters with identical pewter angels, saved from fire, retrieved from a steel vault and delivered only to be locked up again in treasure chests—"

"And Henry's purchase of Jenny's house. He was so excited, claiming to have found his other self, imagining that the lady he bought the house from was Jenny and then, the discovery of the diary to learn that home was in fact really hers!"

"All these things and even their dreams were prompted by the gentle actions and whispered urgings of their guardian angels," concluded Zachariah.

Father shook his head lamentably, "Yes, I can see how heaven played its part. It's rare for a love to be so strong in spite of everything that happened and even their desire to be together and be married is—"

"Well, that's where we come in, David. Since it was our heavenly involvement that created such a deep and lasting wound of love and yearning, we are looking at some way to make up for it. In fact, their guardian angels feel so responsible and moved by the zeal, lasting commitment and desire that these two have for one another, they have gone back and forth with great solicitude to the throne of God, hoping to procure for their protégés, a special request. Especially since sunrise, today the angels are bearing the prayers of Henry and Jenny to our heavenly Father, imploring Him to hear their petitions."

Father didn't know what to say. "Well, it is clear that they are deeply in love and have been so since that moment but, Zachariah, how can they find fulfillment, now? Jenny is gravely ill and about to die, perhaps she has already. And the Bible has taught us that marriage, as we know it, does not exist in heaven. How then can they possibly be united or find any kind of meaningful relationship, now? Surely marriage, which they so much desire, is out of the question?"

"David, you above all people should know that nothing is impossible with God. During your entire life, you have believed in the power and abundance of our heavenly Father."

"Yes, yes, that is true, so what will happen here?" Father quickly asked, revealing his impatience once again.

"That is what we are waiting for. Soon, two people very dear to your heart will come here. And soon, a decision of what is meant to be, will be issued and carried out. As we speak, David, a very important meeting is going on. God the Father, God the Son and

God the Holy Spirit and a whole host of heavenly saints and angels are discussing this matter. Soon, we shall know their answer."

As Father began to question Zachariah further on what he just said, Henry and Jenny, and their guardian angels appeared on the scene. At first they only saw Father sitting on his chair in the sun room with all the residents standing around singing and praising the Lord.

"Oh, that's the group that was praying for me this morning!" Jenny exclaimed.

"But, why isn't Father praying?" Henry asked.

"Look there," said Jenny pointing to where Father and his guardian angel were floating in the far end of the sun room.

"Over here," Father said, waving at Henry and Jenny.

"I knew you'd be here. We are coming to get you," said Jenny.

Father opened his arms as both Henry and Jenny flew into them, their guardian angels stopping just short of being caught in Father's exuberant embrace as well and getting their wings all tangled.

"What a pleasant surprise to see you both," Father exclaimed, as he freed Henry and Jenny from his loving hold of them. "I expected Jenny perhaps, but not you, Henry."

"Yes, for the three of us to meet our Maker on the same day is remarkable. I am still trying to understand it all. The Lord works in mysterious ways, Father."

"Yes, yes, He most certainly does."

Henry studied Father's guardian angel for a moment and then said, "Now, I know what you would look like if you grew a beard, Father. The warmth of your angel's eyes and benevolent smile is just like yours."

"Yes, yes, there is a remarkable similarity."

"It's one of the hazards of looking after someone that has lived as long as David," said Zachariah with a chuckle. "You not only pick up their traits, but looks, as well." He opened his arms towards Henry. "I'm Zachariah. You may call me Zach, if you wish. It's nice to meet you in spirit. Father thought about you so often it's as if I know you through and through."

Henry stood on his tiptoes and still had to reach way up to give and receive a hug from Zachariah.

Jenny greeted Zachariah next and unlike Henry who forgot to

use his flying ability, Jenny floated up into Zach's open arms while Father extended a warm hug to Hannah and Gabriel.

Surrounded by heavenly angels and at last her first love standing next to her, Jenny could no longer contain her bubbling excitement. Her eyes sparkled and flashed as she turned to Father. "Our guardian angels, Gabriel and Hannah brought us here to pick you up. We think that maybe you will be able to marry us before we enter heaven, or perhaps after. A heavenly marriage would be so wonderful."

Father looked compassionately at Jenny, reluctant to reveal yet another impediment which may keep her and Henry from fulfilling their hearts' desire.

"I'm sorry to say, Jenny, marriage in heaven does not exist."

"I tried to tell Jenny that too." Henry confirmed.

Jenny looked lovingly at Henry and then back at Father. "But maybe, just maybe, a rule can be broken. Henry and I have desired this for so long, that perhaps even the good Lord has to make an exception,"

"Yes, that may be a possibility. Zachariah and I were just talking about that before you came—"

"Ahem," Zachariah interjected, "It is not yet time to share our conjectures, Father. That is for the Lord to decide." They all looked at each other, not sure what to say.

Comfort gathered in Father's eyes as Scripture came to mind. "The Lord does remind us in Isaiah 55:9, 'As the heavens are higher than the earth, so are My ways higher than your ways, and My thoughts than your thoughts.'"

"See, there you are, anything is possible with God!" Jenny blurted and then added, "Well, at least we will be together. That's why I am so glad to have you both here. I wouldn't want to lose you up there, but I still feel the Lord is going to do something special for us. I say we trust in the Lord and pass through the tunnel and see what God has in store."

Jenny looked at the angels and then at Henry and Father Engelmann.

"Yes, perhaps the Lord is waiting for us." Father turned to Zachariah and continued, "What do you say?"

"We are here to follow your will. We shall know soon enough if that is what the Lord wants." replied Zachariah.

"Good," said Jenny. Since no-one seemed to have any objection to her plan, she slid between Father and Henry and said, "Quickly, take my hands."

Father and Henry took Jenny's hands in theirs and all six spirits— Father, Henry, Jenny and their respective guardian angels— moved forward through the south panel of windows as if they were not there. Just before them was the bright light which Father had noted earlier. It was the tunnel that they would go through to enter eternity. Once through, there would be no coming back.

Chapter Twenty

"Hello, Mr. Hamilton? Nurse Johnson just called to say you be phoning for me?"

"Look, Matilda, I have one of my staff making arrangements to ship Marjorie's body back to Ottawa—"

"But, Mr. Hamilton, she may have made arrangements to be buried here where her daughter lives and also her..."

"We'll just have to cancel any cemetery plot she may have purchased. Her daughter will just have to come to Ottawa—"

"But, Mr. Hamilton, it's not just her daughter, it's also..." Matti's words trailed off.

"Surely you don't mean that farm boy, Pederson, has any say in this?"

Matti was surprised that Mr. Hamilton knew of Henry Pederson. "Do you know Henry Ped—?"

"Yes, yes, from way back. Marjorie got over him a long time ago. That's why she married me! No, she belongs at home with her family and we're going to have a funeral that she rightfully deserves. J.J sold her home last fall in Regina and so Marjorie doesn't have any ties there anymore."

Matti could feel her employer's sensitivity in the matter. She knew from years of experience with her master that he could erupt at any time. He had been softening up this last while, but she had to say what was in her heart. She knew how deeply her dear friend loved Henry and so desired to be with him.

"But, Mr. Hamilton—"

"There are no 'buts' about it, Matilda. Marjorie is coming back to Ottawa and I will press to have it done by tomorrow at the latest! And since you are there, I would like you to go to the hospital first thing in the morning and do everything you need to do to keep things moving. If there is any problem or matter that needs attention, call me right away and I'll have it attended to. Is that understood?"

Matti was perspiring, "Oh, sweet Jesus, if you be fishing in one them there heavenly streams, I hope you catch Your limit soon. You be needed back on the job. I don't like the way this be movin' forward, that for sure…"

"What are you mumbling about, Matilda. You're not beginning to lose it on me, are you?"

"No, I just be waiting on the Boss, to tell me what to do—"

"I just told you, for Pete's sake!"

"My God, Camilla, look at the crowd up ahead. That's where the accident scene must be. My heart is pounding so fast, I hope I don't have a heart attack."

Camilla reached her hand over to Jeremy's and squeezed tightly. "Maybe park over there and let's walk into the crowd."

"Yeah, that may be best." Jeremy pulled over and parked the car. The three of them made their way through the crowd. They saw the ambulance attendant close the back doors to the ambulance and hurry around to the driver's side.

"There's a police officer. Let's go talk to him. The ambulance may have Dad in the back or somebody else that was injured."

They formed a single line and held hands as they slithered through the crowd.

"Excuse me officer, my name is Jeremy Pederson. I'm not sure if it was you or one of the other policemen that phoned to let us know that Dad was in an accident. That's his red SUV over there."

"You're his son, are you?"

Jeremy nodded struggling to keep his emotions in check. He was much like his dad in that regard; he wore his feelings on his sleeve.

"The ambulance just picked up your father and are on their way to the General Hospital—"

Jeremy lowered his voice, stood in front of Josh, and asked the officer, "Did my dad die in the accident…?"

The senior police officer tightened his lips and nodded, "I'm afraid he didn't make it, son. You can see the condition of his vehicle. That was some accident. We needed the Jaws of Life to remove him. It's a tough break…"

Camilla began to sob. "Why are you crying, Mommy?" Joshua wanted to know.

Camilla simply bent down and picked up her son. "Maybe we should go to the hospital and see your dad, Jeremiah."

"You go ahead with your family. There's not much you can do here. We will put your dad's SUV into our compound. You may be still able to catch up to the ambulance. It's getting close to the noon rush hour and there is no urgency to get to the hospital…" He gazed slowly at Jeremy, not sure if he should have said what he just did.

Jeremy nodded and forced an appreciative smile. He turned to Camilla. "Okay, let's get back to the car and go to the hospital."

THE NURSE HAD difficulty walking into the crowded room. It was filled with family and parishioners to overflowing. Normally visits were restricted to only family and limited to two people at a time in the IC unit but Angie's request to override the hospital regulations was approved by the family doctor. The nurse had to admit she could feel the spiritual power in the room. Perhaps the prayers by those present could bring healing where medical help was no longer effective. Florence went over to Peter's side and picked up his wrist.

The nurse looked at Angie and slowly shook her head. "I'm so sorry," Florence whispered. She looked up at the rest of the family and friends that surrounded the bed and the sadness in her eyes confirmed what she had just relayed to Peter's grieving wife. Florence let go of Peter's wrist and gently laid his hand down on the bed and in the same motion pulled the sheet over Peter's face.

Angie's weeping became more audible but soon was drowned out by the praying sounds of others present in the room. Everyone remained stationary, unable to move, nor accept what had happened. They all expected Peter to be healed; they had been praying so fervently.

Tears filled the eyes of the attending nurse, as well. Florence had not seen such support, love and prayer for someone in a long time. She, too, had come to love Peter in the few days that he had been on her ward. Florence gazed at the monitor and saw the steady line on the screen hoping that a blip would appear, but neither the line nor its eerie sound changed. Just as she went over to the monitor to turn it off, a blip appeared and then vanished.

Florence looked at the monitor puzzled.

Angie had heard its tiny sound and looked up, but only saw the steady, even line. Perhaps it was just her imagination, hoping against all hope that her dead husband was coming back. She stared at it for the longest moment, along with the nurse.

Once again, just as Florence reached up to turn off the monitor, she was so startled she nearly keeled over...

Chapter Twenty One

Father Engelmann, Henry, and Jenny approached the tunnel of light. All three were holding hands and about to pass into a life of eternity. As they neared the light, their clothes turned a brilliant white, much like the angels' robes behind them already had. Their features began to change, as well. They were shedding their old age and miraculously regaining their youth.

Although Jenny had no longer appeared frail and pallid in spirit, she began to look younger and even healthier by the second. Henry, too, was going through a metamorphosis. His beard was shedding at the same time his hair was growing and darkening. He looked forty, then thirty, then… it was an amazing sight.

Father Engelmann's one hundred earth years melted away into dark wavy hair and a rascally look in his eyes. They were so caught up in entering the tunnel of light, they were completely unaware of the transformation that each was undergoing.

The three were now at the very edge of the radiant tunnel. Even in their spirit form, they had to squint; the light was so dazzlingly white and brilliant. Their respective guardian angels walked closely behind each of them, ready to deliver them to their Lord and complete the assignment they'd been given years ago.

Just as they all entered the doorstep, the threshold of eternity itself, another light, even more brilliant than the one they were stepping into, emerged from the tunnel and advanced towards them. They stopped, momentarily frozen in their paths and then retreated, unable to withstand the utter holiness emanating from this emerging light. Was it God, Himself, coming for them?

The closer the light came, the more they had to retreat from the tunnel and so did their youthful transformation. They began to age and assume the appearance they had before. Father's hair began to fall out and Henry's beard grew and turned grey. Jenny's glowing youthful look, her skin so luminous and fresh, turned pale and languid. For the first time they began to feel frightened or was it God-fearing?

Gradually, the dazzling light took form almost as if it were coming out of a mist. The first to emerge, were two hands almost touching at the end of open outstretched arms, as if diving into their presence. These arms led up to broad soft rounded shoulders, from which grew two large wings, moving ever so gently. The magnificent apparition flew directly towards them, much like a white dove with outstretched wings. It became clear the manifestation was another angel of immense size.

Then, almost imperceptibly, the radiant angel raised his wings and fanned them out as a dove preparing to land. He slowed, and the rest of his angelic body hidden behind his shoulders and wings, lowered, and his legs and feet emerged. His wings rose high above him and fluttered effortlessly before stilling. They folded behind him as his feet touched down, his powerful frame coming completely into view with all its majesty.

Henry, Jenny and Father were awestruck and transfixed at the daunting figure before them. They shuddered with fear and clustered together. This was an angel of high rank. Clearly, the persona of an archangel, perhaps, Michael the Archangel.

Everything about him was whiter than the most dazzling pure white, one could ever imagine and beyond. His long, flowing golden hair fell upon his robe and continued in rhythmic glistening motion. It was as if his entire being were perpetual waves, shimmering and glowing in the light. An aura of such radiant, majestic holiness enveloped his entire spirit. It was difficult to make out his face. It was a sight of awe and wonderment. The spirits of Henry, Father and Jenny dropped to their knees in reverence and veneration, bowing their heads.

Zachariah, Hannah, and Gabriel floated off to the side to meet with the archangel as Father, Jenny and Henry dared raise their heads and watched. The angels greeted each other much as humans do with hugs and kisses on the cheek. At times, their wings intertwined as they fluttered in reaction to their joyful reunion. The angels conferred with one another as if in some private board meeting. Hannah's wings flapped excitedly every now and then as the archangel talked. The news must have been good as the angels were smiling and their wings fluttered like three hummingbirds.

After a brief moment, the angels hugged the archangel, once more. Backing away to make room, he turned and moved his immense wings. He easily lifted up and slowly aimed his arms out towards the tunnel of light. With just two flaps of his wings, he re-entered the bright passageway and was gone. The intensity of the light instantly increased and became so blinding, the trio had to look away.

Then, as if consumed by the tunnel of light, the intenseness quickly diminished back to what it was as the archangel returned to his heavenly quarters.

Zachariah, Gabriel, and Hannah braced themselves as the decision of the Lord as revealed to them by the archangel was upon them. Instantly the mountain— the cancer that had ravaged the body of their dear, sweet sister Jenny— shook and crumbled and fell into the sea of God's love with a mighty crash. A towering tsunami of immense power erupted, healing everything in its path. It was coming forth as a mighty wind with lightning speed. The breath of God was blowing to them, in them, through them, their very essence of being renewed, restored.

Jenny, Henry and Father held onto their spirits for dear life, as the hurricane of the Lord passed upon them.

"Hurry." said Zachariah, "Let's get back to them lest they soar into infinity." The angels flew over to their charges, their long hair and robes blowing and fluttering deliriously in the storm. The angels comforted their commissions as they had always done in the past.

Instead of fear, Father, Jenny, and Henry were filled with jubilation and praise. They raised their hands into the wind, their spirits soaring, and rejoicing. Gabriel moved closer, directly behind Henry with his hand firmly upon his shoulder. Hannah hovered a foot or two behind Jenny, struggling against the turbulence. Her arms extended in a watchful, protective pose, ready to catch her.

In the wake of the healing storm, the wind abated and turned into a gentle, warm, summer breeze. They all felt exhilarated having felt the grace of God wash over them. They turned and gazed into each others' eyes, their hearts filled with youthful joy. And like little children, they took each others' hands and danced around and around.

"They that wait upon the Lord shall renew their strength," shouted Father.

"They shall mount up with wings as eagles," cried Henry.

"They shall run, and not be weary; and they shall walk and not faint," chimed in the three angels gleefully completing the rest of Isaiah 40:31.

Their spirits soared with love and affection; the heavens glowed brighter. Hannah's wings flapped so exuberantly she lifted the entire encircled group and spun them into the air.

"Oooh!" Jenny shrieked, her hair like the angels' whipped by the force. Laughter, mingled with buoyant cries of exultation, effervesced into the celestial atmosphere.

"Please stop!" yelped Father. "All this happiness is making me too dizzy!"

Slowly they descended and resumed their carefree prancing. Zachariah and Father stood side-by-side reveling in God's healing power. Both had seen their Lord work mightily before and knew what was in store for them.

And as this awareness inched its way into Henry and Jenny's understanding, tears of impending parting filled their eyes. As they hopped and skipped, one by one, to each of them it began to happen.

First to disappear was Jenny. She was firmly holding both Father Engelmann's hand and Henry's and yet she slid out from between them as easy as a pat of butter dissolves in a warm pan. She was gone and so was her zestful protector. No sooner had Henry turned to his beloved Jenny then he too, vanished into thin air. Only Father Engelmann and Zachariah were left.

Father raised his head towards heaven, "Thank you, Lord, for granting us our hearts' prayer. Their marriage will truly be a match made in heaven."

Father turned and looked lovingly into his life-long friend's gentle eyes and extended his hand. "This has been a wonderful day, Zachariah. I am now ready to see my Anna and parents..." Father's words trailed off as his protector's eyes revealed something else in store.

Zachariah smiled. "Your time has not yet come, David."

Father's face puzzled. "But why, Zachariah? Has the Lord not accepted my life for Jenny's? I am an old man; surely my life on earth is over."

"Did you not say earlier, 'as the heavens are higher than the earth, so are His ways higher than your ways, and His thoughts than your thoughts?'"

"Yes, yes," Father blurted, already re-gaining his earthly impatience. "What else could there possibly be left for me to do that others cannot?"

"You have been a man of God and witnessed many things during your lifetime, David. The Lord wishes for you to record all you have seen in your earthly life as well as what you have been allowed to see in the unseen today. At the heart of all this, will be the story of your two dear friends. It is a love story that the heavens played a part in and will touch the lives of many people and restore their faith."

"Do you mean to write a book!?"

"Yes, David—"

"But, I am no writer, Zachariah, and at my age... my memory is failing, the task is too great..."

"David, all things are possible through God who strengthens him. The Lord shall inspire you. You shall remember everything that has happened to you. Thoughts and words will come to you to clearly express your dear friend's life story."

Father Engelmann gazed at his protector in awe. He enjoyed this visit on the other side with Zachariah so much and couldn't wait to spend eternity with him. Zach's gaze returned that affection. He deeply loved the man before him whose life he had protected and guided.

In the next moment of thought, Father was granted the vision of all that went before not only in the lives of his friends but of all humanity. He was witnessing it all from both an earthly and heavenly perspective. In that split second of eternity, Father was filled with the deepest of sorrow and taken to heights of pure elation.

The sorrowful condition of mankind, the workings of angels, how the divine providence of the Lord is at work to bring His children home… it overwhelmed the holy priest.

"Oh, what has the future in store, Zachariah?"

"Only the Lord knows what lies ahead. Neither man nor angels can see into the future. We are messengers of God and this is what we are here to tell you. Our conjectures, perhaps more astute than yours, are still conjectures. Your days will unfold moment by moment and the wise decisions and choices you make will to a large degree determine your future, as you well know. Your life on earth has been good and close to your Creator. There is no reason for you but to continue to live in peace."

Zachariah gazed tenderly into Father's eyes, hesitant for a moment and then continued. "There is one other task the Lord has in mind and is the second reason for your return—"

"A second task? What is it?" Father quickly asked, the puzzled look on his face returning again. "I wish to stay or return as quickly as possible. I miss my Anna and desire to be with the Lord."

"Yes, we understand, David, but the Lord has a matter that is best accomplished by you. It is a very important mission. It may prove to be your greatest challenge and crowning achievement."

"But the Lord can accomplish all things… surely, He doesn't need me."

"That is true, David. The heavenly Father knows of your desire to come home and so he has allowed you to see into the future and you can decide to either stay, and leave the tasks to God's divine providence, or you can choose to return to carry out these two assignments."

In the next instance, Father saw what his second mission was. Tears filled his eyes instantly and he quickly without any hesitation nodded. "Yes, Zachariah… He will need me."

Father hung his head and shrugged his shoulders at the same time. He lifted his hands and said, "Let the Lord's will be done."

Father Engelmann looked up to burn the image of his protector's kindly, warm eyes into his memory, but his guardian was no longer visible. All Father felt, was the mighty squeeze of his tender hand as his guardian angel pulled him gently through the crossing from the doorstep of heaven, back to earth.

Chapter Twenty Two

N urse Johnson stood by the counter and recalled watching Henry earlier as he walked to the elevator, his right arm had lifted as if he were reaching out to someone beside him, holding their hand. It was unfortunate he came on the day Ms. Hamilton died and not sooner. It was obvious he loved her deeply. The sight of him kissing her so tenderly just before she passed away still sent warm shivers through her. Clearly, it was not just a kiss between friends, but definitely between two lovers. She still felt a little cruel telling him he had to go. He just sat and slept there for over an hour holding her hand as if he were trying to bring her back to life. What a deep love he must have had for her.

Oh, how we all search for love and when it is there, it is snatched away so quickly at times.

As she walked behind the nurse's station, shaking her head she muttered, "It's truly a sorrowful sight."

Empathy and compassion were Nurse Johnson's strong traits and why she was so well suited for the palliative care ward, but following through with the morgue and filling out forms when a patient died were duties she dreaded. Reluctantly she picked up the phone and dialed down to the hospital basement.

"Hello, John. This is Nurse Johnson from Five West. Ms. Marjorie Hamilton just passed away—oh really? That sounds terrible. No, I understand. Good. No, there is no hurry. That will be fine."

Next, Nurse Johnson reached for the forms to write up her report on the circumstances surrounding Marjorie Jennifer Hamilton's demise and also those required for the morgue. Ms. Hamilton seemed like such a dear sweet lady. Nurse Johnson wished she could have gotten to know her better.

"Oh, how I dread to fill out these reports." Nurse Johnson got up and went to the staff room to get a coffee, finding any excuse to put off dealing with the matter for as long as she could.

A good half hour or so passed. Nurse Johnson filled out the necessary forms, had a coffee and a nice chat with the nurse's aide on duty. Suddenly, a light flashed on the monitor before her from room 505, Ms. Hamilton's room. Someone must have found her dead and was pulling the cord alerting the front desk.

"I already know," muttered Nurse Johnson, as she got up and headed to Ms. Hamilton's room. "Ms. Hamilton is my responsibility. I wish other nurses would just keep to their assignments."

Nurse Johnson burst through the open doorway completely expecting to see one of the other nurses hovering over Marjorie Hamilton's body. She was beginning to adopt her "head nurse" posture, as she gathered her resolve to emphatically state that she knew Ms. Hamilton was gone, when she stopped in mid-step. Her eyes opened wide, and her chin dropped to the floor as if she were seeing a ghost.

Sitting up on the bed, with the pillow propped behind her back, was Jenny. Her lack luster, lifeless eyes of just an hour or so ago now flashed and sparkled. She had the sweetest smile on her face. Incredibly, her yellow hair was fuller and longer. The bed covers were neatly folded on top of her legs and waist and her hands rested gently on her lap.

"I was wondering, nurse, could I please trouble you for a cup of chamomile tea?"

But, she couldn't be alive. I watched her die!

"Are you okay nurse? You look very pale… and growing even more so. If you don't feel well, I can do without a cup of tea. I assure—"

Nurse Johnson blinked her eyes several times and shook her

head, making certain she was not dreaming. Finally, regaining some composure, she responded, "Are you okay, Ms. Hamilton?"

"Yes, I'm fine, just had a nice long nap and feel a bit hungry, as well. Perhaps, I should have my tea with dinner. I can wait until then."

"No, no that's fine. I'll get you some tea, right away." Nurse Johnson rushed towards the door just as the attendants from the morgue came in.

"So, where's the corpse, Val?"

"Oh… no… not this room…"

"But I thought you said 5—"

"Ssssh," Nurse Johnson whispered, putting her forefinger across her lips.

"Oh, did someone pass away?" inquired Jenny.

"Yes… I mean no—"

Nurse Johnson was so flustered, she didn't know what to think or say. She shooed the attendants out.

"She was dead and came back to life!" Nurse Johnson exclaimed the moment they were out the door and out of earshot, her hands gesticulating.

Finally out of frustration, she motioned them to come down the hallway with their rolling stretcher where she could fully explain what she herself didn't yet understand. All she knew was that first thing this morning, Ms. Hamilton arrived by ambulance. All her vital signs indicated that she was on the verge of death and would be so within the hour. They were going to put her on life support, but she had signed papers at the care home that indicated she did not wish to have her life sustained by any machinery or medication. Later in the morning, when Mr. Pederson came in, she passed away. And now she was alive and looked in excellent health and years younger!

ABOUT THIRTY MINUTES after Carey's call for an ambulance, it arrived. Dianne heard the siren stop from her spot at the nurse's station as she worked on the requisite paperwork on her desk.

Dianne looked up at the front door as it opened. She expected the ambulance attendants, but it was Tony, the care home's custodian.

"Hi, Dianne," said Tony, "Did someone get hurt? Why is the ambulance here?"

Since Tony was only beginning his afternoon shift, he didn't know yet that Father Engelmann had passed away. Just as Nurse Frowler was about to explain what happened, they were interrupted by the ambulance attendants that walked through the front door carrying a stretcher.

"Hi, Tony," Dianne finally said.

She didn't know how to tell Tony, as he and Father Engelmann became very close friends during the past several months. Tony's attitude towards the residents and his care for their quarters greatly improved since Father arrived, but then Father had that influence on everybody.

"Tony, I have some sad news to tell you. Father Engelmann has passed away. He is in the sun room. Would you mind taking the ambulance attendants to him?"

Tony looked at the nurse with a look of bewilderment. "What? Are you kidding me?"

"No, I'm not. I wish I could say I was," replied Dianne, with a hopeful tone.

"Well, that's impossible, Dianne."

"No, I'm afraid it's true, Tony," Dianne replied, more firmly.

"No, Dianne, it's impossible," Tony repeated, just as emphatically as Nurse Frowler.

"What do you mean that's impossible?" Dianne said.

"Dianne, I just saw Father walk out the door. I saw him get into a taxi. He was just leaving as I walked in. I even said 'hello' to him."

Dianne stared at Tony. "Oh, Tony, that's impossible. Father Engelmann is dead. He is in the sun room. We had a little prayer wake for him during the last hour and a half. I checked his pulse—"

"No, you're kidding me," Tony questioned, his voice rising. "I know what I saw, Dianne."

Dianne was flushed and nervous. She didn't want to continue this insane argument any longer.

"Look, Tony, just come with me and see for yourself."

Dianne dropped what she was doing and marched down the hall towards the sun room. Tony and the attendants followed closely behind. Dianne turned sharply into the sun room and was instantly dumfounded, flabbergasted, so astonished, that she staggered backwards into Tony's arms. The chair where Father Engelmann had been seated not less than thirty minutes ago was empty!

THE AMBULANCE DROVE at a normal speed, towards the morgue at the General Hospital. The guy they just took out of the rolled-over SUV was a goner, so there was no hurry to get him to the hospital. His days of rush and hurry are over. No need to speed and risk another possible accident. It was a good thing in a way, as they had time to stop and examine an elderly lady who had fallen. But she proved to be okay and so they continued on their way.

Normally, when the attendants picked up a dead body, they simply put the corpse in the back and both the driver and the aide drive in the front seat. In their haste to clear out and get the traffic back to normal on Hill and Elphinstone Street, Steve went into the back with the body and Doug jumped into the truck and, out of habit, sped off.

Doug was just thinking about the accident. How the moving van had hit that SUV and it rolled over several times. It was amazing that the driver of the Escalade wasn't crushed in the severity of it all. He only had a slight red bruise on his forehead. That's probably what killed him. A sharp blow to the head when the SUV rolled and the driver's side slammed into the concrete road.

"Oh well, an autopsy will determine the cause," he mumbled, as he fumbled for his cigarettes.

At that moment, his partner buzzed up to him.

"Hey, Doug, you're not going to believe this. You better pull over. The guy who we just picked up at the accident, well, somehow he… he, has just come back to life."

"Ah, come on, Steve, don't give me the gears. The guy was dead, we both checked his vitals. Look, I've only been spooked one other time in my life like this. You can't BS me."

"Honestly, Doug. I'm not giving you the gears. He's alive. Just listen." He turned to Henry, sitting up on the cot. "What did you say your name was?"

"Henry Pederson."

"Holy s_ _ _," yelled Doug, his cigarette flying out of his mouth just as he was about to light it. "The artist? Henry Pederson?"

"Yeah, that's me," Henry calmly replied.

"Geez, I've got one of your paintings in my house and my mother-in-law, she just loves your work. Steve, is he really alive? Is it really Henry Pederson back there?"

Both Henry and Steve were now smiling.

"Yeah," said Steve, "He's wondering if we can take him back to his gallery?"

Doug burst out laughing, "This is so bizarre, too funny for words."

Steve looked at Henry, shook his head and then chuckled.

"Listen, Steve, we better take him to the hospital and make sure everything is okay," Doug said, trying to resume some role of responsibility in all this.

"But he says he is fine. He looks fine to me, too. I checked his pulse and blood pressure and he's very much alive and healthy. He had a serious bruise on his forehead, but I don't see that anymore, either. I don't understand what's going on here, it seems like we must have missed his pulse the first time or some kind of a miracle is going on back here."

"We better check him again at the gallery." interjected Doug.

"Yeah, we can check him over again and make certain he's all right," Steve concurred.

Doug flipped on the siren and with a chuckle and a burst of exuberance in his voice he exclaimed, "This is one time I don't mind turning on the siren. Let's get this guy home."

THE BLIP AND sound on the screen monitoring Peter's heart was so strong it startled the nurse. She turned to Peter but his face was covered by the sheet. Florence quickly made her way over to him and once again picked up his wrist fully expecting not to feel any pulse.

She was wrong!

She immediately felt a pulse and then another much stronger than the one before. The beat was accelerating so rapidly Peter's body began to shake and he abruptly sat up throwing the sheet off him. His eyes popped open and grew wide.

It was like a bolt of lightning was surging through him. Florence tried to pull her hand away from Peter's wrist, but was unable to. The electrical charge zooming through Peter's body kept it stuck. The charge was now flowing through Florence's body, shaking her as well.

Angie and those in attendance looked on in awe, their eyes and mouths wide open. The power of the Holy Spirit was so strong in the room it was palpable.

The blip on the monitor was racing up and down across the screen with blitzing speed; its sound deafening. Suddenly the monitor flashed with glowing sparks and went out. An eerie silence followed. Everyone turned to Peter...

Was Peter healed?

CHAPTER TWENTY THREE

J UST AS JEREMY crossed the intersection of Albert and College Avenue, he noticed the lights of an ambulance up ahead. It had just turned right on 14th Avenue.

"Did you see the ambulance up ahead, Camilla?"

"Yes, I did. It's heading up 14th to the General Hospital, probably."

Jeremy picked up speed, trying to catch up to the ambulance. As soon as he turned at 14th Avenue, it was Camilla who spotted the van.

"Look, there's the ambulance up ahead. It seems to be stopping at the gallery…"

"What on earth for?" muttered Jeremy.

PATRONS IN HENRY'S café looked out of the south windows as an ambulance, with its sirens on, pulled up in front of the café.

"Look, it's Henry getting out of the ambulance!" exclaimed Millie. She said it so loud, customers who were not aware of it turned to look too. Some even stood up and went to the window. "I wonder if someone in the café got sick or had a heart attack?"

asked one. "I hope whoever it was is okay." said another. "Maybe Henry was hurt or in an accident? He seems to be all right though, look how he is joking with the ambulance attendants."

More patrons in the café went to the window. Some, who had heard from Lauren and Justin that Henry had been in a serious accident, looked puzzled. One rushed off to the gallery to get Henry's children!

Henry shook Steve and Doug's hand.

"Thanks for the lift fellows."

"It is our pleasure," replied Doug. "Are you sure you're okay?"

"Yes, I am fine. In fact, I never felt better!"

"That was some accident you were in."

"You say it happened on the corner of Hill and Elphinstone?"

"Yeah, your SUV is totaled for sure. It's amazing that you got out with only a scratch on your arm—and even that mark on your forehead is gone… someone upstairs must be looking after you."

Henry just listened, totally bewildered and dumbfounded. He recalled visiting Jenny at the hospital. After she passed away, he left and decided to go back to his home at Hill Avenue.

"Yes, now I remember… I was driving down Elphinstone and… I missed the stop sign."

A deep wrinkle grew on his forehead, as he tried to recall more.

"Oh Yes!" Henry blurted out to Doug and Steve who were still standing there, a little concerned by the seemingly vacant look on Henry's face.

"I remember a truck coming towards me, as I failed to stop at the stop sign … but that's all I can recall."

"Yeah," said Steve. "A moving van broad-sided you. Your SUV rolled over at least twice. When we got there, you were unconscious. In fact, when we pulled you out of the SUV, we thought you were dead for sure." Steve stared at Doug with a look that asked if this all really happened…

Doug gave his answer to Steve by replying for him.

"Henry, when we took you into the ambulance, you were dead. It's amazing you didn't have any broken bones or more open wounds, other than a bruise on your forehead. By the time we got halfway to the hospital, you suddenly came back to life!"

Henry's head snapped back, still in a daze and trying to understand what happened. "I do recall waking up in the ambulance and you guys kidding about me being dead... are you sure I just wasn't unconscious from the accident?"

"You were a goner, Henry; you had no pulse, no vital signs whatsoever. We have never had equipment failure."

"I was dead and came back to life... how on earth could this be?"

Henry shook his head. "I, I...don't understand it all fellows... but one thing for sure, I'm glad to be here and... alive."

Steve and Doug looked at each other and then back at Henry and sort of chuckled, still amazed and bewildered by it all too.

"Well, we better get back to the station and have all the equipment examined and tested," said Doug and added, "Better check into that Escalade of yours as soon as possible... they probably towed it to the police compound."

"Yes, thanks again, guys."

"Good luck, Henry, nice meeting you!" yelled Steve, as he got into the ambulance and closed the door behind him.

Henry watched as the ambulance sped off, still in a daze. He couldn't believe what he just heard... *I was pronounced dead in an accident and then came back to life?... and Steve said it was some kind of a miracle?*

"Dad! Dad!" cried Justin and Lauren almost in unison as they rushed down the front stairs of the café. Justin flew into Henry's arms. He felt his son's heart beating as they tightly embraced one another. Justin was filled with tears and too choked up to speak. Lauren expressed what Justin couldn't say, "We heard that you were in a serious accident Dad, and that you were... killed. Was someone kidding us? Justin thought for sure it was a police officer that phoned."

Henry opened his other arm to embrace his daughter, as she too, was tearful and in a state of shock.

"I don't understand it all, honey. But I guess I was in a serious accident and somehow came out of it... I'm sure glad I did."

"So am I," Justin finally muttered, as he gained some composure.

Henry turned as Keith, one of his servers, came out the front door of the café, followed by several customers.

"Are you okay, Henry?" inquired Keith.

"Yes, yes, I am fine…never felt better for a guy who was just pronounced …" Henry couldn't finish the statement; *that he was dead and came back to life*. No, he didn't want to go there, it was all too bizarre.

Embarrassment overshadowed his previous thoughts as Henry became aware of the crowd of people standing there, staring at him, wanting to know what this was all about.

"Oh, I just had a little accident and the ambulance gave me a lift home, or rather to the gallery. I'm okay, really…nothing to worry about."

Henry motioned that he wanted to get back into the café. Everyone turned and went back inside. As Henry followed the patrons with his two children, he heard Jeremy running up the street hollering his name. Close behind were Camilla and Josh wiggling through the crowd that had gathered.

"Hey, Dad is that you?" Jeremy slowed, as he approached his father… a puzzled look on his face. He stopped and stared hard at Henry, tears surfaced in his eyes, "We thought you were… the police said you were killed in the accident… what happened, Dad?"

Henry let go of Justin and made his way down the steps towards his son.

"Grandpa, Grandpa," said Josh as he broke away from Camilla's hand and ran to Henry. "We asked your angel to ask God to make you better!"

Henry picked up his grandson and hugged him, "Your prayer sure worked, Joshua, I'm all better."

Jeremy and Camilla were standing side by side with wide open eyes, in a state of disbelief. Jeremy began shaking his head. "What is going on, Dad?"

Before Henry could answer, Camilla came to his side and hugged Henry. "Oh, Dad, we were so worried about you. Did a miracle really happen to you?"

Jeremy approached his father, wanting to make certain it was him, and waited for an answer. When Henry didn't answer, Jeremy continued with more questions.

"Do you remember anything about being—dead? Where you went? They say you see a tunnel of light… did you see it?"

Henry's mind was completely blank. "I don't recall anything Son, other than leaving the hospital, driving back to Hill Avenue, seeing this truck come at me and... after that, all I remember is waking up in the ambulance."

After a brief silence, Henry added, "No, I don't remember anything at all about that time in between."

An uncomfortable, yet pleasant feeling crept over Henry as he tried to remember more. It was all like a dream he wished could go on forever, but sleep could no longer hold him. And once awake, the dream vanished, gone into some abyss... "Perhaps someday it will come to me," Henry murmured.

Henry could feel the eyes of the patrons upon him and he also wanted to let his son know what he still didn't understand. Henry looked at Jeremy and nodded, "I think that is a possibility... let's go inside to the gallery and I'll explain what happened... at least as much that I know."

In an attempt to bring things back to normal and distract attention from him, Henry began engaging in idle talk as he made his way into the café with his children.

"Hi Millie, that's a great hat you have on today."

Millie nodded and cast Henry a warm smile. Not to leave her companion out, Henry continued sincerely, "And that's a nice blue dress, Marie. The colour looks so nice with your grey hair."

"Thank you, Henry." But not so easily distracted, Marie asked, "Are you okay, Henry?"

"Yes, yes, I'm fine. Thanks for your concern, Marie."

Henry quickly moved on and waved to Tom and George at another table. He heard people still talking about the ambulance and wondering what had happened. Henry ignored the curious remarks and comments and didn't stop to explain or listen to people's conjectures. Finally, he and his family made it into the gallery.

"So what happened, Dad?" Justin wanted to know and so did everyone else.

Henry started to explain how the accident happened, but then his words trailed off. His thoughts began to drift back to earlier this morning when he discovered from the diary that Marjorie was Jenny, and how he raced to see her at the hospital... he realized he should really start from the beginning and tell his family everything. He had been through a lot that day and yet, felt surprisingly spry. Perhaps now was as good a time as any to tell his children about the blonde girl that moved into the neighbourhood three doors down when he was fifteen years old…

"Are you okay, Dad? You look suddenly lost in space," Lauren asked on behalf of everyone there.

"Yes, I was just thinking about all this and I think I best start from the beginning. You all have a right to know…" and turning to Camilla he continued, "Especially you, Camilla—"

"Geez, Jeremy, a policeman is writing out a ticket at your car… you didn't park it!" blurted Justin.

"Oh, for Pete's sake. There were so many people milling around the ambulance when we pulled up I couldn't find a parking space so I just double parked."

"Well, you best get out there and explain what happened," said Henry. "In the mean time, Justin, bring up a couple of chairs from the basement as this is going to take some time to tell you this story."

Henry waited until Jeremy came back before beginning. His son was holding a ticket.

"So, he didn't have compassion on you?"

"No, I told him what happened. That you were in an accident and an ambulance brought you back to the gallery and… well, he was sympathetic, but as soon as he saw my name on the driver's license, he asked if I was related to you. When I said yes, he shook his head and said he should have given you a ticket this morning. Perhaps then you would have been more cautious and not been in that accident."

"Oh no, not the same officer…" Henry shook his head and managed a private chuckle.

CHAPTER TWENTY FOUR

WHEN EVERYONE WAS settled and found a seat, Henry began to tell his family about his past. He hoped that his children would be understanding and realize that he loved their mother dearly.

"Two days after I turned fifteen and just started my summer holidays, a new family moved in three doors down…"

Henry started out and proceeded to tell the story of how he met Jenny and how they fell in love. He told of how they spent the summer together and about that fateful day Jenny moved to Ottawa. He shared about how all of the letters they both had written to one another were destroyed, except for two letters with pewter angels inside. He explained how amazing it was for them to each send an identical pewter angel to each other. Henry showed his children the one he had received from Jenny. Camilla made an affectionate sound as she remembered seeing them earlier that morning in the hospital and now it made more sense.

Henry went on to explain that somehow the two letters were kept for years by Jenny's father and so neither he nor Jenny knew that they had written to each other. As time passed, both he and Jenny assumed that the other had lost interest and found someone else. And that is in fact what did happen. Julean came into his life when he was in grade twelve and the rest is history, most of which the children knew.

"How did you know Jenny's dad had the two letters?" Lauren wanted to know.

"This is where this all gets very interesting. Jenny's father's secretary found them in his wall safe after he died. She told me that following the orders of Jenny's dad, she was the one who destroyed all the letters I had written and always felt guilty about doing that. So when she found the last two letters, she mailed them by special delivery directly to our homes. She wanted to make certain that we got the letters, one to me and the other to Jenny. These were the last two letters with the pewter angels inside!"

"Wow..." muttered Lauren. "So when did you get yours, Dad?"

"The secretary mailed the letters in the summer of 1962, just two weeks before your mother and I got married. When it was delivered, I was at work and so my mom received the letter. Mom decided not to give me the letter as it would be so upsetting for me and interfere with the wedding that was going to take place within two weeks. She thought that after all those years from 1956 when Jenny left to 1962, that surely the feelings that Jenny and I had for one another were over and so she hid the letter from me. I really don't know what happened to the letter I sent Jenny, but I have a feeling that something similar must have happened to her as well."

"But...you're wearing the pewter angel, Dad. You must have gotten the letter..." Lauren was totally fascinated by the story and wanted every detail explained.

"That's a good question, Lauren. Just before Mom died, she invited me over for lunch and said she had something she wanted to give me—"

"It was the letter!" blurted Lauren.

Henry smiled, "Yes, it was the letter... at least that is what I later found out. If you remember, I found Grandma, dead on the floor, when I went there for lunch. After the funeral, when I went to clear her things out of the house, I found the letter in her apron."

"Wow..." exclaimed Lauren and then asked, "so you found the pewter angel inside the letter... is that when you put it on the chain around your neck?"

Henry gazed at Lauren, feeling somewhat embarrassed to admit it, since he didn't want his children to feel he loved Jenny more than their mom. He simply nodded and said, "Yes, it is a beautiful angel and I've always loved mine and so…" Henry's words trailed off as if he did not want to really get into it and reveal just how much he still loved his teenage sweetheart.

"I guess Jenny's mom must have given the letter that I sent to her, as well, as Jenny was wearing the identical pewter angel around her neck when I saw her this morning —"

"You saw Jenny, Dad?"Justin piped in, beating Lauren who was about to ask the same question.

"Yes, I will get to that." Turning to Jeremy, Henry continued. "Here's the part you won't believe, Jeremy. The house I bought on Hill Ave was Jenny's. I think that, in part, was the reason I was so fascinated with the home. I must have sensed it somehow… I didn't realize it though because the lady's name on the title was Marjorie. I didn't know that Jenny went by her second name when we met back in 1956. She only used her first name, Marjorie, when she signed the documents—"

"Oh, Dad," related Camilla, "that first and second name of Jenny sure created confusion in my mind, too! Since you only knew of Jenny as Jenny, I only learned later that it was her second name and that her first name was really Marjorie."

"I don't understand what you guys are talking about! I'm getting mixed up!" Lauren exclaimed, wearing a very frustrated look on her face.

Henry went over it all again and tried to explain it more clearly. Henry went on to describe that he had a special feeling for the owner of the house on Hill Avenue, just like Camilla always had a feeling that she was adopted. Anyway, Henry told them how he found Jenny's diary in a secret compartment, which was exactly like the one that Justin stores his money in, in the roll top desk.

Justin wanted to know how he found that out. Henry explained that he believes Julean showed him where it was, but insisted that was another story; how angels and Julean got involved in all this.

"After I had read in the diary early this morning, that Marjorie really was Jenny and that I had bought her house, I raced to Regina this morning to see her as I knew she was critically ill."

Henry paused while thoughts of Jenny dying flooded him. And yet, he didn't feel sad or mournful. He gazed at Camilla. She had tears in her eyes and her gaze was locked completely into Henry's. She was probably wondering why he, too, wasn't more emotional and despondent as he had been this morning.

"So did you get to see Jenny?" asked Lauren again, clearly fascinated with this unfolding love story.

"Yes, I did. She was in the Grey Nuns' Hospital in a special room where they tend to people who are about to die. I got there just in time to see her. She came out of her coma and then she… passed away."

Henry didn't tell them how he kissed Jenny, as he wasn't sure how his children were feeling about their dad loving another woman beside their mother. Again he was surprised at his state of mind. Not at all despondent like he had been that morning.

After a long silence, Camilla spoke. "What Dad didn't tell you is how I come into all of this." Camilla went on to share with her extended family how she had always felt that she was adopted. How she had discovered some documents this past year, which proved that she was in fact adopted. Yesterday she had spoken with the adoption agency in Ottawa, who confirmed that she was adopted and that her mother Marjorie or rather Jenny, Henry's teenage girlfriend was critically ill at the care home in Regina. Jenny however, was moved to the hospital that Dad mentioned.

"Unbelievably, both Dad and I were in the same room with Jenny this morning before she died…" Camilla began crying as she recalled that precious moment. Jeremy moved over to his wife and put his arm around her.

Lauren was crying in sympathy and spoke in between sobs, "That… is all so beautiful. Did you get a chance to speak with her, Camilla?"

Camilla nodded… "both Dad and I just had a brief word with her before she passed away."

Lauren hesitated for a moment and then asked a question burning in her mind, "Camilla, who was your father…?" A concerned suspicion had grown in Lauren's eyes. She looked at Henry and then back to Camilla.

Henry looked hard at his daughter-in-law, ready to explain that he wasn't her father. But then he recalled Nurse Johnson telling him that Jenny's niece and Matilda had explained the circumstances surrounding her birth to Camilla. He waited for his daughter-in-law's reply to Lauren. Slowly, tearfully, and comforted by Jeremy's arm around her shoulder, Camilla told the circumstances encompassing her conception.

Remarkably, Camilla knew everything just as it had happened. Jenny must have shared her rape with her niece and friend, Matilda. Incredibly Camilla also knew that her biological father was Peter. Henry had no idea how Camilla— or Jenny, for that matter— had learned that it was Peter Fraser who had forced himself on...

Tears surfaced in Henry's eyes just thinking about it. He was relieved that Camilla knew the circumstances under which she was conceived. Although she was not conceived in love, she had been showered in the love and forgiveness from Jenny's heart for her whole life. And that no matter how she came into being, she knew that she was nonetheless still a child of God, as precious as every human life, no matter what.

Lauren's concerned expression on her face relaxed once she realized her dad wasn't Camilla's dad, too. She shook her head side to side, obviously relieved that her father wasn't the man that fathered Camilla! "Oh, I can hardly wait to call Allison and tell her all about this!"

Henry looked at his daughter sheepishly; now all of his children knew about the secret girl in his past life...

Jeremy gave Camilla a warm tender hug and looking over her shoulder to Henry, said, "That's a remarkable story, how could this all have happened and be so interconnected? It's almost unbelievable."

Henry nodded, "Yes, and to think that Father Engelmann had been visiting Jenny for the past several months and didn't realize that she was my Jenny..." then looking Camilla in the eye, added, "our Jenny... Unbelievable!"

"You must be exhausted, Dad." said Camilla.

"In a way I am, but I'm surprised that I am not despondent. Perhaps just seeing Jenny and..." He was about to say, *'and kissing her one last time'* but thought against it... "gives some closure to all this..." Henry knew in his heart however, there was something else that he couldn't explain. Trying to draw attention away from himself and his strong feelings for Jenny, he turned back to Camilla, "You must be emotionally drained as well Camilla, finding your real mother and then having her slip away like that."

"Yes, I am. But I'm also thankful that I was able to see her and hear her voice and hold her... I could see how much I look like her."

"The resemblance is astonishing! You can see now why I always stared at you the way I did. Every time I looked at you, I saw Jenny."

"The last few days have explained so much. I feel so relieved just knowing who my real parents are. I am still not one hundred percent sure it's Peter, but it has to be. It's too strange that we have both had dreams about each other... And just the way Chloe and Matilda spoke, it must be him. I feel like I should meet him. It will be awkward, but I'm sure I can handle it."

Henry didn't reply. He suddenly remembered that Peter was critically ill and on the verge of death, himself. *Oh, no... that will be such a blow on Camilla when she learns the news.* She had been through so much today that Henry decided not to say anything. Rather he said, "He's a good man as far as I could tell, Camilla. We all do things in our past that we regret and I know Peter is very sorry for the circumstances in which you were conceived. And yet, look at you and how you turned out; I couldn't be more proud having you as my daughter."

"Daughter-in-law!" Camilla reminded him, as she laughed through her tears. A second later, Henry laughed as well, as the full meaning of her remark settled in.

"Well, it's just past one. I think I will go to the house on Hill Avenue and take a shower. I have a change of clothes there. There is a lot to do this afternoon. I am concerned about the funeral arrangements for Jenny. I think her ex-husband wants her body shipped back to Ottawa."

Henry saw the disappointed look on Camilla's face and shrugged his shoulder to express his, as well.

Jeremy added, "If you have time, you may want to drive to the police compound to see your car. It sure looked like it was a complete wreck. It's a miracle you survived that accident, Dad. Wait until you see your SUV. One side is completely caved in where the van hit you. I still can't figure out how you escaped greater injury. The seat belt must have held you in place and after it rolled it crushed the passenger side... your guardian angel must have been very busy watching over you!"

"Miracles have been known to happen," Henry said, as he shook his head. "One never knows what the day has in store. Make sure you treasure every moment the good Lord grants us."

Henry thought about Jenny almost being hit by that Chev so many years ago and how he almost hit the lady crossing the street just that morning... Angels were involved both times, he was certain of it!

Jeremy broke into his thoughts, "Having a major accident, dying and coming back to life. It's like you've been given a second chance at life, Dad."

Henry nodded. Although it made no sense since Jenny was already gone, he was certain it had to do with giving him and Jenny a second chance.

Turning to Lauren, he said, "Can I borrow your car for the afternoon? You're working in the boutique shop until five and so you won't need it, will you? I should be back by then and we will go home together."

"Sure Dad, just drive carefully, will you?" Lauren winked.

Justin came over to his dad, "I'm sure glad you're okay, Dad. The thought of both you and Mom gone sure scared me." Justin choked up, unable to go on. "Justin's right Dad," said Lauren and gave Henry a big hug.

This was followed by Jeremy and Camilla. Josh, who had been busy colouring in the colouring book they had at the gallery just for such occasions like this, looked up, and saw that group hug. He jumped up and ran over to his grandpa and said. "When I say my bedtime prayers tonight, I'm going to say a big thank you to my guardian angel for making you better."

Henry picked up his little grandchild and gave him a hug and kiss. "You do that for Grandpa and tell your angel a big thank you for me, too!"

CHAPTER TWENTY FIVE

As soon as Henry got up to the office, he called the police station and requested to be transferred to the compound.

"Police Compound, this is Constable Thorpe."

"Yes, good afternoon officer, this is Henry Pederson. I was in a car accident on the corner of Hill Avenue and Elphinstone Street a few hours ago. The ambulance attendants informed me that my car would be towed to the compound."

"A red SUV Escalade was pulled in here about fifteen minutes ago. It's a shame a nice SUV like that was totally demolished."

"Yes, that's the one, that's my car."

"So who was driving your vehicle, sir?"

"I was."

There was a long silence … "Is your name Henry Pederson?"

"Yes, that's me."

"But the report here says, you were pronounced dead at the accident scene …?"

Henry paused for a moment, not really knowing how to answer.

"Yes, apparently I was dead, but came back life." As soon as Henry said that, he knew it sounded crazy and unbelievable. He waited for an answer from the police officer, but there was none.

"I know this is difficult to understand or believe. I'm having trouble sorting it all out too, but believe me, I am Henry Pederson and I am the owner... and I was driving. What should I do now?"

After a long pause, the officer finally spoke. "Yeah... well, call your insurance broker as soon as possible, explain what happened. He'll report it to the Saskatchewan Government Insurance. They will send over an adjuster to view the vehicle. I think you will be getting a new Escalade... there is no way they can even begin to repair this one." And after a reflective moment he said, "And if you say it was you who was driving that SUV, you are one lucky man to be alive ... I'd say it is a miracle."

Henry just shook his head. That was the fourth or fifth time he had heard that.

"Officer, I left a diary in the car. It was lying on the front seat. Is there any way I could get you to check to see if it's there. It's a very important diary."

"I'd be glad to help you out if I could, Mr. Pederson, but that's impossible. Your truck is so squashed I don't think I could even slide my hand in there. When you come to have a look at your SUV you will understand what I'm saying. You'll know why you are one lucky guy... and you say that you are still walking, have no broken legs, arms or fractures?"

"No, I'm perfectly fine. The ambulance attendant said I had a bruise on the forehead where my head hit the concrete, but it's gone. Somehow, when I woke up from it all, my body was in perfect shape. In fact, I have never felt better."

There was a long pause... "You're a walking miracle, sir. That's all I can say. I'd get down on my knees and thank the Big Guy upstairs, if I were you."

"Yes, I've been doing that ever since I woke up from all this."

Henry listened to the dial tone as he held the phone in his unsteady hand. *Something very inexplicable is going on here...* Henry felt dizzy, so perplexed, and almost disorientated as to where he was.

"Was I really dead... and now I am alive?" he questioned himself. "But I don't remember being dead, I have no recollection of anything after I went through that stop sign... has a miracle really occurred?"

Henry began to wonder if Father knew or heard about the

accident. Perhaps he and his prayer warriors had been praying for him. But this all happened within the past two hours, it would have been impossible for Father to have heard about it so soon. Yet... someone had interfered or something very uncanny had happened...

"My dear Lord, what on earth is going on here? I wonder if Father knows of Jenny's passing too? I hope Father's at the care home; surely he will be able to help me sort this all out. I'll call him later when I get to Marjorie's... Jenny's house."

CHAPTER TWENTY SIX

M ATTI RUSHED TO the phone. It was on its fourth ring.
"Hello, is this Matilda Belafonte?"

"Yes... this be she..."

"This is Nurse Johnson, the Supervisor of Palliative Care at the Grey Nuns' Hospital—"

"I 'spect you be calling me. You just wants to say Jenny woke up from her nap. Ain't that so, now?"

Nurse Johnson chuckled, "I'm afraid Ms. Hamilton was more than sleeping. She was deceased—"

"Yes, I know that, but you calling to let me know she no longer be deceased, but come back to the land of the living. Now, that be the gospel truth... ain't that so?"

Nurse Johnson shook her head, "My, my, Matilda... you sure are a woman of faith. But you're absolutely correct; Ms. Hamilton has miraculously come back to the land of the living, as you said. And she is perfectly hea—"

"Praise the Lord! Halleluiah!" Matti yelped! "I just knew Jesus was busy earlier on. He's back and tendin' to business! Halleluiah! I just can't wait to tell Chloe..."

Matti dropped the phone and started to run to Chloe's room

and then came back to the phone.

"I be so sorry, Nurse Johnson, I'm so excited to tell Chloe the news I forgot to thank you for phoning. That be the best news I heard since Harry Belafonte sang in Carnegie Hall!"

"I also wanted to tell you not to come right away as Ms. Hamilton's room is completely occupied by doctors and nurses examining her—"

"I can just see the puzzled looks on their faces! Yes sir, they be scratchin' their heads for a long time trying to figure out how the great Physician does His healing works. He just say, 'Jenny, it be time to get up now, that's right, you wake up and you be openin' your pretty blue eyes and give me one of your sweet smiles. There ain't no-one that can resist that, Ms. Johnson. Even Lazarus after sleeping for four days just got up and walked out of the tomb!"

"Well, I can't argue with you, Matilda, some mighty Power did an amazing job on Jenny. She was so critically ill; the cancer had attacked almost every cell of her body—"

"See now, that's how the Lord works sometime. Not only does He heal the sick, but also heals people who need a boost in their faith. Now tell me, has your faith increased over this?"

"I must admit it has… this is all so unbelievable, I've never seen anything like it in all the years of nursing. And the kiss that Jenny and Henry Pederson had just before she died was so powerful, so filled with love."

"And that is what the Lord responds to. Love touches His heart right away. It draws out His power. We all be so filled with love for Jenny and praying so hard for her, He just have to be listenin'."

"Well, He did, Matilda…He sure did."

"I best be going to the bathroom, I still so excited I better pee before going to Chloe's room… oh, she in for one biiiiig surprise. That young thing feeling so sad over her Auntie being gone, I just can see her face lightin' up with joy! We be singing and dancing so hard the hotel management may throw us out!"

Nurse Johnson and Matilda shared a good long laugh.

"Be seeing you later, Nurse Johnson. Thank you for calling!"

"Oh, Matilda!" Nurse Johnson exclaimed, "Matilda, are you still there?"

"Yes, I be here…"

"You work for Mr. Hamilton, correct?"

"Yes, that be so…"

"He and his staff have been calling nonstop to make arrangements to ship Ms. Hamilton's body back to Ottawa, but since what has happened that won't be necessary. He said that you would be assisting in that matter, as well—"

"That man be in for one big surprise! I forgot all about him. Yes, I'll call him as soon as I tell Chloe the good news. I don't know how he'll take to this. I know he be wantin' her back, but now… Oh sweet Jesus, Your healing business is a long waaaay from being over!"

Chapter Twenty Seven

Henry drove slowly up to Jenny's home and parked the car. After all these months, he still could not call the home he purchased his. It just didn't seem that it rightfully belonged to him. He had come across this home in such an extraordinary way and always felt a twinge of guilt walking in and taking control of someone's life. It just never sat right with him. At least now he knew who the house really belonged to and it explained so many of the strange feelings he had when in the home.

It was uncanny that Marjorie turned out to be Jenny and that I actually bought her home! Truly an angelic occurrence.

Henry got out of the car and made his way up the winding walk. What a difference from the first day he and Jeremy went to look at the house. Snow was piled at least two feet high on the sidewalk and today most of the snow had melted, revealing the amazing landscaping that was hidden under the winter blanket. Either Jenny was a gardener in her own right, or she came across someone that really knew his craft.

It was nearing the end of April and an early spring was definitely in the air. The landscaping was starting to come alive. Most of the junipers looked green and he could see as he stopped near the front door that some of the perennials were beginning to peek through the soil. Henry could only imagine how beautiful the front yard was going to look when everything was in bloom.

Henry fumbled with the lock until he realized that he had inserted the wrong key. Finally, he opened up the front door and walked inside. The fragrance of lilac was especially strong. He detected it right off in spite of all the other scents in the room. It was as if Jenny had been there and just left.

He gazed at the round table which housed the diary. He shook his head and marvelled over the way he had found Jenny's diary and the manner in which his dear wife had led him to it. He was going to sit on the chair beside the table and relive that moment of discovery, but was drawn to the kitchen and then to the window that looked out to the back yard.

The first thing he noticed was that some of the plants in the kitchen had been moved. He was certain that he hadn't touched them. Several of the herb plants had been stripped of some of their leaves… especially the thyme plant. Its odour was strong and competed with the lilac scent for his attention. The lilac was definitely the one that still drew him.

He looked outside. Most of the snow had melted and just traces of snow remained under the low branches that were shielded from the sun. A glare at the very back of the yard caught Henry's attention. The rays of the high sun bounced off the white, marble angel near the gazebo. It glistened and appeared as if ready to walk through the garden and collect more flowers.

"Are more flowers in the basket?" Henry whispered under his breath.

The angel's basket definitely seemed fuller than the day before. *He was drawn to them.*

He made his way to the patio doors and stepped out into the warm air. He took a deep breath and immediately smelled the thyme. He looked down the path and saw that many leaves of the herb had been strewn on the stone path. A puzzled look grew on his face. He partially turned to go back and check the plants again… and then decided to do that later. He walked down the steps and followed the winding lane to the back where the gazebo was. His eyes stayed focused on the angel's basket the entire time. Unbelievably, there were more flowers in the basket! He looked from side to side to see if there was any evidence of someone coming into the yard... but there was none.

He stared at the basket overflowing with wildflowers, but where did they come from? There were some peeking through the ground, or so he thought. The fresh odour of the herbs was growing stronger as if coming from the gazebo. He glanced over and he noticed a pile of thyme leaves on the swing inside the gazebo. The statue was hiding part of the swing. He leaned over slightly and was shocked to see what looked like Jenny's diary, laying on the swing. His heart nearly stopped...

Is that Jenny's diary?

It couldn't be. How on earth did it get here?

He slowly made his way over and picked it up. A pencil was between the pages at the very back. He noticed an entry...It had today's date on it. An eerie feeling crawled up and down Henry's spine. The hair on the back of his neck began to rise. Something so strange had happened and his mind was blocked as to what it was. He felt frustrated, as if he were standing in front of a door that housed secrets and he didn't have a key to open it.

It was Jenny's handwriting, he recognized it right off. The eerie feeling returned as he read the entry. She wanted to make her son aware of her daughter, Camilla. That she was his step sister and that it would be so wonderful if they met and she became part of the family. It would be so fantastic for him to have a sister and for Camilla to know she had a brother.

In the second paragraph, Jenny asked for J.J.'s forgiveness for the way the marriage of his parents went and for the breakup of the family. She hoped that someday he would understand and find it in his heart to forgive her.

Oh Jenny, you had such a heart of gold. No wonder after all these years, I still loved you so dearly... But, how on earth did the diary get here? He was certain it had been in his SUV... Henry shook his head in awe of what he was seeing. And he still couldn't figure out why he was not despondent and in tears over Jenny's passing. He wondered if a miracle could have possibly happened to her, as well. But she had been dead for hours.

Wasn't she?

Her lips had felt warm when he kissed her, yet it wasn't the same when she was awake and he gazed into her blue eyes. He could taste and feel her tender lips just at the thought of it all.

It made him think of Father Engelmann and that he should phone him.

It was the thought of the phone that brought Henry out of his reverie and he realized that the phone in the house was ringing. He ran to get it. He thought for sure the caller would hang up, but whoever it was, *was as determined as Henry to communicate.*

CHAPTER TWENTY EIGHT

AFTER MATTI SHARED the good news with Chloe, Matti's prediction came true as the two women danced and jumped around in glee. Chloe was elated and took the longest time to let the truth sink in that Jenny had really come back to life.

Chloe phoned her dad. Robbie wasn't surprised. He and his prayer group had been praying, as well. Both Chloe and her father were filled with praise and rejoicing.

No sooner had Matilda returned to her room when the phone rang.

"Hello, this be Matilda."

"Matilda!" James hollered into the phone, "What's going on? I just talked to the nurse and she said that Marjorie was miraculously healed and came back to life—"

"That be true, Mr. Hamilton. Ms. Johnson called me just ten to fifteen minutes ago and said the same. Ms. Hamilton be healed! Praise the Lord, Mr. Hamilton, Jesus has restored her life and healed her of all her ailments!"

"Matilda, for Pete's sake, don't carry on so… how can that be possible? She must not have been dead in the first place. Doctors and nurses are known to make mistakes."

"No! Mr. Hamilton, I was in the room the whole time. Nurse Johnson checked her vital signs and confirmed that Ms. Hamilton had passed away. Now, I just knew that the good Lord was going to heal her and so I took it all that Ms. Hamilton just be taking a nap like you be thinking... that's my personal assessment of the matter, know what I'm saying...?"

"No! No, Matilda I don't know what you're saying. This all doesn't make any sense to me. I've already called my doctor and he can't explain to me how this could happen either. I am going to fly him there tomorrow to check Marjorie out himself. I want her to have the best care possible. Is that understood?"

"Yes, I know what you be saying, Mr. Hamilton, but it won't be necessary. When the good Lord heals, there ain't a doctor in the world that can improve upon it."

"Really, Matilda!"

After James let out a sigh that carried a tone of frustration mixed with disbelief, he went on. "Are you going to see her, Matilda?" James wanted to know.

"Chloe and me be waiting until after dinner. Nurse Johnson say the room be filled with doctors and nurses and no-one else can squeeze in until they leave."

"Well, try to get there as soon as possible and call me. Make sure Marjorie is well and okay. I still find it hard to believe that she died and came back. The whole thing doesn't make sense. As soon as you do in fact see her and talk to her and make an assessment as to her condition, you must call me straight away. Is that understood?"

"Yes, sir, I understands what you be saying. I do as you ask, Mr. Hamilton."

"Matilda! Are you still there?"

"Yes, I am..."

There was a long silence as if the phone had gone dead.

"Mr. Hamilton, are you still there...?"

"Yes, there is something I need to ask you..."

"Yes, I be listenin'..."

"When you were at the hospital, did a guy by the name of Pederson come up to see Marjorie?"

Once again there was a long silence...

"Yes, Mr. Hamilton, Henry Pederson did come up to see Ms. Hamilton."

"Was she… you know, happy to see him?" James was hesitant to know.

"Yes, she was, Mr. Hamilton. She be more than happy as far as I could tell."

"Did he kiss her, Matilda…?"

Matilda hesitated to answer. Her master could get very upset when things didn't go his way. She was beginning to suspect where this was going. Mr. Hamilton was beginning to wake up after all these years and see the jewel he had.

"Yes, Mr. Hamilton, Henry did kiss his teenage girlfriend—"

"On the lips, Matilda?"

"Yes, that's usually where two people who are fond of each other kiss—"

"I didn't ask for an analysis, Matilda, just a yes or no will do."

James was getting riled. Jealousy was surfacing. His mind immediately recalled that evening when Marjorie told him of the boy she spent the summer with when she lived in Regina. He sensed it then and he sensed it even more now how much Marjorie liked that man.

James also remembered that night when he called for Jenny. They were just leaving to see a movie in the city. It was a good thing he answered and they were just about out the door. He had made it clear in no uncertain terms that he didn't want Henry Pedersen involved with his girl again. Fortunately, the farm boy didn't bother him nor Jenny after that. And yet, after all those years, *he's back in our lives again*!

He wondered what would have happened had Henry and Marjorie spoke to one another that night he had called for her. That's beside the point; they were conversing with each other now and it concerned James. It concerned him a lot.

Well, he would take one step at a time…

"Mr. Hamilton, are you still on the telephone?"

"Yes, Matilda… call me after you see Marjorie. Note everything. I want to know exactly how she is doing. If there is anything she wants, let me know… flowers? Yes, she would want flowers. What kind does she like, Matilda?"

Without waiting for an answer, James blurted, "Wildflowers, yes, of course, she'd want that kind. Would florists carry wild-flowers or just roses? S…surely they would have something like a wildflower in that small city, wouldn't they? Matilda. For Pete's sake, speak up!"

"I wants to, but you keep prattling on… yes, florists should have some wildflowers. I know she loves daisies. She likes the simplicity of the daisy, especially yellow ones… they remind her of the sun—"

"Yes, I'll send her flowers. Ask her indirectly what kind she likes besides daisies and anything else she might need…Yes!… Books! She always had her nose in a book. Find out what she likes to read… go to her soon and phone me immediately when your visit is over, is that clear?"

"Yes, Mr. Hamilton, it's all clear as a bell what you wants…!"

"And, Matilda…" James was getting desperate. He never thought he would ever see the day when he asked his staff for help. Yet, these past few months had changed his life… and he was sure it was for the better.

"Mr. Hamilton, our connection not working again…you still there?"

"Matilda, I need your help," James finally blurted out. "Do everything you can to convince Marjorie to come back to the estate. She'll listen to your advice. She's my wife and I want her back on the estate where she belongs."

"But Mr. Hamilton, you divorced Mrs. Hamilton, she no longer be your wife, did you forget?"

"For Pete's sake, Matilda, of course I didn't forget. I meant she was my wife but it's the same thing, we need to get her back on the estate. I'm sure you would be much happier if she was and so would Thomas and everyone else. Wouldn't you agree?"

Matilda could see her master be working himself up like he was after some big deal for his company. But this may be one business deal he will not be closing. *Jenny was in love, really in love and I could see it the moment them two kissed this morning.* Finally, Jenny would be free to marry the love of her life, and there was no way under the sun that Matilda would interfere with her precious friend's heartfelt wish and dream for all those years.

"Yes, it would be nice to have Miss Jenny back, but its Jenny's… I mean, Ms. Hamilton's life, it be up to her if she wants to come back or not. And I wouldn't be setting my hopes up too high, Mr. Hamilton… that boy she met a long time ago will have someting to say about all this; that be for sure…"

Click.

Matilda held onto the phone for a long time after James hung up. Matti slowly hung up the phone and muttered, "What one wants one can't always be getting... even a man with all the money in the world has his limits...

"That be for sure!"

CHAPTER TWENTY NINE

"Ah, I am glad you made it to the phone. It's Father Engelmann!"

"I was just about to call you, Father."

"How are you feeling?" Father asked, in a serious tone.

"I'm feeling great, Father. I haven't felt this good in a long, long time—"

Henry wanted to tell Father about what happened to Jenny, but thought he would tell Father of his accident first.

"I have something I want to share—"

Before Father could tell Henry the reason for his call, Henry took a deep breath and rambled on...

"Father, you're not going to believe this! I was in an accident a few hours ago. They said I got killed in the car accident but on my way to the hospital... I came back to life!"

Henry waited for Father to respond with one of his German phrases, *Oh mein lieber Gott* or something like that, but Father remained silent. Henry assumed that maybe his mentor didn't hear him and explained further...

"I was in an accident and got killed! The ambulance attendants said my SUV was completely demolished. They said all my bones should have been broken, but I only had a bruise on my forehead where my head hit the concrete. They said that's probably what killed me…" Henry waited for a response, but still Father remained silent. He didn't react at all like he usually does…

"Father, Father, are you still there?" Henry's voice carried alarm.

"Yes, I am still here Henry… something truly miraculous has occurred—"

There was that word again, "Father you're at least the fourth person who has said that a miracle has occurred. What is going on?"

After a reflective silence, Father's voice carried a tone of awe and wonder, "Henry, the Lord has restored our lives."

"What are you talking about? You mean He has restored my life."

"No Henry, several hours ago, I too, was taken by the Lord. Nurse Frowler found me in the sun room. The residents said they prayed over me for over an hour. After they said their good-byes to me, Dianne ordered an ambulance to come for my body and take it to the morgue."

"What is going on Father?"

Again after a long silence, Father continued. "For the last fifteen minutes the residents were amazed to see me walk through the door. They said I was like Lazarus walking out of the tomb… that the Lord restored my life out of His love for me."

"Yes, of course Father. That would make perfect sense. There is no-one closer to the Lord than you. But, did I hear you correctly, that you died and came back to life as well!?"

"Yes, that is the case, Henry. But I am an old man, I can see that he would restore you two, but to give me renewed life to carry out—"

Henry didn't wait for Father to finish, "What do you mean 'you two' Father? If you're referring to Jenny as well as me, she passed away at the hospital. But it was your prayers Father and those of your warriors that kept her alive long enough for us to say goodbye and even share a kiss."

"Jesus, Mary and Joseph," Father whispered. He was beginning to realize that neither Henry nor Jenny remembered anything of their time on the other side. Only he was able to recall everything and more…

"Father, what is it? I can't take this anymore… what is going on?"

"Henry, when you had that accident, do you recall anything from the time you were struck dead to the time you… miraculously recovered?"

"That's the thing, Father, I don't recall anything. After Jenny died, I decided to drive back to my house on Hill Avenue. I went through a stop sign on the corner of Elphinstone and Hill and a van hit me… next thing I remember I woke up in the ambulance. The attendant was shocked; almost scared him out of his skin! He said I was dead… What I don't understand, Father, is why I am not feeling mournful or despondent over Jenny's death. I am almost feeling guilty that I am feeling so good."

"Perhaps you'd better sit down, Henry, if you are not already."

"I'm sitting on the edge of my chair, tell me Father!"

"Henry, I too am in awe over what happened. The reason I called you was to see if you were alive and what happened to you. What you told me so far confirms what I saw when I passed over to the other side. I saw you and Jenny. I expected to see Jenny as she was on the doorstep to death, but not you—"

"Do you mean to say you saw me when I died…?"

Father didn't want to alarm Henry or have him think that his old age was finally catching up with him and had lost his senses.

"There is something I need to explain to you, Henry, but better in person than over the phone. You have to take my word for now, but yes, the three of us met at the doorstep to heaven. I even met my guardian angel as well as yours and Jenny's—"

"What? Are you serious Father?"

"*Ach mein lieber Gott!* Yes, yes, Henry, I shall explain it all to you later. For now let me finish. Are you sitting down Henry?"

"I'm just barely sitting, Father, tell me what is going on here? I can't wait another minute."

"Henry, after the Lord woke me from my deep sleep, I wondered if Jenny was still alive or came ba—"

"I can tell you that, she died, Father!"

"Henry, please don't interrupt me, I want to tell you what is so miraculous about all this."

"Sorry, Father, please go on."

"As I was saying, I called the hospital to see if Jenny was alive, but there was no answer on the fifth floor. Twice I let it ring, until the line disconnected. The admittance office tried too and couldn't understand why no one was answering—"

"Father, get to the poin—"

"Henry, please…"

"Sorry, Father…"

"I couldn't wait for them to check the phone lines and so I immediately called for a taxi and went to the Grey Nuns' hospital. I thought you might be there, as well."

"They would have removed her body by that time, Father. Did you talk to the nurses and hear about Jenny and me and the last moments we shared?"

"Henry, you must stop interrupting me, I have something very miraculous to share with you."

Finally, it was starting to sink in that Father knew something that he didn't… could it be possible that Je… "Father, please go on!"

"When I got to the fifth floor, I immediately went to the nurses' station, but there was no-one there! The floor was deserted. It was as if everyone had gone home. As if there weren't any sick people to attend to. The thought at the time overwhelmed me, Henry. But as I approached Jenny's room there was a huge crowd of nurses and doctors gathered there. They were backed out into the hallway, as no more could fit into the room."

"What, Father? What had happened?"

"I asked a nurse who was trying to peer into the room, but she refused to look at me. Then I asked a doctor and it was the same. They were so mesmerized by something which had happened in Jenny's room, it was as if everyone had gone deaf."

"Father, what happened? Please tell me, I can't take this anymore."

Father remained silent. Henry suspected Father was purposely getting even with him for all those times he played on Father's impatience and dragged out news. The table had turned and Henry sensed his mentor's glee. "Please, Father," Henry pleaded… "Is Jenny alive?"

"Finally, I pulled a nurse aside and with great difficulty, I got her attention and asked her the very question you just posed to me—"

"Jesus, Mary and Joseph," Henry blurted anxiously. "Father, what did she say?"

"She said that the woman in that room had been completely filled with cancer. She died several hours ago, but suddenly—miraculously - came back to life and… she is totally healed!

"I had to be sure, Henry, so I asked, is it Marjorie Hamilton… or Jenny—"

"And…?"

"She shook her head and shrugged her shoulders saying she didn't know. Everyone in the hospital is talking about it. She had just heard about it and came up from the 4th floor after her shift was over to see for herself."

"Was it Jenny, Father?" You know Father… please, tell me!"

"Yes, yes, Henry… let me finish. I tried to work my way into the room, but it was too jam packed. It was like a can of sardines. I thought I would wait until the crowd dispersed, but even more medical staff came running to the room pushing me further out of the way. I knew I couldn't leave until I knew for sure. We prayed for a miracle so much that the Lord would heal our beautiful sister. It had been revealed to me that she was healed when I crossed over to the other side. But alas, our doubts are a life long struggle… I just had to know for certain if the Lord heard our plea."

A silence followed. The suspense had worn Henry down. He thought he would explode. He got up, and then sat down, and then he paced the floor holding the phone; waiting for an answer.

"Finally, Doctor Kreake and the others began to work their way out of the room. I was elated to finally see a recognizable face. I immediately pulled him over and asked what has happened?"

"What did he say Father!?" Henry was ready to collapse.

"Henry… your beloved Jenny was healed, fully restored! I met with her myself and—"

All Father heard was the clanging sound of the phone receiver as it hit the floor. Henry was up and out the door on his way to the Grey Nuns' Hospital just as fast as he could get there.

CHAPTER THIRTY

I sooo excited, Chloe, I be visiting the toilet every ten minutes to pee. Good thing I'm not at the estate, this be Charles' time of day to be working on his plumbing. Good Lord, I'd have to go outside behind the rose bushes, that's for sure. Don't you be tellin' anyone, but that happened before and that's the gospel truth! More than once I be using a mirror to see my back side and remove one or more of them thorns!"

Chloe laughed. "Yes, I am so excited too, Matti. I just can't believe that Auntie Jen is alive. I need to see her first hand to make this a reality."

"See, there now, you be like doubting Thomas. He too, had to see the Lord when he came back on the third day. I just knew my God would not forsake me."

"You have far greater faith than I… that's for sure," Chloe added for good measure. "I was thinking that we should call Camilla, but maybe we better go see Jenny at the hospital first and make sure everything is as Nurse Johnson said and then phone Camilla. I would hate to call her and not be totally accurate that her mother is completely healed."

"There be no doubt in my mind, Chloe. Our precious little

princess is healed, that's for sure. We could go up and see Jenny first, though. Mr. Hamilton wants me to check her out too, and then call him straight away. That man sure becoming interested in his former good wife. I feels he wants her back so bad he be willing to do anyting. Never thought I would see the day he be asking for my help." Matilda shook her head.

"I'm sure James regrets divorcing Jenny. I think his ailment is giving him time to think and see what is now lacking in his life."

"That's the way the good Lord works sometime. He allows problems to come into our lives and its all for the good. It takes time to see that, but good will come out of all this Chloe, that's for sure."

"I can't wait a minute longer, Matti. Let's go to the hospital. Hopefully the doctors and nurses won't be in Auntie's room any more.

JAMES WALKED UP and down the many paths in the garden and still could not find Thomas.

"Ah, there he is!" James made his way to the storage shed.

"Thomas, can I speak with you for a minute?"

Thomas turned and leaned the spade against the wall of the shed.

"Good afternoon Sir, what would you have me do?"

"Has Matilda been in touch with you about Marjorie?"

"Yes, she did call yesterday to let us know Miss Jenny is gravely ill. We all have been praying for her."

"Your prayers are answered, Thomas, I was just informed that Marjorie was miraculously healed…"

"That's wonderful news, Mr. Ham—I mean James. Praise the Lord for His goodness. So Miss Jenny is fully recovered…?"

"Yes, I spoke with the attending nurse and she was completely taken aback by it all. Doctors from all over the hospital are making their way into Marjorie's room. I'm sending my personal doctor there tomorrow to make certain everything is okay with Marjorie and give me a full report. I wanted the nurse to take a phone into the room so I could speak with Marjorie, but the nurse said that it was impossible to even get close to the door."

James stopped rambling and looked hard into the gardener's

eyes. What he was about to do was way out of his comfort zone, but he trusted Thomas and felt relaxed around him. They had come to speak of many things that he would never dare to talk about with his business associates and friends. There was something peaceful about the man before him that drew him ever closer and allowed him to put his defenses down.

"So tell me, Thomas, what kind of flowers does Marjorie like? I would like to have some sent to her at the hospital. It seems to me wildflowers would be top on her list, wouldn't you think so?"

"Yes, Miss Jenny does like wildflowers, indeed. Her favourites would have to be—"

"Daisies!" James blurted out. "Especially the yellow ones… they remind her of the sun!"

"Why yes, James, that is exactly correct," Thomas said, with a look of surprise on his face.

"I have to be honest, Thomas. Matilda shared that with me earlier. I already asked my staff to call all the florist shops in Regina and send over every daisy that's in the city."

Thomas grinned and nodded. "That's a fine gesture, James."

"So what other flowers does she like? You've been around her when she was in the garden over the years. What would be her favourite?"

Without hesitation, the gardener replied, "Lilacs, James. Miss Jenny loved the fragrance of lilacs."

"Yes, why didn't I think of that? Lilac perfume was what she wore all the time. And you're right it does have a nice fragrance. I enjoyed the odour very much in our earlier years of dating. So do we have some here on the grounds?" James wanted to know.

"We have many lilac trees, but they are not in bloom until late spring. June, when the Monarchs return, is when they flower. Miss Jenny was in heaven at that time of the year. Both the flower and return of the butterflies to the estate, put her into a state of sheer joy. I would say she almost grew wings like an angel and flew around with the flitting butterflies."

"Yes, I am looking forward to the return of the Monarchs as well, Thomas, but we must get some lilacs. Surely there must be some place in the world where they are in full bloom?"

Just then, Charles beckoned from the patio doors outside the kitchen.

"Yes, what is it, Charles?"

"Mrs. Hamilton is here to see you. Shall I escort her out here or to the living room?"

"Send her out here, Charles. Use my wheelchair if she has difficulty walking."

"Yes, sir."

James turned back to Thomas who was just getting ready to get back to work. "Okay, Thomas, use the phone in my den and call around to see if you can locate some Lilacs. Let me know how you make out. I'll get my staff working on it as well after Nancy leaves."

"Good afternoon, Mrs. Hamilton," said Thomas, as she made her way towards the two men.

Nancy stopped and supported herself with her cane. "Yes, good afternoon, Thomas. A beautiful spring day."

"It is indeed, Ma'am. That's a beautiful white rose you have pinned to your dress."

"Thank you, Thomas. Pinning a flower to my lapel seems to give me more life somehow."

"God's creation does have that affect on us." Thomas smiled, nodded and went on his way.

"Glad to see you out enjoying this lovely day, too, James."

James made his way towards his step mother and assisted her to a bench near the gazebo.

"So what brings you here, Nancy?"

"Do I need a reason to visit my son? Just came by to see how you're doing. How are you feeling James?"

"Actually I am feeling fine in spite of the latest news. The doctors think they have detected the start of another tumor. They did a biopsy last Thursday and should know by tomorrow. In any case they will use chemo instead of operating."

"Well, let's hope we have seen the end of that. Jim sure went through a lot in those last months." Nancy shifted on the concrete bench and winced.

"Is the arthritis acting up again?"

"Yes, some days are better than others. Today wasn't too bad and that's why I decided to come for a visit. And besides, the weather is so lovely and I do enjoy the garden on the estate so much. Thomas does such a fine job of looking after everything."

"Yes, he does at that. Can I get Charles to bring out a pillow?"

"That's fine. Perhaps we can stroll slowly around the garden. The exercise may loosen things up and I notice that some wildflowers have already come up near the gazebo."

"Yes, it's a bit early for them but Thomas said that ever since Marjorie came to the estate, her love of the wildflowers encouraged them to come early just to please her."

"Flowers will do that…?" Nancy asked with a look of skepticism.

"According to Thomas, plants and flowers respond to affection and appreciation… I can't imagine flowers coming out of the soil early just to please someone and yet as you can see, there they are!"

James helped Nancy get up and supported her as, they both began to walk towards the gazebo.

"I've noticed a change in you, James. Seems like your time away from the business has been good for you. It's unfortunate that an illness has caused you to slow down and take some time to enjoy what you have."

"You know, Nancy, I've been thinking of that a lot lately, as well. These last few months or this last year as a matter of fact have made me stop and smell the roses. I've never really understood what that saying meant until now. I can see what Marjorie liked so much about the garden and being out here in her gazebo."

"Yes, Marjorie was a special girl, James. I was sorry that it didn't work out for you two. I was always tempted to throw in my two cents worth, but didn't want to meddle."

"At the time, I thought it was for the best. I could never accept the fact that she bore another child before we got married… but things seem different now. I have grown more accepting not only of that, but of many other things. Look…" said James, as they neared the wildflowers peeking through the soil. Many already over six inches high. "I hated these flowers and the disorganized way they grew for years and now I can hardly wait to see which flower comes up. I can hardly wait for the butterflies to return and I even enjoy when they rest on my hand."

Nancy stopped and looked at James, making certain she had heard him right. "That's wonderful, James."

"I was even able to get the sculptor to make another statue similar to the one that Marjorie had here before."

"The one you sent her?"

"Yes, at the time I was glad to get rid of it, but then the more I began to enjoy the garden, the more I wanted to have everything like Marjorie had it. The statue is almost the same except the angel is holding the basket in the left hand instead of the right. The sculptor said he simply couldn't make an identical statue. He only agreed to sculpt another one when I told him that the former statue had such healing power and that it may do something for the illness I have. Apparently he always thought that the statue he created initially had spiritual powers and spooked him. That's why he wanted to get rid of it and it finally ended up in our garden."

"You don't say?"

"Yes, apparently Marjorie's father had it commissioned for her before he died. It's quite a story how Thomas got a hold of it and how it ended up here in the garden as a gift to Marjorie. Anyway, the sculptor agreed to make me another statue based on the condition I told you. The marble was imported all the way from Italy."

"You don't say," Nancy said out of habit, more than thought. She gazed at the sparkling, marble statue; the sun bouncing off its brilliant white surface made her squint.

"It really is lovely, James. The angel almost appears as if it is walking towards you. The flowers in the basket are beautiful; surely they are not from the garden at this time?"

"No, I had Thomas get some from the local florist. I am continuing the practice that Jenny...I mean Marjorie did when she was on the estate."

"Oh?"

"Apparently she called the statue the Angel of Thanksgiving. Every day she would place flowers in the basket all summer long in thanksgiving for someone or something. Before she left the estate at the time we split up, she placed a bouquet in the basket for me in thanks for giving her such a beautiful garden while she lived here. The flowers survived all that fall and even over the entire winter. When I came to the estate last spring to convalesce from the prostate operation in June, the flowers were all still intact. Thomas swore up and down that he didn't water the bouquet for the entire time after Marjorie left or protect them from the winter in any way."

"That's remarkable, James! I've never heard of such a thing. So when did they eventually wither away?" Nancy wanted to know.

"You won't believe this, Nancy. I killed them by allowing hateful thoughts to enter my mind. I'll never forget that day. When Thomas first told me Marjorie did it as a gift of love and thanksgiving for me and that is what he thought sustained the flowers. Nancy, that act of appreciation, after all I put her through hit me to the core. I never felt anything like that and it brought tears to my eyes."

"But those are good thoughts, James…"

James shook his head and went on, "It was the first time I ever felt such care for me…beside you of course. It was something indescribable, Nancy…but then I allowed thoughts of Marjorie's rape and having a child to enter my mind. How deceitful she was in not telling me. Revulsion and anger pushed away Marjorie's kindness and were replaced by thoughts that she was impure and touched by others and how foolish I must look crying in the presence of Thomas…"

James stopped and looked at his step mother with an expression that he was reliving, that time, with regret, slowly continued almost in a whisper, "With each such thought, the flowers began to die, within seconds before my very eyes. I loathed seeing them squirm as if in pain and wither away. It was as if each thought racing through my mind sucked the life out of the flowers. One by one they dried up and turned into dust. Within seconds the angel's basket was empty…*the power of one's thoughts,* Nancy…" James words trailed off.

"That's remarkable, James…" Was all that Nancy could say, as her thoughts drifted off into a world of her own as well. She recalled the day she first met Marjorie and they had that chat together about James' family background. She could see right off that Marjorie was special; she had a loving heart. If anyone could penetrate the hard core of James it would be her. It was so unfortunate James was beginning to realize that now… it may be too late in regards to their marriage, but perhaps it may still be helpful for James.

James broke into his stepmother's thoughts after coming out of his own.

"Something quite amazing has happened, Nancy. I told you last week that I had sent Matilda to Regina to tend to Marjorie. Her cancer had consumed her entire body and she was moved into the

Palliative Care ward with the prognosis that she could die at any time."

James turned to Nancy again and said, "She died earlier this morning and… and suddenly came back—"

"Do you mean she became alive again?" Nancy asked with a puzzled look on her face.

"Yes, apparently some miracle occurred in her life and she came back fully healed. It's unbelievable. The nurse I spoke to at the hospital said doctor after doctor is in her room now examining her. They are all amazed. I've asked Matilda to see for herself and get back to me."

Nancy stopped again and looked at James as she repeated what she had just said a moment ago, "That is remarkable, James."

"Funny thing is, just yesterday when I placed the bouquet that Thomas brought for me into the Angel of Thanksgiving's basket it was in thanks for Marjorie and the years we spent together. I asked that if there is a God, that she be healed. It was just a passing thought … never really believing what I thought. But… perhaps angels do hear our prayers and take them to a higher power…"

James' eyes began to mist. "I would really like to have Marjorie back, Nancy.

I made a big mistake…"

Nancy could barely believe what she was hearing. She was so happy that she lived long enough to hear this. She had always prayed that Jim senior would see the light of day before he died and show some affection or at least some emotion, but it was like there was an impenetrable, steel wall surrounding him at all times. But now, here was his son, with similar traits, letting his defenses down and actually allowing himself to be vulnerable. Nancy was so astounded she was speechless. She just stared at James and slightly shook her head. For a proud Hamilton to say what James just uttered was truly miraculous. Perhaps as big a miracle as what happened to Marjorie!

"You know, Nancy. I've been trying to do everything that Marjorie did on the estate. I'm up early and out here. I try to enjoy the garden, the butterflies when they are here. I am relating to the staff in the way she used to and I must admit that I have never felt better, yet… it's just not the same without her. She gave the estate a life and joy that no amount of flowers or statues can. It was Marjorie, Nancy, that gave the place life and that last gift she placed in the basket for me, woke me up. It took awhile, but I finally realize what I lost, Nancy. I am going to give everything to have her back."

Nancy could see how hard it was for James to say what he just did. She could feel the loss he was feeling. For the first time in all the years since she came into the family, she felt the seed of love begin to sprout. James was changing and changing for the better. He was dying to a way of life that would have killed him with a terrible emptiness inside just like his father. Nancy had always felt that Jim never knew life nor enjoyed its beauty.

"Oh, James, what you are saying is so beautiful; it is music to my ears."

Nancy walked over to the Angel of Thanksgiving and stood in front of it. Her lips moved as if speaking to the angel, but her words were not audible. She then removed the white rose from her lapel and placed it into the angel's basket. Softly she whispered, "Thank you..."

Nancy turned and moved towards her stepson. Never in her wildest dreams or hopes, would she ever think that what she was about to do would ever happen in her lifetime. She opened her arms and James stepped into them.

Thomas' eyes filled instantly with tears as he stopped clearing out the dead brush from just down the walkway. Acts of kindness and love immediately touched the core of his being. He too, never would have thought he would live to see the day the Hamiltons would display such a grand show of affection.

He prayed that Mrs. Hamilton and James would turn to the Angel of Thanksgiving... Thomas had never seen the angel glow so radiantly since the day Miss Jenny left the estate!

CHAPTER THIRTY ONE

HENRY SCREECHED LAUREN'S car to a stop near the front door at the Grey Nuns' hospital. The space was reserved for at least three taxis and since none were there, he decided to take a chance. He parked the car so half was in the cab area and the other half in the no parking section and then quickly made his way inside the main entrance lobby. Jenny was probably still in intensive care. He ran past the admittance area and directly towards an elevator. It was almost an exact replay of what he had done that morning.

His heart was pounding, as the bell rang announcing the fifth floor. He noticed the nurses' station straight ahead. He didn't expect Nurse Johnson to be still on duty, yet there she was, filling out a report and talking excitedly to a group of nurses.

"Hi, Ms. Johnson," Henry exclaimed, as he rushed towards the counter.

Nurse Johnson's jaw almost hit the counter as she looked up at Henry in total surprise. "There he is... it's Henry Pederson! It was his kiss that brought Ms. Hamilton back to life!"

"I hope that's the case... is Jenny really alive?" Henry asked, just to confirm that it really did happen. It still seemed so unreal that such a thing could occur.

Nurse Johnson continued to stare at Henry as if she were entering another world. He began to get worried that perhaps Father was mistaken.

"Yes, Mr. Pederson ..." Nurse Johnson finally said. She almost called him Prince Charming as that is how she perceived him. Only a prince could have possibly given Ms. Hamilton the kiss of life. It surely had to be his yearning, loving, tender kiss that brought that sickly woman back from the other side... she just knew it had to be him... at least in part.

"Yes," continued Nurse Johnson, "Ms. Hamilton is alive! Miraculously, healed! She is very well indeed ... we all can't understand what happened. Dr. Kreake thinks an instantaneous remission and total healing has taken place... but I have my own theory of it all."

Henry's heart soared at the confirmation. He was going to ask Nurse Johnson what she meant by that, but he was too anxious to see Jenny.

"Is she still in room 505?"

"Yes, she is. We want to keep her here overnight and then move her down to a private room in the morning."

"Is it okay for me to see her?"

"Even if I said no, I know wild horses wouldn't be able to stop you. We gave her a sedative a half hour ago. There was such a commotion after I discovered that she had suddenly revived. The news spread so fast throughout the hospital that within minutes, doctors and nurses from all wards flooded the area. "Poor, Ms. Hamilton was inundated with questions. The doctors and nurses should have known better, but it was so miraculous, the medical staff couldn't help themselves. She may be asleep when you go in. Should you wake her, please keep your visit brief. I know her niece and friend are coming up shortly, as well. And perhaps your daughter-in-law has heard the news. I would have called her, but I don't know her number. So perhaps, please do so. The girls may have, but it wouldn't hurt for you to call, as well."

Henry merely nodded, as he simply couldn't wait another minute to go see his Jenny.

"Yes, go right ahead Mr. Pederson. Oh, I'm so happy for you and Ms. Hamilton. I'll try to keep any curious doctor away until your visit is over."

Henry felt relieved to get away from the counter. He could feel the heat rising to his face as the other nurses gawked at him. Henry quickly walked down the hall towards room 505. He wondered if Jenny would remember he was here before she died. *Will she still recognize me? What will I say? This is all so incredible.* He still felt that he had to actually see her to believe deep down that she really came back.

Henry brushed the few hairs on the top of his head with the palm of his hand, took a deep breath, then slowly walked into Jenny's room and hopefully... back into her life.

The bedside lamp was on, casting a warm glow on Jenny's face. Like earlier this morning, Jenny was asleep, but he had to admit she appeared healthier and... he was relieved to note that the sheet on top of her chest gently rose and fell. Her right hand was lying upon her chest, holding something at the end of a chain. He knew what was in Jenny's hand.

Henry thought his heart would pound through his chest as he neared her bedside, his eyes glued to her beautiful face. She looked like Sleeping Beauty. *Perhaps it was his kiss that brought her back.*

He instantly wanted to hold her and kiss her and never let her go again. Yet, an awkwardness was now present that wasn't there this morning, almost as if a courting phase was about to take place. Jenny's impending death this morning cut through all formality. There was no time to be concerned about protocol.

There was immediacy.

They had expressed their love for one another freely... trying desperately to beat death, which was knocking at the door.

But now, the urgency wasn't there. Perhaps it was time to slow down and enjoy this reunion. They could savour it, enjoy every moment of it. This second chance would make up for all the times they were denied and cheated out of being together while growing ever more deeply in love!

Henry quietly pushed a chair beside her bed and slowly sat down. Tears of bliss surfaced as he stared at his first love. He silently prayed in thanksgiving to Jesus for bringing Jenny back to life. Not more than six hours ago he sat in this very chair as she slipped away. Henry wiped a tear rolling down his cheek, still in a state of awe over what had transpired.

He wondered if it really was Father's prayers and those of the residents that brought his loved one back. He smiled at the thought that it might have really been his kiss like that of Prince Charming. It made him recall the dream he had on the day he'd met Jenny. He had dreamt that same dream earlier today again after Jenny passed on and that it was Death coming to take her away. But as he approached her, anticipating the touch of her lips, she suddenly disappeared and in her place was an older man wearing a tan-coloured suit with a yellow flower in the lapel. It was Father Engelmann! It was him who gave his life for Jenny… or was it?

If Father really had given himself as the sacrificial lamb, Henry thought further, then why was Father's life restored, too? This entire matter was so incredible. Perhaps they would never know why or how all three of them had passed away and miraculously came back…

It is all so incredibly, unbelievable!

The important thing was that they had all been given a second chance at life. The thought overwhelmed Henry as he gazed at his dear sweet Jenny. Her eyelashes were soft and thick. Her golden hair had filled in from this morning and spread out on the pillow and shimmered like a halo. Her white nightgown was her own, not the one from the hospital. He couldn't remember if it was the same one he had seen on her that morning. Cut lace outlined her collar and was U-shaped around the front. The silver chain sparkled as she moved slightly, but then was lost in her hand which clutched the gift he had sent her almost thirty two years ago. Henry marveled at the fact that he wore an identical one around his neck and would until his dying breath.

He drew a deep sigh at the very thought he would have to leave her after a short visit. He wanted her in his sight every minute.

Jenny began to stir, as if sensing his presence in the room. It was the same that morning. Her long eyelashes flickered and her eyes opened. She looked over at Henry, her clear blue eyes lit up and she smiled. A warm flush rose to Jenny's face and an expression grew in her cerulean blue eyes as if she was seeing an angel before her. She was so in love with Henry…

"Oh Henry, you came back… it's so nice to see you."

Henry sensed that Jenny felt a bit awkward too; she moved her hand hesitantly towards him. Henry immediately responded and took her hand into both of his. The moment their hands touched,

Henry felt that same surge of pure ecstasy go through his entire being as it did when they first held hands crossing the Avenue when he was 15 years old. It was the same now as it was then and earlier that morning, only more so now. Incredibly, his sweetheart came back and with it all the pent up love, yearning and desire suppressed in the recesses of his heart.

"Oh Jenny," was all he could say as tears welled up in his eyes. He carried her hand in his to his lips and gently kissed it.

Jenny rolled over towards Henry and brought her other hand onto his. Tears had filled her eyes as well. Neither could speak… the love flowing between them said what words couldn't possibly say.

Softly, Jenny spoke. "Oh Henry, Father Engelmann was here a short while ago. He said that you were in an accident after you left the hospital this morning… did you actually die and come back, too?"

"Yes, apparently my SUV was totally destroyed and the ambulance attendants were amazed that I wasn't hurt. They said I did die and came back. When I spoke with Father, he said that he passed away this morning as well and was miraculously healed… I don't understand it all. I don't remember much of anything after I left you this morning until I found myself in the ambulance."

"I don't remember anything either. After I saw you and Camilla, it seems like I went into a deep sleep… it was so peaceful and then, I suddenly awoke. The first thing I noticed was the absence of pain and how thirsty and hungry I was. When I called the nurse to ask for some tea she turned as white as a ghost when she came into my room. She couldn't believe that I was alive. She looked so foolish for calling the attendants in the morgue to come and get me.

"Anyway, within minutes after she and the attendants left, doctors and nurses began to stream in, asking me all kinds of questions and examining me… they all looked so puzzled and amazed. I loved it when Doctor Kreake came in… he's my doctor. He couldn't get over it. He kept saying it was a miracle. He had seen remissions in the past, but nothing like this…" Jenny's words trailed off.

"Did you know that Father was the same Engelmann that owned the corner grocery store?"

"Yes! He told me! I couldn't believe that Father David was the same man that you worked for! I honestly didn't know and who would have thought? He said the same thing and yet, he was upset with himself for not realizing it sooner. He always had the feeling that he knew me from some place before, but couldn't put his finger on it, was the way he put it. We were trying to talk about it more and also his passing today as well, but so many doctors interrupted us that he decided to go. He said he would call you right away."

"Yeah, I couldn't believe my ears when he said that you were healed. I came right away. But that is when I told Father that I was in an accident and had died… yet, he already knew and you just told me as well, that he shared that with you. How is it that he saw those things and we didn't…?"

"He said he came right up here to see you when he miraculously came back, as well. He wanted to make certain that he wasn't imagining it… and that's another thing, did he tell you that he saw his guardian angel and ours, too?"

"I don't know, Henry. He didn't say… perhaps he did see something that we didn't when he died. It's all so strange…"

Jenny grew silent and shook her head in awe of all that had happened since that morning, but her expression carried a more serious note.

"When Father David came in, I immediately told him that I needed to go to confession and ask to be forgiven for the way I kissed you earlier this morning. It had been such a lifelong wish and prayer of mine to see you and kiss you before I died. When I saw you, I didn't think of your lovely wife and that my actions and words might offend her."

Henry was about to explain what had happened to Julean, but Jenny continued—"

"But then Father told me that you knew that I was divorced from my husband and that your wife, Julean, had passed away several years ago. It made me feel less guilty knowing that I wasn't interfering with your marriage. Yet, I don't want you to feel that I am happy she is gone… I'm so sorry for her passing Henry."

Henry gazed lovingly into Jenny's eyes. "It's okay, Jenny. Julean knew of you and before she passed on it was her prayer that you and I might someday find each other again…" Henry's words trailed off. He thought of telling Jenny more about Julean and how she knew of his teenage sweetheart, but now was not the time.

Jenny remained silent, though her eyes told Henry to go on.

Henry shrugged his shoulders and slowly continued. "Since the day we parted back in grade nine, I have always held you in my heart. I never got over you and… apparently in my dreams I spoke of you and that is how she knew."

Jenny squeezed Henry's hand, as he struggled to go on.

"Julean was an amazing person. Although I could never explain why, after all those years you and I were apart, my love for you never lessened, she seemed to understand and accept my feelings."

"That must have been so difficult for her."

Henry's eyes filled with tears again and he remained silent, not knowing what to say. It seemed so awkward to speak of Julean like this with Jenny. He hadn't planned on talking about his former wife and yet it all just seemed to flow out so naturally. He had to admit that he loved them both, deeply.

"I never forgot about you either, Henry. Over all the years, you and Camilla were ever present in my heart. I just can't believe that I saw her and you earlier today; that my guardian angel made my prayer come true. The image of you both remained in my mind when I passed away and was still there when I woke, or rather, came back to life."

"It's all so incredible Jenny! That I indirectly became the father to the girl you gave birth to. Somehow I knew in my heart that you had conceived a child during that evening when Eddy's friends took you to the park, but I would never have imagined that it would have turned out to be Camilla. Yet, the moment my son first introduced me to her, it was as if I was seeing you. She looks so much like you, Jenny."

"I believe that our guardian angels had something to do with all this."

Jenny reached with the hand not holding Henry's and caught the pewter angel hanging around her neck. As Jenny raised it up, Henry took hold of his, as well. The two angels seemed to dance and flit about, catching the light of the lamp.

"It's amazing how we sent each other identical pewter angels and how the last letter containing them survived all the others."

"So you know that the other letters were destroyed?"

Henry nodded. "It's okay, Jenny. Your parents had their reasons and we did receive the most important one of all."

Jenny's eyes misted. She tried to speak… "They were very sorry for what they did…"

Jenny couldn't go on.

"It's in the past, Jen; the important thing is that we are together right now."

And just then, the two pewter angels collided with a tiny clink. It was as if the angels were celebrating their reunion.

Henry and Jenny smiled at one another. "See, Jenny, it's as you said, our guardian angels had a lot to do with our coming back to each other."

Jenny let go of the angel and turned her head towards Henry's hand, holding hers on the bed. She pulled on Henry's hand and brought it to her lips and tenderly kissed it.

"I love you so much, Henry."

Her golden hair fell over their hands and Henry felt the warmth of her tears cascade down through their intertwined fingers.

Henry could no longer speak, his being was enraptured with pure joy and complete happiness, as a quiet peaceful silence fell over the room. No words could even begin to ever capture the love flowing in their hearts and between them at that moment.

Jenny raised her head and gazed into Henry's eyes for but a moment before he leaned forward and their lips softly touched.

All the pain and heartache seemed to melt away in the tenderness of their kiss. All that was left was the promise of a new beginning. They knew in their hearts that their angels had brought them together and somehow a wonderful miracle had happened in their lives.

Their life together would start now … their lives would begin to make up for those days, months and years of secrecy and denial since that memorable summer of their youth. Yes, a new life between two people who were never more deserving and more in love … theirs would be a union that would truly be heaven blessed.

"Oh, Henry I love you so much, I still can't believe this is real."

"I love you, too, Jenny, with all my heart."

They gazed into each other's eyes again with a look of awe, realizing that this was all happening. There was so much to say, so much to explain, so much to tell each other of their lives. But all that would come out in the days ahead.

Suddenly, their reverie was broken by a soft tap on the door and Nurse Johnson peeked in while still holding the door. "I know you two want to be together forever, but others are waiting to see Jenny and both of you have had a very eventful and exhausting day, to say the least."

"Yes, I was about to leave, Ms. Johnson. Reluctantly!" Henry added with a smile.

Nurse Johnson made her way into the room and held the door open. "There are some flowers for you…"

Immediately a delivery man carrying an armful of daisies entered the room. He was followed by another and then another.

The first man that came in spoke, "I assume that you are Marjorie Hamilton?"

"Yes, I am…" Jenny said, her eyes quaking in surprise.

"These are from your husband, James Hamilton."

Jenny wanted to correct the man, but let it slide. It was of no concern to him, yet she knew it would be unsettling for Henry.

"He wanted you to know how much joy it has given him to know that your health has been restored."

As the delivery man spoke, even more flowers were brought in. Soon the room was filled with all kinds of wildflowers, especially daises. The florists had thought of everything; they brought vases and stands for the flowers, knowing there were neither containers nor tables to set them on.

Henry stood there flabbergasted, not knowing what to say. Jenny gazed at Henry, feeling very uncomfortable as well. This was totally unexpected.

As the owners of the florist shops and delivery personnel were leaving, Matti and Chloe came into the room and broke the uneasiness in the air.

"Chloe! Matti!" Jenny shouted as she hopped out of the bed and opened her arms to her dear friends.

"Oh, Jenny, I be so busy praising the Lord ever since I heard the news." "Auntie!" Chloe stepped back to make sure it was her auntie. "I can't believe this!" Chloe shook her head from side to side. "You're completely healed! It's like night and day from the past few days and especially this morning!! You didn't look so good. But look at you now! You look amazing! Oh Auntie! How I wish Mom was here to see this."

"That would make everything even more perfect… I miss her so much."

Chloe moved forward again and hugged her dear aunt. "Oh, Auntie I am so happy for you!" Chloe burst into tears and slowly let go.

Immediately, Matti came forward and embraced her dear friend. "I just don't know what to say." Tears streamed down her eyes. "This be the best day of my life. The Lord be so gracious, Jen. You look so good, and healthy and fine!"

"Yes," interjected Chloe, being more composed, "you look so beautiful and rested Auntie. This is amazing… truly amazing!!"

Jenny noticed Henry standing by the door, somewhat shy being there. "You remember Henry Pederson?" asked Jenny, her gaze falling on him.

"Yes, we sure do!" said Matti. "And I remember the kiss you two had. That was someting soooo special."

Henry turned red and began to blush. Jenny's cheeks tinged with pink as well.

"If we be interrupting you two, we can come back," offered Matti.

"No, no, that's fine Matilda, I was just leaving. Nurse Johnson said you girls might be by and this has been an exhausting day for all of us. I shared with Jenny that I was in an accident as well when I left this morning. She can tell you what happened."

Looking back at Jenny, "Well, I better go Jenny. I'd like to come back tomorrow. What time would be best?"

Jenny walked towards Henry, stood in front of him and placed her hands on his shoulders. Henry began to swim in her blue eyes and his embarrassment of being in the presence of the other two girls vanished. He drew her in closer as if to squeeze her into his heart. He could feel Jenny do the same.

"I still can't believe this. Maybe I am still on the other side! Thank you dear God, thank you," said Jenny as she leaned forward and kissed Henry. "I can't wait for you to come back tomorrow. The earlier the better…"

Jenny's friends couldn't contain their oohing and aahing with Matti praising the Lord in between.

Henry suddenly became aware of their presence and red rolled up his neck once again.

He looked at Matilda and asked, "Does Camilla know what has happened yet?"

"We be calling her as soon as we get back to the hotel, unless you want to deliver the good news."

"Yes, I will call her as soon as I get home. She is in for one big surprise."

"Oh, Henry, I can hardly wait to see her again. Tell her to come as soon as she is able." Jenny's eyes sparkled with joy and delight.

Henry pecked Jenny on the cheek and smiled. He turned to the girls, winked and left.

CHAPTER THIRTY TWO

A
FTER HENRY PICKED up Lauren and Justin at the gallery, they went home to the farm. The first thing Henry did was call Jeremy.

"Hi Jeremy, how are you doing, Son?"

"It's been such a roller coaster of emotions today for all of us. Between Camilla meeting her mom, only to see her die, then learning that you were in an accident and had died sent us into such a tailspin of sorrow. And then to see you alive outside the café… it was like seeing a ghost. We wondered if we were dreaming and had just woken up."

"Yeah, it's been quite a day and it still isn't over with surprises. I have some unbelievably great news for Camilla. Is she there?"

"She went to bed about half an hour ago. She was so emotionally drained that she fell fast asleep… what is the news, Dad? Can I pass it on to her?"

"Yes, perhaps it's best to let her sleep… Well, you're not going to believe this, Jeremy— I hardly do myself— but… in the same miraculous way that I came back to life, so too did Jenny. She's alive, Jeremy! Camilla's mother unbelievably came back to life—"

"What? How can that be? What is going on, Dad?"

"I don't know, Son. Father Engelmann had supposedly died, as well, earlier today at the care home. An ambulance was coming to the care home to pick up his body and he wasn't there. Apparently he came back to life before the attendants came, caught a taxi and went straight to the hospital to see if Jenny was alive. He said the entire medical staff at the hospital was there to see Jenny and the miracle that had happened."

"It's all just unbelievable," said Jeremy in a state of awe.

"I went up to see Jenny as soon as Father phoned to tell me she was miraculously cured. Although frail, she looked beautiful and completely healed. It's incredible that all three of us had supposedly died and then came back! I may phone Father later this evening to find out more details. I think he knows more of what happened than both Jenny and me."

There was a long silence on the phone. Neither man could speak any more. Something had happened that was unexplainable and no words could describe their awe and wonderment.

Finally, Jeremy spoke. "I better wake Camilla and you can tell her all this… this will just skyrocket her emotions…"

"When I left Jenny at the hospital earlier she was exhausted from all the visitors and medical examinations and questions. I think it's best for Camilla to go over in the morning. Perhaps let her sleep and tell her when she awakes. If she wants, she can call me. I may go to bed early as I'm starting to feel the excitement of day catch up with me as well.

"What a day, Son! What a day…"

Lauren made dinner but Henry couldn't eat. He and the children talked about the day briefly and then Henry excused himself and carried his tea to the sun room. He wished it was a bit later and the kids had gone up to their rooms. He wanted to be alone and savour the time he had spent with Jenny. Their meeting was so filled with love. In a way it seemed as if they were continuing their relationship of their youth. As if they had parted for just the weekend and were back together again.

It's all so unexplainable and yet so wonderful…

Henry thought about all the flowers Jenny's former husband had sent to her. What is going on there, he wondered? After reading the diary yesterday, it seemed like they had a distant relationship. Yet, such a show of flowers seemed to convey a different message. He took a sip of tea and closed his eyes.

How does Jenny feel about James…?

Such a thought would normally cause concern for Henry, but fatigue was settling in and in less than a minute he fell asleep.

Henry began to dream the dream he had earlier after Jenny died. There, before him, was the love of his life, lying asleep on a bed of daisies in a vast meadow of wildflowers. He was running towards her to kiss her and bring her back and live happily after ever, but a figure in a black cloak rushed towards him. He braced himself ready to be gripped by the faceless, hooded entity.

But the dream had changed.

The figure ran past him, laughing with glee. He was heading for Jenny and when he was almost there, his hood fell down. He turned back towards Henry. It was James, smiling; victory written all over his face.

Lauren nudged her father and he opened his eyes looking disorientated.

"Are you okay, Dad? You were yelling so loud I heard you over the TV."

"Oh my gosh, Lauren, I'm sorry. I was having a dream… it's been quite the day."

Lauren gazed at her father and said, "We're going to bed, Dad. I love you. Are you sure everything's all right?"

"Yes, I'm fine, honey. What time is it?"

"It's just past ten. Justin went to bed an hour ago. He came to say good night but didn't want to wake you. He sure was tired. He was so worried about you…"

"I'm sure glad everything turned out the way it did. It was quite a day," Henry repeated. "I'll be going to bed right away soon. Good-night and thanks for making dinner."

Lauren bent over and kissed her dad on the cheek. "G'nite, Dad." Just as she turned to leave, she said, "Oh, I forgot to tell you that Camilla phoned. I was going to wake you but she said not to and that she would call first thing in the morning."

"Oh, good. Thanks for telling me. Yes, it's a little too late to call her back. The morning will be fine. 'Nite honey."

Jeremy must have told Camilla the news. *Boy, I would have given anything to see the expression on her face.* Henry could not believe what occurred that day. Not only the physical healings, but the emotional ones, as well.

To have his dear sweet Jenny back sent such soothing throughout his being and for Camilla to have a new life with her real mother...is all so wonderful. *Thank you Jesus, for hearing our prayers and pleas...thank you.*

Henry sat in his chair for about another twenty minutes then went to the living room and turned on the record player. He wanted to listen to his two favourite songs. He turned out the lights and returned to the sun room and gazed out into the sky. The stars were out and there, to the east, was their star... his and Jenny's.

Incredibly, all the prayers he had made to his angel and star had come true. He felt the warmth of the star's rays. He knew that the angel guarding that star was sending him Jenny's love. He had felt the same earlier that day when he held Jenny's hand.

It was unmistakable.

"For you and I have a guardian angel on high with nothing to do but to give to you and to give to me, love forever true..."

True Love had just finished playing on the record player and *Love Me Tender* had started.

"Thank you," Henry softly whispered to his dear wife, Julean. "You said you would help me find Jenny, and along with our guardian angels, you did just that.

"I love you, honey..."

Suddenly, a shooting star shot through the heavenly sky and as the star dust settled in his heart, he recalled what else Julian had said... "A man like you should marry again and not be alone."

His glistening, tear-filled eyes were soothed with wonder and burgeoning hope.

JENNY COULDN'T SLEEP. The light of the moon and stars caught the sparkle of happiness in her eyes as she gazed out of the window, into the heavens above. It had been such a wonderful day, filled with so many surprises. She couldn't stop thanking God for the miraculous healing in her life. There were so many people suffering and dying all over the world. They all had hopes and dreams of being healed, too. Jenny wondered why she was given this blessing. She had been prepared to die. She had accepted her cross.

Her deepest wish and prayer had always been to see Henry and her daughter before she died. She had been granted that wish and more… so much more.

She was so grateful and yet wondered why her?

It was impossible to tell which of the stars was the Star of the East, yet she knew it was there. She could feel Henry's love so strong and warm and tender. It was like it used to be. She recalled the words she had written in her diary on the day of their anniversary, repeated so often over the years… "Even though we are far apart, you are forever in my heart." It was also the last sentence in her letter to Henry with the pewter angel inside.

As tears slid down her cheeks, she thought of their anniversary poem and how she had slightly changed the words when she felt that Henry had moved on to another in his life…

The Star of the East we both can see,
Its warm rays so bright no more caressing me,
If another love has come your way,
Please never forget our special day

Perhaps in the future if it's meant to be
Your love will return and envelop me.
I wish you happiness though from afar
To fill your heart through this, our star.

The moonlight caught a new happiness in Jenny's blurry eyes as she softly whispered, "Even though we may grow apart, you are forever in my heart."

"Only now, you have come back and you will always be in my heart." Jenny wiped a tear sliding down her cheek, its trail glistening in the moonlight.

"Thank you, Julean… Thank you for allowing me to share in your life with Henry. It must have been so difficult for you…"

Jenny felt compelled to add another verse to her poem…

Oh, Star of the East you see all things
Let Julean know on angel's wings
That her love for Henry is welcome here
So in his heart the two of us are forever near.

Suddenly, a shooting star streaked across the sky. It made her think of her friend Tammy who first suggested she make a wish on the star. Her friend had wished that she and Robbie would get married, and it turned out true.

And now Jenny's did, too! Both of her loves had come back to her, as well!

Stepping out in faith, Jenny made another wish... *It was a wish she had always kept buried; a secret ever so deep in her heart.*

Just before the blazing light of the star went out, Jenny sent out her fervent wish.

"Oh star of wonder, star so bright, I wish to the angel guiding your light...*that Henry and I get married and I bear him a beautiful child...*"

And as the glowing light dimmed and faded into the universe, she felt the warmth of the dust settle in her heart. Her sparkling, tear-filled eyes were soothed with wonder and burgeoning hope.

Chapter Thirty Three

Jenny found herself once more at the window in her hospital room. It was as though she had not gone to bed. She was up until well past midnight, gazing into the heavens, searching for the star of the East and feeling wrapped completely by Henry's love beaming in by the light of the celestial sky. She wanted to feel the love of their star forever. And here she was, up again, waiting on the sun to break into another day of bliss.

She had slept so much these past few months that she didn't want to sleep any more. To be free of the pain was another thing. For months, every movement had hurt; every breath had been an effort. She had been constantly on guard for a cough. She had been drained her of energy for so long and hurt with such anguish, there were moments when she didn't think she could go on for another second… nor did she even want to go on at times. How many times did she plead with God to take her? And now, it was all over… She felt completely new; not only was there no pain, there was a flowing energy of love and joyful anticipation coursing through her veins. She felt just like she had when she was 15…

A peace descended upon Jenny. The fragrance of the flowers that James had sent her filled the room and filled her with the same tranquility she felt whenever she sat in her garden. It was so thoughtful of James… and totally out of character. And yet, he seemed to be giving her a message… Jenny hoped this wasn't leading to some kind of reconciliation to have her back. Jenny wondered how Henry felt seeing all the flowers sent by her former husband.

The sun had just come up, exposing the eastern skyline of Regina. From the fifth floor, Jenny could just see the top of the legislative building off to the south. As she held aside the plastic curtain to look out, she marvelled that she even had the strength. Yesterday she couldn't even lift her hand off the bedspread, let alone get out of bed. Gazing out her window, Jenny noticed how small Regina seemed. It's a small city, she thought, not like the skyscrapers in Ottawa or Toronto. But she felt comfortable here; she felt at home.

Suddenly, she squinted as the sun peeked out from behind the McCallum Hill Tower, burning into the tower's southern edge as it moved higher into the prairie sky. The warm rays felt soothing on her face. Rather than move the curtain she was holding to shield her face, she closed her eyes and allowed her celestial friend to assuage her spirit.

Jenny was filled with awe and wonderment as she recalled how she had unexpectedly woke up yesterday as if she had been in a deep sleep and it all had just been a sorrowful nightmare. The doctors told her she had died, yet she had no memory of it. It was as if she fell asleep and awoke totally refreshed and healed and filled with renewed life!

How could she, Henry and Father David all pass away and be miraculously restored to life and good health? Henry did say that Father and his prayer team at the nursing home prayed ardently for her healing… Jenny knew there was power in prayer, but there was more to it… it was also the love between her and Camilla and Henry. It was a love of yearning and hope that had simmered for years and years and suddenly burst into a flame of fire. Jenny felt that surge of love flow through her now.

It was so wonderful to see Henry last evening. *Oh, I love him so much and I know he feels the same about me.* It was so amazing that after all these years of separation, their love for one another had never faded or lessened. Jenny felt certain that this was part of the reason for them coming back… it just had to be. She wondered if Father David remembered anything of yesterday.

She wondered, once more, about the flowers that James had sent her.

Such a change for him. We hardly spoke to one another during those years on the estate. And now this show of care…

It was nice of him and very thoughtful… Jenny was not inclined to be suspicious of others, and yet, she couldn't help but question James' motives… She hoped his intentions were not more serious, as that part of their relationship was over and she had moved on.

As Jenny was thinking on all these things, she sensed a presence… a loving presence. She turned abruptly and there, in the doorway, stood Camilla. Her daughter had a smile on her face and her eyes were overflowing with tears. Jenny let go of the curtain she was still holding and dropped her arms to her side. A rush of love surged through her and tears spilled and rolled down her cheeks. She moved her head almost imperceptibly from side to side expressing her deep longing for this moment…

They stood and faced each other for the longest moment from across the room.

"They told me that you came back to life and were healed… I couldn't wait for daybreak to come and see you…"

Camilla was too choked to say more. She slowly shook her head in awe… they were lost and now after years of separation and searching for each other, they had found one another…

They had come home.

Camilla made a small step towards her mother and Jenny did the same.

"Oh Camilla," was all Jenny could utter as a spiritual bond gripped both women simultaneously. They ran into each other's arms and tightly embraced one another. Tears gushed out as they sobbed uncontrollably. All the years of yearning and love for one another flowed through their hearts into each other.

"Oh, Camilla, I am so sorry for giving you away. Please forgive me… I was too young and thought it best for you to have a mom and dad… I missed you so terribly every day… for so long… for so many years. All I remember were those precious moments of you crying and being held by your feet in the doctor's hand, dangling there. Then you were whisked away… and I never saw you again…"

Jenny couldn't go on and cried even more than before. The pain and anguish of that time lying in the hospital without her baby surged back into her memory. The emptiness of her womb, the swelling of her breasts, the emptiness of her arms…the baby she had carried and grew to love was gone, given to someone else, never to see her growth and development, those precious first steps, those first words, to be called Mommy, to nurture and to hold and to love…it was all gone…only a brief memory of the birth, a flash in an eternity of years.

The sorrow that she had suppressed rose from deep within shaking her body.

Camilla felt Jenny's pain and sorrow and hugged her mother tightly. "Oh, Mom, I'm so glad I found you. The moment I laid eyes on you yesterday, I knew you were my mother. Instantly I saw myself in you. I wanted to crawl in bed with you and be held by you and… I feel your love so deeply. I understand how painful that decision was for you. I see it in the girls I counsel who give their babies up for adoption.

"It's even more difficult for those who abort their baby, only to have the full impact of that decision hit them in the days, months and years that follow. You chose to give me life and the opportunity for this moment when we could be together once more. I love you, Mom, and for me this is not necessary to say but if it's important to you, *I forgive you with all my heart.* I just want, from this moment on, for us to have a mother-daughter relationship."

"Oh, Camilla, I love you so much. Your words are so healing. I promise I will never leave you again…"

Jenny hugged her daughter and they both wept as the rays of the sun streaming in through the window surrounded them, warming their tender spirits.

Chapter Thirty Four

HENRY HEARD A ringing in his ear. At first he didn't know where he was. He still felt the effects of yesterday and it took him a moment for all that had occurred, to sink in. Just as another thought was about to enter his mind, the phone rang again.

"Oh, for gosh sakes, it's the phone!" He rolled over in his water bed and reached over for the receiver as it was about to ring again.

"Hello."

"Is this the Pederson residence?"

"Yes, this is Henry speaking."

"I took a chance. I recall Eddy mentioning that you lived out in the valley near Lumsden. It was the only listing in the phone book."

Henry recognized the voice. It was low and distinctive…

"Is this Peter?"

"You have a good memory, thanks for remembering. I thought I might have some explaining to do as to whom I was."

Henry had received a call from Peter's wife, Angie, just the other day informing him that her husband was critically ill and near death's door. This however, did not sound like a man that was about to enter the pearly gates.

"So, how are you doing, Peter? Last I heard you were quite ill…"

"Yes, I was, Henry… or is it Hank? Which do you prefer?"

"Either is fine, Peter. Most of my friends call me Hank but those I develop through my business and art call me Henry. So either is fine."

"Well, I was just about to say that I was very ill and then something happened—"

"My good Lord, Peter. Did you get healed, too?"

"Why, yes. In fact I was pronounced dead and a little while later my pulse came back. I threw the sheet off me and sat up. The nurse in attendance fainted and Angie went hysterical!

"I couldn't understand what the commotion was all about until they told me that I had miraculously come back from being dead! I've never seen Angie look so surprised. Once it sunk in, she started running down the hallway telling everyone that I was healed and that our prayers were answered. Unfortunately, by that time, parishioners that were there earlier and praying in the hallways had already left. So nurses and patients who didn't know of my condition thought that she had lost it and called for the commissioner to come and restrain her!"

Henry chuckled, "Isn't that something! So you died and were brought back, as well?"

"Yes, the Holy Spirit swept through me with full power. The nurse who was holding my wrist was healed of her injury, as well. She had been in a car accident and injured her back. She could barely assist patients to sit up or get out of bed. But now the petite nurse feels like a 200 pound weight lifter and easily helps those in her charge."

"That's amazing, Peter."

"I am so grateful to Jesus for the healing, too! I know Jenny is alive and was returned from the dead, as well. In fact, I know that you and Father Engel…"

The phone suddenly went dead. Henry could not comprehend what Peter was saying. The words he was hearing were just too far-fetched to be believed!"Are you there, Hank? Hello…?"

"Peter, how did you know Jenny was dead and came back? Did someone call you… who do you know? It all happened yesterday and I still don't know all of the details. Did Matilda by chance call you?" Henry just had to know.

"Oh you mean, Eddy's sister-in law? ...No, she didn't tell me."

"Well, who then?"

Peter took a deep breath and went on. "You may not believe this, Hank, but when I died, I saw you and Jenny and Father Engelmann and all your guardian angels waiting to enter through the portals of heaven. I was about to come over and beg for Jenny's forgiveness when I saw this huge angel appear from that brilliant tunnel of light. There must have been some kind of a reunion amongst the angels because I saw all three of yours go over to the archangel. I became as awestruck as you three over what I was witnessing, that it kept me frozen from moving. Then all at once, I felt the power of the Holy Spirit sweep through all of us. I would have been lifted and carried to some place in eternity if it had not been for my guardian angel, as well. I didn't even realize I had one until I felt his firm grip on my shoulders holding me still."

Peter stopped and took a deep breath. Before Henry could encourage him to go on and explain further, Peter rambled on. "I was going to join you and Jenny and Father and all the angels in your happy celebration over what God had granted, but then you began to disappear one by one. Jenny was the first, then you and finally Father. He had quite the discussion with his guardian before he left. I think he was given the same choice as I."

"What kind of choice, Peter?"

"My guardian angel said that I could choose to stay and continue through the tunnel of light, or I could return to earth. If I chose to stay, I would be welcomed into heaven as the Lord had forgiven me of all my transgressions. If I went back, it would be to serve longer as a pastor, but even more so, it would be to ask for Jenny's forgiveness, as well as my daughter's. There was the risk that the two ladies might not forgive me and hold me in bondage. Or anger or frustration might overtake me in the course of my daily living as is often the case with our human frailty being what it is and I may plunge into sin. So I was taking a chance in returning when the doors of heaven were opened for me... but I so desired to hear Jenny say she forgives me that I had to come back. And the prayers of so many, besides my wife, kept drawing me, as well. I love serving the people of my parish. In the end, I knew what I had to do... and here I am."

Once again the phone was silent. Henry couldn't believe what he was hearing. How was it that Peter, and supposedly Father, as well, could see and remember what transpired after they had died, and Jenny and he were not able to?

Why?

Henry couldn't wait to talk to Father and ask him to relate what happened when he had died, as well. Would it verify what Peter was saying?

"Peter, that is incredible. I don't know what to say. So that is how you knew Jenny was healed, as well, and brought back to life?"

"That's right, Henry. That is also the reason for my call. Angie also told me that you informed her that Camilla knows she was adopted and suspects that Jenny might be her mother. Is that correct?"

"Yes, that's absolutely correct, Peter. As incredible and unbelievable as it is, it does turn out that Camilla is Jenny's daughter."

"I knew it in my dreams, Hank. I just knew that was the case. Well, I want your help in setting up a meeting between Jenny and me and… if possible, for Camilla to come, as well. I need to speak to them. The Lord has given me another chance and He may take me again at any time. I do not want to waste a minute of any part of each and every day from now on. My life will be completely for His service."

"I, I, understand Peter, and I feel the same way. Life's moments are very precious, especially once you see how fragile our lives are and how much of it we waste and squander.

"I am seeing Jenny today and will discuss it with her. Don't expect me to get back to you right away. Jenny and her daughter have barely had time to meet each other and the medical community is swarming to the hospital to question Jenny about her healing. It may take a few days, Peter, but I will get back to you as soon as I can, I promise."

"That's all I can ask, Hank. Do you have my phone number?"

"Yes I do. Your wife gave it to me when I spoke with her last time."

"Great. Thank you for your time and understanding. I know that horrible evening has caused you much pain and anger, as well. Thank you for your forgiveness… please help me get Jenny's and Camilla's as well."

"I will do everything I can. And give my best regards to Angie. That is a wonderful wife you have, Peter."

"I know, and if the truth be known, she was the first reason why I wanted to return. I knew it was her love that drew me and I know her love will help me see this through with Jenny and… our daughter."

Henry hadn't thought of it that way. *Yes, Camilla wasn't just his daughter-in-law; she was also Peter's daughter…*

Suddenly, it hit Henry what happened that night… that this man had taken his beloved and violated her person and showed absolutely no regard for her… or for Henry. Henry recalled how upset and hateful and revengeful he felt for days, months and years over what Eddy and his friends had done. Slowly his anger had subsided and he let go, beginning with Eddy. But now, once again, a slow anger began to surface. For all these years he had suspected Peter was the one who had raped Jenny… but he never was completely sure. Until now.

His uncertainty had held his feelings in check.

But now, feelings he had suppressed and never really felt about that night, mixed with this new knowledge of what had really happened, were suddenly coming to the fore.

Yes, Peter actually did do what he had suspected for years.

Peter's admission that he had violated Jenny and that Camilla was the result of that assault, stared Henry coldly in his face. He could feel the anger and hatred and he didn't like where this was going. A fuse was lit that would travel and burn deep within himself and he knew this matter was far from over. If not dealt with quickly and with compassion, this could all explode into something tragic.

Perhaps Peter's decision to return to his earthly life may not have been in his best interests.

CHAPTER THIRTY FIVE

I T WAS EARLY on the estate. Never would James have thought that he would find himself out in the garden shortly after the sun came up. He had to admit the atmosphere was ethereal… there was a peace and freshness about the early morning that he never knew. It calmed and lifted his spirits at the same time. He was certain that he could even smell the fragrance of the budding flowers and shrubs in the air. Had he only known this healing therapy when he was running the business, he could have been out here every morning before venturing into the corporate jungle. Maybe then, he would have avoided the sickness he had now.

It was interesting to James how life worked. How in spite of ourselves we are forced to slow down and reflect on the direction of our lives. It's a good thing, as he knew for certain that he would have lived and died like his father before him. Thomas would say that God had a hand in all this. James wondered about God. Was there really a higher power out there?

What is it that Thomas believes?

There was something spiritual about the man that drew James to him. It had been the same with Marjorie, only with her it seemed to come through nature, her flowers, her garden, her angel, her need for solace and quietness.

James smiled; she probably needed something to put up with me and all my antics. While God revealed Himself to Jenny through nature, with Thomas it was harder to tell. He certainly loved the garden and nature as much as Marjorie, but he seemed to derive that deep sense of peace from something else. Whatever it was, it reflected in his attitude and overall disposition and demeanor. He was definitely a man of faith. James recalled seeing Thomas's Bible in the tool shed. Every now and then James would catch Thomas reading the book during his break. He wondered if this was Thomas's extra source of inspiration. Could printed words have the same affect on a person as nature does?

James knew of the Bible, but he had never opened one. He knew it was about some man named Jesus, but didn't have a clue what He did. Perhaps he would venture over to the shed and read Thomas's Bible to see what was in it. In the same way he wanted to capture Jenny's spirit and her love of the garden, James was now interested in seeing what motivates his gardener, as well.

James made his way over to the tool shed. If he was going to peek inside Thomas's book, he would have do it quickly as his employee came in early. James often thought Thomas's love for nature was so strong that he would do his work on the estate for free. As James turned the corner on the path leading to the shed, Thomas was already there gathering some of the tools he would need for the day and putting them into a wheelbarrow.

"Good morning, James," said Thomas as he looked up at his employer coming towards him. "Another fine morning."

"Yes, it is, Thomas. I see you're early."

"Seems my cycle is in tune with the sun. I retire shortly after the sun goes down and most times I'm up early enough to greet the sun when it peeks over the horizon."

"I have to say, there is something special about the mornings."

"It's God's time, James… is there anything you would have me do?"

"To be frank, Thomas, I was wondering if I may have a read in your Bible. I forgot my reading material at the house…"

"It's not in the best of shape. It's covered with soil and what not, but you're welcome to peruse it if you wish. Let me get it for you."

Thomas went into the shed and quickly returned. He handed

the well used Bible to James. Normally, James would never touch something that was covered with dirt and looked soiled, but James quickly reached out and accepted the Bible.

"Thank you, Thomas, I'll return it shortly."

"Take your time, sir."

James stood there wanting to say something else, but was hesitant. The perceptive gardener however, was quick to read his employer.

"Seems to me there is something else on your mind, Mr. — James."

"As a matter of fact, there is… I'm going to be calling Marjorie shortly to see how she liked the flowers and to see how she is doing. I have to admit, I'm not much good at this sort of thing and she may find it unusual for me to be calling after our divorce…" James' words trailed off… He wasn't sure how to say what he wanted his employee's advice on.

Once again, Thomas was quick to read his employer. "Why don't we sit down and chat about it for a bit. My start time isn't for another hour and a half."

Thomas went into the shed and brought out two five gallon pails and inverted them on the sidewalk. "They're not fancy chairs, James, but sometimes I prefer these over an overstuffed chester-field… especially when the conversation is good."

James hesitated for but a moment and then sat down on the makeshift chair.

"So, what's on your mind, James?"

"What should I say, Thomas? I rarely spoke with Marjorie towards the end and now out of the blue I would like her back. She won't believe me. What can I do to convince her of my sincerity?"

Thomas thought for a moment and then said, "There is one thing I think would please Miss Jenny and get her attention—"

"What Thomas? Tell me." James sat straighter and leaned towards the gardener his eyes growing wide. Even his ears seemed to bend towards what Thomas was about to utter. James fully expected something profound. He knew Thomas was an educated and well read man who chose a line of work that did not reflect his intellectual abilities and aptitudes. But what the humble man said before him was something James would never have realized on his own, or given it any consideration as being important.

"It has to do with her name, James."

"Her name…?"

"Yes, the name she prefers to be called by; Jenny rather than Marjorie. A person's name is very important. It's the way they are addressed for their life time. To a large degree, it is a huge part of one's identity—"

James still wasn't really listening and cut Thomas off. "When we courted, I used to call her Jenny and Jen but once married I wanted her to go by her first name. It sounds more sophisticated and legal. Don't you agree?"

"Yes, when signing a document one must sign by their birth name but that happens so seldom. It's true, for the most part we go by our first name but on occasion we give someone a nickname or a name they prefer to be called."

Thomas gazed at James and then said, "I have to admit, James, I do prefer Jenny. Both Marjorie and Jenny are beautiful names, but perhaps I am partial to that name since it's what Miss Jenny prefers… and I desire to please her. It would be the same if I called you Jimmy when you preferred James. Out of respect and consideration for your feelings, I would oblige you."

And before James could butt in again, Thomas reinforced his reasoning with a real life example. "I recall the day you brought Miss Jenny to the estate. What a lovely bride she was! I could see such joy in her eyes. You introduced me to her as Marjorie Hamilton and she came right up to me, shook my hand and said, 'Please call me Jenny.' If I remember correctly, you immediately said to me, 'no, it's Marjorie,' and turned to your wife and corrected her as well.

"Instantly, James, the sparkle and joy in Miss Jenny's eyes went out." Thomas was going to add more but he was now bordering on judging his employer and didn't want to cross the line. He hoped James would understand.

James studied Thomas, it was an astute observation. It made James think of later that evening before Jenny and he retired. The issue was brought up again by Marjorie. He recalled how angry he was with his wife for being so foolish and not seeing his point of view.

"See, it's amazing how you see things, Thomas. For most of my life I never bothered to look at things from the other person's point of view. It's always my way or the highway… you know, I never did look into Marj…Jenny's eyes and notice that. In fact, I rarely took notice of Jenny's feelings… Yes, her eyes could have revealed a lot to me if I had taken the time… if I had even understood…" James' words trailed off and then suddenly he blurted, "Thanks Thomas, I shall put that into practice at once! And by the way, were you able to locate some lilacs… surely there are places that are warm all year round."

"Actually James, lilacs need a cold spell in order for them to flower. So we searched in areas that have a cold or winter season. Fortunately, spring came early in Minnesota this year. Some white and purple lilacs are being shipped directly to the florist shop in Regina that delivered the wildflowers to Miss Jenny."

"That's wonderful, Thomas. If only my CEO's were that efficient! So, lilacs need the cold treatment, do they?"

"Yes, sir."

"There's a lot to this flowering business."

"I'm learning more all the time about God's creation."

"Thanks for your time, Thomas, much appreciated. I thought I would give Marj—I mean, Jenny a call first thing before it gets too busy in the hospital."

James got up and as he turned and was about to make his way back to the house, Thomas said, "Oh, James, here's the Bible, if you're still interested."

James looked at Thomas, and nodded, "Yes, Thomas, I am."

The book was soiled and well used. James studied the Bible for a moment and took it from the gardener. He slowly turned and walked away.

JENNY WAS AWAKENED by one of the maintenance men installing a telephone in her room. Shortly after Camilla left, she decided to have a nap. She was up most of the night and knew a busy day lay ahead.

"Sorry to wake you, Ma'am,"

"That's fine. I see you're installing a phone. That's wonderful."

"Yes, we had several calls from your husband and he was adamant we install the phone first thing even if it took the erection of telephone posts to do so. He sure is anxious to speak with you."

Jenny smiled and softly muttered, "Oh, that James."

No sooner had his name left her lips than the phone rang.

"I bet you dollars to doughnuts, that's your hubby calling."

Jenny didn't know how to respond to that remark. Hesitantly, she reached for the phone as the hospital maintenance man left.

"Hello…"

"Hi Marjorie, it's James…"

Oh my gosh, the maintenance man would have won his bet!

Jenny was so startled to hear her former husband's voice, she couldn't reply. The mention of her name as "Marjorie" gritted her and memories flashed through her mind of how much she wished James would call her Jenny. But in all of the years of their marriage, never once did he give her the pleasure of being addressed as Jenny. James must have sensed Jenny's feelings and read her thoughts as he blurted out…

"I'm sorry, Marj—I meant to say, Jenny."

It sounded stiff and deliberate and yet Jenny appreciated the effort and consideration of her feelings…

"Thank you, James—"

"Did you get my flowers?"

"Yes, yes, I did, James. They're lovely—"

"Did the florists send the kind you liked? I can have them changed."

"No, they're lovely, James! So many wildflowers… I'm so glad you remembered that I like wildflowers."

"More are on the way, Mar—Jenny. I'm going to consult with Thomas to see what other ones he would recommend. He knows all the flowers you like."

"Oh, James, the ones you sent are enough, they barely fit into the room. The room is so full of them it's like walking in a meadow… it's so thoughtful of you."

"So what's going on? First they tell me you had died and now you have come back to life and are fully recovered? Did they make some kind of mistake? Doctors make errors all the time, you know."

"No, the doctors here are fantastic, James. Apparently I did pass on and miraculously, I recovered. The medical staff is in awe over what happened… it was truly a miracle."

"It's hard to believe, but I'm very pleased that it turned out that way. I'll be calling J.J. to let him know. I'm sure he will be very happy to learn of the news, as well."

"Oh yes, please call J.J. and please have him call me. I miss him so much. And I would love to visit with Nora and little Jimmy. How is my grandson doing?"

"Well, that's what I was calling about, too, Jen." James hesitated for a moment and decided to come right out and say what was on his mind.

"It would be good for us all to be a family again. I've had Thomas fix up the garden exactly the way you like it. I even commissioned another angel statue… its almost identical to the one you have, except for the basket… it's in the left hand whereas your statue is holding the basket in the right. It's a long story how that happened but anyway, everyone would welcome your return. I know the staff—"

"Oh, James, it's wonderful for you to consider that but, but… it's too late for that. I have moved here to be with my daughter and start up a new life. I love my home… oh my, I sold my home…" Jenny suddenly realized.

"See, that's an omen, Jenny. It was never meant to be. Your home is here, back in Ottawa with your family. J.J. will come around, I'll see to that. You can see your grandson here—"

"Oh, James… it does sound wonderful for us to be a family, but I can't… I need time to sort all this out. It's so amazing that I am even having this discussion with you. My illness had so consumed me that I thought for certain I would be gone and never to return to my home… it's all so…so, up in the air. Like I am floating in limbo somewhere…homeless!"

"You're not homeless, Mar—Jenny. Your home is here and I would like for us to try again… I'm changing, Jenny. Actually, a good thing has come out of my illness. It's forced me to slow down and smell the roses. Something you had encouraged me to do over the years. Well, things have happened and I see what you enjoyed on the estate and… incredibly I have come to like everything that you liked so much when you were here. You, were… you were right, Jenny."

Jenny could barely believe her ears. Was this her former husband speaking? Was this the James that she knew and was married to?

Was it all a front of some kind?

Yet, he seemed sincere. Matti also said that he was changing and how much more relaxed things were on the estate. And
for him to ask was humbling for him… James was such a proud
man… *it was so nice of him to call me.*

Jenny was at a loss for words.

"What do you say, Mar—Jen? It won't be like before—"

"Oh, James, it's too late. I like it here and it's not just my daughter… there is also someone—"

"Listen, Jenny, don't give me your answer now. You have been
through a lot and recovered somehow… I don't understand it all and
you need time to let everything get back to normal. I've asked Dr.
Reiner to visit you. He's flying to Regina today and wants to examine
and talk to you about your near death experience. He's done a lot
of research in that area. I'll call you tonight and we will talk again."

"Yes, we can talk again, James, but to come back is something
that can't be poss…" Jenny's words trailed off. She didn't want to
hurt James. He was trying so hard and this was such a giant step
for him to get out of his self-centered world. Jenny didn't want to
discourage him and yet she didn't want to encourage him to think
that she would even consider coming back to the estate.

"James, please listen to me, I don't want to build up your hopes
in any way—"

"Don't say another word, Jenny. Just think about it. You can be
back on the estate surrounded by all the things you enjoy. I'll have
your Angel of Thanksgiving statue shipped back right away. What
a sight it will be to have them side by side. I'll even build a glass
dome over part of the garden so you can enjoy the wildflowers all
year around… and J.J., just think about him. He doesn't realize it
Jenny, but he needs you… we all need you. The staff here will be
ecstatic when they hear you are coming back—"

Just then the florist, that delivered the wildflowers late yesterday afternoon, stood at the doorway.

"Excuse me James; there is someone at the door…"

"We have more flowers for you, Ma'am." The man turned and
held the door as two other ladies each brought in a bouquet of
white and purple lilacs.

"Oh, more flowers, the lilacs are so beautiful… are these from
yo—"

"Did the lilacs come, Marj?" James hollered excitedly into the phone so loudly Jenny was still able to hear him as her hand rested with the receiver on her bed.

"Yes, James, the lilacs just arrived. How did you manage to get some at this time of the year?" Jenny wanted to know.

"We put out a search party for them, Jenny. Hope they are fresh."

"Yes, they are beautiful. I love both colours. I usually see the purple ones but the white are so lovely, too!"

"Well, there's more where those came from—"

"No, this will be fine. There isn't room for any more."

"Did you know that in order for lilacs to bloom they need to have been subjected to a period of cold weather?"

"I think I may have read about that at one time."

"When Thomas told me that earlier this morning it made me think of something… it's kind of corny, Jenny…"

There was a moment of silence and then James spoke, "Well, it made me think of myself in a way; how cold I have been and so hard to live with. And yet, if a cold winter is needed to make a flower come to life, perhaps there is some hope for me…"

Jenny was speechless. That was one of the most beautiful things James had ever said to her, but…but…

"What you just said, James, touches my heart and I don't want to hurt you, but I just can't come—"

"Jenny, please don't answer now. Just think on it, Jenny. It will all be great! I'll call you later."

James hung up and the line went silent.

Deadly quiet.

Oh, James, can't you see it's all too late for this.

Jenny held the phone receiver for the longest moment and hung up. The only thing that made some sense in that entire conversation was the part that related to her son, J.J. She did want to improve her relationship with him so much. Perhaps going back would do that. J.J. could see that it wasn't her doing that the marriage failed. James seemed so willing to clear that matter up now. And then there was Nora and her grandchild. It was always Jenny's desire to have a beautiful family that loved and cared for one another. *Right now we're all so torn apart and distant.*

But I love Henry and Camilla and my life in Regina and my home…

"Yes, what about my home?" Jenny murmured.

I no longer have a home!

Jenny reached up and clutched her pewter angel. Oh dear guardian angel help me to deal with all these matters so everything turns out for the good.

Chapter Thirty Six

Henry made a cup of coffee and walked out onto the deck. "What a glorious day the Lord hath prepared," he muttered as he surveyed the valley before him. Spring had come early and along with it, the runoff. He was always amazed how quickly the snow, covering the hills, melted and fed the meandering stream. He thought he would find some solace from the peaceful valley, but not this morning. The roar and turbulence of the water, rushing down to the valley floor, complimented perfectly the pandemonium in his mind. One thought after another, regarding everything that happened in the past few days, filled him with anxious agitation.

He took a sip of coffee and concentrated on its soothing warmth, hoping it would help calm him.

It didn't.

There was so much to talk to Jenny about. He couldn't wait to see her! It still was all so unbelievable. Everything came to such a sudden climax so quickly. There was no time to let all that had happened sink in: purchasing Jenny's home, discovering her diary and learning that she and Marjorie were one and the same, racing to see her before she died and…then she died only to come back!

He had to pinch himself to prove that it was all a reality.

It was much like the runoff. Some years, it came slowly, giving time for the snow to melt and calmness to prevail in the valley. But with the advent of the early spring, it all came in a sudden rush. There was no way to slow nature down and Henry knew it would take months of thoughts wandering through his mind to even begin to grasp the incredible miracles that had occurred in a matter of a day!

Henry noticed the road crossing the creek to the Poustinia was already washed out. He would have to get it repaired soon as Father told him two weeks ago he was looking forward to going there for his spring retreat. It was almost a perennial problem, hiring a man with a backhoe to replace the culverts and filling in the crossing with dirt. Perhaps he should think about constructing a bridge and allowing nature to do what it wants; to flow unrestricted as it had done for millions of years before he came along. Maybe there was a lesson for Henry there, as well, but the many thoughts still bouncing around in his head didn't allow him to see it.

He took another sip, but the coffee had lost its warmth. He cupped the mug with both hands, trying to absorb the remaining heat. He pulled in both shoulders to further warm himself. He was beginning to feel the cold. If he had slept better last night he would be able to ward off the cool, freshness in the air. But he was tired and there was so much to do.

He stifled a yawn, as his thoughts drifted to Peter. The anger that arose earlier seemed to be held in check. He had every right to be upset and vengeful and yet here was a man that wanted to straighten things out and make amends. What Peter needed was understanding and compassion… forgiveness.

He wondered about Jenny and if he should tell her about Peter when he saw her. Was it too soon? And yet, she probably thought about it every day anyway. Perhaps getting it out into the open would lead to new insights about the whole thing…

Henry still couldn't get over that the child she had conceived that night turned out to be his daughter-in-law. It was truly amazing how God, in His divine providence, turned all that out for the good and made it all so perfect by restoring all of our lives.

And here I am, playing God, deciding whether or not to forgive and forget. Too many thoughts… he hoped the runoff would soon be over. He much preferred when the stream was calm and exuded a quiet peace.

Yes, he would have to repair the road quickly. He was certain Father would want to go to the prayer house. He also knew what Father Engelmann would want them to do about Peter.

Forgive...

HENRY STOPPED OFF at the florist along the way to the hospital. He held a bouquet, wrapped in colourful paper, behind his back as he walked into Jenny's room.

As soon as she saw him, she hopped out of the bed and ran towards him.

"Oh, Henry! I could hardly wait for you to come! Camilla was here earlier and now you!"

She thrust her arms around his neck and raised herself up on her tiptoes bringing her lips just inches away from his. "I love you so much, Henry," she softly whispered before they tenderly kissed, sending Henry off towards cloud nine. He brought his arms around Jenny to bring her closer and the paper covering the flowers crackled.

Jenny let go and looked at Henry's hands holding the bouquet. "You brought flowers!"

She took the bouquet, hidden by the wrapping, and quickly uncovered the beautiful assortment of mums, daffodils, tiger lilies, and thistles. Before she could see all of them, she excitedly said, "Oh Henry, they're beautiful. Thank you so much!"

Jenny turned to see where she could put them, but there was no room anywhere. Every space was occupied by the flowers James had sent her. Jenny felt uneasy and quickly took flowers out of one vase and stuffed them in another nearby. She placed Henry's flowers in the empty vase and placed it onto the night table next to her bed.

"There," she announced. "They will be the first thing I see when I wake up and the last before I go to sleep and the fragrance from them will soothe my heart and make me dream of you all night through!"

Henry chuckled. He could see the abundance of flowers James had sent was making her uncomfortable, as well.

Just as Jenny picked up the paper wrapping and placed it in the waste basket, she watched as a card fell out of the wrapping and fluttered onto the bed. She picked it up and her eyes immediately misted as she read what Henry had written:

> *Jenny,*
> *If you were a flower, you would be the one I would pick!*
> *I love you with all my heart,*
>
> > *Henry*

Jenny immediately recalled the game they had played that summer. Over the years, she must have relived every word and incidence of those memorable two months they were together.

She made her way over to Henry and once again put her arms around his neck and said, "If you were a tree, Henry, I would carve my heart into your bark."

Henry smiled and gazed lovingly into Jenny's cerulean blue eyes and responded, "If you were the sun, I'd want to feel your warmth all the time. I would never want darkness to ever come again."

"And if you were the ocean, I'd want to be a fish and swim in you all the time."

"Oh, Jenny, if you were the stars I'd be the sky that held you for eternity."

Jenny looked up at Henry and smiled that same smile she had smiled that wonderful evening and said the exact same words, "Oh, Henry, I think you've got me there, I can't top that one."

"Oh, Jenny, you don't have to say anything…"

Henry wrapped his arms around his dearly beloved and lifted her off her feet and began twirling her round and round as they laughed and cried.

"I hope I'm in the right room number," Dr. Kreake said, as he walked into Jenny's room. "Just yesterday morning, you were one of the most seriously ill patients in this entire hospital and look at you now."

"Dr. Kreake!" Jenny exclaimed, as Henry let her down.

"This has to be a highlight in my medical profession. We see so much illness and pain and suffering and just to see you fly around here, like that angel around your neck, makes me very happy indeed."

"It's so good to see you, Dr. Kreake! I'd like you to meet my... boyfriend, Henry Pederson." And as Jenny made the introduction she reached up and clutched the pewter angel hanging on the chain around her neck. Dr. Kreake immediately made the connection.

"Oh, so you're the secret man in Jenny's life. That angel you sent her helped to bring her through some very tough times."

Henry finally caught his breath and extended his hand to Dr. Kreake's waiting hand. "Nice to meet you, Doctor. Jenny said the same thing about you."

"Well, I can't be happier for the both of you. I had a hard time sleeping last night just thinking of the miracle that has happened, Jenny. It's incredible. And I can see that I don't have to ask how you are feeling, it's written all over your face."

"Oh, Dr. Kreake, I still can't believe what has happened, either. I feel like I'm having some dream and I'm afraid to wake up"

"Well, you're wide awake, Jenny. What's happened is completely unexplainable. It's truly a miracle that has occurred in your life and that, in part, is why I am here. We were hoping that you would agree to stay for a few more days. The staff would like to carry out further tests to note the extent of your healing and to fully document what has happened."

"Yes, I can stay for a few more days; in fact, it will give me some time to figure out where I am going to live. My son sold my house last fall and I have no home to go to!"

"Oh yes, you do!" interjected Henry. "I am the one that bought your house!"

"No way!" Jenny's eyes grew wide. It reminded Henry of the first day they started school at Balfour and he told her that Eddy Zeigler was in his home room class. She said the same thing back then. Her expression took him back instantly thirty two years... He loved it then and he even loved it more now...

"You're kidding me, Henry? Did you really?"

"It's a long story, Jenny... just another miracle!"

Then turning to Dr. Kreake and pulling out the pewter angel on the end of the chain around his neck, Henry continued, "Like you said Doctor, it was our guardian angels that helped us through some pretty tough times and brought us back together, for sure!"

After Dr. Kreake left, Jenny hopped on the bed and sat cross legged while Henry pulled up a chair next to her. For the longest time they just gazed lovingly into each other's eyes, unable to speak. Every so often, their eyes misted and they squeezed each other's hand they were tenderly holding. Thankfulness for God's blessings was clearly reflected in their eyes.

Finally, Jenny broke the silence.

"Tell me Henry, how is it that you could have possibly bought my house? I just have to know."

"It's a long and amazing story Jenny…"

Henry proceeded to tell Jenny how it all came about and the incredible feeling he had when he first walked into the home. How everything appealed to him: the furniture, the books, the paintings, the fragrance in the air, down to recipes in the cookbook that was open on the kitchen counter. But perhaps the biggest reason why he purchased the home was because of the white marble angel in the back yard. He felt then and he felt to this day, that Julean directed him to the angel. It reminded him of Jenny and her love of her guardian angel. Incredibly, since his son didn't want the house, Henry just knew he had to buy the home himself.

Jenny listened intently. She was unsettled that her son had simply put the house on the market without removing more of her personal things and yet if J.J. had sold the furniture and removed everything else, Henry might never have purchased her home… or found her.

It was Jenny's next question, however, that sent her heart soaring, heaven bound.

"So, when did you find out it was my home? It must have been just the other day, otherwise you would have come to see me sooner."

Henry didn't know if what he was about to say would upset Jenny but he was finally learning to be open in his relationships.

"That's exactly right, Jenny. Just the other day I discovered your diary—"

Once again, Jenny exclaimed, "No way! You have to be kidding me this time… but you mustn't have. I don't think I ever told you about my diary. How did you find it?" Jenny just had to know.

Henry went on to explain how the day before he came to see her at the hospital, he had this premonition that he was going to discover something in the house. When he had gone in the day before yesterday, he saw Julean's spirit lead him to the round table.

He happened to open the drawer and saw the manufacturer's name that had made the table. It just so happened that several months earlier, Julean had guided him to a shop where he had purchased a roll top desk made by the same manufacturer. At that time, he was informed that all desks, as well as other furniture made by the Kroehler Brothers, had a secret compartment. He thought that the table might have one similar to his.

Henry stopped. Jenny was completely transfixed to his sharing and slowly shaking her head in disbelief. Henry was busy trying to read Jenny's feelings; how would she feel, knowing that he had read her diary?

Henry went on. "Jenny, I was totally shocked to reach in, pull on the brass ring and discover your diary in the secret compartment. I hemmed and hawed for the longest time if I should read it. It was a very personal article. But for some reason I felt prompted to open it up. As if my angel was encouraging me to do so. And by that time, after months of visiting your home, I began to fall in love with Marjorie, not knowing that it was really you!"

"I never knew your first name was Marjorie! I recall the day I took you to Balfour to register and the secretary couldn't find your form because it was under your first name and not Jenny. I meant to ask you what your first or birth name was, but I forgot to. *Had I known I might have made the connection, sooner!*"

Once again, Henry stopped and studied Jenny. She just remained still and silent, her eyes telling him to go on.

"I started to read the diary and then went to the back section in which you wrote things that were more personal. Again I felt prompted to open it. I had fallen so in love with Marjorie, I just had to know everything about her. I dared to open it and read about Marjorie and the bookstore owner... but the part that really got my attention was when you had written that your husband preferred that you go by your first name, Marjorie, rather than your second, Jenny."

When I read that something pierced my heart...

"Oh, Jenny, I am so sorry for reading your diary and yet if I hadn't found it and read it, I might never have come to the hospital. It may have been inappropriate for your son to sell the home with all your belongings and yet, he may not have known of your diary, either. And if he hadn't done what he did, I would never have purchased your home. In fact, the round table could very well be in someone else's home and the diary never discovered by anyone unless they come across a table that was made by that manufacturer and knew of the secret compartments.

"Don't you see, Jenny, it was all meant to be… *it's our angels and Julean that led us back to each other in the only way they could!*"

Tears were flowing down Jenny's eyes. She was completely mesmerized by the story.

"Yes, Henry, it had to be our angels and your dear wife Julean; in life and in death she loves you. I am so happy it was you that bought my home and how it all turned out… and yes, my son's insensitivity turned into the most wonderful good. *"Truly God is so good!"*

"I firmly believe in God's divine providence, Jenny, and this angelic occurrence; buying your home, even makes me believe all the more."

Jenny let go of Henry's hand to reach for a tissue on the night table and dried her eyes.

"I want you to know Jenny that I never felt the home belonged to me. Buying it under such unusual circumstances; to walk in and literally take over someone's life is an incredible experience. You never come to think of the home as yours, because it's still the other person's."

Gazing into his sweetheart's eyes, Henry continued, "So, Jenny, the home is yours and always will be until you decide to sell it. Your guardian angel told me to tell you that…"

Henry smiled and winked at Jenny. She smiled in return.

At that moment, a nurse's aide walked in, carrying a tray with Jenny's lunch. Henry checked his watch and it read five minutes before noon.

"Ready for lunch, Ms. Hamilton?"

"Yes, I'm starved! I slept through breakfast this morning and ever since returning to the land of the living, and not having eaten for months on end, all I think about is the next meal."

Just as Henry was about to excuse himself, another nurse walked in.

"Ms. Hamilton, there's a Doctor Reiner from Ottawa that wants to see you. He wanted you to know that your husband has asked him to check in on you. Also, at one thirty, Dr. Miller and his associates want to run some tests."

Jenny couldn't believe James sent a doctor to check on her… *really, James.* Jenny hoped it wasn't too unsettling for Henry.

"Yes, tell Dr. Reiner he can see me at one o'clock. That will give him a half hour."

"And I should be leaving, Jenny, There were a few other matters I wanted to discuss with you, but there will be lots of time for that."

Henry got up and leaned forward at the same time towards Jenny. She in turn leaned towards him and they kissed.

"I love you, Jenny."

"I love you, too."

"You must be wearing your favourite perfume; I smelled it as soon as I walked in this morning."

"Actually, it's the lilac flowers on the window sill."

Henry turned to the window and saw the white and purple lilacs. "How on earth did you get those, Jenny? They're not in bloom for at least another month or so?"

Jenny was hesitant and then said, "James had them sent; apparently his staff or someone was able to track down where some were in bloom…"

Turning to the flowers Henry had brought in, Jenny added, "Thank you so much for the lovely flowers and the note. It was so thoughtful of you…I love you,"

Henry threw her a kiss and began to turn and leave, but he just stood there. He wanted to throw her another kiss and another or better yet, go back again to her bedside and kiss his dear sweet Jenny once more. It didn't bother him that he would look silly in doing so, but rather, it would be even more painful the next time he went to leave. Reluctantly, he mouthed, "I love you" and tore himself away.

AFTER LUNCH JENNY got up and went to the window and looked outside. Since it faced the parking lot, she wondered if she could see Henry. The fragrance of the lilacs James had sent her sitting on the window ledge wafted up to her nostrils. As she drew near to the flower to inhale a deep breath of its wonderful scent she noticed a card in between two lilac flowers. She pulled it out and read it:

Jenny,

*Thomas told me how much you like lilacs. I should have
known that too, but I have to start from somewhere and so
here they are. I like the odour of them; they remind me of
your perfume, which I always liked. I hope you enjoy the
flowers.*

James.

The note touched her heart, just like his words did earlier when
they spoke. It perhaps was the most sincere thing James had ever
said to her. It was authentic and genuine.

*What if James had been this way from the start? Would they still
be together?*

Although she had lived with James for years, most of that time
was like living alone. And yet, they had a child together... there
was something...

Can that something still have any meaning or life?

More than anything, Jenny wanted to start a new life with
Henry *and now James wants to start again?*

'*Oh dear guardian angel, please help me, help all of us...*

Chapter Thirty Seven

Accoring to catholic doctrine, a miracle is a sign of God's grace, manifested as a sudden event that defies rational or scientific explanation. This case has all the earmarks of an event attributable to a supernatural intervention."

"There is no doubt, John; the Lord's healing power is clearly evident. When I administered the last rites to Jennifer that early morning, she was so consumed with the disease that several times I thought she had already expired. When I left her side that morning, I knew it would be the last time I would see her alive. Just before I left, her doctor came in to check on her and he also indicated there was no further hope for the sickly woman and was surprised that she was still breathing."

A contemplative silence fell over the room as both men reflected over the happenings since that eventful day. The Archbishop had immediately conducted an investigation while the events were still fresh in the memory of those involved. Archbishop John O'Neil and Father Engelmann had met every day since the miracles occurred, going over and over the facts.

In the far corner of the room sat the Archbishop's secretary, taking notes of their conversation.

The two men sat, facing each other in comfortable chairs, in front of the Archbishop's large mahogany desk, as was usually the case when he invited someone to his office. The sun, streaming through the large windows, revealed the grain in the desk's surface, then bounced off towards the two men warming their faces.

"So, David, let's go over this again—"

"John, I cannot say anything different from what I have already told you the last three times."

"I understand David, but my report must be accurate to last the word. Miracles are not taken lightly by the Church. Once my report is sent to the Vatican it will be scrutinized and gone over by many cardinals and experts in the field. They shall not stop in just reading about this incidence but shall send an emissary to investigate, perhaps a delegation. What has happened has not only affected Jenny, but also you and seemingly many others."

"As you wish, John…"

So Father recounted the events all over again; from the time he gave Jenny the last rites, to when he received Henry's phone call that Henry had discovered Jenny's diary and how concerned he was that Jenny may die at any time. Henry had asked that he and the care home residents pray for a miracle to keep her alive and to heal her.

"I immediately went to the chapel and told the residents Henry and Jenny's amazing love story and that Henry had just discovered a diary in the house he purchased several months ago which showed incredibly that it was Jenny's home! He had also learned that Jenny was in the hospital dying and asked that we pray for a miracle."

Father paused for a moment and shook his head, "I have never seen anything like it, John, how heartfelt my sharing was received by my prayer warriors. It must have stirred their memories from their earlier lives, of their loved ones because the response to my request to pray for Henry and his beloved, Jenny, was so overwhelming it could have moved a mountain… and, as we can see, it did! Our faith that God would heal Jenny was palpable. I could feel the power of the Holy Spirit. He was already at work amongst the residents, as well. When I saw Johnny getting out of his wheelchair and stand up, in praise of God, I prayed all the more fervently and so did the others."

"The Church most often investigates miracles that involved the intercessory prayers to Saints or those that were beatified and waiting for a miracle to be attributed to them, so they might be canonized. Tell me, David, were any petitions directed to certain holy persons that might have interceded on behalf of you and the group to the Lord?"

"Not directly, I did at one point cry out to Padre Pio and Father Seelos, both holy men that I had read about. Padre Pio is especially known for healings."

"Yes, I know of Padre Pio. He is being investigated as having received the stigmata of Jesus and a very holy man indeed. In any case I shall make a note of it."

"Did Henry direct any pleas to saints when you spoke with him, John?" Father wanted to know.

"Indirectly he did, David."

"To whom did he ask to intercede, John?"

"It was you, David. Henry considers you to be a very holy man, as do many others in the parish. Henry said he cried out that the Lord might hear your prayers as being more receptive to the Lord than his."

Father simply gazed at John, with a neutral look, not wishing to be elevated in any way over others.

The archbishop paused, looking down at a sheet resting on his lap and continued. "So tell me once more what happened to you after you left the prayer meeting."

"I went to my room, got my Bible, and then made my way to the sun room. I felt weary, John. Visiting Jennifer, for the last two weeks, drained me emotionally. I was ready for the Lord to take me home. I recall reading the 23rd Psalm. I nearly made it to the last stanza when I passed on."

The archbishop gestured for Father to continue. "When I spoke with Henry, he said after Jenny died, he fell asleep in her room and dreamt that he saw you offer up your life to God in exchange for Jenny's life. Did you make such a covenant with the Lord?"

"Yes John, prior to meeting with the care home residents, I did make such a plea to the Lord."

"You see, David, these details are important. I understand your reluctance to make public such personal matters, but in this case it's most necessary that we know all the facts not only surrounding this event, but for future reference of your life. Over the years I have received many letters from your parishioners expressing your holiness and the power of your confessionals."

"Come now, John, it's nothing more than my love for the people and the Lord coming through, no more than in other parishes."

The Archbishop was going to say more about David's holiness and how he was an outstanding moral example to everyone he met, but thought better of it. David would interpret it as an attack on his humility. He would strive all the more for others not to apply such glowing attributes upon him.

"Now, my committee assisting me upon this matter has interviewed the nurse who found you in the sun room as well as all the residents who participated in a celebration of your passing..." The Archbishop paused and smiled at the holy man sitting across from him. "It was not that they were celebrating your death and happy to see you go...it was to celebrate your going home to the Lord."

David knew what His Eminence was referring to, but smiled and nodded to show he appreciated the archbishop's efforts to inject some humour into this matter which was becoming tedious.

"In any case, all those at the care home said you had clearly died and then miraculously came back. Initially they found you gone...apparently that is when you went to see if Jenny was alive and then they all were elated to see you return to the care home fully restored. That part of the event seems well substantiated however, if the Vatican sends a delegation to our fair city to further investigate these miracles, they usually send what is known as the 'General Promoter of the Faith,' or 'Devil's Advocate'. His role is to raise objections and doubts which must be resolved. For example, one member of my committee has already stated that the deaths of all three of you was pronounced after taking your pulse. In your instance, Nurse Frowler took your pulse as was the case in Henry's death by the ambulance attendants. No actual monitor was used and thus opens the door to doubt that your heart and Henry's stopped beating. Could it be the pulse just slowed down? Perhaps the blood pressure was so low, the pulse wasn't detectable. You were all more or less in a deep, deep trance and came out of it."

"But what of Jenny, John? Whether she died or not is not even an issue. Her body was completely overtaken with cancer and then instantly healed. Only the Lord's hand in all this can possibly explain what has happened here."

"Yes, I don't discount what you say, it's just that I know how rigorous it will be . You may be annoyed and frustrated by my questions but you have not seen anything of the interrogation that lies ahead. You will be questioned again and again if they see fit to do so. As I have told you, miracles are not taken lightly. Many are reported every year but most can be accounted for and readily dismissed."

"I assure you, John, I did pass on to the other side and so did Henry and Jenny."

"Yes, let's go over that again. You say you were met by your guardian angel...Zachariah. Is that correct?"

"Yes, after my spirit left my body in the sun room, I immediately saw my lifelong protector. We watched as the residents came into the room and began a prayer meeting celebration on my behalf as we have already discussed. It was at that time Zachariah informed me how Henry and Jenny's love for one another was so ardent and long lasting."

"And he said that their angels were involved; that Henry and Jenny's guardian angels imparted of their heavenly energy to the two young people at the moment they gazed into each other's eyes..."

"That's correct, John. I know it sounds incredible, yet perhaps, even angels can be seduced to go beyond their assigned duties when a union that is so close to heaven is found on earth. Apparently, Henry and Jenny's very souls were united due to their angels' involvement."

The archbishop remained silent. This part of the story was almost unbelievable and yet, David appeared to be in command of all of his senses. He had known David for most of his life to be a man of God and of such high integrity. If it had been anyone else, he would have discounted or doubted this happening almost immediately.

"Yes, and then shortly after you say, Jenny and Henry and their guardian angels appeared on the scene."

"We have been over this three times, John, and I must admit my patience is running low. However, I shall tell you one more time. I expected to see Jenny on the other side, but was surprised to see Henry. I met Jenny's guardian, Hannah and Henry's lifelong protector, Gabriel as well. Jenny shared how much she wanted to marry Henry and suggested we all go through the tunnel of light and hoped God would make an exception in their case to marry in heaven. Clearly the Lord indicated that marriage does not exist there, but Jenny was adamant. Just after we decided to go, an archangel emerged from the tunnel, bearing news to our protectors. It was a decision that Zachariah said would be coming to determine our fate. It was then that the healing power of God swept through us and we were all three returned to earth fully restored to life. In Jenny's case not only to life, but completely healed of the cancerous disease that had totally invaded her body."

"Now, David, I understand that you are tiring of this matter. However, I must to a degree play the Devil's Advocate, as you will surely be asked this upon future investigation of these happenings. When I spoke to Henry and Jenny about their after death experience, they both have no memory of any of this. The only thing they know is what they have been told; that they died and miraculously came back to life. It seems definite that in all three of your cases, death was established by some medical attendant. In your case, it was Nurse Frowler, the ambulance attendants in Henry's case and Nurse Johnson that witnessed Jenny's death. The only thing that cannot be verified is what you have said happened in the afterlife…

"*Could it have all been just a dream, David?*"

"No, John, I saw what I saw. I am still elated and dizzy by the celebration we shared after we knew of the Lord's workings in our lives. I never expected to be returned to earth—"

"That's what Henry said, too. After he dreamt that you had given your life for Jenny, he was surprised that your life was restored as well."

"The Lord has further work for me to do, John. This is another reason why I know that it was not at all a dream. I have communed with my angel and the Lord all my life, John, and I know when His will is revealed to me. He wishes for me to carry out two missions."

The archbishop sat up in his chair. He was glad now that he had decided to go over this with David once more. This was the second time his dearly benevolent friend had withheld pertinent information unintentionally.

"I understand, David that you may think this has solely to do with Jenny, but what has happened to you and Henry is also of vital importance. It may be connected to the Lord's decision to perform this miracle or it might very well help us to understand this entire matter more clearly when we know all of the facts."

The archbishop uncrossed his legs and planted both feet squarely on the floor. He leaned forward towards David as if not to miss a word the holy man might say in response to his next question.

"David, tell me, what further work does the Lord wish for you to do?"

"I can see by your look, John, that you are as surprised as I was to learn that at my age, what was there that the Lord could further possibly want me to do? The Lord is the God of all possibilities. Surely, there are countless others in the peak of their lives that could carry out any mission the Lord requires."

"And yet, He asked you!"

"Yes, this may be as hard to believe as the miracles themselves, John, but the Lord wishes for me to write a book that encompasses my life and that of Henry and Jenny. I told him that I was not a writer, but Zachariah said that he and the Holy Spirit would assist me. My protector said that Henry and Jenny's story would touch the hearts of many people and bring many back to the faith. Earlier, when I had shared Henry and Jenny's story with the care home residents it was evident that the love story touched their hearts, too. Their response was truly overwhelming. Perhaps, yes, just maybe, such a story would have such an effect on the faith of a larger multitude of people."

The archbishop's eyes grew wide as he nodded his head.

"Yes, David, the more I learn of this story, the more astonished I am over what has transpired over the years and what finally has happened to bring these two together. Yes, it is truly all miraculous, indeed."

The archbishop paused for but a moment and then continued. "There is something else which hasn't been substantiated yet which supports and gives further credence to what you have shared with me, David. When I spoke with Henry the other day, he said he had received a call from a man by the name of Peter. Henry said that he was the man who had fathered Jenny's child, Camilla. Apparently he was quite ill and died that same morning as Jenny did. He informed Henry that he had seen him and Jenny as well as you,

David, when he passed over to the other side. He saw everything which you described about meeting Henry and Jenny and their angels. He too, saw the archangel bring a message to the angels and the resulting healing power of God sweep over all three of you. He too saw Henry and Jenny disappear and return to earth and that you stayed behind for some time speaking with your guardian. He said you had been given a vision in which for a split second, you were surrounded with a light that blinded him. When it diminished and went away, you had tears in your eyes and agreed to return to earth. Perhaps, it has to do with your second mission…"

And just as His Eminence sat back to relax and get more comfortable, he quickly resumed his former alert position, but now expressing even greater interest to what Father would say to his next query.

"David, please share with me what the second task is that the Lord requires of you?"

"You have a keen perception, John; I was allowed to see all that went before, not only in the lives of Henry and Jenny but of all humanity. It was to prepare me for the task of writing their story. It was at that point, however, that I still desired to come home to the Lord and see my Anna and parents and friends. Zachariah understood and anticipated that I might not wish to carry out that task and leave it up to God's divine providence to accomplish that mission. However, I was then allowed to see into the future and why it was that the Lord saw it best that I carry out that task. I recall seeing what it was and immediately said yes, that I would do it. Upon my return to earth, it vanished from my memory. I recall Zachariah saying that neither man nor angels see what the future has in store. While memory of it was taken away from me, I have the feeling that I will know what it is that the Lord wishes of me as soon as that time comes into my present existence."

John sat back but wasn't relaxed. He was clearly disappointed in not knowing what the Lord further required of the holy man before him. He had no idea of what it possibly could be. He hoped to be alive to see that day. It must truly be something that only a man dear to the Lord is capable of carrying out.

"There is no mistake, John, I have been brought back for two reasons. I didn't mention this before as I thought it was not related to Jenny's miraculous recovery. And I suppose, the offering of my life wasn't necessary as the prayers of the nursing home and those of Henry and Jenny and the solicitations of their angels were sufficient to be heard by the Lord and bring about these miracles."

The Archbishop nodded, his countenance still carrying the look of disappointment over not learning of what Father's second mission might be.

"There is one other issue, David. Henry mentioned something that has puzzled him and now me. When he went to Jenny's home later that day of his accident, he still didn't know of her miraculous recovery until you called and told him. But before you called, he said he walked in the back yard and noticed Jenny's diary laying on the swing in her gazebo. Henry swears that the diary was in his SUV at the time of the accident. He recalls seeing it when he left the hospital. He was curious about two matters. First, how did it get there? And second, he noticed that Jenny had made an entry earlier that day about family matters and asking to be forgiven by her son. He has no memory of how either of those things could have happened. Just by chance, David would you know anything of this?"

"Yes, John, when I was given the vision of everything that went before in order for me to write about all that happened to Henry and Jenny, I saw after Henry left the hospital, both his and Jenny's spirits were in the SUV with the diary between them. Immediately after the accident, Jenny went to her home and took the diary with her. When Henry arrived there he saw Jenny writing in her diary. After she made her entry, she took Henry back to the accident scene to see what had happened to him. After that, they came to see me and Zachariah as I told you earlier. Why Henry and Jenny were not allowed to recall their stint on the other side eludes me as well, John."

"Well, that does explain that mystery and further substantiates your stint on the other side and what you have seen. Do you now see why it's so necessary to go over and over this matter, David?"

The two men sat in silence for several moments until they heard the secretary in the corner of the room turn several pages of her notes.

"Well, I shall write up the report as you have told it to me and submit it. I believe all you have told me David; however, there are skeptics who do not know you as I do and will play the Devil's

Advocate. As we know David, the Lord is in perfect control of the universe at all times. The workings of His divine providence are a most incredible miracle. How He works with the laws of nature to perform miracles (many of which are never acknowledged) in the lives of people all the time. His purpose; to restore their faith and to bring healing, is both astonishing and totally incomprehensible. So many of the challenges and trials that come into our lives are dealt with in this way and yet, there are times when He chooses to work without secondary means and intervenes directly against the natural order of life He created. Clearly, David, this is one of those times. Perhaps we will never know the complete repercussions of the Lord's work in this matter..."

"Or perhaps, John, the full repercussions are yet to be revealed..."

CHAPTER THIRTY EIGHT

WHEN JAMES GOT off the phone with Jenny, his mind was buzzing. Over the years he had always been able to outwit any competitor and secure contract after contract. He was now going after the biggest acquisition of his life; he wanted Jenny back. Surely he could outwit a farm boy. He recalled talking to Henry once. The conversation had been brief but James recalled every word… "Look, bud, I'm James Hamilton and Jennifer is mine. She's my girl and we intend to get married, so get lost creep and don't call her again." He remembered slamming down the phone and that his innards ached for hours and days afterwards. He could barely watch the movie that he and Jenny went to. Well, that approach worked then but a different approach was needed now. Perhaps James would call Henry, feel him out and see if he could be persuaded once again to butt out.

James' mind was getting into gear… his next move was already taking shape. A plan was forming, however to get others to cooperate in the plan was a different matter. He picked up the phone and called Regina once again.

"Hello, this be Matilda."

"Glad I caught you in; did you see Marj— I mean Jenny— yet today?"

Matti checked the clock on the night table. "It's only seven thirty, Mr. Hamilton, I be seeing Jenn—I mean Ms. Hamilton later today. I told you everything last night, how she be and how the hospital is in such an uproar over all this healing business. I 'spect she don't be changing much from last evening until now."

"Yes, yes, of course… and you don't have to keep saying Ms. Hamilton. I know you have been calling her Jenny… is that clear?"

Matilda just didn't know how to take Mr. Hamilton anymore, he was changing by the minute. "Yes, sir, that's clear. I will try to—"

"It's okay, Matilda, I'm really calling about another matter… we talked about this before, but I would like you to consider staying longer and try to influence Jenny to come back. I can pay you extr—"

"I'm sorry Mr. Hamilton; I leave it all up to Miss Jenny to decide how she want to spend the rest of her days. That be her business and not mine. Chloe and me are going to visit with her one more time today and then we both be flying home first thing in the morning…"

There was a brief silence and then Matti continued, "I wish to come home now, if you'll have me. I appreciate from the bottom of my heart that you allowed me to come here and be with my mistress and friend. I'll never forget this special time and the miracle that be happening. You be a good man for allowing me to come."

Matti never thought that those words would ever come out of her mouth… but the Lord can do strange powerful things. Thomas be right after all. Maybe, just maybe, a little of Miss Jenny be creeping into Mr. Hamilton's soul. *Soon I 'spect I be accepting Mr. Hamilton just like Jen.*

"Are you certain, Matilda? Just think how the estate would be with her back."

"Yes, it would be heaven, that's for sure. But I came to give whatever support I could to my friend and will continue for the rest of my life. Now, I know what you want me to do, but I can't. There be no way I can interfere with Miss Jenny's life, or anybody else. I need to come now. My work here is done."

The words, 'you be a good man,' stuck in James' mind. He couldn't remember anyone ever saying that to him and he felt the sincerity of it. He had no choice but to agree with his employee.

"Matilda, I understand what you're saying, it is Jenny's life and you're welcome for what I did. It was for my benefit to get her back. I realize now the wonderful lady I had in Mrs. Hamilton and for the rest of my life, I will regret the way I treated her and drove her away… but I'm no fool Matilda, I would like to have her back in my life and I will do anything to do so.

"Yes. Come home, Matilda."

NEXT, JAMES CALLED the office to speak to his son but he wasn't in. He left a message for him to call or drop by the estate. J.J. would be a key player in getting Marjorie to consider coming back. The kid had a serious attitude problem… he reminded him much of himself.

Maybe he's at home, James thought as he dialed the number

"Hello," said Nora softly. There was a hesitancy in her voice, as if she was almost afraid to know who was calling or… hoping someone would call.

"Morning, Nora, it's James. Is J.J. in?"

"Oh…hi, James. No, J.J. isn't at home."

"I tried the office but he wasn't there. Is he on his way to work?" James wanted to know.

A silence hung over the line…

"Nora, where is J.J.?" There was urgency in James' voice and it was rising. It frightened Nora; she had seen James lose it many times.

"We, we had a fight two nights ago and he may have gone to some hotel. I don't know where he is, James."

This time it was James who didn't answer promptly, but for only a moment.

"What the hell is going on, Nora? J.J. isn't fooling around is he?"

Nora didn't answer. James faintly heard her crying. The sound was muffled.

"Nora, I'll see if I can find him. If he calls or comes home tell him I want to see him. It's urgent! … Are you okay…?"

Nora was surprised to hear James express concern. She wanted to tell him that things hadn't been going well for months. J.J. was working way too long almost every day and many times he didn't make it home. Nora suspected that he was seeing someone but wasn't certain. She was afraid that if she mentioned it to James, J.J. may resent it and get even more distant.

"No, I'm fine… if you do get a hold of him please, tell him to call home."

"Yes, yes, I will. Goodbye."

"What the hell has gotten into that kid?" muttered James, as he made his way out the back onto the patio. The sprinklers were on and the morning sun caught the moisture on the blades of grass. He had often heard Jenny say how the lawn glistened like millions of diamonds. At the time, he thought she was getting carried away by some fantasy world, but she was right… the entire scene before him sparkled with a calming freshness. It soothed him.

James sat down at the patio table and picked up his pen. He wondered if Jenny liked the card he sent with the lilacs. He forgot to ask and she didn't say. Maybe she didn't notice. It took him forever to write that short note. If it had to do with a business letter, James would have been done in minutes but to write a note on a small card was like writing a five hundred page manuscript. He tore up note after note. He had thought of hiring a writer but he knew Jenny would detect its artificiality. No, he had to do it on his own and he was glad he did. It gave him an unusual sense of accomplishment and…something more. He didn't know what that "*something more*," was, however. He thought he would try to write another note, perhaps longer. He had just written her name down, "*Jenny*" when he heard talking in the kitchen through the screen door. It was J.J. He was announced by Charles.

"Your son is here to see you, Mr. Hamilton."

"That is completely unnecessary Charles," said J.J. as he walked out directly behind the butler.

"Hi, James. The office said you wanted to see me."

"Did you see Nora?" James looked hard into his son's eyes.

"What does she have to do with it? She doesn't have to tell me to see you."

"I'm not referring to that, J.J., she said you haven't been home for a couple of nights—"

"What the hell did she tell you that for? It's no-one's concern what I do."

James shook his head. He could see himself in his son: arrogant, proud and cocky. J.J. was on the road that James had prepared for his son, but now he needed a sharp detour. His son clearly had an attitude problem, but James was aware enough and honest enough to know that it was part of his doing. He was reaping what he helped to sow.

Anger was growing within him and normally it would have found an outlet by now. He would be tearing a strip up and down his son's hide, but he put a hold on it and instead said, "Look J.J., I mean, look, Son, Nora is a good girl and you have a son that needs a father. I thought I knew best when your mother and I lived together but I was wrong and I am now paying a heavy price for my mistake. I turned on your mother and I got you to turn on her, too."

James looked hard into his son's eyes and said something that surprised even himself…

"J.J., I was wrong. The reason your mother and I split up was all my doing. I did a good job in convincing you differently, but now I want you to know the truth. If you want to turn against me, go ahead, but I want you to forgive your mother. In fact, there is nothing to forgive. I am finally realizing what a wonderful woman she was and I will give anything to have her back. And J.J., Nora is the same; don't make the same mistake that I made. You will regret it for the rest of your life."

James stopped trying to read J.J.'s reaction. But his son held a cold glare. At one point in his life, James would have considered what he just said as words to manipulate and win over. He hoped J.J. wouldn't interpret his past actions and words in that light. For the first time, James meant every word he just said. James continued in an attempt to add more truth to his words.

"Look at Susan. I took her over your mother and look what is happening. She is blackmailing me for millions. How I could have taken her over your mother was an unbelievable mistake on my part. If you are seeing someone else other than your wife, please stop immediately. You have a wonderful family, J.J., don't blow it."

J.J. was having a very hard time standing there listening to his father. He couldn't believe his ears! He knew his dad had softened since he got sick, but this was ridiculous. James sensed J.J. wasn't swallowing his words.

"J.J., listen to me. Something wonderful has happened to your mother and she couldn't be more deserving. She had died yesterday morning and suddenly she came back to life as the attendants from the morgue were coming to get her. She is completely cured and apparently as good as new if not better according to Matilda. The doctors can't explain it. They claim it was a miracle."

James stopped to make sure J.J. was giving him his full attention… to see if his words had any impact at all on his impervious son.

"J.J., I want your mother back and I need your help. I want you to make amends with her—we both want to straighten things—"

"Forget it, James. Since when has it ever been *we*. That's a joke and with Marjorie it's over between us. For as long as I can remember it's been over. I don't know her. I have little feelings for her. In fact, I could care less if she lived or died. You always took me away and discouraged me from having anything to do with her. And now you ask me to forgive her and like her. It's like a stranger coming up to me on the street and saying, 'call me Dad, I love you.' I can't respond to that, James. I spent most of my upbringing apart from Marjorie and when I saw her kissing that store owner, I knew she betrayed you. It all but destroyed the little that was in your marriage, as far as I'm concerned —"

"No! It wasn't Jenny that kissed the man, it was him that kissed her. And it was wrong of me to take you away from her for all those years. It was my mistake and I want to make it all better. Surely I didn't turn you away from her to that extent. Surely you realize that she is your mother, your own flesh and blood and not just some stranger you met on the street. She has always showed care and concern for you. It's just that you have never reciprocated. I never allowed you to or discouraged you from doing so. It's my fault, J.J., not hers. I am admitting and taking full responsibility."

"Well then you tell her and make amends. Do it without me. There is no relationship between Marjorie and me. There has not been for as long as I can remember. It's always been you and me. And the only way I could reach you was to do what you wanted just like all the other CEO's. Well now I'm tired of it. I will do what I want to do."

"Look, son, try to—"

"No! You look! it's too late for that and I would appreciate it if you would stay out of our marriage. What's going on between Nora and me is our business and no-one else's. Didn't you always say that? That you can handle your own affairs and didn't need anyone to butt in?"

"I might have said that, if fact I know I have, but in this case with family, I was wrong, J.J… How can I convince you of that?"

"That's up to you, James. If you think it was wrong, then that's fine for you. You can live your life the way you want and let me live mine the way I want. If I want your advice I will ask for it."

"Ahem," Charles said.

Both men turned to the butler standing at the doorway.

"Are you ready for your afternoon tea, sir, and can I get a cup for your son?"

"No, Charles, I was just leaving." J.J. turned to his father and was going to say something, but seemed to think better of it and stormed back into the house and out the front door.

"I hope I wasn't interrupting, Mr. Hamilton."

"No, no, that's fine, Charles … *I am just reaping what I have sown.*"

Chapter Thirty Nine

It was such a sad farewell scene to see Matti and Chloe go back home. Jenny appreciated their love, prayers and support so much. Perhaps it was a blessing they had left however, as in the days that followed Jenny was confronted with one medical person after the other. Doctors and scientists from all over the world made their way to Regina in an attempt to explain the unexplainable. Well known writers who had written on the subject of life after death and of patients who had died and returned back to the land of the living also flocked to her in the hope of another story. And when they heard about the kiss and about her relationship with Henry and the ensuing miracles, Jenny was offered lavish contracts … it would be the greatest love story ever told!

After the fourth day however, Jenny felt so wonderful and healthy that she wanted to go home. She had enough of the interviews, probes, tests and examinations. She was elated to get the report from one of the gynecologist's who had thoroughly examined her that her womb was completely free of cancer and she was perfectly healthy to bear children in all respects. He did express concern over her age but other than that, she could conceive a child.

When Dr. Kreake came in later that afternoon, Jenny shared with him that she felt like some freak show at a circus. While she wanted to help the doctors understand what happened, she had had enough. Doctor Kreake agreed and said he would get the release papers in order and everything approved in a day or two at the most. Dr. Kreake couldn't thank her enough for her cooperation and said that in a few months her case would be written up in one of the Medical Journals.

Jenny agreed to stay for just two more days. She ached to get home. Spring was here early and all signs indicated that it was here to stay! March was in like a lamb and out like a lamb. It just seemed that winter had completely lost its grip on the prairies and wasn't about to have its last hoorah this year! It couldn't have complimented Jenny's spirit more perfectly.

The flowers seemed to sense spring's victory as well. Henry told her just yesterday how he noticed the perennials coming up. Soon, the yard would be filled with the beautiful array of colourful flowers and herbs and saturate the air with fragrances that she loved. She was sure she had seen a robin sitting on her window ledge the other day and soon the butterflies would be returning. Jenny felt ecstatic and didn't know if she could make it through another day cloistered in her hospital room.

The only consolation during all this commotion and activity, were the visits from Camilla and her wonderful family. They actually had to make appointments to visit in between the tests and examinations carried out by various physicians. She had loved meeting Jeremy and her grandson Joshua. *My, Jeremy was tall, dark and handsome and their little son, Joshua, an angel.*

Jenny would never forget what Josh said when he saw her. "I prayed to my angel to send me another grandma. I miss Nana Pederson so much." He looked at his mommy and said, "See, my angel asked God to heal Grandpa and he sent me a new Nana!"

Both Jenny and her daughter looked at each other with tears in their eyes.

Henry and Jenny had decided to wait until she got home to meet his other children. Jenny smiled when she heard that Lauren was dying to meet Dad's teenage girlfriend and that Justin had his reservations. He wasn't so sure he wanted someone to replace his mom who was still missed so much.

Jenny couldn't wait for Henry to call. It was a long and tedious day and hours seemed to drag. Perhaps it was her anticipation of her beloved's call that made minutes turn into hours. This would be the first day Henry wasn't able to make it up to see her and he said he would phone later that evening so as not to interrupt any meeting she might be having with doctors during the day.

She wondered how his meeting went with the archbishop. His Eminence visited her briefly the other day and said he would like to speak to her again on her miraculous recovery when she got home. He was not only astonished at her recovery but by so many others as well. Both Henry and Father Engelmann had passed away that same day and came back to life in perfect health and then there were several residents in Father's care home who had miraculous healings, too! "The power of prayer is manifested all the time. However, at times like this it defies everything we know and understand. Truly God's ways are higher than our ways," the Archbishop said before he left.

Jenny had to admit that what happened defied all reasoning like so many other happenings in her life. She could hardly wait to put flowers in her Angel of Thanksgiving's basket!

As soon as the phone rang, Jenny knew that it was Henry and answered the phone accordingly.

"Hi Sweetheart, I so missed not seeing you today and kissing your tender lips!"

Henry quickly lowered his voice and replied, "Ahem, this is Dr. Kreake, just wanted to check in on you…" Henry couldn't contain himself longer and burst out laughing.

"Henry! You had me going there for a minute! I must say I'm glad you pretended to be Dr. Kreake, I do have a crush on the man."

"I better not pretend to be him in the future, then. I wouldn't want that to become an ongoing concern."

"No worries honey."

"So how is my sweetheart tonight? Still baffling all the most intelligent doctors and scientists in the world?"

"Yes, I'm afraid so. Most just shake their head and find it hard to believe the reports that I was so sick. Dr. Kreake restricted my visits to just doctors and scientists and excluded others like writers and journalists. One pretended to be a doctor today until one of the nurses caught him as he was about to come into the room and asked that he leave. It was hysterical hearing him plead with Nurse Johnson. He even offered her money."

"Well, you're quite a story, honey, in more ways than one."

"So, how did your meeting go with the archbishop?"

"Apparently the Vatican is thinking about sending an emissary or delegation to investigate all that has happened here. There wasn't just one miracle but several and wait until they find out about Peter…"

Henry's words immediately trailed off. He wasn't going to mention Peter until Jenny got home and settled in. Henry knew from what Camilla shared with him the other day that Jenny apparently knew it was Peter who fathered her child.

"I hope mentioning him doesn't upset you, Jen?"

"No, I know who you are speaking of and I was hoping we could talk about it sometime. Camilla knows as well and expressed to me the other day her wish to meet Peter some day." Jenny hesitated to go on. She wondered how Henry was feeling about her being raped that night.

Would he have similar feelings that James had?

It was as if Henry had read her thoughts. "It must have been so difficult for you to find out that you had been assaulted that night, Jenny. When I learned about it, I wished over and over I had been there to comfort and support you. If only you had phoned, I would have been there in a flash…" Henry couldn't go on as words began to get caught in his throat.

Jenny, too, couldn't speak. She just felt a rush of warmth flood her body hearing Henry's words of support and empathy. Thoughts of calling him so many times flooded her mind. Her fantasy that Henry was the father, over that brute, helped her to cope with her pregnancy time and time again.

"Oh, Henry, there were so many moments, so many times, I picked up the receiver to call you but I didn't want to complicate your life. We were so young and how would you have reacted to this?"

"Jenny, I would have done anything to support you…oh, Jenny, I love you so much and Camilla, too. In a way she is our daughter. It's amazing how this all turned out! It's just another incredible miracle. The archbishop was in a state of awe for most of our meeting."

"What did you mean when you said a few minutes ago, about Peter being healed as well?"

Henry went on to share how he first heard from Eddy how Peter was dreaming that he had fathered a child that night and the incredible dreams and meetings that resulted. The phone calls from Peter, his wife, and their meeting at Father Engelmann's anniversary. It was Peter's dreams that had especially haunted Henry.

Henry shared about Peter's guilt over what happened and his resulting illness, death and miraculous recovery. He told Jenny that Peter had called just the other day and so desired to see both Jenny and Camilla and seek forgiveness for what he had done.

"When I realized the full impact of Peter's confession, as to what actually happened that night, I felt all the anger and hatred I had for those guys return, Jenny. And just as the grip of vengeance started to take its hold on me, thanks to Father Engelmann's teaching, I asked, 'to what end and for what purpose would it serve to get my mind caught up in all those negative feelings. I have been there and it isn't a good space to be—'"

And then Jenny added to his thoughts, "And why allow the beautiful birth of Camilla be tainted with thoughts of anger, sorrow or regret. I love her so much Henry, I just want good and beautiful thoughts to surround her—"

"That's so true, Jenny. Something so incredibly good has come out of this and even if Peter wasn't such a good man and so desirous to be forgiven, we would still have to do it…we just have to forgive and move on."

"Oh, Henry, God has given us renewed life. We cannot allow not even one precious moment of our lives to dwell on thoughts that are not loving and forgiving."

"Jenny, Peter so desires that we meet him. Apparently he had died as well that same morning you did. Unbelievably, he saw all three us on the other side; you, me and Father Engelmann. He said he saw our angels and how we almost entered the tunnel of eternity and then a healing act of God took place. He knew that our lives had been restored! I was going to mention it to the archbishop, but thought I would talk it over with you and also Father Engelmann. I wonder if Father saw what Peter did and why was it that we didn't see what they saw?"

A calming peaceful silence hung over the phone line. Both

Jenny and Henry were lost in a world of the unseen and the incredible happenings of the past few days.

"Oh, Henry, I love you so much and thank you…thank you from the bottom of my heart for being so understanding and supportive."

"I love you, too, Jenny with all my heart. I wish I were there to hold you and comfort you…"

Once again, a peaceful quiet settled over the phone. Soon, Henry heard Jenny sobbing and his heart went out to her. He recalled one of the notes that she had sent him via the fence gate post so long ago and softly whispered, "If you were a bed, I would want to be a blanket and cuddle up with you all night through."

He could picture, Jenny's bright blue eyes light up and her sweetheart lips curl up into a warm smile."

"And if you would send me the pillow that you sleep on, Henry, I would dream, dream after dream of being held in your loving arms forever and ever."

"'Nite, Jen."

"'Nite, Hank."

HENRY HUNG UP the phone and Jenny's last remark conjured up images of his dear sweet wife, Julean. "'Night, Hank" was what she had so often said just before they went to sleep. It was funny how Jenny always called him Henry and Julean had referred to him as Hank. Somehow it suited both of them and gave each a special relationship with him. He had to admit he loved the name each woman called him.

"Oh, Julean, I know I will never stop loving you, either. What would Jenny think or say if I dreamt of you in her presence like I did of her when you were alive? The Lord has blessed me with two beautiful women. How will Jenny react when she knows that I can't let go of you, either?"

It slowly drifted into Henry's consciousness, that James must be entertaining similar thoughts about Jenny. Henry still didn't understand all the circumstances surrounding their relationship and yet they had drifted apart to the point where a divorce ensued. Did Jenny still have feelings for her former husband? Obviously, Mr. Hamilton wanted to restore their relationship. They were married for a long number of years and raised a child. There must have been something, as a lengthy marriage took place and yet, the circumstances didn't seem that good.

Can their marriage be salvageable? What was his role in all this?

Henry felt agitated and concerned. When he and Jenny spoke and were with one another it seemed so clear that they were deeply in love with one another and yet, he too, still had such deep loving thoughts of Julean.

What if she came back, what would he do?

The decision to just abandon one's spouse and move on with another is not that easily done. He knew the Church didn't approve of divorce and favoured reconciliation at all cost. An annulment was only allowed under very strict conditions. It was all so unsettling.

Henry got ready to retire for the day and gently settled into the water bed. His weight displaced a large quantity of water, forcing it to the other side of the water mattress. He always thought Julean enjoyed that moment of being lifted as much as he did when the water gushed back lifting him, too. In that split second of time when the hidden wave crested and was about to fall, he felt a weightlessness in which his mind let go of all thoughts. He was immersed in the feeling and tried to extend that moment of freedom; that moment of not having to worry or feel guilty where his heart lay or the challenges of what may lie ahead or the worries of the day. Back and forth he swayed, relishing those few seconds as the rocking motion played itself out and stillness settled in. He wished it would have gone on longer and lulled him to sleep, as the peace didn't last.

He picked up Julean's rosary that he had tossed on the bed before taking off his trousers. He pulled the pillow next to him, close to his chest. It always reminded him of his dear wife's presence, but tonight, he prayed that it was the pillow that he dreamed on; that it was the pillow that he could send to Jenny and together, it was the pillow that they all could dream on.

Chapter Forty

IT WAS ALMOST a replay of the other morning when Peter called. Henry was in a deep sleep when the irritating sound of the telephone rang again and again. He thought it was the phone ringing in his dream, when he finally realized it was the phone on his night table next to the bed.

"Oh, God, I hope that's not Peter again." Although he had spoken to Jenny just last night about setting up a meeting with Peter it was still far from being finalized.

It must have been on the eighth ring, when Henry finally picked up the receiver.

"Hello," Henry said, still half asleep.

"Is Henry Pederson in?"

There was something about the voice that recalled an immediate unpleasant memory. Some conversations one never forgets. Especially when they have to do with a matter that involves one's heart and soul. Instantly Henry recognized the voice. He tried to sit up, but the flexibility of the water bed made him lose his balance and he fell back onto the bed pulling the phone at the end of the cord with him. He quickly rolled out of the bed and sat on the edge, trying to untangle the cord from the phone.

"Sorry, are you still there? Hello…"

"Yes, I'm still on the line. Is this Henry Pederson?"

"Yes, this is Henry."

"I'm James Hamilton, Jenny's former husband. I phoned to thank you for helping to restore Jenny's health, if not her life. I understand a lot of people prayed for a miracle and it happened. I saw it here on the estate as well when Jenny lived here. Some of the strangest, most unexplainable happenings occurred; flowers lasting for months without water, a statue her father commissioned turning up in the garden under the most unusual circumstances…"

James continued to ramble on about other incidences. Although it sounded like gibberish, Henry knew what James was talking about. He had seen the same kind of unusual happenings in Jenny's home and yard as well. But Henry was no longer really listening to the man on the end of the phone. His mind began to analyze the motives for the call. What did James really want?

Henry didn't have to wait long for the answer.

"What I called about was to try and get your help or better yet, your cooperation in assisting me to get Jenny back to her home in Ottawa. You may know that we divorced, but that was all my doing. Boy, I have made some mistakes, not too many mind you, but letting Jenny slip away was my biggest error and I want to correct it.

"She belongs back home here," James said forcibly and went on, "She has a son and daughter-in-law, a grandson, a mother-in-law that's aging and they all need her. I'm not trying to draw sympathy but I am suffering from cancer and the prognosis isn't that good. It would be wonderful to have Jenny back here…who knows, maybe her presence will create another miracle and have me healed as well!"

Henry only heard bits and pieces of what James had said. As soon as he stated that he wanted Jenny back and that she belonged back home in Ottawa, a heavy cloud covered his thoughts.

"Are you there? Mr. Pederson…"

Fortunately, Henry had listened enough to grasp the gist of James' rambling and slowly began to respond.

"I see…" said Henry, not really knowing what to say in the light of all this.

"I know, Marjorie, that is…Jenny, has fond feelings for you

and may be interested in reviving an old relationship with you…I would like you to discourage that. If there is some money or anything you need or desire I will do anything to help you."

Henry remained silent. This was such an unusual conversation and the furthest thing from his mind was to lose Jenny. She had come to Regina for her daughter, Camilla, but hopefully also for him. They had already expressed such love for each other that had never been lost. And yet, he was speaking to her former husband who had a right to express his desire to have her back…

"Well, really Mr. Hamilton—"

"Please call me James. Better yet, Jim, if you prefer."

"I think this all up to Jenny, James. You will have to ask her what she wants to do. I really have no say in the matter."

"How long have you been seeing Jenny since she returned to Regina?" James wanted to know.

"Not very long; less than a week. I just discovered the other day that I had purchased her home and made it to the hospital just before she passed away." Henry suddenly realized that he didn't need to divulge that information. Yet, to give their relationship some depth, he quickly added, "We have known each other since we were fifteen, however."

James couldn't believe that Henry Pederson had purchased Marjorie's home and yet he felt relieved that they had just started seeing one another.

"Like I said, Henry, since you're only beginning to see one another, it should be easy for you to discourage her…you know, tell her that you are not interested; it will help sway her to return. Do you understand what I'm saying?"

"I know exactly what you are saying, James, but I could never do that because I am very fond of Jenny…in fact, deeply in love with her. To be honest, I was hoping since she was no longer married that we might get together after all these years."

"How could you and Mar—Jennifer possibly be serious? You haven't been in touch for years. It should be easy for you to cut things off. You're dealing with her husband who was married to her for twenty two years. Surely that should take precedence over just a few days?"

Henry could hear James' breathing get heavier; his frustration and growing anger were intense. He fully expected to get a blast like he had years ago when James had called to speak to Jenny.

"It may be just a few days, however, our feelings go back a long way before you and Jenny met. Something…" Henry's words trailed off. He didn't need to explain how this relationship remained intact over all these years. He loved Jenny and wanted her more than anything…even more than considering her former husband's desire to have her back. It felt right and yet it didn't feel right…he felt confused and remained silent.

James had already gotten his staff to get some background information about Henry. James knew Henry was an artist and owned a gallery and gift shop in Regina. He now resorted to tactics he and his CEO's sometimes used in their business dealings. James was reluctant to do this, but he was getting desperate.

"Look, Henry, I know a lot of people and have many connections. I could very easily stop a lot of product coming to your shop. I could do a lot to put you out of business… Look, I wouldn't do that…sorry, it's something I perhaps would have done." James hesitated for a moment, to allow Henry to absorb what he could be capable of doing, just so he understood the gravity of the situation. It was a scare tactic that he never employed, but it sent a message of what could possibly happen. James went on.

"Look, Henry, I need your help and will do anything to get it…I don't mean to sound tough but it's a cruel world out there…"

"I told you before, it's all up to Jennifer and I will do everything I can to win her love. You had your chance and obviously it didn't work out. And please don't call me again if it's in regards to this matter."

Henry hung up the phone. He heard James yell some profanities at him before the connection was terminated.

JAMES STORMED OUT of the house onto the patio. He failed to understand how some guy who had seen his wife for a few days could stand in his way to saving his marriage. Surely, their relationship of some thirty years ago couldn't have any real value. It wasn't as if they had been divorced and Henry had been seeing Jenny for years after the fact.

What could he possibly do?

He thought for sure if he got Matilda's help, his son on board, and got this Pederson guy to lay off, that he could persuade Marjorie to return. But so far all of his efforts were failing.

He still hadn't got the results back from the tests and x-rays he had undergone a week ago. He knew however what they would find. His cancer was returning. He could sense, it, feel it, smell it; he was in a race against time. Life support and freezing his body would buy him time if it came down to that. But how much time would it give him? And how meaningful would it all be?

Perhaps he would talk to Thomas some more on the matter. What was it that drew him back again and again to the gardener? It was difficult for James to accept the fact that his employee knew more of life than he did. And yet James didn't feel he was lowering himself, in fact, just the opposite. The thought sent a soothing feeling through him, which he didn't quite understand until his discussion with Thomas centered on *pride.*

CHAPTER FORTY ONE

"THANK YOU FOR helping me tidy up the place, Mable. It needed a good vacuuming and dusting."

"No problem Henry, I'm just so happy that Jenny is coming home. She was so excited when I went up to see her yesterday. For awhile there, I thought she would never see her beautiful home and yard again. Who said miracles don't happen?"

"Well, I'm a perfect example of one, too. This has all been an incredible two weeks."

"I think you have put everything in its place Henry. The home looks to me exactly like it did the day Jenny left for the hospital. I looked after it for weeks and I can't see anything out of place."

"Ever since I purchased the home, I left it as I bought it. I loved everything about the home so much. I never dreamed of changing anything. I always felt like I was a guest, privileged to have such a wonderful place to escape to from the business. Except for the odd book I may not have put back exactly in the same place on the book shelf, I would agree with you, it's exactly as I found it."

"It's amazing that you were the one that purchased the home. Anyone else and God only knows what might have happened to this or that."

"Yes, Mable, I believe it was all pre-planned. Jenny and I are big believers in guardian angels and we attribute most of these incredible happenings to their involvement."

"Well, I can't argue with you … someone upstairs was definitely working to bring this all together almost like a fairy tale. In any case Henry, I am so happy for you and Jenny."

Henry checked the clock on the kitchen wall. "It's one thirty, time to pick up Jenny. I think I will just drop her off when I bring her back. Give her a chance to be alone and re-orientate to her life."

"Yes, that's considerate of you. Things have been so hectic for her since her recovery. She was elated, when I saw her yesterday, that Dr. Kreake said she could come home.

"See you later, Mable, and thanks again for your help."

Henry held Jenny's make up case with one hand and unlocked the front door with the other. He removed the key from the door latch and handed it to Jenny. He stepped back, allowing Jenny to open the door. She walked into the foyer and Henry followed. The beep of the security system sounded, piercing the stillness. Jenny turned and automatically keyed in the numbers and the beeping stopped.

"You didn't change the code."

"Actually Jenny, I didn't change a thing. When I first walked into this house it was like coming home. I loved everything about it exactly the way it was. It should be like the day you left and admitted yourself into the hospital."

Jenny turned towards Henry, filled with gratitude that words could not possibly express and whispered, "Thank you so much."

Tears welled up in both their eyes. Jenny set down her overnight suitcase and threw her arms around Henry's neck and they warmly embraced.

"I'm going to go now Jenny and leave you to settle in. You have a beautiful home. It gave me such peace over the past few months. I knew it was special, I knew it belonged to an angel."

Henry kissed Jenny tenderly and then turned to leave. Just before he closed the front door behind him he said, "When you have a minute, check the angel's basket in the backyard, you'll see something amazing. I think it's another miracle."

Jenny smiled, a twinkle in her eye suggested that she knew already what she would find there.

As soon as Henry closed the door, tears of joy and thanksgiving flowed from Jenny's eyes. "Thank you dear Lord for bringing me home again."

She walked into the living room and made her way to the fireplace. The book, Mere Christianity by C.S. Lewis was lying open and face down on the end table next to the sofa. The HB pencil was beside it just as she had left it. She gazed at the painting above the fireplace but her vision was too blurry to make it out. She wiped the tears with the back of her hand, turned and went into the dining room. The surface of the table shone in the light coming in through the window. Jenny knew it must have just been dusted. The odour of lemon wax still wafted off the surface. Mable or Henry must have done it. She slid her hand over the walnut surface near the edge as she walked towards the kitchen.

The sun was just making its way to the back yard between the tall fir trees. Rays of light snuck into the kitchen window, brightening the room. A sliver of light fell on the open cookbook lying on the counter. Jenny went to it and smiled … she was going to make chicken marsala with mushrooms that evening. Memories, good memories were coming back.

Henry knew they would, that is why he left me be. He must have walked through this home so many times and wondered about it all. I know he sensed my spirit, I just know it … and I sense his spirit here as well.

I feel his love…

Resting beside the cookbook, was an envelope addressed to her. It was Henry's handwriting. She opened it and noticed the title to her home and accompanying letter. She unfolded it and read:

Here is the title to your home. It's a gift from me to you.
Never have I ever purchased anything that has given me
so much joy. I hope someday you will let me become a per-
manent resident! Thank you for letting me into your home.
Love you with all my heart, Henry.

Jenny gazed out the kitchen window. A very light snow had fallen that morning, covering everything with glistening snowflakes. The snow on the winding path to the gazebo had already melted. However, the brightness of the sun drenched snow, surrounding the Angel of Thanksgiving, was glistening so brightly it made her squint at first glance. She smiled through tear filled eyes as she saw what Henry had alluded to just before he left. The angel's basket was filled with a beautiful bouquet, looking fresh and alive. She recognized the flowers; they were the very same ones she had picked and left there on the day she went into the hospital last fall.

"Oh thank you my angel so dear for granting my prayer to bring Henry and Camilla back to me. And thank you for having Henry buy this house. Where would I have gone if he hadn't and someone else had? Everything that I have loved and had given me spiritual sustenance over the years while living with James would have gone and, and…I would have been homeless."

Jenny looked at the bouquet again as well as the flowers peeking through the snow. She marveled at the number of times this miracle had happened when she lived at James' estate both during the summer and winter. Jenny was so overwhelmed that she began to twirl around in the kitchen. True happiness had finally come to her. She prayed that Henry desired to marry her as much as she desired to marry him. What if he wants to live alone? Or his family doesn't want him to marry again? Jenny felt certain Camilla would have no objections. They had already had some good talks when she came to visit her in the hospital.

These thoughts made Jenny think about her son. How would J.J. react to her getting married? The way he had acted towards her when he visited was so uncaring. And the manner in which he handled the sale of her house, without discretion or concern for her privacy, was very disappointing. For a moment Jenny realized that she should be upset with J.J. but then what good would it do other than rob her of the immense peace and joy she was experiencing?

No, she decided to deal with it in the same way she dealt with all the nonsense that James threw at her. She simply refused to allow other people's shortcomings and lack of considerations to control how she felt or her fate in any given precious moment the Lord granted her. In time people will get their just rewards. For now, she was just so grateful for all that had befallen her way.

A waterfall of tears gushed forth as Jenny thought about all the blessings she had been showered with. She raised her hands in praise and thanksgiving, twirling once again in her happy kitchen which seemed to have just grown brighter with each passing moment.

As Jenny swayed to the new music playing in her life, she gradually made her way to the bedroom. She flicked on the light and gazed around. Everything was as she had left it. She went to the bed and sat on the edge. Her fingers ran over the floral bedspread. She wondered if Henry had slept in it. She tried to feel his warmth. She was sure he had. Slowly, Jenny leaned forward and placed her head on the several pillows piled against the headboard and raised her feet on the bed. She was so happy; she felt as if she were on a magic carpet, floating into paradise. She closed her eyes, and wept tears of joy, until a brilliant white light, filled with the peace of her ever present guardian angel, Hannah, surrounded her.

JENNY AWOKE SHORTLY before seven o'clock p.m. She decided to take a shower and perhaps make the recipe that she had planned the day she left for the hospital. Sure enough, two chicken breasts were in the freezer. Jenny took one out and put it in the microwave to thaw. Henry had thoughtfully placed a bottle of white wine in the fridge. She would need it for the chicken marsala. She poured a glass of wine and went into the living room and opened the door to the console. She noted Henry had left a classical record in the changer. She turned on the player and immediately recognized "Dreamings" by Schumann, one of her favourite solo piano arrangements.

Jenny marveled at their similarity in tastes, in music, books, furniture but most of all, in their respect and consideration for each other. She noted that Henry had placed kindling and paper in the fireplace so it would be ready for her. She lit the paper and stood back, as the flames quickly caught the logs and danced before her.

She recalled when he came to the hospital, he read her diary and that was how he knew the house he purchased was her home. She wondered if it was still in her secret hiding place or if Henry had it. She opened the drawer and pulled on the ring. The partition opened and … yes, the diary was there just as she had left it. Henry was so considerate of everything. Trying to make certain that he in no way invaded her privacy.

Jenny also remembered that when she checked out of the hospital the letter she had received from Henry was no longer in the drawer of the night table. She wondered at the time if had been thrown out. She asked Nurse Johnson but she didn't know what happened to it. She meant to ask Henry when he came up to visit her but forgot. A sudden thought came to her that maybe Henry had found the letter that morning he came to her…if he had… she felt prompted to make her way to the bedroom. She opened the closet door and took down her mother's chest and placed it on the bed. As soon as she opened the lid, there it was, Henry's letter emitting a special glow.

Down to the very last detail, Henry made certain everything was in its place. But how did he know that the letter should be placed there? This is all so angelic, Jenny thought. There was just no other way to explain all the wonderful happenings. If only she had this kind of relationship with her spouse and son…but she also knew James was changing. She wondered if he was part of the miracle that had happened to her and Henry and Father.

The latter thought made her think about calling J.J. and Nora and let them know of her miraculous recovery. She felt Nora would care but hoped her son would too.

LATER THAT EVENING Jenny nervously dialed J.J.'s telephone number. After several rings, Nora answered the phone.

"Hello."

"Hi Nora, this is Jenny."

"Oh, hi Mar … Jenny, I've been thinking of you so much recently. How are you feeling?"

"Nora, I have had a miraculous recovery. I had passed away in the hospital and then when I returned to the land of the living, all the cancer that had ravaged my body was gone!"

Nora remained silent for a long moment. "Jenny that is wonderful …and you are completely cured? When we visited you last October you were so ill—"

"Yes, I recall…but it's all gone. I'm totally healed. I believe it was Father Engelmann's and Henry's prayers and of course our guardian angels that were responsible for it all."

"Father Engelmann, Henry…who are they?"

"Of course Nora, I'm sorry, I should have explained who these people are. Father Engelmann is a priest who came to visit me in the hospital and Henry was a boy I met when I was 15 years old and my parents and I lived in Regina for the summer. It turns out that when J.J. put the house up for sale, it was Henry who purchased it. I should explain that Henry was my first teenage boyfriend …" Jenny chuckled embarrassingly. "Oh, Nora, this all gets very complicated. I'll explain it all to you when we visit."

"Well, Jenny … visiting may not be that easy. J.J. has moved out of the house and, and he is trying to get Jimmy Junior away from me—"

"Oh, Nora, how could this be happening?" Jenny's voice carried a lamenting tone. She immediately thought of what had happened to her with James and that the same scenario was playing out.

Jenny could hear Nora begin to cry and longed to be with her so that she could console her in person. "I'm so sorry to hear this Nora, is there anything I can do?"

"J.J. is so critical of me and everything I do, I…finally told him to leave. I'm afraid now that I may lose Jimmy. J.J. is seeking custody through the courts and my finances are so limited. I had to sign a prenuptial agreement when we married and everything we have is owned by his company." Nora burst out crying again.

Jenny couldn't believe that what had happened to her, was replaying in the life of her daughter-in-law. "Nora, I will help you. It would be disastrous if J.J. were to take control of Jimmy. We will deal with this matter together. Perhaps I could begin by calling J.J. Do you have his number?"

"Yes, I have both his office number and home number, but he never answers the phone and only calls when it is convenient for him and he wants to talk to Jimmy. Oh Jenny, I am so worried about what might happen."

"I understand exactly what you are going through Nora. I went through a similar experience with James. In fact, James is probably behind all this."

"Well I don't know Jenny. James' cancer has returned and he is going through some legal concerns with the lady that was living with him."

"Is that Susan?" Jenny asked.

"Yes, I've met her several times. She seems like a nice person but for some reason or other James seems to want out of that relationship."

"I see. Well, perhaps I will call J.J. first and see what I can do there. In any case, Nora, I want to assure you that I will assist you in every way I can."

Nora gave the two numbers to Jenny.

JENNY DIALED J.J.'s home number and let it ring until the answering machine turned on. The machine caught J.J.'s character, "Leave a message."

Jenny paused for a moment and then said, "Hi J.J., this is your mother. I have some good news to tell you. A miracle has happened and I am totally cured of cancer. Please call me as soon as you can. I would love to talk to you and share the great news." Jenny left her return number and hung up. If he didn't phone by noon tomorrow, she would try his office number. She would ask Father and his warriors to pray for J.J. and Nora and ... James and Susan as well.

I wonder if James would help...he seems so different...

Chapter Forty Two

OH MABLE, how do I look? I feel like a teenager going out on a first date!"

"You look as beautiful and ravishing as ever, Jenny. And this isn't exactly your first date. Henry has made a steady path to your hospital room every day for the past week."

"Yes, I know. It's just that I get so excited each time he comes and this time we are really going out on a date. Does the dress look okay? I have lost so much weight my body doesn't fill it in just yet."

"Jenny, I would die to have your problem. As I said, you look gorgeous. Henry will be swept away the instant he sees you."

Just then went the doorbell rang.

"That's Henry!" Jenny's face flushed a soft shade of pink.

Mable got up and went to the door.

"Hi Mable, I'm here to pick up my girl."

Mable stepped aside, bowed and swept her arm towards Jenny. "Here is your princess."

Henry's heart melted at the sight of her.

"Jenny you look beautiful…" His words trailed off as he stood there speechless.

"Oh Henry, you look so handsome. I see navy blue is still your favourite color."

"It compliments the shade of your blue eyes." Then turning to Mable, "Don't you think so too, Mable?"

"Absolutely! You both make such a lovely couple."

"I made reservations for dinner at seven at the Hotel Saskatchewan, so perhaps we better be off."

"And so must I, Jen. I'll call you tomorrow." Mabel winked at Jenny and rolled her eyes at Henry as she passed him in the foyer.

"See you, Mable, and thanks for looking after the house and plants on those days I couldn't make it here."

"It was my pleasure, Henry."

After Mable left, Henry approached Jenny and took her in his arms. He gazed into her eyes for a long moment holding his breath.

"Oh Jenny, I love you so much. How I have longed to hold you and swim in your blue eyes."

"I love you so much, too... it finally seems like the ache I felt so long for you is subsiding."

Henry brought his lips close to Jenny's and tenderly and softly kissed her warm lips. He then drew Jenny more closely into his arms with a warm embrace. The feel of her body against his filled him with passion and desire. An inner happiness swept through his being, as he struggled to hold back tears of joy. It was hard to believe that his beloved, Jenny, was in his arms.

After what seemed like an eternity, they reluctantly withdrew from each other and made their way to the front door. Henry took the coat that Jenny chose from the closet and held it for her. As she went to slip her arm into the coat sleeve, he twirled her towards him once. She fell into his waiting arms and he pulled her in. "Oh, Jenny, I love you more than words can say."

"I love you, darling." Was all Jenny could utter before their lips met sending them both into a state of sheer ecstasy.

"Here's to you Jenny, to us," said Henry as he raised his wine glass towards Jenny and gazed lovingly into her sparkling eyes.

"I can't believe this is real, Henry. It seems as if I am just a step away from this side of heaven. I have to pinch myself each time we are together and I look into your eyes."

Henry shook his head from side to side, "It's a long dream come true Jenny. Since that first day we met in Mr. Engelmann's store, you were forever in my heart. It was as if my heart was pierced with a wound so deep that nothing over the years could heal it."

"It was the same for me Henry. Like a torch that went on fire and never burned out. Over the years I felt so guilty being married to James and having you in my mind and heart."

"And isn't it something Jenny that since that incredible day we passed away and came back to life, I have these strange dreams that I met my guardian angel and he, in part, was responsible for my returning to earth."

Jenny's mouth fell open as she listened to Henry... "My God, Henry, since that day, I dream of my guardian angel, too. It's so hazy and sketchy ... and exhilarating. Last night I dreamt that you, Father Engelmann and I held our guardian angels' hands and spun around and around in the star studded sky, just outside of the doorway to heaven."

"I dreamt that too Jenny...do you think that we were really all together?"

For a moment neither of them paid any attention to their officious waiter standing stiffly at the table with their meals.

"Here is your filet mignon sir, and your salmon, madam."

"Oh, this looks wonderful!" said Jenny as the server set the plate before her.

"May I top your wine madam?"

"Yes, please."

"I'll have some more, too...thank you."

The waiter returned the bottle to the ice filled bucket and left.

"This is delicious, Henry. So succulent!"

Henry concurred, nodding as his mouth was filled, as well.

Just as Henry was going to talk more of the dreams he had, Jenny spoke. "I'm sure happy that it was you who purchased my house—"

"Amazing, isn't it? I'll never forget the day the realtor took Jeremy and me to view it. It was supposed to be a revenue property for him and yet it was I who ended up purchasing it. Truly it was all planned by our angels."

"Yes, yes, I'm certain they did! The other night as I lay in bed going back over time and all the events that occurred, it is easy to see their angelic involvement."

"I wonder what Father Engelmann thinks of all this? I spoke

with him briefly yesterday and he remains fairly quiet on the matter. His only comment is that he praises the Lord for restoring our lives and giving us a second chance."

"He is such a wonderful man. His eyes are so kind and full of understanding and compassion. I've never met anyone like him before. I was so fortunate to have him at my side as I underwent all the treatments."

"Yes, he truly is a saint, Jenny. I think you said when I visited you at the hospital that you didn't recognize him at all as Mr. Engelmann from the corner grocery store?"

Jenny swallowed and then took a sip of wine. "Now that I know, I do see a resemblance in my memory. It was such a long time ago and when I came into the grocery store, I was mainly looking for you. And when he visited me the first time in the hospital he introduced himself as David. I didn't even know his last name… but I must say, he certainly has retained his youth."

"He's ageless, Jenny. Did you know that he celebrated his hundredth birthday a few weeks ago? He seems as if he were in his seventies or even younger."

"Yes, it is truly remarkable. I just love him, Henry."

"He's my hero and lifelong mentor, Jenny. Without him I would be long gone. He asked if he could use the Poustinia later this week and just have some peace and quiet. The excitement of all the miraculous happenings, his daily discussions with the archbishop and so many people coming to him asking for healings in their lives is having a huge toll on him."

"Ah, yes, it must be tiring him out. He is always so willing to help everyone."

"He rarely says no unless it goes against the wishes of his Lord's teachings. He also wants to have a serious talk with the Lord as to his purpose for the remaining years of his life. He seems to know what part of his work is going to be, but always waits on the Lord for instructions. You'll soon see that no matter what happens to Father, he tries to see it in relation to God's purpose and plan for him."

"Yes, he is a holy man. His aura of peace when he came to visit me always helped to sustain me and relieve the pain I was undergoing." After a brief pause Jenny asked, "What is a Poustinia, Henry?"

"A Poustinia is a small simple prayer house. The idea originated in Russia and was introduced to western society by a Russian lady named Catherine Doherty. She came penniless to Canada in the 1920's and within a short time became wealthy again. She was haunted by the words of Christ to sell all that she had, give to the poor and to follow Him."

Jenny stopped eating and listened intently.

"In 1931 after her husband died, she sold all she had and went to live with the poor in the slums of Toronto. There she founded the first Friendship House and gained many followers. From there, she went to work in Harlem, New York and later in the 1940's, she and her new husband purchased some land in Combermere, Ontario and founded Madonna House, a spiritual centre."

"What an interesting story. Is she still alive and what do they do there?"

"She passed away a few years ago, but the community she formed is very much alive and active. The community is based on prayer, silence, and the honest love of all who come to them for help."

"Henry, that's wonderful. I would love to go there ... so, this is what prompted you to build the Poustinia?"

"Yes, after Catherine founded the community on the property that she and her husband purchased, she came across an abandoned shack which reminded her of the Poustinias in her home land. Since then she has built several more one room Poustinias and she and other members of the community go into the huts for a day or two, or maybe even longer with just a Bible, water and bread and pray to the Lord ...so this is what prompted me to build a Poustinia down in the valley beside a pond."

Henry hadn't noticed but Jenny had stopped eating over five minutes ago totally entranced by Henry's story. Tears were in Jenny's eyes, she was so moved. Henry put his knife and fork down and reached across the table and took Jenny's hands.

"Oh Jenny, your heart has only grown softer and more beautiful over the years."

'I've always wanted to do something like that Henry, to help the poor or people in the third world. We have so much and they have so little ... the hunger, disease and poverty, that so many people suffer with, is almost unimaginable."

"Yes, it has moved me so many times as well, Jenny. In fact, the real reason that the Lord had me build the Poustinia was for me to examine my life and the direction I am going. I so love to build and make things beautiful—"

"Oh yes, Henry, that is what I have always remembered about you over the years ... your desire to make the world a better place."

"Well, what I was getting at, Jenny, is that I seem to be stuck in the wealth that I enjoy and have accumulated. Along with that, I enjoy the admiration of others for what I have accomplished. I try to be generous and kind and serving but I know the Lord wants more from me. Father tells me frequently that one cannot serve two masters."

Unbidden tears now welled up in Henry's eyes. "I'm afraid to go into the Poustinia for fear of what the Lord will request of me ..."

Jenny squeezed Henry's hands, "Oh Henry, what are you afraid of?"

"Excuse me sir, madam, are you finished with your meal?"

Henry and Jenny began to laugh. Their hunger had left them, replaced by another kind of hunger.

"I hate to waste food, but I'm really no longer hungry, Henry."

"Neither am I. Perhaps you could package this; I have two dogs and several barn cats that would love the remains of this fine meal"

"Very good sir. May I interest you in our fine desserts?"

A sparkle glinted in Jenny's eyes that Henry recognized instantly from patrons of his own fine café who desired something sweet.

"Well, yes, surprise us. Bring us what you would have, if you brought a feminine friend to this fine establishment."

The server smiled broadly and his shoulders relaxed. His pretentious manner dissolved and he exclaimed with a wink in his eye. "Leave it in my good hands sir, you shall not be disappointed."

It's still early, would you like to come in for awhile?" Jenny asked as they pulled up to the house.

"Yes, I would like to very much."

Henry quickly got out of his new SUV and skirted around to the passenger side and opened the door.

"I see chivalry hasn't left you."

"Not in the least Madam."

Henry opened wide the door and gave Jenny his hand as she stepped down from the extra high running board.

"You certainly won't get stuck in the snow or mud with this vehicle."

"That's exactly why I buy an SUV. Winter snow and storms can create quite the drifts on farm roads. I've never been stranded or stuck so far."

They were silent as they made their way up the winding walk. The light snowfall earlier that day had melted but left a cool chill in the air. Jenny leaned into Henry as they walked and he quickly responded by wrapping his arm around her.

Once in the foyer, Henry helped Jenny with her coat and then took his own off. He followed Jenny into the living room feeling a little awkward. For months he had come in freely and now that he returned the house to Jenny, he felt out of place.

"Would you like some wine or tea, Henry?"

"I've come to enjoy your chamomile tea over the past several months … that would be fine."

"Why don't you start a fire in the fireplace while I get the tea ready?"

"I know how to do that, as well. I've even done so in mid afternoon during some of the more blustery days."

"I guess you know everything about this home and perhaps, some secrets about me as well?"

"I must admit Jenny, this has been an extraordinary experience, to come into someone's home and literally take it over."

"Normally, Henry, I would be a little upset with my son for being so careless as to put up my house for sale without taking any consideration to my privacy, but the more I think on this … it was meant to be. The angels knew that it would be you that would purchase the home and eventually bring us back together again. So how can I fault my son? In his inconsideration, he brought me the greatest blessing life can bring to anyone."

Henry lit the kindling and walked into the kitchen. "My God, Jenny, for months I was upset with your son for that very reason and suddenly it all turns into this great gift!"

Jenny drew near to her loved one and gently slipped into his open arms. Henry tenderly kissed Jenny and embraced her warmly. The familiar whistle, that Henry had become accustomed to, could be heard, blowing in the kitchen.

"Have a seat in the living room and I'll bring your tea in momentarily."

Henry sat on the sofa facing the fire which was burning as brightly as his heart. The light from the fireplace revealed the joy and happiness in his eyes.

Jenny sat his tea on the coffee table in front of him and hers beside and then sat next to him. Henry put his arm over her shoulder and drew her in as they gazed at the fire.

"It must have been quite an experience for you to take over someone's home."

"It was Jenny, it's amazing what you can learn about a person from the little notes they leave around, the furniture they buy and especially the books they read...it tells a lot about the person."

"Did you ever sense that it was my home?" Jenny was curious to know.

"For the first month or so I felt more of a spiritual presence that angels were in the house. Gradually the home, the books, the music, the plants and flowers grew on me and I began to fall in love with Marjorie, the owner of this amazing home. One thing that reminded me of you was the lilac fragrance over and above all the scent of the other plants. I especially noticed it in your bedroom."

"So after all those years, you still remembered my favourite perfume."

"I never forgot that nor anything we said and did that summer. But, I think it was after I discovered the letter you sent me with the pewter angel, inside my mother's hope chest, after she died, was when I could no longer contain my desire to have you back. I began to fantasize that Marjorie was you, never once realizing that she was really you!"

"And then you discovered the diary and read all my secret entries."

"Jenny! You have no idea the exhilaration that swept through me when I realized that Marjorie was you. There was a time when I wanted to visit Marjorie in the Santa Maria Home, but the nurse said only family was allowed and that you were too ill. But then knowing who you really were and that you were on the doorstep to dying, such an urgency to see you, overtook my being."

Henry drew Jenny closer to him and couldn't speak for the

longest time. "So many times before I became ill I wanted to come into your gallery and see you—"

"Oh, Jenny why didn't you?"

"At the time I thought you were married and I didn't want to interfere with your family. My son, J.J. blamed me for breaking up our marriage and I was so afraid that some misunderstanding might happen again and perhaps get Camilla upset with me…oh, I just let it get too complicated…and then I became ill and entered the hospital and the rest you pretty well know about."

"It's all so astonishing how everything is connected: the home, Father Engelmann visiting you, your daughter turning out to be Camilla, Eddy's wife Coreena being the sister to Matilda, Peter… and I could go on with other incidences."

"Unbelievable," whispered, Jenny, "Truly unbelievable."

Jenny snuggled closer into Henry's arm once more and both watched the flames dance to the fire they each had burning for one another. Slowly, the excitement of the day and their wonderful evening lulled them into a dream that they wanted to last forever. They didn't notice that one of the burning logs collapsed sending sparks like shooting stars into the air.

"Oh my Henry, it's two thirty! We must have fallen asleep."

For a moment there, Henry thought he was in heaven as he opened his eyes to see Jenny smiling at him. She leaned forward and gently kissed him on his lips.

"You can crash out on the couch if you want …"

"You may not find me on the couch in the morning …" Henry winked at Jenny. "No, I better go, Ginger and Coco are waiting to be fed and I have a painting to bring in for a client."

"I can hardly wait to come to your acreage and see your studio, and the Poustinia sounds so intriguing."

"Father is coming out Friday to use the Poustinia, so why not come out Saturday and we can visit him and I'll show you around the farm and valley."

"That sounds wonderful Henry, I can hardly wait. And I am anxious to meet your children, too." Jenny said excitedly.

They walked to the front door and Henry put on his coat. He held open the front flaps and motioned for Jenny to snuggle in.

The feel of her warm, soft body next to his sent throbs of desire throughout his being. It had been years since he had made love; the last time had been with Julean in their hotel suite in Minot just prior to her passing.

Jenny raised her chin off Henry's chest and brought her lips next to his. They tenderly kissed. Almost instantly, Henry felt his maleness. He recalled the struggle he had with his urges before his marriage to Julean. It seemed far more intense now. He squeezed Jenny and pressed himself more into her. Jenny didn't back away. He wanted so much to make love to her. How many times did he recall that time in the park when they almost made love? How many times did he wish he had?

And then he recalled that wonderful wedding night with Julean and the precious gift of their total selves that they had saved for each other under the umbrella of the sacrament of matrimony. He would never forget that special moment. *He wanted no less for him and Jenny.*

"I love you so much, Jenny." Henry said dreamily, struggling with his sensual longings.

Jenny pulled away slightly and looked deeply into Henry's eyes, "I love you so much too…one of the things I so remember about us that summer is how safe and sure I always felt around you."

Henry nodded and softly whispered, "Yeah…I better go … for now."

Henry smiled and kissed Jenny lightly one more time. "I'll call you in the morning."

Jenny rested the side of her happy face on her hands that held the edge of the door and watched the love of her life make it to his SUV. Just before he ducked into his truck, he stood high on the running board and waved to his dear sweet Jenny.

She, in turn, blew him a kiss from the doorway like she had so many times from the steps of her house on Broder Street during that memorable summer of 1956.

At that moment, his forty seven year old heart beat as if it were fifteen years old again.

CHAPTER FORTY THREE

AFTER HENRY FED the dogs and went to bed, he couldn't sleep. His thoughts went over the date and how the evening went. He was aware of how everyone turned their head towards Jenny as they made their way to the table. It made him recall a similar scene of the day when he made a special plan for Julean and him at the Hotel Saskatchewan for their 18th anniversary. All the men having a business lunch had turned their heads that day too as Julean was escorted to the table. He knew what a lucky guy he was then and what a fortunate man he was now. He looked at the ring on his finger as it caught the moonlight that was entering through the window.

What happens when Jenny and he marry? Should he take the ring off?

Henry didn't think he ever could.

Henry wondered about James and the phone call he had received from him. How was this all going to play out? He knew that they needed to talk about it, but tonight wasn't the time.

But when would there ever be a good time? He loved Jenny so much and didn't want to ever lose her again. And, and…here was her former husband wanting her back, too.

Henry could feel an anxiousness stealing away the wonderful evening that still lingered in his heart. He searched for Julean's rosary in the darkness. As soon as he found it, he pulled Julean's pillow towards him and began to pray. One of the similarities between Jenny and Julean was they both had a solution for every dilemma that came up. He looked at his ring again and knew one or the other would have an answer to his concern.

Perhaps he would wear two. Yes, two rings; the two sweethearts in his life. He thanked his dear wife for guiding him back to Jenny and for being such a wonderful understanding wife.

Normally he would fight tooth and nail for Jenny's love, but this was a special case with so many others involved.

They had briefly talked about her and James at dinner. But it was too soon, too uncomfortable to discuss. Was he interfering? Would a marriage between Jenny and him estrange her family, especially her son whose love she wanted badly and also, her grandson and daughter-in-law? It would not be easy for Jenny, that was for certain and…on his part, what was the morally right thing to do? He began to feel tense…

He pulled Julean's pillow close to him and rested his hand with the rosary on the pillow and began to pray. And just before sleep overtook him, the thought of his teacher came to mind. Yes, Father Engelmann would know what to do…yes, his mentor was always there. Thank you Jesus and thank you Julean and thank you to my guardian angel…

Hail Mary, full of grace, the Lord is with… his prayer trailed off.

Oh blessed mother, mother of God, you know families, you and Joseph and Jesus were a holy family, pray for me. Let me be sensitive to the needs of others. Let me allow my Jenny to be free to make decisions that are true to her heart. Let me know what the Church requires in situations like this. Does the Church recognize Jenny's divorce? Oh, blessed Mary, ask your son, Jesus to guide my steps in the following days, so there are no regrets, no hurts. Help us all to be compassionate and understanding with each other…and most of all dear Lord, let Your will be done in this situation.

JENNY TOSSED AND turned in bed. It was so late and yet she knew sleep would not come easily. *I love Henry so much and there are so many obstacles in the way.* What would happen to her relationship with J.J. and James if she married Henry? James seemed to be changing and coming around in such a wonderful way. She had always seen him so different when they were married; refusing to be affected by some of his inconsiderate actions and words. Jenny wondered if he was touched by all the miracles that happened, too. It was such a sudden change for him to be so considerate and to admit that he was wrong and plead for her to come back. It was *a miracle*. He was such a proud man.

Jenny rolled and tossed again, the dilemma was growing in her mind and she saw no real solution in sight. All she had thought about over the years was to be reunited with Camilla and Henry and now it had finally come true! She thought she would be free when it finally happened and yet, was she really? Could she just sever her relationship with James and the rest of the family?

"And I love Henry so much." Jenny whispered into the darkness. "I can hardly wait to get married and so want to give him a child. How I wished and fantasized that it was Henry who had fathered Camilla!"

In the early stages of her pregnancy, she had wished it so deeply it was the only way she could keep the child within her womb. But then she learned to love the baby growing within her. And slowly, she began to accept the baby as her own, and even allowed her mind to dwell on the man who assaulted her. But now, everything could be a reality, if only the road was clear for her and Henry to get married.

Jenny began reliving those minutes before Henry left. She could tell that they both desired to make love. Their bodies ached to be together and yet, there was that something special that kept both of them in check. To do so outside the bonds of matrimony seemed to equal losing something…it was more for themselves. To be married was such a holy and sacred sacrament. A wedding day, was such a wonderful day when it would all come together and begin a momentous journey. Courting was a time of enjoying one another and getting to know one another and yes, it was not without sacrifice. And yet that seemed to be the wonderful part about it all; that willingness to wait for that special day.

She had never given in to James all the time they had dated. She was certain it was because of Henry and the restraint he showed. No, she would wait. She knew that was what Henry wanted, too, even though their desire for one another was so strong. *Henry showed his strength again tonight.*

Oh dear guardian angel, clear the road ahead of all obstacles so we are free to carry out our hearts' desire.

CHAPTER FORTY FOUR

"Hi, Camilla, this is Mom! I know you know who it is, but I just love saying it."

"And so do I, Mom. It's so good to hear from you, Mom!"

"Yes, it's been over three hours since we last spoke! So much must have happened to you since I last called!"

The two ladies giggled and laughed, their faces aglow with joy.

"This may not give you enough notice, but I was wondering if you and I could go out shopping tomorrow and if you would like to sleep over at my house? I could take you home Sunday morning and pick up Joshua and take him to church with me. Would all that be possible?" Jenny wanted to know.

"I would love to go shopping with you, Mom. I can get Susan, next door, to look after Josh until Jeremy gets home from work. Saturdays are pretty busy at the café, so I know he won't be able to book it off."

"That's great, Camilla. We will go to Henry's for lunch so you can see your wonderful husband and do some shopping there, as well, if you'd like."

"You have it all planned, I can see."

"Yes, I do. So, I will pick you up around nine thirty and we'll start at the Bay and work our way through all the stores. I always dreamed of taking you shopping and buying you outfits."

"That sounds wonderful, Mom. See you at nine thirty."

"The yellow summer dress looks so nice on you, Camilla. I can just see Jeremy with his mouth wide open in awe when he sees you!"

"It is nice, but you already bought me a floral jumper at Eatons."

"Oh, Camilla, let me spoil you a little. I have been waiting for this for so long."

Camilla held it up in front of her as she looked in the full length mirror. "I really do love it…are you sure, Mom?"

"Of course, I'm certain; you look stunning in it."

Jenny took the dress and handed it to the sales clerk and checked her watch. "Well, it's 12:45 p.m., which just gives us enough time to get to Henry's. I made reservations for one o'clock so we miss the noon hour rush."

"Oh, Mom, thank you so much. I can't believe this!"

Jenny and Camilla waited for three patrons to come out of the café before entering through the front doors. They were immediately greeted by Joshua who came running up to Camilla.

"Mommy, Mommy," he cried, as he broke away from his dad's hand.

"Josh! What are you doing here?" Camilla looked up to ask her husband the same question, when there behind Jeremy was Henry, his family, Camilla's neighbour who had brought Josh to the café and off to the side was Father Engelmann wearing a broad smile and a twinkle in his eyes.

"What is going—" were the only words Camilla could utter before everyone began singing happy birthday.

Camilla just stood there as they all sang, and even some of the patrons joined in. She shook her head in disbelief, tears filling her eyes. "I thought everyone had forgotten my birthday. Jeremy, I was upset with you for not remembering when Mom picked me up." Turning to Jenny she continued, "Did you plan this, Mom?"

"Every May 24th, since the day you were born, I celebrated your birthday and this is one that I have been looking forward to for a long, long time." Jenny went to her daughter and hugged her tenderly. This was followed by the rest of the family.

Henry introduced Justin and Lauren to Jenny. She wanted to hug Henry's children, but thought she better just shake their hands. She could sense a little hesitancy on Justin's part, but Lauren's eyes lit up to meet her father's girlfriend.

"It's so good to meet you, Jenny, Dad was telling us all about you and how you met and…oh, you and Camilla look like twins. You look so much alike!"

"I do have another daughter, Allison," said Henry, "but she is at college and will be home in about two weeks."

"It's so wonderful to meet you—" Jenny started to say to Justin and Lauren before Henry interrupted.

"Okay, let's get to our tables and away from the front door." Jenny felt a little relieved as Justin still had not spoken to her and she was struggling with what to say to him.

Three tables were put together in the back section which was just about empty except for two patrons at the window holding hands and too much in love to really pay any attention to the birthday party. Jeremy had decorations up and a special head table designated for his dear wife at the centre with Jenny and Father Engelmann to her right and Henry to her left.

"This is all so wonderful! Mom and I had a great morning shopping and wait until you see the new outfits she bought me."

"Your eyes will never be the same again, Jeremy. She looks stunning but really, she would make anything look great." Jenny added.

"I recall a morning when your mom came into Engelmann's Grocery store and she too had been shopping with her mother and came in to show me her outfit." Turning to Father, Henry asked, "Do you recall that, Father?"

"Yes, yes, how could I forget? Jenny looked more lovely than a princess, all dressed up with her new blouse and skirt and shiny black shoes—"

"Oh you even remember my new patent shoes!?"

"Yes, yes, but even more so, I remember the awestruck look on Henry's face when he saw you…he was too speechless for words. I had to help him out."

"That's exactly right Father, and I will never forget what you said when she left, 'A happy heart, makes a cheerful face.'"

"Ah yes, Proverbs 13:15. You reminded me of the proverb every time you entered the store, Jenny. I still cannot get over not recognizing you when I met you in the hospital and started to visit you."

"Nor, I you," concurred, Jenny.

Just then two waiters came to the table with soup and an assortment of sandwiches already prepared and waiting for the party.

"Father, would you please say Grace?" requested Henry.

Father made the sign of the cross and then extended his hand to those next to him and the others followed. Soon the entire birthday party was holding hands. "Thank you, dear heavenly Father, for the food we are about to eat and for all of our blessings. Thank you for the gift of life each day but especially on the day we come together to celebrate the day we were born. This is Camilla's day! Thank You, Lord, for this beautiful woman and all the joy she daily showers on her family and on others. You have truly blessed the world with her presence. Let us sing and enjoy this wonderful celebration of Camilla's life!"

"Oh, thank you, Father, for that beautiful prayer and I just want to add that it's Jeremy's birthday today, too! Isn't that amazing we were both born on the same day!"

Everyone extended their birthday wish to Jeremy, as well. He simply nodded appreciatively and remained silent.

Camilla blew him a kiss and turning to her mother, she added, "Dear Mom, thank you for choosing to give me life and after thirty one years this is the most precious birthday gift I will treasure this day forever, to have you here to celebrate our first birthday together!"

Those sentiments were already in Jenny's mind. Her tears were clearly revealing the joy in her heart!

After the delicious lunch, not only one waiter came carrying a birthday cake with thirty one lit candles, but all the rest of the staff joined in with the party to sing once again a happy birthday to Camilla.

"Every year as your birthday rolled around, Camilla, I baked a cake and put one candle on it. I promised that as soon as we were together, I would put all the candles on for your age that we were celebrating and, I might add, I plan to do so for the rest of our days!"

After a lovely party, the ladies browsed through the gallery and clothing boutique on the second floor. Once again, Camilla found an irresistible outfit: a black dress that accentuated every curve of her body. Jenny, too, found some jewelry that she liked, as well as a white scarf with blue polka-dots to tie around her hair when driving her convertible.

Since it was only three thirty, the women decided to continue their shopping spree at the mall. This time they shopped for the children. Jenny bought some toys, a sweater and pair of trousers for Josh and also decided to buy a necklace for Lauren and a wrist watch for Justin, both at Birks Jewelers. She wasn't sure if it was too soon to buy him a gift, as all through the lunch party she noticed both Lauren and Justin had kept eyeing her. It was Justin's stare however, that carried an unsure look. Jenny could sense it would take some time to win him over.

After a late candle light dinner, Jenny and Camilla decided to have a pajama party. Both showered and then met in Jenny's bedroom. Jenny was already seated on top of her bed cross legged, waiting for Camilla to come in. Camilla also assumed the lotus position towards the end of the bed and the two just stared at one another for the longest time.

Finally Jenny broke the silence. "Oh, Camilla, I fantasized for so many years doing this with you. I still can't believe that it has finally happened. I would love for you to tell me about your growing up years with the Breckharts. What were they like and how did you get along and when did you start thinking that perhaps you were adopted? If you don't want to talk about it, I understand. I just want for you to feel free to share what you want and when you want, okay?"

Camilla reached for her mother's hand and began to share her earliest memories growing up with her adoptive parents. They were very loving and caring, a bit old fashioned and strict, but always loving. Camilla shared certain incidents to support some of her judgments, but on the whole, Jenny got the sense that her upbringing had been very good. But then Camilla added something that made her feel still better about her daughter's rearing and adoption.

"You know, Mom, there is a perception out there that adoptive parents are just fill-ins until the real birth parents are found. But I didn't ever feel that about my parents. Had our appearance not been so completely different, I might not have felt out of place.

There wasn't a day I didn't feel loved and well cared for. I was so fortunate to be in a home that instilled good values, with parents who so wholeheartedly gave me of their lives, just like natural parents would have…" Camilla gazed lovingly at Jenny and said, "They truly loved me as their own. Many times I felt so guilty for even thinking that I was adopted. In a way, I feel special to be blessed with two sets of parents."

Jenny nodded, "The value of one does not outshine the other, Camilla. Yes, you have been specially blessed; you have both real parents and birth parents who love you dearly. And, I too, feel specially blessed to have you come back into my life to love, honour and value you just as the Breckharts did. I so wish I could have met and known them. In spirit we will always be family."

It was just after one o'clock in the morning, when Camilla began sharing her teenage years and the several crushes she had with boys throughout high school. She also thought that it was during her early teens that she began to suspect that she didn't belong to the Breckharts. She could never understand why her parents and relatives looked so different than her in all respects. She would spend hours studying family photos, searching for any kind of similarity and sense of belonging…but there never was one.

"I always felt out of place and deep inside I could feel a void. I recall when we moved to Saskatoon, at first, I didn't want to leave my friends in Ottawa. But I soon came to love the prairies and even more so when we moved again to Regina."

Camilla paused and gazed more intently at Jenny who also was listening so intently to every word her daughter said.

"It was here, Mom, when we came to Regina that I knew I had come home. There was just that unexplainable feeling that told me this is where I wanted to spend the rest of my life. Mom and Dad tried their hardest to convince me to go to Victoria with them when they moved to B.C. but I felt prompted to stay put and soon I found out why."

"It was Jeremy, wasn't it?" Jenny's eyes looked assured that her guess was correct.

Camilla's eyes brightened, further confirming Jenny's assessment. "Oh yes, I remember to this day when he walked into the tuxedo shop to rent a suit for the weekend. He was so tall and handsome and when he tried on the suit, I thought I would die. A few weeks later we started to date. We were a bit shocked at our age difference, but even more to realize that our birthdays fell on the same day and we were exactly seven years apart in age."

"That's amazing, Camilla, I didn't know it was Jeremy's birthday today!"

"Yes, I don't think he wanted to draw attention to himself and he quickly agreed that I should spend the evening with you; that it was more important for us to celebrate the day being it was our first birthday together."

"You love him a lot, Camilla."

Camilla undid her legs and lay back on the bed. She rolled over facing her mother, "I love him with all my heart, Mom. Even though he is a lot younger, he is so mature and loving and considerate. He's always there for me and places my happiness over his all the time."

Camilla's words trailed off as tears of a deep love filled her eyes. She rolled on her back once again and rubbed her tummy. Very softly she said, "I have a wonderful secret to share with you, I am pretty sure I am expecting another child. I've missed my period for two months now. I have an appointment with our family doctor next week just to confirm it."

"Oh Camilla, I am so happy for you. That is such wonderful news. It will be so good for Josh to have a little brother or sister. After I had J.J., I always wanted to have another child to give him a sibling, but it was not meant to be."

Jenny's words trailed off. She didn't want to tell Camilla that once James knew about her and the circumstances of her conception, he never slept with her again. But Camilla wanted to know Jenny's background and so for the next two hours, Jenny shared her life with James and J.J. and some of the challenges she had faced. She did mention that all through her marriage, Camilla and Henry were in her heart, never far below her daily thoughts.

"You still love Henry a lot, Mom?"

"Yes, with all my heart and if I can share a secret with you, I would love to give Henry a child."

"I could tell! In fact, when Henry came to visit you at the hospital, all of us could tell how much he loved you…how much both of you loved each other. There was such a glowing light around both of you that morning."

"It was our angels shining through us, Camilla." Jenny winked as she made the comment, but was very serious.

"Absolutely, you and Henry were making reference to your angels that would explain the aura. Jeremy and I are the same. We are always saying the little guardian angel prayer. Ever since I met Jeremy, I am so much more aware of my guardian."

"That's so true, the more we acknowledge our angels, the more we become aware of their presence in our lives."

Although it was approaching three-thirty a.m., neither of the women were tired. Camilla sat up and crossed her legs and inched towards Jenny. Once again, she took her mother's hands in hers and asked, "How do you feel about the man that fathered me, Mom? If you don't want to discuss it, it's okay. I can only imagine what happened and how terrifying it must have been for you."

Jenny was a bit shocked at the question. She knew it was just a matter of time before they would have to discuss Camilla's conception. She was relieved that Camilla was informed on what happened, through Matti and Chloe. Even that part, which would have been so difficult for her to share with her daughter, was already looked after by her earthly angels. And just the thought of angels gave Jenny the perfect way to talk about it.

"We were just talking about angels, Camilla, and I do believe it was my guardian that saved me from the trauma of it all. When the boys took me to the park, I completely passed out. I didn't even know that anything had happened that evening until I started to put on weight and began feeling so tired. Mom took me to the doctor and after a few tests I was told that I was with child."

"That must have been such a shock for you…to know that you were violated and carrying a baby."

Jenny could hardly believe how receptive and empathic Camilla was being. Instead of just thinking of herself and the horrible, hurtful circumstances of her conception, here she was helping Jenny to work through it all.

Jenny tightened her grip around Camilla's hands and went on. "Yes… yes, Camilla, it did shock me and hurt me and—"

"Did you want to abort me? It's okay, Mom, please talk about it and let me know it all. It's important for both of us to deal with every aspect of it."

Jenny took a deep breath. She had always imagined that she

was going to would have to be so careful in how to approach such a sensitive subject with her daughter, and suddenly--unexpectedly the tables were turned. Here was Camilla, her daughter, leading Jenny to get it out... Hesitantly, Jenny went on...

"Yes, Camilla, it did cross my mind and it was suggested to me by counsellors as well, but I couldn't do that. Over the weeks I grew to love you and the thought of killing you became unthinkable."

Camilla just nodded, gesturing for her to go on. Tears surfaced as Jenny relived that insufferable time.

"What became so unbearable, Camilla, was that I had decided to give you up for adoption. My mother didn't feel she could raise another child and felt I was not only too young, but that it would complicate my life too much. For days we discussed it and down deep I knew that you would be better off to be raised by loving parents that could give you a home and a proper upbringing."

Jenny began to cry. She didn't realize how deeply she still hurt by that decision. Jenny suddenly remembered how in the days that followed Camilla's birth and giving her away, she had fallen into a deep depression. Jenny could feel those buried feelings surface now and could no longer speak. When Camilla came to the hospital the morning after she was miraculously healed, Jenny thought that most of her feelings over the adoption of her daughter had surfaced and been dealt with. *But she was wrong.* There were still so many deeply repressed emotions.

Camilla tightened her grip on her mother's hands. Jenny suddenly realized that as a counselor herself, Camilla understood what Jenny went through. Jenny was so grateful for her daughter's support and understanding. She knew that everything was okay. That Camilla had accepted it.

Camilla rose to her knees and knelt beside her mother and put her arms around her shoulders. Both women began to openly cry.

"Oh, Mom, I love you so much. Thank you for giving me life and making that huge decision at such a young age. Thank you for going through all that suffering and pain of loss, thinking it was in my best interests. Oh, Mom, I am so fortunate to have you as my mother. From the bottom of my heart, thank you, thank you."

Jenny reached up and squeezed her hand around Camilla's arm, conveying her love, too emotional to speak.

"I still didn't answer your question though, Camilla, about how

I feel towards Peter. For the longest time I couldn't think of him and what he did. I even imagined that Henry was the father…but gradually I let go of all those feelings, Camilla. I didn't want to associate anything negative connected to your birth. I just wanted good memories. Even though it wasn't the most desirable way to conceive you, I accepted what happened and in my heart, I forgave Peter. Henry told me a little about him and that he feels so guilty over what he did. In fact, Henry said that Peter's conscience bothered him so much that it made him terminally ill. Apparently he, too, died that same day that I, Henry and Father Engelmann passed away. And he too, came back and was totally healed. I feel all our coming back in part, was to give all of us a chance to resolve this…

"How do you feel towards your father, Camilla?"

"I don't have any feelings towards him, Mom, just that I do want to meet him and get to know him. It helps to know that he has lived with such remorse over what he did to you. I…I'm not sure I would be as able to forgive him, Mom, but knowing that you have made peace with it in your heart is helpful. I'm curious about him…he is my father…I wonder if he would want to meet with us?"

"Oh yes, he does, Camilla. Henry told me the other day that he wants to meet with both of us and ask for our forgiveness."

"Then, we should meet with him, Mom. Would you want to do that? It will be difficult for all of us, but I feel that it would be healing for all of us."

Jenny took a deep breath. "Yes, Camilla, it will be difficult, but I could get Henry to call him and set up a meeting."

Camilla tightened her embrace and whispered softly, "You are such a brave, wonderful woman with such a forgiving heart. I love you so much."

"I love you, too, Camilla. You are so forgiving and understanding as well. Thank you for helping me share all of this with you. I really didn't know there was still so much pain in my heart about it all."

The women remained silent for the longest time, until Camilla noticed that it was almost four thirty in the morning.

"Oh, Mom, you will never guess what time it is…four-thirty! Pretty soon we can watch the sun come up!"

"My gosh, Camilla, where did the time go? I prepared the bed for you in the guest room."

Both ladies got up and went to the washroom. They hugged each other and said good night as each went to their respective bedrooms.

Jenny went to her room and left the door ajar and climbed into bed. She wasn't tired, even though she felt emotionally drained. She was relieved to have been able to discuss such a delicate subject so openly. It reminded Jenny of some of the conversations she had had with her friend, Tammy, many years ago. In many ways, Camilla was like her. Camilla was perceptive and able to so skillfully draw out her feelings. A surge of love swept through Jenny just thinking about it all. She turned off the light and lay in the dark.

Shortly, Jenny heard a light rap on her door and it swung open. Jenny could see Camilla's silhouette in the doorway, standing there like a frightened child. Softly, her daughter whispered, "Mom, can I come and sleep with you?"

"I hoped you would ask, Camilla."

Jenny tossed the blankets aside and like an excited child, Camilla ran to the bed and hopped in. Jenny put her arm around her daughter and drew her in, near to her heart. Soft tears, sliding slowly down their cheeks were caught by the moonlight coming in through the bay windows. Had they been gazing out of the window they would have noticed several shooting stars. Wishes and dreams, long held by both of them were coming true and the star dust was settling into their hearts.

"Mom," Camilla softly asked, "can I read your diary?"

Jenny patted her daughter's shoulder, "Yes, you can, honey, in fact, I gave an envelope to Father Engelmann to pass along to my lawyer in which I wrote a little about myself. It was intended for you in case I didn't make it. I willed my diary to you, Camilla. But now that I'm here and we're together, I certainly won't make you wait until I'm gone to read it!"

"Oh, that's good, I want to know as much about you as possible. You can read my journals as well, if you want."

"Yes, Camilla, I would love to read your journals and talk to you about treasures you've carried in your heart over the years."

Camilla snuggled in closer to her mother's chest and the peace of the moment descended upon them.

And then, softly, gently and ever so sweetly, Jenny's little girl began to whisper the Guardian Angel prayer into the advancing early morning:

"Angel of God, my guardian dear,
to whom God's love commits me here,
ever this day be at my side,
to light and guard, to rule and guide
my life...my Mom and Dad's...
and my Mom and Dad Breckhart
who I know are looking down and so
happy that I have found my birth mother
to continue the love they have given me.
I ask my guardian angel to fly up and give
Them a big hug and kiss...
forever and ever.
Amen

"Oh, Camilla, you have the heart of an angel," Jenny murmured as they both finally drifted off to sleep, exhausted.

CHAPTER FORTY FIVE

MATTI STEPPED OUT onto the patio and took a deep breath of morning fresh air. "My, my, what a glorious day the Lord has prepared. I shall be glad and rejoice in it, that be for sure. My, that air smells good...all them flowers and herbs drifting here and there. Yes, hmmm, it sure be good to be back on the estate."

Matti held a plate of cookies in one hand and the coffee in the other and began heading for the shed. James had told them to use the kitchen for their breaks, but they still preferred the shed. There was just something about sitting close together amongst the tools and the odour of earth in the air... 'Just seems more cozy and friendly' was the way Thomas put it. Matti had to admit she loved the smell of potting soil in her nostrils as much as the fragrance of her home baked cookies.

Thomas had just finished cleaning the dead leaves out of several Dogwood plants when he saw Matti.

"Ramon and I will be along momentarily, Matti."

"Make it quick, Thomas; I know how much you like the cookies warm out of the oven."

Matti entered the shed and set down the coffee and plate of cookies and proceeded to turn over another five gallon pail to sit on. Two were already overturned.

"Morning, Matti, it's sure good to have you back," said Thomas as he entered the shed. "Oh, that sure smells good. No-one makes coffee like you do and I don't rightly know who I missed more, you or the hot cookies!"

"It best be me, Thomas, them cookies would never visit your taste buds if it weren't for my baking abilities and know how. I be the one puttin' them in the oven and don't you be forgetting that."

"That's for sure," Thomas said with a wink as he sat down.

Matti poured a cup of coffee for Thomas and passed the plate of cookies in front of him. "Is Ramon coming soon?"

"He may be a while, Matti. He wants to finish setting up the sprinklers. So, tell me, Matti, how was Regina?"

"Oh, Thomas, that sure was someting else. When I first got there, Jenny wasn't doing so good. Every day, me and Chloe could see she be going downhill. When they could do no more for her at the care home, she was moved to the hospital and put in one of them wards where your days be numbered. That same morning, who should come to visit, but her daughter Camilla and teenage sweetheart, Henry. Thomas, their timing couldn't have been more perfect, as poor Miss Jenny was minutes away from meeting her Maker—"

"You will have to fill me in on her daughter and what's this about her teenage sweetheart?"

For the next ten minutes, Matti told Thomas about the boy Jenny met when she was fifteen years old when she lived in Regina and the incident Jenny had with a group of boys that resulted in her conceiving a child. Thomas knew about Jenny's daughter because he recalled that day when Mr. Hamilton found out Miss Jenny had a daughter as result of a rape. There was such a ruckus and after that, things on the estate were never the same. Thomas, however, was not aware of Henry and how much Miss Jenny still loved him in spite of their separation.

"I tell you straight, Thomas, when them two looked at each other minutes before Jenny died, it be the most beautiful vision between two people in love I ever did see. Why those two went to heaven and back. The light around them glowed and brightened as if the sunrise be coming up in the room. All of us there be spell-bound. And then when Miss Jenny passed on to meet her Maker, a sadness filled the room like the sun going down and we be carrying a huge load of cement on our shoulders."

"That must have been quite the sight, Matti."

"Ain't seen not'ing like it before and never will again. It be one of those moments that one never forgets, that for sure. It didn't last long though and the sun came up again even brighter than before. The good Lord done bring Jenny back! The entire hospital was in such an uproar as if it be the fourth of July! Why, Chloe and me couldn't get into her room to see for ourselves how Jenny be doing. Every doctor in the hospital and all over the city came and squeezed into Jenny's room to see for themselves what the good Lord had done."

Thomas was so entranced by Matti's sharing, he hadn't taken a sip of coffee or sampled the cookie in his hand. He was just about to speak, but Matti beat him to it.

"Them two are sure in love, Thomas. Even though they were separated for all those years, it seemed like they never were apart. You'd have to be there to see the way them two kissed. Theirs is a match made in heaven, that's for sure."

Thomas swallowed the cookie he was chewing and took a sip of coffee, "I didn't know about Henry, Matti. That may complicate things for Mr. Hamilton."

Matti gazed at Thomas and her eyes brightened. "You and me on the same wave length. Mr. Hamilton wants Jenny back in the worse way and she has a man she be deeply in love with. I knows that don't sit right with Mr. Hamilton. He already asked me to encourage Jenny to come back to the estate. But, I told him that I can't do that. That be up to Jenny."

Thomas, nodded, tightened his lips and simply said, "Hmm."

"I remember you saying in this very same shed a few years ago, one day that man is going to realize the gem he had. He be awfully sorry now he didn't polish it like a good husband should."

Matti shook her head and added, "Mr. Hamilton be changing some, Thomas. He be more relaxed, kinder... if only he'd of been that way back when Miss Jenny was here, I 'spect we wouldn't be having this discussion."

Thomas nodded. He lifted his coffee mug, gesturing for more. Matti quickly got up and obliged him while at the same time said, "Jenny gave Mr. Hamilton a gift, that's for sure. By her presence and acceptance of him, she planted a powerful seed of goodness that we see sprouting and growing now."

"It's all part of God's divine providence, Matti. James' illness may have forced him to slow down and convalesce, but without Miss Jenny in his life to give him some direction, I dare say the man might have very well focused on his disease and how horrible it is. He could have become very angry like many people do and blame God. But you can see he has accepted his illness and he seems devoid of anger. Jenny gave the man a gift of love, Matti, all the while living in an intolerable situation. He learned how to see God's beauty and get outside of himself and grow. Remember God wants all of his children to come to Him. The sun shines on the good and those that err are still struggling. The good Lord worked through Jenny because she was obedient to His will and command to love, and not judge, and to accept. Yes, the man received a gift of true love. And now look at the result."

"She be a saint, Thomas."

"Yes, she definitely has saintly qualities, but her traits are possible by all of us if we just see the beauty and strength in her approach to life. She accepts what is, changes what she can and she has the wisdom to know the difference. She goes to the well, the fountain of life, constantly. She goes to her heavenly haven and restores her soul and mind just like it says in the 23rd Psalm… He leads me to the still waters; He restoreth my soul."

"Amen, brother, the good Lord be giving you a special gift too, Thomas; the gift of wisdom. Every time I talk to you, my life goes up a notch. Soon, I hope to develop wings and fly off into the garden with them butterflies. Can't you just see it Thomas? Why, with my good looks and well endowed body, them wings have to be mighty big for a lift off!"

The two laughed. A reflective silence fell over them, but soon Matti spoke softly.

"Mr. Hamilton sure be trying hard to get his Missus back. The flowers he sent to the hospital was one big surprise for all of us, especially for Jenny. It was like a piece of her garden grew suddenly out of the floor. Everywhere you looked were beautiful wildflowers. It lifted Jenny's spirit some… but I don't know." Matti shook her head and continued, "I can sure see why Mr. Hamilton be wantin' Jenny back, but it sure makes things difficult for Jen… and that other man, too. Why, Jenny and Henry have an entire future ahead of them and all of a sudden they be asked to give it all up for the sake and happiness of another."

"That's right, Matti. And it's not only James, but other members of the family are affected, as well. It's become a very powerful moral issue."

"See now, here it be getting too complicated. It's here I be turning it over to the Lord."

Thomas nodded, "I think you're right, Matti. I 'spect, you're right."

Matti got up and said, "Tell Ramon to come by the kitchen. I have fresh coffee for him and will warm up some cookies."

"That's great, Matti. I'll send him along straightaway. And by the way, did James talk to you yet about the guest house?"

"Guest house? What you mean, Thomas? We be expectin' someone?"

Thomas smiled and winked with a twinkle in his eyes. "You're in for one big surprise, Matti, that's for sure!"

CHAPTER FORTY SIX

THIS WAS THE third time the phone rang. Jenny knew it was James calling and she knew what he wanted. Yesterday and first thing this morning, Jenny was certain that every florist in the city had delivered flowers to her home. It was a good thing early summer was here and she could put some of the flowers onto the back patio. There wasn't any more room in the living room, kitchen or bedroom.

"Dear guardian angel, help me," Jenny whispered as she picked up the phone. "Hel… Hello…?" Her voice was barely audible.

"Jenny… is that you?"

"Yes, James, this is me, Jenny." She hadn't heard James call her Jenny since before they were married.

"Geez, I've been trying to reach you since yesterday… I was getting worried about you. Where have you been?"

Jenny was surprised that he didn't scold her for not answering the phone.

"I've been out in the yard much of the time… you know how much I love the garden."

"I do, Mar… Jen, and that's why I'm calling. The garden has never looked more beautiful. I'm out in the yard right now and want you to know, the Monarchs came yesterday; hundreds have arrived. We are all so excited to see them. I have to admit, Carlos is almost ecstatic. I've never seen anyone so excited to see his Mexican butterflies. He keeps raising his hands and spouts words in Spanish. I don't understand a word he's saying, but it must be good the way the butterflies swarm around him."

Jenny smiled. She could vividly recall her friend raising his hands that day when the Monarchs came and she was so worried over Tammy and not hearing from Henry… The sight of Carlos and the Monarchs was so uplifting then… it had given her such hope.

"Yes, I recall Carlos singing praises of joy when the Monarchs came to my parents' estate. He knows the area where they migrate back to and hibernate in Mexico."

"He was telling me about that; very interesting. He's concerned that a lot of the villagers are cutting down the trees for lumber where the Monarchs come home to."

"I saw a documentary on TV about that. It's so sad that people have to resort to destroying their habitat in order to live. There must be some other solution."

"I agree, Jenny. I have been talking to Carlos about how that can be curtailed. Perhaps there is something we can do."

Jenny couldn't believe her ears. James seemed so different; and to be concerned about butterflies? Unbelievable!

"The flowers you sent are beautiful, James. Please don't send anymore though, there is no more room to put them!"

"As long as you like them, Jen. But I have to say, they are nothing compared to the flowers that are blooming on the estate. Thomas agrees that the garden has never looked more beautiful. The only thing that is missing is you…"

A warm chill ran up and down her spine… she had anticipated this. She feared it and yet, just the way he was expressing himself seemed so warm. She was at a loss as how to respond.

"When my illness returned last year and I was forced to come back to the estate, I began to see things in a much different way, Jenny. At first it drove me crazy to slow down, but I have to admit, it was the best thing that ever happened to me. I began to see what you had enjoyed on the estate. It was all under my nose and I couldn't see it. I didn't take the time to see it. It took this damn cancer to force me to open my eyes. At first I thought it was all the flowers, the statue, the gazebo and butterflies that made the estate so beautiful and seemed to give you so much joy and peace. I tried to emulate and do everything that you did on the estate to see if I too, could capture that special something that was here…" James paused and then slowly said with such feeling that his words instantly touched her heart.

"One day, Jenny, while sitting on the swing in the gazebo, like I had seen you do many times over, it suddenly came to me at the core of my being, that what had awakened me had nothing to do with the flowers or the garden or the statue or any of these things… it was you, Jenny, and your unwavering acceptance of me. All the money and power I have at my command is nothing compared with—"

"Oh, James, please stop…" James' words were so sincere and Jenny knew where this was all heading. She could no longer travel down that path. She was so happy to finally come back to Henry and thought for certain they would soon wed. But now so many obstacles were in the way.

James was startled by Jenny's reaction and spoke with caution. "Jen, I don't mean to upset you…"

"Oh, James, I… I can't come back to you like we were. I have moved on with my life and am making a new start here in Regina. I have a daughter and—"

"But you have a son here as well, Jenny. Don't you see? I now realize that it is you who I want and need back in my life. You can restore my life and health. I am different now, we can be a family again and I will straighten things out with J.J. Jenny I need you, we all need you… don't you see?"

Jenny was becoming overwhelmed. James was making such progress and she didn't want to discourage him, but she had now given her heart to Henry and so desired to marry him. Dizziness began to overtake her… she had to let James know and not give him any hope.

James interrupted her thoughts, "I suppose it's that Pederson guy." She took a deep breath and dared to let it all out…

"Yes…"

"You have only known him for a few weeks, Jenny. Why would you want to give us up for him? It doesn't make sense."

"I love him, James. I have always loved him."

"So you don't love me, or J.J. or… your grandson?"

"I do, James, and I always will… but things are different now and I have a daughter here and Henry…" Jenny's words trailed off. She could hear James' breathing get louder.

"I am so sorry, James. I can't come back and try again. You will have to let go…"

"Geez, Jenny, I can't. I won't let you go; I don't want to lose you. I am ill and your love can restore my health and we can travel and be a happy family. I will straighten things out with J.J."

"I can't heal you, James. Perhaps prayer can."

"Then teach me how to pray. Come back and I will follow your example. I know you were out here every day, praying to God and—"

"James, it can't be the same as it was before. I now have others in my life that I just can't discard."

"You can see them, Jen. Bring your daughter here, and Henry is welcome anytime, we can all be together."

"James, I will support you and be here for you and help you in any way I can, but we can't go back."

"What about J.J. and Nora and Jimmy… can you discard them?"

"No, I can't do that either. I was hoping to talk to them and I would need your help… Of course I still want us to be family and for us to be friends. J.J., Nora and Jimmy are the only real parts of our marriage. You and I never developed a relationship." Finally, Jenny let out what she had been holding in for so many years. Finally, she felt James might actually be able to hear what she was saying.

"The day after we were married, I woke up to an empty bed. You were already gone and for most of our marriage it was the same. I often wondered how we were together long enough for me to even have conceived a child. Oh, how I loved J.J., but even him, you took from me. For most of the years after I gave birth to your son, we drifted apart. I was alone… if it had not been for the garden and staff who became my friends, I don't know what would have become of me." Jenny's voice rose almost imperceptibly while she spoke.

"But Jenny, I can repair all of that. I see the errors of my ways. I'm sure once you come back, so will J.J. We can be a real family… give me another chance."

Tears filled Jenny's eyes. She could hear the sincerity of James' words and she would have given anything for him to have said them years ago. But now... it was too late. She didn't want to hurt James with her next words, but at this point, she had no choice but to express them.

Jenny took a deep breath. "I've been given a second chance at life, James. My health is restored and the man I truly loved has come back into my life—"

"But you were mine first, Marj-Jen! You married me!"

"Yes, I did because Henry and you were the only men in my life. I think I saw in you some of the traits I saw in Henry."

"See, I have the same traits, Jen."

"It's not the same, James. The feelings I have for Henry are different! I'm so sorry James, but I cannot. I pray we can be friends and that J.J. comes back to me, too. Please, please, James, let me go... I don't want to hurt you..."

"I'm ill Jenny; having you back will restore my life. A miracle will happen like it did with you." As sincere as James was, Jenny realized he hadn't changed yet as much as it appeared; his motives for having her back were selfish. Jenny could see that what James wanted most was to restore his own life and was trying to use her to do it. Still, Jenny was filled with compassion...

"I can't, James, but I will be here for you. I will tend to you as much as I can. But it's Henry I truly love... I will be your closest friend, but I cannot be your wife any more..." Jenny said with a finality that hid the weakness she felt in her knees.

They were going around in circles and she was beginning to feel faint. She could hear James pleading over the phone and wanted to shut it all off. She laid down the receiver and walked away. She heard him calling her name as she opened the patio doors and stepped out onto her deck and closed the doors behind her. The sound of a chickadee came from the fir trees and soothed her. The sight of her garden began to seep into her spirit and calm her troubled heart. She felt so sorry for James. He was coming out of his shell and he needed her support and love, but she had none to give. She shook her head as she waded through all the flowers the florists had placed on the patio from James. He was trying so hard, *but what could she do*?

CHAPTER FORTY SEVEN

IT WAS EARLY Friday morning and the air was filled with new life. Henry couldn't help but notice the barn swallows zipping back and forth through the air. He knew they were building a nest between the floor boards underneath the deck. He loved watching their agility. As soon as they saw Henry standing on the deck, they zoomed towards him, threatening to strike him down if he dared come near their nest. He marveled at their boldness.

Henry loved this time of the year when everything was bursting with life. The drab colour of the trees during the winter was gone and their skeletons covered with fresh, green leaves to announce yet another season of life on his acreage. This was a perfect time to be down in the prayer house. The thought made him check his watch. He had to pick up Father and bring him back to do exactly that; spend time in God's creation.

In less than an hour, Henry and Father Engelmann were back at the acreage and slowly descending around the winding road that was carved into the side of the hill leading down to the valley bottom where the Poustinia was situated. The road was narrow and at times Henry's SUV came precariously close to the edge that dropped off into a deep gorge.

"You picked a great time to come to the prayer house, Father. Most of the runoff is finished but there's still enough to feel the power of the water rushing down the stream."

"Yes, it's all truly beautiful, Henry. You have been blessed with a slice of heaven," Father replied as he gazed out the truck window, overlooking the beautiful valley before him. Father never tired of seeing this scene as it came into view while the truck travelled around the hill. The pond in front of the Poustinia was like a sheet of glass reflecting perfectly into its mirror-like surface the small hut and clouds above. It immediately reminded him of the 23rd Psalm and he could hardly wait to sit on the deck and take in the peace of the still waters.

"Are things still pretty hectic at the care home?" Henry interrupted the silence.

"Yes, so many people coming for prayers and healing. They do not understand that it is not I who have the power to heal, but the good Lord."

"It's only natural, Father, that people would do that. They see you as a very holy man and expect God's power to be flowing through you." And before Father could respond with a more humbling tone to what he just said, Henry continued to ask, "Are your meetings coming to an end with the Archbishop?"

"For now, they are. John flew to Calgary to meet Peter, the man who fathered Camilla. The Archbishop said he will want to speak with me further on that, as a miracle has occurred there, as well."

"It's truly amazing all the healings that occurred that day."

"The Lord works in mysterious ways, yet what seems to be happening here is, in part, obvious, no. The Lord not only wants to heal physical illnesses, but deep emotional ones, as well."

"Jenny is coming out here tomorrow. We plan to come down and visit with you, if that's okay, and one of the things we wish to discuss is a meeting with Peter."

"Yes, please come down and, by all means, we must discuss Peter and how this affects both Jenny and her daughter and… you as well."

Henry slowed as he came to the bottom of the valley and cautiously travelled over the repaired road that was washed out by the spring runoff. Henry felt his tires sink slightly into the soft, fresh dirt. Once over, Henry followed the narrow trail to the Poustinia and parked the truck. Both men got out and walked onto the deck and breathed in the fresh air and soothing calm before them.

"Quite the sight, Father."

"It is, indeed, Henry. God's creation: the sky, land, water, birds, smell, taste and sound is perfect. Only an almighty God could have imagined it all and created it. Man is daily blessed with spiritual sustenance if he but takes the time to acknowledge it."

"So true, Father. It's hard to understand how daily we neglect our blessings or acknowledge our gifts."

Father Engelmann didn't respond. He turned and sat on one of the deck chairs and continued to gaze upon the still water of the pond. Henry mimicked Father's movements and pulled up another chair beside his teacher and sat down. The men remained silent, unable to speak, or rather not wanting to interfere with the growing peace seeping into their being. The scene before filled them with awe.

"So, you and Jenny have spent some time together and are getting to know one another again?"

"We have, Father, it's as if we were never apart. It's wonderful to have her back again."

"It is incredulous, Henry, that I didn't connect Jenny as the girl next door to you. I knew there was something special and familiar about her, but never would I have conceived that she was your teenage sweetheart."

"It is truly astonishing how this all turned out and how we all are so connected."

"Only the Lord, in His divine providence, could have worked it all out so beautifully."

"I gave Jenny her home back and everything in it exactly the way she had left it. That's another incredible part of all this, as so many other potential buyers saw the home before I did."

"Yes, it is as you have said several times before, an angelic occurrence, that it was you who purchased the home." Father shook his head in amazement of it all.

There was a brief silence and then Henry broke the quiet of the surroundings. "I was going to ask you Father… Jenny and I had our first date the other night and it was wonderful, but I can see that I would like marriage to be soon in the offing. What is the Church's position on this since Jenny is divorced?"

"Yes, I was thinking of that as well, and did discuss it with the archbishop the other day. The church does not recognize divorce but will consider an annulment of the marriage under very strict circumstances."

Henry's face immediately carried a concerned look. "What kind of circumstances, Father?"

"First of all, the Catholic Church's teaching, or position, on divorce is based upon a time-honoured interpretation of the words of Jesus, "What therefore God has joined together let no man put asunder." (Matthew 19:6). "The Church views marriage as a covenant for life that cannot be severed. However, some marriages are entered into without the necessary maturity or full knowledge and ability to keep such a permanent commitment, or without full free will because of external pressures. If it can be shown that the marriage bond was less than such a covenant for life because it was lacking something necessary from the very beginning the Church can declare an ecclesiastic annulment of the marriage.

"During my visits with Jennifer, we did talk about her marriage, but I am not at liberty to discuss that with you, Henry. It is best that she speak to me or if you and Jenny decide, we can all look at the issue. Annulments are not easy to come by and can take considerable time."

As Father spoke, Henry's heart began to sink, yet he tried to find some reason for hope. "I do know that Jenny's marriage was not a favourable one, Father. I, too, do not know all of the circumstances yet, but I'm sure there must be some way Jenny can get an annulment."

Father just nodded, not ready to commit himself until he knew all of the facts. He did recall Jenny sharing with him the uncertainty and pressure she felt the day of their marriage and that she fainted after saying 'I do.'

"If it could be shown that she did not freely agree to the marriage, then, that could be cause for an annulment." Father added out loud.

Henry didn't hear Father's words and asked, "Do both parties have to agree to the annulment, Father?"

"Yes, agreement by both the wife and husband more readily facilitates the annulment—"

"That may be another problem." Henry swiftly interjected. "I already received a phone call from her former husband, James, asking me to discourage my relationship with Jenny as he wants her back. He said that he was sorry for his behaviour and for not only his sake, but that of his son and family, he desires for them to try again."

Father tightened his lips, his expression growing more serious. He knew of all of the impediments that Henry and Jenny had endured during their lives. Now, when it seemed so close to their getting back together another one, a major one in fact stood before them.

"The Church always encourages reconciliation, Henry. If the husband refuses to grant an annulment and informs the Church or the tribunal in charge of the case that he seriously wants to try again and can show by a sincere confession supported by witnesses that he is serious, the Church may not grant the annulment."

"But Father, they have to! I don't think I could take it if Jenny and I could not be wed."

Father's position was firm. "Without annulment, the Church will not grant you and Jenny consent to marry in the Church."

"I would never want to leave the Church, Father, but... I don't know what I would do. I already desire Jenny so much now, that I don't know if I can wait much longer." Henry wished he hadn't blurted out that last remark. He wondered if Father understood what he meant. It didn't take long for Henry to know Father's mind.

"If you are referring to having sexual relationships with Jenny, you both would be engaging in an adulterous affair. Since divorce is not recognized by the Church, she is still considered married—"

Henry shook his head and muttered, "I can't believe this, I just find this all so incredulous..." His words trailed off.

Father could sense the deep disappointment in his adopted son. "There is one other consideration. Jenny married outside of the Catholic Church. Did she receive dispensation from the Church to do so?"

Henry looked at Father and shrugged his shoulders, "I don't know."

Father nodded, "Henry, we are putting the cart before the horse. Let us take one step at a time. Discuss this with Jenny and encourage her to come either alone or the two of you, which I prefer, and we shall review the facts and what steps we should take."

Father was hesitant to ask the next question, but felt it was key to even considering going forward.

"Has Jenny's former husband approached her about reconciliation; wanting to try again?"

"We didn't discuss it in detail, but I would have to say yes. He called her when she was in the hospital and also sent her flowers... so, I would have to say yes to your question, Father."

"Then the next question has to be, Henry, how does Jenny feel about his request? Would she consider going back? There are others involved. She does have a son and I understand a grandson—"

"Yes, yes, I know!" Henry blurted out in frustration. "I was thinking about that the other night... it's all getting so mixed up. I'm certain Jenny wants to marry me, but there are now so many complications, so many impediments. Oh Father," Henry lamented, "I love Jenny so much, but I would want for us to be married in the Church and I would want for everyone to be at peace about it all, especially Jenny. *How on earth can this all come about?*"

Henry gazed hard at his mentor and dear lifelong friend, hoping he would say something that would give him hope in all this. Suddenly, the calm, serene scene of the valley before him no longer pacified his dark and stormy mind.

"All I can say, Henry, is that God is the God of all possibilities. Nothing is impossible to Him if we put all our trust in Him. But, we must accept His will in the matter. This I know, Henry, if you do trust Him, He will turn it all into good."

Henry just shook his head; he didn't want to discuss it any further. It was too upsetting. "Well, I better get going Father. I have an appointment at the gallery."

Henry got up and made his way into the Poustinia. "I want to check if there is enough water in the fridge."

Father got up and followed Henry inside.

"Did you want me to bring down any food?" Henry asked as he opened the fridge.

"No, I wish to fast for a few days. There are so many concerns—"

"Well, you have enough water for three or four days. I can bring more tomorrow if you like."

"I think that is fine, Henry. I will let you know tomorrow. I am not sure how long I will be staying this time."

Henry walked into the living room. The first thing that struck him was the large cross hanging on the wall and the small altar below. He knew Father would be saying Mass as soon as he left. "Everything looks like new, Father; hardly lived in."

Henry peeked into the bedroom and noted the desk in front of the picture window exposing a panoramic view of the valley. He turned and forgot Father was carrying a satchel. Henry grew curious. "Got your Bible, Father?"

Father lifted his satchel slightly, "Yes, it's here and…"

"Have you got more than one, this time?" Henry further wondered, as the Bible was all Father usually carried with him.

Father could see Henry's curiosity and so he decided to share what he had in the satchel. Father walked into the bedroom and took out his Bible and placed it on the table. He then reached into the case again and brought out several pads of paper and a pen.

Henry knew Father never wrote a homily and always relied upon the Holy Spirit, so he asked, "Making notes on scriptural readings?"

Father was a bit hesitant to reveal that he was about to write a story about them; he, Jenny and Henry and thoughts about life. Father simply said, "Perhaps I will be noting some Scripture as needed and… well… I am going to write a story, Henry. For now, I am keeping it to myself… you shall soon see what it is about."

"You mean, an actual book, like a novel?"

Father nodded, "Yes, Henry, it's a story about life. In fact, it's a love story involving miracles and angels and all the things that happen in God's kingdom." Father smiled, "It's going to be a story that may have an effect upon a lot of God's children."

"Now you really have me curious, Father, I never knew you wanted to write a story and, a love story at that."

"Neither did I, Henry. One never knows when one wakes up in the morning what God has planned for their lives. Suffice it to say, God sent his messenger, my guardian angel, to let me know that this is part of the reason for my coming back from the other side."

"To write a love story?"

Father nodded and smiled with a twinkle in his eye.

"Yes, Henry, an epic love story."

Chapter Forty Eight

Thomas took off his cap and with the back of the same hand, wiped the perspiration from his brow. It was a hot afternoon on the estate and now he wished he had mowed the grass that morning. On his way to the shed to get some gas for the lawn mower, he saw James sitting on the swing in the gazebo. He knew his employer was troubled and his heart went out to him. He recalled only too well, the struggle he, himself, had gone through growing out of a life style that would have killed him. He suspected James was struggling with many of the same issues.

"Afternoon, James. It's another fine day. How are you feeling?"

James closed Thomas' Bible that he was reading and looked at the gardener. Rather than answer as to the state of his health, he said, "Can't make much of what's in here," as he lifted the Bible towards Thomas. "Nothing but a bunch of small stories about a man named Jesus, travelling around the country with His buddies teaching His philosophy of life."

"Yes, He is teaching the people a way to live that will bring peace and harmony into their lives, but there is a little bit more to it than that—"

"The part I really want to know, Thomas, is how to get Marjorie back on the estate and into my life again. Is there a part in this Book that may show me… specifically?"

Thomas smiled and entered the gazebo. He sat on the ledge of the railing surrounding the gazebo and asked James, pointedly, "Has Miss Jenny declined to come back to the estate, James?"

James smiled, "Can't sidetrack you from the real issue, can I? Yes, as a matter of fact, I was speaking with her the other day and she flatly refused to come back. I sent her flowers and told her I was a different man and wanting to try again, but…" James shook his head and looked down at the Bible.

Thomas could feel the pain James was going through, not only physically but the sorrow of a great loss in his life. He was still so confused about what it is that brings two people together and keeps them together.

"I don't wish to speak out of turn, James—"

"No, say what's on your mind. You're the first person I could ever talk to about stuff like this… actually, stuff that really matters. Look, Thomas, I'm desperate, what the hell can I do?"

"There was a time when you and Miss Jenny were attracted to one another… to the degree that you married. The thing is, James, this attraction wanes in time and couples grow distant unless their relationship is nurtured by care, kindness, acceptance, forgiveness, commitment and… I could go on and on."

James could see right off that he didn't do any of what Thomas just rattled off. At that time, he lived in the world of business. He not only didn't have time, he didn't take time and even if he had, didn't have a clue how to show love and commitment. Yet, what Thomas said, struck a chord. It was what Jenny exhibited all the time… only he didn't reciprocate. She had pointed that out to him when they last spoke, too. Her words came to mind, "We never developed a relationship. The day after we were married I woke up to an empty bed. You were already gone and for most of our marriage it was the same. I often wonder how we were together long enough for me to even have conceived a child. Oh, how I loved J.J., but even him, you took from me…" James couldn't handle the truth that was exposing his gross failure. In self defense, he blurted, "Look, Thomas, I don't want to make excuses, but at that time I was running a huge corporation… I didn't have time to nurture our relationship."

"But you do now. You may have been forced to stop, but perhaps it's good in the sense you are beginning to realize what you missed. The Bible you're holding may not give you a step by step list of how to get Miss Jenny to reconsider to come back, but it will show what it takes to love and care for another. Like I said, I don't want to speak out of turn, but could it be possible that had you lived by the philosophy of what you have been reading about Jesus, that we may not even be having this discussion? It's up to you, James, but what that Book will do is expose who for you are and what you need to do to find peace and direction in your life. As I said, there is a lot more to it, but for now, that may be a start to assist you with your relationship with Miss Jenny."

"What do you mean, Thomas?"

"Well, the Bible pointed out to me, for example, something I was very guilty of that kept me from enjoying life and my fellow man—"

"What was that?" James was eager to know.

"Perhaps I can answer that better if I tell you a bit about myself. I wasn't always a landscaper, James."

"That's right, Carlos mentioned to me the other day that you were a lawyer at one time. How the hell did you end up as a landscaper, Thomas?"

"I'm glad you asked, James. I was about to share that with you. It may be hard for you to believe, but there are similarities in our lives." Thomas shifted on the railing, trying to make himself more comfortable.

James shifted to one end of the swing. "Here, sit down on the swing, Thomas."

"My pants are soiled—"

"No matter, Thomas, please, sit."

Thomas sat down and began to tell James about his background.

"My parents sent me to London in the late fifties to study law. They both worked hard and wanted a better life, so they thought, for their son. I did have two siblings but they died during one of the hurricanes that hit the island."

"Was that the same storm that killed Matilda's parents?"

Thomas nodded. "Yes, it was the same one; literally wiped out the island. Dad was determined to get me off the island perhaps even more so, to prevent nature from taking his last child should another such hurricane hit Jamaica again. In any case, I worked hard and grades came easy to me. I graduated at the top of my class. Many firms wanted to hire me, but were concerned about my colour and worried that many clients would not accept me. There was one firm however, who took a chance and eventually offered me a position as one of the partners…" Thomas paused and then added, "I'll get to that part of it.

"At first, many clients by-passed me, but for those who didn't, my success rate as a trial lawyer was one hundred percent. I worked hard and thought of every angle and anticipated every question or issue that would arise by the defense attorney or judge. Soon, clients were clamouring to get me to represent them…"

Thomas paused and looked hard at James. "I don't say this in a boastful manner, but more-so to let you know that I was very successful and made more money than I ever dreamed possible. My income in a few days was more than what my father made in a year on the island. I was living high and fast and was accepted in high society circles. I considered myself a very important man and rubbed shoulders with many important people of influence."

"Well now, if I haven't seen it all," muttered Matti as she walked down the stone path and saw Thomas and James sitting on the swing together. "Never in all my years would I have thought I would live to see such a sight!"

Both men looked her way as she walked up to them carrying a tray with a glass of water, several plastic vials and a pot of tea.

"Afternoon, gentlemen, you two be looking mighty comfortable. I brought you your medicine, Jim, and some tea."

"Thanks Matilda, I'll just have the water. Perhaps Thomas might enjoy the tea?"

"Why yes, if James doesn't care for it, I would enjoy some tea, Matti." Thomas held the cup and saucer while Matti filled the cup with tea all the while almost imperceptibly shaking her head in disbelief.

"I suppose you two be wanting some of my fine cookies?"

Both men politely declined. "Well then, I best be on my way. I wouldn't want to be interrupting an important discussion."

Thomas took a sip of his tea and reached over to the ledge and set it down. "You were saying how you made all that money and became a man to be reckoned with."

Thomas grinned and shook his head trying to tone down what James said.

"Interesting thing is, James. I had the world by the tail, but I wasn't happy. In fact, I could tell I was losing my health. I couldn't sleep… much of it had to do with getting clients off that I knew were guilty as sin. I even got two men acquitted who were guilty of murder. I knew deep down that most of the people who I considered friends were interested in me only because of my success… but to make a long story short, James, I had lost my way in life and even though I was living a life that many would consider far above that of my parents, I knew they were much happier than me. I realized this even more when something happened."

This time, James shifted on the swing and took another sip of water. Thomas took that as a cue and reached over for his tea and took a gulp. As he sat it back on the ledge, James asked, "So what happened, Thomas?" James was eager to know.

"You may have heard about the case. It was a modern day Jeckyll and Hyde murder case. A prominent doctor, who was afflicted with a mental disorder, selected certain patients of his to terminate their lives during operations he performed on them. It was a colleague of the doctor who eventually noticed what was different in his procedure with some patients that led to their untimely death. After studying the reports and cases, I came to the same conclusion as the doctor who reported my client. He definitely was guilty. Day in and day out I would walk into the court room and see the many spouses and family members who had lost a parent or child under the hands of my client. My conscience began to get the better of me. It was my mother's death that saved me. I asked for week adjournment to fly back to the island and it was granted."

Thomas paused and started to reach for his tea and then stopped short and continued. "As soon as I got off the plane in Jamaica, the island air hit my nostrils and a peace that I had forgotten swept through me like a healing balm. At that instant, I knew I could never return to the life I knew in London. Unfortunately, it took my mother's death for me to realize it. In the days that followed, that peace began to grow deeper. The first week passed and I called the firm and told them I needed more time. Reluctantly they agreed. They needed me more than I needed them. My client was furious and threatened to sue the firm. After the second week, the firm offered me a full partnership if I returned immediately and still, I refused.

"It was during that third week, however, that my decision was made. I began to work side by side with my father helping him with the landscaping on the estate he looked after. I had never seen so much beauty. The colours of the flowers, the aroma and different species began to open my eyes to the beauty of nature and the spiritual sustenance it provided. The wind and air and scent of the sea, was like opium to my frazzled mind, filling me with peace. The clouds lazily drifting in the blue sky calmed my troubled spirit… not only had I forgotten all this, but its beauty hit me to the depths of my being, even more so than as a young lad before I left for London. I had taken it for granted back then, but now, I realized to my very core what life was all about. And it was the peace that I was beginning to feel that confirmed it."

"Had you told me this over a year ago, I wouldn't have understood a word you were saying. But I know exactly what mean, Thomas. This past year on the estate has made me realize the same thing. Who would have thought slowing down and looking at nature and examining one's life could possibly have such an effect upon one's personal wellbeing! I thought that was for philosophers or people that have too much time on their hands."

The two men shared a knowing smile of something they had in common and James asked, "So did you leave the firm?"

Thomas nodded, "I called the firm and submitted my verbal resignation. They threatened to sue and blackball me; claimed I would never practice law again. And that suited me fine. After that telephone conversation I was floating like one of the clouds in the sky. The next day I was kneeling in the dirt wearing one of my Italian made trousers and white shirt. By the end of the first day when I took my clothes off and looked at the soiled condition they were in, I actually picked up my pants and kissed them and laughed and laughed. Something I hadn't done in years.

"In the months that followed, I learned more about plants and herbs and where to place them than I could ever have learned in the finest, horticultural school, anywhere in the world. I still don't claim to ever coming near to what my daddy knew."

Thomas paused for a moment in memory of his father and then

continued, "I couldn't believe that the owners of the estate never came to their island mansion, but wanted it maintained for that odd week or two that they came to enjoy what they owned."

James squirmed on the swing. It was becoming painful for him to sit on the swing.

"We can continue this another time, James."

"No, I'm fine, doesn't matter where I sit, it will be the same. Anyway, I can relate to what you were saying, Thomas. I never realized either the treasure that I had right under my nose… I was too busy… or rather, chose to be."

Thomas nodded. "Yes, it's sad that so many of us fail to enjoy what we have and more importantly, the beauty of God's creation that surrounds us each and every day. My momma used to write and scold me for not coming home; that I was always on the run and never took time for family and to enjoy life. 'Life is short, Tommy,' she used to say to me, 'soon you will grow old and all the good moments are gone.'"

Thomas stopped and nodded, "It was this awareness that I had forgotten since leaving the island that opened my eyes again. It was as if I had fallen into a deep sleep and was on a train that moved so fast that I didn't see the beautiful landscaping the train was travelling through. The journey only focused on winning, making money, being at the top, success, the challenge of another case and more accolades. I was becoming a very proud man and more powerful and influential by the day. This was what held my vision, my attention, and was my goal in life."

James' eyes clouded as he identified with Thomas. He knew only too well that train trip. He had been on it for all of his life. His father had, too, and certainly now, J.J. was following their lead. James began to understand himself through the gardener's sharing of his life. James was seeing what Thomas was doing by opening himself up… it was for him. James was touched and softly said, "Go on, Thomas."

"I was a very proud man, James. My desire to be the best consumed me."

"You don't appear to be proud though, Thomas, rather the opposite…very humble."

"As soon as I quit the rat race, my desire to be the best was no more. I was no longer in competition with everyone, just myself. I now had a different goal. I wanted to grow and be the best human being I could. I wanted to be better than I was the day before. As soon as I quit competing with others, pride slid off me and was replaced by a peace I hadn't known. I saw it in my mother and father. They just accepted others and lived with them side by side just like the flowers in a field or the trees in the forest. They simply bloom where they are planted. One flower may be prettier than the other, but to the flowers they just are. They give all glory to their creator and when their time under the sun is over, they simply accept their death, as well, and return to the soil."

A silence descended upon the men. Thomas looked down at his hands as if counting his fingers and thanking God for the gift of being able to hold and touch the earth and make the world more beautiful by the gift the Lord had given him. James, on the other hand, appeared to be calm, however, his mind was swirling. Everything Thomas had said revealed his own character. He was the best, and was in competition with everyone, every moment of his life to prove himself better and with more power. He recalled how he competed with his brother for his father's attention. He felt pangs of guilt as flashes of his brother's hatred for him dimmed his eyes. His competition with his class mates, his professors, his colleagues… everyone was inferior. Even when one of his executives challenged him, for days he would snub him and prove him wrong until the man lost his confidence.

Could his entire life have been wrong? All the anxiety, frustration, anger, endless hours of work, struggling and conniving, and manipulating…for what? It never gave him any inner peace, happiness or love…what's that? He thought power and wealth would give it to him, but it all betrayed him. It was all an illusion that continuously left him empty.

This past year was the first and only year he had come close to experiencing what life really was all about. It took an illness to open his eyes. It took a disease to make him see and appreciate the beautiful woman he had been married to. She had exhibited all the qualities of life right from the start of their marriage that could have helped him out of his self imposed prison. She was devoid of competition, devoid of pride, devoid of judgmental attitude and criticism. She accepted others and softly spoke her side just openly and not defensively, unless others' actions caused harm or injury in some way. It was Marjorie who had given him the first inkling of being accepted and having to look at himself and his behaviour because there was nothing to attack. How do you fight and quarrel with someone who shows love and acceptance? It's the most frustrating experience and yet transcends normal understanding because we live in a world that functions primarily upon conditional love and acceptance.

He owed Marjorie his life!

James gazed hard at Thomas and nodded his head. *Could there be promise for him?*

"What must I do to win Marjorie back?" James blurted. "That farm boy just might steal her away from me!"

Incredibly, James had just experienced such incredible insight into himself through Thomas's sharing yet, he didn't see how trapped he still was in his old world.

"It's a process James, growing out of the old habits and perceptions, into new ones; it takes time. But if we stick to it and …"

"And what, Thomas?"

"I prayed a lot, James, for the Lord to help me. I believe we need His strength to grow out of ourselves."

Thomas stared hard at James and dared to challenge James' thinking. "I see getting Miss Jenny back as just another competitive venture of yours, James. Pride is rearing its head. You see Henry as inferior to you. What could Miss Jenny possibly see in a man from the farm? Could it be James, that that's the very thing that Miss Jenny sees and understands and drives her away from you? You wish to own her; she is just another possession in your eyes. Do you really want her back because you love her, or do you want her back to prove that you are better than Henry; that you own this precious lady and for the whole world to see just how lucky you are?"

Thomas stopped and dared to glance at his employer, fully expecting a blast, but what Thomas saw was a man whose light just went on; an 'aha' moment. James was speechless.

"Yes, Thomas, yes… how can Jenny love me? She often said that I consider her as another possession, an acquisition… yes, but… but how do I love her Thomas? I don't know how to love… I love in the only way I know how."

"You have made the first step James. You have become aware of who you are and the need to become who you really are. It takes some soul searching and total honesty. It hurts to look at ourselves honestly, but the struggle is worth it all. Gradually, you will come to know what it means to love. It's within you. Jenny saw it all the time and that's why she accepted you. You see, at the core of your being is love… a reflection of your creator. As you grow and come closer to this core you will draw love from it… true honest to goodness love.

"At the start of our conversation, I said that the Bible pointed out to me something I was very guilty of that kept me from enjoying life and my fellow man—"

"Most of what you were talking about seemed to centre around your pride. Was that it?" James was eager to know if his assessment was correct.

"Yes, James; pride. It's our pride, James, that is truly the root of all our problems. Overcome your pride, James, and I will guarantee you heaven on earth."

"Is that what you have gleaned from the Bible?"

"Yes, Jesus Christ taught us how to love. He laid out the map for us; how we should live with one another. As we yield our will more and more to Him and discipline ourselves with His strength to follow Him and His teachings, we grow to love. You will soon see, James, as you read the Bible, His example to love, to forgive, to accept, to not judge, and to even go the distance to die for us in spite of our sinfulness—".

"That's the part I was just reading when you came by earlier. It makes me skeptical of the whole thing, Thomas. If Jesus is God's son, why on earth would He come down to earth and put up with all that crap? Allowing Himself to be tortured, scourged, and crucified and… what kind of Father is God to allow this to happen to His Son? If my son was in that position, I would zap all those involved in a minute. It doesn't make sense."

"Once you understand the entire picture, James, it will. Out of love for us and to open the gates of heaven so that when we die, we may join Him for eternity, His Son agreed to die for us in payment for all our sins. Trust me, James, when the full impact of that hits your mind, heart and soul you will understand the tremendous sacrifice Jesus made for us. We were talking about pride. What you just described about Jesus putting up with all the abuse and torture is the perfect example of humility. There isn't an ounce of pride to be found in what Jesus and God the Father did for us."

Thomas said those words with such depth of meaning, tears surfaced in his eyes.

"You know, Thomas, when I sit here and look back over the years and how I treated Marjorie, in many ways she was like that Christ guy. She put up with a lot of crap that I threw at her almost every day and yet, she just accepted it and returned kindness and acceptance of me. And now look, here we are years later and I am begging to have her back. Clearly, in spite of the hell I put her through; she was the happier, the stronger, more at peace and better off."

James shook his head, "I'm confused. I just don't understand it, Thomas."

"You're doing fine, James. Just keep working on the pride and it will all come together."

A silence descended upon the two men. The air was cooling off and Thomas sensed it. He checked his wrist watch and made a motion to get up, but then sat back. There was something further he wanted to say.

"In our discussions, James, it seems to me you are expressing sorrow for the way things were between you and Miss Jenny…?"

James nodded, "Yes, I regret a lot of things, Thomas, but most of all was the way I treated Marjorie."

"Have you ever told her that, James?"

James reflected for a few moments and then said, "Not in so many words. I have asked her to come back and that I need her and that we all do. I suppose that implies I was sorry for the way I treated her, but… it's not the same as if I came right out and said I was sorry…is it?"

"Well, James, if you recognize pride within yourself and want to work on that and your relationship with Miss Jenny, it seems to me that would be a mighty big step to take."

Chapter Forty Nine

HI Matti, I was hoping you would answer the phone."

"Good, Lord, it's my sweet Jenny, the miracle girl! I best be sitting down, I feel all the blood rushing to my head and there's none left for my feet!"

"Oh, Matti... so, how are you doing? I sure miss you."

"I miss you, too, Jen. Every morning as soon as I get out of bed I get on my knees and thank Jesus for giving you back your life and restoring your health. It be just as big a miracle as He did for His beloved Lazarus. I just knew He was going to do it!"

"Well, I not only got my health back, but my house, too, Matti. Henry gave it back to me. Everything is turning out perfectly... well, almost."

"I know what you are leading up to, Jen. That former husband of yours is feeling so sorry for divorcing you. He'd give anything to have you back on the estate."

"I could never hide anything from you, Matti. James has asked me to come back, but I just can't do that anymore."

"That's what I keep telling him. You be a free woman now and I keep telling him that another man be callin' at your door. But he won't accept that and keeps asking me to convince you to come back."

"Oh, Matti, I don't want you to get involved in this—"

"I tell him that over and over; that it's your life and best thing is to just let you be."

"What I meant was that I don't want to worry you or make you upset over our affairs."

"Jen, you be family to me and when someting ain't right then I want to be there for you and help anyway I can."

"Thank you, Matti. And I do feel like you're family and free to discuss things with you… has J.J. been to the estate lately?" Jenny wanted to know.

"Charles say he be here when I was in Regina with you. The boy and his daddy had a big fight. I 'spect part was over you. Mr. Hamilton wants his son to make up with you."

"That's so good of James, but I still haven't heard from J.J. and apparently he and Nora have separated."

"Yes, Jim be tellin' us at the supper table the other night. He's very upset about that."

The phone grew silent for the longest moment and then Jenny dared to ask, "When you said Jim just now, Matti, did you mean… Mr. Hamilton… James?"

"Sorry, Jen, I should be explaining; a few things been happenin' around here. You might want to sit down, Jen, this be hard to believe."

"Tell me, Matti, I'm on the edge of my seat."

"Well, first of all, we all be having dinner together, with Mr. Hamilton… me, Thomas and his wife, Charles, and sometimes the new gardener, Carlos, joins us as well."

"Just wait a moment, Matti, you said so much I can't take it all in. You said, all of you are having dinner together?"

"Yes, Ma'am! Mr. Hamilton decided he wants company when he eats! And another t'ing, Jen, he gave me one of the guest houses all my own, and Thomas and his wife the other, and he's having the storage house renovated for Charles. It's so beautiful near the lake, I don't want to come to work anymore. We each have the lease to the house until we die or decide to leave—"

"I can't believe what I'm hearing, Matti. James actually gave you and other staff guest houses on the estate?"

"Yes, Jen. We all thought, like you, the man be fooling with us, but he's dead serious. I have to say, Jen, that man be changing some.

He be a different man from the time you were here on the estate, that for sure. In many ways it be a bigger miracle than yours!"

"And you are all having dinner together...?"

"Yes, just like we be one big happy family. He says I should call him Jim or James and he leave it up to me to decide, or I can call him both. First time I calls him Jim, I braced myself for the biggest scolding since I broke my momma's tea pot that belonged to her momma. But, no sir, he be as calm as a low cloud driftin' slowly in the sky on a warm summer evening. Why, we be talking lately like we be the best of friends. I be more surprised than you! Never in all my days, would I have imagined sittin' at the table with the master of the house like he was one of my kin... that's for sure!"

Jenny was flabbergasted. She didn't know what to say. Perhaps James really was changing and not just putting on a front to entice her to come back.

"And, did you say Carlos is now at the estate... the one that used to work at my parents' residence?"

"The very same one. How Carlos goes on and on about how much he loved it when you were at home on your momma and daddy's estate. He claims you were just like a butterfly. I think the master hired him because he knows how much you like Carlos. It may be a strategy of his... his mind be going all the time, Jen... but in a good way... know what I'm saying?"

Jenny chuckled, "Yes, I know what you're saying." Jenny paused briefly to catch her breath. If only James had done that when they were married, she would doubt very much she would be here in Regina. This was all so hard to believe. Perhaps James was already working on the concern she had about her son, too.

"Part of why I called was to talk to you, Matti, but also to tell you that I am thinking of coming to Ottawa towards the end of August. I would like to see Nora, and also visit with my grandson. Hopefully I will see J.J. as well. I am going to ask Henry to come with me and so we would plan to stay in one of the hotels nearest the estate."

"When Mr. Ham... I mean, James, hears about this he will insist on you staying on the estate... I don't know about Henry, if he be welcome here or not. I think James might just be determined enough to buy all the hotels in Ottawa and say, 'no vacancy' just to make sure you come here."

Jenny chuckled, "Oh, Matti…"

"Maybe talk to Henry and see if it's okay for you to stay here."

"I'm not sure if that will work. It's all still in the planning stages and I will let you know what I decide. I am seeing Henry tomorrow; I may discuss it with him then."

"You give him one big hug from Matilda. I could see all the way through you when you be living on the estate that Henry was the man in your dreams. When I saw the two of you kiss when you lay dying on your death bed, I just knew there was a love between you that heaven made. Why, when your lips touched his, there was such an aura around you both. It was a light from Jesus himself, I just knew it, Jen. I even heard a choir of angels sing in the room. I knew it right then and there that you would be healed. There ain't not'ing, no sir, not'ing that a love like that can't do. I knew Jesus be healing you and He did."

Before Jenny could respond, Matti rambled on. "As much as I like the way the master be changing and wanting you back at the estate, you make up your own mind, Jenny. You were alone for years and years; I saw how lonely you were so many times, and how that young boy of yours be taken away from you. Your heart broke in so many places, I can't even count, Jen. No, you follow your heart…"

If only it were that easy, thought Jenny.

"Yes, I am very fond of Henry. I am so excited; he is taking me to his home in the valley tomorrow. I can't wait to see it, especially his studio where he paints!"

"You mentioned before he be an artist. I done forgot. Why, you be the perfect model for him, Jen. I 'spect he pick up the brush straight away as soon as he have you in the studio!'

Jenny chuckled. "He's more of a landscape painter, Matti. I'm sure he's not interested in painting me."

"Don't you be selling yourself short. One look at you and any man be wanting to paint you in his mind. Best you keep them clothes on!"

Jenny laughed again and then quickly changed the subject. "Camilla, Henry and I are thinking of flying to Calgary to meet Peter and his family."

"You mean the man that fathered Camilla?"

"That's right, Matti. Apparently he was very ill with cancer and died and miraculously, he too, was brought back to life and fully restored. He called Henry a couple of weeks ago and wants very much to see me and Camilla and make up for what he did."

"Praise the Lord, Jen. This be one big healing party. I just know you be forgiving that man. I recall the look of sorrow in his eyes when I met him at Father Engelmann's anniversary. He recognized his daughter for sure and I could feel the ache in his heart. At the time I didn't 'spect that he be Camilla's daddy. Well, if that don't take the cake. My, my, how the good Lord works... my, my... and that ain't the end of this story, that's for sure..."

"What do you mean, Matti?"

"Last Sunday evenin', my sister, Coreena, called to let me know she and that man of hers be flying to Regina to see his momma. She said she and Eddy may also go visit his friend, Peter, in Calgary. She told me that Eddy was with the boys that night when they took you to the park. My heart nearly fell open, Jen, when she told me that. I knew Eddy be Peter's friend, but didn't know he was in with the boys that done you wrong that evenin'."

"I recall the first time you told me that your sister met this man from Regina whose name was Eddy. When you described how short he was and wore his hair in a high wave, I suspected it was Eddy, but wasn't sure. I do know now, however, that it was the same Eddy. In fact, Matti, Henry called me an hour ago to tell me that Eddy and his wife are in Regina right now and that we are planning to have dinner together. Henry also said that Eddy wants to talk to me and apologize for what they did that night."

"I be praising the Lord from now until kingdom come. And here I thought the Lord be out fishing and not tendin' to business and not healing you sooner. Why He be laying back on one of them fluffy clouds and thinking how on earth He be bringing this entire situation together! Whoopee! Now ain't that some creative thinking!"

"It truly is amazing how all of our lives are connected and all working together for the good!"

"Couldn't have said it any better myself, Jen. That's the way God works! He causes all things to work together for good for those who love Him, to those who are called accordin' to His purposes. Yes, sir, this all be one big healin' party! Whoopee!"

CHAPTER FIFTY

JENNY GREW SILENT as Henry turned his vehicle and drove slowly down the lane to his cedar log home. Ginger and Coco had already greeted him and were nipping each other as they escorted the SUV past the red barn and down into the valley. Two horses in the pasture looked up briefly and then hung their heads and resumed eating the green summer grass.

What a difference in estates, thought Jenny, between the Hamilton Greystone Manor and entrance to Henry's farm. She felt instantly as relaxed as the two horses she just saw grazing in the field under the warm sun. Every now and then she saw glimpses of the valley between the huge fir trees that lined the road. No wonder the entrance read: Sudden Valley Ranch. One didn't expect to see a valley dropping off so suddenly from the flat prairies.

"This is beautiful, Henry," Jenny said, as the truck turned the bend in the lane at the bottom of the hill, exposing the home and the valley all around. Jenny was spellbound by the view and remained speechless.

Henry pressed the garage door opener. "I'll close the garage door behind us to keep the dogs out, otherwise they'll lick you to death. We'll meet them later when we go down into the valley."

"Yes, they're such beautiful dogs, I want to meet them."

Henry led Jenny through the mud/laundry room and then into the large foyer which led in three directions: a stairway leading to the upper level, the living room to the left and the kitchen straight ahead.

Jenny made her way to a wall and touched its smooth surface. "Henry, I just love the cedar log interior, it feels so warm and looks so inviting."

"Yeah, I like it too. Come on, I'll show you where I usually hang out in the sun room."

Henry walked into the kitchen and then detoured through the dining room and into the sun room. He turned, but Jenny was still in the kitchen area looking everything over. "Just go slowly, Henry, I want to take everything in."

Henry walked back. "Oh, I'm sorry Jenny; I just take it all for granted."

"What a beautiful kitchen and I love how it overlooks the sun room and the valley beyond. Julean must have been in heaven living here."

"Well, she grew into it. She was a city girl and so adjusting to the life style of an acreage was a bit of a challenge for her. But she soon grew to love it as much as the children did."

Jenny gasped when she walked into the dining room, which opened up to the living room. She instantly loved the mahogany antique dining room set. She ran her fingers across the surface, cutting through the slight layer of dust. And the grandfather clock in the corner immediately caught her attention. "This is all so beautiful, Henry!" Jenny exclaimed as she walked further into the room. The north wall was all glass overlooking the valley. The adjacent wall was covered with natural stone picked from the fields in the area with a huge wood-burning fireplace in the centre. Comfortable chairs and sofas were formed into a conversational setting. And against the far back wall of the living room was an upright piano, with two antique arm chairs on either side. Jenny was in awe as she walked around the room and took it all in.

"What on earth did you see in my house when you have such an incredible log home?"

"It is quite a contrast, but that is what appealed to me and especially all your antique furniture. It puts my small collection to shame. But then, most of all, I think I loved your home because I felt your presence… it was like coming home, Jenny."

Henry drew near to his beloved and embraced her. "I'm glad you like it. I love you so much, Jenny."

"And I love you so much, too."

With his arm over Jenny's shoulder they made their way into the sun room. Jenny stopped in her tracks. There must have been at least fifty plants in the room if not more. For someone who loves plants it was like Henry had brought the outdoors inside. The room was filled with Jenny's best friend; nature.

Jenny was silent as her eyes took it all in. Gradually, she noticed another theme emerge; hidden behind or interspersed amongst all the plants, she realized that most of the furniture and wall hangings were Native artifacts or related to the outdoors in some way. The table between the rocker and the reading chair had legs carved with an elephant head at the top of each corner, with its foot at the bottom of each leg. The standing lamp beside the arm chair grew out of an elegant water bird. An original bow and arrow set enclosed in a glass framed case hung on the wall, along with tomahawks, horse sculptures, wood carvings of bears and Native Indian faces.

As she walked further into the room, she noted a portrait of a Native Indian chief painted on the gut of a bison's stomach, hanging on the wall. It was stretched between a frame made of sturdy branches and the way it was nestled between a spider plant and huge fern was breathtaking. Hidden behind the large fern, up high towards the ceiling, she was startled to see a realistic looking hawk sculpture growing out of the high wall, as if to spring on her at any moment. As she followed the gaze of the bird, she noted the prey it was really after: a fish as if diving out of the water, growing out of the wall a few feet below the hawk. *Would that be its last glimpse of the world outside its habitat?*

Jenny backed away and turned to where she knew straight away must be where Henry read. It was a comfortable looking, slightly reclined arm chair, upholstered in a Navaho print. Right beside was a free-standing fireplace, to keep him warm and heat the room. She could just picture Henry reading during a winter snow storm or rainy day, yet warmed by the fire.

Just as Jenny was going to sit in his chair, she gasped as her eyes suddenly took in what was behind his chair filling the entire corner of the room. There stood a huge eagle sculpture at least four feet off the floor with wings spanning five feet. It appeared to be flying out of a forest of ferns, a variety of different plants and tall dieffenbachia, as if frightened by the towering totem pole just behind...

"Oh, my gosh, Henry, what a scene. I would almost be afraid to sit down in your chair...it looks so real."

"The sculptor did a nice job on the eagle and the tall base it's suspended on almost looks like a tree trunk and blends into the plants."

"Yes, it appears to be in flight...it's all so unbelievable."

Jenny had never seen such a room designed so creatively. "Oh this will take days to take in, Henry. Everywhere you look, there is something of interest."

She twirled around and stopped with her gaze focused through the patio doors leading onto a large deck. Henry slid open the door and led Jenny out. She just shook her head in awe; the view of the valley was breathtaking. But when she turned to the right and looked down into the valley it was as if she had entered paradise. She immediately knew she was looking at Henry's Poustinia surrounded with wildflowers. The meandering creek opened into a large pond beside the prayer house. It reflected quietly into the still water. It was the perfect picture of peace. She compared the Poustinia to her Angel of Thanksgiving.

Henry drew near to Jenny and wrapped his arm around her shoulder. "That's the Poustinia, Jenny."

"Yes, I know, Henry," Jenny softly replied.

"Father is there. I took him down yesterday. I'm sure glad spring came early this year. Most of the flowers are out and I love when the old dead grass is covered over with fresh green grass. It does turn brown as the summer progresses, unless there is a lot of rain."

"Yes, look at the green hills and all the wildflowers surrounding the pond! It's all so beautiful...oh Henry, look at the three deer behind the Poustinia!"

"Yeah, I see them. They always come when Father is there. I've even seen him feed the deer by hand. I'm telling you, Jenny, Father is another St. Francis."

"This is amazing Henry, I just love it all."

Henry squeezed Jenny. "I'm happy you do. Come on, I'll show you the family room on the other side of the kitchen and then the studio upstairs.

"There is no end to this place. It's similar in size to James' estate but more rustic and so natural with nature all around."

The hair on the back of Henry's neck bristled at the mention of Jenny's former husband's name, but he decided to pretend not to have noticed.

"It's comfortable here and even though I have lived alone for many years with just the two kids, I like a large home to ramble in."

Jenny hoped she would be sharing it with him soon.

After Henry showed Jenny the family room, they made their way up to the bedrooms and to where Henry painted. At the top of the stairs, they turned right and followed the railing around to the studio. Jenny held her breath as they entered.

It was filled with light. Immediately to the left were two stairs that settled into a seating area much like a family room. The walls were completely covered with paintings from floor to ceiling. But to the right was the artist's easel, accented by a soft north light coming in through three huge picture windows. The walls were lined with a counter and storage shelves and drawers below. In the small wall space area were book shelves that displayed art books on master painters and technical books related to watercolour, acrylic and oil painting.

As Jenny made her way to the easel, she held her breath as she looked outdoors at the panoramic valley view. Wherever she looked there were uninhabited hills and valleys and streams and pockets of water surrounded by trees and flowers.

"What inspiration this must be for you, Henry," Jenny softly muttered, trying to take it all in. As she passed by the easel, she now saw the canvas that Henry was working on. It was of a young girl balancing on a log that projected out over a turbulent stream in the valley. It was early morning, as a soft mist covered the distant trees. Her arms were extended like wings and her right foot was raised and reaching forward as she dared to go out further over the water below.

"Oh, Henry, that's beautiful. Is that one of your daughters?" Jenny wanted to know.

"Yes, that's Lauren. She is always the one to take chances. I recall one spring a few years back, she tried to come down the rushing waters with a dingy. Fortunately, Justin informed me and no sooner had we got to the valley bottom that I saw her hurtling down the stream, yelling for dear life. The dingy tipped over not too far from us and down she went. Our angels must have been with us that morning, as I rushed into the turbulent water and saw her come up. Before she went down, I was able to grab her and make it back to the shore."

"That must have been so scary..."

"It was, but it didn't seem to deter her from doing other risky things. I guess that's why I did that painting of her on the log...to capture her spirit."

"And you did!"

Henry wrapped his arms around Jenny and they made their way to the windows that faced slightly east.

"Look!" Jenny pointed, "There's Father coming out of the prayer house. Is that a brown robe he's wearing?"

"Yes, it is a Franciscan habit, I know how much he admires St. Francis and he finds the hood keeps his head warm in the fresh early mornings."

"Does he know I am coming with you?"

"Yes, he's expecting us. Perhaps we should stroll down there. He may be waiting for us to join him when he says Mass if he hasn't already done so."

Jenny turned to Henry, "Yes, let's g—"

Jenny couldn't finish her sentence as Henry's lips touched hers and they warmly embraced.

JENNY AND HENRY decided to walk down in into the valley rather than drive down. They didn't want to disturb Father with the sound of an engine roaring through the valley. Jenny slipped on her sweater and runners and together, hand in hand they began to stroll down the winding hill road leading to the Poustinia and valley below. The dogs settled down after a bit of Henry's scolding and eventually left their new found friend in peace.

"They're lovely dogs, but will take some getting used to. James never allowed any animals on the estate or in the house. I think he would have shut out the birds in the sky if he could have," Jenny chuckled.

"Well, pretty much anything goes out here, Jen. You're free to do whatever." Henry left out a loud exhilarating yell, startling Jenny, and waited for the echo to come back. "Oops, I hope that didn't disturb Father," Henry said and quickly added, "Well, when he's not here you can scream all you want."

As they descended, the air became cooler and fresher. The wildflowers stood out so colourfully against the lush, green trees and shrubs.

A beaver flapped its tail at the sight of the dogs. Coco was the first to dive in, followed by Ginger.

"Oh, that water must be so cold, Henry."

"Their fur protects them somewhat. Not like that of a beaver for sure... It's hard to tell as they seem to enjoy the water so much."

The dog's movement in the water obliterated the still reflection of the Poustinia that was there before they entered the water.

"I can't get over how beautiful this is. The view from the top of the hill is wonderful, but from down here it seems as if you are entering a different world."

"I get that feeling each time I come down here. You get so close to nature, the absence of civilization, the wild animals...you almost become one with the glaciers that passed through here millions of years ago, carving out the valley and creating the foundation of the valley we see now. And it's still ongoing and changing as the flowing waters continue to carve and reshape the valley floor."

"Were the wildflowers here all the time, too?"

"Some were, but most of them we planted by hand over the years. It was Allison's idea. Of all the children, she loved the acreage the most as soon as she saw it. She loved the flowers and also the butterflies. I don't know if you noticed all the milkweed plants around the log house and they are also interspersed amongst the flowers. The monarchs should be coming soon."

"I love wildflowers and butterflies, Henry."

"Yes, I know. I can still recall when you chased after the butterflies when we went for walks during that memorable summer of '56!"

"You remember that, do you?"

"I remember everything we did, Jenny. Those were such

precious memories and I replayed them in my mind a million times."

Jenny squeezed Henry's hand, "I did, too."

She bent down and picked a white daisy alongside the road. She brought it to her nose and breathed in deeply. "Oh, Henry, we had wildflowers at the estate as well, but to see them grow in the open like this in such a natural setting is incredible. What a feeling of freedom; so exhilarating!"

"Well, you haven't seen all the flowers that are yet to come. By midsummer it does take your breath away, especially if accompanied by a lot of spring rain."

Jenny could no longer contain herself. She let go of Henry's hand and began running towards the prayer house, twirling the daisy in her hand like a magic wand. The valley before Henry was transformed into a picture of beauty as she ran down the winding lane. He was momentarily mesmerized by her golden hair glistening in the sun and flowing freely in the breeze. He fully expected her to fly like an angel at any moment; he started to chase after her just to dispel the surge of love overwhelming his racing heart.

CHAPTER FIFTY ONE

W HEN THEY CAME to the Poustinia, they still didn't see Father.
They assumed he was inside. Rather than enter through the
front door, Henry quietly slid open the kitchen patio door and
took Jenny's hand as they entered. Jenny's grip on Henry's hand
tightened and she slightly gasped at the sight. They saw Father
kneeling before a small altar and a huge cross with Jesus crucified
hanging just above. Henry still couldn't get over the size of the
cross when he hung it for Father; it was at least five feet high. Both
Jenny and Henry looked on in awe at the sight of the holy image
before them and the feeling of holiness all around.

Father was so deep in prayer that he was still unaware of their
presence. Henry noticed the brown habit Father was wearing and
couldn't help but feel how well it suited him; another St. Francis,
thought Henry. He felt the fire of perfect love. Jenny felt it too, as
tears streamed down her face.

Henry took hold of Jenny's hand and together they softly tip-
toed into the living area and knelt down behind Father. He sensed
his loved ones and while still facing the cross, Father extended
both his hands back to Henry and Jenny. They each brought forth
their free hand and took hold of Father's. Instantly, an electric

spiritual energy flowed through all of them in a perfect circle of love with their creator. The power and presence of the Holy Spirit filled them all to overflowing. Vague flashbacks of their stint on the doorstep of heaven was before them; spinning round and round with their guardian angels as if flying into the arms of Jesus.

Father let go of their hands and reflected quietly for a moment. He placed both hands on the edge of the altar and pulled himself up to the standing position and continued to pray. It became apparent to Henry and Jenny that Father was saying the Mass and was just beginning the Consecration; the holiest moment of the Mass. Just as Jesus did at the Last Supper and requested that we do the same in memory of Him, Father took the bread in the form of a Host and said, "This is My body." He elevated the Host and gazed at it for the longest time, placed it down and genuflected. Then he took the chalice of wine, and said, "This is the cup of My blood." Once again, Father raised the cup and then genuflected.

When Father came to the Lord's Prayer, rather than face the altar, Father turned to his children and took their hands and together they prayed:

> Our Father, who art in heaven,
> hallowed be thy name
> Thy kingdom come, thy will be done,
> On earth as it is in heaven
> Give us this day our daily bread
> And forgive us our trespasses
> As we forgive those who trespass against us.
> And lead us not into temptation, but deliver us from evil,
> Amen.

After receiving Holy Communion and Father's blessing, they hugged one another and made their way out onto the deck. After all were seated, Father began, "Who would have thought that just a few weeks ago, the three of us would be sharing Mass and sitting on the deck of Henry's prayer house on this beautiful summer day! Clearly, as the Lord says, 'My ways are not your ways.' It's as if we're still just on this side of the portals to heaven."

"Oh, Father, you simply must share with us what you saw that day. Henry and I have no memory of it, but we both are having dreams that don't make too much sense. Perhaps you can enlighten us and at the same time we may be better able to interpret our dreams."

"Yes, I do not fully understand why you and Henry have no memory of your stint on the other side. I have complete memory and before I returned to the land of the living, my guardian also permitted me to see all of mankind and into the lives of all the people that I've known, including you." Father raised his right hand to gesture that he referred to both of them and continued. "I was not allowed to see into the future, only into the past, and right up to that moment before I left to return to earth."

"How could you see everything in such a short period of time?" asked Henry.

"There really is no time, Henry; it's all in the present. Within a thought, one can see and understand lifetimes. One experiences how God's mind works. He knows all things past, present and future; now. It is difficult for man to comprehend with his finite mind."

"That reminds me of another matter that Jenny and I were wondering about, Father. If you saw everything up until the time we all came back to life, how did Jenny's diary get to her backyard when it was in my truck before I had the accident? And did you see Jenny write an entry in there?"

"Yes, the archbishop asked me the same question…"

Father went on to tell them exactly what he told the archbishop. Henry and Jenny were amazed that Father had seen that and just as the archbishop's belief of what Father had seen increased, so did theirs. Jenny, however, was more interested in her celestial guardian.

"Oh, this is all getting too heavy for me to understand, Father. Henry says that you saw our guardian angels. Please tell us about them, I am dying to know!"

"Yes, when I first crossed over, Jenny, I met my protector, Zachariah. Our spirits hovered over the sun room in the care home. We talked a bit and watched the residents in the care home celebrate my passing. Shortly, you and Henry came to the site, along with your guardians."

"Oh, Father what did they look like and did they tell you their names!?" Jenny was so excited; she was on the edge of her chair.

"Yes, yes, your angel's name is Hannah and Henry's is Gabriel."

Looking at Jenny, Father continued. "Your angel is younger and more petite than Henry's. Her wings were always in motion, almost like a hummingbird." Father paused and gazed towards the morning sun, "Now let me see, yes, she wore a blue robe with white straps that crossed over her shoulders and then around her waist. Her hair is yellow, like gold, long and flowing. And her eyes are blue like yours, as well. Henry's angel is more masculine. He wore a brown robe that matched his brown hair. I can't recall what color his eyes are, but he is tall, but not as tall as Zachariah. Mind you. My guardian was the most mature of the three and did most of the talking. In fact, it was Zachariah who explained to me why you and Henry were so smitten with one another and why your love for each other has been so long-lasting".

"Oh Father, this sounds so mysterious and intriguing, you just have to tell us every detail."

Although Henry hadn't said much, he too, was at the edge of his seat. He also wanted to know everything that had transpired.

"Do you recall the morning you two met in my grocery store—"

"I'll never forget that morning," Henry cut in sharply.

"Nor will I, Father. The moment I looked into Henry's eyes it was love at first sight. I was completely lost in the moment. It was as if we were lifted and something travelled through the gaze we were sharing."

"Yeah, it was almost like something was caught in my eyes."

"And mine too," concurred Jenny.

"Ah, das erklärt es, yes, that clearly explains what Zachariah said. Apparently, when the two of you looked into each other's eyes that morning, not only was there an earthly attraction, but there was a heavenly one as well. Both of your guardian angels were so excited when you two met that they also imparted some of their spiritual energy into the gaze you both shared with one another. As a result, not only were your hearts united, in the earthly sense, but also your very souls, in the heavenly sense. It was quite something to see. I recall a bright aura around both of you that morning as you gazed into each other's eyes."

"That would explain why I felt something caught in my eyes," said Henry.

"Yes, yes, I remember now. Zachariah explained it this way;

love between two people in most instances begins in the eyes as they see and are attracted to one another. That morning when you and Jenny met, it was as if the angels' energy entered into your eyes in the form of shooting love darts which not only penetrated your heart, but going still deeper, wounded your soul, as well. You pained for one another. It was plain to see not only that day, but in the days and weeks that followed until the day Jenny left. Oh, how much you yearned and desired one another."

"Oh, that sounds so powerful, Father. That morning is so clear in my memory. I can just visualize our angels doing that, like two cherubim's flying near us with their bow and arrow!"

"That's amazing, Father," said Henry, in awe of it all. "That would explain both the strength and duration of the love between us."

"Oh, Henry!" Jenny exclaimed again, "I would have loved to see our guardians. I would have given both such a big hug for all they did for us."

"But you did embrace them, Jenny, very warmly, I might add. And another thing, they played a huge part in getting you both back to earth. Since they felt responsible for creating such an ardent love between you both which led to the depth of your hearts' desire to marry one another, their solicitudes to God were continued on your behalf, especially on the day you both passed away. I surmise that it was a combination of their pleas, our prayers and yours that swayed the Lord to create all of these incredible healings."

"It's all so amazing Father. There seems to be so many reasons why we were all allowed to return to our earthly lives," Jenny said shaking her head.

"Yes, you have been blessed to see and return to your loved ones, your family and of course, Henry and Camilla. There is Peter, too, and perhaps reasons that you may not be aware of until years in the future. It's all part of God's divine providence."

Jenny thought for sure that it had to do with bearing a child for Henry…the name of her guardian angel, Hannah, resonated in her mind.

"You mentioned Peter, Father. Jenny and I were discussing him the other day and his desire to see Jenny and Camilla to seek their forgiveness."

"Yes, this is an area that needs healing and the sooner the better," Father quickly added.

Turning to Jenny, Father asked, "Are there any concerns in this area, Jennifer that you wish to talk about? Are there any obstacles that may impede reconciliation?"

"In my heart, over the years, Father, I have forgiven the man who fathered my child. Yet, now that we plan to meet with him, so many memories arise; the night Henry and I were assaulted, the boys taking me to the park, fainting and not knowing what happened and what they did. And now, to face him seems scary and I must admit, feelings of hurt, anger and violation are surfacing again. I thought the other night when Camilla and I spoke about it, I was free of these feelings perhaps not..."

"Yes, of course, all these things, many which you have repressed for years, are now coming to the fore once more. These are human feelings that demand understanding, justice or even vengeance. But we must face each and every one of these feelings and yield them to Jesus to heal. If you don't, the feelings will arise again and both you and the beautiful child that came out of that horrific act will always be surrounded with these feelings.

"Henry and Camilla have to do the same. Each of you must come to Jesus and ask him to bring your memories to the fore for healing and with His healing grace, let them go. Forgiveness must be your goal..."

"I have already spoken to Henry about this event. What about Camilla? You said you spoke with her the other night?" Father wanted to know.

"Yes, I was both surprised and grateful for how well Camilla is taking this. I think many women who become pregnant through rape or violence feel justified in their decision to have an abortion; they can't bear the thought of carrying a child who was forced upon them. For so many women in this position, it is a wrenching decision. Even for those who decide to carry and birth their child, under these circumstances, often the child ends up feeling unworthy of living. I was so relieved to see that Camilla has accepted herself so wholesomely as she should and not feel she has to prove or justify her existence to herself or to anyone."

Reaching out to Jenny and taking her hands in his, Henry added, "She knows the truth about herself, Jenny. She knows that her value is not based upon how she was conceived, who raised her or what other people think. She knows she is a child of God and that alone is what gives her value, as it does all of us."

Father Engelmann's eyes brightened. "That is a wonderful observation, Henry. God values and loves us so much that He asked His son to make the infinite sacrifice and die for us that we might have life. That's how much He values each one us!"

"I am so happy that Camilla was raised in a Christian home and has that understanding. She is so beautiful and is doing such good work. Perhaps, too, it is her counseling background and that she works with girls who have had similar experiences that helps her understand the big picture. In fact, when we talked about it the other night, she even helped me to further accept my feelings around it all. I was so happy that Chloe and Matti had explained to Camilla the circumstances surrounding her conception. It would have been difficult for me to tell her. I had held it in for so long and was ashamed to bring it up...but talking about it with Camilla was so freeing..."

"Your guardian angel is helping you to deal with it all, Jenny," Henry observed.

"Oh, yes, I could feel my angel's presence as Camilla and I spoke."

"In a way, it's good that Camilla has already seen Peter so it won't be totally new for her when we all meet," said Henry.

"Yes, that is a blessing. She told me she had already seen Peter at your anniversary party, Father. When she saw him there, she saw herself in his features. For the first time in her life, she felt like she belonged in the physical sense. Now that she knows that he is in fact her birth father, she wants to meet with him to promote healing."

"That is wonderful, Jenny. Camilla sees the enormous benefits to forgiveness and moving on. The good Lord has already blessed her with wisdom and understanding. She is a peacemaker."

"When Peter called and also when I spoke with his wife, Angelika, they both expressed how sorrowful Peter is and wants forgiveness," Henry added to the conversation.

"Yes, of course, his conscious has plagued him for years. Not only does Peter want this matter to be healed, but his wife and children do, too."

Father shifted in his chair and closed his eyes as he looked up towards the sun. Henry recognized that move and look. Father was trying to recall something that would bring clarity into this matter. Henry didn't think it was a Scripture as it would have been spouted out already. No, it had to be a story…Henry was right.

"I recall an incident that happened in the old country when a man broke into a home, tied up the husband and raped his wife in front of him. The wife conceived a child. The health authorities approved for the woman to have an abortion. Before she carried out the termination of her baby, the husband said to his wife, "I understand that man violated you, but the child within your womb is half yours and half his. I love you dearly and should you decide to have this child, I will love it like our own because of my love for you. I know that even if that man did an evil thing, he is still a child of God. I will see that child as coming from the man that God loves and created."

"The wife decided to have the child and true to his promise, the father loved the child as his own. When the child was grown, she found out what had happened and wrote a book in honor of her father and that she would not have had life if not for the example of his true love."

"Oh Father, that was such a powerful story. In many ways that was what happened with me. I, too, considered abortion, but I grew to love the baby growing inside my womb. At first I imagined Henry to be the father so that Camilla would be surrounded by loving thoughts. But, slowly over the years I allowed Peter into my life and forgave him. To fully love Camilla, I knew I had to accept the man who fathered her. I just hope when I see him I will feel the same."

"Jenny, you were given a forgiving heart. Much will depend on you. Pray for strength to lead all those around you to the path of reconciliation, peace and freedom."

Tears sat on the edge of Jenny's eyes and almost in a whisper, she asked, "Would you pray for us all, Father, so we receive the strength we need to do what is right? Pray for another miracle."

"Yes, yes, of course."

Father reached over with both of his hands and they were quickly received by Jenny's and Henry's hands. They bowed their heads…

The morning sun was rising higher into the sky, warming the air around them as well as their hearts. The sound of the water bubbling nearby as it flowed over the beaver dam seemed to recede, but soft enough to soothe and cleanse their spirits. Even the chattering of birds in the trees quieted as a peaceful silence descended upon them.

As soon as Father felt the Holy Spirit moving amongst them, he softly began to pray...

"My dear Lord, come, enlighten our hearts with Your Holy Spirit. Grant us the wisdom to know Your truths and apply them to the lives of Jennifer, Henry, Camilla, Peter and his family. There is a connection between these, Your children, that requires understanding and compassion. At the root of this connection was an act done by Peter, that should not have happened, but it did, and now needs acceptance and healing.

"Help us all to see, dear Lord that Peter is not the act, Peter is Your child just like Jenny is, Camilla is, Henry is, and as all of us are. There are times in the lives of each of us when we err and sin. Some of our sins are small and some are large, but we are not the sin: our choice was, our thought was, our action was. Grant Jenny, Henry, Camilla and Peter and his family the wisdom to separate the act from the person; the child of God who You created.

"We are all brothers and sisters in Christ, who are good and beautiful, who at times need forgiveness. And just as we ask for Your forgiveness or seek and receive forgiveness from others for our transgressions, we in turn must give our forgiveness to those who trespass against us. You have given us free will, the power to choose to stop the pain and to heal the hurtful memory that struggles to survive in our hearts. Come now, oh Holy Spirit, and fill us all with the strength and grace to do what we know is right; *to forgive.*

"Yes, forgiveness is the path to reconciliation, peace, freedom, and even friendship. All of these elements of healing are ever present if only we choose to be open enough to let such Christ-like thoughts into our hearts and minds.

"Let Jenny, Henry, Camilla and Peter and his family, when they meet, choose such a path. Let them know that Christ is ever there to instill peace and forgiveness for the most grievous of offences and atrocities. That is the extent of God's love. We can choose to tap into it and find peace or we can rebel and continue to fill our beings with hatred, resentment, bitterness …hell.

"Tremendous power to do good will be present when they meet. Let them know the power of the choice they can make in that moment; the power to choose three little words. *I forgive you*…and perhaps, it will lead to the most powerful words…*I love you.*

"Fill them with Your grace, dear Lord, so they can all experience the exhilarating freedom that comes when *we choose Your will and Your ways.*

"We ask this in Jesus' name. Amen."

Jenny and Henry just sat there in silence contemplating the wisdom of Father Engelmann's prayerful words. The sounds of nature around them were so soothing, it only further increased their desire not to disturb the peace of the moment. It was good to let go of all thoughts and just allow the spiritual sustenance of God's creation to do its work.

Perhaps it was the openness of the moment that enlightened Jenny's spirit to feel compelled to share how she coped with her pain and suffering in the hospital in the days and weeks leading up to her death and miraculous recovery.

"I am so thankful for my illness. It brought me closer to the Creator than anything else in all my life. Suffering is such a mystery and yet, in some small way, Father, I understood it in the light of a vision I had. I saw the connection between suffering, pain, joy and gratitude, all at once. How my suffering along with Jesus' suffering brings the joy of heaven and salvation to all of us…"

For the next half hour Jenny shared how she fell into a darkness in her dying days and when she thought she could no longer handle it, she had a vision which helped her to understand Jesus' suffering, her suffering and that of others. It taught her how to love at a greater level than she had ever known before. And she discovered the joy that is possible in suffering and was filled with deep gratitude to Jesus for laying down his life for her and her brothers and sisters.

"You know, Father," Jenny concluded, "I know God does not cause the suffering, but He permits it. We can fight it and turn our back on Him and gain nothing but the added pain of separation and rebellion, loss of hope and despair. Or, we can come to Him and trust Him and invite Him into our hearts. He is ever waiting to give us comfort, grace and strength. I know with all my heart Father, that suffering has made me stronger, more fulfilled, more loving, compassionate, and humble. Most of all, I realized the tremendous sacrifice that God the Father and His Son made to open the gates of heaven so that we, too, may be partakers of the joy promised in eternity. I could see that my suffering was nothing in comparison to the suffering Jesus was called to endure."

Father shook his head and finally said, "Jennifer, you have been granted such an extraordinary blessing from God. In all my years, I have never heard of a clearer explanation of the mystery of suffering. Perhaps, Jenny, this is but another reason for your return; to let others know of what you saw. Next Sunday, I will be filling in for Father Knuka while he goes on a three week vacation. Would you consider sharing what you just said to Henry and me about your view on suffering to the congregation of St. Mary's church?"

"Yeah, Jenny," Henry interjected, "That has really helped me to understand pain and suffering so much better. Others would greatly benefit from your sharing."

"Yes, Father, I am honoured that you would ask…if it helps others, I will certainly share it, Father."

Henry checked his watch and then looked up at the sun. "I didn't realize how long we've been here Father. It's mid afternoon and the sun sets earlier down here in the valley."

"Yes, I can feel the air cooling off," concurred Father. "That's why I like this hooded robe so much. Helps keep the heat in when the shingles have flown away," Father added, making reference to the loss of most of his hair.

Henry and Jenny chuckled. "You look very distinguished, Father, with your receding hair line." Jenny observed.

"I have to agree wholeheartedly with that," added Henry, now making reference to his hair loss, too.

"Well, I'm getting very hungry, Jenny, and we certainly won't get anything to eat in Father's kitchen. He's on a fast and the only thing he's offering is water. So, we better get back up to the house." Henry gazed into the sky again, as a buildup of heavy clouds covered the sun. "We may get wet before we make it back, Jenny."

Jenny gazed up and rolled her eyes.

They all rose and hugged Father. "Thank you so much Father

for everything. It was so wonderful being here with you. It's so peaceful…like paradise!" said Jenny.

"It's so good to see you healthy and happy, Jenny, and to see you and Henry together filled with such love. We praise the Lord for his kindness and blessings."

Father picked up his Bible on the table beside his deck chair and opened it. "Just this morning before you came, the Lord gave me a Scripture that he wanted me to share with you both. Isaiah 55:12 says, 'For you shall go out with joy, and be led out with peace; The mountains and the hills shall break forth into singing before you, and all the trees of the field shall clap their hands'".

"Oh, Father, that's so wonderful, thank you!" said Jenny.

Henry nodded, "Yeah, that's great, Father. Thanks for sharing!"

Father watched Henry and Jenny step off the deck and make their way back to the house holding hands. He could see Jenny pull Henry into the meadow of wildflowers beside the road and begin to run.

"So spontaneous, so full of life, even when she was on her death bed, she never lost that sparkle for life." Father murmured.

A tear surfaced in Father's eyes as the happy image of Henry and Jenny reminded him of Anna and him climbing the hills and mountains in Austria. His Anna was always full of life, too. Her brown hair was much longer than Jenny's and he could see it now in his mind's eye, blowing in the wind as she raced up the mountain side, "Komm schon, David, die Aussicht wird immer besser und besser."

Yes, thought Father, the view of his dearly beloved will get better, too, as soon as he finished the two tasks the Lord wanted him to do and he could return to his heavenly home.

How will this all play out, Lord? Father thought further, as he watched Henry lift Jenny high into the air and twirl her round and round amongst the flowers. They were so much in love and yet, so many obstacles lay ahead for them. The heavens rumbled and thundered almost in agreement. Within moments, Henry and Jenny were soaking wet.

Wrinkles of amusement and joy gathered at the corners of Father's eyes as a favourite Scripture, John 10:10 came to mind, "I am come that they might have life, and that they might have it more abundantly."

Father's eyes misted as he faintly heard the two love birds shout in glee and raise their hands to the sky like two little children. It was almost as if they were back just on this side of heaven spinning round and round with their angels.

I shall say another Mass for them for the Lord to give them strength and not lose hope as they journey in the road ahead.

Father turned and went inside, but the sky continued to rumble and cry.

CHAPTER FIFTY TWO

H EY, HANK, HOW are ya doing, ole buddy?"

"Eddy! What brings you into town?"

"Pop passed away six months ago and Mom ain't doing so good. I should have come home for his funeral…but we never got along, so, I decided to pass. It hurt Mom not seeing me at the funeral and so I thought I better come home and try to straighten things out."

"Yeah, that's a good idea, Eddy…" Henry's words trailed off, not sure what to say under the circumstances.

"So, how long are you in town for and is Coreena with you?"

"Yeah, the wife came along, Maybe we'll stay a week or two, see how things go, know what I mean?"

"I think I understand what you're saying, Eddy. Sounds like you have a cold? That's quite the cough you have."

"Afraid it's more than that, Hank. One of my lungs is going… guess, the smoking is catching up with me."

"Well, I hope you stopped."

"Na, not yet. A tough one to let go of. So, how are things going with you, ole buddy?" Eddy asked trying to steer the subject away from his bad habit.

"A lot has happened lately. I was in an accident and apparently died and came back to life without a scratch and…" Henry wasn't sure if he should talk about Jenny as it was Eddy and his friends that assaulted her back in high school. But Henry decided to push on. "Do you remember the girl I dated back in grade nine—?"

"You mean the blonde chick, Jenny?"

Henry was surprised by Eddy's response. He didn't think Eddy would remember. "Yeah, that's right, Eddy. She came back to Regina and you will never believe this, but she had cancer real bad and like me, she died and came back to life, fully healed as well!"

"Geez, that's powerful, man. Same thing happened to the Padre says Mom. She heard he died and came back. All the old folks are going to him for healings…maybe I should pay a visit to St. Engelmann, see what he can do for me."

Henry smiled, "So you heard about Father Engelmann, too!? It's unbelievable, Eddy, that Father died and was restored on the same day as we were"

"No kidding! What's going down, Hank? God doing that Lazarus thing?" Eddy tried to make a joke. But Henry didn't know how to respond and so he said, "We're still trying to sort it all out… and did you hear that Peter was very sick, too, This sounds crazy, but he also died and was brought back to life…"

There was a long silence. "Geez, Hank, something's happening here. I spoke with Peter about three months ago and he was sure hurting over what he had done to Jenny. He would do anything to see Jenny and…I would, too, man"

There was another long silence, "Well, we are going to meet with Peter and his family in the next few weeks and try to straighten things out, but…did you just say you would like to see Jenny, as well?"

"Yeah…It's always bothered me, too, what me and the boys did that night to you and her. I think an…geez, this cough is annoying, give me sec. I'll light up. Seems to help for some crazy reason…" Henry heard the snap of a lighter and then click as Eddy closed it. Henry could visualize every movement Eddy was making.

Eddy blew out and then continued, "Yeah, as I was saying Hank, an apology from me is in order as well. Is she still in town?"

Henry could hardly believe his ears. All he could think of was God's divine providence at work. "Yes, she is, Eddy. As a matter of fact I'm hoping that we will get married…there are a few hurdles we have to meet, but I'm optimistic."

"That's cool, man. Well, tell her..." Eddy stopped to cough and clear his throat and continued, "yeah, tell her I would sure like to meet with her, perhaps introduce her to the missus...maybe go out for dinner, the four of us. What do you say, Hank?"

"That sounds great, Eddy. Let me take down your phone number where I can reach you and I'll set something up. This is unbelievable Eddy," Henry said again, as he copied down the number. Just before he hung up he added, "Check into that cough, Eddy, doesn't sound good."

HELLO, HANK, THIS is Angelika, Peter's wife, Angie."

"Hello, Angelika, it's good to hear from you. I was planning to call Peter."

"I hope it's to tell us that Jenny is okay and that she will see Peter."

"Yes, that's exactly what I was going to call about. All three of us plan to fly to Calgary in the next two weeks...that is, myself, Jenny and her daughter, Camilla."

"Oh, Hank, that is such good news! Peter is so worried that his healing may have been in vain. Lately, he seems to be getting ill again. I told him to call you, but he didn't want to be a nuisance and he wants forgiveness to be given freely and not forced. I decided to take it upon myself to call...this makes me so happy that the three of you are coming. Do you have an exact date in mind yet?"

"No, Angie, we are still working on it. Jenny is free to go at any time, but Camilla is working and will have to arrange some time off."

"We will be happy to share some of the expenses if need be."

"No, that's fine, Angelika."

There was a momentary silence on the phone and then Angie spoke softly, "We have been praying that Jenny and her daughter will forgive my husband, I so hope that is her heart's intention. Is there anything I can say to her beforehand? To explain how sorrowful Peter feels and what kind of man he is?"

"That will not be necessary, Angelika. Jenny is a very understanding person. I can't say how she will respond to Peter...or, how Camilla will either. We'll just have to see when we all meet."

"Yes, it's best to leave it up to the Lord. So, you will be calling and let us know when you will be coming?"

"Yes, I will let you know as soon as possible. Thank you for calling, Angie."

CHAPTER FIFTY THREE

THIS WAS FATHER Knuka's first break since Father Engelmann retired from St. Mary's Parish. Another priest had come to help on a part time basis but fell ill and wasn't able to assist Father Knuka for several months. Father Engelmann jumped at the request to look after the parish for three weeks while his dear friend went home to visit his family and mother who was also critically ill.

Henry could hardly wait to attend church nor could he wait to pick up Jenny. The service would be special not only having Jenny there, but also to see Father Engelmann at the pulpit again. It would be like old times. Henry knew what the topic of today's sermon was going to be about. Father had asked Jenny if she would share with the parishioners the days leading up to her death. Father was profoundly touched by what she had said on the deck in front of the prayer house last week and felt it would also touch the hearts of the people at St. Mary's Church as well.

As Henry neared Jenny's home, his heart began to flutter in anticipation of seeing his loved one. It reminded him of the days when he first met Jenny in the neighborhood. Some days he just couldn't wait another moment and dashed to her place as soon as dinner was over. He loved it when she was out sitting on the steps waiting for him. Her warm smile and sparkling eyes greeting him; melting his heart.

Jenny must have read his thoughts, because as he pulled up to her house, there she was sitting on the landing. He thought for sure his heart would burst. The same thoughts that had entered his mind back then seemed to return now. An angel, he thought, she looked like an angel with her blond hair glistening gold in the bright morning sun and her smooth skin shimmering in the warm light. For a moment Henry envisioned himself parking his red bike in front of the yard, rather than bringing his SUV to a stop. Henry waved as he got out of the truck and made his way up the winding sidewalk. He wanted to say 'hi', but his mind was so transfixed by Jenny's smile and sparkling blue eyes, he was speechless. He was mesmerized and lost in a world of love. *Love* — what a wonderful gift the good Lord gave mankind.

Jenny's right hand was near her chest and Henry could see part of the pewter angel sticking out of her closed fist. Instinctively he raised his right hand and clutched the fluttering angel hanging from a chain around his neck as well. Henry let the angel fall and dangle at the end of chain. He reached out both hands as he stood in front of his dearly beloved and took hold of both of her hands and lifted her up to her feet. She let go and swung both her arms around Henry's neck and within seconds their lips met and both were lost in a world only lovers would understand. Henry's heart exploded with such a rush of affection, he could no longer contain the joy welling up in his being. He picked Jenny up and twirled her round and round in an attempt to dissipate the surging feeling of ecstasy sweeping through him.

Slowly, he stopped and set Jenny once more on the walk. The scent of lilac perfume mingled with the fragrance of the flowers and herbs and sent Henry into oblivion. He shook his head from side to side and with all the heartfelt emotion he could put into words, he softly whispered, "Oh Jenny, I love you so much."

Jenny was only able to respond in part before their lips met and their spirits soared.

As was his customary practice, Henry took Father's parking space in the church parking lot near the rectory. He could never understand why no one else did. Everyone knew Father didn't drive a car, but Henry was glad it worked out that way as the church was always packed. Today was no exception. Even though Henry and Jenny were early, the lot was filled and so were the streets for at least two blocks in either direction.

Since Jenny had come out of the hospital, she attended the church near her home, but as soon as they came near the parish, she recalled the times when she and her parents came to St. Mary's Church. She had to hold back the tears as memories of her mom and dad crossed the screen of her mind. She had to admit that as a young teenager she never got that much out of Mass as her eyes were always searching for Henry.

"Oh Henry, I'm so excited to hear Father's sermon. He is such a wonderful priest and his visits, when I was in the hospital, were so comforting. Just his presence seemed to fill the room with a healing balm."

"I'm looking forward to your sharing too. You and Father will give a talk that the parishioners will never forget."

"I am so nervous, I hope I don't collapse."

"If you do, it will be in my loving arms—"

"Hi Henry," said one of the ushers as he and Jenny entered the foyer of the church. "We knew you were coming, Father requested that we save a seat for you right up front," the attendant added with a wink.

"Thanks Mel, that's very much appreciated." Henry felt a little strange walking in with Jenny as Mel had always seen him with Julean. Even though the parish knew she had passed away, Henry always felt a sense of faithfulness to his first wife even though Jenny was his first love. *Julean would always hold a special place in his heart.*

Henry could see Mel staring at him and seemed to relax as Henry finally said, "By the way, Mel, this is Jenny Hamilton, a very special friend of mine."

"Very pleased to meet you," said the usher as he extended his hand.

"It's so nice to meet you too, Mel. I can hardly wait to see Father and listen to his sermon. I am so happy you were able to save a pew for us up close."

"Yeah, thanks again, Mel. Well, we better get in there. We're kinda blocking the path." Henry sidestepped to allow several parishioners to pass by and then they followed Mel to the front of the church.

After Henry and Jenny entered the pew, they both knelt down and made the sign of the cross almost in unison. Instinctively, Henry reached into his pocket and pulled out Julean's rosary. He kissed the cross and began to pray. His eyes were closed as he always said the first Hail Mary in dedication to his wife. Julean and the Blessed Mother had such a close relationship.

For a moment there, he thought it was Julean whispering to him, but it was Jenny.

"What a beautiful rosary, Henry."

Henry was momentarily startled out of his reverie… "Yes, it's Julean's" Henry whispered…his words died off. He wondered if Jenny would be upset with him for holding his first wife's rosary and kissing it. He also noticed his wedding band on the finger that was also holding the rosary. Many times when they were together he tried to cover it up with his other hand. Perhaps they should talk about it. Jenny never seemed to mind and yet…

Henry turned towards her but Jenny remained silent. She reached over and squeezed his hand holding the rosary ever so softly. The gentle touch said what words couldn't …*It's okay, Henry, I would always want you to love your precious wife.*

No sooner had Jenny sat down when the door to sacristy opened and out came the altar boys followed by Father Engelmann wearing the biggest smile he could muster. Henry could see how much he loved to be back home in his parish. This was expressed by the parishioners as well as they all rose and no one could hold back from applauding their long time beloved shepherd. The clapping went on and on and finally Father raised his hands, gesturing it was time to begin the entrance song. The choir began a rousing rendition of *City of God* and the parishioners' voices swelled with enthusiasm as they joined in the singing.

Henry was thrilled that they were right up front and could see the nuances on Father's face. It was apparent his teacher was struggling hard to hold back the tears. Henry could feel that his dear mentor's heart was filled with joy and gratitude.

Finally he opened his arms and welcomed everyone and all those visiting.

"My dear friends, I was so elated when Father Knuka called to ask if I would look after the parish for the next three Sundays while he went back home to the Maritimes for a long overdue visit. This was my home for so many years and I have to admit it still feels like home…"

Henry could see Father struggling for words and choking up at the same time. He just shrugged his shoulders as if to say, *you know how much I love you,* and began the Mass, 'In the name of the Father and Son and Holy Spirit…"

Soon came the part everyone was waiting for; the reading of the two epistles followed by Father reading the gospel for that Sunday and then his sermon. As usual, he asked the parishioners to pray that the Holy Spirit would speak the sermon. The congregation rose and raised their hands and began to pray with boldness. Ever since the day when Father Knuka stood in front of them and asked for the Holy Spirit to touch his heart as it did Father Engelmann's, the Holy Spirit touched the hearts of the people there as well. Many parishioners, in such sympathy and empathy for Father Knuka that day, also received the gift of tongues as Father did. Henry could hear many speaking in tongues as the parishioners prayed.

"What a beautiful sound," commented Jenny.

Henry couldn't respond, the power of the Spirit filled the church and his spirit as well.

After everyone was seated, Father surveyed the congregation from one side to the other; his eyes inviting each and every one to listen to the Word. A hush fell over the church, the complete antithesis of the exuberant prayers moments ago. An anticipation for Father's sermon was building; it was palpable. Like a flock of sheep, the parishioners yielded their senses to gather closely around their shepherd. The momentary silence waiting for Father to speak was…holy.

Chapter Fifty Four

MEINE LIEBEN KINDER, today I want to talk about a subject that has been discussed down through the ages; suffering. Why is there suffering and pain? How can God allow war, sickness, rape, murder, adultery, loneliness and so many hardships? If God is just, why is there injustice? People on one side of the planet live in abundance and freedom, while on the other side, people are dying every second, of starvation, sickness and unthinkable atrocities. If God is merciful and good, how can He stand by and allow innocent children to suffer and die, while their parents look on in anguish? Or a man or woman lying in pain for days and months with some terminal disease; surely, an all powerful God could have created a more perfect world?

"These are questions to which there are no easy answers. They present deep struggles in our minds that have caused so many to turn away from their faith and question the very existence of God. To try and come up with some comforting answer that suffering is only temporary and happiness awaits us forever in the hereafter, is unacceptable in the midst of one's pain or that of a loved one. They would be quick to suggest that you sleep in my bed or walk in my shoes for even one hour and the promise of some distant paradise to me is meaningless, along with the many other platitudes that try to offer comfort.

"Yes, we can sympathize with the sufferer or if it is us who are in pain, we can engage in self pity and turn our backs on God, but all of these prove to be empty. No, there must be a more meaningful way to deal with the pain and hardship surrounding suffering, when it comes into our lives or is already either in our own or those of loved ones.

"To glean some understanding of suffering in the world, we have to look at the big picture. Besides gifting man with a free will to choose his own destiny, God created a world that is governed by laws and principles. There is cause and effect to everything. To every action there is an opposite reaction and each carries consequences. Thus, we can understand that if one places their hand on a stove, a burn and pain will result. If one stays out in the sun too long, they will also get a burn or even contract skin cancer and thus suffer the consequences. If someone commits murder, it will cause pain and death to someone and suffering to all those involved. This is part of the human condition. Understanding the world we live in helps to some degree, to deal with suffering, but how do we cope with it? To the one in pain, it can be so unbearable and senseless that it goes beyond their comprehension that God does not intervene. 'Surely, if I were God,' they might think, 'I would be quick to heal everyone.'

"The question that arises is the matter of free will and an orderly world based upon predictable laws. If God were to heal everyone who becomes sick or intervene every time things go awry, then there would not be free will and we would be puppets dangling at the end of the string. The laws of life and the cause and effect of our actions, would quickly become chaotic and meaningless. Life would lack order and natural consequences. Furthermore, how would we learn and grow and mature and deal with life's challenges?

"No, we must live in the world that God created for better or worse. For the most part, suffering is understandable as a natural consequence in our lives, but as I said, it can be so horrific and go on so endlessly, that it strikes such a deep chord in mankind that God's wisdom in this area is viewed more harshly and at times as senseless and cruel.

"It demands that we examine more closely how suffering fits into God's plan for the world beyond being part of the human condition and why is it that some even see joy coming out of their suffering?

"In trying to understand the mystery surrounding suffering and how we can cope with it, I have found some degree of insight as I examined the suffering in my own life and that of others. Sometimes, an example or a story is more revealing as it allows us to relate and identify with similar challenges that others have undergone and how they have dealt with it.

"I remember the day Karl burst into my store and related to me how his son was in a car accident and in critical condition in the hospital. He asked me to pray for a healing and that God would spare his boy. His son was in his mid twenties, married with two children, with a bright future as a lawyer. For years Karl and his wife scraped and struggled to save enough money to put their son through college and were so proud of him. Karl even offered his own life to God to please heal his son. On the fourth day following the accident, however, Karl's son died. Not only did Karl hate the man whose carelessness caused the accident, but he was deeply angry with God for not saving his son. In the days that followed, I saw Karl become more and more imprisoned.

"I and my wife Anna could relate, because for years our hearts were filled with the same destructive emotions of hate, hurt and anger towards the Nazis for killing our loved ones. We too were trapped with a spirit of unforgiveness and almost every living moment of our lives was tainted with the horrific memories of the past. We were only partially alive and the anguish was unbearable. It was Anna who saw the light before me. We were paying a heavy price by reliving our hurt and stirring our anger, hurt, and want of vengeance. She knew the only road to freedom was to accept what happened and to forgive.

"One morning, Anna and I found ourselves on our knees in the back storage room of our store and pleaded with God to soften our hearts and help us to forgive. He answered our prayers and a peace that surpasses all understanding swept through us and remained from that day until today. We experienced the power of love and forgiveness.

"I shared our experience with Karl and the need for him to

accept, forgive and move on with life. God was not the cause, but due to an unfortunate accident, the boy was now in the good care of the Lord.

"He would have none of it.

"Many times, he would come into the grocery store and see my Bible at the end of the counter and he would hiss at it. "How, can you believe in that Book, David? There is no God." He would clench his fist and shake it skyward. In vain, Anna and I pleaded with our friend to see what he was doing to himself and his family, but he would not listen. He would not allow our words to penetrate his hardened heart.

"Daily, he would relive his sorrow and anger and spout curses at the Lord. His days were filled with darkness; his emotions fed with anger, unforgiveness and rebellion. Not only was he suffering, but all those around him suffered too. Instead of giving love to his spouse and other children, they received a father that had chosen to be loveless. He had shut out God and the healing benefits of receiving His peace, grace, strength and comfort. He could not see that the pain his son experienced in the accident was far less than the pain he inflicted upon himself. He was a prisoner of his thoughts and lived in his own hell daily.

"This is not a good portrayal of a man's life and unfortunately has no happy ending. Over the years, Karl's anger and unforgiveness never lessened and he grew old before his time and eventually became physically ill. Shortly, his heart gave out and he followed his son to the grave.

"Now, let us look at another person's approach to suffering and hardships. Here today is a woman I visited in the hospital this past year who was dying of terminal cancer."

Almost simultaneously Henry and Jenny squeezed each other's hands.

Father gazed at Jenny and smiled tenderly and lovingly.

"When I first met Jennifer, her disease was being treated with both radiation and chemotherapy. The cancer had shrunk and was arrested to a degree, but only for a brief time. In all the weeks that I visited her, Jennifer never complained, even though her pain was great. Finally, the disease consumed her body and in her dying days, she stopped all treatment, knowing that the pain ahead would be difficult to deal with. She died, but miraculously was brought back to life, fully restored. Seldom does the Lord intervene this way, but He did.

"Recently I spoke with Jenny about the days and months leading up to her death and how she coped with her debilitating disease and its accompanying pain. Rather than share what she told me and give it to you second hand, I have asked Jenny to tell her story to you this morning." Father gazed at Jenny and swept out his hand to her, "Please let us welcome Jennifer Hamilton."

Jenny made her way slowly to the podium. She adjusted the microphone and then looked at the congregation with a radiant smile. Henry thought he would burst as his loved one stood there, a picture of utter beauty.

Jenny turned and looked at Father. "Thank you, Father Engelmann, for asking me to speak today. I am so grateful to God for restoring my life and returning me to the land of the living, but I must say that an even greater miracle occurred for me while I lay in the hospital as the cancer spread more and more throughout my body. At first, I did feel sorry for myself and asked God why this was happening to me. I thought perhaps I was being punished for giving up my first child for adoption, or for my failed marriage. I begged and pleaded with God to heal me and fought hard daily to combat the disease. But I only grew weaker, and the more I rebelled, the worse it seemed to be.

"As I lay there, I began to think about the story of two angels, each carrying a basket go out each morning. One angel gathers requests from people of what they need and want. The other angel collects thanks from people for the blessings they have received. Very soon the basket gathering requests is filled to overflowing, while the other angel's basket at day's end is barely filled with thanks, sometimes none at all. It just so happens that I have a life size angel statue carrying a basket in my backyard at home that is surrounded by wildflowers . "Every day when I was there, I would pick a flower or several flowers and place it into the basket in thanks for a blessing I was thankful for or a blessing for someone else.

"I realized that I had not been practicing gratitude at all since I had gotten sick. All my thoughts were filled with what I wanted and needed to get well. I decided it was time to fill up the angel's basket with thanks for my blessings. I pictured myself in my backyard and I mentally began to pick flowers of thanksgiving and placed them into the angel's basket and I said, "Thank you, God, for blessing me with this disease. I don't know why you allowed it into my life, but it has helped me to understand and appreciate the suffering of others. Reveal more to me why You have bestowed this blessing upon me." It felt strange to say such a thing and yet, I drew comfort from it. It made me think of my guardian angel, beside me in the room with her hand on my shoulder, soothing my spirit. In turn it reminded me of a picture I saw of Jesus in the Garden of Gethsemane, praying to God with an angel standing behind Him, too. The angel's hand was also on Jesus' shoulder, comforting Him as well, in the face of His impending death. I remembered reading in the Bible that Jesus too, asked the Father if it was possible to take this cup away from Him, but not what He wanted but what the Father wanted.

"*Let Your will be done.*

"It brought tears to my eyes. Jesus was showing us His humanity; even He didn't want to go through the suffering, if it was possible. Jesus could have said, no. After all, He is God, too. Surely there was another way to reconcile the sins of mankind with the Father that didn't require all what lay before Him. But the Father said no, and Jesus was obedient.

"*It made me think further on this.*

"Why would both the Father and Son see this as the best way to open the gates of heaven knowing the pain, suffering and anguish that both would go through? Jesus would be tortured unmercifully and then crucified, while His Father looked on, allowing it? To the many who lived at that time, clearly, it made no sense. If Jesus is truly the Son of God, surely the Father would never allow this to happen to his Son! Why would the King of kings and the Creator of the universe agree for such an atrocity to happen?

"But then I realized that this is earthly thinking and many at that time didn't see the big picture to God's plan or all the good that would come out of it. Through Jesus as mediator, in his own self, He healed the breach between all of us; the entire human race and His heavenly Father. Through His death and crucifixion, Jesus laid down His life for us to show how much He loved us. That awareness pierced my heart like never before. I could feel the nails going through Jesus' hands and feet and the weight of his body tearing and stretching the nail holes and the excruciating pain as the cross was lifted higher and then jarred into a hole to support it. It made me think of the Scripture: Greater love has no man than this that a man lay down his life for his friends. What more could our God do than to give His life in order to save us? But perhaps, even more so, was the love that the Father had for me that He would put His own Son through such great physical pain and suffering. Yet, still more than the physical pain, Jesus also suffered complete separation from His Father. Moments before Jesus died, he cried out, "Father, why have you forsaken me?"

"My heart was filled with such indebtedness and at the same time, repentance gripped my soul and spirit. I was so sorry for having offended my dear Lord and that I had caused part of His suffering because of the many times I turned against His love. I pleaded with God to forgive me from all my sins while at the same time I uttered my deep thankfulness, over and over again. My tears of sadness and sorrow turned into tears of happiness. Never, would I have thought that out of suffering could come such joy and bountiful blessings."

Jenny paused, and brushed away a tear. She breathed deeply and continued, "As I lay there in my hospital bed, weeping, I mentally drifted back to my garden and placed more and more flowers into the Angel of Thanksgiving's basket in thanks to Jesus for what He did for me and for all of us. With each flower I placed into the basket, I received His grace and strength.

"As my pain began to subside, I heard Jesus whisper to me. "I love you, Jenny and want you and as many others in the world to come to heaven. Such unimaginable beauty and joy await you and your brothers and sisters. Eye has not seen, or ear heard, or mind imagined, the things that my Father has prepared for those who love Him. Please, Jenny, help me. Please continue the redemption I have started. The gates to heaven are now open, the debt has been paid once and for all, but man must still choose to come in. Jenny, people need to pray for one another, to be beacons to one another, to lead one another, to be kind and do good works for one another, to always be forgiving and to offer our suffering up for one another—

"It was that last request that touched the deepest recesses of my heart… In the same way Jesus laid down his life for us, we too, must offer ourselves to Him and others. I fully realized my value and purpose as a child of God. We are all family in Jesus and every act of love we do for others counts! Yes, He is the vine and we are the branches…

"All at once, everything was connected! Jesus' crucifixion and death, my repentance and forgiveness, my pain and suffering, my joy and gratitude! It was all there!

"*Suffering was no longer a mystery…*

"It was at that point that I said, 'Yes,' and surrendered my suffering to God. I knew at that point, in the depths of my being, that my suffering and pain would not be wasted. God would use and turn my suffering into good like He did His Son's and be used to help in the continuing redemption of mankind.

"*At last, I found meaning in my pain. I fell freely into His open arms and placed all my trust and hope in Him.*"

Once more, Jenny paused and the light, power and truth of what she had just said, penetrated the hearts of all those present. Many in sympathy with Jenny's revelation were in tears as well. Taking another deep breath, Jenny continued.

"After the vision, I knew the end was near and I wanted to die as close to Jesus as I possibly could. There was considerable pain, but the grace and strength I received from God was sufficient for me to bear it. And that is the message that I want to leave with you today. Yes, there is incredible beauty in the world that God created, but there is also pain and suffering and hardships. As Father David said, such is the world we live in.

"*But God does not abandon us.*

"He knows the world is imperfect and He is always there to give us grace and strength and turn even our greatest trials into good. *It's up to us to choose to turn to Him and accept His offering.* It is then that our trust, faith, hope and understanding of love grows and works at the deepest and most meaningful level.

"I am so grateful to God for healing me, but even more for the wonderful vision that brought me to this understanding before I died. Without that, I would not be here today sharing how you, too, can be used for His purposes."

When Jenny finished her sharing, Father got up and picked up a bouquet of wild flowers from the table beside him. He took them over to Jenny and with tears in his eyes, he said, "My dear, Jenny, that was a most heartfelt sharing. The Lord has so richly blessed you. We know how much you love the beauty of wildflowers and the symbol of freedom they represent. As you spoke, this bouquet beside me seemed to brighten and fill the air with evermore fragrance. Jenny, you too, are like the wildflowers. In the same way, the flowers give off this wonderful aroma, the words you spoke were like incense filling the air in this church with a spiritual fragrance that has touched the hearts of us all. You have found in Jesus, the secret to beauty, to peace and freedom. On behalf of all those present here today, thank you, thank you, thank you."

Jenny took the flowers as tears slid slowly down her cheeks. She simply nodded and returned to her pew bedside Henry who was bursting with pride and love. He took her hand and ever so tenderly transmitted all that was within him to his dearly beloved.

Father watched Jenny as she returned to her seat. Tears were flowing down his cheeks as well. His love for Jenny, her sharing, and the Lord for the redemption of man overwhelmed the holy priest.

When Father spoke again he said, "When my Anna was ill, I too, knew she was in intense suffering and often I expressed my sorrow over her condition. But she would often say, "David, it is nothing compared to the suffering of our Lord. It is the least I can do." Although I understood what she said intellectually, it wasn't until I heard Jenny's sharing that Anna's words travelled to my heart.

"Yes, there is nothing that can compare to the depth of suffering of both the Father and Son in those dying moments of Jesus on the cross. His suffering with the Father watching on, culminating in the complete separation of Father and Son was the height and depth of all pain and all love. "Why have you forsaken me?" Jesus cried out as He entered death alone, bearing the sins of all mankind, from the beginning, to the end of all time. When this fully reaches our heart and soul as it did Jenny's, we begin to realize the immense love that the Father, the Son and the Holy Spirit have for you and me, despite our sinfulness and ingratitude.

"My dear brothers and sisters, listen with your heart as Jenny did to our Lord's plea to come to Him and offer your life. If you say yes, He will set fire into your heart for Jesus to help His Son continue the atonement for us all."

CHAPTER FIFTY FIVE

TEN MINUTES HAD passed since Henry and Jenny had finished their dinner, and neither of them had spoken a word since. The candle in the centre of Jenny's dining room table flickered, catching the love they had for each other in their eyes. Henry ached to hold Jenny and make love to her. Jenny felt the same and yet neither made the next move that would find them both in Jenny's bedroom. Father's words stung in Henry's heart. Jenny was still considered a married woman and to sleep with her would be an adulterous affair. Henry was not aware whether or not Jenny was familiar with the same knowledge.

Although they had talked about their relationship and knew where it was headed, so many issues had come into play that a more serious discussion was warranted. Was their relationship in jeopardy? Henry knew James wanted Jenny back, and then there was the annulment issue and even if it was possible for them to ever get married. What about her son and grandson and daughter-in-law? Henry knew how much Jenny desired to have that situation healed. All through the meal, their conversation skirted around any of these issues until Jenny finally opened the discussion.

"Did you call Peter, and let him know that we are coming?"

Henry nodded; his thoughts oscillated between the obstacles they faced and how much he desired Jenny. Her words caught him in the latter pleasurable world of caressing Jenny and kissing her warm sweet lips.

"Yeah, he's very happy that we are coming next Tuesday and thanked me for our consideration of his weekend obligations at the church. He said that he, his wife and two children would be there to meet us. He also admitted that he is extremely nervous, but even more anxious to get the healing process started."

"I feel nervous, too. I am so glad that both you and Camilla are coming along."

"I think we all need each other's support. That was some discussion we had with Father the other week. He sure has a handle on life and especially forgiveness. For as long as I can remember, he encourages forgiveness time and time again."

"It is a main obstacle to peace and moving on with your life."

"Yeah, I dealt with it all the time when I was counseling students and met with their parents. Many times the discussion starts out with problems the student is having and quickly grows into a discussion on the difficulties that the parents are dealing with in their marriage. It's unbelievable how after a few months or a year or two, couples begin to take each other for granted and even forget the vows they made to one another. I've witnessed so many times how spouses' treatment of strangers, colleagues or customers at their work place receive more consideration and respect than the person they vowed to love, honor and cherish."

"Oh, yes, I keep thinking of you as an artist and gallery owner, I forgot about your counselling career. Just what you said, I see in what Mable tells me is happening in their marriage. She shared with me that the romance seems to have gone out of their relationship. Her husband Ben spends a lot of time at work and mainly watches TV when at home and then goes to bed with the cycle repeating itself."

"Yeah, marriage requires effort, commitment and nurturing. But like you just described in Mable's case, many couples settle for a mediocre relationship and just take each other for granted."

"Oh, Henry, I would love to do counseling, too. When Mable talks about their marriage, there is so much I would like to discuss with her and help draw out her feelings like Camilla did with me when we spoke of Peter. In fact, I was even thinking that I would like to open my home as a meeting place for women to discuss their marriage and family concerns. It could be so healing."

"Like daughter like mother?"

Jenny smiled, "Yes, I think what Camilla is doing to help troubled girls find their way again is commendable and must be so rewarding as well…and it's what we are supposed to do to help others…" Jenny gazed at Henry waiting for his response.

"I think you have found your calling, Jenny."

"I know I am getting on in years, but late forties is still young enough to begin another career. Since being healed, it feels like I have been given a new lease on life, which I have and I want to serve others and God in some way…and I do feel called to help and serve in this way."

Once again, Jenny stopped and turned to Henry, "What do you think, Henry?"

"I think it's a wonderful thing to do, Jenny. You have so much to offer and give. You're sensitive, accepting and empathetic; you would be perfect for that job! Not only do you have the skills, you would also be such a positive role model. Yes, by all means, Jenny, if you want my opinion, absolutely, go for it. I would be the first to want to join if males were permitted!" Henry added with a wink.

"Before I can be a role model, I will have to fix my relationship with my son, I am at a loss as to how to reach him."

Henry was aware of some of the problems Jenny had with J.J. from reading her diary. But for the next half hour, Jenny shared more of her relationship with James and a similar scenario was occurring with Nora that had happened to her.

"I would hate to see Nora go through what I did and not receive any compensation from the marriage or financial support to look after Jimmy if it should come to that."

"Well, from what you told me about your marriage to James, the sooner we deal with Nora's situation the better. At least she hasn't invested as many years into the marriage as you have. They've been married four years, is that correct?"

"Yes, but with J.J.'s present attitude, it could seem like ten years to Nora. She was very upset when I spoke with her the other night; I hope she can cope with it. I've already told Father about it and asked him to say Mass for them and perhaps get his warriors at the care home to pray as well. If the results are anything like what has happened to us, they don't stand a chance."

"Prayer will help but from the sounds of it all she most likely will need your guidance and support. Not everyone can handle a failing marriage like you did. By your very nature, you are accepting and can tolerate others' shortcomings and not be adversely affected by them. But this is not the usual case, for one that is not centered and confident within themselves, such a relationship can have disastrous effects."

Jenny smiled at Henry and softly said, "It's so nice to be understood and affirmed."

Henry reached across the table and took Jenny's hands into his. He looked lovingly into her eyes and posed the question. "What's happening to us Jenny? Where is our future heading? I would love for us to consider marriage…there are a few obstacles—"

"I think I am aware of the main one," Jenny interjected. "I have to get an annulment from James."

Henry was surprised by what Jenny just said as he was going to bring up that very topic. "Were you talking with Father about that?"

"No, I spoke with the parish priest at the church I go to in this area. He told me that the Church does not recognize divorce and that the only way I could remarry was if James died or we can show in some way that the marriage wasn't valid in the first place."

"I recall you telling me how unsure you were of marrying James and that you fainted as you struggled to say the marriage vows. Father thought that might have some bearing in the sense that you were pressured into the marriage or didn't fully realize what you were doing."

"But I did Henry; I knew what I was getting into, although I did feel pressured by my Mom and James…"

"The other thing Father asked me was if you had received dispensation from the Church if you could marry outside the Church. Did you?"

"We were supposed to be married in a cathedral and had a huge wedding planned, but James' father died and James was involved in a major deal or merger and pleaded with me to just elope. Suddenly, everything was in such a rush. He promised that on our first anniversary we could receive the blessings of the Church and have friends and family present, but that never happened. To answer your question, yes, I did get dispensation from the Bishop due to the circumstances and that the Justice of the Peace was a retired Pastor from James' mother's church. Mom was so anxious for us to get married that she agreed and thought too, that a special church ceremony down the line would be okay..."

"We just need James to agree now to an annulment..." Henry offered with a tone of hope.

"I don't think James will agree to it. We spoke a couple of times since my life and health was restored and he is adamant that I come back to the estate. He seems so different from when we lived together. When I spoke with Matti the other day, she too, cannot believe how different James is. By the sounds of it, he and the staff have become the best of friends."

Henry wondered if he should tell Jenny that James called him as well. It was unsettling to say the least with the threats James threw at him. Jenny would be very upset to learn her ex-husband had the nerve to do that...and yet, Henry couldn't blame him for trying to get his former wife back. He thought it best to just leave it for now. Instead he asked, "How do you feel about James wanting you to come back, Jenny? Do you want to go back to him?" Henry moved closer to the edge of his seat and held his breath.

"I told him over and over that I could no longer do that and I had moved on with my life."

"How did he feel about that?" Henry already had a good idea but still was anxious to hear it from Jenny.

"He wouldn't accept it and kept going on how he has changed and that he is ill and needs me. The one thing that did affect me more than anything he said was that J.J. needs me and that if I come back, I would be instrumental in restoring J.J. and Nora's marriage...and I do miss my grandson."

"Oh, Jenny, what a position you are in...what do you want to do?"

"I would love to fly to Ottawa a week or so after we see Peter. Nora needs some support and probably some advice on how their financial affairs are set up if it's not too late. I do want to spend some time with my grandson and hopefully be able to talk to J.J. and for us to make up. Oh that will be so difficult trying to resolve things with that boy of mine...do you think you might be able to come with me?"

"Yes, of course I will come with you." Henry said, showing immediate support.

"That makes me feel better and perhaps when I see James in person, I'll ask if he would agree to an annulment. If he does, then we at least stand a chance the Church might grant it. Without his consent and the fact that he wants to try again, will definitely impede the process."

Henry's mind barely heard Jenny's concern with her son and family...what if James refused to go along with the annulment?

"I don't like to see this as an option, Jenny, but the only way we might be able to get married is if James should die."

"Well, he is ill and that could be a possibility, but knowing James he might consider life support to keep him alive until a cure is found. In fact, Matti told me a while back that James is having his body frozen upon his death for the same reason."

"I've read about that. Apparently scientists are still working on how to bring the person back. That is, how to thaw the person quickly enough and not destroy the cells along the way...something like that."

Henry paused for a moment to reflect and then cautiously continued, "So even if his illness would bring him to his death, he could be kept alive for years. How would the church view a situation like that...would he be considered dead or not?"

"Just talking about it gives me the shivers, Henry. I hope things don't come down to any of that. I do want the best for James."

Henry nodded, "So do I, Jenny, so do I."

CHAPTER FIFTY SIX

THEY WERE ALL so nervous as they boarded Air Canada for Calgary. The sky was overcast, reflecting their somber mood. Jenny sat in the middle seat of row seven. Her elbows rested on the armrest, but her hands were tightly wrapped around Camilla's who sat in the window seat and Henry's, who was next to the aisle. They were finally on their way to meet the man who had assaulted Jenny over thirty two years ago and fathered a child that fateful night. Henry had called Peter over a week ago and made arrangements for the meeting as soon as they landed in the Calgary airport.

Henry recalled the conversation he had with Peter. He was so thankful for the call and that the ladies had decided to come and meet with him. Henry already knew that his wife, Angelika, knew of the matter and that his parishioners did as well. What Henry did not know, however, was whether or not Peter's children were also aware of their father's daughter and that they had a half sister. Peter said that his wife and children would be with him at the airport.

During their conversation, Peter also told Henry that the reason he was so haunted by what he did was due to the aches and pains he had in his stomach just like Henry did prior to Jenny giving birth to Camilla. Amazingly, on May 24, 1957, Peter, like

Henry, also threw up on the day of Camilla's birth and on each and every year that followed up until last year. Early on, Peter realized that there was something to this as the thought of his assault on Jenny was so strongly associated with the pain and nausea that he felt. Further, when he made the calculations in his mind, the day he first threw up was in that ninth month period after he and his friends had taken Jenny to the park.

Over the years he was continuously haunted by the fact that he had fathered a child that evening. Finally, after all those years, the day of reckoning, reconciliation and hopefully healing was upon them all. It was now Henry, who squeezed Jenny's hand as a chilling tingle ran up and down his spine.

JENNY, TOO, WAS immersed in thoughts about that fateful night. One flashback after another crossed her mind; the boys coming out of their car and grabbing her and forcing her into the back seat. She could feel the fear seeping through her now as the car sped away. She tried to look back at Henry but the boy's grip on her wrists was too strong. She remembered pleading with them to take her back and let her go, but all she heard was laughing and obscenities. The fear that rushed through her when they parked the car and pulled her out, terrified her.

Jenny began to shake in the seat. She wanted to grab the angel hanging on the chain around her neck, but didn't want to let go of either Henry's or Camilla's hand. *Oh guardian angel please help me,* Jenny screamed in her mind now, as she did back then.

Jenny squeezed her daughter's hand and felt Camilla's love transmitted back with a tender hold. Next to her sat a beautiful child, a daughter that she loved deeply; the result of that fateful night. How could she mar that image of her child due to the manner in which she was conceived? She must do as Father Engelmann said; separate the act from the person whom God created. At the core of the assailant's being is the love of God. Father Engelmann was right. She could not give in to her feelings, she must be like Jesus and forgive. Forgiveness was the only answer that would heal and give freedom.

Jenny felt the power of forgiveness growing within her...

As the plane hurtled through the sky, each second bringing

them closer to their meeting, Jenny's nervousness returned. She agitated in her chair, her feet started to bounce. It was the same when she was waiting in the doctor's office for the test results. Every sound was like an explosion; the doctor's footsteps coming down the hall, the turning of the door knob, the click shut. She recalled every move the doctor made; entering his office and avoiding eye contact, the swirling of his chair and pushing it next to her, his furtive glances, movements, his facial expressions, it all revealed what words would come out of his mouth. He sat down in front of her. Instantly, the flashbacks of that awful night and the naked truth of what had really happened was written in the doctor's eyes.

Oh angel of God help me, please don't let me faint again.

"Mom, are you okay?" Camilla asked, concern written all over her pretty face.

Jenny nodded and forced a smile. She squeezed her daughter's hand.

God had worked miraculously in her life by healing her and bringing her back. She believed it was for her and Henry to be together, but she could see that this might be another major reason for her return. *She had to love.* She could forgive now, this minute, she was certain of it, but when she faced him, could she still?

Please come into my heart, dear Jesus. Give me Your heart, Your strength, Your mercy, Your compassion, Your spirit of forgiveness. Give me the grace and strength to do what I must...

CAMILLA TURNED TO her mother, and noticed Jenny's eyes were closed. She wondered about all the thoughts that must be running through her mind. Girls who have been assaulted are so emotionally distraught; the trauma of that event plaguing them for days, months and years. She could only imagine what her mother went through at age fifteen and how she coped with it all of those years.

Camilla was surprised how well her mother did cope with it. Perhaps it was Jenny's closeness to her guardian angel which provided so much comfort from her protector. But then again, it was also Henry's love and imagining that it was he who was the father. Perhaps it was all these factors as well as her nature that gave Jenny the ability to accept what happened without too much trauma.

How would she react when she saw Peter, Camilla wondered?

It was at Father Engelmann's anniversary party that she had first seen Peter. Immediately, she knew there was some connection. She could see it in his stare; his features, the way he talked. Although she had always felt that she was dearly loved by her adoptive parents, she felt a sense of belonging that she had not felt before… even though he was a complete stranger.

Camilla had those feelings now, but with understanding. She now knew why she was so drawn to him.

Peter was her father.

A mixture of excitement, nervousness and fear sizzled through her body. How would the meeting go? She knew she could accept her father and what he did. She should be angry with him and what he did to her mother, but she wasn't. Perhaps it had to do with the way Jenny had accepted it and her birth and the deep, genuine love she felt from her. Her mother had not allowed the event to destroy her or control her life.

Maybe that was it.

She had seen and heard of so many cases of sexual assault and the devastating effects it had on so many people. Camilla wanted this to be different. She could see the pain that girls went through and how they relive the trauma over and over, unwilling to let go through forgiveness. Many girls did not realize the power they had given to their assailant by allowing themselves to be controlled by another's actions and shortcomings, sometimes for years. Camilla did not want to imprison herself like that nor her mother and father. She wanted healing more than anything and she wanted it now. She hoped and prayed her mother did, too.

Tomorrow, it may very well be too late!

Suddenly the voice of Captain spoke through the intercom, "Please fasten your seat belts. We are entering into turbulent skies as we begin our descent for landing and may experience some bumpy spots."

No sooner had the man in control of the plane uttered those words then the aircraft began to rattle and shake as it hurtled through the sky. "Flight attendants please take your seats and fasten your seat belts. We will be landing in Calgary in ten minutes."

Jenny couldn't help but feel the road ahead would be turbulent as well, but prayed that soon there would be smooth sailing and clear skies. The minutes and seconds were speeding up, bringing them closer to their impending meeting. *Please, dear Jesus, help me to trust completely in You. Oh, Hannah, protect us and bring us safely to the ground.* She squeezed Henry's hand.

Henry knew it wasn't the bumpy ride through the sky that was giving his loved one jittery nerves, but what lay just ahead. Similar thoughts were growing in his mind as well.

Their hearts raced as they felt the tires come out of the plane's belly and lock into place for the landing.

"Oh, Mom, I feel so nervous, I wonder how Peter and his family must be feeling."

"I can just imagine, Camilla. This is going to be hard on all of us, but it will be worth it, honey..."

Jenny's words trailed off as the plane hit the tarmac. Their bodies were thrust forward as the brakes and wing flaps were applied reversing the thrust.

As SOON AS the sliding glass doors opened into the main terminal, Jenny knew instantly that the man in the distance next to a woman and three other adults was Peter with his family. He didn't look at all like the huge muscular man that had assaulted her, but thin and frail. But then, like her, he was plagued with cancer and the disease had taken its toll on his body.

His arms hung at his side and when he saw Jenny, he slightly raised his right hand and waved. It was a hesitant movement, an unsure one, not knowing if the person it was intended for would reciprocate.

Before Jenny could respond, Camilla had already raised her hand and waved back. While Jenny wanted to slow their approach to the nervous waiting family, Camilla tightened her grip on her mother's hand and quickened her pace, pulling Jenny forward and Henry along with her. When they were a few feet from each other, they came to a halt, as if to rethink what was about to happen or should happen.

For years and years, Jenny had this image of a strong man forcing her to the ground, his eyes filled with a raving, frenzy look, and now, there before her was a man whose eyes were filled with sorrow and remorse. She could read the pleading in his face and the way he stood there asking for her forgiveness.

He appeared broken.

He waited and the momentary hesitancy on her part must have been like a year to him. His wife's hand wrapped around his was white. In a flashing glance, Jenny saw the woman's pain and pleading, too, and all she had gone through to accept what her husband had done. Her support of her husband, stung Jenny's heart.

Jenny had gone over and over how her reaction would affect all those present, but now she was in the moment; this moment. If she was cold, they would think evil of their father. Jenny wanted to send the message that he was a good man who had made a mistake. It was not only for them, but for her daughter as well.

Jenny wondered now if she could convey that kind of forgiveness from her heart to the man who violated her. Father Engelmann's words entering her mind were comforting and encouraging. '*Somewhere between your heart and Camilla's and Peter's is a connection that never died nor ever will. At the root was an act that shouldn't have happened, but did, and now needs compassion and forgiveness; a forgiveness that is a path to reconciliation, freedom, peace and friendship. All these elements are ever present if only we are open enough to let such Christ thoughts enter into our relationships and meetings. Christ is ever there to instill mercy and forgiveness for the most grievous of offences and atrocities. This is the extent of God's love. We can tap into it and find peace or we can rebel and fill our beings with hatred, resentment, bitterness... hell.*'

A radiant smile began to cover Jenny's face and she thought of her angel and Peter's and Father Engelmann's description of how they met their protectors with a warm embrace instead of a handshake when they had gone to the other side.

Yes, this was the moment that was filled with power, with hope, reconciliation and forgiveness; she would not walk away and lose this moment in time...

Jenny stepped forward ever so slightly and let go of Henry's hand to her right and Camilla's to the left.

They were waiting for her, to follow her lead.

Peter made a slight move, but waited for Jenny, to be sure, to be certain... Jenny stepped still closer and her arms began to raise towards her assailant. But he was no longer the man who had harmed her; she chose to see a brother in Christ. She chose to see the man God created and loved too. This was why He sent His only

Son to die for our sins out of love for us. Yes, Jesus died for her so that in moments like this she would continue to see His redemption upon all of God's children. He came to save sinners. She saw it all when she was ill and suffering. It all tied together whether it was suffering an illness or a deep emotional scar in life…it was all the same; we must accept our cross and forgive or do whatever is required to continue the atonement that Jesus had started.

Old, sluggish, feelings tired of being replayed over and over that wanted justice and revenge struggled to rise up, but didn't stand a chance. A surge of love and complete forgiveness swept through Jenny's being as if Jesus himself had flooded her spirit.

As she inched closer, Peter dared to raise his arm to shake her hand, but Jenny saw Jesus raise both His arms, His heart radiating mercy and peace. She was drawn to both Peter and Christ, *they were one*. Jenny could no longer hold back as she was filled with God's grace and strength to love beyond her capacity.

The next step brought them together. Jenny could feel Peter's touch and the nearness of his body next to hers. It was no longer repulsive, but warm and caring. She heard his words, "Please forgive me, Jenny."

Jenny chose to love; to reflect Jesus' mercy… softly, she whispered back, "I forgive you, Peter… I love you."

Peter and all those in attendance felt the power of God's love penetrating each of them through Jenny's act of forgiveness. It was as if heaven was on earth. A joy swept through them all as Jenny and Peter cried and embraced.

Camilla could no longer stand back, as she too, rushed forward and embraced her father and mother. Like her mother, she softly whispered, "I love you, Dad. It's so good to finally meet you." She didn't want to dwell another minute in the past nor give it any further power.

This was the moment of a new beginning!

And one by one, Henry, Angelika and Peter's children all crowded in on Peter, Jenny and Camilla, huddled together, embracing one another.

An aura shone around them as the heavens rejoiced along with them. If only the angels around and above them were visible, what a joyous, spectacular sight could be seen!

Passers-by in the airport could feel the love and energy; many wept. They were caught in a deep moment of pure love.

The odour of victory over sin freeing imprisoned spirits enlivened the air!

AFTER AN ENJOYABLE meal in Peter's home, they sat around a warm fireplace and continued to share their lives. They talked of their background and the incredible way Camilla came to find her mother and how she ended up marrying Henry's son! Camilla loved learning more about her step brother and sister and they all vowed to write and see each other twice a year if not more and talk every week on the phone. Before the evening was over, it was as if they were all family. Joy, laughter and singing pervaded Peter's home.

As THEY FLEW back to Regina, Henry, Jenny and Camilla sat side by side as they did before, on their way to Calgary. And as before, the three were silent, immersed in the memories of the weekend. The memories and thoughts this time however, were different.

Jenny never looked more radiant and at peace. Camilla's head rested on her mother's shoulder and Jenny was stroking her daughter's hair. There no longer was tension or nervousness in the ladies. Their thoughts were filled with a bright future.

Henry, on the other hand, was overwhelmed with all of the insights he had gained from what had transpired. He could hardly wait to see Father and share the wonderful experience he had the past couple of days and it was all because of Jenny.

Henry couldn't help but squeeze Jenny's hand. He was so proud of her and the example she exhibited. He never would have thought Jenny could ever be any more beautiful than he already thought. *But he was wrong.* This past weekend Jenny became beautiful beyond words because she allowed Jesus to live through her. Jenny had the heart of an angel, it was pure and loving, perfect for Jesus to enter and shine through.

"Wow," was all Henry could utter.

CHAPTER FIFTY SEVEN

HENRY AND FATHER Engelmann retired to the sun room at the care home after the morning Mass. It took almost an hour until the crowd of people dispersed and left. Doris was getting concerned over the number of visitors coming to the Nunnery. It was not just to attend the morning service, but also to ask Father to pray for them or to touch him hoping for a miracle in their lives. Word of the healings that occurred in the care home the day Father had died and came back to life spread quickly beyond the neighborhood, the city limits and into neighboring provinces.

"I see the care home is as busy as ever, Father. Soon you will need a larger chapel," observed Henry.

"Yes, it concerns me, Henry. No matter how many times I let people know that it is the Lord that heals and not me, many still think I have special powers to do so. You may find that my stay at your prayer house may become more frequent and my stays longer. Perhaps if I am not here so often in the next while, people will get discouraged and stop coming. And yet, I want to lead people to the Lord and not avoid them…"

"Yeah, I know what you mean, Father. I'm sure in time things will settle down."

"Yes, I hope so. Now, tell me, Henry, how did the meeting go with Peter and his family?"

"Yeah, that's why I came to see you this morning. It went incredibly well. I wish you could have been there. Jenny was like a saint, Father; the perfect example of the Saint Francis prayer of peace that you say everyday:

Lord, make me an instrument of Your peace.
Where there is hatred, let me sow love.
Where there is injury, pardon,
Where there is doubt, faith,
Where there is despair, hope,
Where there is darkness, light, and where there is sadness, joy.

"I have to say, Father, Jenny was an instrument for peace all right, and it reflected her nature in the last part of the prayer as well. Father joined in with Henry and together, in unison, they completed the beautiful prayer:

Oh Divine Master, grant that I may not seek to be consoled,
As to console;
To be understood, as to understand;
To be loved, as to love;
For it is in giving that we receive—
It is in pardoning that we are pardoned;
And it is in dying that we are born to eternal life.

The two men gazed at one another and smiled. "Every word of that prayer, describes Jenny to a tee, Father." Henry reiterated once more.

"Yes, Jenny is truly a peacemaker at heart. Peter is very fortunate to have had such a forgiving person to deal with and I suppose it was good for Jenny, as well, that Peter was so contrite and seeking her forgiveness."

"I thought that, too, Father. The fact that Peter is a pastor and turned out to be such a fine man would make it easier for Jenny to forgive and accept him. However, when I mentioned that to her, she quickly corrected me. She said, she would have loved and forgiven him regardless if he showed remorse or not, regardless whether he was seeking forgiveness or not, because of her desire to please God. She said your words, when we met at the prayer house that Saturday how we must separate the deed from the person who God created, was very helpful."

"Yes, whether the action or behaviour results in a huge hurt or small one, the decision is the same; we forgive the sin, but love the sinner. God does that all of the time. If He didn't, I'm afraid there wouldn't be very many of us who have a hope of getting into heaven. In the same way God forgives us, we too, must forgive others. If we don't, God cannot forgive us as our hearts are filled with unforgiveness. We hold the key to peace. Turning it open to the door of our heart that is imprisoned, allows us to walk out a free person."

"And that's exactly what happened. Jenny's choice to forgive created such a feeling of freedom, it was almost palpable, Father. I'm certain that everyone in the airport must have felt the power of it all. And just think, Father, it could have been so different, had Jenny withheld her forgiveness. By worldly standards, many would say that Jenny should never have forgiven Peter, rather, she should have beaten him and scolded him for all the hurt, anger and sorrow he caused and she had every right and justification to do so."

"But what would have been the gain for her or anyone else?" Father quickly questioned. "No, Jenny didn't allow pride to enter; she chose to die to herself and to all those feelings. By doing so, Peter and all those present were blessed to witness the power of letting go and letting God shine and seeing the tremendous fruits of forgiving."

Henry nodded and continued, "It was wonderful to witness that, Father. The power that was released when Jenny said, "I forgive you, Peter," was like an explosion of incredible good in everyone's hearts that witnessed it. I am still reeling over it all."

"Jenny used her free will perfectly, Henry. She chose to let Jesus live through her and what incredible results were witnessed by all those present. The power of our free will elevates man as the highest being on earth and when used wisely yields amazing fruits. What joy and freedom awaits a person when choosing Jesus' ways!"

Father Engelmann had learned the secret to yielding his free will to the Lord long ago and look at the results, Henry thought as he gazed lovingly at his mentor. He is like Jenny was the other day, all of the time; twenty four seven.

Father broke into his thoughts, "Why live in hell when you can live in heaven on earth? The choice is ours. We can live for Him all the time, part of the time or never. If we yield our will to Him, all of the time, pick up our cross daily and trust that He will turn everything into the good then we, too, can live in perfect peace all of the time. That is what Saint Francis calls, *perfect joy*, to do God's will in all circumstances. It's a complete trust in God's divine providence, Henry."

"That's precisely what I was thinking about on our way back to Regina, how God's divine providence was working for years on this situation to bring it to a head."

Father nodded, "God allows struggles and challenges to come into our lives constantly in order that they work together for our good so that we become more like Jesus. When we truly believe that God is constantly at work in our lives, we can rest knowing that God is the one orchestrating the events of our lives. It is His plan. When we know and accept this, we become less frustrated with circumstances and people and everything that challenges us. God is behind it all and in perfect control, constantly at work for our good. Just submit to Him and trust Him with all your heart. "

Henry shook his head from side to side. "Why are we so foolish to do it our way when there is an all knowing God who can guide us perfectly through life? "

"We lack faith, and trust and we want control. For the most part, it's because we haven't taken the time to develop a relationship with Him. To know Him, is to trust Him, is to love Him. This can only come through spending time with Him each day and study his Word and teachings. Gradually, we learn His truths and what is best for us. Gradually, we turn our will over to Him because we see the enormous benefits from doing so. We pick up our cross daily and begin to live with eternity in mind."

"Yeah, it makes such good sense, Father. It really hit home to me what you have spoken of so often; dying to yourself. In the Prayer of Peace, Saint Francis describes it perfectly and like I said, Jenny captured the essence of that prayer. Although I see it in you all of the time, I take it for granted. Seeing it through Jenny's actions, I really understood what it means to die to oneself. Like I said, Jenny could have chosen the opposite of what she did…"

Father just nodded and waited for Henry to go on.

"But rather than allow her feelings, her pride, her sense of justice to dominate and control her thoughts, she humbled herself like Jesus and accepted her cross just like you encouraged us to do in your sermon last week. I clearly recall you looking at the cross and instructing the congregation that it all has to do with the cross. Crucifying ourselves along with Christ and continuing His redemption, Jenny showed us exactly what that means and the fruit of doing so. She was a beacon of light in the darkness. Such a perfect example of the power we have to live a life with assurance, purpose and meaning!"

Henry shook his head once more as God's plan for mankind became clearer in his mind. He could see the power of free will; to choose to love or hate, to be forgiving or unforgiving, to be kind or cruel…with free will there is an opposite to everything and God gave us this gift and the complete freedom to choose one or the other. He had seen it so clearly in the choices Jenny had made that weekend. The results could have been so drastically different had she chosen not to love! *The life free will offers is staggering if used in the way God intended.* Henry could easily see in his own life when he ran into trouble or messed up or worried and had a guilty conscience was when he chose to disobey the teachings of Jesus and His commandments.

Father gently spoke, reinforcing the insight Henry was grasping at a deeper level. It was as if the teacher had read the student's mind.

"To the degree we *choose* to die to our self interests, our ways, our pride, is the degree to which we allow Christ to come into our lives. This is what it means to pick up our cross each day, to follow Him and live with eternity in mind."

"Yes…" Henry whispered as the Scripture Father had said so many times and one that he had read over and over sprang to life: in John, 12:24-25 Jesus said, "I say to you, unless a grain of wheat falls into the ground and dies, it remains alone. But if it dies, it produces much grain. He who loves his life will lose it, and he who hates his life in this world will keep it for eternal life."

It felt as if Henry was sitting out back of the old grocery store with his mentor, learning truths. Mr. Engelmann was right then and continued to show his wisdom now. It was all in the Bible! Psychologists, philosophers, psychiatrists have not really discovered anything new. It was all there; Jesus laid out the map for us so beautifully and simply; if we but only choose to follow it!

That was what it was that was so appealing about Father, thought Henry. He lives the teachings of Jesus so perfectly that he emulates the words of St. Paul, "I have been crucified with Christ: it is no longer I who live, but Christ lives in me. And the life which I now live in the flesh I live by faith in the Son of God who loved me and gave Himself for me."

"Did you and Jenny discuss the possible annulment of her marriage, Henry?" Father asked, changing the subject to one that was becoming more pertinent to Henry and Jenny's future.

Henry shuffled in his chair; he didn't expect Father to bring up that topic.

"Yes, we talked about it. Jenny already knew much of the information as she had discussed it with the parish priest in the neighbourhood where she lives. He informed Jenny pretty much what you and I had discussed."

"What about the matter of asking for dispensation to marry outside of the church?"

"I did ask her that and she said she was able to obtain a dispensation from the local Bishop. Apparently they had planned a big wedding in the cathedral in Ottawa, but it didn't materialize due to James' father's untimely death. They were going to have a special celebration in the Church at a later time, but that, too, didn't pan out either."

"I see," said Father.

"She is planning a trip to Ottawa. Her son and his wife are having marital difficulties and Jenny is concerned about that. She would like to try and help out and see her grandson. She would also like to speak to James in person and ask for an annulment. I will be accompanying her for support."

Father nodded and once again said, "I see."

A lengthy silence descended upon the men. The morning sun suddenly peeked in through the windows, drawing Henry's and Father Engelmann's attention to the courtyard. The perennials were in full bloom and many were surrounded by annuals that some of the residents had planted. The petunias and pansies were doing very well, as were the marigolds. Henry didn't recognize the others as they hadn't flowered yet or lost their bloom. He momentarily pictured the nuns watering and caring for the plants, when the care home was a convent, when Father interrupted his thoughts with a troubling question.

"What if Jenny hadn't come back to life, Henry? What would you have done with the rest of your life? Would you have continued to run your gallery? Buy more rental property? You are still a young man..."

Henry shrugged his shoulders. "I don't know, Father. I suppose I would do more painting. The kids are taking over the operation of the business...the only thing that seems to stir any other interest is when I receive a letter from Gary and he talks about the missionary work he is doing."

"Yes, both John and Gary seem to be very committed to serving the Lord in that capacity. Would you consider going abroad, too?"

"I don't think I could do that, Father. What appeals to me is to make the Western world more aware of their responsibility to help meet the needs of their brothers and sisters in the third world. I recall the talk Gary gave that Sunday you had asked him to speak about his work before Mom died. He indicated that there was a need to do that."

"Yes, Mother Teresa has done similar tours to make North America aware of that need. She did say however, that loneliness is even a greater concern. I believe she was referring to the treasures in our heart which lack purpose and meaning to serve God and others."

"Yes, it's all connected..." Henry's words trailed off.

"Perhaps the Lord wants to talk to you about it, Henry. You have such a magnificent retreat house in the valley. Have you considered doing a retreat there?"

Henry was hesitant to answer and then dared to go on. "I think I am afraid of what the Lord might ask of me, Father. I still am too connected to the world and its ways. I struggle with what I have and the identity it gives me. I enjoy the recognition, prestige and accolades of my accomplishments. I know it is all an illusion and has no eternal value except for how it is used to serve. What it comes down to, Father, is that I still serve two masters."

"It's good that you recognize that. You remind me of the man in the Scriptures that Jesus asked to sell all and follow him."

"Yes, and he walked away sad because he was a very wealthy man. I think of that Scripture all of the time. Surely, He doesn't want me to go that extent? Does He?"

"We have discussed this many times amongst ourselves and also in sermons. It's not the wealth so much as it is our attachment to it and our pursuit of it that is a very serious problem for the western world. Simplifying our lives, giving of our riches, is a start. The closer we come to a true sense of poverty; the realization that nothing is ours, not only our wealth, but our very lives, the freer we become. We must become less and less until we know deep in our heart that we are nothing without God. Everything is His, it all belongs to Him. Don't be seduced into worldly ways any longer. Don't blame the world that it has too hard of a grip upon you. It's all up to you to take responsibility for your life and choose His ways over yours. It comes back to the power of free will that you just spoke of. Everything you choose to do in your life must glorify the Father. Keep in mind that our lives on earth are very short; just an infinitesimal blip in the vastness of eternity. The closer you get to this sense of poverty and realize how short our existence really is, the freer you become to your attachment to the world."

Father could see that Henry really wasn't listening, he had an idea of what was troubling his son and Henry's next words confirmed his assumptions.

"I know what you are saying is true, Father, but my mind is too troubled…what if I lose Jenny again?

Father had already been thinking of such a possibility and that is why he asked Henry what he would do with his life if Jenny had not returned to life.

"It seems to me, Henry, we have had this discussion one time before when Julean came into your life."

"Yeah, I recall that time in the back storage room you talked to me about God's divine providence and trusting in Him to turn it all into good."

"Yes, we have to yield our will to His, Henry and trust in Him. You just explained such beautiful insights about trusting Jesus like Jenny did and waiting on Him."

"Yeah, I know it comes down to that all the time. Trust

in the Lord with all your heart and don't rely on your own understanding."

Henry wondered if he would ever be able to do that. He worried so much about Jenny and him. Could he just give it all to God? *Oh dear Lord, give me the grace and strength to submit our lives into Your care and trust You with all of my heart to turn it all into our good.*

Father peered at Henry over the rim of his glasses, "Why don't you come and spend a weekend with me at the prayer house? There are things that the mind cannot answer, Henry, only the heart can."

Henry nodded. Father thought his son was finally agreeing with him to make a prayerful retreat, but Father was wrong.

Once again, Henry posed the question...

"What if Jenny decides to go back to James?"

CHAPTER FIFTY EIGHT

THE DOORBELL RANG for the second time. Jenny thought she had heard the chime as she sat on the patio. Good thing the doors were open. She looked outside and saw a delivery van with Regina Florists written on the side. "Oh no, I hope James isn't sending me a bunch of flowers again." Jenny opened the door and saw a huge grin on the delivery man's face. He was holding a small package. It was long and narrow. Jenny suspected perhaps a single flower or two and definitely not from James. It's probably from Henry.

"Morning ma'am, I'm glad you answered, I'm always afraid to leave flowers at the front door when no one is at home. Hope this makes a happy day for you," said the young man.

"Yes, thank you very much…and you have a nice day, too!"

"That was so thoughtful of Henry, I wonder what it is? A rose? It could be a wildflower," Jenny said, as she made her way into the kitchen.

She laid the package on the kitchen table and opened the wrapping. It was a single white daisy with a deep yellow–orange centre. Attached to the stem was a card.

Jenny carefully removed the elastic securing the card and slowly opened it up.

An eerie feeling began to sweep through her body. Instinctively she knew this wasn't from Henry…it was from James:

Dear Jenny
It came to me that a single flower would capture your
attention more than a showy bunch of dozens of flowers.
It's simple, plain and honest. I want you know that I'm
trying to be like that. I know how much you love flowers
and see such beauty in them. I hope someday to grow just
a little bit so that you see in me what you see in this daisy.
I will call later, hope you are home.
I love you Jenny.

James

Jenny felt weak. She made her way slowly outside to the deck and sat down.

Oh James…my dear, James. Can't you see that it is over between us?

Jenny shook her head and tears surfaced in her eyes. She had planned to call him this very day to ask for an annulment. She so much wanted to be free to marry Henry and now…this.

Oh dear guardian angel, what am I to do?

The back yard garden was in full bloom and looked so beautiful and serene. The Monarchs were back and Jenny felt like she was in paradise. Usually it was such a sight that restored her calm and gave her such peace especially when she lived on the estate, but now it had lost its healing power. Sadness was seeping into her heart. She didn't want to hurt James. He was growing…he was becoming like a flower ready to bloom.

The ring of the telephone startled her. Panic gripped her heart; she couldn't move. She brought her hand to her mouth and muttered, "Oh Lord, what am I going to do?" She had to answer the phone. The phone rang again and again. Slowly, Jenny got up. Her knees threatened to collapse. The phone rang again as she made it into the kitchen. She reached for the receiver but couldn't pick it up. It rang again…

"Hello," Jenny said almost in a whisper.

"Hi Jen, I was just about to hang up. Bet you were outside in that haven back yard of yours."

"Oh, Henry, I am so relieved that it is you!"

"Yup, it's me. Were you expecting someone else?"

Jenny held her breath; she had to be truthful...

"Oh, Henry, I don't want to upset you, but I just received a flower from James. He said on the card that he was going to call this morning and I thought that when the phone rang, it might be him."

There was a long silence on the phone. Finally Henry spoke, "Is he asking for you to come back, Jenny?"

"Yes..." Jenny said softly, but quickly added, "But I don't want to and I won't. I had planned on calling him today and discussing an annulment of our marriage but...he keeps asking for us to try again."

"Geez, Jen...I love you with all my heart and there isn't anything I want more for us than to be married..."

"And that's what I want too, but how can we with so many obstacles in the way?"

"We will just have to take one step at a time, perhaps ask him about an annulment when he calls."

"I know what he will say, Henry, and he won't even understand what I'm asking."

"You will have to explain it to him—"

"Oh, Henry, I don't know how to handle this. If it was just James it would be easier but with a son and grandson and daughter–in–law and all the problems that are going on there...it's just so overwhelming."

After a long silence, Henry spoke softly, "Jenny, as much as I love you, I don't want to force you to make a decision. I will support you in any way I can but you are going to have to decide... you can do it. I will accept what you decide."

"See, you always give me this freedom, Henry. Can't you just come and sweep me away and lock me up and let's just shut out the rest of the world?" Jenny blurted out of frustration.

"Jenny, please, things are going to work out...we just have to have faith and trust in God to turn it all out for the good. As hard as it is for me to see that, I just don't see any other way."

"I suppose so, Henry. Did you call to tell me you're coming over?"

"Actually, I was going to pick you up and bring you to the farm. The kids are home and Jeremy and Camilla are coming for dinner…but maybe some other time would be better?"

"No, I think that would be wonderful. Yes, I would love to come. I hope Justin warms up to me."

"Oh, it's just a matter of time, Jen. He and Julean were very close. He'll come around."

"He's such a nice boy. I see a lot of you in him; he wears his heart on his sleeve."

"Yeah, well, I'll pick you up around two thirty or so. Maybe we can go for a walk in the valley. I was surprised how you ran over all the wild daisies when we were visiting Father in the Poustinia."

"It doesn't hurt them. Daisies spring back even when they are trampled."

"See, Jen, you're like a daisy. I know when James calls, you'll spring back too. I love you, dearly, sweetheart."

"I love you, too."

No sooner had Jenny hung up when the phone rang again. Hopefully it was Henry and he had forgotten to tell her something, Jenny thought. Since talking with Henry, Jenny felt stronger. She answered the phone on its second ring.

It was James!

"Hi Jenny, did you get my meager, lone daisy?"

"Yes, I did and it's beautiful, James, and so was the note."

"I must say that one only took me a little over an hour to compose. Pretty soon Hallmark Cards is going to hire me."

Jenny laughed and felt a welcome relief to her tension.

"So, how are you feeling, James?" Jenny sincerely wanted to know.

"To be honest, Mar-Jenny, not so good. The test results came back and so did the cancer. A lump is growing next to the prostate gland and they see another smaller one near the liver."

"Oh, James, I know how all that feels. Are you on chemo or radiation?"

"Yeah, I go in every three days for both. Also taking some wonder drug, but so far don't notice a damn difference. Doctor wants me in the hospital, but I don't want to leave…in fact, Jenny, I'm waiting for you to come home."

Jenny's tension returned instantly. She was gasping for breath. She didn't want to hurt him and yet…

"Are you still there, Jenny?"

"Yes, yes, I am, James. Oh, James, I am so sorry that you're ill and I want to support you as much as I can but…I can't come back there anymore."

"Look, just give it a week…check out the difference on the estate, in me, in the staff. Everything is the way you wanted it when you were here Jenny."

Jenny took a deep breath and slowly said what she had been rehearsing for three days. "James…I want to move on and… and…I need to ask you for an annulment of our marriage…"

There was a long silence on the line as if it had gone completely dead.

"What…? What the hell are you talking about, Marj. What is an annulment?"

Jenny knew he wouldn't understand and she dreaded the thought of having to explain it to him.

"Oh, James, please try to understand…to annul our marriage; that there never was a marriage in the first place. We were married on paper, but never really married."

"For Pete's sake, Jen, of course we were married."

"You may recall how difficult it was for me to say the wedding vows, 'I do.' I fainted, do you remember?"

"You were nervous! It happens all the time! So was I, but we were married!"

"In name only, James. The very next day you were gone and from then on, it only got worse. We spoke of this last time you called. You were married to your company, not me. And when you learned that I had a previous daughter, you wanted nothing to do with me after that. All you wanted from me, was an heir. After I was able to give that to you, you cast me away."

"But it is different now; I was wrong and too engrossed in the business. This illness has stopped me in my tracks and now I see what a beautiful person you are and I want to start over again. I want you back…and, why do you want this annulment thing? Where did this come from, anyway?"

Jenny didn't want to bring Henry into this and so she answered this way.

"I am a Catholic by faith, James. We were going to get married in the cathedral, remember? When your father died, you convinced me to elope and we were married by a Justice of the Peace."

"So, what has this got to do with an annulment?"

Jenny knew she was beating around the bush and continued. "Well, since I had received a dispensation from the Bishop to be married outside the Catholic Church, the Church recognizes our marriage as valid—"

"Of course it was valid—"

"The problem is, I cannot re-marry in the Catholic Church since I am divorced. The Church does not recognize divorce... that's why an annulment is required; to show that the marriage was not valid in the first place."

A long silence ran through the phone line. Jenny knew what thoughts were running through her ex-husband's mind. James was no fool.

"I suppose that Pederson guy is of the same faith, Jen?"

"Yes, James, he is..."

"So you want to marry him?"

"Oh, James, I so don't want to hurt you...but, yes, I do want to marry him."

"You don't love me anymore...you don't want to at least try?"

Tears filled Jenny's eyes. James was trying so hard. Had he been this way before, she just knew that they would still be together. She did love him at one time...but it was never like Henry, yet... how would she really know? What would it have been like to be married to Henry? She just knew at the core of her being it would have been so wonderful.

"Mar—Jenny, are you still there? You didn't answer me."

"I do love you, James, but not in the same way. But I do want to be there for you in any way I can."

"Then come back just for awhile, Jenny. Please come and see how I have changed. For so many days, I have imagined you sitting here on the gazebo swing like I used to see you. I dream of watching you again. Every day I place flowers in the angel's basket in thanks for bringing you back...I just know it will happen. I placed flowers in the basket for your healing and a miracle happened...I just know it will happen again."

"Oh, James," was all Jenny could utter.

"And...and, there is one more thing I want to say to you...I...I, am very sorry for how I was during our marriage...please let me make it up to you. Please say you forgive me..."

For the first time, James truly spoke from his heart and Jenny could feel his sincerity. It touched both Jenny's and his heart. Neither could speak and James began to weep. Jenny was too overwhelmed to continue. Her heart was too forgiving, too compassionate, too kind, too generous…too sacrificial.

"I forgive you, James…please, let's talk again…I have to go…bye…"

Jenny waited for a response, but there was none…just heartfelt tears streaming through the line.

Jenny hung up the phone and picked up the daisy that James had sent her. It was still lying on the kitchen table. She read his card once more and began to cry. Her heart was breaking…

Still holding the flower, Jenny went outside for some air and solace. She stood on the deck for the longest time and tried to seep in the beauty before her as she done earlier. Then, she stepped off the deck and slowly strolled along the paved path that led to her gazebo.

A ray of sun caught the Angel of Thanksgiving and it beckoned her. When she got to the angel's side, she placed the daisy from James into the basket.

"Oh, thank you Jesus for all my blessings. Thank you for James, for healing him and giving him new life. What is it that I should do? What is Your will for me, dear Lord? In my heart, annulment isn't the answer. I did give my vow to James and the Church does encourage reconciliation…but, I love Henry so dearly, Jesus."

Tears began to surface and Jenny wept. She was so elated to come back to life and so thankful to be healed. She thought for certain it was so that Henry and her could be married and live the life they dreamed of for so long and now…*was it that she should return to James?*

Jenny made her way to the swing in the gazebo and sat down. Everything was beautiful and serene in the garden, but her spirit was so troubled. Monarchs flitted about her, but neither the butterflies nor the wildflowers, nor the fragrance of the herbs in the air could soothe her heart. For the first time, nature seemed to grow distant.

She began to feel alone. In some small way, this is how Jesus must have felt, moments before he died on the cross. He felt abandoned, too, and yet He was obedient unto death.

Am I to pick up this cross, Jenny wondered? I did so many times during my marriage. So many times I died to myself. But Henry coming back into my life is what I have dreamed and longed for, Jesus…It's all so close and near to fulfilling my dreams and heart's desire.

Must I die again?

Rays of sun covered Jenny's face and brought some soothing relief of hope, but it only lasted a moment. The warm, midmorning summer breeze carried another message; the soft whisper of Jesus…

Yes, Jenny, that is My will for you.

CHAPTER FIFTY NINE

For over an hour, Jenny drifted back and forth on the swing, unable to move. She replayed the conversation she just had with James over and over. Life had lost its direction and her heart searched for hope...A cloud of confusion surrounded her. It was mingled with so many emotions that they were no longer definable. Her dreams were shattering as the realities of life worked their way into the cracks of her heart. Oh where was this all heading?

Suddenly, Jenny felt a soft touch on her shoulder. Normally it would have startled her, but she instantly recognized its warmth. It was more of a loving caress.

"I hope I didn't frighten you, Jenny?"

Jenny reached back and touched Henry's hand. "I knew it was you."

"James called, didn't he?"

Jenny nodded and tears surfaced. She couldn't speak. She squeezed Henry's hand. He came around and sat beside her on the swing. He raised his arm and Jenny collapsed into his chest.

"Oh, Henry, I am so confused. I love you so much...I am so afraid what the future might bring."

Henry felt a rush of love sweep through him. He wanted his

dear sweet Jenny more than life. He felt her heart pounding and her chest heaving and didn't know how to console her…she was caught in between so many conflicts; pressure coming from him, would only add to her troubled spirit. He remained silent and stroked her shoulder, setting the swing into motion.

It was the sound of nature that eventually promoted Henry to speak. "Isn't the sound of that meadowlark beautiful, Jen? Of all the birds I hear, it's the sound of the meadowlark that is the most melodic and soothing of all. So many times I walk down the country dirt road, I hear the buzzing of bees, the hum of the wires overhead, but every now and then I am fortunate enough to hear a meadowlark sitting on the telephone wires singing a song for me. The melody instantly touches my heart."

Jenny and Henry gazed skyward and there it was sitting on the wires.

"The tune it sings is so beautiful. Its name is beautiful, too… meadowlark, such a soothing name. I can just see it singing in the meadows at your farm. Imagine walking through all those beautiful daisies listening to that."

"It reminds me of a Scripture I once memorized; in fact, I used to memorize a lot of them when I attended university. Julean was amazed how I would spout Scripture after Scripture. But it helped to calm my nerves when I was worried about things."

"What were some of them, Henry?"

"Like I said, hearing the meadowlark reminded me of what Jesus said in Matthew 6: 25-26, I think it was that we should not be worried about life. And later on in that Scripture, He comments on the birds in the sky and that they do not fret or worry about their food or life and God makes sure they are fed and He asks, 'Are we not considered of more worth to the Father?' And still later in that same chapter, Jesus says, 'Do not worry about tomorrow; for tomorrow will care for itself.'"

"That's beautiful, Henry…can you recall some others?" Jenny found it soothing.

"Yeah, Matthew 11:28, 'Come unto Me, all who are weary and heavy-laden, and I will give you rest.' And verses 29 and 30 are helpful too, Jenny. 'Take my yoke upon you and learn from Me, for I am gentle and humble in heart, and you will find rest for your souls. For My yoke is easy and My burden is light.'"

"Henry, that's amazing that you can remember and quote those Scriptures!"

"I have to admit I used to say them over and over…it almost became a way of life."

"Tell me another one…"

"You'll like this, Jenny, it has to do with bringing you peace—"

"Oh, tell me quickly…I sure can use that."

"It's John 14:27: 'Peace I leave with you; My peace I give to you; not as the world gives do I give to you. Do not let your heart be troubled, nor let it be fearful.'"

"Oh, Henry, that's beautiful. I can just feel the peace of Jesus calming my heart. I bet that's what the meadowlark was singing."

Henry squeezed Jenny and they fell into a silence once more.

"Do you have a favorite Scripture, Henry?" Jenny wanted to know.

"I do Jenny, the one that has helped me cope with situations more than once is Proverbs 3:5: 'Trust in the Lord with all thine heart; and lean not unto thine own understanding.'"

"That's exactly what I need to do right now, Henry." Jenny sat up and looked at Henry. "It's our thinking of all the worst case scenarios happening that gets us all so bogged down. What you just said made me think of a favourite of mine as well. I can't think of the Scripture like you can, but it has to do with trusting God as well to turn all things into the good."

"That's Romans 8:28, Jenny. That's the one Father Engelmann quotes all of the time. You know, Jenny, why don't we pray about that right now. I know exactly what Father would say if he were here."

Henry reached out with both of his hands and Jenny's were right there for him to take. He smiled so lovingly at his dear sweet Jenny. Henry closed his eyes and squeezed Jenny's hands, "Dear Jesus, give us the grace and strength to do and accept that which reflects Your will in this difficult situation. I love Jenny so much and yet she has a husband and family that love her too and want her back. Please help me, Jesus, to let Jenny be free to decide what is best for her to do. And help us both to trust in You knowing that You will turn it all into good for all concerned."

"And I thank you too, dear Lord, for my darling, Henry, for His love and understanding and support."

Jenny squeezed Henry's hands, then let go and walked over to the Angel of Thanksgiving. She bent down and plucked a yellow daisy in the wildflower patch. "Thank you so much for Henry."

Jenny placed the daisy in the angel's basket next to the one from James.

"I gave the Angel of Thanksgiving a name, Henry..."

"I bet it's Hannah..."

Jenny nodded. "As soon as Father David told me the name of my guardian, I knew right then that's what I would call the Angel of Thanksgiving. It's perfect. My angel is always surrounding me with blessings."

Jenny's face brightened "Before you came, Henry, I was so troubled and now I feel like such a weight is lifted off me. Thank you so much for coming..."

Henry gazed at his sweetheart lovingly. He knew as did Jenny, that this was just a momentary respite in the difficult journey that lay ahead. What was she really thinking and feeling?

Please dear guardian angels, help us...

Henry got up and made his way to Jenny. He couldn't keep his eyes off her, "I love you so much, Jenny."

"I love you too."

They warmly embraced and parted.

"It's such a beautiful day, Jenny, what do ya' say, we go for a drive in the country?"

"Yes," Jenny responded, her eyes flashing, "And let's get out and walk down a country dirt road with our guardian angels at our side."

"Yeah, and maybe, just maybe, we all might be serenaded by a meadowlark!"

"Yes, and maybe, just maybe, there might be two of them sitting on the wires, wouldn't that be something! Just think, a duet!"

"Now, that would be a miracle, Jenny!"

Jenny looked straight into Henry's eyes, "I believe in miracles, sweetheart...don't you!?"

CHAPTER SIXTY

"YEAH, OKAY NICK, let's keep it in abeyance for the time being should she initiate the procedure."

James couldn't believe that Jenny asked for an annulment of their marriage. He barely made it to the kitchen table and sat down.

"Can I get you some tea, Jim?"

"Yeah…" answered James, clearly sounding dejected and in pain.

"Couldn't help over hearin'…and, ain't none of my business, what's this annulment t'ing or whatever that Miss Jenny be asking for?"

"Never heard of it before either, Matilda. That's why I called one of the lawyers in our legal department. Apparently, the Catholic Church doesn't allow a divorced Catholic to re-marry in the church. They must have their first marriage annulled. That is, to show that there wasn't a valid marriage in the first place—"

"How can that be!? Of course you two be married…why I recall to this day you be bringin' that fine little t'ing to the estate. My, my, never seen such a pretty lady. First thing I be saying to myself, Mr. Hamilton sure done hit the jackpot! Now, the Bible say, Jim, when two people swear before God they be loving each other come hell or high water or heaven or bliss they got to work things out one way or the other. All too many, now days don't take their marriage serious; know what I'm saying—"

"Enough, Matilda, I know what you're saying but in some cases it doesn't work out and separation is best for all concerned."

"Now, you look at your marriage, Jim. You be wanting back in. Now...I may be speaking out of turn, but if you be trying to get along with Jenny right from the start maybe, you wouldn't be in this predicament. What I'm sayin', too many people just don't try. Why if I get married and swear to love and honor in good times and bad, why I be throwin' away the key. There be no back door for me to back out of...that be for sure."

"Well in my case, it might work to my advantage. My lawyer says for an annulment to be approved, it's best for both parties to agree. The Church further promotes reconciliation and trying again and that's exactly what I want. And, as far as I'm concerned, it would be impossible to show that there wasn't a marriage in the first place. Marjorie did have trouble saying the vows but...everyone's nervous when they make a commitment like that."

"I be agreeing with you a marriage took place, Jim, but I have to say...and I don't mean no offense... but it sure didn't seem like you two be married. You hardly be home and when little J.J. come along...oh, Jim I be speaking out of turn. Sometime, my mouth just don't know when to keep closed."

"Oh, Matilda there was a time when I would have fired you on the spot for saying something like that, but you're right. There really wasn't a marriage and I regret deeply treating Marj—I mean Jenny the way I did—"

"Here... you best be taking your medicine, I can see you need it." Matilda handed James a plastic vial and some water.

"The doctor says you be better off in the hospital."

"To hell with them damn doctors and that research...they still can't figure out how to cure a simple disease..."

"I 'spect it be more complicated than that, but I do agree it be best to stay in this lovely estate for as long as you can than be lookin' at four walls—"

"And waiting to die...ooh, geez, Matilda, maybe give me some more of that red pill and where is Doctor Reiner, anyway?"

"He be making a call and picking up more medicin'. He insists that you allow more medical staff on the estate if you plan to stay at home. I be agreeing with him, Jim, and what about them two technicians from that company that are going to be freezing your body. The tall one say the contract be no good if you are not in the hospital."

"Those two guys give me the creeps, if the truth be known…"

"Amen…"

"To be honest, Matilda, I like having you look after me better than any stranger might. There is more care…you know what I mean?" James added with a wink.

"Now, ain't them be the kindest words I be hearin' all day." Matti made her way over to James and rubbed his shoulders.

Just then, there was a tap on the patio door and it opened, "Matti, just checking to see if you're coming to the shed with coffee. Oh, hi James…I hope I'm not interrupting."

"My, my, Thomas, I done forgot to make you coffee. Jim and me having a discussion and I got distracted. I get it going straight away. Be no more than ten minutes."

"Come on in, Thomas, have a chair."

Thomas closed the patio door and sat down at the end of the table next to James.

"I was just telling Matti that Marjorie asked for an annulment of our marriage. Are you familiar with that?"

Thomas nodded. "Yes, I am, James. I'm also of the Catholic faith and I do recall lawyers on our staff back in London working on one or two of those cases. Annulments are very difficult to come by; it must clearly be shown that the marriage contract was invalid. That is to say, in some cases one of the parties was forced into the marriage, or wasn't aware of what they were doing, some mental deficiency and I can't really recall all the conditions that might be relevant."

"So in the case of Marj and me, it would be difficult to annul our marriage?"

"I would say so, Jim…now, I don't know all the facts, but seems to me it was valid."

"It was valid on paper, but Marjorie doesn't think it ever was in our marriage…and unfortunately I would have to agree."

No one spoke or responded to James' truthful analysis of his marriage to Jenny. A calm silence fell in the kitchen. The ticking of the wall clock, although not loud enough to be irritating did announce that with each tick, time was running out for James in more ways than one. His illness was progressing rapidly, especially this past week and most of the time he was unable to walk around the grounds, but still managed some in his wheelchair.

The silence was broken by the coffee pot percolating. The water kettle was also steaming and just beginning to whistle. Matilda made her way over to the counter and unplugged the urn. She took two cups and saucers from the cupboard and set them on the counter. One she filled with coffee and other she placed a tea bag and added steaming water.

"What about Ramon, Thomas?"

"If you give me two mugs and the pot I'll take it out to him. He and Carlos are in the shed."

"How about you chat with James for awhile? I'll take it out to the boys."

"That would be fine, Matti, I'd enjoy chatting here a little longer."

After Matti left, James was the first to speak. "You know, Thomas, I never thought my life would come down to this. For years I thought I had the world by the tail. I could buy and have anything I want and now I see it was all meaningless. I enjoy sitting here and chatting with you more than all the corporate meetings and impressive speeches I made and…well, I've learned a huge lesson…a little late, but at least I've learned it. This is what life is all about. Friends, helping each other out, taking the time to enjoy what you have and sharing. I have to say this last while, having dinner with you folks and talking around the dinner table have been the best and most fruitful board meetings of my life. I just wish Dad could have lived to see what is happening here on the estate."

Thomas took a sip of coffee and smiled.

Suddenly the patio door opened and Matti returned.

"Met Ramon comin' up the walk looking to see what was keeping you. He took the coffee back to the shed. It be getting late, thought I best come back and get dinner started."

"Dinner can wait, Matilda, sit down, maybe you can give me your two cents worth; I know you will even if I don't ask…" James looked at Matilda and nodded with a slight grin forced over his pain.

Matti took a chair next to Thomas and across from James.

"There may be just one other way I could convince Marjorie—I mean Jenny…no, damn it, I do mean Marjorie, I like calling her by her first name and is more sincere coming from me than Jenny… anyway, how the hell do I get that kid of mine to come around, Thomas? I'm afraid I taught him well. He's more stubborn and arrogant than I could ever be. The thing is, I know down deep he wants his mother back as much as I do…"

"I agree, James. Most of what he's doing is acting out, defending himself—"

"From what, Thomas?"

"Well, it may be from being further hurt, not wanting to disappoint you, fear, angry with Miss Jenny or blaming her for not making the marriage work. It's hard to say."

"What do you mean defending himself from further hurt? No one hurt him?"

Before Thomas could reply, Matti jumped in. "One thing I did see right from the start, Jim, was little Jimmy didn't know who to love. More than once he tell me he would like to call Marjorie, Mommy, but he was afraid to disappoint you or get a scolding. He may not have been able to say it in so many words. He still be caught in between—"

"You may be right, Matilda, the other day when I spoke with him, he said he sees Marjorie as a stranger and doesn't know how to relate with her."

"He might be blaming Miss Jenny for that and that she didn't get more involved," offered Thomas.

"But she try again and again, but Mr. Ham—" Matti looked at James, and said, "I be so sorry, Jim, I don't want to say something. I be sorry—"

"No, hell, it's true, it's all true and I told J.J. that it was all my doing, but he says it's all too late. I was ready to take a strip of hide off that boy, but for some reason I held it in."

"That might be the best thing, Jim. Fightin' and screamin' ain't going to win him back or make him listen. He be a young man now and don't want to be told what to do even if you be right."

"It's that damn Hamilton pride…Thomas and I were talking about that the other day."

"Tell me, James, what do you think got you started thinking more about your past marriage and your life in general?" Thomas was interested in knowing and now Matti was, too. She sat up and moved closer to the edge of her chair.

James looked at Thomas wondering about his question and how it was relevant to their present discussion. James barely moved in his chair when a sharp pain made him wince.

"Can I be getting you something, Jim?"

"No, not now…thanks, Matti…well, Thomas, you were there that day I noticed a bouquet of flowers in the angel's basket. When you told me that Marjorie placed them in there for me the year before when she left the estate, in thanks for giving her the garden, I would have to say that touched me…it touched my heart. But like we were talking about, my pride wouldn't allow me to accept the gift of love as you called it at the time, but I never forgot it. After all I did to that woman over the years and for her to still thank me…"

James couldn't go on as a surge of emotion overcame him. Unbidden tears surfaced. Normally, it would have embarrassed him, but somehow it didn't matter anymore; he was beginning to adjust to talking to his newfound friends. Matti reached across the table and patted his hand resting beside the tea cup.

"I suppose the illness made me stop and not only think about that, but it brought into my mind, all the acts of kindness Marjorie showed me at other times and her downright acceptance of me, despite my behavior and attempts to provoke her. Half the time I felt silly standing there spouting off and Marjorie simply accepted it.

"At first I thought it was stupid on her part, but then…I saw it as a deep inner strength that I didn't have. It unnerved me, to tell you the truth. But to answer your question, Thomas, I suppose what it all comes down to as to what it was…I would have to say it was this question: *What did Marjorie see in me that she liked?* What was it that despite my rude behavior and all the other stuff that made most people fear me, hate me or dislike me at the very least, that she could accept and love? How could one be so blind as to not see the real James Hamilton!?"

"But the real James Hamilton to Miss Jenny, James, was not how you were everyday with her or others. The real James that Jenny saw was the James that God created. That's what she focused on. When you were reading the Bible the other day, you asked why would Jesus , the son of God, be so foolish to come down to earth and put up with us humans and allow himself to punished, tortured and crucified? It's the same reason, James. He loves us, He hates our sins, but He loves all of God's children and wants us to be with Him when we pass on. Jenny was being Christ like all those years, James, right up until the day she left. And even then on the last day, she gave thanks for your kindness.

"Look at the power of that act."

James nodded, "Yeah, it got me thinking..." James suddenly stopped and gestured for Matti to fill up the empty vial on the table. She quickly got up and brought more medication to James and a full glass of water. After he swallowed the pain killers, he spoke. "Why did you want to know how I got started thinking about my past marriage and myself, Thomas? And how is this related to getting J.J. to come back?"

"It came to me that the way Miss Jenny brought you around to reassessing things in your life; you might also apply to your son. I've seen him talk to you disrespectfully and it can test one's patience, but I'm thinking that maybe you might just show acceptance and kindness to J.J. Like Miss Jenny did to you. You say you have already asked him to be more forgiving of his mother and that she was not at fault and you took full responsibility, so what more can you do? The other day when he acted out, you said you almost took a strip off his hide. What would that have accomplished...?"

"We would have ended up in a big fight, that's what."

"That be for sure—" Matti concurred.

"Exactly, he would leave and probably spend the next few days fuming over what you said and what he should have said and on and so on. But, you didn't. You reacted much like Miss Jenny; with patience and acceptance. Now, it may appear as if nothing was registering in that boy, but perhaps there was in the same way Miss Jenny got you thinking about yourself and your behavior. Loving another can be difficult, but we are called to do it. Sometimes tough love is needed, but in this case, the boy is confused. I have a feeling he knows what he should do, but..."

"His damn pride is getting in the way." James winced hard as he spouted out the words.

"Amen, brother," interjected Matti.

"Whenever I have concerns, James, I give them up to God to solve and ask for His direction…if you're in agreement, I'd like to pray about this matter."

James didn't look up; his gaze was still focused on Matti's hand resting on his. He felt the love and care flow through her touch and it overwhelmed him. Over the years he had treated her badly as well, and here she was showing such care…he was glad that she still hadn't removed it.

"Y…yes, Thomas, go ahead…I suppose it couldn't hurt."

Thomas shoved the coffee mug aside and slid his chair closer to the table and to James. He placed his left hand on top of Matti's which was resting on James' and his right hand on James' shoulder. He bowed his head and quietly reflected before he began, "Lord, You said where two or three are gathered in Your name that You are here amongst us. We give You our brother's concerns about his marriage and family."

"Yes, sweet Jesus…" echoed Matti.

"We ask You to come into their hearts and bring Your healing and peace and understanding and forgiveness. Help James to love his son and to accept him where he is at in life. Let him be a beacon of light that brings his family together—"

"Oh, yes, Lord, You be bringin' bountiful blessing to this family…"

"We also ask You, Lord, if it is Your will, that You heal our brother of his illness. And we further ask that You reveal Yourself to brother James in a special way that he receives You in his heart—"

"Do Your healing, sweet, Jesus…"

"We ask these things in Your name…"

Almost in unison, both Matti and Thomas said, "Amen."

They all sat back and no-one spoke. Matti looked like she was still in prayer…her lips were moving.

James was deeply touched by the prayer and heartfelt concerns of his employees…his friends. He brushed away a tear sliding down his cheek and said, "Matti, could you fetch the wheelchair and wheel me out to the garden…I'd like you to come along, too, Thomas, if you will."

Matti and Thomas helped James out onto the patio and set him in his wheelchair.

"Let's go the gazebo," ordered James.

Matti pushed James in his wheelchair and Thomas walked along side of James.

"What's that smell in the paving stone, Thomas? It's appealing somehow."

"Yes, it's the thyme, James. It's a herb that we plant in between the paving stones and as one walks on it, the herb releases its fragrance. Miss Jenny loved the smell, too."

When they got to the gazebo, James turned the wheelchair so it faced the Angel of Thanksgiving.

"There's something about that angel that I can't quite explain. Thomas, would you pick several of the wildflowers and place them in the angel's basket? You can pick a couple too, Matti if you wish."

"I love the red poppies and white daisies. They go together so nice."

"Thomas snapped off several wildflowers and placed them in the basket alongside the ones Matti had just placed there.

"When Marjorie was ill, I placed flowers in the basket for her and the next day Matti, you called from Regina to tell me that Marjorie was healed. I don't know how much there is to all this prayer stuff, but I would like to ask the angel to take our thanks to whoever does the healing, and ask that my son forgive his mother and me…and I would like to ask a special favor, to…to, have Marjorie come back…"

Once again, unbidden tears filled James eyes. It was evident, the Holy Spirit was softening James' heart. Thomas was going to add a prayer, but he didn't think it was necessary. Anything he would say now would never carry such a heartfelt prayer to the good Lord.

Matti must have been thinking the same thing. She softly, whispered, "Amen."

CHAPTER SIXTY ONE

IT WAS A gorgeous, September fall day. The leaves were beginning to turn into their golden colours and along with it, came the smell of another dying season. The odour of green trees and grass was gone and the scent of wheat being cut down over a mile away, only confirmed the death of another year. Many of the barren trees before him in the valley, exhibiting their skeletons, testified still further to Henry's senses. Soon the prairies would be covered with a blanket of white snow and the swirling winds would churn snow-flakes obliterating the valley view before him.

As much as he loved the fall, he had to admit he loved the cold blizzard winters too. He loved to be cocooned by the fireplace and read a good book or lose himself in a landscape painting in the warmth of his studio. Henry felt certain if he lived in a more moderate climate, he would never have been as prolific a painter as he was. As a gallery owner, he had to say, Saskatchewan, perhaps more than any other province, had many artists that produced vast amounts of art for others to enjoy. He was certain it was the hardy winters that were behind it all.

Henry tried to guess what his mentor would be preaching about as he sat in the front pew with Jenny. He could feel the gentle squeeze of her hand in his. He knew she was probably thinking about the same thing.

It never failed to amaze Henry how Father's sermons always cut to the heart of life and seemed to speak directly to each and every parishioner in attendance. Truly, when Father spoke, his lips moved but the words he uttered were guided by the Holy Spirit. Father Engelmann was the closest person he had ever met who seemed to fit the Scripture reading by St. Paul. "It is no longer I who live, but it is Christ who lives in me" (Galatians 2:20).

"Good morning my dear brothers and sisters in Christ. Once again, it is such a joy to be back in this beloved parish. Father Knuka had to return home this week as his mother is critically ill and was hospitalized. We shall be offering up this Mass for her and the family.

"When I lived here with Father, he often spoke of his home in New Brunswick and how he missed the beautiful fall colours. He would often say how the landscape in the Maritimes was blessed with such a variety of trees. So many different species growing side by side and their identity revealed in the fall by each possessing a different color. The result was a vibrant, dazzling display of God's creation and beauty. He often said that one day he and I should make that trek.

"Well, I can just imagine the beauty of Father Knuka's province, but I have to say, the colours in the valley, where Henry Pederson's acreage is situated, perhaps contain a little slice of that beauty in the Maritimes. The colours of the trees and the quiet repose of the prayer house beside the pond is a feast for my eyes as well."

Gazing at Henry, he continued, "I am so grateful to Henry for allowing me to spend so much time there."

Father nodded to Henry's smile and added, "Just this past week while at the prayer house, contemplating what the Holy Spirit wanted me to say, I recalled one word in Jenny's beautiful sharing a few Sundays ago that stood out in my mind; *repentance. Ach, mein Lieber Gott*, of course, that would be the perfect sermon to follow up on our talks on suffering. Jenny so beautifully and powerfully shared how she was led to repentance and joy as she fully realized what God and His Son had done for her. Yes, repentance is at the heart of the Gospel and when one has a contrite and repentant heart and comes to Jesus, there is great joy and jubilation as Jenny so beautifully expressed. I could only imagine the wings of Jenny's guardian angel flapping like that of a hummingbird!"

The congregation chuckled over such a happy image! Jenny leaned towards Henry and whispered, "I wish I could have seen my guardian angel like Father did. I can just imagine Hannah flapping her wings like that."

"Yeah, it would have been really something to see mine too, like Father described to us. I wonder why we can't remember." They sat back and listened to Father explain why heaven is so happy over a repentant sinner.

"Repentance, especially if it's sincere, humble, and we come before our Lord, broken in our sin and plead for forgiveness, our contrition goes straight to the heart of God. To one who recognizes his sinful nature and the gravity of what he has done, to him much is forgiven. And when He forgives, it releases such immense freedom within us, we feel like floating. The joy that erupts inside, sets the heart on fire for the Lord as Jenny so aptly said in her sharing. This is the kind of warrior the Lord wants and needs. One that is fully alive with the Holy Spirit!

"Only through repentance can others see the *light* in your eyes and your being. Without it, your faith is only partially alive. How can we be co-workers with Jesus to continue the redemption He started unless we have fallen on our knees and begged for forgiveness for what we have done? Then, we are prepared to spread the joy of forgiveness to others! The *light* within you is contagious and instills faith and hope and spreads God's love.

"Daily, we must repent and humble ourselves. The more we do so, the more we will be raised and receive His grace and light. God works through broken people, not the proud or arrogant who feel self righteous. No, people who know they are sinners and how far they fall short of God's goodness and come before Him and when necessary, to our fellow man and say, "I am so sorry," will be richly rewarded. Just like a seed has to die and be buried in the earth to bear fruit, so too, we must die to ourselves and bit by bit, we too, will grow out of our imperfections and faults and become soldiers for the Lord. In such repentant sinners, God can show His glory and light.

"As I was thinking on these things in front of the prayer house, I was gazing out at the beautiful valley before me. I too, had a beautiful vision like Jenny. I could visualize John the Baptist standing next to the meandering stream feeding into the pond, shouting for us to repent because the Messiah was here and that the kingdom of heaven was at hand. This was the image that was before the people at that time when Jesus began His ministry. John was introducing us to the Good News! The Messiah was here; He will open the gates of heaven and repentance was the way to enter and go straight to the heart of God!

"As my vision expanded, the sight of John the Baptist standing by the stream faded. The pond before me became the Sea of Galilee, I could almost smell the salt in the air. Off in the distance, great throngs of people were climbing the hills. My ears began to hear a soothing, commanding voice echoing ever so clearly in the valley. There on the hillside, was Jesus preaching the Sermon on the Mount that was so beautifully recorded in Matthew's Gospel in the 5th to the 7th chapters. It was as if I were there amongst the crowds of people listening to the Messiah as He expounded upon His laws of Love. His words were radical and filled with truths. What He was saying was so different from what the people had known and heard before. The beatitudes brought tears to my eyes; blessed are the poor in spirit, blessed are those who mourn over their sins, blessed are the meek, the merciful, the peacemakers...

"As His teachings went further, I soon found myself upon my knees. The wisdom of His words pierced my heart. To forgive, to love your enemies, to be faithful to your spouse, handling money, not to worry and live for today, how to pray. He laid out the map that we must follow as a guide on how to approach God and deal with other people! His words were the path to the fullness of life!

"It grieved my heart that over all the years since our dear Lord spoke those words, there are still so many who have not taken them to heart. There could be such peace and love in the world if people would be obedient to His teachings. We are little different today from the people back then. For three years, Jesus chose to live in poverty, rather than riches and comfort, and travel from town to town, region to region telling us over and over how we must live in a fallen world and by living that way for Him, promises us eternal life. How foolish it is that many people still have not listened and taken such wisdom to heart? There are still many Christians and church-goers who have shut out the Lord or are lukewarm to His love and teachings. What more could the Lord have done to not only lay it all out for us how we should live but then went on to lay down His life for us so that we can come to the Father and spend eternity with Him!

"Tell me? What more can He do?

"I have come to see that this is the dilemma of mankind right from the beginning and not just a modern day phenomenon. Man has always been secular, more drawn into worldly ways, than God's ways. Man has always lowered God's standards to man's standards to make being a Christian more comfortable. Perhaps it is more so today than before, but we are still dealing with many of the same issues. Clearly, the message of the Lord's teachings have not sunk in and really taken hold of the hearts of mankind!

"Please don't be offended or perceive my next remarks as judgmental, rather use my comments to search your own heart as to where you stand with the Lord. If a man comes to church still bearing unforgiveness towards someone, what is the point of coming? Did Jesus not say, if you come to the altar to give me a gift and hate your brother, first go seek reconciliation and then come and give your gift? If one has slandered his or her neighbour, was dishonest in their dealings, told lies, was covetous and has any sins in their heart, they must first repent; otherwise the light of Jesus Christ will not be in you. He wants so desperately to come in to your life, but it is you who shuts Him out!

"It is plain to see that what we lack is Jesus in our hearts and the truths of His words. He did not become man and teach His message for three years prior to His death for nothing. There was deep purpose and necessity for Him to lay out the map for us to follow to ensure our journey in life leads us to our heavenly home. Unless we are transformed by the renewing of our minds, we will never enter through the gates of heaven that He opened by laying down His life. Were His efforts to teach us how to enter heaven in vain!? Will we be lost in a world that is passing and we along with it!?

"Over and over, through the years I have heard man accuse God for the troubles in the world. That if he were in control, things would be so much better! No! It is our self-righteousness and arrogance that makes us so blind that we do not see that man alone is entirely responsible for all the misery here on earth. Look how feebly we give to our brothers in need both here and abroad, look how we abandon and ignore the sick and shut-ins. Look at how our leadership is in the home; our mothers and fathers exhibiting little or no faith or love for God and Jesus? Is there daily prayer or respect for the Sabbath? Do we talk about Jesus with our family and instruct our youths His teachings as the basis for living a Godly life?

"Can we not see the disservice we do to our children who will suffer needlessly in future trials because of our shutting out our Lord or halfhearted faith? Look into your own past life, is it not true when troubles come along who is it we eventually turn too? God made us this way that we come to Him. Sooner or later we all do. Is it not best that we and our children come sooner?

"Listen to me; if we obeyed God's commandments and the teachings laid out for us by Jesus and lived according to them, my friends, we would never fall under His judgment and heaven would be here on earth. *We would never again blame God for the injustices or problems in the world!*

"Listen to the voice of John the Baptist, please repent and come back home. The kingdom of heaven is at hand. Time is passing and sooner or later one of us will meet their Maker. Don't be caught without the light of Jesus in your heart. To say you have no time for God is to say you have no time to eat. Receiving the nourishment of God's Word is more important than the food you need to sustain yourself.

"*Man cannot live by bread alone!*

"My dear friends, the main reason why not too much has changed from the time Jesus came to teach us how to live is because we don't take the time to establish a close relationship with Him. The way you can do this my friends is to do what I have been telling you over all the years I have been your parish priest. You have to get up early every morning and sit quietly with the Lord and read His Word. This is how we get to know Him and to know Him, is to love Him. You will quickly learn that His teachings have life. They are based upon truth, reality, justice and love. He did not come to walk the regions for three years and teach mankind just to get exercise. He did it out of concern and love for you to point out a path to follow that would lift you out of the world that you live in and into His world that leads to eternal life!

"Yes, we must live in the world of the human race with all of its problems and challenges, but rather than live in it with our own perceptions and efforts and faulty thinking, we do so by inviting Jesus into our lives to show us how to really live. We begin to pray, read the Bible and study and meditate on His word.

What we are doing is developing a new habit of living and thinking that gives us inner peace, purpose and meaning while at the same time living in the world man has created. Without Jesus as our guide, we live in the darkness of man's world. Clearly He tells us, "I am the way, the truth and life."

Father paused and allowed his gaze to sweep through the church. He raised his hand, gesturing for their attention:

"Now this is important to understand, my children. When we repent and accept Jesus into our hearts as our Lord and Savior, it doesn't mean that our sinful nature is now gone or that life will be without struggle. No, there may be a brief honeymoon, but life goes on. God gave us a free will and He respects that and never forces His will on us. *In every moment of every day, for all the days of our lives, we have to choose to live either for Him or against Him.* Even though we are made of love and for love, we also have inherited a nature that is sinful from our first parents which is a part of us all the days on earth. As Jesus said, we must take up our cross daily and follow Him.

"The good news, my friends is this: the more we come to know Him and accept Him into our lives, the more grace and strength we receive to live according to His teachings. The greater and closer our relationship with Him becomes, the more peace and inner joy we receive. Coming to the Lord daily develops a new habit of living and thinking and acting until eventually it dominates the world of man and its worldly values and ways. Thoughts, actions and emotions that got us in trouble before and sent us into a frenzy now are overcome with peace. *We are transforming our lives, renewing our minds, becoming a new creature in Christ!*"

Father's voice was now rising, sending shivers of excitement into the congregation.

"By coming daily to the Lord and developing this powerful relationship with Him, we are building our life; our home on a rock and no longer on the sand that washes us away as soon as a problem comes into our lives."

Father raised both of his hands as his voice came to a crescendo.

"To say you do not have time to learn how to live a life that creates inner peace is not only foolishness of the first order, but your life will lack purpose and meaning!"

Father paused, took a deep breath and continued softly, "We have an extremely important job to do. Jesus needs all of us to come on board. He gave us all talents, abilities, and gifts and we are to use them to achieve His purposes. Recall what Jenny revealed to us in her sharing after she was overjoyed to realize at a deep level what Jesus did for her. As she shed tears of joy and gratitude, it was then that Jesus came to her and whispered, "Please Jenny, I have paid the price and opened the gates of heaven, but you and others must choose to come in. You must help Me to continue the redemption I have started. I will send you the Holy Spirit to help you, I will continue to intercede with the Father for all of you, but I need your help. Pick up your cross daily and follow me."

"This is what the Church is all about; God's children coming together with this common purpose to worship Him and give thanks and praise. In the Mass we celebrate what Jesus did for us in memory of Him. On the day before He died at the last supper, He took the bread, gave a prayer of thanks, broke it, and gave to his disciples. 'Take and eat it,' he said, 'this is my body.' Then He took the cup, gave thanks to God, and gave it to them. 'Drink it, all of you,' he said; 'for this is my blood, which seals God's covenant, my blood poured out for many for the forgiveness of sins.'

"Do this in memory of me".

"My children, we offer Christ's sacrifice on our behalf, up to God the Father, along with all our prayers, thanks and petitions at each Mass. At communion we receive His body and blood in the form of bread and wine to give us nourishment and strength to go out and continue His redemption."

Father turned and pointed to the cross. "That, *meine liebe Brüder und Schwestern in Christus*, we must never forget. When you walk into the church, that must be the first thing you see and the last image you take out with you when you leave. Never take Christ's crucifixion for granted and what He has done for you and all mankind from the beginning to the end. The cross is at the heart of Christianity; the core of our faith and belief. Never allow the cross to be removed from the Church. It is a constant reminder of what the Lord did for us; the depth of love that the Father has for you and me.

"I say this again; don't leave without the image and memory of the cross so that it is in your mind throughout the week. You need the strength of the cross. Ask the Lord to give you the grace to get down on your knees and thank Him until you weep, are broken and empty of self. Then, *meine liebe Brüder und Schwestern*, you will be filled with peace and full of joy. Then and only then, can you be used for His purposes."

Father gazed hard at the congregation, as his eyes slowly swept from one side to the other. "Promise me this. Come to Him each day, just as you are and do as I ask and I promise you that eventually you will be filled so full of grace and strength and His light that you will shine before men brighter than the sun!"

Father opened his arms to his beloved people and said, "May God richly bless you and moving his right hand in the shape of the cross, he said, "Glory be to the Father and the Son and the Holy Spirit."

No sooner had father returned to his chair, than Margaret Tearhorst stood before the altar and as usual, sang with the voice of an angel, a song that captured the essence of what Father was saying to his sheep.

Just as I am, without one plea,
But that thy blood was shed for me,
and that thou bidst me come to thee,
O Lamb of God, I come, I come.

Just as I am, and waiting not
to rid my soul of one dark blot,
to thee whose blood can cleanse each spot,
O Lamb of God, I come, I come.

Just as I am, though tossed about
with many a conflict, many a doubt,
fightings and fears within, without,
O Lamb of God, I come, I come.

Just as I am, poor, wretched, blind;
sight, riches, healing of the mind,
yea, all I need in thee to find,
O Lamb of God, I come, I come.

Just as I am, thou wilt receive,
wilt welcome, pardon, cleanse, relieve;
because thy promise I believe,
O Lamb of God, I come, I come.

Just as I am, thy love unknown
hath broken every barrier down;
now, to be thine, yea thine alone,
O Lamb of God, I come, I come.

CHAPTER SIXTY TWO

"I SUPPOSE YOU WILL never guess who this is calling?"

"I know exactly who this is. I can still remember that spell-binding conversation we had at the estate prior to marrying James. Hi Nancy, it's so nice to hear from you!"

"I was a bit concerned about phoning since we've lost touch over the years. When I realized that things were not going well with you and James, I decided to withdraw and mind my own business. However, in retrospect, I don't think that was such a good idea on my part. Perhaps if I had meddled more or been more supportive of you, the marriage might very well have worked out."

There was a lull in the conversation. Jenny could tell that James' mother was finding it hard to speak. Where is this going, Jenny wondered?

"I suppose you are wondering why after almost ten years I am calling?"

"It is crossing my mind, Nancy. Is it about James?" Jenny offered, trying to help open up the conversation.

"Yes, as a matter of fact it is. Do you recall when we spoke at our Manor about James and his background?"

"Absolutely, I remember almost the entire conversation. You had me sitting on the edge of my chair the entire time. That's why I recognized your voice so quickly. I think I must have recalled what you said over a thousand times…"

"I can only imagine it was to try and find some justification for having married into this family. The Hamilton men are a tough bunch, Marjorie. They wear an iron clad shield around them and don't let too many people enter into their lives. I never was able to with Jim. We had a relationship that was all surface…very businesslike and never showed emotion and rarely affection. I think I told you at the time that James followed very closely in his father's footsteps and there was something else I mentioned—"

"I think I know what you are going to say, Nancy. I found it strange at the time, but you said that I have a loving heart, something which James is not used to. As you explained more of James and the family background that day I began to understand what you meant."

"Yes, that's right, Marjorie and I'm sure over the years of living with James, that insight was confirmed over and over. I can only imagine how difficult living with James at times must have been for you. I can say that because I too had to undergo a major adjustment to try and understand and accept Jim. It's not easy living with a stone."

Jenny was somewhat taken back by the analogy, yet had to admit that the metaphor was accurate.

"I recall thinking after we parted that day that I was prepared to accept the challenge. I so empathized with James after learning of his upbringing and his brother that more than anything, he needed someone who would love him. In fact, it helped me make the decision to marry James. The feelings of abandonment that would attack his heart if I were to leave him would be devastating and only reinforce his past. And, and…I loved him enough to help him find his true self…the real James, I already loved."

"My dear, Marjorie, I am so grateful, that I was granted the years to see my stepson take such a dramatic turn in his life. I can honestly say that you have done what I thought was impossible. You do have a heart of gold. Through your untiring acceptance of, James, unconditionally, you have broken through the iron curtain surrounding his heart…Marjorie, you have ignited a spark within

James that is new, so totally different, that it is almost unrecognizable because I am so used to seeing the other... Marjorie, the spark is...*the spark of love...*

"You have helped him truly find his true self."

Jenny was speechless; she didn't know how to respond. She had been getting little snippets of this from Matti noticing how different James was becoming. And, the flowers, cards and conversations with James had shown a totally new side of James...she could see it, too. But it was all too late...

Rather than be elated over what Nancy was saying, Jenny's heart was cracking further.

"I suppose you are beginning to understand the reason for my call."

Mrs. Hamilton hesitated, waiting for some response from Jenny, but there was none and so she went on, "I was over at the Greystone Manor yesterday. The estate looks so beautiful with all the wildflowers and butterflies...it looks so heavenly, but even more so, I was flabbergasted to see James. Marjorie, he is a changed man! His illness, though life threatening and painful has turned out to be a blessing. It slowed him down long enough to examine his life. I saw it in his father those last few months before he died. I could see regret in his eyes and I suppose if I had been able to love and accept him as you did James, he too might have died in peace and having at least some glimpse of what life is all about. But it was too late for Jim...but with James, there is promise. Marjorie, James sees what he has lost. He sees what a wonderful girl you were in his life. Marjorie, James wants you b—"

"Oh, Nancy..." Jenny was already in tears, her heart was aching. She knew now what Nancy was about to ask...she struggled with it in the garden the other day. Jesus was asking the same. No, no, no she couldn't go back...

I love Henry so much...I want to marry him...I want to bear him a child...

"I'm so sorry if I am upsetting you. I know you have been through a lot with the divorce and the estranged relationship you had with James and your illness...you need time to think this all out. But I just wanted you to know, if you have any love left for my stepson, you would make him the happiest man in world if you were to go back...and I would love to see the two of you together again. These damn divorces come all too easy. No-one seems to try anymore…Marjorie, you have done the impossible…you, you are in my books, a saint!"

"Oh, Nancy, I have been ill for months and miraculously I have been healed. I moved to Regina to start over. My daughter is here and there is another man who has been in my life since I was fifteen. It's a long story, Nancy, but incredibly he was healed as well, His wife passed away several years ago and a day before I died, he found me and since then we … have started to court …to see one another…"

"I understand, Marjorie. But please, consider what I have to say. The relationship you have with this other gentleman is just starting whereas with James it was a relationship you had for over twenty years. It may not have been under the best circumstances, but you have family, a son, daughter in law and grandson. It would be wonderful for you all to start over—"

"Oh, Nancy, it's more than a teenage romance that I have with this man. It's a love that I can't explain, it's a deep love, a true love… oh, you won't understand, no-one can…Nancy, I can't carry on this conversation any longer. It aches my heart just to think on it at this time…I'm sorry. Nancy perhaps we can speak in a few days. I am just getting my life back together and I need time…I need time to think this all out…" Jenny's words trailed off.

"Marjorie, I didn't want to say this unless I had to. I don't want to pressure you and was hoping you would decide freely, but James' prognosis isn't good. The doctors had ordered him to go into the hospital last week, but he refuses to go. He firmly believes that you are going to come back. He wants to see you in the garden on the estate one more time. He wants to see you on the swing in the gazebo surrounded by the wildflowers. He wants to see you strolling down the different paths in the garden. He wants to see you chasing the butterflies and the sun on your face and the wind flowing through your golden hair. I've never seen a man so full of imagery and desire for a woman. He is so firm on staying on the estate. If he is going to die, he wants to see these images of you one last time…"

Jenny could barely listen to another word. But Nancy's last remarks pierced her soul.

"What a wonderful statue sits in the garden by the gazebo. James shared the wonderful story behind the Angel of Thanksgiving. Who, but you, would have started to place flowers in the angel's basket in thanksgiving for your blessings? Usually it would be for requests. Anyway, Marjorie, every day for the last week, he makes it to the garden with great difficulty and gives thanks that you have come into his life and all you have done by accepting him and showing him true love. But most of all, he places flowers in the angel's basket in thanksgiving for your return."

"Oh, Nancy…I just—"

"Marjorie, I know how difficult th—"

"And, please don't call me, Marjorie, my name is, Jenny… Oh, I'm sorry, Nancy, it's just that…oh, I just have to go…I'm so sorry…bye."

Jenny hung up the phone and ran to her room. She collapsed on the bed and began to cry uncontrollably. She was so happy these past few days; it was like being in heaven. She thought the other day when Henry came to her after James had called that she just might have imagined that Jesus wanted her to go back to James.

Is this really and truly the cross I have to carry? Is this the real reason for my healing and return?

But what about Camilla, and my family here…and what about Henry?

My dear, sweet Henry, whom I love more than words can say.

CHAPTER SIXTY THREE

JENNY WAS SO exhausted after her call from Mrs. Hamilton that she fell into a deep sleep and didn't wake up until the next morning. She was surprised to find herself still dressed from the day before. As she slowly orientated herself, she hoped that what had happened yesterday was all a dream, but slowly the reality of Nancy's call glared in her mind.

Oh, what should I do?

Oh how I wish Tammy was alive, Jenny thought. She would be on the phone to her in a second. Perhaps she would call Camilla and talk it over with her. And then there was Matti and Chloe… she would start with her daughter.

Jenny got up, washed herself and made a cup of tea. She looked outside and noted the blue sky. There was a slight breeze in the air. She could tell by the swaying of the tops of the tall fir trees in the backyard.

It was early, just a few minutes after seven. It was Thursday and Camilla would be getting ready for work. She didn't start at the tutorial school until nine-thirty, perhaps she would have a few minutes to talk. Jenny didn't think she could last until after dinner. She needed to talk with someone…her daughter was used to speaking to girls in difficult situations. Yet, what she had to share involved her, too. It had to do with family and she might find it difficult to be objective. No, she would call her daughter; they had talked about her relationships with James and Henry before. She would understand.

Jenny picked up the phone in the living room, sat down and dialed the number.

"Hello…"

"Hi Jeremy, I hope you were up?"

"Oh yeah, for over an hour. I'm an early riser, a practice Dad drilled into me. You have to start the day right."

Jenny wished she could say the same for her day. "Is Camilla up and around?"

"Yeah, she is just coming out of the washroom, hang on."

Jenny heard Jeremy calling his wife and Camilla exclaim, "What does Mom want so early?"

Camilla's footsteps could be heard rushing to the phone.

"Hi, Mom! This is an unexpected call so early. Have you got something exciting to share with me?"

Jenny held back her tears… "Do you have a few minutes to talk, Camilla? If this is a bad time…you may be getting Josh ready for play school and all…"

"No, Jeremy usually does if he notices I'm running late. I have time, Mom, what's up?"

"Oh, Camilla, I am so torn over what to do. James, my ex-husband has been calling for me to come back and yesterday his mother called and said James is critically ill and pleaded with me to come back too…"

Jenny could no longer hold back her tears…

"Oh, Mom, what a difficult situation to be in. I know how much you love Henry and your plan is eventually to marry him. Would this be just a temporary visit to go back?" Camilla wanted to know more facts.

"I think James wants more than just a visit and he is trying so hard. All the years we were married he was never there. It was always his business that took priority, but now, with his illness he so regrets it all and wants to try again. My heart goes out to him and yet it is really Henry that I truly love."

Camilla was silent as the full ramifications sank in of what all this would mean, if Jenny returned to Ottawa.

"Camilla, I truly believe he needs me at this time…I don't know what the future holds, but I have to go."

"Oh, Mom, I don't know what to say…usually I can come up with some solution, or advice, but…oh my gosh, this must be so terribly difficult for you to be caught in between like this."

"It's heart breaking, Camilla. I want to stay and get married to Henry but that's another problem. The Church doesn't recognize the divorce between James and I, which is another hurdle. There is the possibility of an annulment, but that's remote if not impossible. Even if I don't go back, what is the future for Henry and me? I know for certain Henry wouldn't go against the wishes of the Church. And even if we were able to get the annulment and get married, I may feel guilty for abandoning James. He is so filled with regret over our failed marriage and seems to be trying so hard to change…and then there is my son, J.J. and grandson…Oh, Camilla, I am so torn as to what to do!"

Jenny could hear Jeremy in the background asking what was wrong…

"Just a minute, Mom…please get Josh ready and take him to school. Mom is having some difficulties, I'll explain later…Yes, love you, too…sorry, Mom…I would hate to see you go away, but that is selfish of me. But then I think about Josh as he is beginning to love you so much. I know how much he missed Grandma Pederson and now to see you go away…oh, these are all such selfish thoughts, Mom. Even if it's how I feel you shouldn't have all this pressure on you… I just don't know what to say."

A silence hung on the phone. Both women began to cry.

Slowly, Camilla began. "Mom, I have to meet with one of the girls that is going through a crisis, too. It may take me most of the morning and then I will take the afternoon off and come over. There has to be something that we can do…usually when we see doors closed, there is always another that opens…just hang in there, Mom. I'll be at your place as soon as I can. Are you going to be okay…?"

"Yes, Camilla, I'll be fine. Do what you have to do. If you can take some time off later, I would love to see you."

JENNY WAS ON the way out to the patio deck with a cup of tea when Chloe called.

"Hello, Auntie Jen! Is that you? I can hardly hear you."

"Yes, it's me, Chloe," Jenny said, catching her breath and trying to compose herself. "It's so good to hear from you. In fact, I was thinking of calling you."

Chloe didn't pick up on the troubled tone in Jenny's voice and began sharing an experience she just had.

"I've sure had an unsettling morning at the centre, Auntie. A pregnant girl, Gail, who I have been counselling to keep her baby came in to the centre this morning with her sister. Boy, was her sister ever upset with me!"

"What happened, Chloe…?" Suddenly, Chloe's problem gave Jenny some relief from her own dilemma.

"Well, Gail's sister said I had no business talking Gail out of having an abortion and that it was her right to do what she wanted. She went on and on how the fetus wasn't anything more than a mass of blood cells and that it was Gail's body and I should be minding my own business. This led into a confrontation that lasted for over an hour."

"What did you tell her, Chloe?" Jenny wanted to know.

"Whenever I could get a word in edgewise, I tried to explain that our viewpoints had some middle ground. I tried to explain to Gail and her sister that we care deeply for both; the baby and the mother. The question I asked her was, "Why can't we love both? Why do we have to destroy the one?"

"That's a good question, Chloe, what did she say to that?" Jenny was eager to know.

"She didn't answer my question but kept following the argument that it was Gail's right to choose to do as she wanted with her own body, as she claimed earlier. So I asked her again, 'To choose what? Is it Gail's right to choose to kill the baby in her womb? Doesn't the child have rights, too?'"

Jenny remained silent, hoping Chloe would go on.

"It's just a fetus, it is not a human being," she went on to say. So, I asked her, "When is it a human being?" "When it's born," she responded "and takes its first breath." I tried to explain something I knew she already knew, that the moment the sperm fertilized the egg, a human being was created. In a matter of days, the identity of a human emerges and soon a separate tick of the heart can be heard, two different brain wave patterns can be identified, as well as two different blood types and in some cases, two different sexes! What further proof does one need? Some babies are born three months premature and what comes out of the womb...a human being!"

"It must be so frustrating for you at times, Chloe."

"Well, discussions like this usually end up going around in circles because there really is no case or justification. Abortion is simply choosing to terminate the life of a child and in all too many instances, is nothing more than another form of contraception. The argument that it is a woman's right to control her own body just doesn't make any sense. In all other areas of our society, the rights of individuals are limited when they infringe upon the rights of another. Sadly, abortion is an exception; women have the legal right to kill an innocent, defenseless human being simply because that human being is within their womb."

"Oh, Chloe, if I had terminated the life of Camilla, it would have haunted me for the rest of my days. I just know I would have been devastated."

"Unfortunately, most women know that what they are about to do is wrong and what the consequences will be. However, they don't see any other options. They feel trapped by circumstances: their boyfriend wants them to, their parents encourage them to, or their future will be affected. The list goes on..."

"But there are so many alternatives and support agencies—"

"Exactly, Auntie! That's why we are here to show girls that there are better choices to abortion. That's what I tried to show Gail and her sister. There are thousands of helping centers that provide financial aid, medical services, legal advice, counselling, a place to live, a job, education, assistance to parent the child or make an adoption plan."

"I remember you also telling me there are retreat centers to help women who have had an abortion..."

"Yes! The one we spoke of was Rachel's Vineyard Retreat, but there are many others. Fortunately, we are getting the message out that we are here to help women who are suffering from Post Abortion Trauma. We are here to help them, not condemn them. We are here for the mother and the child. And this is what we ask of abortion defenders, to be the same. How can one say they love the woman without loving the child in her womb? How can one say they can harm the child without harming the mother?"

"Why can't we love them both, Chloe?"

A long silence travelled over the phone line as both women reflected upon the senselessness of abortion.

"Millions upon millions of babies are terminated each year, Auntie. So many lives affected. The pain and heartache we see is so sad and devastating. If only people would realize that by remaining silent, they are not helping women who are considering to choose abortion nor helping women who have had an abortion. Both perceptions convey the message that they don't understand the woman's pain, the issue, that they simply don't care or there is no hope—its legal, can't do anything about it! So, at the end of the day, most remain silent and allow this holocaust to continue."

"Yes, as you said, in all too many cases it's the silence which has led to make such a disastrous choice in the first place."

"Gail's sister's argument that it was none of my business to interfere may be sincere, yet lacks understanding. It's everyone's business. We never hear someone say, 'I would never abuse my child, but if you want to, that's your choice.' No, we would intervene out of care and love for each other…Oh, Auntie, it's such a huge concern for society and somehow we must wake people up to voice their opinion! I am so glad Mom got me started in all of this and made me aware of what is going on and the need to cry out."

"Yes, I was just thinking of Tammy the other day and how much I miss her and the chats we used to have. She was such a dear, dear, close friend."

"You were like sisters, that's why I call you Auntie! Do you ever hear from Uncle James? I barely remember him. He was never at home when I came to visit you on the estate."

"Yes, I have heard from him quite a bit lately, Chloe. It's interesting that you should ask. I was actually thinking about calling you to talk about James and discuss a choice I am struggling with."

"Oh, Auntie, here I've been rambling on and forgot to ask how things are going with you! What choice is troubling you?"

"James is ill, Chloe. Apparently he's as sick with cancer as I was. He has called me several times asking for me to come back and try again—"

"But what about, Henry? You two are so much in love. I thought you were going to get married? Oh Auntie, what a position to be in!"

"Apparently, from all reports, he's a changed man and I must admit he sounds so completely different from the way he used to be when he calls."

"And what about J.J., gosh, I haven't talked to him in ages nor met his wife or seen his son! There just were never any family ties created."

"That's right, Chloe. And J.J. still isn't talking to me. I thought if I do decide to see James, I could perhaps talk to J.J. and see my grandson. It's just that, I don't want to give James the wrong message…"

"And you don't want to hurt or worry, Henry."

"Yes, I've prayed so long for us to be together and now this has come up and there are other complications that have to do with the Church. The Catholic Church doesn't recognize divorce and so this is a major impediment for Henry and I to get married."

"Oh, my, Auntie, isn't there anything you can do?"

"The only option is to have our marriage annulled. To show that there was never a marriage between James and I."

"Well, in a sense that's true, Auntie."

"But I did make a vow to love, honour and cherish, in good times and in bad, until death do us part and so did James to me."

"I hate to think this, Auntie, but that may be your only hope, that Uncle James passes away. Oh, that doesn't sound right, does it?"

"No, I am actually praying for his healing, Chloe. I do want the best for him and yet…" Jenny's words trailed off.

A silence fell over the line again. Neither Chloe nor Jenny saw any solution in sight. Jenny did however feel better than before. Chloe's concern took her mind off her matter and just talking about it more calmly gave her a different perspective.

"The best solution is to take one step at a time and deal with challenges as they arise. Fretting and worrying won't help the situation."

"I agree, Auntie Jen. Things have a way of working out…"

"Henry and Father Engelmann would say to trust in God's divine providence. He knows all things and can make what seems impossible, possible!"

"Daddy says that all the time—"

"Yes, how is Robbie doing? I haven't spoken to him since I got out of the hospital. I wanted to thank him for all his prayers and his prayer partners. I'm sure all those prayers from everyone were heard by the good Lord."

"You can count on it, Auntie. I'll tell Dad you called and ask him to phone you, he might have some suggestions. By the way, how is Camilla? It was so nice meeting your daughter when I was there. She looks so much like you and such a lovely lady. We had so much in common when we spoke. We're both counsellors, and we were born out of wedlock and…we both could have been aborted!"

"The thought makes me shiver, Chloe. I thank God everyday for blessing your mom and me with such lovely girls. Oh thank you, thank you, thank you Lord!"

"Oh, Auntie, I am so elated that you were so miraculously healed. I would have missed you so terribly. I love you so much!"

"I love you, too, Chloe. Please say hi to Robbie and tell him to call me when he has a minute. Camilla is coming over after lunch, so I'd better get going."

"Say hi to her for me. I'll keep you in my prayers that everything works out for the good, Auntie. Bye…"

Jenny slowly hung up the phone and looked at the kitchen clock. It was still early. There was another half hour before the gallery opened, she had to talk to Henry and tell him what she had decided to do.

Chapter Sixty Four

H ENRY WAS WORKING on a framing order when he felt a presence. He looked up and was startled to see Jenny standing at
the doorway that led to the café side.

"Jenny! It's so good to see you! What brings you here?"

Henry put down the mat board sample he was holding and
walked over to the love of his life. Unbidden tears were sitting on
the edge of her eyelids and it took only one more blink for the tears
to begin sliding down Jenny's cheeks. Henry knew what might be
troubling her, but he so desired to kiss her and hold her that everything else could wait. They warmly embraced and kissed tenderly.

"Come, let's sit down." Henry led her to the bay window in
the back section of the café. A few patrons were having coffee in
the front section. They could vaguely be heard but not seen from
that area. They sat at a table for two and immediately reached out
their hands to each other. They gazed into each other's eyes for the
longest moment and then Henry asked, "What's wrong, Jenny?"

He knew what it might be troubling his sweetheart, but hoped
that his assumptions were wrong.

They were right!

"It's James, Henry. He wants me to come back. Late yesterday, his mother, Nancy, called and pleaded with me to come as well. Apparently, James' condition, although stable, is not very good; he should be in the hospital but refuses to go. He is adamant that I return and wants to see me on the estate again before he will agree to be admitted to the hospital."

Henry squeezed Jenny's hands and shook his head. "That puts so much pressure on you, honey…what do you want to do?"

"That's why I'm here. I want and need your input."

A concerned look grew on Henry's face, "Your marriage with James was never fulfilling and he was the one that divorced you…are you sure you want to go back and…this would be just temporary, wouldn't it?"

Jenny slightly shrugged her shoulders and nodded. "Yes, that's what I'm thinking…to just take one day at a time. Our marriage was so one sided and he was rarely at home. Yet, I know he could use my support. When I lay in the hospital for days on end, friends came to see me, but I would have loved if family came. And when my son did come, it was such a whirlwind visit. That was also the time he put my house up for sale and…he was so unfriendly towards me. That's another reason, as we discussed before, that I want to go and see if we can patch things up."

"If this didn't involve family, I would fight tooth and nail to keep you here, but with family and James' illness…" Henry shook his head and continued, "As much as I don't want to say this, I think you have to go, Jen. Our relationship would always have something between us if you didn't go. You're the kind of person that would feel regret and guilt for not reaching out…and, he was your husband."

"James has had such a difficult upbringing. To many it may appear he has the world on a string with his wealth and power, but what he needs most is to be accepted and loved."

For the next half hour, Jenny shared with Henry, James' background: his mother's alcohol addiction and never being there for him and his twin brother, the cold business nature of his father and the feelings of abandonment James felt when his mother died and guilt over his brother's suicide.

"The last thing James needs right now is to feel abandoned and alone. The staff on the estate notice such a change in him and so do I. It took years for James to find himself and—"

"I've seen it in others and those who I counselled in the past; there are so many who are crippled in this area of giving and receiving affection. Many do not know what to do, how to show it, how to begin. We, who are more blessed, either due to our upbringing, or by nature, must be understanding and compassionate and help lead…"

"Oh, Henry, we all want to love and be loved. I think it was learning of James' background that was part of my motivation to marry James."

Henry shook his head and allowed his compassionate side take over, "I can see why you don't want to abandon him now and encourage him in that direction so that he does not lose hope…"

Henry shrugged his shoulders, "And I understand you want to be supportive in his illness, but…Jen, you have to come to terms with your son and James and the entire family for us to have a relationship that is not encumbered with all these unsettled issues. You would always feel torn between our family and yours. I love you too much to see you unhappy in any way. You have my blessings and support to go back and do what you need you to do."

"Oh, Henry, that is what I have always loved about you. You have left me free. I recall that day in the park when we could have made love, but you considered my feelings above yours. I was sorry we didn't and yet I felt so free afterwards that you didn't force me to make a decision that I would regret later. And here again, you offer me that same freedom…your love is so wonderful…It reminds me of a saying. 'If you love someone, set them free. If they come back to you, they are yours. If they don't come back, they never were'…"

They both leaned forward over the table top and tenderly kissed.

Although Henry was putting on a brave front, his heart was already aching. He never anticipated this to happen after they both were miraculously brought back to life. He thought for certain they would be married and already living together and suddenly all of these obstacles popped up!

Jenny gazed at her dear Henry, so thankful that he understood. She nodded and tears surfaced in her eyes again. "I know he needs me, Henry. I have to go and… I feel it's God's will somehow and part of His plan for us to bring our families together."

"Well, God is the God of all possibilities…you never know."

Henry stared at Jenny trying to burn the image of her in his mind and heart. He didn't know if he could possibly live without Jenny, he was missing her already. "I suppose you will be going alone? You don't want me to come along anymore, do you…?"

Jenny shook her head, "No, I think it's better I go alone. I don't know how long I will be there and your presence might complicate any kind of reconciliation with J.J. at this point and…somehow, I feel being with James for a few days might be the way to reach J.J."

Henry nodded, "I think you're right, Jen. So when do you plan to leave?" He hoped it would be never.

"I will call Air Canada as soon as I get home and see if there is a flight out this Saturday morning."

"That's just a couple of days…Oh, Jen, I will miss you so much…" Unbidden tears surfaced in Henry's eyes. He was too choked up to say more.

Jenny brushed away a tear sliding down her cheeks. "Camilla is coming over this afternoon for awhile. I'll pack later so that I can have tomorrow off. Perhaps we can spend the day together."

Just then as she spoke, her every word filled Henry with sadness over her impending departure. He thought his heart would explode.

Neither wanted to get up and part. They just tenderly held hands and continued to gaze at one another. If it hadn't been for a customer wishing to see Henry, they may have gone on that way for the rest of day…

Henry turned to the framer, "Be right there." Turning back to Jenny, he shrugged his shoulders, "Well, honey, perhaps phone me later when you have everything settled and under control. I may drop by on my way home for a bit as well."

"Oh, yes, please do, Henry."

They got up and embraced one another and tenderly kissed.

"Love you with all my heart, honey. See you later…"

Jenny shook her head side to side, "*I love you more, Henry.*"

Chapter Sixty Five

A s soon as Jenny came home, she called Air Canada to secure a ticket. There were two seats left on the seven-forty five a.m. flight to Ottawa. Just as she was about to begin packing, Camilla was at the door. They had lunch together and discussed all the obstacles that were now facing Jenny and Henry. The talk with Camilla went much better than that morning. Jenny had made the decision to go to Ottawa and felt in her heart that it was the right thing to do. She was so relieved that Henry had supported her on this as well. They chatted for over three hours until Camilla had to leave to pick up Josh at his school.

"Oh, Mom, I will miss you so much. Please phone as often as you can."

"Yes, I will…I love you," Jenny called out just before Camilla ducked into her car.

Camilla leaned forward and waved before pulling away. Jenny threw her daughter a kiss and then wiped away a tear rolling down her cheek with the back of her hand.

For the next two hours, Jenny began packing. She wanted to have everything ready to go for Saturday morning so she would be entirely free to spend all day tomorrow with Henry. There was one more thing to do and that was call James and let him know that she was coming and arrange for someone to pick her up at the airport.

Jenny was both nervous and excited as she called the Hamilton residence. She was relieved when Matti answered. Matilda almost hit the roof when Jenny told her she was coming to the estate for a short visit. Jenny gave Matti the flight number she would be on and the time of arrival.

"Oh, Jenny I be so excited that you're coming, I have to pee. Jim will be one happy man to hear that you're on your way. Are you sure, Jen…? As much as I want you back here, I know how much in love you are with that man of yours and all the plans you made."

"Yes, Matti, I feel it's the right thing to do. Tell everyone I am so excited to see them. Are the monarchs still there?" Jenny was anxious to know.

"It be thinning out a bit, but there are still lots here. More than usual at this time of the year, I would have to say…perhaps, they know you be coming!"

"Oh Matti, I love you. See you Saturday."

"Yes, and I be making sure the Chauffeur be picking you up on time in the limousine."

THOMAS POPPED HIS head up from behind a bush he was trimming when he heard Matti hollering for him.

"Thomas, Thomas, where you be hiding?"

"Over here, Matti."

Matti stopped and saw Thomas waving near the gazebo. She hurried over to him."

"Thomas," she gasped. "Thomas, I need to talk to you…"

"Come let's sit in the gazebo and slow down, Matti, catch your breath."

The two walked over to the gazebo and Matti sat on the swing while Thomas rested on the railing ledge surrounding the gazebo. "What's the problem, Matti…? Now take it slow and easy."

"Thomas, Jenny just called. I can't believe it, Thomas, Miss Jenny be coming back to the estate. She wants to visit and give some support for James. I know he be calling her and wants her back real bad and… she has decided to come and see him. I never thought I would see the day that I would say that I feel for Mr. Hamilton. I've grown to like the man and feels sorry for him and yet, I can still picture how he was back then. How he be treating his Missus so cruel, Thomas. She owes him nothing. He owes her everything. When I see the unkind words he say to his precious darling; hire a nanny to feed her own child, denying the mother from giving the nutrients the child needs from her breast as nature intended, steal the boy while growing and even refusing to allow the boy to call his mother, mama. I be a good woman, and I have grown to like the master, but I have a long way to go to love like Jenny. She be a saint, that for sure."

"True, Matti, Jenny has a heart that is governed by love."

Thomas paused for a moment and then went on, "You know, Matti, both as a lawyer and an observer of life, I have listened to many heartbreaks, stories of cruelty, complaints by the hundreds that if only that person could be this way or that and the list goes on and on. I have learned that it's not what happens to us, it's not what the other person did or said, *it's how we respond to it.*

"Jenny is a perfect example of one who is control of her heart. She had every excuse and right to be upset with James' words, actions and deeds and yet, she always chose to be a peacemaker, to love, to forgive. She is the freest person I know.

"Most people's minds would be filled with memories of anger, hate and resentment for the way he treated her. The tape in their mind would play again and again, justifying their want for vengeance." Thomas added.

"Yet, she be forgiving and acceptin', all the while the man shuns her. Mr. Hamilton has grown a lot and he be easier for me to forgive now, but back then…" Matti shook her head disgustingly, "there be no way I could say lovin' words to him. And now to come back and be there for him…" Matti shook her head.

"That's right, Matti, Miss Jenny's mind was always so focused on the James we see now. She bypassed his behaviour and planted the seed of love in James' heart. What we are beginning to see in Mr. Hamilton is what was covered over by layers of pride, power, and possession; *Jenny was able to see it then.*"

"My, my…" was all Matti could utter.

"I see Jenny's willingness to come here to complete her work out of compassion and care for another human being who had lost his way. She has brought peace and freedom and love to James in his dying years at the expense of her own happiness with another.

She has saved his soul, Matti. What greater gift can one give, besides laying down their life for another?"

"Oh, Thomas, so many times I see Jenny standing there like a meek little lamb being slaughtered, unwilling to fight back and stand up for her rights…but now, I be confused…"

"Many would consider gentleness or meekness as faint-heartedness, timidity, or lack of strength. To me, Matti, it is a peaceful, willing submission to God and others without the defiant, bitter, retaliatory aggressive behavior that is typical of human nature.

"As we can see, gentleness is the key to wisdom and has great power. Jenny knew that choosing the worldly way to respond would only worsen her dilemma and make her miserable in an environment that she chose to live in. By withdrawing regularly into her garden, she received daily spiritual sustenance. Some days, she was filled with such light of God's wisdom that was pure, peaceful, gentle, and full of mercy, I couldn't tell who was the brighter, Jenny or the sun! Miss Jenny was such an inspiration to me, Matti. A living example of a peacemaker. She always chose to forgive those who hurt her and seek gentleness instead."

Matti nodded, "Miss Jenny is pure of heart just like, Jesus. He just stand there, too, and suffered a lot of abuse, that for sure."

"I couldn't agree more, Matti. Look how the Lord humbled himself: accused of this and that, tortured, scourged, giving up his rights and on and on and what did He do? He asked the Father to forgive them for they know not what they do. It may have appeared foolish to many back then and even today, but look what Jesus did for mankind through His humility. He showed us the path to peace and good will. It's a hard path to follow because it requires death to self. In many ways, Miss Jenny is pure of heart just like, Jesus."

"I see Miss Jenny doing that day in and day out. Many days it be like Jenny lives in the eye of a storm. Turbulence and trouble is all around and yet at the centre there be calm."

"That's a beautiful description, Matti. We were not only witnesses to that when she was here, but I predict we shall see even greater fruits of such an attitude when she comes back."

"I think you be right, Thomas. Best I hold my tongue about Jenny coming back…I know that be rare, Thomas…but we have seen a saint before us and not only Mr. Hamilton be benefittin', but so have we all."

"It took years for this to happen, Matti. Transformation comes over time. It is a process and not instant like the world today would want it. No, building character; allowing Jesus into our lives, requires us to choose again and again and again. Dying to ourselves is an endless task and Jesus was the perfect example of one who was obedient to the Father's will unto death. Miss Jenny is a beacon of light to us, too, a living example that it is possible to be like Jesus."

Matti was going to speak, but Thomas beat her…"Now, don't get me wrong, Matti. Gentleness in attitude doesn't mean that we can never be angry. Our anger must be under control and should occur only for the right reason. Even the Lord got upset when he noticed the money changers in the church. He overturned their tables and cast them out!"

"Now, that be more like it. All too many times, my fuse be too short and quick to explode. I still have a long way to go, Thomas, for all this understandin' to travel from my brain to my heart."

"We're all on that journey, Matti." And after a short reflective pause, Thomas said, "You know, Matti, what I have come to discover over the years is that *underneath everyone's shell, no matter how hard and tough, is someone who wants to be appreciated and loved and… wants to love.*

"All of us have been fortunate enough to be witness to someone who not only understands that, but lives it and is willing to put another's happiness before her own regardless of the costs. Had Miss Jenny chosen the path that most of us would have followed, we would not see Mr. Hamilton transformed like he is. Isn't that something, Matti?"

There was a long, long silence and tears surfaced in Matti's eyes.

"Oh, Thomas, to live like that and heal another's soul be asking for one big sacrifice, that for sure, but it can be done…you be right, we be seeing its life changin' power before our eyes…that's for sure…"

CHAPTER SIXTY SIX

HENRY HELD JENNY's hand, as he slowly drove to the airport. The traffic was light; hardly any other motorists out at six a.m. on a Saturday morning.

"Are you nervous, Jen?'

"Yes, I am feeling all kinds of emotions, Henry. I don't want to leave and yet, I feel obligated to go. It was so nice to have friends and support when I was in the hospital and especially Father Engelmann's visits were always so uplifting. I know James could use someone with him who has been through what he is going through."

"Yeah, not only that, you're so supportive to begin with. He's a very fortunate man, Jen. There are not many women who would be doing what you are," offered Henry.

"It feels right, somehow Henry. Like God has a plan for all this and as Father David encourages us to do, I am going to trust in Him to turn the many obstacles and difficulties I see into good."

Henry quickly added, "And all things are possible through God! Trust in Him with all your heart and don't lean on your own understanding."

"That is such a beautiful Scripture and offers such hope. The things which are impossible for us are possible with God." Jenny squeezed Henry's hand tenderly...

A silence fell in the SUV as Henry came to a stop sign. Since no cars were in sight, Henry bowed his head and said a prayer that reflected what they were just discussing. "Yes, Jesus, help us to trust in You. Help me to accept Jenny's leaving to help her family who is in need. Give me the strength to let her go freely and be such a beacon of light for them all to see. And through Jenny's graciousness, compassion, and love, let it draw the entire family to come together and also to You. Help us all to realize that with You at the centre, families grow and flourish. We pray for a safe trip for Jenny and that the Holy Spirit and her guardian angel guide her heart to accomplish Your will whatever it may be."

Henry turned to Jenny, smiled and drove on.

"Oh, Henry that was so beautiful, I love you so much. I will call you every day and let you know how things are going."

"It sure was a lot of fun yesterday at the farm. I hadn't ridden a horse in over two years and my aches and pains testify to that."

Jenny chuckled, "Yes, my bum and back were quite sore when I tried to get out of bed this morning. The last time I rode a horse was before I came to Regina from Vancouver. It was in seventh grade when the class was taken on a tour to a local riding club. I recall how much I enjoyed riding and bugged Mom and Dad to get me a horse."

"I was born on the farm and there were plenty of horses, mainly work horses, but there was a small quarter horse that all of the kids were allowed to ride. When you're at my place next time I will show some pictures of me sitting on Sandy, wearing a six shooter, cowboy hat and a black mask."

"I bet you were the Lone Ranger?"

"That's right, except my horse was a sandy colour and not white."

"I'm sure you were the hero and saved the day, regardless of the horse's colour." Jenny squeezed Henry's hand and leaned into him as he came to a stop. "I will miss you dearly, Henry."

Henry leaned forward, trying to read the overhead signs as he entered the airport. "I guess we will take this road...it leads to the passenger and luggage drop off."

Henry made another turn and pulled up in front of the entrance to the airport.

Before getting out, Henry turned to Jenny, put his arm around his sweetheart and drew her in as close as he could. They kissed and would have gone on longer if the guy in front didn't honk his horn for Henry to back up a bit. He was sandwiched between two cars; Henry's and the one ahead of him.

Henry quickly backed up, stopped and got Jenny's two suitcases from the trunk. Jenny was out of the car and waiting for him. Henry handed the small case to Jen and pulled out the handle of the larger one and led Jenny into the airport. The Air Canada check-in was just off to the right.

"I think my car will be okay in the drop off area for five minutes or so. Come, I'll help you get checked in."

There were four people ahead of them in line. Good thing they had come early, as many more people were coming in the few minutes they were standing there.

"Next, please," shouted the lady at the desk.

Henry carried the suitcase over to the counter and placed the case on the weigh scale. Jenny decided to take the small one on board with her. She had several magazines inside which she wanted to read during her flight.

Just as Jenny and Henry turned to make their way upstairs to the departure area, Jenny noticed a very striking, attractive lady staring at her and then at Henry. The lady's gaze was bold and penetrating. Jenny found it hard to divert her gaze from her.

"Henry, there is a lady over there that seems to staring at us. I don't think I know her, but perhaps you might…she is beautiful."

Henry turned and blushed, "That's Ivania!"

"You know her, Henry…?"

Henry's face flushed revealing a tinge of red especially on his neck. He could feel the heat…and now even more so as Ivania began to make her way over to them…

"*Oh, God…*" muttered Henry

When she got within speaking distance, Ivania blurted out, "Hendry, I didn't see you at first; I was so taken by the beautiful blonde lady standing beside you. I couldn't believe that was you next to her!"

Ivania stood directly in front of Jenny with a bold stature and looked her over. It was obvious Jenny was unsettled and her cheeks grew a tinge of pink as well. For a moment neither could speak…

it was an awkward moment for Henry to have a former girlfriend face the girl who had captivated his heart over Ivania's.

Finally, Ivania spoke while looking directly into Jenny's sparkling blue eyes, "Now I don't feel so bad, Hendry. I was upset for days, no…months that you left me for some teenage sweetheart who you hadn't seen for years. I thought you to be crazy for living in such a dream world when you had such beautiful, real girl at your disposal…but now, I can see why and I apologize for questioning your judgment at the time. There is no need for you to introduce me to this lovely creature, I know this must be the Jennifer of your dreams…your first and it seems your only love."

Ivania stuck out her hand and Jenny immediately responded and the two ladies shook hands.

"Very nice to meet you. Ivania, I must admit, Henry hasn't told me about you."

"There was no need for him to, there was never another in his life. Oh, I tried to seduce him. I used all my feminine wiles, but when a man has a love in his heart for someone as deep and strong as Henry does for you, not even Cleopatra would be able to lure such a man away for the woman in his heart and dreams."

Henry chuckled nervously. He turned to Ivania and rather than shake hands, he approached her and gave her a warm hug."

"I bet you were in Toronto on another insurance seminar?"

"No, this time it was to finalize a promotion. I will be overseeing all of Western Canada and not just Saskatchewan as I used to. The sales have improved so much over the last two years they want to see if we can accomplish the same in the other provinces."

"They have the right person at the helm, that's for sure. I wish you all the best of success, Ivania."

"So are both of you off somewhere, a honeymoon perhaps?"

"I wish we were," said Henry and added, "Jenny is off to Ottawa. Her ex-husband is quite ill and Jenny wants to give him her support. She also has a son and grandson she wishes to visit with."

"That is so kind of you, Jenny. Are you staying long?"

"I'm not sure, it all depends on the circumstances that develop."

Ivania turned to Henry and said, "I don't mean to alarm you Hendry but a similar situation happened with a friend of mine. It was the ex-wife that had cancer and the husband who was considering marriage to another woman went to visit his ex-wife who was ill. Low and behold if they didn't fall in love again and he never came back. I am still consoling my friend…"

Ivania noticed the alarmed look on Henry's face, "But such a thing could never happen between you two. If I can't lure you away, I'm sure Jennifer won't be lured away that easily either…but if she is…" Ivania winked, "I am still here for you, Hendry."

They all laughed nervously except for Ivania…she was dead serious.

"Well we better check in upstairs, Jenny, I hope I don't get a parking ticket. It was great seeing you again, Ivania. I'm not in the shop or café as much anymore, but I will keep an eye out for you and maybe we can have coffee."

"Yes, I would love that, perhaps while Jenny is in Ottawa I can prepare a nice home cooked meal for you…I'm not all business you know."

"Oh, I don't know if that is such a good idea, Henry." Jenny chimed in with a nervous tone in her voice.

"Believe me, Jenny, you have no need to worry. Somehow you have wrapped an iron shield around his heart which no woman is able to penetrate."

"I hope that's the case." Jenny said, with a smile.

Henry was blushing more and more by the minute. He took Jenny's hand and led her off to the check in area upstairs. "See you, Ivania."

"Yes, bye, and it was so nice meeting you, Jenny."

They had spent so much time chatting downstairs that there was only a few minutes left before boarding time was over.

"You better hurry, Ma'am, if you're on the Ottawa flight. The doors close in two minutes."

"Oh, Henry, I love you so much."Jenny dropped her suitcase and wrapped her arms around his neck.

Henry pulled her in hard against his body and a surge of love passed through them both. Henry wanted all of her. He ached to hold her, to kiss her forever, to make love to her and never stop. His mind, heart and soul screamed out for his Jenny and now, she was going away once more…

"Jenny I don't know if I can take this. I don't want to live without you anymore. Please make this a temporary visit and come back soon."

"Ma'am, the plane is closing its doors. You'll miss your flight if you don't go now."

Jenny picked up her case… "I love you, Henry I will call you tonight…"

"I love you, too, Jenny… I love you, too."

Henry wasn't sure if Jenny heard his last words as she was running down the hall towards the plane.

Henry went to the window and watched as the plane began to back out. With each foot it travelled away, his heart sank deeper and deeper …"Oh Jenny, please come back to me…"

The plane turned and made its way to the take off runway. Henry's heart beat faster and faster. He didn't want to watch and yet he couldn't move. He recalled the day Jenny left Mr. Engelmann's grocery store and made her way to the corner to cross Victoria Ave. He had sent out a prayer to surround his sweetheart with his love and keep her safe as she crossed the busy Avenue. And it did. She was almost killed by a racing car but her guardian angel saved her.

Henry prayed again as the plane picked up speed as it raced down the tarmac. "Oh guardian angel, keep my Jenny safe while she goes on this mission. Guide and protect her and shield her from all harm. And …please bring her back to me."

The front of the aircraft lifted and then the back tires. Higher and higher it ascended. The clouds were low and the plane quickly disappeared into the sky. *And Henry's heart sank.*

Father Engelmann's words immediately surfaced as they always did to give him comfort…

Life on earth is bright and sunny even though some days may be cloudy and stormy. Right behind the heavy dark clouds, the sun still shines. It's there waiting for us, bursting with life and renewed hope.

Chapter Sixty Seven

J ENNY STILL FELT more at home in Ottawa than Regina. Sure it was a much larger city, but she had lived here for a good part of her life and probably had driven down almost every street in the city at one time or another. She loved Ottawa at this time of the year. The maple leaves were turning into their fall colours and everything looked so colourful and beautiful. She especially liked it when the sun struck the trees directly from one side increasing the brightness of the hue. It was almost as if the sun was caught, trapped in the leaves themselves.

She hoped to have lunch with Nora and walk alongside the Rideau Canal. Jenny recalled many fond memories of walks with her mother when shopping and those rare times when they went skating on the canal in the winter.

If only Daddy had taken more time off.

A tinge of nervousness swept through Jenny as the chauffeur turned into the gated estate. The driver pushed a button and the gates opened to Greystone Manor. She recalled the first day James brought her here. It was the day after they got married. All the while dating James, he had never taken her here or mentioned it... it was one of the few pleasant surprises that James gave her in all the years they had been married.

The grounds looked beautiful as the black limousine wound in between the trees on the curved road, leading to the front of the mansion. Yes, thought Jenny, just one more turn and the mansion would come into view. She held her breath almost the same as she did that first day she came. The sight of the mansion was so huge and overwhelming. To this day, she didn't think she had explored every nook and cranny of the immense structure.

Thomas was working out front and Jenny could see Matti peeking out the window. As soon as the car came to a stop under the canopy, Matti opened the door and ran out…

"Oh, Jenny, Jenny, you're here! I have to visit the bathroom so often I thought I may not be here to greet you when you drive up. Good thing I held it for one more minute!"

Jenny didn't wait for the driver to open the door. She had already rushed out of the back seat and into the arms of her dear friend.

"It's so good to see you, Matti!"

"I be going around in circles all morning, I be so excited. I be givin' the boys a fork with their cereal and spoon to cut their bacon, Oh, Jenny, I just couldn't keep my mind off you. We all be so happy to see you!"

Matti embraced Jenny once again.

Jenny turned and there was her dear friend, Thomas, wearing his usual warm smile. His hair had grayed at little at the sides, but made him look even wiser and kinder if that were possible. He had his hand extended to shake her hand as he approached Jenny, but she bypassed it and gave Thomas a warm embrace.

"Oh Thomas, it's so good to see you. I can't begin to tell you how much I missed our chats in the garden."

"I did too, Miss Jenny, right up to today. Perhaps I'll have a reprieve from my daily distress over your absence."

"Oh, Thomas, your words were always able to touch my heart. I hope we can have many chats while I'm here."

The driver had taken Jenny's suitcases out of the trunk and was waiting for instructions. Matti noticed it the same time Jenny did.

"Please take the suitcase to the head of the stairs. I will have Charles take them to Jenny's room."

"I'm in the same bedroom and not the guest room?"

"Yes, James thought you would feel most comfortable in the room that you are used to. We all agreed with him. Well, let's not just stand here, come on in, Jenny. The house is in a little disarray. James tried to get a few antique furniture pieces for the living room to make you more comfortable and feel at home. But we don't know where to put his gleaming furniture as the guest houses are now all occupied. Don't matter none, things don't need to be so organized as they used to be. Jim be more accepting of things from day to day."

Jenny walked into the living room and looked around. Matti was right. Not nearly as neat and precise as the first day she came here over twenty three years ago. There was a pleasant mix of modern and old furniture. Some didn't seem to go together, but Jenny didn't mind at all. She appreciated the effort and gesture more than the furniture anyway.

"I can't wait to see the garden, Matti—"

"Jen, it be more beautiful than ever. We all cannot believe how James is becoming a gardener. I never thought I'd see the day he be getting on his knees and planting marigolds and petunias! And they ain't in no straight lines anymore. They go where he feels like putting it…much like an artist. Sometimes I think the old way looked better, but no-one cares anymore…if it be giving joy to Mr. Hamilton that be more important to us than anyting, that for sure."

Jenny shook her head in amazement over what she was hearing. There seemed to be such a camaraderie growing on the estate. She immediately felt a much more relaxed atmosphere confirming what she was seeing.

"Where is James, Matti…?" Jenny was hesitant to ask but was surprised he still hadn't greeted her.

"He be waiting for you out in the garden, Jen. This morning at breakfast he say how beautiful the garden is with all the flowers, the angel, and shrubs but the thing that will give it all its real beauty will be when Marjorie comes walking through the garden."

"Those words are so wonderful, Matti…"

"You be seeing a big difference in the master, Jenny. He sure has changed some. We all be living just this side of heaven most days."

"How is he doing Matti?" Jenny wanted to know.

Matti shook her head. "He be a lot worse than he looks. Doctors say he should be in the hospital over two weeks ago, but he refuses to go. Says he won't leave until he sees you in the garden one more time. He be in his wheelchair much of the time, but many days he forces himself to get up and walk around. He be in a lot of pain, but he's enduring it somehow. I 'spect he wants to keep strong for your return."

"I'd like to go out and see him, Matti."

"He be waitin' for you. Jen. He either strolling around in his wheelchair or sitting on the swing in the gazebo like you used to do. In fact, he be doin' what you used to do almost every day when you were here; stroll along and take in God's creation, rest awhile on the swing and gaze at all the different wildflowers coming up and every now and then get up and place a wildflower in the angel's basket in thanksgiving for someting that comes to mind. Yes, Jen, you be surprised just how much that man be changin'…he be putting flowers in the Angel of Thanksgiving's basket more than once a day in thanks for your return…and look, you here! Almost as if he knew you be coming."

Jenny didn't know what to say. This all overwhelmed her and touched her heart deeply. She walked over to the patio doors and peered out, but could not see James. As soon as she opened the patio doors, several monarch butterflies greeted her. She raised her hand, trying to entice one to land, but they just kept flitting about and then proceeded down the stone path as if to ask her to follow.

Jenny stepped outside and closed the door behind her. The grounds never looked more beautiful. It was a gorgeous September day, just a gentle breeze in the air. She immediately smelled the Thyme and faintly, some of the other herbs.

Although the grounds filled her with peace, a tinge of nervousness inched her way through her body. She felt a little anxious to see James. Their parting several years ago was so cold and abrupt over the phone and the last time she saw him was in the court room. The circumstances were now so different. She had talked to him the last couple of weeks and noticed such a difference. Jenny couldn't but help think of God's divine providence at work. He was always trying to work things out for our good. 'Trust in the Lord with all your heart and don't lean on your own understanding' was a Scripture Henry had quoted that morning. Jenny found it soothing now as she slowly strolled down the path towards her beloved haven.

As soon as she turned the corner just past the fountain, she saw James sitting on the swing in the gazebo. It appeared as if he was reading a book. Jenny only took two more soft footsteps for James to detect a presence. He looked up, his eyes brightened and smiled…

Jenny smiled back. He looked so frail and had aged. His hair had thinned and grayed near the temples. He still looked handsome, but seemed to have lost some flair.

Jenny liked the new look.

"I knew you would come, Marjorie." James made some effort to get up but he winced hard and sat back down.

Jenny hastened to his side, "It's okay, James, don't get up."

Jenny sat next to James on the swing and took both of his hands in hers, "It's nice to see you James. How are you doing?"

James shrugged his shoulders, "Some days are better than others. When Matilda told me you were coming, it made me feel good, Marj. *Awfully good.* I could hardly sleep last night, just thinking on it. Maybe that's why I feel more tired today than usual. Tomorrow will be better."

Jenny squeezed James' hands. "I'm glad I came, too, James. What you are going through is such a struggle and I do want to be there for you as much as I can."

James nodded. He wanted to say more; that she had come more for him than his illness, but decided not to, rather he said, "How do you like the grounds, Marj-Jen? Damn, here I go again. I know you like to be called Jen or Jenny, but would it be okay if I called you Marjorie or Marj? I don't mean that out of any disrespect, it's just that to me Marjorie carries more affection that I have for you than Jenny. Everyone calls you Jenny or Jen…can this be something different between us? I will call you Je—"

"Actually James, I love the way you just put that. Yes, please call me Marjorie or Marj. I do like the way you call me that and it will be special…thank you."

Jenny leaned forward and kissed James on the cheek and then let go of his hands and sat back against the swing. "Yes, James, the grounds look beautiful." Jenny said, as she gazed at the garden before her. "The wildflowers look so full and beautiful, too, James."

"It's a funny thing that keeps going on here, Marj. Several times a day, I pick some of the wildflowers and place them into the angel's basket in thanks for your coming back and sometimes within hours, another wildflower seems to come up to take its place."

Jenny looked at the Angel of Thanksgiving. It did look odd to see the basket in the angel's left hand, but otherwise it was identical.

But it did shock her to see the large number of flowers in the basket…it was overflowing!

"Oh, James, I've never seen so many flowers in the angel's basket…" Jenny's words trailed off as she realized that they were all for her coming back.

"I knew you would come, Marjorie, I was too foolish to see it when we were married, but in this last while, I have come to see and understand a lot of things. As I thought about how you coped all the years of our marriage and how you treated me, I began to understand your heart, Marj. You are one of a kind…I knew you would come. *Your heart would give you no choice.*"

Jenny turned back to James and just smiled.

"The doctors want to admit me into the hospital. They can provide better care and then there's much ado about life support and a contract I have with a company that's going to freeze my body until a cure is found. An emergency response team is already at the hospital ready to prepare the body for transport to the suspension facility."

"Are you sure you really want to do that, James?"

"I know it sounds silly…right now I'm not concerned about it. Now that you are here, I want to spend as much time as I can on the estate with you. I hope you will be staying awhile. I asked Nora to bring Jimmy over tomorrow. I sent a message to J.J. to come also, but that, I can't guarantee."

Jenny reached out for James' hand and squeezed it. "That was so thoughtful of you, James. I would love to see Jimmy. It's been almost a year since I last saw him. He must be running around all over by now."

"Yes, he sure is. It's quite the sight to see him running up and down the paths. I bought him a tricycle this summer and he's learned to ride that pretty good. Wait till you see him."

Jenny found it hard to believe James talking about his grandson this way. He never took time for anyone. *Once more, God's divine was providence at work. In God all things are possible*!

"How is Nora doing? Is J.J. back at home yet?"

"Nora is doing okay, but sure would like it if J.J. came home. I don't know exactly what is bothering that boy. I've tried talking to him, but he has the Hamilton traits: pride and arrogant as all hell."

"He'll come around, James. I so hope while I am here, I will be able to work things out with him."

"I've tried to encourage him in that direction, too, and I don't know how much plainer I can be with the boy to let him know that our marriage failed and was in trouble all because of me."

Jenny squeezed James' hand, "He'll come around, James, I just know it. Perhaps now that I am here, we can start to place flowers in the angel's basket for J.J. to come home, too…you know, in the sense of truly coming home to his wife and to us."

James nodded and remained silent.

Jenny noticed the soiled Bible resting on the swing beside James.

"Is that a Bible you are reading, James?"

"Yeah, it's Thomas'. He lent it to me. Most of—"

Jenny and James both looked up to see Matti coming down the path carrying a tray with a glass of water and several plastic vials.

"I held off as long as I was able not wanting to interrupt the chat you two be having. But it's best you be taking your medicine, Jim."

"I suppose you're right Matti." James took the glass from Matti with one hand and one of the vials with the other and tossed the pills towards the back of his mouth and swallowed some water. He repeated that procedure with the next two vials.

"It's the small white pill that will put me to sleep in about ten minutes so I best be getting back to the house. I'll be as sharp as a whip at dinner time. You have to be to keep up with all of the folks at the table."

Jenny recalled Matti telling her that the staff shared dinner with James. She had to see it to believe it.

Matti wheeled the chair up to James and with great effort, he lifted himself. Jenny tried to help by lifting on one arm and Matti on the other. James half turned himself around and fell into the wheelchair.

"Well, Marj, I won't be much good to you in a few minutes. This pill seems to put me to sleep in no time." James looked up at Jenny and as tenderly as he could, he said, "Thanks again for coming, Marj. I knew you would. He lifted his right arm and Jenny received it with her right hand.

"I'm glad I came too, James. Have a good rest and we'll talk some more later."

Jenny watched as Matti pushed James back to the house. Tears surfaced in her eyes.

Yes, she murmured, the real James has come out.

CHAPTER SIXTY EIGHT

"THE FLIGHT WAS great; no turbulence at all and I even had a little nap," said Jenny, her voice filled with excitement.

"I left the gallery early this afternoon and had a nap, too. I didn't sleep too well last night—"

"Yes, and then getting up earlier than you needed to, to get me to the airport."

"So, tell me, Jen. How is James?" Henry was eager to know.

"He's so different, Henry. The antithesis of how he was; much gentler and very communicative. I think the staff here have drawn that part out of him. He never gave anyone much of his time. Every second chatting with someone he considered as time and money wasted. It's all so different now, things are much more peaceful, relaxed and the grounds are so beautiful."

"How is James' illness? Should he be in the hospital or is he still able to get around at home?"

"He should be in the hospital, but says he will hold off for as long as he can. It's obvious he is in a lot of pain and has difficulty getting up on his own. He went to his room for a nap around four this afternoon and that's the last we have seen of him."

"Is he okay…?"

"Apparently when he was told I was coming, he couldn't sleep last night either. He looked very tired when I came to the estate. I suspect that he will sleep the whole night through. I remember when I was really sick, a good night's sleep really helped to pick me up. I hope that will be the case for him tomorrow."

"Do you have plans for tomorrow?" Henry was interested in knowing.

"I am going to take one of the cars in the garage and head to church. There's one about eight miles from here and has a ten o'clock Mass. And, I am so excited to see Nora and my grandson! James invited them over for the day. I can hardly wait to see them."

"Is J.J. coming?"

"We don't know. Apparently he is still living on his own. James asked the office to tell him to come over. So I am praying with all my might that he comes."

"You know, Jen, visiting with James as you are may be the best way to reach J.J. in a family setting."

"That's what I kept thinking after Mrs. Hamilton, James' mother, called and asked me to come. I was so troubled by her request and didn't want to go. I went out to the gazebo in the back yard and that very thought came to me. That Jesus wanted me here. Perhaps that is part of the plan...I sure hope so."

"I do too. I will pray that things get resolved. You don't need this kind of family turmoil in your life. If only family members realized how foolish it is to carry on with the cold shoulder and not speak to one another. Life is so short...it's our stupid pride hanging on to literally garbage, day after day until it stretches into months and years, and for what?"

"I feel the same...that's why I am so excited to start up a women's group that addresses some of these issues when I get back. We can be so supportive to one another. You know the old saying, two heads are better than one!"

"And even better when a group of women get together; why you can change the world!"

"Now that, my dear Henry, is a very wise observation. Oh, I must tell you about dinner time. Apparently James gave Matilda, Thomas and Charles, the butler, each one of the guest homes. They are going to show me their homes tomorrow. Not only that, I don't know if I told you, they all have dinner together like one big family.

It's absolutely lovely, Henry. There is prayer at meal time, and discussion, and joking and fun…in all the years I lived on the estate, except for the times Matti and I went out for lunch, there wasn't once, that I had such an enjoyable dinner. Thomas' wife, Neela, is petite and quiet and I love her warm smile. They are so in love and so considerate of one another. And I dare say, it seems to me, Charles may have a fancy for Matilda! I am looking forward to seeing James at the table tomorrow. I can't imagine him being in this kind of a setting."

"That's great, Jen. It warms my heart to hear it. In a way, with all of his money and power, this is probably the most he ever got out of it that gave him true happiness."

"I couldn't help but think the same thing, Henry. I think this was a brilliant move on his part. If the good Lord is going to take him soon, at least he will be exposed to what family life is really all about!"

"It all sounds good, Jenny. It sounds to me like the big challenge is to get that son of yours on board."

"He'll be a tough one all right, but I don't think he will stand a chance against all of us. *We will win him over with love.* And please tell Father to say a Mass for us and request his warriors to pray as well. Pretty soon that son of mine will have his head spinning, he won't know who to hug first!"

Henry and Jenny chuckled, knowing in their hearts it just may not be that easy.

"Oh, by the way, Ivania is such a gorgeous woman, Henry. Was she your lady friend for awhile?"

Henry really didn't want to discuss her, but said, "Yes, she was a customer at the café and we sort of hit it off and dated for awhile but…" Henry's words trailed off.

"But what?" Jenny wanted to know.

"Well, all the while I dated her I couldn't get neither Julean nor you off my mind. She noticed it right away and eventually confronted me on it. I told her about you and Julean and after that we just became good friends."

"She certainly is a striking woman and very bold I might add."

"Yeah, I don't think she would be able to do what you are doing, Jen."

There was a long silence and Henry found it easy to break the silence with feelings that were more true to his heart…

"I miss you a lot Jenny. I know you are where you are supposed to be, but the selfish part of me wants you here."

"I want to be with you too, Sweetheart. Let's take one day at a time and as you said this morning, all things are possible through God. Let's trust Him to turn all this into good."

"I love you with all my heart..."

"I love you even more, Henry. Good night."

CHAPTER SIXTY NINE

WELL, HERE THEY are!" exclaimed Matti, as Thomas, his wife and Jenny walked into the kitchen. "You all be just in time for some smoked bacon and my Aunt Jemima's pancakes. Why they be so fluffy and delicious with some apple slices and syrup on top you be begging for more!"

"Could smell it soon as I came in," said Thomas and Jenny quickly concurred.

James was sitting at the table and looked very rested. A smile covered his words as he said, "So the three of you went to church together? I hoped you prayed for me."

"We did indeed, James. Offered up the Mass just for you!"

"Did you take the Mercedes or the Porsche, Marj?"

"Neither, we took a car with a lot more class and character. We took Thomas' 73 Dodge."

James looked surprised. "Did you really, Marj?"

"Of course, it's a lovely car; much roomier than the Porsche and besides, the company was much better than the radio."

"Well, you all sit down and continue your chat over a fine warm breakfast. It be ready in less than five minutes."

"It's not often I see you in Sunday duds, Thomas, you look very distinguished," observed James.

"That's what the wife keeps telling me too, so there must be some truth to it."

"Now that ain't quite so, comments like that travel fast to a man's head," replied, Neela with a wink.

"That for sure," piped in Matti.

"So tell me, what do you three get out of church anyway? How important is it really that you have to go?" asked James.

"You know James," began Thomas. "For the longest time, I thought going to church was fulfilling your obligation. It was the day for the Lord so I thought, but it came to me for all the church attending I was doing over the years, the thing I was missing was a close relationship with the Lord. Without that, I was simply going through the motions, only kidding myself."

"I agree with you Thomas," chimed in Jenny. "I came to know God through His creation. I am at awe at everything in the world and God created it all! When I am alone in the early morning and out in the garden, I feel His presence in everything, especially the silence. That's when I hear him whisper to me."

"So is one better than the other and can you do with one and not the other?" James was interested in knowing.

"You need both, Jim," Matti piped in. "Like Thomas be saying. If you just go to church and the good Lord is not alive in your heart like your closest friend, you be just sitting and singing away. When church be over why you forgot about the Lord before you get to the car.

"Now, going to church can get you more interested in knowing the Lord. Seeing your brother and sister at church, who have a relationship, act like beacons of light that encourage you to seek what they have. It's much like you be taking an interest in the Bible because you see Thomas be doing it. So you go home and start reading and you ask, 'okay, Jesus, I want what my brother has.'"

"What Matti says, sums it up James. When one has a close relationship with God, you want to go to church and praise Him and get nourishment from the service and your brothers and sisters. We are all in this together to support each other. We want to share the light, not hide it." added Thomas.

"What's that song? *To know Him is to Love Him* and to know Him you have to spend time with Him. Look at Miss Jenny and the hours she be spending with the Lord. Why someday, I swear I see Jesus walkin' right beside her..."

Jenny smiled, "I don't think I can wait much longer for those pancakes, Matti!"

"Oh my, me and my big mouth get talkin' and I soon forgets I've got to feed you all!"

"When are Nora and Jimmy coming over?" asked Jenny.

"First thing this afternoon. She called while you be at church to say they be going to her momma and daddy's place for breakfast first. They may stay for dinner."

"Oh, I hope they do! I can't wait to see Jimmy."

James got up and got some water and took his medication. He returned to his chair.

"I'm so glad to see you up, James and able to move around," observed Jenny.

"Yeah, that long sleep helped. If I watch myself, I can go for most of the day on my own."

Jenny smiled brightly. "That's wonderful."

During lunch they continued their previous discussion, however, after a bit, Jenny tuned out and just sat there to take in the wonderful thing that had happened in the Hamilton residence.

It was becoming a home.

In the strangest way, James was growing up all over, but in a family setting that was healthy and normal. Unbidden tears came to her eyes. She wondered if this had been the way it was when she was here, would she still have felt so strongly about Henry.

After lunch, they all helped to gather the dishes and then retired outside and sat around the patio table.

Soon Charles announced that Nora and her son were here. He directed them to the patio. When Jimmy came out, he walked over to James with an erect posture and his hand extended as he had been taught by J.J., who in turn was taught by James.

"Hi, James," said little Jimmy, as he stood in front of his grandfather. What happened next astonished all of them present, but most of all Jenny.

Rather than shake Jimmy's hand, James with some degree of effort picked up the child and set him on his knee. "Remember when you were here last week, what did I tell you to call me?"

Jimmy put his forefinger to his mouth as if to help him

remember, "Grandpa, but J.J. said I should call you James… it is more grown up."

"But don't you recall what I said to that?"

"You said it's nicer to call you Grandpa because it's a special name you call someone you like a lot."

"That's right. You see Jimmy, when you call me James, it does sound grown up, but it's not as friendly as when you call me Grandpa. It's special because it means we are part of this family. Which do you like better? Here, let's shake hands." James stuck his hand out stiffly and shook Jimmy's hand abruptly and said, "How do you do, Jimmy? Or we can do it this way." James gave Jimmy a big hug and shook him lovingly and tickled him at the same time. "Now isn't that more fun and friendly, Jimmy? Which one tells me that you like me more…the handshake or a hug?"

Jimmy shook his head. "Yes, Grandpa, I like the hug better but don't tickle me."

"But I like tickling you…" James grabbed Jimmy again and warmly hugged him.

"See, Jimmy, I am your daddy's father and I would like him to call me Dad from now on, too. We are family, Jimmy and call each other in ways that are special. So please, from now on call me Grandpa. Don't forget."

"Can I tickle you when I do?" Jimmy tickled James' tummy to which James let out a loud howl. And immediately he tickled Jimmy back.

It was evident that James was in pain, but he ignored it and once again he grabbed little Jimmy and hugged him so as to keep his arms still.

Once James had caught his breath and Jimmy settled down, he asked Jimmy, "Who is that lady over there?"

"That's Marjorie!"

"That's right, but she is your daddy's mommy. So what makes her special to you, Jimmy?"

Jimmy looked confused and turned to his mother and asked, "What should I say, Mommy?"

Nora came over and knelt in front of him. "What do you call my mom, Jimmy?"

"Grandma."

"That's right, you call her Grandma because she is my mommy

and Marjorie is daddy's mommy and so what should we call her?"

Jimmy looked at Nora and whispered… "Is it Grandma, too?"

"Yes, Jimmy we call her Grandma, too. We are all family and like Grandpa said, we have special names for each other."

"Why does Daddy want me to call him J.J.?"

James piped in, "Here's how it is, Jimmy. You tell J.J. to start calling me Dad and you start calling J.J., Dad or Daddy, too. When I see him next time, I will tell him so, too. From now on, we are family and we want to call each other by our special names. In no time you will get the hang of it."

Jenny got up and went over to Jimmy who had his hand extended, but Jenny ignored it and gave him a warm hug and a kiss on the cheek. "My goodness you have grown since I last saw you, Jimmy." Jenny brushed the boy's hair with her hand. "Do you remember coming to visit me when I was in the hospital?"

Jimmy just nodded.

"I was so happy to see you. I wish you could have stayed longer and I could have played with you. But we can now…"

Jenny stood up and turned to Nora. "It's so good to see you again, Nora." Jenny went to her and the two ladies hugged one another.

"You can call me, Jenny, if you wish, Nora, but I would love for you to call me, Mom. What do think Jimmy, wouldn't that be nice if you called me Grandma and your mom called me Mom?"

Jimmy looked at his mom, "Is that all right, Mommy?"

Nora, nodded, "Yes, that's okay, Jimmy. We will all be part of one big family."

Jenny knelt in front of Jimmy once more. "Come-on, let's go and see if we can see some butterflies before they go back to Mexico."

"There's one, Grandma." Jimmy pointed to one just above James' head.

"Here, give me your hand, Jimmy. Come on, Grandpa, take Jimmy's other hand and let's catch some butterflies."

James quickly responded and the three strolled down the path with Jimmy, hopping and swinging on his grandparents' arms. They quickly disappeared along one of the paths, but their laughter could still be heard.

CHAPTER SEVENTY

M ATTI WAS SHARING with Nora the miraculous healing that Jenny had received, when J.J. came out onto the patio.

"You just missed breakfast, but I can dish someting real quick," offered Matti.

"No, that's okay." He turned to Nora and nodded.

Nora looked at her husband and said, "Hi, J.J., it's nice to see you."

J.J simply nodded again and looked down the path to see if he could see his son. The three came into view, but just for a moment before his son, still swinging in between his grandparents, disappeared behind a group of shrubs. J.J. remained expressionless.

"Jimmy is having a lot fun with his grandparents. Your mom was so happy to see Jimmy."

Once again J.J. just nodded. "How long are you going to stay here, Nora?"

"We were invited for dinner and so are you. I hope you can stay."

J.J. shrugged his shoulders. "So I can't take Jimmy with me today?"

"Your mom came all the way from Regina to see him and your dad gets such joy from watching him play in the garden. It would

439

be best for him to spend some time with them and it would be nice for you to do the same. Your mom would love to see you, please stay."

I be baking your favourite dish, J.J.: roast chicken and baby back ribs. That be quite a combination! You always told me how much you liked them and to be honest, I had you in mind when I made up the dinner menu. Please join us, son."

"J.J. shook his head, "I have things to do. But I want Jimmy next weekend for sure, Nora."

He turned and walked back into the kitchen without any further ado. Matti followed and just as he was at the door and about to leave, Matti went up to the landing. She looked him straight in the eye and said, "J.J., its none of my business, I knows that, but I helped raise you along with your momma and that nanny and so I feel I have the right to say what I have to say. Listen, son, you be missing out on a lot of joy and holdin' back from giving a lot of happiness to your family and mommy and daddy. It be so good for Jimmy to see love between all of you. If you need to talk anyting out, I be here for you. Oh, J.J., one of the heaviest burdens a man can carry is a chip on his shoulder. Your mommy and daddy want so bad for all of you to be family. Your mommy come all the way to see you, your daddy is sick and soon the Lord may take him. They made mistakes just like their children. Nobody's perfect J.J., not even you. What do you say, come back in and let's work on being a family…please."

"They had twenty years or more to do that Matti…I remember year after year going over to friends' places and both their parents were at home and there for their kids. They had holidays, birthdays and Christmas together and with us, there was nothing. It's too late for this family thing."

"See now, you be seeing what a family should be like, and that is what they be trying to do. They be seeing the light and want to make up for the past and have a new future. Don't you see?"

J.J. stared at Matti and just shook his head from side to side.

Matti went on, trying desperately to find an opening into the boy's hardened heart.

"Sometimes one walks in the shadows of life for so long all they see is darkness. But I tell you J.J., what I see today, is a lot of people coming out of the shadow. Look how hard your daddy is trying and he be sick and all. You would make him so happy and your mommy would fly to heaven if you come and say hello and give her a warm hug and call her Mommy. This first name stuff is not for family, it's for strangers and friends. For family we show more love and caring and respect as we should for all people, but with family there be a special connection. Know what I'm sayin'? Please, come back and show caring for your family, J.J. Come, please come and join us, do it for Matti."

Matti reached for J.J.'s hand, but he sharply pulled it away and walked briskly out the door.

"It's too late, Matti, tell Nora I want Jimmy next weekend for sure."

"Yes," said Matti as she continued to follow him. "Yes, next week may be too late. Your daddy awfully sick, J.J."

J.J. didn't answer and began to walk down the steps to his Porsche.

"You should be minding your own business, Matti. I'll see to it that you get fired."

Matti was losing her calm, "Now you see here, young man, I wiped your bum more than once and I have a right to talk to you this way because we be all family and care for each other. You say your mommy and daddy weren't there for you but what about you now, you be doing the same t'ing...you talkin' out of both sides of your mouth, J.J."

Matti looked up and saw a girl sitting in J.J.'s Porsche. "Who's that young t'ing in your car J.J.?" Good, Lord, J.J., you not be unfaithful to your wife and child are you? Should I bring little Jimmy out here and show him what his daddy be doing!? And you have the nerve to judge your parents so harshly when you be doing something even worse...shame on you, J.J."

Matti walked down the remaining steps to the car. "What's your name young lady?" Do you know he be a married man with a child? You have no business getting involved with him."

Turning to J.J., Matti continued, "J.J., I be so disappointed in you. This be not right. Now you drop this young lady off at home and you get right back here and be with your wife and family, hear me!?"

"Mind your own business, Matti."

J.J. turned the key, revved the motor and screeched away.

"My, my, what the world be comin' to, bringin' a lady friend to the very doorstep where his wife and family is? Oh Lord, that boy need a spanking. Reason and commonsense don't do no good. Why he got heaven at the doorstep and he chooses hell."

Matti turned and muttered once again as she made her way back up the steps, "What the world be comin' to?"

When she got to top of the landing, she stopped before entering. She was so riled up, she began to shake much like a dog coming out of the water. Instead of getting rid of water, Matti was shaking out the tension and anger. "Ooooheeee!!!" She shrieked and shook some more.

"There now, that be better to get it out of my system or the entire day be in the shadow. Jenny may look at her garden to get rid of annoyances, but I just shake them away."

Matti wiped her feet on the mat, grabbed her dress from both sides of her hips and pushed the gathered parts down. "There, that be feeling a whole lot better." She raised her head and went inside as if nothing out of the unusual happened.

Nora was sitting alone at the patio table watching Jenny and James trying to catch a butterfly for little Jimmy. She had tears in her eyes.

Matti pulled out a chair and sat beside her.

"Did J.J. go, Matti?"

"Yes, he's gone, Nora. I 'spect he be hurting inside. He's one confused young man and needs some growin' up to do. But sooner or later, he be comin' around. *The Lord will see to it.*"

"He is just so hard to reach Matti and I do love him so. Jimmy misses him a lot and asks for him all the time."

Matti put her arm around Nora. "He be working things out, Nora. Like I say, he's confused and needs a little time. I 'spect his mommy and daddy be talkin' to him, too. All we can do right now, Nora, is be praying for him. *God knows how to bring him around.*"

A silence fell between the women as they listened to Jimmy playing with his grandparents.

"Oh, you're playing us out, Jimmy. Come let's sit on the swing for awhile." Both Jenny and James were out of breath as they flopped on the swing in the gazebo.

"That was so much fun," said Jenny, as she hugged Jimmy and tickled him like James did before.

Almost at the same time, a monarch landed on James' hand and another on Jimmy's.

"Oh, look!" exclaimed, Jenny. "A mommy and daddy butterfly. Look, Jimmy, see the two dark spots on the back wings of the butterfly on Grandpa's hand, that's a male butterfly, a daddy."

"There are no spots on mine," observed Jimmy.

"That's right, Jimmy, because it's a female butterfly, a mommy!"

Jenny was so excited to share with Jimmy that she hugged the little boy and frightened the butterfly off.

"Oh, she will come back again, Jimmy. I still have the male. The girl butterflies can't resist the boys. She'll be back, guaranteed!"

"Oh, James!" Jenny gave him a poke.

Matti and Nora were still sitting quietly at the table when Jimmy came running up the walk. Jenny and James were just behind.

"Mommy, Mommy! A butterfly landed on my hand. It was black and orange and Grandma said that it was a girl butterfly because it didn't have any black marks on the wings like Grandpa's did."

"Are you ever smart, Jimmy. Mommy didn't know that. Next time you can show Mommy how to tell the difference."

Jimmy ran off down the path trying to catch another butterfly.

"Oh that was fun," said Jenny, as she sat down. "I thought I heard J.J.?"

"Yes, he be here, but had to go."

"Go where?" James bellowed.

Matti just shook her head and shrugged her shoulders.

"I'll have a talk with him tomorrow."

Jenny wanting to change the subject, said, "Oh, Nora, if you have time this week I would love to go shopping with you and Jimmy. I'd love to by him an outfit or two if I could. He's just about two years old, right?"

"Yes, he'll be two next month, October, 21. And, yes, Jen... Mom, I would love to go shopping with you. We could go Tuesday or Wednesday."

"Let's go Tuesday, the sooner the better. I'll pick you up around ten and we will make a day of it. Perhaps we can have lunch in a café along the Rideau Canal walkway. It's so beautiful there this time of year."

"Sounds wonderful, Mom."

"I best be getting your medicine, James, and it be a good time for a nap soon." Matti interjected.

"Yeah, I suppose I could use a rest after keeping up with this little guy. Have we some ice cream, Matti?"

"We have strawberry and chocolate."

"What would you like, Jimmy?" asked James. "Chocolate or strawberry? Mmmm both sound good, don't they?"

"I don't know…can I have both?"

"Both it is for Jimmy and me. I haven't had ice cream in years." James rubbed his tummy. "My tummy can't wait, how about yours, Jimmy?" James grabbed the boy and rubbed his tummy, tickling him at the same time. Jimmy cringed away and tucked his arms in to protect himself. James grabbed him and gave him a big hug.

Jenny couldn't believe how James had changed and knew how to be an absolutely great grandfather. "Where did you pick up such wonderful Grandfather skills, James?" Jenny was dying to know.

"Instinct, Marjorie, just instinct. Once you stop and take the time for family…it just naturally comes to you. But then again, it could very well be a Hamilton trait." James winked and lifted his shoulders gesturing that it would be more believable if he added, "a trait that they had a long, long time ago…"

CHAPTER SEVENTY ONE

"Hɪ, ʜᴏɴᴇʏ, ꜱᴏʀʀʏ I didn't call last night. James was quite ill and there was quite a commotion here for a few hours."

"Did they take him to the hospital?" asked Henry feeling relieved that Jenny called.

"The doctor tried his best to convince him to go, but James refused. He said he'll know when he has to go and was firm in staying home. James' doctor isn't the only one who wants him admitted. There is an emergency team of doctors ready to transport him to some facility where his body will be frozen."

"Yeah, you mentioned that to me before. He is still serious in going through with that?"

"I think he agrees it's a bit farfetched, but he hasn't put a stop to it. Money is no object to James. He may do whatever he can to postpone his death. I'm sure he has a series of life support measures in place as well."

Henry remained silent, not really wanting to go there. He was more concerned about Jenny and their relationship.

"How are you holding up in all this, Jenny?" Henry was eager to know. He listened to her response carefully.

"Surprisingly well, Henry. James has changed so much and …

445

for the better, I hardly recognize him as the same man. Our grandson, Jimmy, was over Sunday with Nora and we had such fun with him chasing butterflies. Except for yesterday, when James had a spell, everything is going fine. J.J. was over to the estate on Sunday but I didn't see him. James and I were taking Jimmy for a walk when he came and he left right away. He's going to be a hard one to reach, I'm afraid. Anyway, Nora, Jimmy and I spent the whole day today shopping. We had so much fun. Nora is such a lovely girl. J.J. should consider himself fortunate to have her as a wife. I hope he realizes it before it's too late."

"Did you chat with Nora about her financial arrangement with J.J.? Is it set up the same way yours was? I recall you were concerned about that."

"Yes, while Jimmy was colouring and playing with a small toy the café supplied, I asked Nora about that. Apparently, she too, entered into a prenuptial agreement which was similar to the one James and I had. But two months ago, James changed all that. He formed a trust for Jimmy and a bank management arrangement such that for each year that J.J. and Nora are married, the account increases substantially. It goes hand in hand somehow along with an agreement that dictates how a settlement would be made. Nora had her father take the agreement to his lawyer. After review, the lawyer apparently said the agreement outlined a very generous and fair division of assets between the husband and wife should a settlement ever be required." Then Jenny added something which twigged at Henry's concern receptors.

"I just cannot believe how wonderful James has become…it's another miracle, Henry."

"Yeah," Henry said, hesitantly, "It sure sounds like it. Change doesn't come easy, Jen. When I was a counsellor it got very discouraging at times when clients came back time and again still dealing with the same self defeating behaviours. And yet, when one is ready to change, it can happen. I can see in James' case, his illness stopped him in his tracks and forced him to examine his life and where it was all heading."

"And it could have gone either way. He could have remained cold, hard, aloof and blaming God and life for his situation but rather his old ways seem to be replaced by a sincere attempt to reach out and be kind. I never would have thought that the garden would have such a healing effect on him either. He never ever gave a flower, a shrub or tree a second thought and now when he passes them, he stops to touch a flower or smell a herb and at times even tastes both!" And after a reflective pause, Jenny added, "The acids within him that so corroded his spirit have been miraculously neutralized by an alkaline dose of nature."

"That's beautifully put, Jen. But I think the real truth of the matter is that you are primarily responsible for James' incredible recovery and he realizes it, too. Your prayers for him, your unconditional acceptance and the fact that you never lost hope. You always saw in him the child of God who the Lord had created. "

"That was beautifully put, too. Thank you, Henry."

Henry paused, dug deep into his compassionate nature and continued, "I am so happy for James and your growing appreciation of him...just don't forget me, sweetheart..."

"Oh, Henry, never! I will love you to my dying breath...oh here I have been talking about myself, how are you doing?"

"Keeping busy at the gallery. The fall weather is beautiful. I was thinking about driving around the country and doing some sketches of the harvest. I love the smell of straw in the air...almost as much as you like the fragrance of thyme."

"Oh, I can't wait to go out with you and watch you draw. Do you ever paint outdoors?" Jenny wanted to know.

"Actually, I trained under a plein air painter. I loved painting outdoors and the challenge of capturing the landscape in front of me. Unfortunately those are rare occasions on the prairies as it is usually too windy. On days when the wind is calm and it's pleasantly warm, with or without the sun being out, there's nothing like outdoor painting. Ask any artist and they will say, nature is the best teacher."

"I would love to watch you paint!"

"That reminds me, Jen, of one early spring morning, my art instructor and I went to Wascana Park to paint when the sun came up. It was the first Saturday in May and we were at the park and all set up at the crack of dawn. Snow still covered the ground and the runoff and melting ice created a mirror-like surface on the lake. Both of us had our easels set up and paint out ready to capture the light in the landscape in front of us.

"It was an amazing experience, Jen. How quickly one has to

paint to capture the changing light and how the hues change by the second. I can only imagine God as a Master Painter creating the world this way. Just imagine all over the world, thousands of His paintings are seen in the eyes of those who stop to look. *God's creation is the largest gallery all over the world."*

"Oh, Henry, you truly are an artist at heart. It's so true. When I look at nature or the garden, I am just overwhelmed…it constantly brings tears to my eyes."

"You will like this, Jen. A month later after this outing, my art instructor, and I went out again to the park. It was a humid morning and a foggy haze rose off the lake partially obscuring the landscape before us. I will never forget what happened next."

"What? Tell me quickly!" Jenny asked like an excited child wanting to hear a secret.

"As the fog burned off by the heat of the rising sun, I noted a path leading to the water's edge. It brought back a memory deep inside—"

"I bet I know, Henry! Was it the path that we cycled down that day we went to the park?"

Henry was taken aback by Jenny's intuition. "Yes, Jenny, it was the same."

"I remember that scene so clearly. I played it over and over in my mind. The legislative buildings on the other side of the lake, the sail boat…I imagined we had made love and that was when I had conceived Camilla. It was my way of coping at first…"

"Oh, Jenny, I can't begin to count the number of times I played that scene over in my mind as well."

"Did you see the tree Henry?" Jenny just had to know.

"Yeah, I was just getting to that. The tree was still there and so was the carving of the heart. The edges had crusted over and the pale yellow bark had weathered and browned, but the inscription was still intact- H loves J."

"And could you still make out the tiny angels under each curve of the heart?"

"Yes I could, Jen. It brought back so many wonderful memories."

"Someday when I'm back, I want you and I to visit that place again. I have a secret to tell you, Henry…"

"What? Tell me now."

"You will have to wait; it will be something very special."

"I sure wish you were here, Jenny. I can't wait to hold you and kiss your tender lips."

"I can't wait either, Sweetheart."

"It's such a warm beautiful evening, I am actually out on the deck talking to you on the extension phone."

"Is Father at the Poustinia?"

"Yes, he is. He says he might stay into the winter and see what it's like. The house is heated and he is beginning to accept a little food. And even if I can't get down there with the truck, I can with the skidoo."

"It's amazing how he spends his days and nights in prayer like that."

"Yes, he is very close to the Lord...oh, I just noticed he lit a candle."

"There is electricity, isn't there?"

"Yes, but he prefers just the basics, and besides praying all the time, he is also writing a book. Did I tell you about that?"

"No. What kind of a book?" Jenny wanted to know.

"Father shared with me earlier this spring when I first took him down to the prayer house that he was going to be writing a story his guardian angel asked him to write when he was on the other side."

"You mean Zachariah asked Father to write a book? What kind of a book?" Jenny asked again.

"You're not going to believe this, Jenny. He said it's a story about life. In fact, it's a love story involving miracles and angels and all the things that happen in God's Kingdom."

"That's incredible, Henry."

"Yeah, Father said, it's going to be a story that may have an effect upon a lot of God's children."

Jenny was in awe over what she just heard. "That's truly amazing...and Father said it's a love story?"

"Yes, and an epic one at that!"

"Oh my gosh, a love story involving miracles and guardian angels... in a way it's similar to our story..." Jenny's words trailed off.

"I visited with him for awhile on Sunday evening. When he was in the bathroom, I went into the bedroom where his writing desk is to see how he was coming along. I was amazed to see how much he had written already. One manuscript lay off to the side. It was in the form of a large binder and had, Book 1, printed on the outside cover. When I opened it up I was thoroughly shocked to learn what the title was. You will never guess what the title of book one is, Jenny…?"

"I can't imagine, Henry. This is so intriguing; tell me, what is the title?"

"Pewter Angels."

CHAPTER SEVENTY TWO

Henry remained on the deck after he finished talking to Jenny. He reached up and took hold of the pewter angel hanging on the chain around his neck. "Isn't that something that Father would call his book, Pewter Angels?" In a way, he thought what Jenny had said about what Father was writing about was similar to their story. Henry wondered if there was any connection.

Henry gazed to the east and there was their star shining ever so brightly. Since Jenny's return, he didn't bother to look at the star as he used to for solace. She was here in real life and much preferred to feel her arms around him and the warmth of her lips on his. But as he gazed at the star he wanted to feel Jenny's love. He wanted the assurance that all was okay...

He still felt Jenny's love in the stars' rays but the strength had diminished. Could it be that Jenny's love was slipping away or were his feelings just covered over with too many concerns about their future? So many obstacles and such a huge one glaring at him; in the eyes of the Church, Jenny was still married to James.

How could he possibly fight for Jenny's heart in such an arena?

The thought of trying to steal away another's wife was too unsettling. He didn't want to dwell on this any longer, anxiety was at the doorstep and he fought hard to keep it from entering his mind and heart.

But…but, what would he do if Jenny were to stay with James? The thought felt like a knife stabbing through his heart. The pain surged through his being like a bolt of lightning.

Fear was inching its way into his body. He had felt that emotion many times before and he struggled to keep it at bay. He thought of the letter he received from Gary on Friday. His friend was thinking of becoming a priest. He wanted to offer people who were dying the bread of life. He wanted to give them communion and the promise of what awaited them. Henry knew the Lord was calling him in that direction as well.

Here he was, still struggling with worldly values and attachments and worldly glory. Oh, when would he ever be free of it? Father understood his struggles. These were such shallow goals and had no meaning and purpose. Henry knew better. He should be down there in the Poustinia with Father searching for God's will. How many times had his mentor encouraged him to make a retreat with him?

Henry looked into the starry night, ablaze now with millions of stars. As the darkness of the evening grew, he could almost see more and more stars blossoming in the infinite meadows of the sky. It made him think of their stint on the other side when Jenny, Father and he had died. He wished he could recall more like Father had. Perhaps his faith would be stronger.

The thought of heaven gave him a temporary reprieve from his troubled mind. A calming quietness began to sweep through his body; the tension of moments ago was leaving. The sounds of the valley were drifting back into his awareness. The babbling water trickling through the beaver dam was becoming audible.

His thoughts drifted to Julean and he felt her presence. Even while he was with Jenny, Henry knew she was ever near. He reached into his pocket and pulled out her rosary and kissed it. He wished she were here. There were many nights that they stood out on the deck just like he was now with his arm around her shoulder next to his chest. He wished she were here now. She was always there ready to talk and comfort, just like Father.

As Henry began to pray the rosary, the eerie sound of a coyote shrilled through the air. The dogs were immediately out of their house to the edge of hill, barking in response. It brought him back to the reality of the moment.

What was in store for him in the future? It looked so bright, yet so bleak. What did the Lord want of him? Yes, he could give up his wealth and worldly ways. Yes, he could free himself from attachments but could he give up Jenny?

Henry stared into the heavens, ablaze with twinkling diamonds and pleaded to his Lord...I just cannot do that if this is where this is all leading to...please don't ask me to give up Jenny...please, don't ask that of me.

Chapter Seventy Three

S EPTEMBER HAD LONG gone and October was nearing an end. James' condition, although stable, was worsening. He loved to be with Jenny on the estate so much that he flatly refused to be admitted into the hospital. He still went in for radiation treatments three times a week. However, he asked that they stop the chemo treatments so as to have more energy while at home and would start again as soon as he had no choice but to be admitted.

Jenny's stay on the estate had become much longer than she initially planned. She asked Camilla to get more clothes and things from her home and send them off to her. They spoke regularly and missed each other terribly. The family back in Regina, was getting concerned where this all might lead to and how it would end, most of all Henry.

Jenny kept thinking she would stay for just another week, but then it passed and another week still found her on the estate. She decided to trust God and had the sense that she was exactly where she should be even though she wanted to be desperately back in Regina with Henry.

She was taking life day by day.

Ottawa was blessed with an extended autumn that year.

Although the monarchs had left on their trek back to Mexico, many of the flowers still bloomed. They shouldn't be. Thomas attributed it all to the love that was floating so freely on the estate. Many times he said it felt like he was just on this side of heaven. He had never experienced such peace and bliss in all the years he had worked on the Hamilton estate. Perhaps the flowers felt it, too, and it was the reason for their longevity and why they continued to bloom.

It was mid morning and both James and Jenny wore sweaters and long pants, as they strolled through the garden. They were on their way to the Angel of Thanksgiving to do their daily ritual: pick flowers that were still blooming and place them in the angel's basket in thanks for all their blessings. Although he didn't verbalize it out loud, Jenny knew that James' daily prayer was for her to come back to him.

James held Jenny's hand more as an excuse to do so rather than support for his condition. He felt surprisingly strong. Perhaps it was the discontinuation of the chemo treatments that gave him that extra boost of energy. But then again, it could be coming from the one whose hand he was holding.

Just as James was about to speak, Carlos was making his way up the walk.

"Oh, Carlos, I finally get to see you!" said Jenny excitedly.

"Si, Miss Jenny, it is so good to see you, too. It's been many years."

Carlos lay down his shovel and extended his hand but Jenny bypassed it and gave Carlos a warm hug."

"I recall so many wonderful discussions we had at my parent's estate."

"Si, my wife and I just returned from a vacation in Mexico and we spoke of you and how much the Monarch butterflies loved you. I see they have all returned to my native land. Perhaps we passed some in the sky as we flew back here."

"Do you remember me sharing with you about my little girl I had?"

Carlos looked at James and then back at Jenny, "Yes, I do recall and Maria and I prayed a novena for you and your baby that someday you would meet each other."

"And we did, Carlos. She is such a lovely lady, I so hope you will meet her one day."

"Tonight Maria and me will give thanks that our prayers were answered. That is wonderful news."

Turning to James, Carlos said, "How are you feeling today,

Senor James? It is so good to see you strolling with Miss Jenny in the garden."

"It's one of my better days, Carlos."

"Thomas and Ramon are waiting for me so best be on my way. It is a pleasure to see you, Miss Jenny. The Monarchs would be so sad if they knew they left too early..."

Jenny smiled and nodded as Carlos tipped his hat, nodded and went on his way.

"He is such a kind hearted, perceptive man, James."

"I must admit I enjoy talking to him, too. In fact I enjoy talking to all of them..."

As they strolled along, James asked, "So, tell me, Marjorie, how did you and Henry Pederson meet and...what is so special about this guy?"

Jenny stopped and turned to James. "Are you sure you want to know?"

"Yes, tell me all the ugly details. I deserve all of it. Don't spare me anything."

"Oh, James, everyday you surprise me all the more. It may be more painful than your illness when I tell you how head over heels I fell for this guy."

"Ooh, that hurt already. Okay, smooth it over a little so that it's more palatable."

"Well, let me see, perhaps I'll start right from the beginning. It was the summer of 1956, when I, my guardian angel and parents moved to Regina from Vancouver into a house three doors down from Henry's home. While we were finishing the unpacking, Mom sent me to the corner grocery for some baking supplies. On the way..."

And so Jenny began to tell James how she and Henry had met; that it was love at first sight, but something very special also happened (that James found hard to believe). Their guardian angels were involved when they met and imparted their heavenly energy into the gaze they shared when they first looked into each other's eyes. Jenny went on to tell James of the wonderful summer that followed; how they grew deeper in love, how she was raped and conceived a child, their parting, the letters, the birth and adoption of her daughter and the incredible way they came back to each other again in Regina.

James was enthralled and totally fascinated by the story. They didn't even stop for lunch. Matti brought his medicine at the regular times and cookies and afternoon tea which they were now enjoying as they sat on the swing in the gazebo.

"That is some story, Marjorie. The part where you, Henry, and that priest die and meet up with your angels is a bit hard to swallow, but it does sort of explain how you are still hooked on this guy after being apart for all those years."

"It really all happened, James. I may not have any memory of it like Father David does, but it explains and clarifies so many things that have happened."

"Tell me, Marj, would a non-religious guy like me have a guardian angel, too?" James was now curious to know.

"Yes, James. I believe we all receive a guardian angel when we are conceived who stays with us from that moment until the day we die."

"Really?"

"Yes, they are a gift to us from God. Our angel's assignment is to protect and guide us and help us get to heaven. The more we acknowledge them, the more aware we become of them in our lives. I consider mine my best friend!"

James was silent for a moment trying to take it all in. Jenny then added something which swayed James more than anything she had said. Perhaps there is some truth to this angel thing.

"James, why are you putting flowers in the angel's basket?"

James was startled by the question. To a degree, he already believed in the existence of angels, otherwise, he wouldn't be putting flowers into the basket in thanks for the blessings he had received from God!

James shook his head, "You got me there, Marj. I must admit, I've seen some amazing things happen here over the past year: flowers surviving over the winter, shriveling and dying seemingly by the power of my negative thoughts, your miraculous healing the day after I put flowers in the basket in thanks for your healing…yeah, as bad a guy as I am, I just might have a guardian as well that has an 'in' with some big guy." James said as he rolled his eyes heavenward.

Jenny squeezed James' hand and with a wink and a sparkle in her eye, she replied, "You're not such a bad guy after all, James."

Chapter Seventy Four

J ENNY HAD TROUBLE reading the book she had started over a week ago. Normally, she would have it finished it in two evenings, but so many thoughts sweeping through her mind interfered with her concentration.

Her thoughts oscillated between the conversation she had with Henry an hour ago and the day she had spent with James. She missed Henry and she could tell he was getting concerned with her staying longer than she had planned. Yet she felt that this was where she was meant to be.

She couldn't get over the interest James was showing in her life and even Henry's. She recalled how jealous James had been when she and Henry had dated and felt certain that he would erupt at any moment as she told of the love she had for her teenage boyfriend. He remained surprisingly calm during their entire conversation.

How he listened and participated in the conversation at the dinner table was so out of character, yet every day during meal time, a new James was revealed. Truly, a miracle had happened in James' life and Jenny was certain he was part of the miraculous healing that happened when she was brought back fully restored that day.

James went to bed shortly after dinner. Jenny could see he was spent after their long extended talk in garden. He was trying to squeeze out every moment of life that he could in the time he had left. She recalled having days like that, as well, when she was sick. She had fought so hard against that disease until it snuffed out all of her energy.

As Jenny was laying there holding the book she had tried to get into for the past half hour, there was a light rap on her bedroom door.

"*Who would that be?*" She looked at the clock on the night table: 11:25. She put down the book she was reading and said, "Yes, come in…"

The door slowly opened and Jenny was surprised to see James standing in the doorway.

"James, I thought you would be sound asleep, you had such a long day and looked so tired at dinner time and…how did you make it up the stairs?"

James smiled. "Love conquers all, Marjorie…actually, my guardian angel helped me. Do you mind if I come in?"

Jenny propped her pillow up against the headboard and sat up. "No, come in James."

James went to the chair next to the bay window and with effort, pushed it beside Jenny's bed and sat down.

"I was thinking over what you told me today…"

James paused, and then asked, "If I had been more like Henry, would there have been a chance for us?"

Jenny looked compassionately at James and nodded, "Yes, I think there would have been. However, there was always the three of us, James."

"Why does it take a lifetime to learn what is really important, Marj?"

Jenny lifted her shoulders slightly, tilted her head and smiled.

"What keeps you so happy, Marjorie? I don't think I have ever seen you down…"

"The only true joy in the world, James, is to do God's will. Especially since my healing, I am convinced more than ever that, that is what we really want. We are God's children. He made us. He is the light at the core of our being and the more we can let it out and shine in our lives we are doing His will."

"And less of what we want."

Jenny nodded. "God is bringing you to a very beautiful point in your life, James. He and your guardian angel, I might add, are leading you so wonderfully to the truth of it all."

"It's taken me all of my life to get to this point."

"It's mainly because we don't take the time to reflect on our lives and why we are here. The important thing is, James, is that you are learning this now. Many live and die, never knowing their purpose or experiencing peace. It makes me so happy to see you enjoying and coming to terms with your life…"

"Yeah, the little I have left…"

James fell silent. Jenny thought he was thinking on their rather philosophical discussion, but she was wrong.

Suddenly he asked, "This afternoon, Jenny, what did you say the song was that you and Henry shared?"

Jenny was reluctant to hurt James and yet she found herself answering James' question. "True Love…" her words trailed off.

"You know, I hardly ever listened to music. I wouldn't even know the name of a song to suggest…the only time I listened to the radio was to find out how the stocks did that day. Tell me, Marjorie, do you know the words of that song…do you remember them?"

Jenny nodded.

"Say them to me, please."

Tears surfaced into Jenny's eyes and softly, almost in a whisper she began:

> *"Well, I give to you and you give to me*
> *True love, true love,*
> *And on and on, it will always be,*
> *True love, true love…"*

Jenny stopped; she didn't want to go on. She could see the hurt in James' eyes.

"Is there more?"

Jenny nodded.

"Please, say it all…"

Jenny brushed a tear rolling down her cheek and spoke faintly again:

"For you and I have a guardian angel on high with nothing to do,
But to give to you and to give to me,
Love forever true."

Jenny tilted her head and lifted her shoulders slightly and said, "That's all, James."

James had tears in his eyes as well. "That's a nice song, Marjorie."

Jenny just nodded and looked down at the book on her lap.

"When you talked about the letters you and Henry sent to one another, was the pewter angel that you're wearing the one he had sent to you?"

Jenny immediately clutched the angel with her right hand hiding it from view. Once again, she just nodded.

"What did you do with the wedding ring I gave you…throw it away?"

Jenny looked up and turned to James, "I have it in my jewelry box at home…"

"Would you ever consider wearing it again, Marjorie?"

"Oh, James…" Jenny stared at James tenderly, her expression remaining neutral and then looked down at the book on her lap.

A silence fell over the room for the longest time. Every now and then, Jenny looked over at James. He seemed to be resting peacefully.

She could tell he was becoming more tender-hearted…Nancy saw it before she did. The day Nancy had called, she related to Jenny that she never thought she would live to see the day a Hamilton would grow soft. Jenny didn't think so either, until today.

She wondered when he was going to leave. It would be too painful for him to sleep in that chair all night. She was going to ask him if he needed some help to go back to his room which was downstairs. The den had been converted into a temporary bedroom for him.

Suddenly, he spoke. Jenny had to strain to hear what he was saying.

"I'm afraid of dying, Marjorie…I feel alone. Did you feel alone when you were sick in the hospital?"

Jenny turned to James and said with empathy, "Yes, James, I felt alone and abandoned by everyone; even God. But I really didn't believe that…I was tired of being sick and in so much pain and couldn't see the sense in any of it. It came to me one day that my suffering wasn't in vain…it's part of life and the cross we must bear and can all be offered up to God. It all makes sense, James, if you believe. I am so happy to see you reading the Bible and getting to know Jesus. When you fully appreciate and understand what He did for us and why, you won't feel alone anymore."

James responded with a request that shocked her.

"Can I sleep with you tonight…? I really am quite harmless?"

Jenny turned to James and nodded, "Yes…"

James kept his housecoat on and lay down next to Jenny. She slid down on the bed, placed the book on the night table and turned off the light.

Jenny lay flat on her back while James lay on his side facing her.

Gradually their eyes adjusted to the moonlight entering through the windows. There was enough light to make out Jenny's silhouette. Jenny just stared towards the ceiling, hesitant to look at James. It felt awkward and yet…so right.

"Camilla, that's a nice name, too. And she married Henry's son…how about that… Who does she look like, Marj?"

"She does look a lot like me, James. We're quite the pair."

"She must be very beautiful…so, that would make her J.J.'s half sister…?"

"Yes, it would be so nice for him to meet her one day. Actually, I wrote that in my diary the day I died. That was my final wish and prayer that J.J. meets his sister."

James didn't say anything for the longest moment and then he said, "And…the man who fathered Camilla, you forgave him…?"

Jenny didn't answer right away and then replied, "Yes, James, I did."

"You were doing God's will…"

"Yes."

Almost twenty minutes elapsed without either saying a further word. Jenny thought James had fallen asleep. She was going to turn over away from him and try to sleep as well when she faintly heard James' weeping.

She didn't know what to do.

"Marjorie," James softly began, "I'm so sorry for hurting you all those years, please…please, forgive me…I was such a damn fool…"

James' words pierced her heart. She turned over and faced him with tears in her eyes as well. She reached out and put her arm around him and drew him close to her."

As soft as a feather, she whispered…

"I forgive you, James…"

CHAPTER SEVENTY FIVE

HENRY TOSSED AND turned for well over two hours and knew that he would never find sleep. He might lose the love of his life and he wondered how he could possibly cope if that happened. The clock on the bedside end table read 3:15 Father Engelmann would be awake, probably reading his breviary. Henry had planned to see him first thing in the morning, but he could no longer wait. He had to speak to his mentor; his heart ached too much.

Henry decided to drive down to the prayer house. The sound of the truck would alert Father that he was coming rather than just walk in without warning. He marveled that Father had no fear in staying down there alone. So many nights, the coyotes would howl and work themselves into a frenzy if they downed a deer or caught a rabbit. There wasn't any light on in the prayer house as Henry pulled up beside. He got out and made his way to the deck. The sky was beginning to lighten in the east. The sun was slowly approaching and gradually filling the valley with warm light. In all the time he owned the prayer house, only one other time was he there this early. It was to capture the morning light on the pond and how it lit up one side of the valley. It was a study he wanted to do for a painting. It made him recall his art instructor who used to take him outdoors to paint first hand.

"In the same way," thought Henry aloud, "twilight is such a special time between when the sun goes down and when the night is beginning. There is a morning twilight as well, only in reverse. Such a powerful peace fills the air."

Henry now understood why his mentor got up so early and why he enjoyed the early mornings as the best part of the day. Henry peeked through the kitchen window and made out a dim light. It was the light coming from a candle. Father preferred that to electrical lighting.

Henry softly tapped on the door and entered. "Father, it's me Henry."

There was no answer and Henry entered further into the living room and peeked into the bedroom. Father was in his hooded robe. He was writing into a large coiled binder. What an image to see his teacher writing under the light of candle. This is what it must have been like when his patron, Saint Francis, wrote his thoughts as well.

There was such a strong similarity between the two.

Everything Henry had read about Saint Francis, he saw those same attributes in Father Engelmann.

Suddenly, Father stopped writing and looked at Henry. "What brings you here so early, Henry?"

"I couldn't sleep, Father, I want to talk to you. Have you read your breviary, yet?"

"Yes, I have. I wanted to write some thoughts down before saying Mass. Is something concerning you?"

Henry nodded. "Jenny has decided to stay longer in Ottawa, Father. James is quite ill and could go into the hospital at any time. She feels the need to support him."

"Yes, yes, that is understanding and compassionate of her, Henry."

"But Father, what if she stays permanently?"

Father set his pen down on the table and arose. He came to Henry and placed his hand on his shoulder, "Come, let us sit by the window and watch the sun come up. Perhaps the light from the heavens will illuminate our thoughts."

Father and Henry made their way to the two chairs in front of the patio doors that overlooked the pond. Although it faced south-east, it was evident that the sun was already nearing the horizon. It would have to climb higher to make its way up to the hill tops. It was still too dark to notice the clouds near the horizon even though the sky above seemed clear with twinkling stars still in view.

It was strange speaking with Father in the semi-darkness, almost like he was in a confessional booth. In a way it was like going to confession. He had to admit that he was very frustrated and some of his thoughts did reflect anger and ill will towards his adversary. Henry turned to Father, the dim light catching Henry's concerns written all over his face.

"It just seems there is always another problem or obstacle to surmount, Father. Jenny asked her husband for an annulment, but he refused. And really that was just a shot in the dark. It probably wouldn't have worked anyway."

Henry paused and then continued, "James is adamant to have her come back and that they try again. And, like I said, Jenny decided to stay for the time being.

"*But for how long?*

"And, what if she decides to go back? Everything seemed to be working out so well after we all were miraculously returned to life…and for what? I thought it was mainly for Jenny and me to get together again!

"I just don't know what to think, anymore."

Father listened carefully, allowing Henry to express his feelings and then he responded, "I understand your frustration and disappointment, Henry. Both you and Jenny are in a very difficult situation. If Mr. Hamilton, or rather James, wants to try again, the Church will look upon that in a favourable light. Remember, Jenny did agree to marry James and I surmise that what she is struggling with is the commitment she made."

"But she said she was never very certain that she really loved him; that part of the attraction was that he reminded her of me… and even on the day they married, she had difficulty saying the marriage vows. She felt under so much uncertainty and pressure that she fainted."

"Yes, I recall you mentioned that before. It's true that a person must be free to choose their mate. If a decision to marry is forced; the woman is pregnant, parents force the marriage, immaturity, lack of mental capacity, an annulment could be granted. There may be grounds here, Henry, but as you already noted, annulment does not come easy and is a lengthy process. In this case, it is further complicated by the reluctance of the former spouse to agree to the invalidation of the marriage. Do not get your hopes up too high."

"But surely if a marriage didn't work and there was neglect or abuse, isn't divorce the best solution?"

"When two people vow in front of God and the Church to love and honour each other in good times and in bad, until death do they part, what does that mean? That they can separate just like that? Yes, if abuse is present, then separation is warranted. In most cases, though, marriages break up due to unfaithfulness, immaturity, the 'grass looks greener on the other side' living in a fantasy world. More and more couples today are walking away from their commitment and promise to one another without even trying. It seems to me Mr. Hamilton is taking the first big step to making a marriage work; he is dying to himself."

"But she doesn't love him—and, and he divorced her!"

"Jenny is a very responsible woman and is looking at this situation very seriously even though her marriage might not have been the best. We have to assume that there was love present, at least at the beginning. True, they are divorced, but are they really?

"I know how difficult this is for you to accept, Henry, but it may be best not to interfere. Jenny must be left free to decide."

The sun was just a few moments from peeking over the hills. The rays were painting the low clouds in a spectacular array of colors. For just a moment, the sight seized Henry's full attention. The artist in him capturing its beauty and burning it into his mind. But not even the glory of the impending morning could hold his gaze for long. Instantly he returned to the reality of the moment and the heavy weight he would have to carry in the days ahead; not knowing what the future held.

Father was better able to read his son in the growing light. His entire body language exhibited sorrow and forlornness. Perhaps he could get Henry to change his perspective.

"Henry, look at the wedding ring on your finger and think about the oath you and Julean made to each other on the day of your wedding. As I just said, all too many these days consider their vows meaningless. There is a lack of commitment. The world is changing wherein we ourselves have become like any other commodity. If it's no good, we throw it out and get a new one. All too many live in a fantasy world that the feeling that brought them to make their vows is gone and thus feel they are no longer in love.

"*Love is not a feeling in the final analysis; it is a decision.*

"Couples who are married for forty, fifty, and sixty years did not always have it easy. They had their trials and I'm sure many times were ready to quit, but they didn't because they made a commitment to love in good and bad times.

"Marriage is a relationship in which we can grow up or stay proud and self centered and think that our spouse is no longer worthy of them. They feel they deserve better and think the grass is greener on the other side. They have failed to take this tremendous opportunity to die to themselves.

"Just a few weeks ago, you noted how Jenny had died to herself in forgiving Peter. That through her actions, you more fully understood the Scripture in which Jesus said, 'unless a seed dies, it cannot bear fruit.' When a person wants the best for his partner, he looks for the good in others who God created and is more concerned for the happiness of their partner than themselves, they are then realizing their commitment to love. They will see the grass can be even greener on their side if they water it enough through acceptance, understanding, compassion and forgiveness.

"Henry, your dear Jenny may love you with all her heart and yet, she may sacrifice it for the sake of the man she married and to keep her family together."

"Oh, Father, I don't like what you're saying or where this could be heading."

Henry shook his head struggling to hold back his emotions of despair.

"I could offer you words of hope and say all will be fine, but you have to face the eventuality of what might occur. Consider this; what if Julean were still alive? For years she stayed with you despite her awareness of the love you had for your teenage sweetheart. What if James had died and Jenny suddenly came along? What would you do? Would you abandon Julean? Is your love so great for Jenny that you would now turn your back on your wife? Or, even if your marriage with Julean was mediocre, what would you do? When you stood at the altar and you and Julean exchanged vows, did you not vow to marry each other for better or worse?

"Henry, is divorce ever an option?"

"But if Julean and I were divorced, it would be different, Father."

"But what if Julean wanted you back? What if the children you both gave life to, wanted their mother and you back together? What then?"

What Father just said struck Henry hard. It really hit home.

"Jenny is facing such a decision, Henry. When she said, 'I do,' Jenny recognized that does not automatically mean that they were going to live happily ever after and that the road would be free and easy. No, she decided to love her husband and accept him even when the feelings that stung their hearts for one another faded away. Jenny planted deeper seeds and I believe it was because of her faith in God and His creation; she loved whether she felt like it or not, she accepted her husband when he was not deserving of it, she cared and showed understanding and compassion when she could have hated and spouted angry words. She stuck it out, Henry. What Jenny did for all the years that she was married was plant the seed of a love that now has sprouted. Even though her husband did not have Jenny's faith and loving acceptance, she had Jesus at the centre of her life. I think that is what kept her centered and sustained her. Had Jenny not been planted on such a rock, her life would have been in disarray and James would have died as a lost soul."

"Jenny's capacity to die to herself and see the good and potential in others, is a powerful example. *That is a remarkable trait.*"

Father paused and after a long moment went on to say, "If a married couple places Jesus at the center of their marriage and truly has their partner's best interests always at heart, the divorce rate would quickly decline. Counseling helps in marital difficulties and may help for awhile, but unless the counseling promotes to have Jesus at the centre, the struggle for all too many is too great. It draws them back to their selves and self-centeredness. We love for Christ's sake. We obey His commandments; we live out His teachings and we need His strength and grace to do so."

Henry no longer spoke. He simply closed his eyes and let the rays of the sun streaming into the prayer house warm his face and soothe his spirit. If James now wanted to make amends and save his marriage, was it right for him to stand in James' way? And what about J.J.? Henry recalled reading in Jenny's diary how much she wanted to reconcile with her son. Henry's stomach began to churn as he was beginning to see the other side. Should he put up a fight and try to win her…? Henry knew the deep decision Jenny was facing and his role was to simply be supportive and give Jenny the freedom to choose. Henry was realizing what it meant to love and yet he struggled against it. Father's words that followed were not hopeful.

"So you are free to re-marry, but Jenny isn't. The only options are an annulment or Mr. Hamilton dies."

"But that's the thing, Father!" Henry exclaimed, suddenly coming to life again. "James could outlive us all!"

"I thought you said the man was gravely ill."

"He is, but he plans to have life support and a group of doctors to stand by and make sure he lives as long as necessary until a cure is developed. If life support fails, he plans to have his body frozen—"

"What do you mean, Henry, frozen? I have not heard of such a thing."

"This is new to me as well, Father. Apparently scientists have developed a way to freeze one's body at the point of death while there is still life in the brain. They still haven't figured out how to thaw the person safely after a cure is found. However, scientists think within a year or two they shall know how to bring the body back quickly without damage to the cells or brain."

Father shook his head. "*Mein leiber Gott*, what will people think of next?"

Father slapped his knees, startling Henry. "It is time to turn this matter over to the Lord. Let us celebrate Mass together, Henry. Let us offer up this Mass for Jenny and her family and for you and your family as well. I have said it before and you will probably hear me say it again: Trust in the Lord with all your heart and not your own understanding. Over and over, during the years, my son, you have seen how the divine providence of God works and turns all situations into good."

Father got up and clapped Henry's shoulders. "Come, let us receive the Lord into our hearts, our bodies, and souls."

Chapter Seventy Six

THE DOCTORS WERE amazed that James was able to stay home without the full care and attention provided by a hospital. Something beyond the medication he was taking must be assisting him somehow. A person in his condition with that many tumors growing within his body and travelling back and forth three times a week as an outpatient for his treatments astounded the medical profession at the General Hospital. In the next month that followed, James' condition, although stable, demanded more vigilance. The doctors insisted that if he wanted to stay at home an attending nurse around the clock was absolutely necessary. Even though Matilda provided exceptional attention and support for her employer, a trained nurse could detect signs sooner than Matti and would be qualified to administer medical care if required.

James finally agreed. He was adamant to beat the disease until Christmas which was only three weeks away. He wanted desperately to have one Christmas with Marjorie, J.J. and his family. Of all the memories he had of his own childhood there was only one Christmas that stood out. It had snowed heavily that year and his father had no choice but to be at home at that time. And for some reason James' mother was there for the family as well. Perhaps it was because it was early in the day and she hadn't started to drink yet. It was the only happy memory James had of his family all being together in front of the Christmas tree opening gifts.

He admitted to Jenny that he had been guilty of carrying out that same pattern in their family. Within the first few years after J.J. was born, they rarely spent a Christmas together and the times they did were not very memorable.

Could he stave off death for the next few weeks and achieve all the goals he wanted? His biggest challenge was to get his son on his side. He had talked to J.J. over and over during the last month but to no avail. The boy wouldn't budge. In the weeks Jenny had been back at the Manor, J.J. would not come to visit since that day she had first arrived. Even then, he left before saying hello. Each time James spoke with his son he needed to take sedatives to keep him calm as it only aggravated his condition. Neither Matti, Jenny nor Thomas knew exactly what was ailing the boy and even in the face of the impending death of his father, J.J. was unwilling to soften his firm, hardened position.

What was it that kept her son so cold and rigid? That was the last thought Jenny had before she drifted off into a deep sleep.

Jenny wasn't sure if she was dreaming or if she really was hearing a siren. She looked at the clock on the end table: 3:25 am. A flashing light coming through the windows echoed in the room.

"What is going on?" Jenny muttered as she got up and made her way to the window. The front portion of a vehicle was visible but the rest was hidden under the canopy of the entrance to the front doors of the Manor. Just enough showed so as to partially expose a flashing light.

It must be an ambulance.

Jenny's heart began to race; *were they picking up James?* Last week he had been deteriorating and complaining of abdominal pains. Jenny turned on the lights and quickly put on her housecoat.

Matti was just closing the front door and Charles was making his way into the kitchen when Jenny came down to the front foyer.

"What's happened, Matti?" Jenny asked with concern covering her question.

"They be taking Jim to the hospital, Jen. He's not doing so good. The nurse called me over an hour ago. He be throwin up and in considerable pain. We tried to help Jim up but the pain be too

472

much for the man. Best let the ambulance people tend to their business. They know how best to move an ailing man and get him to the hospital."

Jenny didn't know what to say. She just stood there shaking her head. How quickly one's condition could change for the worse. *Would James make it through the day? Was he dead already?*

"Oh, Matti, I just have to get ready and go. He needs someone there... I know what it's like..."

Jenny quickly turned and ran up the stairs to get dressed.

JENNY FELT SORRY for James as she drove to the hospital. He talked about Christmas everyday for the last week and what it would be like to have the family together. Everything now had suddenly come to a halt. *Death waits for no man* was a phrase that crossed Jenny's mind but for only a fleeting moment. She quickly started to pray for James and that God would heal him. She would ask Henry to pray for James and perhaps call Father Engelmann to do so as well.

Jenny parked her car and made her way into the front entrance of the hospital. She went to the admittance desk and asked if they might know what room James Hamilton would be in. The information had just been entered minutes ago. James was up in the I.C. ward, room 4C.

When Jenny came up to the nurse's station, she was informed that James was taken down to the second floor for x-rays. Jenny was instructed to sit in the waiting area and that she would be notified as soon as James was settled back into his room.

No one was in the waiting room when she entered and sat down. There were several magazines lying on the chair next to her but she didn't want to read. She just allowed her mind to drift over all that had happened since she came to Ottawa. She was still in awe of all the changes for the better that had been made on the estate. She had to hand it to James, when he made up his mind to do something, he forged ahead, nonstop. That was one of James' traits that had always reminded her of Henry.

And what about Henry; last night when they spoke he asked if she would be home for Christmas. She would love to spend her first Christmas with her daughter and her family and with Henry and his family but Jenny had family here, as well. She felt like a butterfly caught in a spider web, unable to fly in either direction. If only they all lived in the same city and this marriage problem was resolved.

How will this all end?

Jenny wondered what caused James pain; was it the existing tumors or a new one? She recalled only too well her bouts with the disease and how tumors can pop up just about any place in the body and even in the head. She had hoped that she wouldn't see the inside of a hospital for a long time since her healing and release but here she was again.

It should have been unsettling for Jenny and yet she realized this was the nature of life and how fragile it can be. Yesterday, she and James strolled through fresh fallen snow in the garden, marveling that the flowers in the Angel of Thanksgiving basket had survived the first week of the real onset of winter. Now, here today, they both were in the hospital, awaiting the prognosis and fate of James.

Jenny shook her head; *one just doesn't know what tomorrow will bring.* She was learning to take one day at time and live it to the full.

Just then, Jenny heard a woman scream. The lady was shouting out someone's name. Perhaps her husband, child or close friend had passed away. She would find it difficult to work in a hospital day in and day out and tend to illness and peoples hurts of all kinds…and death.

"Excuse me, Miss Hamilton… Mr. Hamilton is settled in his room if you wish to see him now."

Jenny immediately stood up, "Yes, which room is he in?"

"I will take you. Please follow me."

James had several monitors attached to his chest and an IV tube going to his right arm.

"Oh, James, how are you feeling? I was so concerned about you."

"I didn't think I would make it a couple of hours ago. The stomach pain was something else, Marjorie. The x-rays they just took show a growth inside of the wall of the intestinal tract. That's why I was finding it harder to keep things down. The doctor is not certain if the growth was malignant or not. He said my regular doctor would check it out when he comes in later in the morning and decide if they want to do a biopsy at this point. Anyway, they gave me a pain killer and are feeding me with this thing…" James looked at the tube going into his arm.

"Geez, I hate being in the hospital… I hope I can get well enough to get out of here again. I was doing okay until this damn stomach problem… maybe they can operate and remove whatever it is."

Jenny took the chair next to his bed and sat down. She reached for his hand and squeezed it. She knew all too well the nature of this disease and what it could do, not only physically, but mentally, emotionally and spiritually as well.

"We'll keep praying for you James. Hopefully, you will be out for Christmas."

"If only J.J. would come around. I never thought there could ever be anyone more stubborn and proud than myself. I guess it's true what they say, 'the apple doesn't fall too far from the tree.'"

Jenny smiled, "I might call him later when I get back home—"

"Yeah, tell him I'm not doing so hot and that I would like to see him about a couple of matters. And please call Nancy as well to see if she can make it up for a visit. I would like to run a couple of things past her, too."

James took a deep breath and let it out slowly. Jenny could see he was beginning to relax.

James squeezed Jenny's hand, "It was good of you come right away, Marj. I'm glad there is still someone who cares about me."

"I do care for you, James, and I understand what you're going through… I hope you continue to read the Bible, it will help you to understand things better."

"I know we have talked about this before, but if there is a God, surely he could have created it so there is not all this pain and suffering."

"He does allow suffering, James, but He is there to comfort you. Trust me, I know. Just think, James, if this illness hadn't fallen on you, you would still be leading the life you were living. In spite of your pain, can you see how all this has drawn you closer to Him and the truth about life and what is important? It's all part of the cross we must bear in an imperfect world, but even out of suffering comes such good. I see a much happier James than before…"

James tightened his lips and nodded slightly as if to agree with her.

"The important thing is, James, that you don't turn your back on Him. Now is the time that you need God the most. If you chose to go against Him, your pain will multiply…"

"How is Mr. Hamilton doing?" asked a cheerful nurse as she walked into the room.

James rolled his eyes as the nurse went to check the quantity of fluid left in the IV bag.

"Dr. Reiner and Dr. Fritz want to examine you in a few minutes. There are also two other technicians from a Cryonics facility that wish to see you as well."

Turning to Jenny she continued, "You will have to wait in the waiting area. It shouldn't take longer than a half hour."

"Yes, thank you."

As soon as the nurse left, Jenny said, "I think I will go home and freshen up. I'll call J.J. and Nancy and tell them you are here and that you would like to see them. I will be back right after lunch."

Jenny smiled tenderly at James. She got up, bent over and kissed him on the cheek. "I'll see you in a couple of hours."

"Thanks for coming, Marjorie…and, could you bring up Thomas's Bible when you come back?"

Jenny nodded, smiled and left.

CHAPTER SEVENTY SEVEN

WELL NOW, IT'S not often one sees a Hamilton lying on his back. It's good to see you, James."

James turned towards the door and lifted his head slightly to see Nancy and J.J. walk in.

"Glad both of you could come. I guess Marjorie got a hold of you?"

Nancy sat down at James' bedside while J.J. stood behind his grandmother. "Yes, she got in touch with both of us. I called J.J. to come and get me."

James looked at his son and nodded, "I'm glad you came, J.J., I want to discuss a few things with you."

"How are you doing, James?" asked J.J. stiffly.

"Fine, but I would feel a hell of a lot better if you would call me Dad from now on. I don't know how much time I have left but I'm trying hard to put our family back together again and I need your cooperation. I want to see you make up with your mother and you know how much she would appreciate it if you called her Mom as well…I can see now, half of the time we were like strangers or business associates—"

"That's what you brought me up to say. For as long as I can

remember you said, 'no hugs, that's for sissies and call Mom, Marjorie'; that it was more grown up. I was doing what you asked me to do—"

"I take full responsibility for that and admit for the tenth time it was a huge mistake on my part. How we call each other in a family connects us. I see that now, J.J. and I plead with you to help me…"

"I've never approved of this first name—"

Nancy was cut off by the nurse entering the room. "Mr. Hamilton, the doctor wishes to see you again. He wants to go over the blood tests and your treatments." Turning to Nancy and J.J., she said, "This shouldn't be too long. Can I ask both of you to please wait in the waiting area? I will call you as soon as the doctor is finished."

Nancy got up slowly and supported herself with her cane. "Let's go J.J. I don't know what is so important that family can't listen in to what is happening…okay, James, we'll see you shortly."

J.J. was going to offer Nancy some assistance but she shrugged it off.

Nancy was the first to speak as they both sat quietly in the waiting room. "You know J.J., it's quite possible that I could die before your father. I am an old lady and getting more cantankerous by the day. If I could trade places with James, I would gladly do it. I haven't been able to do much in my life time. The money was there and supported me so generously whether I did something or nothing. Most times I did the latter. Now, I can see the hurt in your father's eyes and your mother's heart over your unwillingness to come to them. Would you give me the opportunity to die knowing that I was able to do something meaningful with my life?"

Nancy shifted in her chair and rested her cane on the chair beside her and turned to her grandson.

"Talk to me J.J. I may be old but I still have all my marbles and I would like to help. Can't you see what your mother is doing to help your father? You know only too well the life they shared. It wasn't a happy or fulfilling marriage and here they are trying to make up for it in the dying moments of your father's life and unfortunately your stubborn Hamilton pride is holding up this beautiful homecoming.

"Your mother didn't need to come back. She didn't owe James anything and yet she is here. In fact J.J., she was always here. If the truth be known, Son, your mother lived for years and years in an almost intolerable situation for your sake. She knew James' understanding of life was flawed and James openly admits it now. And yet she stayed primarily for those precious times that she was able to hold you and spend time with you or to offer you some sense of what a family should be like. Many women would have been long gone, but she stayed…she didn't abandon you and she tried to be a mother through it all primarily for your sake J.J."

Nancy looked at J.J. who was staring at the floor. At least he was listening and didn't get up and walk away. Nancy continued…

"She sacrificed the prime of her life for you, J.J. She was faithful to your father through thick and thin. She lived up to the commitment she made when they married. And you know it was your father who divorced your mother, not her. That book store man was nothing to your mother and James knew that. There was absolutely no affair going on there whatsoever. Ask your father and he will tell you. He had that entire matter investigated and he knew there wasn't anything he could use against her and so he used you and your testimony against your own mother! James recognized it as an opportunity to get a divorce and nothing more. And what did he get? A woman who blackmailed him. He deserved what he got."

Nancy glanced furtively towards J.J. hoping he was taking some of this in and once again, continued…

"I recently learned that since her divorce there is a man in her life who she knew from her youth whom she loves and could spend the rest of her days with. Since her miraculous healing, J.J., she now has the opportunity for some happiness and yet… here she is once again. She is sacrificing her life for a man who treated her as if she didn't exist and hoping against all hope that she can reclaim her son who is still doing precisely what the father had done!

"J.J. you have a wonderful mother, far better than I could ever be. Your mother possesses a heart that was able to break through a shield of steel. Both my husband, your grandfather, Jim, and your father were never exposed to a home that was filled with love and care. All they knew was the cold life of business, power and wealth and I'm afraid your father has been an excellent teacher in that regard for you, too. I can see, so clearly, your life being imprisoned in the Hamilton clad of armor.

"Can't you see what your father is trying to show and tell you in the dying days of his life? Don't make the same mistake as he did."

Nancy stopped and looked at her grandson. "Look at me J.J., please. If you don't come out of your shell, one day you will regret this decision for the rest of your days. There is no time for the past my son, forget it. It's nothing more than sour memories kept alive by our brains which can be very stupid and self defeating at times. The mind is such a wondrous gift, yet when used this way is more destructive than an atomic bomb. At least then it's over in a flash! This way, it's a slow death over years and years of self inflicted pain. Give it up, J.J. You have a beautiful wife and child who is in many ways like your mother. *Don't ruin your life.*

"Well, here I am gabbing away and I should be listening so I'll shut up. If you want to talk to a dying old blabber mouth, go ahead."

A silence fell over the room. Nancy thought of more to say, but thought better of it. She kept her mouth shut and waited. She was startled by J.J.'s words. She didn't expect him to say anything.

"If only she would have got upset with James and fought with him. Many times I was at friends' homes and their parents argued and showed affection for one another, did things together, had family holidays…"

Nancy decided to speak. "You're right J.J. In most normal families, there is discussion and heated ones at times, which is healthy and good, but trust me, son, to argue with a Hamilton is like arguing with a stone. The only thing that will happen is they will throw it at you in the end. When I first married your grandfather, I soon learned you don't argue with them. Their minds are made up before you even begin. The Hamiltons are proud, arrogant and know power. No one dares to talk to them in any confrontational way.

"Ask yourself this J.J. Did you argue with your father when you were growing up? What happened to any of the staff that did? They weren't around for long. Most relate to the Hamiltons in an atmosphere of fear.

"Listen to me. What good would it have done for your mother to argue with James, tell me? You were in a home where there was peace. If Marjorie had fought with James, and she could have at every turn, there would have been sheer hell in the home. But look what that accepting, peaceful approach did to your father? It transformed him!

"What you and I are witnessing is a miracle! Rather than abuse and arguing and fighting which would have gone nowhere, your mother planted the seeds of love in your father's heart. Don't you see the change in the man before you? Don't you see the power and strength your mother has through her patience and love and acceptance of your father? J.J., don't be blind to it.

"*Your mother is a saint!*

"When your father was at his most undesirable and miserable behaviour, your mother looked past it and saw the James that we are now seeing. She is the most forbearing person that I have ever known. Truly amazing!

"For God's sake J.J. don't blow it! I have made many mistakes in my life that I am so sorry for, but if you don't stop and try to make a go of this, you are missing out on the biggest and most important deals of your life!"

Nancy paused, "I don't know what else to tell you, but I am four times older than you and I may not be as smart as you, but think on what I said and think hard, but don't be too long. Your dad could die any second and when he does, your mother will be gone. She will be deeply hurt that she was unable to reach you…"

Nancy knew she was talking too much but she just had to add, "For God's sake J.J. Don't be stupid like James was. Don't wait twenty years to grow up! Go in there and call him 'Dad' and your mother, 'Mom' and talk to them. Swallow that damn Hamilton pride and live for once in your life… They need you and love you… be there for them now, and please go home to your wife and son before you lose that, too!"

The strain of the discussion was too much for Nancy and she felt faint. She took hold of the chair beside her to support herself.

"What's wrong…Grandma?"

J.J. rushed to her side and panic crept up his spine.

Nancy gasped, "It's my heart… open my purse…J.J… take out my nitro glycerin in the small brown bottle. Quick… give me one to put under my tongue."

"There's three bottles… oh here it is…"

J.J. quickly opened the bottle and gave Nancy a small white pill. "I can't move my arms… put it into my mouth…"

"Do you want another one?"

Nancy shook her head and breathed sharply through her nose

and leaned forward as if to fall over. J.J. stood there ready to catch her should she keel over. Her breathing began to be more rhythmic and relaxed.

"Are you okay, Grandma…?"

Finally, Nancy nodded. Faintly she said, "Yes, it's that blood pressure of mine… I got over-excited… but did I hear you calling me Grandma or was I on my way to heaven and one of my grandchildren from the grave was beckoning me?"

J.J. smirked… "Are you okay? You had me worried for a minute."

"Say it again, J.J. That was like music to my ears… That, more than that damn pill was what helped me. Make me proud, son."

Tears welled up in Nancy's eyes. J.J. sat down beside her and bent forward placing his bent elbows on his knees and rested his chin on his hands that were closed into fists. He began to cry and couldn't stop.

"I thought you were going to die, Grandma…"

Nancy put her hand on his shoulder and wept along with her grandson.

"Death can come at any moment. That's why it's so important to do everything we can to make things right. *This opportunity may never come again.*"

Nancy paused for her words to reach and touch her grandson's mind and heart and then said, "We're going to remember this day, J.J. Come, let's go see how your dad is doing."

When they got to the door of the hospital room, Jenny was there with James. Nancy looked at J.J. and said, "Go in there, I'll wait outside. Make me proud, Son. I want to remember this moment on the day I die. Let this be the day the Hamiltons start living as a family."

Nancy stood at the doorway and listened. There was a long silence, then she heard J.J. say, "I'm sorry, Mom." He mumbled something else but Nancy couldn't care what it was. J.J. had already said the magic words she wanted to hear.

A nurse came and was about to enter but Nancy blocked her way. "You don't want to go in there now. They have all the medicine they need."

Nancy shifted and rested more of her weight on her cane. She looked straight at the young nurse and added, "You could help me though, what I sure could use right now…is a double scotch on the rocks!"

Chapter Seventy Eight

THE NEXT DAY Nancy took a cab to the General Hospital. She found James to be in excellent spirits. He went on and on how J.J. suddenly changed. He suspected Nancy had something to do with it.

"What's the secret, Nancy? What did you say to him that got him on side so quickly and completely, I might add? He said he was worried that you were having a heart attack and might die. He was glad that he was there to get your pills for you. What pills? There's nothing wrong with your ticker, Nancy. Hell, your heart is stronger than a horse's!"

Nancy winked at her step son and said, "If the truth be known the white pills are sucrose tablets to keep my blood sugar level stable…and the rest of it, well, the moment needed a little shock therapy."

James stared at his dear stepmother; his eyes suddenly brightening, "You old devil, you!"

"Yes, I know, I could have been a big star in the movies and yet, I chose be the dull wife of an unappreciative Hamilton."

Nancy paused, "I think he really likes the way you and Marjorie are getting along. Down deep, James, he's been angry for a long time because he was denied that and just didn't know how to express or show affection to either of you—"

"Until you gave him some motivation."

Nancy shrugged her shoulders. "J.J. is still a very young man, James. He grew some yesterday, but when you're gone, he's got a big load to carry. Quite the responsibility…"

"He'll manage, Nancy. It will be tough, but he's a Hamilton and for better or worse, he has acquired a lot of my traits and skills."

Nancy nodded and decided to change the topic. "So, you look good, James. What do the doctors have to say?"

"It's not good news. The tumors are still growing. The radiation doesn't seem to be helping and they're hoping that starting up with the chemo treatments again might help to arrest the disease or at least delay its terminal effects."

"Well, let's hope for the best. If I could change places with you I would. I'm just putting in days that are not that fulfilling. I must say my talk with J.J. yesterday gave me the first spark of life in years. Perhaps I should do more of that… you know, visit people in care homes or something like that. Probably be good for my arthritis to keep on moving."

"Yes, Nancy, something like that might be good for you and if you can give motivation and life like you did to that son of mine, you just might close down some of the hospital wards!"

They both smiled at one another. Nancy patted James hand, "That was nice what you just said. It was encouraging."

James nodded to acknowledge his mother's words and then grew more serious. "Nancy, I don't know how long I have left. I'm hoping till Christmas…maybe longer. I didn't think Marjorie would stay this long and it has been wonderful of her to do so. I know she is torn between staying here and going home for Christmas. I know she'll stay… it's her nature. If there are angels, she has to be one."

Nancy nodded. "I couldn't agree more, James. She is truly a very special woman. One of a kind, I would say…"

"Well, here is what I was thinking. Matilda knows Marjorie's daughter, Camilla. They met in the hospital when Marjorie was there. I asked Matilda a couple of days ago when I was still at home if she still knew how to get in touch with Camilla. She said yes and when I told Matilda what I had in mind she thought it would be a nice surprise for Marjorie."

"What did you have in mind, James, you have me intrigued?"

"Well, if Marj can't or won't go home for Christmas, why not see if we can bring Camilla and her family and… if they will come, the entire Pederson clan to the estate for Christmas?"

Nancy's eyes widened. "That's a wonderful idea, James, to bring the families together. It would be lovely for us to meet Marjorie's daughter."

"That's one of the main reasons I am doing this besides the obvious selfish reason to keep Marjorie here. She shared with me a few weeks back that the last wish she wrote into her diary when she had died was for J.J. to meet his half sister. I would like to help make Marjorie's wish come true for her two children to meet."

Nancy shook her head, "What a marvelous thing to do, James…" Nancy paused to reflect on what she was going to say next and decided to ask, "Didn't you say to me one time that Camilla married the son of the man that Marjorie is sweet on… Henry, is it?"

"Yes, that's him all right… one fortunate man. The two would probably be married by now if it weren't for their Church's rules about divorce."

"What do you mean, James?"

"The Catholic Church, to which they both belong, does not recognize divorce. The only way it can be dissolved is through some kind of an annulment, which really doesn't apply in this case…"

Nancy was reluctant to say it but she did, "And the only other way is through your death…"

James nodded. "That's quite the spot those two are in… and I have to be honest, I'm still hoping that I can win Marjorie's heart… wishful thinking, isn't it?"

"Well, you have come a long way in exposing your heart, James. If I were a young woman and not your mother, of course, I would easily fall for you, even with your thinning hair."

James smiled. He raised his arm and touched his hair with his fingers, several strands immediately fell out.

"Funny, how important looks and hair are until all of a sudden it doesn't mean very much… if you haven't got your health, what does it matter? What does anything matter? I have enough money to buy half this city… so what? What does any of that do for me?"

"Make wise choices in the days you have left. I must say, what you did for Matilda, Thomas, and Charles is wonderful, James. That was a very fine gift you gave them."

"Even before I gave them anything like that, they were becoming such close friends to me. I finally realized it all had to do with me. The moment I started to change they found it easier to approach me. I must say, Thomas is the first man I was ever able to talk to in a meaningful way. I was surprised how I opened up to him and was able to discuss personal matters that I would never discuss with my colleagues."

James paused and shared an insight, "You know, Nancy, it came to me that I never much trusted my staff or colleagues and I wondered the other day if I had been less judgmental and more approachable and considerate of others, I think I would have found some friends there amongst the corporate jungle. It really depends on how we choose to relate to people that determines the response we get. I am amazed at Marjorie's ability to be so accepting. Why she could be talking to anyone and they would fall in love with her in an instant and openly share their life story."

Nancy nodded, "There is an aura of warmth and calm around people who are at peace with themselves. They know how to love so easily; it just flows out of them. But I have to say, James, she cracked into your armor and it all fell off. It took quite a spell, but not even you were a match for Marjorie's special qualities. In my wildest dreams I would never have envisioned us discussing life like this. Why I just love talking with you, Son…I just have to say, how proud I am of you and… how dearly I love you."

Tears surfaced immediately in James eyes, "Ooh, that was nice…I love you too…Mom."

Chapter Seventy Nine

H I, DAD, IT'S me, Camilla."

"Just one word is all it takes to recognize your voice, Camilla. There is only one voice sweeter and that is your mother's."

"Mom would like that, that's for sure."

"So what is on your beautiful mind, Camilla?"

"Well, I gave you a clue when I added, "that's for sure." Do you remember who likes that phrase more than anyone I know?"

"It does sound familiar…"

"Do you remember Eddy's wife's sister, Matilda?"

"Yeah, that's right. Seems to me she did say that a lot. I do sometimes, too. It's good when wanting to emphasize something.

"So, what does this have to do with Matilda?"

"Well, first let me tell you about the call I received from Mom last night. She really misses us, especially you, I might add. But you already know that. She wants to come home for Christmas so bad but is afraid to leave James. He is in such poor health and feels that he needs her there. Now, she asked me to do something for her. She didn't say I shouldn't tell you, so I feel free to let you know…"

Henry didn't like the sound of that for some reason. "What is it, Camilla?"

"She wants me to go to her house and pick up her wedding ring. The one she got from James…"

Oh, no, what next…?

"Dad, are you okay?"

"Yes …why does she want the ring? What for?" Henry was eager to know.

"She didn't say and I didn't think it was any of my concern to ask her. I just thought I would let you know. I will need a key to get into her house. I know you have one and so does Mable next door—".

"I can pick it up this afternoon and send it home with Jeremy… where did she say it was?"

"In her jewelry box in the bedroom. She said that I would recognize the ring right away."

"Yes, I'm sure it must be quite something…"

"Are you sure you want to do this? I can easily slip by there after school."

"No, that's fine… it will help me to accept whatever is going on… and there was something else you wanted to tell me about that had to do with Matilda calling. What was that all about?"

"Well, here is where this all gets very interesting. Apparently James wants to fly all of us to his estate for Christmas as a surprise for Jenny. He knows how much Jenny misses you, and will all the more at Christmas, and so he wants our family and his to spend that special time of the year together."

"My good Lord…"

"Now, you just said another phrase that Matilda says a lot, too. I suppose it's when something awesome is about to happen or has happened," Camilla said, trying to make light of it all.

Henry smiled, "That's about the size of it, Camilla. That is really something. I don't know what to say… and first thing that comes to mind is that we will never get a flight. Christmas is less than three weeks away."

"That's no problem, Dad. Matilda said James would send his private jet to pick us up and a limousine would be waiting at the airport to take us to the Manor… and I know what you are going to say… 'my good Lord!' Right?"

Henry chuckled, what else could he do or say? It almost was hilarious. James inviting the man who was waiting for him to die so that he could take his wife. Henry shook his head and softly muttered in the phone, "That's quite a change for that man… to even think of doing something like that."

"Well, what do you think? I ran it by Jeremy and he's all for it. He's looking forward to some royal treatment. When he said that, I told him it will be a let down from the royal treatment I give to him all the time!"

Henry chuckled again. "Well, let me run it by the kids… what about Father Engelmann? He always spends Christmas with us."

"She especially said to be sure and bring the holy priest along. Matilda loves Father Engelmann. Why she went on and on how the Holy Spirit works in that man and attributed Mom's coming back to his prayers and that powerful kiss you and Mom shared that morning."

"Well, if everyone else is game, I'm all for it, too. I would love to see Jenny, even if it's under such extraordinary circumstances!"

HENRY UNLOCKED THE door and entered Jenny's home. It was kind of eerie coming in after giving back the home to Jenny. He no longer felt that freedom, but rather hesitant and cautious what he looked at and touched. He was here to get Jenny's wedding ring and leave and yet, like before, everything spoke to him in such a powerful way.

He smelled the lilac fragrance right off along with her presence. It was so strong now. Perhaps it was because he knew for certain that it was Jenny who resided here and not some unknown Marjorie who kept him guessing for months. His quick survey of the room told him the home was exactly as he found it when he first purchased it. Nothing had changed and why should it? It was perfect in every way. It had the touch of someone who cares for every plant and piece of furniture as if it had the owner's personality indelibly stamped on it.

He recalled that last day he had come in and was guided by Julean to the round table that housed Jenny's diary. Henry wondered if it was hidden there and if she had written any personal thoughts in the back section. Perhaps it would reveal where her heart was at…

He walked by it, dismissing the temptation, and made his way into the kitchen. He gazed outside at the yard all covered with snow. The Angel of Thanksgiving's basket held flowers but only soft contours of their shape was revealed by the snow that lay on top. He wondered if the flowers underneath were fresh and alive? He would never forget that miracle… nor all the ones that followed.

If only Jenny were here. He desired to hold her. The smell of her presence made him ache inside. He had better get the ring and leave. Too many memories, too many scents, everywhere he looked he saw Jenny.

The door to her bedroom was partially open. He switched on the light and there it was; the jewelry box immediately to his right on the dresser. He turned on the lamp on the dresser nearest the white, leather covered box. A key was sticking out of the lock. He turned it and the latch sprang open. He lifted the top and it swung back and locked into place. None of the many sections in the top layer resembled anything like a ring; mainly earrings, necklaces, pins and one or two coins that represented some commemoration.

He pulled out the second drawer and it was filled with mainly necklaces and two silver bracelets. He fished through the necklaces to make certain he didn't miss the ring. There was one bottom drawer; he hoped it would be there. If not, perhaps there was another box in the closet near where her mother's chest was on the top shelf.

The third and bottom drawer didn't open right away. It was stuck shut, perhaps from lack of use. He gave it a sharp tug and it pulled free. As soon as more of the interior was revealed, the light caught the huge diamond. It sparkled like something he had never seen before. He felt nervous to touch it. It had a sacredness about it. It represented the love a man had for a woman. *A woman that he loved deeply, too.* It carried a vow to love that man though, not him *and that thought stung his heart.*

He picked up the ring and brought it close to the light of the lamp. He squinted to see if there was an inscription inside the gold band. *There was.* He crouched closer and brought it still nearer the source of light: *May, 8, 1965.*

He and Julean married September 9, 1962. Almost three years before Jenny and James. The thought of Julean brought him back to the reality of the moment. He looked at the wedding band Julean had given to him. They had uttered the same vows or similar ones that James and Jenny did. *That's some commitment two people make to one another. To love, honour and cherish in good times and in bad until death do they part.*

Unbidden tears surfaced in Henry's eyes. "Dear Jesus, please don't allow my mind to harbour thoughts of James' death. Heal him as you did Jenny. Restore his body whole and give him life."

Henry pulled one dresser drawer open and then another and found what he was looking for; two small square boxes. One had a brooch in it and the other was empty. He kissed Jenny's ring and placed it into the box, covered it with a cotton pad, closed it and put it into his jacket pocket. He raised his left hand, looked at his wedding band and kissed it as well for a long moment. He knew what his dear sweet Julean would do if she were in the same position as Jenny.

"Yes," he softly whispered, "yes, Julean, this is the right thing to do." Henry now knew in his heart what Jenny would do should James live. She was preparing the way... not only for James, but for him as well.

CHAPTER EIGHTY

IT WAS DECEMBER 23, the day the Pederson clan was to arrive. The flight came in just before noon and they would be at Greystone Manor by three that afternoon, depending on traffic. James was hoping to have Marjorie with him at the hospital during that time and be in for the surprise when she usually left around four o'clock. James wished he could be there to see her face when she arrived home to see Henry and his family at the estate.

When Jenny came to visit James just before eleven, James' two doctors were just leaving his room. Dr. Reiner, who knew Jenny, nodded, but didn't stop to talk. The first thing Jenny noticed when she entered James' room was the absence of the IV tube going to his arm.

"Hi Marjorie," said James, his face brightening. "I swear, Marjorie, just seeing your presence does more good for me than all the medication and treatments."

Jenny smiled tenderly and sat down next to James' bed. She reached out and took hold of his hand. "I see the IV tube is gone, are they getting another for you? Don't you need the medication and nutrients?"

"I told them that I can live on love…" James smiled. "So how was the driving? The day nurse said it had snowed quite a bit."

"It was slower than usual but still okay. The city crews were out with their equipment. I'm sure it will be better when I go home... So how are you doing?"

"Oh, about the same. I'm hoping to be home for Christmas Day. I have asked that the chemo and radiation treatments stop until after Christmas. Hopefully it will give me more energy."

Jenny studied James carefully. She had the feeling that things weren't just right with him.

"J.J. was here first thing this morning. He sure has made a turn around. It is nice of him to call me Dad. I never knew how a word can make one feel so good."

"Words carry love, express kindness, affection, respect, belonging, the list is endless, James."

James nodded, "For some of us it takes an entire lifetime to recognize that. Every day I see it all, plainer and more clearly, that the real essence about life is love. I don't understand it and yet I know it. We want peace, to let others know that we care for them and love them. The closer we approach death, that becomes our main focus... all else is non-existent and meaningless."

James paused and gazed tenderly into Jenny's eyes, "You have lived a life filled with love, Marjorie, it was well lived. Your forgiving heart has kept you free to live a life of love... unbelievable, that I should begin to see and understand that now. Keep no record of wrongs... that was you, Marj; kind, patient, never dwelling on hurts... forgiveness always on the edge of your heart... you held the key to inner peace."

Jenny squeezed James' hand; tears surfaced in her eyes. She didn't know what to say. It sounded like he had read St. Paul's letter to the Corinthians on love...

"You know, Marjorie, I see such a difference in the way you and I love. I love you for the sake of being loved in return. You love just for the sake of loving. That has been your life focus."

Jenny gently changed the subject, "Did J.J. tell you that he went back home?"

James nodded, "Yes, he's becoming a man, Marj."

"Nora called this morning and said they would be over for Christmas Eve. It's all so wonderful how things are coming together. It's something I have prayed and wished for, for so long.

I so hope you will be able to come home for Christmas Eve as well as Christmas Day."

"I do, too, Marj."

Jenny noticed Thomas's soiled Bible lying next to James. It seemed so out of character for James to be reading the Bible. It amazed her that he was handling such a soiled book after being so concerned with cleanliness all of his life. *It's all so miraculous... everything was turning out for the good.*

"I see you have been reading the Bible."

"I read the part where Jesus was crucified and I could relate to one of the criminals that was hanging beside Him that day. The one who acknowledged Jesus as the Son of God was saved while the other didn't..."

Jenny looked at James with compassion. "At the end of the day, James, that is the decision we have to make. You may doubt that there is a God as one of the thieves did or you can choose to believe, as the other did." Jenny paused for but a moment and went on, "Even if there is no God, James, which of the two thieves was the wisest and made the best choice?"

A smile crossed James' lips. "And I always considered myself smarter than you..." James shook his head and whispered, "*For you to come back to me and stay with me and love me, Marjorie, that is what makes me believe there is a God.* Only someone from heaven could have created someone as wonderful as you. You could never have come from this earth."

Once more James' words touched her heart, "James, we are all children of God. I have always seen Him in you."

James closed his eyes. Jenny knew he was in pain; she could feel it through his hand. She squeezed his hand ever so slightly and it seemed to draw James' attention.

He raised his head and looked down at Jenny's hand that was wrapped around his. He raised his hand bringing hers along with it and gasped. He threw his head back in disbelieve, "Marjorie, you're wearing your wedding ring!" James shook his head and lifted his shoulders, "How did you get it?"

Jenny smiled. "I had Camilla send it to me."

James gazed into Jenny's eyes, "Does that mean you are coming back to me?"

Jenny shrugged her shoulders. "I don't think I ever left... looks like I'm stuck with you for better or for worse…" Her words trailed off and tears came to her eyes once more.

James couldn't speak as tears surfaced in his eyes, as well. He brought Jenny's hand in his to his lips and kissed her fingers. "I love you, Marjorie."

"I love you, too, James."

CHAPTER EIGHTY ONE

J ENNY WAS CONCERNED about James as she drove back to the estate. During the entire time that she was with him, not once did a nurse come into the room to check on him. She did, however, see his doctors leaving when she came earlier. Perhaps he is getting better, but she could sense his pain. He tried hard to hide it but *she knew that pain only too well.*

James told her not to come up tomorrow and to spend Christmas Eve with J.J. and his family and the rest of the staff. He would make every effort to be there, as well. He had already made arrangements with an ambulance service if he felt well enough to come home. He did, however, say that this would be a Christmas that she would remember for a long time, maybe even forever.

I wonder what he meant...

Thomas was out clearing the road leading into the Manor when Jenny turned into the estate. She had to slow down and follow behind the snow blower that crept along slowly. Thomas was unaware of her presence due to the wind swirling the snow emitting from the blower.

Jenny didn't mind as the image before her had a mesmerizing effect which calmed her.

Thomas turned the machine onto the circle drive leading to the front of the mansion. Jenny chose to drive around the other way and picked up enough speed to beat him to the garage.

When Jenny entered the foyer she hollered out, "I'm home, Matti!"

Jenny heard footsteps and turned... she nearly fainted. There in front of her stood her daughter, wearing a radiant smile.

"Camilla, what on earth are you doing here!?"

"I just had to come, I missed you so much!"

The two ladies rushed towards each other and warmly embraced.

"I can't believe that you are here!" Jenny stepped back still with a look of disbelief... "How did you get here and are you alone?"

"It's a long story, Mom, well, not really. Matti called me a week or so ago and asked if I could come and spend Christmas with you. Apparently it was James' idea. He knew you would be lonely. I was to bring Joshua and Jeremy, as well, if I wanted but we decided under the circumstances I should come alone."

A puzzled look grew on Jenny's face. "What do you mean...?"

"Well, Matti said that James informed her that it was one of your deepest wishes for me and my half brother, J.J. to meet and get to know one another. James wanted to surprise you and at the same time send you someone from home so you wouldn't be lonely."

Jenny was speechless. She just shook her head. "So maybe that is what James' meant when I left today that I was in for a surprise. That James, my, my."

"I see you two have met," said Matti as she walked out of the kitchen.

"I should have known you and James would be up to something. This is some surprise."

"Ooh, I be wantin' to tell you every day. I be so careful not to let out the secret. I knew you'd be so happy to see your daughter. Come, let's sit in the kitchen and visit for awhile. We be havin' dinner as soon as Thomas finishes clearing the road."

Jenny wrapped her arm around Camilla as they followed Matti into the kitchen. "I can't wait for you to meet your brother and his—"

Camilla stopped in her tracks and said, "I've already met them,

Mom! They were at the airport to meet me. J.J., Nora and their son, Jimmy. They came in the limousine because their car was too small and didn't know how much luggage I had."

Once again Jenny shook her head… "J.J. came to meet you…?"

"Yes, why? Is something wrong with that?"

"No, it's wonderful! It's just that… it's so out of charac…well, that's another story…or perhaps even better, another miracle!"

Jenny wrapped her arm around Camilla once again and continued into the kitchen, "Well, I'm dying to hear, how things are back home…? I know I should be asking about Josh and Jeremy but I have to know… how is Henry doing…?"

"I'm doing just fine, Jenny!"

Jenny looked up and saw the entire Pederson family standing behind the kitchen table! She looked so shocked she didn't know if she was in the right home… she staggered backwards and Camilla moved to her side just in case Jenny should faint. Jenny's eyes grew wide and she brought both of her hands to the sides of her face… still in a state of disbelief.

"Oh, my good Lord!" Jenny exclaimed, while everyone began to laugh and cheer and move towards her. Jenny greeted them all with open arms, and even Justin accepted a warm hug from Jenny. Many went on to rave about the house and the look on her face.

Finally, Henry made it up to his dear sweet, Jenny. More than anything he wanted to embrace and kiss her lips forever. The ache to hold her was almost unbearable. He had to draw upon a stronger power: *I can do all things through Christ who strengthens me.*

He simply stepped up to her and said, "It's so good to see you Jenny." They both looked at one another intently as if lost in another world and then Henry went towards her and kissed her cheek. He gave her a brief hug and then stepped aside for Camilla to hug her mother once more.

"The look of shock and surprise on your face, Mom, would make picture of the year in any contest!"

"It's incredible, Camilla, that all of you should be here… unbelievable."

Jenny stepped back and waved her hands in front of her face for more air. She was still overwhelmed to see Henry here in James' home! That had to be another miracle!

"Well, if you folks would retire into living room for a half hour,

Charles and I can serve the dinner in the dining room. It be a good thin' that James' dining room table still be here. Next to the antique table, it's perfect for the entire two families."

Jenny took Camilla's hand and led everyone into the living room that easily accommodated all the guests.

Just before Henry stepped out of the kitchen, Matti said, "That's mighty nice of you to come, Henry, considering the circumstances and all. You be a fine man."

Henry turned and said, "Well, Matilda, I do miss Jenny and it would be good to meet Mr. Hamilton. Of course, it's hard to turn down a request when it comes from a charming lady like you."

"My, my you sure know how to sweet talk a lady."

Henry winked. "I meant what I said, Matti. You are a very dear friend to Jenny and it was a pleasure meeting you when you came to support Jen."

"I was hoping Father Engelmann would be comin'. I recall him praying over Miss Jenny… It be giving me shivers just to think on it. The Holy Spirit be movin' in that man so powerfully."

"Yes, Father mentioned that he had felt the strength of your faith as well, Matilda. We are all so blessed to have had the Lord work so powerfully not only in Jenny, but all of us… the miracles just keep going on and on. Who would have thought I would be spending Christmas in Ottawa with Mr. Hamilton's family and friends?"

"Every day be like watching an exciting movie when you let the Lord be the Director."

"I can't agree with you more," said Henry as he walked into the living room.

The first thing Matti noticed as she walked to and from the dining room past the living room, was that Jenny sat next to Camilla and had her arm around Joshua, and Henry was sitting on the other side of the room with Justin. Matti admired the respect Henry was showing for Mr. Hamilton. Matti knew only too well what Henry's heart desired. Allison was sharing stories about the Bible School she attended and whenever Lauren could get a word in edgewise she shared about her love of dancing and that she was planning to go to Montreal to further her training.

Henry was surprised when everyone came and sat around the two tables that were slid together so that everyone could be accommodated. It was easy to see why Jenny loved the staff at the estate and why she considered them her friends. It was one of the liveliest and most enjoyable dinners he had ever had outside of his own home. The meal lasted for over two hours.

When it neared bedtime, Matti exclaimed, "This be the first time since I be livin' in the Manor that more than half of the bedrooms are being used. Charles be workin' most of the day making up the beds and he pinned your name on the door to which be your room when you're ready for retirement. It's been a long day, so no need to be polite; when Mr. Sandman comes knocking, you just get up and Charles be ready to escort you."

Henry was the second to get up and announce he would be heading for bed. Justin and Josh had left about an hour ago. "I can't tell you all what a pleasure it has been to meet you. Now, when Jenny speaks of you I will be able to put a face to the person she is talking about. This has been a most delightful evening and I understand a day of sightseeing is planned so I better hit the hay."

Henry went over to Matti and thanked her again for such a delicious meal. He turned to Jenny who was still sitting next to her daughter and just raised his hand. "Night, Jenny, it's so nice to see you. Give my best to James when you call him and how much I appreciate his kind hospitality."

Henry could detect Jenny's eyes getting blurry as she softly whispered, "Good night, Henry, thank you so much for coming!"

Chapter Eighty Two

I

IT WAS JUST before eleven p.m. when Jenny called the hospital. James had a private phone but he did not answer. Perhaps he was in the washroom. She called again ten minutes later but there still wasn't any answer. Concern began to creep up her spine. She called the hospital again but this time asked for the nurses' station in the ward James was in.

"Ward C, Nurse Rushmer."

"Hi, this is Mrs. Hamilton. I have been trying to reach Mr. Hamilton but he is not answering his phone. Can I ask how he is doing?"

"Mr. Hamilton was given a strong sedative an hour ago. Last we checked he was asleep."

Jenny was about to hang up and then asked, "If I can keep you a moment longer... is he still being fed and medicated intravenously?"

"No, he requested that be terminated."

"How...how is he doing...?"

"You will have to discuss that with Dr. Reiner. He will be making his rounds first thing in the morning."

"This is his wife; please call me if there is any down turn or emergency."

"Yes, we will."

Jenny slowly hung up the phone in her room and sat in the chair by the bay window. It was the same chair James sat in the other night when he came to visit. Jenny wondered why James stopped taking his meds and he needed to be fed intravenously as he could no longer keep food down the normal way.

Was he dying or was it no longer necessary?

He had asked her not to come up Christmas Eve day but to enjoy it with Nancy and J.J. James said he would make every effort to come home Christmas Eve or Christmas day for certain. He wanted to spend it with J.J and his family... but he must have meant all the guests, too! She marvelled at what James had done to keep all this planning secret and to surprise her.

Jenny got ready for bed and decided that she would call the hospital first thing in the morning before going on the sightseeing trip that James also had the staff arrange.

Jenny slid into bed and turned off the lights. So many thoughts were travelling through her mind. She thought of taking a sedative, too. Would she ever find sleep?

It was so good to see Henry. She could hardly contain herself from jumping up and flying into his arms. He showed such restraint and consideration for James and the position that she was in. He was being so careful not to interfere and give her complete freedom...

"*I love you so much Henry,*" Jenny whispered.

Jenny turned over and buried her face in the pillow. Tears began to gush out as she thought of James. He was so loving, too. She still couldn't believe that he had sent for the entire Pederson family! What an incredible thing to do; allowing Henry and her to be in his home together without his watchful eye was... amazing. His heart and nature had changed so much. Jenny couldn't help but recall the Scriptures in the Bible she had read when she was ill in the hospital. When one grows in Christ, their mind is renewed and they become new creatures. The old self falls away and a new one is born...

"*Oh dear Jesus, please heal James. Whatever the future holds I am prepared to live out Your will. Although in a different way, I love both Henry and James.*"

EIGHT ROOMS SOUTH of Jenny's room lay Henry in his bed tossing and turning, as well. Henry wasn't quite sure where Jenny's room was. He suspected it was on the same floor. He had never seen such a long hallway. It was similar to that of a hotel.

He would love to steal down the hallway and enter her room. He could just picture them together in bed with her in his arms softly caressing her. He could hardly keep his eyes off her as she sat across the room. It was like torture of the worst kind. Henry felt guilty over having such thoughts but he couldn't seem to help himself, he so desired Jenny.

What if James was healed like they were? Henry was certain he knew the choice Jenny would make. He had noticed she was wearing her wedding ring.

Henry knew his dear, sweet, Jenny's heart… he knew what she had to do… there really wasn't any choice in the matter.

Father Engelmann's words rang in his mind, "Is divorce ever an option?"

"Yes, of course it is…" Henry screamed in his mind yet, his heart carried a message that was so different.

"Oh Jenny, I love you so dearly. I don't know what I will do without you should it come down to this." And yet, he thought the same when Julean had passed on. His world had collapsed as he knew it… Life was so beautiful and yet held so many, many, challenges…

Father Engelmann was right. Only in eternity will we be free of strife… *Live each day, Henry, with eternity in mind. Make certain you enter the right door.*

Henry got out of bed and made his way to the chair over which he had tossed his trousers. He had forgotten to take out Julean's rosary. On his way back to his bed he walked over to the window which overlooked the garden. The moon was full and the landscape before him was lit up and sparkled brightly. He saw the gazebo and pictured Jenny sitting there for all those years. But something even more dazzling caught his eye. Just in front was another Angel of Thanksgiving, its white marble glistening in the moonlight. Henry immediately noticed that the angel was carrying the basket in the opposite hand to the one Jenny had in her back yard. He marvelled at the sculptor's skill to capture the lifelikeness of the angel, as if walking through the garden.

He kissed Julean's rosary and began to pray. His fingers slipped slowly over one bead after the other. He felt Julean's fingers intertwine in his as he prayed for James and that he would be healed. He prayed for Jenny and lastly, Henry prayed for...Jenny and James' happiness.

JENNY WAS UP before six a.m. She kept thinking about James and that something may be wrong. She didn't know if she should go with Henry and his family on the sightseeing trip. It was three hours away from when the limousine would be picking them up.

Jenny couldn't wait a minute longer; she just had to know how James was doing. She dialed the phone in his room. On the second ring, James picked up the phone.

"Hello, James? Is that you?"

"Hi Marj. Yeah, it's me. The nurse told me you called last night. They gave me quite a heavy duty sedative and I was out for most of the night."

"Why have you stopped the IV, James? You need the nutrients..." Jenny asked in a concerned tone.

"I told you, Marjorie, I can live on love. Your coming back to me has helped me more than you know. Tell me, did the Pedersons come?"

"Oh, James, I was so concerned about you, I forgot to tell you how surprised I was to see Camilla and Henry and his family there when I came home! I thought I was dreaming. James, that was so thoughtful of you! How you arranged all that is amazing."

"You can do a lot just lying on your back. Did J.J. go out to meet them?"

"Yes! I couldn't believe that either, James. J.J., Nora and Jimmy were there to greet the entire Pederson entourage. Camilla couldn't say enough over what a wonderful host J.J. was and how happy he was to meet his half sister. Camilla said he even gave her a hug! Oh, I am so proud of J.J., James. This is like a dream come true. What you have done has made me so happy, James. Thank you so much."

"Take it easy Marj, I'm growing too soft. Talks like this blur my eyes pretty quick. So is everything planned today for the Pedersons?"

"Yes, but I don't think I should go. I won't see you the entire day and I am concerned about you…"

"I'm okay, Marj. It's amazing how a good night's sleep restores one's energy."

"I remember that too, James, but I still—"

"No, please, Marj, go out and enjoy your guests. I will try to make it home for an hour or so this evening to meet everyone. I have an ambulance booked to take me and wait to bring me back. So it's all arranged. Please, Marj, just go and enjoy the day, I will be fine. There is one thing you can do for me. Ask Thomas to come up if he can. I would like him to do something for me."

"Yes, I will… is there anything else I can do…?"

"Marjorie, you have done more than anyone could ever do. I love you and… thank you for wearing the wedding ring again. I just don't know how to tell you what that means to me…"

Jenny was in tears and couldn't answer at first… "I love you, too, James. I so hope you get well. Please listen to the doctors and please get them to hook up the IV… you need the nutrients."

"I'll talk to the doctors about it. I'm saving it all for the big turkey dinner tomorrow. Isn't that what normal people have on a special day?"

"Yes, Matti will make you something special…"

"Will you say hello to Henry for me? I hope I get a chance to meet him later this evening or tomorrow, for sure. He's a lucky man, Marj. And thank him for letting you come back… He must be quite the guy."

Jenny didn't say anything. She didn't know how to respond. She loved both men each in their own way.

"Dr. Reiner just stepped into the room, Marj. I don't know what the hell good he does…" Jenny heard the doctor laugh in the background.

"Have a good time, Marj. Hopefully I will be strong enough to make it to join the party tonight. Perhaps Dr. Reiner has some tricks up his sleeve."

"Take, care, James… I love you."

"I love you, too, Marjorie."

CHAPTER EIGHTY THREE

After a hearty breakfast everyone was ready and waiting for the limousine to pick them up. Henry checked his watch; five minutes before nine. No sooner had he looked up when he spotted the rays of the sun bouncing off a shiny black car as it meandered through the trees leading up to the Manor.

"Wow, what a long car!" observed Justin as the extended vehicle pulled to a stop under the canopy to the front door entrance. The limo easily accommodated all the passengers. They decided to leave Josh at home with Matti. J.J. was going to bring Jimmy over later in the morning with some toys for the two boys to play with. Camilla and Jeremy thought the fast paced tour might be too exhausting for their son and may not hold his interest.

Their first stop was at Parliament Hill for a quick tour of the building and architecture. They stopped to listen to a story or two of Canada's history. They were disappointed that the house was shut down over the holidays and so they couldn't take in a session, but then again it may have been a good thing.

Next, they went to the Canadian Museum of Civilization. Henry had read so much of the complete story on human history that was portrayed by the four permanent exhibition galleries.

They had a light lunch at a café along the Rideau Canal. It was such a colourful sight to see so many people skating on the Canal. Henry had read that the Canal was considered the largest outdoor skating rink in Canada. As he gazed down the Canal he could see why. People were skating as far as he could see.

Jenny slipped away for a few minutes to call home and speak with Thomas. But he was still up at the hospital visiting James. Jenny instructed Matti to tell Thomas to call the driver of the limousine on the radio phone if James' condition was urgent…

THOMAS HAD JUST finished writing a note for James that he was to give to Jenny via the Angel of Thanksgiving.

"Do you want me to read it back to you, James?"

"No, that's fine Thomas. Thanks for writing it… perhaps I should sign it."

Thomas took the tray off the table and placed the letter on it. He held it in front of James to sign. It was evident James was in considerable pain. His signature was barely legible.

"I'll stop by and pick up flowers on the way home as all the shops will be closed tomorrow."

"Yeah, that's a good thought, Thomas."

"Are you still planning on coming to the Manor this evening?'

"I don't know, Thomas, I would like to… So, Marjorie was surprised to see her daughter and Henry and his family?"

"I wasn't there at the time but according to Matti, she had never seen such a look of surprise on the face of anyone in all her days. Yes, James, Miss Jenny was very happy to see her family from Regina."

"What's Henry like, Thomas?" James wanted to know.

"He's a fine gentleman, James. I think you would like him."

"It would be nice to meet him…we'll see…"

THEIR LAST STOP was a highlight for Henry; the National Gallery of Canada. They managed to see some of the abstract paintings, Italian art and some photography. However, being Christmas Eve, the gallery closed early and just as well, as they were all getting tired and hungry and looking forward to getting home.

"I'VE BEEN DOING a lot of thinking on this Jesus fellow, Thomas. I recall the day that you and Matti prayed for me as we sat around the kitchen table. Do you remember?"

"Oh, yes, James. I wouldn't forget that nor the prayer you said later when we went into the garden and placed flowers into the angel's basket in thanks for the good Lord to restore your family and bring Marjorie back to the estate"

"It seems to me, Thomas, our prayers have been answered on all accounts. Marjorie has come back to me, completely... I never dreamed she would. J.J. has come around and is treating me and Marjorie as Mother and Father, as a son should. And I think the Man upstairs has healed me, as well. It may not be a physical healing, but it might be what you call a spiritual one. I have the feeling that you would consider this healing, coming closer to the Creator, the most important healing."

Thomas just nodded and smiled softly.

"All of you have been such an inspiration to me. There is something special that you have that I haven't got. Perhaps the biggest beacon of light, if we can call it that, would have to be Marjorie. For all the years I have known her, she carried that light and offered it to me day in and day out and I preferred the darkness just like I read in the Bible the other day. Something about the light has come into the world but men love the darkness rather than the light..."

"Yes, that's John 3:19."

"See, you know that book inside out, Thomas, and both you and Marjorie live it out, as well, and that's what draws me to the Bible. Like I said, Marjorie stuck with me when I was at my lowest... she never gave up on me for all those years... And look, here I am in my last days and finally at peace. She gave me the gift of experiencing true love. Amazing! Thomas..."

James stopped and asked for the some water. Thomas took the glass and directed the straw to James' mouth. "There's some ice here if you want some..."

"Water is fine...when J.J. was here before you came I talked a bit about this and asked him to consider taking the family to church with you and Neela on Sunday. He needs your guidance Thomas... be a father to him..."

Thomas nodded, unbidden tears surfacing.

"You have been a dear friend to me, Thomas. You're a good man… I like you…I like you a lot. Tell Matti the same…"

Thomas gave James some more water and said, "We all love you, too, James…"

"Tell me, Thomas, what do I have to do or say to commit to Jesus? Would something like what the thief who hung next to Jesus said be sufficient for me to say to get up there to what you folks are aiming for?"

"Yes, James, something like that would be just fine. The Lord is more interested in what is really in your heart. He knows where you are at and accepts and loves you just as you are. He knows if you are sorry for your sins and your desire to accept him as your Lord and Saviour. If you would like, James, I can lead you in a prayer…"

James just nodded, tears were filling his eyes. Thomas could feel the Holy Spirit moving powerfully in the room. Thomas took James' hand in his and said, "I will say a little prayer, slowly, and you simply repeat what I say…

"Lord Jesus Christ,"

"*Lord, Jesus Christ,*" *repeated, James.*

"I am sorry for my sins."

"*I am sorry for my sins…*" said James, tears flowing…

"I acknowledge You as the Son of the Living God."

"*I acknowledge You… as the Son of the Living God…*"

"I accept You as my Lord and my God."

"*I accept You as my Lord and my God…*"

"Lord Jesus Christ, I receive You as my personal Savior"

"*Lord Jesus Christ…I receive You as my personal Savior…*"

James was weeping…

Thomas' tears were falling on their hands clutched together…

"Fill me with your Holy Spirit."

"*Fill me with your Holy Spirit…*" an aura brightened around James…

"Heal and strengthen me."

"*Heal and strengthen me.*"

"I love You, Jesus."

"*I love You, Jesus…*"*James softly whispered.*

Chapter Eighty Four

Ⅰт тоок ᴸᴼᴺᴳᴱᴿ than usual to get back to the estate. The traffic was heavy with last minute shoppers and the snowfall slowed the traffic movement even further. Everyone was tired and anxious to get home. Jenny hoped Thomas would call the limo driver and let her know how James was doing. She felt pangs of guilt to be sightseeing and thought she should be at James' side. He was adamant, however, when she left yesterday to stay at home and host her guests.

J.J. and Nora had come over early in the afternoon to help look after Josh and Jimmy to free up Matti to prepare dinner for all the people, as well as get the turkey ready for the Christmas Day celebration.

Joshua missed his mom and dad and kept looking out the front window for their return. Suddenly he shouted, "They're home!"

J.J. and Nora rushed to the front door to greet them and help with their coats.

Josh ran to Camilla as soon as she entered the door. She picked her son up and gave him a big hug. "Did you have fun playing with Jimmy?"

"He has neat toys, Mom. Come, I want to show you!"

"Okay, just wait until I get my coat off…"

"Here, Camilla, let me help you," offered J.J.

"Thanks, J.J., so how was Josh?"

"He was great. He and Jimmy entertained themselves most of the time. It was fun watching them play together."

As J.J. spoke, Camilla could see his eyes and mouth carried their mother's genes. His hair was a different matter—jet black. Yet, she could see that J.J. and she were related.

Camilla went to her brother and gave him a hug.

"Sure smells good," said Henry, as he hung up his coat and walked into the living room to make room for the others.

They all greeted one another and slowly they made it into the living room to enjoy refreshments which Charles had already prepared.

Jenny wanted to know how James was and if Thomas was at home yet.

J.J. answered all of Jenny's questions. "Thomas is still up at the hospital or on his way home. I was up before noon and Thomas came in just as I was leaving. Dad said he was fine, but you know him. He's pretty good at covering up his pain. I wish he would let the doctors feed him through the IV tubes. He's losing so much weight and it's obvious he is growing weaker each time I see him. I did see the nurse give him a shot just before I left. Thomas can fill you in from there on when he gets home…"

"Thank you, J.J., the nurse probably gave him morphine…"

"Come, Mom, I want to show you Jimmy's neat toys…"

Camilla was listening to J.J. about James' condition… "Okay, let's go Joshua."

As the foyer cleared out and Jenny saw Charles already carrying drinks in to the guests, Jenny decided to excuse herself and make a quick call to the hospital. She ran upstairs to her room.

Jenny called James' room, but like last night there was no answer. She decided to call the nurses' station. She wondered if James would be able to make it out that evening. The snow fall was getting thicker… probably not. Thomas and Neela were still at their guest house and should be along any moment. Thomas would know how James was.

"Ward 4C"

"Hello, this is Mrs. Hamilton. I tried to reach James Hamilton but there was no answer in his room. How is he doing?"

"He thought you might be calling, Mrs. Hamilton. He said he will not be making it home this evening, but will for certain tomorrow, on Christmas Day. He asked for a sedative just a half hour ago and is sleeping soundly."

"Would you please ask him to call should he awaken... please?"

"Yes, I will and also relay the message to the next nurse on shift at eleven."

"Thank you..."

Oh, James, what are you up to...

She recalled his last words when they spoke this morning, "I love you, too, Marjorie." There was such a tone of finality...

Oh, I hope and pray he's okay...

JUST AS JENNY came down stairs and entered the foyer, she ran into Thomas.

"Oh, good, you're home," Jenny said with a sigh of relief. "How was James, Thomas?"

"As best as can be expected, Miss Jenny. I don't know if he will make it tonight. He was very tired when I left and the nurse gave him a sedative and pain killer. He said he wants to be here tomorrow and has something for you."

"What, Thomas?"

"You will have to wait until then, Miss Jenny, those were my instructions."

The gathering was so beautiful. It was wonderful to have everyone sitting around the tree and roaring fire. It was so soothing to everyone to listen to the Christmas carols playing in the background after a tiring day. Henry thought he and the family might go to the Notre Dame Basilica for midnight Mass, but winter conditions outside and exhaustion from the long day hit them all early. It was so nice to see the children play and how excited they were to open some of their gifts. Henry could see most people were tired and decided that perhaps he should initiate the bedtime ritual.

"Well, everyone, that was quite the day. Thanks again for the wonderful tour, Jenny. I know we only hit the tip of the iceberg of tourist attractions, but perhaps another time we can come for a longer visit. I sure hope James is able to make it home tomorrow.

I would like to meet him."

"It is wonderful having you and your family here. It's all so supportive." Jenny smiled at Henry from across the room. She so much would have loved to be held in his arms.

"Coming, Justin?"

"Yeah, I will go up with you, Dad."

"I can see the girls chatting for another hour or two. Good night girls."

Camilla, Lauren and Allison were reading the back of one of the records Lauren got for Christmas.

The girls jumped up and hugged Henry and Justin. After saying good night to everyone except Jenny, Henry made his way over to her. She rose and they hugged and Henry kissed her on the cheek. "Night, Jenny."

"Don't forget to set out milk and some of those fine cookies that Matti makes for Santa Claus!" Henry waved again to everyone and he and Justin exited the living room.

HENRY THOUGHT OF calling Father Engelmann when he got to his room. They would be two hours behind, but Father was probably getting ready for midnight Mass. Father said if Father Knuka didn't need help he would have an earlier Mass at the Nunnery. Henry decided to call him in the morning and wish him a Merry Christmas.

At first Henry thought coming here wasn't such a good idea but perhaps James' plan for the families to meet would prove very beneficial and may prepare the way for a better future for all of them. Henry was pleased that J.J. was friendly towards him. He felt the young man's eyes on him most of the evening and they did chat several times. Henry was glad Jenny was wearing her wedding ring. He wondered if J.J. and Justin noticed it…

Yes, Henry thought, as he reflected on coming, *it was good to get to know one another.* As Father often said, "If only we could see that we are all connected through Jesus. We are all brothers and sisters."

Henry could see Jenny was distracted most of the day. She tried so hard to be present to everyone, but Henry knew she was concerned about James and would have much preferred to be ministering to him.

Jenny's heart was so compassionate. Rather than feel left out or slighted at Jenny's focus on her husband, Henry loved his dearly beloved all the more. Despite such a loveless marriage, her heart went to James so completely. There was no holding back.

What kind of heart did Jenny really have?

She was able to sacrifice her own happiness out of sheer loving without even knowing it. She considered it all gain. She and Father Engelmann had so much in common.

Henry turned over and kissed Julean's rosary. He began to pray for Jenny, for James and his family...Henry hoped that perhaps tomorrow he might meet James...

CHAPTER EIGHTY FIVE

Morning could not come soon enough for Jenny. She had tossed and turned most of the night. Shortly after three a.m. she finally drifted off into a light sleep. Around six a.m., about the same time as the day before, Jenny got up. She just had to phone and see how James was doing and if he would be well enough to come home for at least part of Christmas Day.

"Ward C, Nurse Rushmer speaking."

"Hi, Nurse Rushmer…this is Mrs. Hamilton. Can you please tell me how my husband is doing?"

There was a long silence on the phone.

"I am so sorry to let you know…Mr. Hamilton passed away moments ago. He was still in his sleep when he expired. We were checking on him every 10 – 15 minutes and he was breathing restfully. For most of the night, however, he seemed to be dreaming—"

"Is he still in his room?"

"Yes, he will be moved shortly."

"Would you please leave him in his room until I get there? I will be there as quick as I can."

"Well… yes, Mrs. Hamilton, I will see that they don't move him until you get here. His son called just before you and requested

515

that we leave Mr. Hamilton here, as well."

"Thank you."

Jenny quickly got dressed and made it downstairs. Matti has just come in from the guest home.

"Jenny, you be up early…"

"Oh, Matti, James passed away," Jenny cried. "I am going up to the hospital to see him before they move him. I should be home around noon."

"Do you be wantin' Thomas or me to go with you?"

"No, no, I will be fine…" Just as Jenny turned to leave, the phone rang. It was J.J.

Matti looked at Jenny, "It's your son. He wants to let you know his daddy passed away."

"Tell him I'm on my way to the hospital."

Jenny raced to her car and sped out of the estate.

More than an hour had elapsed since she spoke with Nurse Rushmer.

I hope she was able to keep him in the room.

She dreaded to go to the morgue.

She took a deep breath as the elevator came to a stop on the fourth floor. She turned right and walked rapidly to James' room. A nurse saw her and was about to holler out but caught herself as soon as she recognized Mr. Hamilton's wife.

The door to James' room was ajar; Jenny slowly pushed it open.

The sheet had been drawn up over James' face. Tears surfaced instantly. Her heart went out to him.

"Oh, James…my dear, James."

She walked slowly over to the bedside and stood beside him. She took a deep breath and slowly pulled the sheet down, exposing his face. She didn't know what to expect. His eyes were closed and he looked peacefully at rest.

She hadn't noticed the other day how frail and sunken his features looked. Perhaps, when one is alive and talking one doesn't notice that death is just a breath away.

Yes, his time had come.

James had had a hard life. To many people, he may have had the world by the tail, but Jenny knew it was not all what people thought. As soon as Nancy had shared James' background, she loved him all the more because that was what he needed. James had lacked love in his life. That was always Jenny's main goal regardless of their relationship: *James needed love.*

Jenny placed her hand over James'. It was still warm. She bent over and kissed his forehead. "Good bye, James… I love you. I know you are here in the room. I was up there where you are now. Floating around, ready to meet your guardian angel. Perhaps you already have and your angel is ready to escort you to your Maker." Jenny gazed up and turned thinking that she might see James. "Someday we will meet again. Thank you for sharing your life with me…"

Nurse Rushmer walked into the room. "Is everything okay, Mrs. Hamilton?" she asked compassionately.

Jenny nodded, "Yes. Thank you for keeping him here until I came."

The nurse came up to Jenny and placed her hand on her shoulder, "I came in at twelve o'clock, the midnight shift. I think I mentioned that he was dreaming quite a bit."

"Yes, you did say that earlier when I called…"

"He kept saying how happy he was to give the gift of freedom to Marjorie… that it would be the only meaningful gift he could give to return the love he had received… Do you know who she is, Mrs. Hamilton? Is that you…?"

Jenny didn't answer…her heart was too touched for words.

"It almost seemed as if he wanted to die today. He kept asking the nurses and doctors how long it takes after the IV is removed for a body to exist without the nutrients…"

Nurse Rushmer shook her head and stared at the body. "His wish to pass away on Christmas day came true."

"Didn't he have life support planned?" Jenny wanted to know.

"Oh no, he signed off on that a week ago and his son also canceled some contract he had with the Cryonics company."

The nurse shook her head once more and added, "He knew he was going, Mrs. Hamilton, and he planned as best he could, how he would leave and when. All I can say is that he accomplished his goal, but at the expense of considerable pain."

"Oh, James, my dear James…"

Suddenly, J.J. came bursting through the door, startling Jenny and Nurse Rushmer. J.J.'s eyes were red and filled with tears. He stared at his father lying there and made his way slowly to him. He never took his gaze off James; it was as if no-one was in the room. Jenny and the Nurse stepped back and allowed J.J. to get nearer. He looked down and began to openly weep. "Oh, Dad, what will I do without you…?"

He threw himself across James' chest and continued to cry.

Jenny drew near her son and placed her arm over J.J.'s shoulder.

Nurse Rushmer, with tears in her eyes, quietly withdrew from the room and closed the door.

CHAPTER EIGHTY SIX

JENNY DROVE SLOWLY home. At times she had to pull over, stop and let a fountain of tears fall. She never realized just how much she had cared for and loved James. It almost took an extra hour for her to make it home. Thomas was sitting in the kitchen, expecting her.

He got up when she entered the kitchen. He could see the sorrow and sadness in her eyes. She approached Thomas and fell onto his chest. He was hesitant but then wrapped his arms around her and hugged her tenderly, as if she was one of his own. He began to cry in sympathy with his dear Miss Jenny.

"Oh, Thomas, James was such a good man. I am so happy we all saw the real James."

Thomas didn't speak.

Slowly, Jenny gained some composure. "Where are Henry and his family?"

"Neela took them to church. They should be home in the next half hour. Matti went along, too."

Thomas paused and then continued, "There is something James wanted me to show and give you, Miss Jenny."

Jenny looked tenderly into Thomas's eyes; her gaze was questioning enough without words.

"Come, it's outside."

Thomas put on his jacket. Jenny still hadn't taken hers off.

The first thing Jenny noticed was that Thomas had cleared the snow off the walkway right down to the paving stone. They stepped out of the kitchen doors onto the patio and began to stroll down the path that Thomas had cleared. It was free of snow all the way to the gazebo, including the interior of the gazebo itself. It appeared as it would have on a summer day.

Thomas led Jenny to the gazebo and entered. He asked Jenny to sit down and once again after a brief hesitation, he decided to sit next to Mrs. Hamilton.

Softly, Thomas began, "James knew how much you loved this haven and the garden and the Angel of Thanksgiving and so it is only fitting that he would want to give you his final farewell here."

Thomas paused to collect himself and went on. "I have to say, Miss Jenny, that James planned to die today. He wanted to give you a Christmas present that was meaningful in the only way he knew how. He wanted to give you his life in exchange for all you did for him. I have to say, I am deeply moved."

Jenny didn't look up at Thomas, she leaned into his side and rested her head on his shoulder.

"He asked me to buy you a bouquet and put them into the angel's basket so that fresh flowers would be here for you. I placed them in the basket when I came home last evening after visiting with James. As you can see the flowers are still fresh, I knew somehow they would survive the night. But, Miss Jenny, after clearing the walk this morning I noticed that I didn't need to buy any flowers."

Thomas got up and walked a few feet to the wildflower patch that surrounded the Angel of Thanksgiving. He brushed away the snow over the wildflower patch and miraculously the flowers beneath were as fresh as if they had just bloomed!

"Isn't that something, Miss Jenny? I have seen more miracles in this garden which just overwhelms me, time and time again. But this one, well…"

Thomas paused to compose himself and said, "I am going to leave you. When you are ready, you will see a letter I placed in between the bouquet of flowers. James had me write it as he dictated it to me yesterday when we visited for the last time. He signed it as best he could. When you are ready, you go ahead and read it... all I can say, Miss Jenny, is that in all the years of my life, I have never read a letter that was more from the heart."

When thomas came back into the house, Henry and his family had returned from church. The kids for the most part were interested in the gifts they had received and were presently occupied, which was a good thing as it left Henry free. Matti was bustling around in the kitchen getting ready to prepare breakfast.

"Hi Thomas," said Henry, when he saw Thomas enter from the kitchen. "Is Jenny up or did she go to the hospital?"

"I have some sad news for you, Henry, James passed on early this morning. Miss Jenny was already up to see him and she is now out in the garden sitting on the swing in the gazebo. If you don't mind to put your jacket back on and go out there, I think Miss Jenny could use your support at this time."

Henry walked slowly along the path, not sure if it was the right direction. He decided that the cleared walk of snow must be an indication of where to go.

He wasn't sure how to feel about James' death. He would have liked to have met James. He had thought about going up to the hospital but didn't want to put undue stress on James to see him and Jenny there together. And yet, James had invited him to come...It was an odd situation Henry found himself in and also one that could have altered his life for the rest of his days.

Henry sensed that Jenny had grown fonder of her husband since returning to the estate...the Church is right...if both parties in a marriage really try, it's surprising the obstacles that can be overcome.

Jenny had seen something in James that drew her love. Henry trusted that love. If Jenny had decided to go back to James, Henry would have understood. It may have broken his heart but he knew down deep he would have had to let her go. Their relationship had to be based upon freedom...

Henry would soon see that James felt the same way, too...

As SOON AS he turned the bend around a lilac bush covered heavily with snow, Henry saw Jenny sitting on the swing in the gazebo.

As he neared, he saw she was holding a letter and was crying. He walked into the gazebo and sat next to his dearly beloved. He raised his arm and Jenny fell into his chest and once again burst into a waterfall of tears. Her hand holding the letter rested on his lap.

He tenderly squeezed Jenny. Without looking at Henry, Jenny offered the letter she had been reading to him. Henry took the letter from her hand and began to read:

Dear Marjorie

Yesterday, for the first time in my life, I said a prayer to Jesus. Oh, I talked to Him before, but this time it came from the heart. I want you to know that I decided to choose to be like the thief that believed in Him.

I feel the end is near and so, I will soon know if I made the right choice. Deep in my heart, I know I did. How could I not? You often said that we are children of God and…it was in you that I saw the Father.

Marjorie, thank you, from the bottom of my heart for coming back to me in my last days. Thank you for wearing the wedding ring and being my wife. I know my days on earth were extended because of your love.

Truly, there are angels. There is no doubt in my mind that they are gifts from God. If only I could be sitting there with you now on the swing giving thanks. The angel's basket could never be big enough to give thanks for all the blessings you have brought into my life. If there ever was an earthly angel, it has to be you.

Please accept my leaving as my last gift to you. Marjorie, you are now free to follow your heart. I always knew right from the start when we started to date there was somebody in your heart that kept you from loving me completely. If you recall, there were many times I asked you and once you shared your heart…it was Henry. He's a lucky man. And I wish you both all the happiness in the world.

This may sound out of character for me, but this past summer when I strolled through the garden and sat on the swing in the gazebo, I often heard music from the radio that Thomas and Ramon carried around with them as they did their landscape work. One day, there was a song that a lady by the name of Dolly Parton sang. I think the name of the song was 'I will always love you.'

It caught my attention right away. I think the first verse was something like this:

If I should stay
I would only be in your way
So I'll go but I know
I'll think of you every step of the way.

That about sums it up, Marjorie, I will always love you as best I can and know how…let this be my last gift to you… Fly, Marjorie, fly like an angel and a butterfly…you were born to be free.

With love,

James.

Chapter Eighty Seven

Henry and his family stayed an extra day and went to the funeral home to pay James their last respects. It was good for all of them to put a face to James, the man Jenny had been married to.

Camilla stayed an extra week. She supported Jenny through the funeral and spent more time with J.J. and his family as well.

In the days that followed, Jenny helped J.J. settle the estate matters. J.J. and his family moved into the Manor and continued living exactly the way James did when he was on the estate the past two years. J.J. didn't want to change anything. This was the first time he felt the love of family. He knew exactly what his father had discovered and wouldn't want it any other way.

Henry and Jenny talked everyday on the phone. They expressed their deep love for one another, but never once talked of marriage. They just took one day at a time.

At the end of January, Jenny decided to return home to Regina. She had established a close relationship with J.J. and Nora and loved to play with Jimmy. She felt so good about how everything turned out. She now fully realized why Jesus had wanted her to come back to James. It was such a beautiful homecoming and healing for the entire family. It only confirmed God's love for His children and how He always works to turn everything into the good in an imperfect world.

The flight home was smooth and peaceful. She could hardly wait to see Henry. They had been separated for over four months with just those few brief days at Christmas when he and his family surprised her with their visit. That was so wonderful of James to bring the families together like that. She would be forever grateful to Henry, too, for being so understanding and supportive and not once pressuring her into making any kind of choice or decision. She had sensed that he was even prepared to step away if she had decided to go back to James if he were healed.

Oh, it will be so good to see him.

Jenny felt a bit of nervous excitement as the wheels of the plane hit the tarmac and came to an abrupt stop. She could see mounds of snow everywhere; much more than in Ottawa. She wondered how difficult it would be to drive home.

As she entered the terminal, it was easy to see Henry. His face was beaming, as if struck by the sun. Tears came to Jenny's eyes and quickly blurred her vision as she ran to Henry who was already hurrying to her, as well. Jenny threw her arms around her sweetheart and was immediately swept off her feet as Henry twirled her around and around.

"Oh, Jenny… it's so good to see you; to hold you…too…" and their lips met and both lifted into a world of ecstasy.

When they pulled up to Jenny's home, the walkway leading to the front door was neatly shovelled.

Jenny turned to Henry, "Did you do that?"

"Yeah, I came early enough before the plane arrived. You'll have to get used to our winters… you will get a lot more exercise here than in Ottawa."

Jenny jumped out of the SUV. She didn't wait for Henry to open the door.

"Oh, it's so good to be home!" she exclaimed, as she ran up the winding walk to the front door. She unlocked the door and entered her domain… it was on a much smaller scale than the mansion she just came from, but it was her home.

Jenny walked further into the living room just as Henry was coming in the front door with her luggage. There, on the dining room table, was a crystal vase filled to overflowing with wildflowers. The room glowed with colour and… love.

Jenny went over and took a deep breath, filling her senses with the mixed aroma of the different scents of each flower. It seemed as if she was elevated. She removed the card attached to one of the flowers and read:

> *My dear, sweet, Jenny, whom I love more than words can possibly say. My heart bursts at your return. I recall each moment of you running through the meadow of wildflowers near the Poustinia. So free, as if lifted by the summer breeze; your hair glistening gold in the bright sun… you're an angel, Jenny.*
> *Welcome home,*
> *With all my love,*
>
> > *Henry*

Jenny felt Henry's hands gently on either side of her waist. She spun around and gazed into his eyes, "I'm so happy to be home, Henry. I love you so much."

"I love you more, Jenny."

CHAPTER EIGHTY EIGHT

"THIS MEAL IS delicious, Henry," said Father Engelmann as he took another mouthful of the Chicken Parmesan.

Father sat in between Jenny and Henry who sat at each end of the table in Henry's sun room on the farm.

"I have to admit, Honey, this is delicious. And I love the texture of the rice. It's so nice and fluffy rather than sticky like mine usually turns out to be."

"It's all in the technique," Henry winked.

"I was surprised to learn that you were still at the prayer house, Father. There is so much snow in the valley."

"If it wasn't for Henry's skidoo, I wouldn't be able to get out, like today, for example. But I enjoy it just as much in winter as the other seasons. Winter has such a pristine quality; so clean and fresh and the moonlight sparkling off the snow at night is heavenly."

"I have to agree. When I lived on the estate, walking in the garden covered with snow was so wonderful. I tried to guess which flowers were hidden just below the white, glistening cover," said Jenny.

"How are you coming along with your writing, Father?" Henry wanted to know.

Jenny's eyes instantly brightened and sparkled. "Yes, yes, Henry told me you were writing a love story, Father! That's amazing. Who is it about?"

Father's lips curled at each end and grew into a smile. "Oh, it's a love story that involves both of you and also about life and how we choose to live it."

"About us, you mean? Henry and me?"

Father nodded and kept eating.

"And it's a love story…?"

"Yes, Jenny. I know that may surprise you. It did me as well when Zachariah asked that task of me. I am surprised how much I enjoy writing and how easily the words and thoughts come to me. Sometimes, thoughts of my Anna generate pages and pages of writing. Sometimes thoughts of you and Henry fill the book with such love my heart rejoices. And sometimes, my guardian angel and the Holy Spirit inspire me with the wisdom and truths of Jesus' teachings to such depths my eyes are filled with tears of gratitude; I can no longer see the pages. At times, as the day comes to an end, I am astounded even more than you as to what came to life on the pages."

Father looked at Jenny and added, "It's another miracle, Jenny. That is all I can say."

Henry and Jenny gazed at Father in awe over what he just said. A silent hush fell over the room.

"I noticed you titled the book, *Pewter Angels*. Is there another book or just the one?" asked Henry, as he held a mouthful of food on the end of his fork.

"Yes, it will be a series of books. I am nearing the completion of the second book and there is still much to say."

"Have you decided on the name of the second book, yet?" Jenny was at the edge of her seat.

"*Another Angel of Love*," replied Father.

"That's a beautiful name… how did you come up with it?" Jenny wanted to know.

"The title is supposed to capture what the story is mainly about. The name came to me in a dream. When I awoke in the morning that was the first thought I had. I just nodded and said, "Yes, Zachariah, that is good."

Henry was intrigued with the name. It stirred a memory of

the time when they sat in the back storage room of the grocery store... Father, or rather, Mr. Engelmann, at the time, explained what God's divine providence was. He had said a prayer at the conclusion of their talk, which Henry recalled to this very day... "Together we ask that You will provide a sign to Henry that will put his heart at peace in his relationship with Julean; that she is *another angel of love...*" Yes, that's what he had said. Henry wondered if there was any connection to the title of Father's second book.

Father swallowed the last of his food and sat back. "That was a wonderful meal, Henry. After one fasts for several days, food has more flavour and every mouthful such a blessing."

A silence fell as the last light of day slipped behind the hills and darkness moved swiftly across the valley. The candle in the middle of the table seemed to know and grew more brightly in response. A feeling of warmth and peace permeated the air in the room.

"It is good to have you back home, Jenny. Henry tells me your trip to Ottawa was very worthwhile and rewarding?"

"It was very good, Father, I am so happy that I followed Jesus' will in the matter. I would never have known just how powerfully God works in our lives to bring us home. The transformation in James was truly miraculous."

"Your presence, Jenny, was needed to lead your husband home. You were a light reflecting Jesus."

Jenny recalled James last words, *I see God more in you than anything I have read in the Bible.* Jenny was going to comment on this when Henry shared much of what she was going to say.

"Yes, I remember so many times Father," concurred Henry, "you saying how important we are to one another in our words, deeds and actions, which can either lead others to Christ or away from Him."

Father nodded. "If we only realized our tremendous responsibility and purpose to be beacons of light. As Jenny so beautifully stated in her sharing on suffering that day, Jesus asks us to help Him in continuing the redemption of mankind. We can never underestimate how one act of kindness and compassion affects another who in turn passes it on. The repercussions can be mind boggling and even result in saving another's soul."

"You know, Father, I think I have to agree with the Church's position on divorce. Initially, it upset me. And yet it is based on what Jesus' said. We do make a vow before God to love and honour in good and bad times until death do us part. There may be instances when separation is definitely required but in most cases it's a matter of dying to oneself, maturing and taking responsibility for your life." Henry nodded, "Father and I spoke of this a few months back; dying to oneself and caring more for the happiness of the other is key to making a marriage work."

Jenny looked at Henry and then at Father. Her eyes seemed to redden, "You know, when Henry and his family came to Ottawa I was so happy to see Henry and yet his presence made me nervous. I wasn't sure how to be dealing with James at the same time...and yet, everything just seemed to be so natural..."

Jenny paused and looked tenderly at Henry, "Although you were there, you accepted the situation unconditionally and allowed me to just go with the moments as they came. I felt free to be myself, Henry, as if you were ready to accept whatever happened."

Jenny softly whispered, "Thank you."

Henry's blurry eyes returned the tender gaze.

"Yes, when Jesus is at the centre of our relationships and in our lives, all things are possible," added Father.

Jenny turned to Father, "That's so true. I was so amazed to see James change before my eyes and he even started to read the Bible! I could see the Holy Spirit working so powerfully in his life."

"It is faith-building to witness the power of Lord work in our and others' lives. You mentioned earlier that you also witnessed this in your son's life and have reconciled with him."

"Yes! It happened so suddenly. I think James' mother had something to do with it, but it just confirms how God works through us to resolve conflicts and restore love... It's amazing. I'm certain, too, that James' changing and trying so hard to be a father toward the end strongly influenced J.J. as well."

Jenny paused for a moment and her eyes brightened, "And I couldn't believe it when Camilla came and met J.J. It was all so incredible how in a matter of a few weeks such harmony and peace prevailed between us all! See, I was meant to go. If I hadn't, none of this would have happened. All I can say is praise God. I can hardly wait till spring to fill my Angel of Thanksgiving basket with flowers of thanks."

Father reached over and patted Jenny's hand resting beside her plate. "The Lord is very pleased with you, Jenny. Despite a one sided marriage, you have brought a family back together. It is so beautiful if each partner accepts the other and a home is a place of love and security. In all too many homes, unfortunately this is not the case as it was in yours—"

"That is why I want to start a women's group of some kind! When I was on the estate, I felt so alone at times. I'm sure other women are searching for companionship and help in dealing with all the challenges we face in our families, marriages, loving and accepting one another, developing our spiritual lives…" Jenny's words trailed off. She shrugged her shoulders, tilted her head, smiled and then added, "I feel called in this way…"

"See, the Lord has been preparing you, Jenny. More than ever this kind of support in the community is needed. This is a wonderful idea—"

"I couldn't agree more," Henry interjected. Looking directly into Jenny's eyes, he added, "You mentioned this before, Jenny. And now that you're back home, it would be great for you to pursue developing such a group. You are such a good role model and could be so helpful in rebuilding marriages, offering insights and learning from the experiences of other women, as well."

"Yes, that's right. We can be there for one another… and, yes, now that I'm home, I think I will start exploring what is out there…" Jenny wriggled in her chair and added, "I'm so excited to start!"

AFTER TEA, FATHER asked if Henry could drive him back to the Poustinia. It was past his bed time and he had many prayers to say.

It was a calm February evening. The sky was clear and a full moon hung low in the heavens. Henry sat up front on the skidoo, Jenny right behind with her arms wrapped around Henry and Father sat perched at the end of the long touring snowmobile. Father gripped the side rails beside his seat as Henry started the motor and pressed the accelerator.

As soon as the dogs heard the revving of the motor they were out of their doghouse in a flash. Henry flicked on the lights and slowly moved forward. Ginger and Coco knew where Henry was heading and ran towards the road that would take them down the hill to the Poustinia.

It was different driving at night and more caution was needed. Henry felt Jenny squeeze his waist as the skidoo began to descend around the hill. It was too dark to see the bottom of the gorge but Henry stayed well clear of the edge of the road that dropped off. Soon they were at the bottom and gently sliding over the rolling drifts of snow. The tracks made by the skidoo earlier when Henry picked Father up were hidden underneath fresh fallen snow. It looked like a winter wonderland.

Henry turned off the motor as soon as he stopped by the deck. Father got off first, then Jenny and last, Henry. They stood on the deck and looked out over the sparkling valley. Each snow flake seemed to glisten like a diamond. Jenny wrapped her arms around Henry, "This is so beautiful… no wonder you love it here, Father."

"Yes, truly a paradise. Well, my dear children, I must get ready for prayers and bed. I have a lot to do. Thank you for that wonderful dinner, and evening, Henry. It will be hard to fast after that. Oh well, just the discipline I need…"

Father hugged Jenny and then Henry. He made his way to the door and turned on the interior light. "Good night," Father said, just before he closed the door.

Jenny and Henry turned and looked out at the valley before them again. Suddenly, the light cast by the prayer house went off. Henry turned to see just the dim glow of a candle inside.

Just as suddenly, the heavens seemed to blossom with millions more stars. Henry and Jenny squeezed each other ever more tenderly.

"We were out there somewhere spinning around with our angels, Henry. It seems like it was all a dream. I wish we had memory of seeing our angels, like Father does. I am starting to dream more about that… I see us holding hands and spinning around somehow… it's still so vague…"

"It's all so incredibly amazing… not only our dying, our guardian angels and returning back to life on earth, but just the magnitude and wonderment of it all… Human beings with the gift of sight, hearing and touch, love… it's all so overwhelming and to think the universe has no beginning or end. Our conception of God is so limited and restricted by our finite minds…" Henry's words trailed off.

"In moments like this, it's easy to sense the divine nature of God in everything; so huge, magnanimous, almighty…so utterly overwhelming."

Coco nudged Henry's hand which was hanging loosely at his side. It startled him. He patted his friend.

"I wonder if Julean and James are looking down on us?"

"I wonder about that, too, Jenny. So often I feel her presence."

"That's good. That's how it should be. Our loved ones are always a part of us, even though we feel a void when they go."

"That's another thing, our memory and how we can retain the past and bring it to life to help ease the sorrow of their passing…"

"And the power to choose our thoughts… to remember the loving thoughts and to let go of the others," added Jenny.

"Yes, only when love is present is it real and touches God's heart… everything else is just our earthly thinking, for better or worse…"

"Oh, my gosh! How did we get so philosophical and lofty all of a sudden?"

"It's moments like this, Jenny, when I realize we are all at one with the Divine."

CHAPTER EIGHTY NINE

For all of February and most of March, Henry and Jenny went about their daily living. Henry was still involved with the gallery most days and Jenny was slowly getting back into her routine, as well. Henry knew Jenny needed time to mourn and let her life slowly come together again. For the most part it seemed as if Henry and Jenny had entered into a courting period in which they began to know each other even more intimately. They both desired one another but had made the decision to wait. But to wait for what…?

Since Jenny returned from Ottawa, neither brought up the topic of marriage. Jenny thought perhaps Henry avoided this subject as it was too soon after James' passing. But three months had elapsed and still Henry hadn't brought it up. Jenny wondered if perhaps she should. Maybe he no longer wanted to marry. He had been talking quite a bit about supporting the missionary work that his friend was doing.

All such thinking, however, was about to change.

It was the first week of April and a chinook was moving into the prairies from Alberta. The weather for most of March was very cold but with the news of this forecast and evidence of it warming in the last couple of days lifted everyone's spirits. It showed on people's faces and how they greeted one another. The hibernation season would soon be over.

Jenny was gazing out into her backyard when the phone rang. She knew it would be Henry. He called at pretty much the same time each day and was as dependable as clockwork… but not always…

"Hi Honey, I bet you were standing by the kitchen window looking at your back yard and visualizing it filled with all the beautiful flowers."

"See, I am as predictable as you. I was just thinking that it would be you calling as you do so at this same time each day."

"Well now, I better change my pattern… wouldn't want to be taken for granted. Perhaps what I have to say will get you guessing again."

"And what could that be, Henry?"

"There's something I want to show you that will lift your heart to the highest height. It's something filled with so much wonderment that it will lift you instantly off your feet…"

"Now you have my interest, Henry. I'm very intrigued. What is it that you want to show me?"

"It's something that must be seen just at the crack of dawn. This Friday is April 1st and the sun rises at six forty nine. So we have to be at a certain location at least an hour before…"

"Henry, April 1st is April Fool's Day… are you going to play a prank on me?"

"Yeah, that's right! Friday is April Fool's Day. That makes it all the better! Yes, it will be a lighthearted celebration, indeed!"

HENRY YAWNED AS he drove into the city to pick up Jenny. At precisely five a.m. Henry pulled up in front if Jenny's home. Her outside light was on. Just as Henry was about to get out, he noticed the living room light go out and the front door open. Henry's heart raced just at the sight of her silhouette. But even more so, Henry's heart pounded in anticipation of what was about to happen.

Jenny ran to the SUV and opened the door and hopped in. She turned to Henry and with her most serious stare and tone said, "Henry, are you certain this isn't an April Fool's joke?"

"Jen, I am so sorry, I got my dates mixed up. It's actually tomorr—"

Jenny punched him in the shoulder, "Please don't keep me in suspense any longer! I've been racking my mind trying to think what you want to show me."

"Fasten your seat belt, Jenny. You will soon know."

Jenny leaned over and kissed Henry on the cheek before she fastened up. Henry pulled away and made his way to Albert Street and then headed north. Jenny kept looking at Henry to anticipate where he was going to stop but he went straight through the city. Once on the outskirts, he took the turn off ramp to Lumsden and Saskatoon.

"Henry, where on earth are you going? Not back to your acreage?"

"No, not quite, about five miles more and we will be there."

At exit A, Henry turned off the main highway and headed down a gravel road. It was clear of all snow as were much of the fields. Henry was amazed at how much snow had melted in the last few days.

Just a mile or so before Tragarva, a small town just outside of Regina, Henry and Jenny saw the lights of several cars in a field. It looked eerie. Henry slowed his truck and muttered, "That must be them—"

"Who?" Jenny exclaimed.

"You'll see…"

Jenny turned to Henry and punched him again. "Don't be so cruel! Tell me!"

Henry chuckled and turned off the gravel road onto the field. At least seven people were working on something and their car lights were positioned to light up what they were working on.

"What is going on…Henry?"

Suddenly, Jenny knew what was happening as they pulled up nearer to the site. "Oh, Henry we are not going to go up in a hot air balloon, are we?"

"We're going to fly high today, Sweetheart."

"Oh, my gosh, Henry!"Jenny shrieked. "I can't…ooh, Henry, I just can't!"

"Yes, you can, Jenny…" It reminded Henry of the little nursery rhyme, *The Little Engine That Could* and the words he repeated, *I think I can, I think I can,* that early morning he was rushing Julean to the hospital.

"Jenny, did I ever tell you of the time I delivered Justin?"

Jenny wasn't listening. She was staring intently at the deflated balloon.

Henry got out of the car and made his way over to someone that was already approaching him. Jenny saw them shake hands and whispered, "Oh my dear guardian angel help me, I don't know if I can get in that basket."

Henry and the other man approached the SUV on Jenny's side. She rolled down the window.

"Morning. You're Jenny, right?'

"Yes, I'm Jenny, and a terrified Jenny, at that."

"I'm Sam, Jenny, and believe me there's nothing to worry about. It's very safe and once you lift off it will be the most exhilarating experience of a life time. Trust me."

"Oh, Sam…how high will it go?" Jenny wanted to know.

"As high as you want. There is a limit of course. But we can stay low if you wish, but I guarantee you that once you start ascending, you will want to go higher. You're in for a heavenly ride."

The word, heavenly struck a chord. It gave her a sense of security.

"We are all set to start inflating the balloon. We would like to have you and Henry up in the air before the sun rise. To see the sun come up, Jenny, will take your breath away. It's a spectacular sight."

Jenny saw several men hold the balloon open at its neck and start up an inflator fan. The sight of this immense balloon inflating took Jenny's breath away. It was as if the balloon came to life; the fabric billowing slowly lifted off the ground, air easing into its edges and rippling through to its tip. "Oh my God, please help me." She felt her heart rise along with her stomach. She put both of her hands to her mouth and shook her head.

Henry came to the door, "Come on, honey, I told you this would lift your heart and sweep you off your feet!"

"Oooh, Henry…" Jenny gasped, her breath hanging in the cool air.

Henry held the door open and gestured for her to come out. Sam had a huge smile on his face and offered his hand to help her down from the high SUV. Slowly, Jenny shifted in her seat and swung her legs to the opening of the door and stepped down on the frost covered stubble. The balloon was growing enormously in front of them. Henry had to admit his heart was racing as well but tried hard to conceal it and avoided speaking to cover any nervousness in his voice.

Once the balloon was half full, the men attached the basket and burner. As soon as the burner was fired up, the balloon expanded more rapidly.

It was spellbinding to watch this huge monster grow and lift off the ground. Henry and Jenny had seen hot air balloons up in the sky but not at this close range. They never would have believed it was this gigantic. They looked like ants beside it. Henry estimated that it took up more space than a fifty by one hundred foot city lot.

"Wow. It's taking the shape of a million watt light bulb!"

Sam chuckled over Henry's analogy, "They get a lot bigger than this one, Henry."

"Is the material fire proof?" asked Jenny cautiously.

"It is coated with a chemical substance," replied Sam. "Once the balloon is inflated with hot air, it's very fire proof and safe, Jenny."

Sam pointed to the pilot and added, "Don has been flying balloons for over 12 years. He's very skilled and takes your safety and enjoyment as the prime consideration. You are in excellent hands."

Sam's reassuring words and calm voice was soothing and instilled confidence in both Jenny and Henry.

"Will it be cold up there; maybe I should have worn something warmer?" Jenny asked, her nervousness chilled her, adding to the brisk, cool air she was feeling.

"You will be fine. It's not any colder up there than here and in fact, you feel warmer as the heat from the inside of the balloon radiates out towards you."

Jenny grabbed Henry's arm and hugged it.

The balloon was fully inflated and upright. It pulled on the basket which was still firmly anchored to the ground.

"Oh, my gosh," Jenny muttered in anticipation of getting into what appeared to be no more than an oversized picnic basket!

Don came over and Sam introduced him to Henry and Jenny.

"This is a perfect morning for a flight," said Don, "just a slight breeze and we'll be up there just in time to see the sun come up."

Don climbed into the basket and motioned Henry and Jenny to follow.

Jenny pulled back on Henry's arm as he stepped forward. If the truth be known Henry was every bit as frightened as Jenny. Bravely, he muttered, "It will be okay, Jen... let's go for it."

Somehow those daring words instilled courage into Jenny's trembling body. Henry climbed in first and then helped Jenny from inside the basket and Sam helped lift her from the outside.

The basket was made ideally for four people. Henry looked around for some kind of seat belt or life jacket or parachute but there was none; only ropes and a railing on the basket to hold on to. Jenny placed one hand on a rope and the other hand tightly gripped onto Henry's arm.

Sam and another man began to free the basket from the anchors. There was a sudden loud blast as the torch was turned on startling Henry and Jenny. Yellow flames emitted from the burner snarled into the interior of the balloon like crazed snake tongues.

The roar of the burner was deafening and gave Henry and Jenny a momentary respite from their apprehensiveness. Before their fear could regain its foothold they were surprised as the earth seemed to fall away from them. They had both braced themselves to shoot off the ground in an upward, driving thrust, but instead it felt motionless; surreal. They wouldn't have even known that they were rising, if it weren't for the image of Sam waving and the cars on the field growing smaller and smaller.

Within minutes they had ascended high into the brisk morning air. Soon they would see the rising sun from that perspective before the men on the ground. Their anxiety and foreboding was turning into a feeling of exhilaration that neither had felt before.

The sky above the eastern horizon was catching more and more light. Streaks of red, pink and orange slowly overcame the dark blue and purple of the twilight sky. As Henry and Jenny drank in this breathtaking display of radiant colours, suddenly, there was a deafening silence. The pilot turned off the burner. He had reached the height he wanted. Although they were drifting with the wind, it seemed as if they were standing still; suspended and caught in a thrilling feeling of awe.

Henry leaned over the edge of the basket with a smile he hadn't felt since that day he had met Jenny. He shook his head as they glided, silently, weightlessly, serenely through the sky and recalled those precious memories. He had retrieved his bike from Mr. Engelmann's store after walking Jenny home. He felt now like he did then speeding down the road passing 13th, 14th and 15th Avenues in a flash, taking the long way home. Memories flooded back of gazing into Jenny's eyes that first moment at the store; how beautiful she was and how wonderful it was to hold her hand. Elation had soared through him as he pedaled along. He recalled vividly how it had felt like he was in a hot air balloon, instead of on his bike, coasting over the streets and intersections, fuelled by the torch in his heart!

Perhaps, Henry thought, this was why he had decided to take Jenny on this memorable adventure…

"Henry," Jenny gasped, breaking him out of his reverie…"This is absolutely wonderful! I feel like I'm floating in the sky!"

"I always knew you were an angel!"

"Look, the sun is coming up!" Jenny exclaimed excitedly.

Henry let go of the rope and turned to catch an orange slice of sun peek over the horizon and begin to burn into the edge of the earth. Rays shot upward and then down towards them and down still further as the sun ascended. The dark snow-covered fields came to life, reflecting a kaleidoscope of colours. Shadows scampered in all directions with no place to hide. Farms that dotted the landscape as tiny twinkles of light suddenly lit up.

The scene before Jenny was so breathtaking, it broke into a memory of her stint on the other side. The heavenly, joyous feeling she had then was re-captured now. Hannah had been waiting for this moment to awaken her protégée's memory of when Jenny had stood next to Henry and Father Engelmann before the brilliant tunnel of light. The memory intermingled now in Jenny's vision along with the blazing sun as it grew brighter and brighter into the morning sky…

Jenny could no longer contain her bubbling excitement as she stood next to her first love. Closing her eyes as the warmth of the rising sun caressed her face, she allowed the full impact of the memory to invade her mind. There she was, with Henry and Father Engelmann at the gates of Heaven, bathed in a brilliant light. In her mind, Jenny saw her eyes sparkle and flash as she turned to Father and said, "Our guardian angels brought us here to pick you up.

Perhaps you will marry us before we enter heaven, or perhaps after. A heavenly marriage would be so wonderful…"

"I'm sorry to say, Jenny, marriage in heaven does not exist."

"But, Father, maybe, just maybe, a rule can be broken. Henry and I have desired this for so long, that perhaps even the good Lord will make an exception."

"Yes," Father admitted. "The Lord does remind us in Isaiah 55:9, 'As the heavens are higher than the earth, so are My ways higher than your ways, and My thoughts than your thoughts.'"

"See, there you are, anything is possible with God!" Jenny blurted…

Suddenly, Jenny was pulled from her vision as she felt Henry take her hand now in his and raise it before him. He gazed lovingly into Jenny's glistening blue eyes and, as if they were back standing on the doorsteps to heaven, Henry asked the words Jenny had longed and yearned to hear over the years…

"Jenny, will you marry me…?"

Tears of ecstasy streamed down Jenny's cheeks as Henry slipped a narrow gold band onto her finger next to James' wedding ring and she cried, "Yes!…yes!…Yes!"

Their spirits soared with love and affection; the sun glowed brighter than even the dazzling tunnel of light. Laughter, buoyant cries of exultation effervesced into the celestial atmosphere. The balloon began to spin!

For a moment, the pilot thought he had lost control of his craft. If only the unseen were visible, he would have known that the sudden, rapid rotation of the balloon was due to Hannah's wings flapping so exuberantly in sympathy with Jenny's over joy!

Don couldn't help overhearing the proposal and waited as long as he could before starting up the burner. The flames leaped into the balloon, lifting it once more into the glorious sky as if propelled by Henry and Jenny's love.

They no longer had to relive memories of that memorable summer of 1956. Their guardian angels had fulfilled their promises!

"Yes!" Henry shouted into the warming prairie sky, just as he had on the day he had met his first love…

"This, is what it feels like… to be in love!"

CHAPTER NINETY

T HE BALLOON RIDE and Henry's creative proposal was just what Henry and Jenny both needed to get their spirits soaring again. The next day Jenny woke in panic.

"My gosh, we are getting married in just two months! There is so much to do! What will I wear? Will Father David agree to have the wedding ceremony in the garden in my yard? Where will we live? In my home or Henry's, or both? And what about the women's group to discuss family and marriage concerns? Should I start it up before or after we get married?" Jenny flung off the sheets and dashed into the kitchen, got a pen and paper and began making a list.

It was only six-thirty. She would wait until seven before calling Camilla; she would be up by then. She just had to tell someone she and Henry were getting married!

"Oh thank you, dear God for restoring our lives and turning everything into such good!"

Who would they invite? She didn't know that many people in Regina. Perhaps it would just be family. "I know Matti would come and so would Chloe. But what about Thomas and Carlos? Yes, they should all be invited and of course J.J. and Nora… oh, the list is growing!"

Jenny got up and twirled around in the kitchen, her eyes sparkling with joy and love in her heart!

"Oh thank you guardian angels for bringing us together!"

And what about Peter and his wife and family? Yes, they should be invited, too. She recalled Father Engelmann's words: "Yes, forgiveness is the path to reconciliation, peace, freedom, and even friendship. All of these elements of healing are ever present if only we choose to be open enough to let such Christ centered thoughts into our hearts and minds."

"Will the garden have enough room for all these people and Henry's family?" Jenny thought out loud. "It's a big back yard... yes, it will work. I just know it will. It will be so wonderful to have everyone in the garden ablaze with flowers and butterflies in the air!"

A surge of happiness swept through Jenny. She felt as though she were back in the hot air balloon soaring in the heavens. She just had to call someone. She would have last night but she and Henry were talking and gazing at the stars in his SUV until almost midnight.

"Yes, they are two hours ahead of us..." she blurted.

Jenny went to the phone and dialed the number.

"Hello, this be the—"

"Oh, Matti," Jenny cut in excitedly. "It's Jen...guess what? Henry and I are getting married!"

It took a few moments for Matti to orient herself and figure out who was calling and for her ear to stop ringing and...finally she squealed, "Whoopee! Jen, the wish in your heart for such a long time be coming true... I be so happy for you!" Matti began to cry out of joy for her dear friend.

"And guess how Henry proposed to me!!"

"He went down on bended knee and pleaded for your hand in marriage?"

"Yes, he did ask, but where were we when he did...?"

"Oh, Jen, don't you be telling me he take you to heaven and back again—"

"You're so close, Matti! Yesterday morning he picked me up around five o'clock in the morning. It was still dark outside and we drove out of the city and then off the highway into a field—"

"Good Lord, Jen, where the man be takin' you... sounds so

mysterious to me. My heart already be jumping out of its cage just listenin' to your sharing."

"There were several cars in a circle with their lights on shining at something in the field. It almost looked like aliens had landed out there... Matti, it was so spooky!"

"Chills or someting are running up and down my spine... what be happenin', Jen?"

"You would never guess—Matti, the men were preparing to inflate a hot air balloon. Henry made arrangements to take me up in the balloon and that is where he proposed to me!"

"Oh, my sweet Jesus. What that man be thinking!? I remember seeing one of them balloons floating up in the sky with a little basket holding a bunch of people...there be no way he get me up there. And you went into that little basket?"

"I was so frightened at first, I thought I would faint. As soon as I got in, the pilot started the burner and away we went."

"I can just see you, holding onto that man of yours for dear life... ain't that so?"

"Yes, but it's so exhilarating and serene you soon lose your fears. And just as we were high in the sky the sun began to rise. Henry and I thought we had died and gone to heaven again. What a breathtaking sight to see the sun come up and change the colours in the sky and fields. The artist in Henry held him spellbound the entire time. I think he may have forgotten all about proposing to me."

"Now that where you're wrong, honey child. There be not'ing in the world that could distract Henry from loving and wanting you as his bride every moment."

"It was all so romantic and beautiful, Matti. The landing brought us back to the reality of what we were doing, though. It was bumpy and scary and thrilling, all at once, if you know what I mean. When the basket landed on the ground it fell on its side and Henry and I fell on top of one another. My heart is still soaring!"

"Mine be up there with yours, Jen. There be no one more deserving of happiness and that man be just right for you. Just the way he ogled you and kissed you at the hospital... Oh, Lord...that be powerful!"

"I am going to call Camilla right after we hang up and see if she can go shopping with me this Saturday. I thought I would get a new dress and shoes…nothing fancy, but pretty."

"You lookin' good in just about anyt'ing, Jen… tell me, when is the big day or are you two still deliberatin' on that?"

"We were thinking about July 6. That's the day when we first met, but it's too long to wait. We decided on June 3rd. It's spring, new life, new start, summer begins, the flowers are in full bloom, the monarchs are back—"

"Perfect time for a wedding, I have to agree…" Matti chimed in.

"We are hoping to have the Mass at the church and then do the marriage ceremony in my back yard garden."

"I recall your yard, Jen, its paradise. That be the perfect place to carry out your vows…it will be so beautiful!"

"What will make it all the more beautiful, Matti, is if you, Thomas, Carlos, Ramon and Charles, all come with J.J. and his family. You are all family to me. It would make me so happy and make the wedding just perfect with your presence."

"Whoopee, Jen. I be comin' if I have to walk all the way. This be one wedding that I will never forget. I am so happy for you, I be holding on the table to keep me from floating in the sky without even being in a hot air balloon!"

"Oh, Matti, you are such a dear friend. Let Thomas and everyone else know. I am going to call Nora right after I speak with Camilla. I hope J.J. takes the news kindly."

"Jen, he be changin' just like his daddy. He becomin' one sweet man. Even coming home in time for dinner with his family. We all still be sittin' together and have a great ol' time. Have some lively discussions and all. Why I can honestly say, we becomin' one big happy family. I just know J.J. be happy for his momma. You done a good job, Jenny, that's for sure…"

As soon as Jenny got off the phone with Matti she called Camilla, Nora, then Chloe and finally her friends Mable and Joan. They talked over much the same as Jen had talked with Matti. Everyone was elated over the news.

Her last call was to Henry. That would get her day started off perfectly.

"Hi sweetheart, I was about to call you. So, have you come down to earth yet?"

"Oh Henry, only you could have thought up something so wonderfully creative. I was so frightened and excited to go up in that balloon. I thought I would get dizzy but there was no vertigo whatsoever."

"It's an amazing experience, just being suspended in the atmosphere like that going gently with the wind. I didn't feel any sensation of movement whatsoever."

"Yes, so true… just so exhilarating. I'm glad you just went ahead and booked the flight; I might have chickened out and missed out not only on the experience, but being proposed to up in the heavens!"

"Exactly my thoughts, honey. The only thing is, I don't need to be up in a balloon to feel that I'm in heaven. Just being near you does it all the time!"

"Oh, Henry, I love you so much."

"I love you more, sweetheart."

"I called Camilla this morning and we are going out to start shopping for what I am going to wear for the wedding. We have several shops in mind and there is a new wedding boutique that just opened up which we want to check out. I don't want anything fancy, just something special for you."

"Was Camilla surprised?"

"No, she was expecting this, just thought you would have asked sooner. But I told her you wanted to just let me be for awhile after coming back from Ottawa. Both your timing and the way you did it was perfect! It just gave me that lift that I needed. I almost flew out of bed this morning."

"I can't wait to be in bed with you every morning! There will be days we may not even get out of bed!"

"I can see that happening and as Matti would say, 'that's for sure!'" And by the way, I called Matti and Chloe and Nora, as well, to tell them the news and also to invite them to the wedding as we discussed last night. We will have to rent some rooms at a hotel. I think J.J. and his family can stay here with me—"

"So who else is coming?"

"Well, the only family I really have is J.J. and his family and I do consider Matti, Thomas, Charles, Carlos and those who have spouses to come as well."

"We have a huge house, Jenny, and can easily make room for them. I think they might enjoy staying on the farm for a few days."

"Oh, Henry that sounds wonderful and yes, Matti and Thomas

and Carlos especially, would love to see the Poustinia. Oh, I can just see Matti's expression when she walks into the prayer house. Why she'll fall to her knees straightaway and give thanks to Jesus!"

"In fact, if Father isn't using it, she can even stay there." Henry offered.

"Yes, she might at that. I would be a little nervous being all alone down there, but she just might enjoy it. We'll see. Now, that only leaves Chloe and Robbie. I might be able to make room for them. Chloe could sleep with me and Robbie on the couch or I could rent an inflatable mattress."

"If not, I'm sure the both of them could stay here as well. I could easily convert one of the rooms in my painting studio as a temporary bedroom. I see no problem, Jen."

"Perhaps you can check with Father Engelmann to see if we can have the marriage ceremony in my backyard garden after the Mass."

"I think that can work, too. So, we are still planning a small wedding; just immediate family and your extended family in Ottawa?"

"Yes, we could go larger if you want. I think there is enough room in the garden for just the immediate families if that's okay with you. It may be a little crowded…"

"That's fine, Honey. I just want to get married and hold you in my arms forever. I'm sure Eddy and Coreena will come. Gary should be calling or writing back to me if he can come and the only other two couples will be Julean's parents and her Aunt and Uncle Jacob. If we want to have more friends and relatives, we can always hold a reception at the café at some future time. But I think having the ceremony in your garden couldn't be any more beautiful and I'm certain it can easily accommodate all the people we plan on inviting." After a pause, Henry added, "On that day, I especially want to fill the angel's basket in thanks for you!"

"And leave some room in there for my thanksgiving flowers as well, for you my dear, sweet, Henry, who I love with all my heart."

"And I love you all the more."

CHAPTER NINETY ONE

THE MONTH OF April went by in a flash and the second week of May was almost over. The excitement that Henry and Jenny were feeling was palpable. Everything about their entire being exuded a radiance that was indescribable. When they walked hand in hand it was as if they were being lifted by each other's angels. Their eyes sparkled and shone like diamonds, their faces radiated the sun and an aura surrounded them that captured the essence of what God gifted mankind with when that loving attraction pierces their hearts.

Henry had gone through this before when he had courted Julean. He couldn't wait until the wedding night. His passion level was almost uncontrollable at that time and was now once again the same. He desired Jenny more than anything and he counted the minutes until he could finally hold her and express his love completely. Jenny felt the same and they were glad they made this choice.

There was a special excitement that would be hard to describe waiting for the wedding night. The discipline that was required just made it all the more rewarding. With each advancing day there was an anticipation of fulfilling their desire for one another. The attraction was so strong and building up to a crescendo like a fine piece of music; the actual fulfilling of their hearts' desire.

Henry thought age and maturity would give him more control but passion springs eternal in the heart of man. Every day, Henry wished their special day was today!

Everything was working out as they had planned. J.J., his family and the staff at the Hamilton household were all flying to Regina on the company jet the day before the wedding. J.J. and his family would stay at Jenny's home, as well as Chloe and her father. All the rest would be hosted by Henry at his farm. Camilla was going keep Matti at their home, but when Matti heard about the Poustinia and where Father Engelmann prayed, she just had to see it.

Henry parked his car outside of the Nunnery care home and made his way up the walk. One of the residents opened the door. Father was at the care home to say Mass but also to submit an article for the monthly newsletter that was still thriving and growing in the community.

"Hello, Henry, it's so nice to see you."

It was Edith. Henry always found it hard to believe that this ninety four year old woman was so agile and healthy. Henry had to agree with Father's tender description of her. She looks like a raisin good enough to eat. Her wrinkles had character and her kindness was indeed edible.

"Hi, Edith, it's very nice to see you up and around. Is Father in the Chapel?"

"He was, but he is expecting you in the sun room. I hear you are getting married to that lady we prayed for. Oh, how your story touched our hearts. It brought back so many memories..." Edith's words trailed off.

Henry could see by the look in Edith's eyes that his assumption that love springs eternal was dead on.

"Yes, thanks to your prayers, Edith, she has been restored by the Lord and in perfect health. I can't wait to marry her."

"It sends shivers of excitement up and down my spine, Henry. It reminds me of the day Sid and I got married. Oh my, what a special day... I can only imagine how you are feeling. I am so happy things have worked out for you and that we were a part of this miraculous miracle."

"Ah, here is my adopted son. Come, Henry, sit in the sun and look at God's creation. I have never seen the courtyard look more beautiful. The perennials are up and the annuals are all blooming. It's wonderful to see the residents so lively and healthy and able to walk in the court yard. It's all a blessing."

Henry came to Father's side and patted his shoulder as he was still sitting. He looked outside and had to agree with Father's observation. The courtyard looked dazzling with brilliant colour and at that moment the sun came around the corner and struck radiance into each plant.

"So the wedding plans are all coming along, Henry?"

"Yes everything is coming together. It will be a small wedding; just immediate family and few friends. We are very happy that you have agreed to have the Mass and ceremony in Jenny's back yard garden."

"It is always preferable to have the Mass and ceremony together because of the connection of the sacrament of matrimony with the Eucharist. After you and Jenny exchange vows not only do the two of you become one flesh but receiving communion, the body and blood of Christ, both you and Jenny form 'one body' in Christ. You and Jenny go forth as living examples, beacons if you will, of this spiritual relationship with each other and your Creator."

"That's beautiful Father, what more perfect way to seal our consent to one another and to make Jesus the centre and heart of our marriage."

Father nodded.

Henry continued, "We will set up a small altar beside the gazebo and we have already placed a cross above the entrance to Jenny's sanctuary." Henry paused, his eyes brightening. "Yes, Father, everything couldn't be more perfect."

"See, the Lord turns everything into good, Henry, but I have to say His plan, from the day Jenny was on the verge of dying until now and all the happenings that have occurred have me awestruck. What a good God we have!"

"So, only eight more days until the wedding, Father. You know me better than I know myself. I don't need to tell you how much I am looking forward to June 3, 1989! We thought about marrying on July 6th, the day we met in your store... but we both decided it's just too long of a wait!"

Father looked compassionately into Henry eyes and knew only

too well his protégé's struggle. He simply nodded. "Yes, I think the third of June would be a fine day for a wedding."

"It's funny how I was so worried about taking off the ring that Julean had given me should Jenny and I marry and it all worked out so beautifully. We both decided to keep our wedding rings and simply give each other a narrow gold band to slide beside the ones that our previous spouses gave to us."

"See, Henry, once again God has worked so beautifully in your lives. That is a wonderful idea and allows each of you to cherish the love and memory of the one you spent your life with. In Jenny's case it may only be in the last few months of her marriage, but Jenny is a rare lady. She knows how to forget and let go of thoughts that are not loving... love is the only thing that counts in the last analysis."

Henry nodded. "Yes, Father, love is the only thing that counts and has any lasting value... or I should say eternal value. You have taught me well."

Father nodded. "Tell me, Henry, how are the children adjusting to Jenny?"

"The girls love her but Justin is still having trouble. He and Julean were so close, Father. But he'll come around...I know my son. That's one of the subjects Jenny wants to raise in the women's group that she is organizing. She thought perhaps one of the other ladies may have gone through a similar situation or know of others who might have. But like I said, I'm sure Justin will come around and I know, there is no-one that can't help but fall in love with Jenny.

"Lauren has been around Jenny more than Allison, but I'm surprised how quickly Allison and Jenny hit it off. Allison's heart is similar to Julean's, and to Jenny's, for that matter. They look more at the present and making things work out for the good...much like our good Lord...right!?"

"Have you decided where you are going to live once married?"

"Yeah, we're going to live at the farm, however, Jenny would like to keep her home to conduct the ladies women's group. So she might continue to come in once or twice a week. There is the possibility that Carlos, one of the landscapers in Ottawa who used to look after her parents' estate, and his wife might be interested in moving to Regina and live in her home and look after the yard and upkeep."

Father nodded, the wrinkles in the corner of his eyes smiling along with his benevolent smile. "Yes, Henry, God is good and great. He truly does turn all things into the good for those that trust Him."

A peaceful silence fell over the sun room. Henry had always loved these moments chatting with his mentor from the time he worked at the store, either inside across the counter or sitting out back on the old grey crates. What a deep friendship they had built over the years. Unbidden tears surfaced in Henry's eyes just thinking on it. He was so happy that God restored Father's life.

Henry gazed outside at the flowers in the courtyard; he didn't want to think of that day his beloved teacher would go to the Lord.

CHAPTER NINETY TWO

Henry's SUV was filled to capacity for first time since he bought it two years ago. Matti sat beside him while the rest of the guests sat in the three back rows. Lauren, Justin and Allison drove in their car and were just up ahead. It was shortly after one p.m. and they were all heading to Jenny's home for the wedding celebration.

Everyone was in such a joyous, festive mood. Jokes about marriage and what goes on in the bedroom on that special day were flying back and forth in the vehicle. Although Henry chuckled along with everyone, he didn't really have a clue as to what he was laughing about. His mind was fully occupied with his impending marriage to his teenage sweetheart. Thirty three years ago they had met and with the help of their angels they were now finally coming together in Holy Matrimony.

The number thirty-three caught Henry's attention. That was the age Jesus was when He started His ministry. For thirty three years He prepared for this life's mission and in a way, so too, did Henry. He was about to wed another love of his life and their angels were true to this day: angel promises fulfilled.

"Thank you Gabriel and Hannah," Henry whispered…

"You be saying someting, Henry?"

"Oh, just talking to myself, Matti. I was thinking how our guardian angels brought Jenny and me together thirty three years ago, and how after all these years, true to their promise, they've brought us to our wedding day."

"You can always count on your guardian angel, Henry. They be there for you day and night…they be your best friend. And… oh your prayer house in the valley be so beautiful. I felt angels flying all around, that's for sure."

Henry just nodded. He began to think about the guardian angel prayer that he and Jenny shared…

> *Oh Angel of God*
> *My guardian dear*
> *To whom God's love*
> *Commits me here.*
>
> *Ever this day*
> *Be at 'our' sides—*

Matti broke in to Henry's thoughts. "I just can't wait for you two to be married; you both love each other so much. That's why the good Lord took you both to heaven and back. He wants to let you know that this be a marriage He ordained in heaven and now blessing on earth. Why He even brought back and prepared one holy man to carry out the wedding vows!"

"Yeah, I'm so happy that Father is here to perform the ceremony."

"You two be an example of how young folks be loving one another. I see when you come at Christmas time how you just let Miss Jenny be free to love the man she be married to. You respect the man's home. I just know how much you love Jen and yet, I could see you be prepared to let her go if she decides to stay. That be a deep love, Henry, that you and Jenny be sharing. Oh, I'm gettin' so excited, I hope there be a washroom nearby and nobody using it, I can just feel I may be in trouble…"

"You just may be, Matti," Thomas said from the back seat, "and there may not be a rose bush outside to hide behind!"

They all laughed.

CHAPTER NINETY THREE

"QUICKLY, HOLD MY hand. They are waiting for us."

Henry turned to Jenny and took her hand as they stood at the edge of the deck at the back of their house on Hill Avenue. Their eyes were filled with burning fires of love, overflowing with happiness. In the huge back yard before them was a small gathering of family and friends who had come to witness their marriage vows.

Standing in the archway of the gazebo was Father Engelmann dressed in a white robe and his usual saintly smile. His arms were folded and he held a red book in his hand pressing against his chest. This was one ceremony above all others that he considered very special. Who would have thought that he would be here, officiating at this marriage, which itself was nothing short of miraculous? He thanked the Lord for restoring his life to allow him to serve Him longer and be present for this happy occasion.

Just a few months ago, Father had visited Jenny in the Santa Maria Home. He had given her the last rites and was certain that he would never see Jenny alive again and there she stood with her husband-to-be in all her stunning glory. But as he saw many times in his lifetime, the Lord works in mysterious and powerful ways.

Rumour in the hospital had it that an instant healing had occurred when Henry entered Jenny's room and kissed her moments before she died.

"It was like a fairy tale; as if Prince Charming, so filled with love, entered her room and gave the kiss of life to the Sleeping Beauty," maintained Nurse Johnson. "I've never seen such a tender kiss and will never again during the rest of all my days. There she was, on the edge of death, moments away, in and out of a coma, and yet so filled with a desire to kiss her first love one last time... She managed to kiss Henry as if it were their very first kiss! Where she got the strength and passion from only heaven knows. I no longer saw a sickly woman or a grieving man, but rather two lovers deeply in love. It was the most incredible scene I have ever witnessed!"

Each time Nurse Johnson told the story, she embellished it all the more. Soon it was the talk of the town: Prince Henry and Princess Jenny and how they conquered death.

The doctors were dumbfounded, as well. Just one of those unexplainable, instantaneous remissions. When Dr. Kreake had examined Jenny the morning of her transfer to palliative care at the Grey Nun's Hospital, her X-rays had shown tumours throughout her body. It was a miracle in itself that she lived as long as she had. She was already entering into a coma, the final stage just before death. Many of her organs had already shut down. It was truly an amazing, unbelievable, miraculous, occurrence.

In any case, Dr. Kreake couldn't have been happier to be there, as he sat in the second row of chairs in the beautiful garden. He had seen enough sickness and sadness in his occupation that he welcomed this happy event with open arms. He was thrilled they had invited him to the special occasion.

Next to Dr. Kreake sat Eddy and his wife, Coreena. And next to them were Peter and his wife, Angie, John McBryne and Henry's closest friend Gary. Who would have thought that Eddy, Peter and John, Henry's most hated enemies would become his friends and invited to his wedding. Father Engelmann's words that anything is possible through Christ rang true... "Forgiveness is the path to reconciliation, peace, freedom, and even friendship. All of these elements of healing are ever present if only we choose to be open enough to let such Christ-like thoughts into our hearts and minds."

Just in front of Dr. Kreake in the front row were Jeremy and his family. Camilla was thrilled to see her mother and Henry get married. He would now be her father-in-law as well as her step-father. Tears of joy rolled down her cheeks as she waited for them to be pronounced husband and wife.

Henry was so pleased to see Julean's parents and Aunt and Uncle seated beside his family and their expression of happiness for him and his bride to be. Jenny, too, was elated to see J.J. and his family present, as well. Everything couldn't be more perfect.

Jenny and Henry glowed as they stood on the deck. They were blessed to retain some of the youthful transformation they had gone through as they were about to enter the tunnel of light. This blessing and the fact that they were together again enhanced even more the youthful, joyful look on their faces. The outpouring of love they had for one another was palpable and the people gathered to witness this occasion couldn't be happier for them.

Like Henry and Jenny, Father also looked younger. However, with Father, it wasn't nearly as noticeable. He had been living such a saintly life for so long, he literally stopped aging years ago. At one hundred and one, he still looked to be in his seventies. He just never seemed to age externally or internally, only numerically.

Father beamed with a radiant smile. The sun streaming through the tall fir trees brightened his face still further. All the weariness was gone. He literally had died and gone to heaven and back again. Word had it that he was destined to live to the ripe old age of two hundred! And if one were able to see the unseen, standing directly behind Father was Zachariah nodding his head acknowledging that possibility; his wings concurring with a slight flutter.

Jenny looked so elegant and beautiful in her white dress as she stood by her man. She wore a small white hat with a veil that came just above her slightly turned up nose. She held a small bouquet of wild flowers in her left hand, while her right was firmly wrapped around Henry's. After her miraculous healing, her hair grew back in its original golden wheat colour and glistened as the mid-afternoon sun shone through the outer strands. Her cerulean blue eyes sparkled as she turned to Henry.

"I love you," Jenny whispered, with her sweetheart lips as she gazed into her future husband's eyes, just minutes away.

Tears of happiness welled in Henry's eyes. An expression of

great rapture had spread across his face. There were no words that could describe or capture the joy Henry held in his heart. He looked so handsome and distinguished in his dark navy suit. Blue was definitely his colour, it complimented perfectly with his white-grey beard and ruddy complexion.

Hidden below their attire, hanging at the ends of silver chains from around their necks, were the pewter angels resting warmly against their hearts. They were blessed that day Henry proposed to Jenny high in the heavens to see a bit more of what happened when they were on the other side. They still had no clear memory of their brief time at the edge of eternity, when the unseen became visible, however, they acknowledged that it was their guardian angels who brought them back together.

Their angels had completed their mission. Despite all the obstacles, the blankets of secrecy and the storms of life that came their way, since those memorable days of their youth were now gone. The angelic letters were delivered as promised and Henry and Jenny were now finally about to be wed. The beginning of a new life was at hand between two people who were never more deserving and in love.

And if one looked closely, the glowing aura around Henry and Jenny was not just from their radiant happiness. Rather, it was from the glow of both their guardian angels. Hannah and Gabriel stood excitedly behind their assigned charges. The protectors couldn't be happier as they watched on in their best shimmering white robes.

Hannah looked unspeakably lovely with a special garland of wildflowers in her hair. She picked them from one of the many meadows in heaven just for this occasion. She was so excited for her Jenny, she had difficulty containing herself. She felt certain she would dart away like a hummingbird at any moment.

A tear or two bedded Gabriel's eyes as he rested his hand on Henry's shoulder as he usually did, guiding him to his ultimate heart's desire— to be wed to his first love. Gabriel and Hannah were so elated that things finally worked out and that the wound to their earthlings' hearts which they helped inflict had been mended.

At that twinkling instant, however, the aura of happiness surrounding the blissful couple grew even brighter. Floating quietly in the background was the spirit of Julean, tears of gladness rolling gently down her radiant cheeks. She was elated that Henry and Jenny were about to be wed. If the truth were to be known about what had influenced the Lord more than anything else to restore the lives of Henry and his first love, was the pleading of Henry's dear wife. Overflowing with joy, Julean brought the tips of her fingers to her soft lips and then thrust a loving kiss out to them carrying a fervent prayer.

As Henry held Jenny's hand he felt Julean's presence along with the comforting words of her sweet voice whispering to him, "I wish you and your bride true happiness, Henry. Someday we shall all be united, again."

Jenny, too, felt James' presence beside her. He had given her the gift of freedom. He could have extended his life for awhile, perhaps, even years. Jenny would remember their time together and what he did for her in his dying days.

It was a gorgeous summer day, the first Saturday of June. The sky was clear from the horizon to the zenith and even the prairie wind relented and bowed to this Holy Matrimony. Only a slight breeze in the air, just enough to carry the scent and natural perfume given off by the numerous array of flowers and herbs, wafted throughout the garden.

The fence in back of the gazebo was covered in a blanket of green and flowering vines. The mixture of the honeysuckle, morning glory, rose and wisteria combined to give a profusion of colour as a backdrop for the wedding ceremony.

Not to be outdone, the wildflowers next to the gazebo were in full bloom setting the yard ablaze with colour. The lilac trees to the right and left of the deck had blossomed just in time for this glorious occasion and their scent mingled with that of the rest of the flowers.

The sound of cherubs laughing and rejoicing amongst the daisies could be heard as soft gusts in the gentle breeze. Their presence was revealed by tiny sparkles of sunlight on the tips of the bright poppies. The Angel of Thanksgiving's basket was especially full as there was so much to be thankful for. And no one as yet had noticed that the Angel of Thanksgiving's Mona Lisa expression had turned into a radiant happy smile, revealing her true heart's desire and answered prayer, as well…that Jenny and Henry be wed.

Jenny and Henry took a step in unison as they descended the

stairs of the deck onto the winding stone path gladdened with fragrant herbs strewn all about, especially thyme. The monarch butterflies suddenly took flight giving off a cornucopia and appearance of colourful little angels flitting about.

All eyes turned and looked across the sea of a breathtaking festival of incredibly coloured flowers, as the radiant couple made their way towards Father Engelmann.

When they were almost halfway there, Margaret Tearhorst began to sing her solo. Her angelic voice was perfect, for the perfect song, for the perfect couple: *True Love*.

> *"Well, I give to you and you give to me*
> *True love, true love,*
> *And on and on, it will always be,*
> *True love, true love."*

As Margaret sang, a hush fell for blocks around the neighbourhood. People stopped and listened, spellbound by this pure, clear, angelic voice giving honour and praise to this miraculous marriage. And then, as if heaven itself opened up, all the choirs of angels on high joined in on the chorus of this memorable song, on this unforgettable, momentous day:

> *"For you and I have a guardian angel*
> *on high with nothing to do,*
> *But to give to you and to give to me.*
> *Love, forever true."*

And as heaven and earth looked on and the angels on high hummed the melody, Henry, at long last, slipped the golden ring onto Jenny's finger, his gaze returned to hers for but a moment, before they tenderly embraced and their lips softly touched.

As they kissed, they began to sway in front of the gazebo. The ceremony halted as Father and those present, their eyes filled with joyful tears, watched Henry and Jenny in their own world, so in love, dance before them.

Father, so caught up in this moment of bliss, concluded the ceremony by saying, "I now pronounce you man and wife!"

In a burst of youthful, joyous, exuberance, Henry scooped

Jenny up off her feet, as if they were on the threshold of heaven itself… for theirs was a match made in heaven, a heavenly marriage now fulfilled on earth!

Henry twirled Jenny, his dear sweet bride round and round in his arms. They looked deeply and lovingly into each other's eyes, their lips met once more and for them, the world stopped spinning. All time stood still…

It was truly…love, forever true.

Future Book

THE ANGELIC LETTERS SERIES

THE HOUSE WHERE
ANGELS DWELL

1991–

HENRY K. RIPPLINGER
Best Selling Author of Pewter Angels

THE FOLLOWING IS A NOTE TO READERS

A Note To My Dear Readers

I<small>T WAS MID-JUNE</small>, 2005, when the inspiration came to me to write this epic series. Never would I have ever dreamed that I would still be writing on this same story. I thought in 2010, when I released the first book in the series, I had pretty well finished the story and each manuscript for the five books just required some editing and fine tuning.

Wow, was I wrong.

In between the release of each book I felt inspired to add to the original transcript. New characters came into the story seemingly out of nowhere only for me to discover down the road how much they played a part not only in advancing the story, creating more interest and depth but more importantly portraying further life lessons.

Since the release of book two, *Another Angel of Love*, the original manuscripts of the last three books have tripled in size. This placed an enormous pressure on me to keep up the pace of not only publishing, marketing, distributing the books and conducting book signing tours and events but to also to ensure the timely release of the next book. This worked out to be one book per year.

Initially, as indicated in the blurb of book one, *Pewter Angels*, this saga was intended to be a five book series and conclude with a one or two page epilogue describing briefly what happens to the main characters in the story. However, it seems to me that the Lord wants me to write a final book. What I thought was a two page epilogue has grown in my mind's eye to be another novel!

As I have barely started the sixth book, I know, considering all the challenges of book signing tours, marketing and introducing the series to a broader market it will take me one to two years to write the epilogue which I have titled: "*The House Where Angels Dwell.*"

I have now brought the story to a conclusion to give some closure and satisfaction to you the reader. At the present time I need to take some time off, recoup my energy and just enjoy the process of writing without undue pressure to produce another book. I can only ask for your patience and understanding. I encourage all of you to please join or check periodically my Facebook or blog on my web site: www.henryripplinger.com for updates of the sixth book and also news of signing events; dates and places. I also intend to do readings as time permits.

Thank you for giving me of your time, love, encouragement and loyal following of the Angelic Letters Series. It is my sincere hope that the contents have brought many hours of enjoyment and in some way enriched your lives. I am very grateful and appreciative of your support!

As always, I thank the Lord for the gift of this story. I am thankful daily for His inspiration and guidance through His angels and Holy Spirit and divine providence.

God bless,
Henry K. Ripplinger
February, 2014

About the Author

Henry Ripplinger is the bestselling author of *Pewter Angels, Another Angel of Love, Angel of Thanksgiving* and *The Angelic Occurrence,* the first four books in the six-book series "The Angelic Letters." The overwhelming response by readers to Henry's novels gives testimony to Henry's gifts as an author to write books that touch human hearts and offer direction to their lives.

Henry's empathetic abilities, combined with his lifelong experience and eclectic career as an educator, guidance counsellor, professional artist and businessman, prepared him to craft this inspirational, spirit-filled love story and indirectly realize his aspirations of writing a self-development book.

Henry is also one of Canada's foremost prairie artists. His work is on display at private and corporate collections across Canada, most notably in Saskatchewan, his home province, and can be seen in the critically acclaimed book, *If You're Not from the Prairie.*

As both author and artist, Henry communicates from the heart, painting pictures with words that are so vivid and real that readers can feel and visualize every aspect of their own lives intertwined with the lives of his beloved characters.

Henry resides with his wife in the panoramic valley setting of Lumsden, Saskatchewan, Canada.

Please e-mail Henry at: **henry@henryripplinger.com** or visit **www.henryripplinger.com** for more information about Henry's work and art. He would love to hear from you!

ALSO BY HENRY RIPPLINGER

PEWTER ANGELS
BOOK ONE OF THE ANGELIC LETTERS SERIES

*"He hath given his angels charge over thee; to keep thee
in all thy ways…In their hands they shall bear thee up:
lest thou dash thy foot against a stone."*

PSALM 91:11-12

The summer of 1956 starts out like any other summer for 15 year old Henry Pederson: hot, long and boring. That all changes when Jenny Sarsky, along with her guardian angel and her family move into the house three doors down. From the moment their eyes meet, an earthly attraction unites their hearts while the spiritual energy travelling the length of the gaze they share joins their souls—spinning a web of love that transcends time and Heaven itself.

Mr. Engelmann, an endearing and wise mentor living out the word of God, comes into Henry's life, providing him with powerful insights and valuable life lessons that carry strength, wisdom and hope.

Pewter Angels the first book of *The Angelic Letters Series*, starts Henry and Jenny and their families on an inspiring yet tumultuous journey through life's struggles and victories, and the miracle of deep, enduring love.

Pewter Angels will grab your heart, squeeze it
and hold it to the very last page.

ANOTHER ANGEL OF LOVE
BOOK TWO OF THE ANGELIC LETTERS SERIES

"God causes all things to work together for good to those who love God, to those who are called according to His purpose"

ROMANS 8:28

It was as if Jenny had vanished from the face of the earth. Two years after she and her family moved out of Henry's life, Henry still longs for her, their whirlwind romance gone from his life but not his heart. He was certain she would respond to his last letter, a pewter angel tucked inside —but there have been no letters, no phone calls. Nothing. A country apart, Henry and Jenny are unaware Jenny's parents have burned all the letters but the last... it is protected, it seems, by an angelic power.

Henry continues to rely on the love, support and powerful insights of his mentor Mr. Engelmann, and his secret plan to seek Jenny out sustains the hope that one day his love will return—until he meets Julean Carter.

But, is their new-found love deep enough and strong enough to overcome the heavenly touch that entwined Henry and Jenny's spirits when they first gazed into each others eyes?

Another Angel of Love...glows with moments of tenderness... deeply inspirational....will captivate the heart of every reader!

ANGEL OF THANKSGIVING
BOOK THREE OF THE ANGELIC LETTERS SERIES

This may be the single most moving book you will read this year—or in your life time.

Henry and Julean couldn't be happier. With a new baby, a new home and Henry's new job, everything is turning out perfectly for the young couple. Or is it? Henry can't seem to shake the memory of Jenny from his mind or the love he still feels for her. Little does he know, his wife is all-too-aware of Henry's hidden thoughts and feelings. Meanwhile, Father Engelmann, back from seminary school and creating a sensation as the new parish priest, is caught in the middle when both Henry and Julean confess to him about Jenny.

Will Jenny finally give in to James' persistent proposals, knowing that once married her chance to reunite with Henry would be gone forever? Spanning two decades, Angel of Thanksgiving takes the reader on an incredible journey of faith, hope and love. As we see Henry and Jenny's lives unfolding separately and so far apart, *will destiny bring them together again?*

Timeless Biblical themes as surrendering to God's will, forgiveness, and unconditional love are beautifully portrayed through unforgettable, real-life characters in this compelling, hard to put down novel.

Make a huge space in your heart before you begin to read Angel of Thanksgiving as it will quickly fill with love's beauty and wonder.

THE ANGELIC OCCURRENCE

BOOK FOUR OF THE ANGELIC LETTERS SERIES

Hailed by readers as one of the most inspiring works of fiction they have ever read, *The Angelic Letters* series is a story that is both riveting and life-changing...

After decades apart, Henry and Jenny's lives are poised to intersect yet again, when Henry's oldest son brings his new girlfriend home to meet the family. Bearing an unusual resemblance to Henry's first love, her name, Camilla, is not just unusual, it's also the same name Jenny had vowed to name her own daughter one day. Did Jenny get pregnant that fateful night in the park? Everything about Camilla seemed to confirm Henry's belief that she is Jenny's daughter.

As Henry struggles with this and other memories of his lost love, he also strives to pick up the pieces of his life after his wife Julean's untimely death. Can the lovely Ivania fill the void left by both Julean and Jenny? And what about Jenny herself? If only Henry knew that Jenny had been trapped for years in a loveless and lonely marriage, and that, more importantly, she has never forgotten her first love.

The Angelic Occurrence, book 4 in the series, is a thrilling and heart-stopping adventure of love. The twists and turns of fate will keep you gripping the book tighter and tighter as you witness the ever widening circle of influence Henry and Jenny's guardian angels bestow upon them in an effort to reignite a love that never died.

The Angelic Occurrence will touch your soul...
the essence of your being where faith is born.

If You're Not from the Prairie, written by David Bouchard and illustrated by Henry Ripplinger, is a poetic and visual journey depicting the prairies and the people who have made this diverse land their own…a treasure for the mind and soul.

To contact the author and for further information about these books as well as other artwork, limited edition prints and other products, please visit:

www.henryripplinger.com

THE ANGELIC LETTERS SERIES

NOW IN:

AUDIO-BOOKS

Book One -Pewter Angels
Book Two - Another Angel of Love
Book Three - Angel of Thanksgiving
Book Four - The Angelic Occurrence
Book Five - Angel Promises Fulfilled...coming soon

Available for purchase at www.henryripplinger.com

EBOOKS

All five books in the series are in ebook format and available for purchase from Amazon, Kobo and iTunes.

JOIN FACEBOOK

Join Henry's Facebook for words of wisdom from Father Engelmann, book signing tours and schedules, blog posts, future books and more.

VISIT THE WEB SITE: WWW.HENRYRIPPLINGER.COM